legik Seá-mein
Seán Ó Roideacháin
1/8/13

SHANAGOLDEN

Seán Ó Roideacháin

KEEPER

Published in 2013 by **KEEPER BOOKS**

through FeedARead.com Publishing – Arts Council funded

Copyright © Seán Ó Roideacháin

First Edition

Part One

Glory

July 1914 – October 1914

The cold winds from the mountain
are calling soft to me.
The smell of scented heather brings
bitter memories ...

1

H^{E ROSE} to pluck the kickout from the sky, he made a beeline for the opposing goals, he rode two lungeing challenges intent on separating his head from his body as he sucked in the defence. But beyond that, Willie Hartnett didn't remember much about the end of the football game. Sandwiched between the late frontal charge, the flying tackle from behind and the haymaker appearing from nowhere, he was out for the count when Ned Reidy collected his lay-off, danced through a gap between the goalkeeper and full-back and slid the ball over the unprotected goal line.

Nor did he see his captain continue his run straight up to the barbed wire holding back the ecstatic Shanagolden following as the referee blew his whistle and ignored the dire threats of vengeance from the Castlemahon players and officials. It was only when the fence broke down and the entire roaring parish spilled out onto the pitch that he came to.

'A mighty goal, Ned!' he could hear. 'And just in the nick of time.'

And his vision returned as they mobbed Ned, lifted him up on their shoulders and strutted up the length of the field to rub the result in on the opposing supporters.

'Come on, Shanagolden!' shouted the crowd. 'We'll be champions before the spuds are dug up!'

'Are you all right?' asked Dick Mullane, grasping his arm and dragging him up. The players gathered around Willie as he wiped the sweat from his brow, spat the blood from his mouth and pulled himself slowly to his feet.

'We done it!' screamed Jimmy McCarthy. 'Except you done all the work and Ned gets all the credit.'

'Are you sure?' He goggled.

'Last minute goal and we win by a point,' nodded Dick. 'Couldn't have been closer.'

Drug Donovan, hired to rub down the team on the strength of his reputation with the greyhounds, shuffled over and extracted one of the many blue-coloured bottles protruding from the pockets of his coat. The concoction stung as it was pressed into the pores of his forehead but the effect on Willie was immediate.

'Jesus, where did you get that stuff?' sniffed Jimmy. 'There's an almighty stink off of it.'

'Mixture of dandelions and dog shit,' explained the normally silent Drug.

Whatever was in it allowed Willie to watch Ned's eyes fire up with rapture as he raised his fists in the air.

'There's a championship in us this year!' he thundered to the crowd. 'By Jesus, there is!'

Now that they'd qualified for their first ever final, everyone was talking about going the whole way in the Limerick county championship. After trailing the coat and letting neutrals, the people of Castlemahon and the local townies of Newcastlewest know that they'd arrived as a serious footballing force, the cavalcade stumbled out of the hostelries and headed off on the ten-mile journey back home. On an occasion as momentous as

6

this, serious drinking was reserved for Shanagolden as dreams of immortality took shape.

Had they less porter and less whiskey inside them, they might have noticed that the road of their travels straddled one of those faultlines in a land trying to turn its back on a memory decimated by famine and evictions; a land not quite sure whether its future lay in making the best of what it had or in striking out on its own. If they wanted to see the past, they'd only to turn their heads to the left where the fields climbed up to the sour brown slopes of the West Limerick hills for the meagre reward to be squeezed from unforgiving soil. If they looked right, it was over the broad green meadows of the Golden Vale, stretching eastwards to the far side of Munster.

Time and place converged on the straggly town of Shanagolden as it rolled down the scarp between fertility and poverty. Change was in the air on that July Sunday of 1914, dividing the community between those who dared to hope and those who would prefer to forget. Fifteen lads of the one age who had stayed around the parish for the football instead of taking the emigrant boat at the first opportunity, were vaguely aware that they were a generation upon whom the responsibility of decision had been thrust.

For over a year, they had followed a dream. America might have beckoned for most of them but, once a patron came up with the money to get a trainer for the team and work was found on the roads, on the farms and down in the docks of Foynes for any of them that needed it, they were willing to wait until their pursuit of glory had been spent.

Yet what had started off as a wealthy publican's ambitions for his son soon took on a life of its own. Inspired by Ned Reidy's way with words and driven by the ferocious though unspoken determination of Willie Hartnett, the players found the power within themselves to turn effort into a wave of ambition. And along the way, they found a mind of their own that wasn't weighed down by centuries of deference to established order.

'D'ye think ye'll do it?' asked a drover moving his herd of mountainy cattle in the opposite direction.

'You'd never know,' answered the player nearest him.

'I don't doubt that ye will. Ye haven't let us down so far.' The drover watched his neighbours pass him by. Half the county was talking about full-forward Ned Reidy whose magic feet manufactured scores from the impossible and whose dark, dapper good looks had ladies sneaking into the coarse jungle of the grass banks behind the goals. Others saluted the solid unflappable bulk of Patie Fitzgibbon holding the defence together, the flame-haired aggression of pint-sized dynamo Jimmy McCarthy, the cuteness of roly-poly centre-back Mossy Noonan or the menace of stocky hardman Dick Mullane who'd take an opposing star out of the game before the victim or the referee realised what had happened. And those like the drover who fancied they knew a thing or two about the game, recognised that the team's heart lay in the long loose limbs of Willie Hartnett.

Up to then, he'd known them only as boys. Nearly all of them were still under twenty, rowdy, uncomplicated and searching for the limits to their aggression. But as the sun set on that warm summer's evening, they were transformed before his eyes into men.

Dusk was descending by the time the victory party hit town and blazing tar barrels lined both sides of the road to guide their approach. Lured by the prospect of a night's free drinking, the Martyrs of Erin Fife and Drum Band from Newcastlewest led the shoulder-mounted team and their riding, cycling, walking and

8

staggering supporters past a hastily-erected platform at the crossroads in front of the landlord's monument and around the corner into the main street.

Those who hadn't made it to the match spilled out of the pubs and the houses and stretched hands of congratulation to the parish's heroes. Shouts, roars and battle-cries split the slightly off-key notes of Let Erin Remember. Bottles of whiskey, black porter and poitín swung through the air and were passed from mouth to mouth. Wide-eyed children, awestruck by their first ever sight of their town lit up at night, snuck out of their beds to witness the head of the procession halt outside Jack Noonan's pub and dump Ned Reidy on its doorstep.

'Pour them out, Jack!' ordered the skipper as he led the charge to the bar and banged his fist off the counter. 'Pour them out! 'Tisn't every parish that makes it to a county final!'

The crowd behind him lifted the roof as Jack laid glasses along the entire length of the bar and topped them up with whiskey as fast as the flashing hands could grab them. But just as he was about to reach for another bottle, he clasped his fingers around a thin darting arm.

'Players only, Flint.'

'But sure wasn't I was minding the jerseys,' pleaded the small bony frame of uncertain age swimming inside his ill-fitting, hand-me-down clothes. Michael Barrett, known even to his mother as Flint, gazed sorrowfully at the drop extricated from his grasp.

'You weren't even at the game,' observed the landlord.

Flint looked imploringly at Mossy standing beside him.

'Leave him off, Dad,' interceded the son.

'Oh, all right then. But just the one.'

Flint downed the glass in one gulp and finished off a second before Jack had uncorked the bottle.

9

'And what about the band?' came a voice from the back. 'We were promised, so we were.'

'Then ye'd want to leave yer flutes on the counter so as we know who ye are,' another shouted back.

Ned escaped from the backslappers passing him by who wanted him to relive the winning goal in his own words and found a place at a table beside Willie, Mossy, Dick Mullane and Patie Fitzgibbon. Supporters had piled up pints of porter and glasses of whiskey in front of them.

'Your father's being very flúirseach, Mossy.' Ned acknowledged another handshake of congratulations. 'That band that followed us look as if they'd drink the Estuary dry.'

'You mean the Martyrs of Erin?'

'Martyrs for the Liquor more like it.'

'He can well afford it.' Dick poked his head through the curtain to view the street outside. 'I heard he made a packet on the game.'

'Five to one,' answered Pat between sups that left creamy daubs of porter head stuck to his moustache. 'Lunatic odds. I'd have taken them myself if I had've had the money.'

'Castlemahon thought they'd only to turn up.' Mossy tapped Dick on the shoulder. 'What are you looking at?'

'What's looking at us.' He drew back from the curtain. 'No sign of the peelers outside.'

'They're all down in Foynes waiting for Redmond,' explained a passing supporter. 'The Volunteers are holding a public meeting here tonight. 'Twas them that lit the bonfires and put up the platform.'

'And I thought they were doing it for us,' sighed Ned. 'Lads, we're not famous yet.'

'Ah, but we will be!' Willie pushed aside a rambling earful of unwanted advice and smashed his fist off the table. 'When we win the final!'

Not everyone welcomed Shanagolden's success. Were it any other year, Thomas Hennessy would have been the first to bask in the glory but, this time, the wrong people were in charge. And much as the owner of the biggest grocery, the second biggest public house, the post office and the only drapery, hardware shop, funeral undertakers and ticket agency in the town loved his money, he craved control even more. Not only was his finger was stuck in every commercial pie of the parish but, as the local representative on Limerick County Council, he had its politics tied up as well. And where his rod didn't rule directly, fellow souls like Canon Murphy kept an eye on matters spiritual, Doctor Molyneaux on matters medical, Sergeant Stapleton of the Royal Irish Constabulary on law and order and James Horgan minded his patch in the creamery.

But Councillor Hennessy had lost out on the football. Ousted from his twenty year reign as club chairman by that returned Yank of a publican Jack Noonan, his standing was further threatened by the team's unexpected success. On and off the field, names of note were emerging that owed nothing to his patronage or influence. Without a diversion, the people of the parish might start listening to the wrong voices.

So, before the final whistle had blown in Newcastlewest, he'd sped down to the telegraph office and wired an urgent message to a colleague in Limerick to add a stop in Shanagolden to his party leader's tour of the county. And with a generous lump of cash down and the promise of more to follow, a gang of carpenters had erected a platform at the crossroads fit to welcome the Uncrowned King of Ireland before the the triumphant supporters began their raucous descent on the town.

The sound of a pipe band emptied the pub. Patrons finished their drinks and made their way down the main street to the excitement. Realising that there was another attraction in town, the team got up and followed. Only the musicians from Newcastlewest remained on the premises as they steadfastly held Jack Noonan to his promise.

Willie brought up the rear of the crowd, more curious than moved by the occasion. Everyone had been talking for months about the Irish Volunteers, about these great recruitment drives criss-crossing the country in Nationalist Ireland's response to the arming of Ulster. But until then, they had never shown their faces in Shanagolden, as Hennessy made sure that no other political influence encroached on his patch.

Six uniformed Volunteers stood to attention under the torches on each side of the platform that had been decked out in the meantime with green bunting and ribbon underneath an ornate banner of the Ancient Order of Hibernians. Holding their upturned hurleys like rifles, they faced the impassive RIC detail on the other side of the road under Sergeant Stapleton's command.

'That's not Teddy Neville, is it?' asked a girl's voice ahead of Willie.

'Well, I wouldn't have believed it,' answered her companion. 'Doesn't his uniform look only gorgeous?'

The baby-faced Volunteer blushed with embarrassment. A mother spotted three of her children's heads pressed against the window of the house and raced off to give them a scolding before her husband noticed them and reached for his belt. The pipe band finished its rendition of A Nation Once Again with a flourish that coincided with Hennessy's ascent onto the platform.

Willie waited for the ceremony to begin.

Accepting Canon Murphy's handshake, the councillor signalled to his adjutant James Horgan down in front of him that he expected applause. The guard of honour took the hint, banged their hurleys off the side of the platform and cheered loudly enough for the less sober in the attendance to join in. Once the volume had reached an acceptable level, Hennessy waved his hands to command silence.

'It gives me great pleasure,' he began, 'to welcome our guests who have come here at such short notice. Ye all know Mr. PJ O'Shaughnessy, Member of Parliament for the West Division of Limerick and Honorary Commandant of the West Limerick Brigade of the Irish Volunteers.'

Aware that his presence was only on the sufferance of a rival who had eyes on his seat in Westminster, the MP climbed up the platform from the back, modestly waved to the crowd and took his seat.

'Mr. Patrick Pearse, Director of Military Organisation,' continued the master of ceremonies.

Pearse, wearing a Volunteer officer's uniform, took his place beside O'Shaughnessy.

'And ... the man we've all come to see. Upholder of Ireland's cause in the House of Commons. United our Party after the split. People of Shanagolden, the leader of our Volunteers, the Uncrowned King of Ireland ...,' Hennessy gasped for effect, '... John Redmond!'

With the composed importance of a successful barrister, Redmond framed himself in the torchlight and waited for the cheering to subside.

'People of Shanagolden. People of West Limerick.' The powerful baritone captured the attention with practised ease. 'We are on a mission. We will have our Home Rule!'

They began to clap but the leader of the Irish Parliamentary Party silenced them with a flourish of his wrist. 'I speak here tonight not to your good selves but to Mr. Asquith, Mr. Carson and Mr. Bonar Law. And if I may be so bold as to presume your support, I speak on behalf of the people of Ireland ...'

'He's got a mighty way with the words,' whispered Ned as the Shanagolden team, their moment of fame temporarily eclipsed, edged their way over towards a gaggle of girls of similar age lingering hopefully at the back of the crowd.

'... And I'm telling them that we will never allow the division of Ireland against its will ...,' continued the voice from the platform.

'Will you stop that, Ned Reidy!' snapped Mary Hourigan, directing her unconvincing irritation at the pressure on her rear. 'I'm trying to hear what Mr. Redmond has to say.'

'He's saying we're the finest footballers in Limerick and we'll be county champions in a few weeks time.'

'Would that be the whiskey talking and not Mr. Redmond?'

'... And we will not be denied by threats and intimidation from Belfast and from their allies in London.' Redmond stepped forward to the edge of the platform to amplify his determination. 'Nor will we be thwarted because an Army refuses to uphold the sovereignty of Parliament and permits an unrepresentative minority to impose their will on the majority ...'

Ned's sister Josie detached herself from her companions and drifted up beside Willie. 'I hear you were the star of the show, Willie Hartnett.'

'All fifteen of us, Josie,' he answered without averting his gaze from the speaker. 'All for one and one for all.'

14

She leaned up as close as possible to his shoulder without actually touching. 'And good enough to win the final?'

'A match for any team,' he whispered into the hot breath between them. 'As long as we don't get carried away with ourselves.'

' ... When Mr. Asquith hears of our resolve, he will not waver on commitments solemnly given to us in the Mother of Parliaments. So I ask you to pledge your support once again to our demand for Home Rule.' Redmond raised his right arm in salute. 'Erin go braugh! May God save Ireland!'

The cheers rang out. The pipe band jumped to their feet and began to strike up God Save Ireland but Hennessy, holding his leader's arm aloft with one hand, frantically signalled them to stop with his other.

'Doesn't Teddy Neville look smashing in his uniform?' remarked Mary in an attempt to divert Ned's attentions from her bottom. 'Makes a real man of him, so it does.'

''Tisn't what a man wears, Mary.'

Hennessy remained on his feet as Redmond sat down. 'Now which of you will join the Volunteers?'

He scanned the crowd. A thin scatter of hands slowly raised themselves from the mass.

'Are these the only men of Shanagolden willing to pledge themselves to Ireland's cause?'

He waited. Only one more hand rose to the bait before heads turned to catch a figure barging his way through the crowd, to stand directly beneath the platform.

'I'll stand by Ireland!' shouted Ned.

'Ned Reidy is joining us!' shouted Hennessy back. 'Ned Reidy is joining up just hours after leading Shanagolden to our historic victory in Newcastlewest! Come on up here beside us, Ned.'

The front row of the crowd grabbed the football captain and hoisted him up under the torchlight where, swaying ever so slightly, he shook hands with Redmond, O'Shaughnessy and Pearse and wrapped his arm around Hennessy's shoulders in an unsteady embrace.

'Come on, Ned!' roared the crowd.

He raised his outstretched arms in acclamation.

'Come on, Shanagolden!' they boomed.

'The whole team's joining up!' he shouted back.

'Shanagolden has answered the call!' added Hennessy.

'Come on up here, boys!' Ned fell back on the Councillor for physical as well as moral support.

Willie, Dick Mullane, Patie Fitzgibbon, Mossy Noonan, Jimmy McCarthy and the rest of the team stared at each other. So did the crowd around them.

'He's drunk,' said Josie.

'Who isn't?' asked Dick.

'For God's sake, Mary,' she scolded her friend. 'You shouldn't have been going on to him about those uniforms. Especially the state he was in.'

'He'd have gone up anway,' answered Mary. 'Ned could never miss a chance to show off.'

'Are ye afraid to join up?' Ned roared from the platform. Hennessy smiled behind him like the spider welcoming the fly to his web.

And Willie knew that he couldn't refuse, not when the invitation was put up to him by the team's captain in full view of a parish intoxicated with the exuberance of victory.

'No, he's right,' he muttered to those waiting on his lead.

The rest of the side followed him as he opened a passage through the crowd. The pipers resumed their rendition of God Save Ireland as they climbed up one by one to line up behind Ned.

16

'Edmund Reidy ... William Hartnett ... Richard Mullane...' announced Hennessy as Pearse wrote down the names in the enrolment book and Redmond extended the hand of welcome. 'Maurice Noonan ... Patrick Fitzgibbon ... John O'Brien ... Michael Culhane ... Cornelius Greaney ... Jeremiah Curtin ... Michael Fitzgerald ... Daniel Hourigan ... Timothy Curtin ... Bartholomew Mullane ... Denis Lyons ... Jesus, what are you doing here?'

Flint straightened his bearing by as much as his alcohol intake would permit. 'I'm minding the jerseys.'

Sergeant Laurence Stapleton and his police detail remained in place as the crowd broke up, Redmond departed to a hotel in Adare and Horgan oversaw the dismantling of the platform so that it could be moved on for the following evening's meeting in Rathkeale. Despite the post-match celebrations and the Volunteer recruitment rally, it had been a surprisingly peaceful night.

And that was the way the sergeant liked it. No sign of the young bucks who might start a drink-fuelled fight over some trivial incident or a few careless words. No indication of long-standing feuds simmering to the surface or long-forgotten insults being dredged from memory. Maybe they'd decided that joining up with Redmond's quasi-military force meant an unaccustomed acceptance of discipline, or that reaching a county final was grounds for moderating their indulgence of the bottle.

It wasn't that reasons ever mattered to Stapleton. His main concerns were orders. Keep a lid on the situation, the District Inspector had told him. His superiors were forever worrying about any outbreak of unrest that might find a focus. Authority was still fragile in this remote corner of His Majesty's United Kingdom of Great Britain and Ireland and a firm hand was

17

needed to prevent the anarchy of the Land War, the boycotts and the cattle drives from returning.

The young fellas were always the problem. It took time to realise that you couldn't have prosperity without stability and it didn't matter a toss to them yet that tenants could now buy out their holdings, and that the co-operatives were delivering a fair price to the emerging class of freeholder farmers. And even if they did, there would never be enough money or enough land or enough work to go around.

The emigrant boat was the only way out. Most of them left for America or England before they could cause trouble and farmers with a few bob put by might invest it in the second son to start a holding of his own in Australia or New Zealand. But that wasn't happening in Shanagolden. An entire crop had postponed their departure and, in doing so, had laid the seeds for future unrest.

In such turbulent times, there was plenty to distract them. Up in the hills that overlooked the town, whole layers of the economy remained outside the rule of law where they rustled their cattle, distilled their poitín and dispensed their own brand of justice on anyone associating with agents of the Crown. In the back rooms of bars, secret societies were plotting revolution against His Majesty in their pursuit of an independent republic. In the schools, in the halls and on the playing fields, Gaelic scholars, musicians, dancers and sportsmen were stoking up nationalist sentiment. In the mud cabins and cottages along the lanes, agitiators from the city were inciting labourers to strike for better pay and conditions.

And enveloping them all was the political stalemate as Unionists armed themselves to resist Home Rule and Nationalists formed their own Volunteer force in reply.

Back in district headquarters in Newcastlewest, they were always looking for information. Who was seen talking to whom?

When they went off training, was it with guns or with footballs? Could the teacher or the curate be trusted or had their heads been filled with misguided notions of sedition? Were there realiable sources in the pubs, in the club, in the sodality and in the creamery?

Stapleton pressed his back against the wall, expanded his ample chest and pulled the front pockets of his tunic out with his thumbs as he sucked in the soft night air. Just a pair of flickering lights broke the darkness and only a single set of horse hooves could be heard in the distance. The trickle leaving Jack Noonan's wasn't going to cause any disturbance. The sergeant could report to his superiors that Shanagolden was still under control.

He was on the point of shutting up shop for the night when the motorcar arrived from Newcastlewest.

'Anything to report?' asked his boss, District Inspector Nicholas Sullivan.

'Fifty of them joined up, sir,' the sergeant told him. 'Nothing much happened until the footballers stepped forward.'

'Anyone we should be keeping an eye on?'

'We won't have a problem at this end. Hennessy should see to that.' Expecting to find a drunk sleeping it off, Stapleton poked his baton into a rag-covered shape lying in the darkness of the street but there were only lumps of horse dung underneath. 'But there was another fellow down from Dublin I didn't like the cut of. Pearse, I think his name was.'

Sullivan, a career policeman with over thirty years service in the hot spots of Munster, didn't share his superiors' complacency regarding the Irish Volunteers. While the private army, set up eight months previously in response to the Ulster Volunteer Force, claimed over 100,000 members, it had neither the arms,

19

the financial backing nor the military leadership of its Unionist opponents and the ragged collection of recruits parading with hurleys or ash-plants was treated with derision by the colonial authorities. And when Redmond and his Irish Parliamentary Party colleagues took over the leadership, any remaining fears that they had dissipated entirely. Crown rule certainly wouldn't be threatened by a group of elderly politicians who, after thirty comfortable years in Westminster, had been stripped of all pretensions and inclinations towards radical action.

But then again, those civil servants and military men in Dublin Castle did not spring from the land that they ruled. They came, they saw and they implemented according to the same rulebook that was applied in Surrey and in Scotland, in Somaliland and in the South Sea Islands. All very logical, no doubt, and refined over centuries of bureaucratic administration, but it took no account of local sentiment.

The District Inspector, on the other hand, knew full well what made the inhabitants of John Bull's other island tick. While he might have been as loyal a subject of King George as any blue-blooded English aristocrat, he was still an Irish Catholic of humble origins and understood the hold that silent suffering could exert on a people who had been through revolution, ruination and starvation within living memory. Where England could be roused into action by the appeal of the Empire, nothing spurred the soul of Ireland as effectively as the spear of resentment.

As keenly as those he was employed to keep under control, he could sense the inequalities in how the law was administered. When the Unionists of Ulster formed their own private army, the military leaders stationed in the Curragh refused to march against them. And when the Ulster Volunteer Force imported 25,000 rifles and three million rounds of ammunition through

20

the port of Larne ten weeks earlier, the authorities had turned a blind eye. Yet if the people that he had sprung from tried the same stunt, official reaction would be swift and unambiguous.

From the moment he had signed on as a constable at the height of the Land War, Nicholas Sullivan had pledged his allegiance to upholding the law and he had been too long on the beat even to know any more whether it was just or unjust. But he still retained enough contact with his origins to see that the flames of resentment were driving the population into the hands of those seeking to destroy it.

2

LTHOUGH the creamery manager normally turned up for work at least two hours after his hirelings began their day, Mr. Horgan, as he insisted that everyone should address him, made an exception on that Monday morning and greeted the throbbing heads with the same relish as Satan welcoming sinners at the gates of Hell. And instead of having the agitator on the butter-maker stripped down to replace a defective bearing, he insisted on running it so that Willie Hartnett, Dick Mullane and Jimmy McCarthy could have their ears pounded with the undiluted intensity of its amplified vibration.

They had to be pulled back a peg. Immediately. Otherwise they'd get notions that fame on a football field counted for something in the greater scheme of life and they might start demanding things to which they were not entitled. Even worse, other impressionable fools in the yard might begin to look up to them. Within the kingdom of his rule, happiness was James Horgan's alone to dispense and, on the whole, he preferred that the labourers employed by the Shanagolden Co-operative Society should enjoy as little of it as possible.

Much to his disappointment, however, his pleasure lasted little more than ten minutes, as the machine seized up with a piercing screech and a Richter scale tremor and spewed the floor with a sickly-stinking mixture of butter, buttermilk and smouldering axle grease. When the grumpy fitter demanded that the entire dairy be cleared out so that he could grieve in peace for his beloved mechanical creation, Willie was sent out to wheel the milk churns off the carts lined up at the landing.

Into the midst of his sufferings descended vague recollections of a night that had ended only a few hours previously when he managed to stagger home to his bed. They were in the county final, he was sure of that, and they'd only a couple of weeks to prepare for it. He was also fairly certain that he'd signed up for the Volunteers, although the reason for doing so quite escaped him at that particular moment.

And in between Horgan screaming at him to hurry up and stop wasting the suppliers' time as they waited in the queue, fragments of conversations with various people peppered his brain but he failed to put them in context. There was even something there at the back of his mind to stoke his anger but it, too, would have to wait until his head was functioning properly.

Ned Reidy wasn't too bright either as he tapped the ass's backside to edge him up to the landing for unloading.

'I didn't think I'd see you alive this morning.' Urged on by the manager standing over his shoulder, Willie grabbed the nearest churn, rubbed his hand down the side to check whether it was the cold milk of the night or the still-warm yield of the morning and wheeled it over on its base to the separator bath. Jimmy took it from there, removed the lid, tipped it over and rolled the empty churn back outside to Willie.

'Check,' shouted the assistant manager at the scales. 'A hundred and sixty seven pounds.' He wrote the amount into the log. 'Chalk it down.'

The chalk fell from Willie's fingers as he recorded the weight on the churn and it crushed under his heel as replaced the lid, left the container back on the cart and wheeled off the next full one.

'One of them mornings,' he muttered, waiting for the assistant to toss him another stick before Horgan noticed and delivered a lecture on the cost of chalk.

Ned took his delivery book from his coat pocket. 'I've been worse and I've survived,' he whispered as he passed Willie by. 'By the way, will you be around tonight?'

'A hundred and seventy three,' announced the assistant manager. Horgan moved over his shoulder to make sure that he entered the same amount in the creamery's log as he noted in Ned's delivery book. Even though the figures had never failed to tot up in over twenty years, the manager was still convinced that his number two was up to some fiddle or other.

'Are you looking to run the poison out of the system?' Willie asked as Ned returned to his cart. 'Like a few runs up the slope?'

'No. Something else entirely. There's someone who wants to see you.'

Willie motioned his head in the direction of Horgan returning to make sure that no private conversations were taking place on company time.

'Call into the yard after you've finished up here,' continued Ned. 'And bring Dick and Jimmy along with you.' He tapped the ass to bring the cart round to the landing on the other side of the building where Dick filled the empty churns with skim milk for feeding to the pigs.

Knowing that they were up to something that evening, Horgan decided that the creamery yard did not measure up to his standards of hygiene and insisted on Willie, Jimmy and Dick

25

staying back to wash the place down a second time as well as cleaning up the mess left in the dairy by the seized agitator bearing. By the time they got away, the sun was picking up colour and descending towards the horizon. Making their way up the main street, they passed by Stapleton outside Jack Noonan's, repeatedly jabbing Flint in the back with the point of his baton.

'You're loitering, Barrett,' grunted the sergeant. 'Get a move on or I'll pull you in.'

'There's some fierce brave men around here,' said Jimmy over his shoulder, loud enough for half the length of the town to overhear. 'They'd take on anyone.'

'I heard that, McCarthy,' answered the policeman. 'I'm keeping an eye on you as well.'

'While you're taking your nice shiny shilling from King George of England.' Jimmy slowed down as two street-corner regulars and a dog ambled over to observe the exchanges.

'Just watch yourself, sonny. Some day you'll give me the excuse and I've all the time in the world to wait for it.' Stapleton grabbed Flint by the soulder. 'Come on, you! Get moving!'

'Will you stop acting stupid.' Willie's long silent arm pulled Jimmy back into line. 'You're only bringing notice on yourself.'

In between mouthing on about Stapleton, Jimmy kept asking where they were going, as they walked the half-mile out of town and then cut back over the fields once they were out of the policeman's sight. Weary from the game, from an extended day of shifting milk and washing down the yard, from the last reminders of the skinful that they had sunk, Willie wouldn't have minded going home and falling straight into bed; the monologue of complaint was getting on his nerves. Even Dick, who rarely spoke unless he had to, was being unusually talkative.

And if he was going up to Reidy's, he would have preferred to be on his own. It was always easier to get sense out of Ned when he didn't have a crowd around him to impress.

Still a month short of turning twenty, they had been born within days of each other, Ned in the farmhouse and Willie in the labourer's cottage down the road. Ned's mother had died giving birth to his sister Josie and Willie's mother had taken care of him until he was of an age to begin school. And when he was old enough to walk the fields that some day he would succeed to, it had been in the company of Willie's father, the lead hand on the farm.

Over the years, the difference in station had pulled them apart but the bond of childhood remained. While Willie had left school at thirteen to take up the job that Ned's father had found him at the Co-op and Ned went off to boarding school for an education, they still treated each other as equals in a society that had only recently assumed the trappings of class when tenant farmers were able to buy out their holdings.

Ned was waiting as they entered the twilit farmyard and directed them to the cowshed.

'Any chance ye were followed?' he asked as he lit the Tilly lamp.

'No,' answered Willie. 'Stapleton was busy with Flint.'

'Do you remember Mr. Pearse from last night?'

Now clad in civvies, Patrick Pearse emerged from the shadows and shook hands with the three arrivals.

'The entire team of ye joining up. It looked good.' His one good eye immediately fixed on Willie, sizing him up as if he was a horse at a fair. 'We need that sort of commitment.'

'No shortage of commitment in Shanagolden.' Ned glowed in the reflected importance of his visitor.

Willie held the soft hand in his clasp. He could have crushed it but Pearse didn't flinch. 'No offence, Mr. Pearse, but I wasn't too impressed.'

'No need for that ...' said Ned.

'No, let him speak,' interrupted Pearse. 'What didn't you like about it?'

'No one will take any notice of ye.'

'We've numbers. Over a hundred thousand and counting.'

'But ye haven't any guns.'

The Volunteer commander scanned the expressions of the other three before settling back on Willie. 'Supposing we got some?'

'It wouldn't matter a damn. We're the wrong crowd.' Yet despite his suspicion of outsiders, Willie sensed the infectiousness of the Dubliner's charisma.

'Go on.'

'All right. Carson and the UVF got their way because the ones in power are all Unionists. After the Curragh Mutiny, they know that the authorities won't stand up to them no matter what they do.'

Pearse nodded, half-amused.

'Anyway, what are ye fighting for? Home Rule? Who's going to lay down his life for a glorified county council?'

'So why did you join up, then?'

'Yeah, tell us why,' added Jimmy.

'Better than doing nothing at all,' was all Willie could think of. 'What else have we got?'

The lamp flickered. Ned tapped it to shake up the paraffin. Unseen wings fluttered under the eaves.

'So we should be looking for more?' asked Pearse.

'Of course we should if we're serious. We'll never get sorted out until we get full independence.'

'You're not the only man thinking that way.'

Willie finally broke into a smile and slapped his hand off Pearse's shoulder. 'Well in that case, we could be talking business.'

'Jaysus, you sure put it up to him.' Dick led them out of the moonlit farmyard into the laneway bordered by thick hedges on both sides. 'I thought Ned was ready to piss in his pants the way you took Mr. Pearse on.'

'Better to find out now if he's sound.' Willie closed the gate behind them. The argument had stripped his tiredenss away. For the first time that he could remember, a man of learning had recognised that he had a view worth listening to.

'Still, I'd have to say he impressed me,' continued Dick.

'He did that ...'

'Willie!' whispered the hedge.

'I knew we were being followed!' Jimmy's startled head turned around.

'It's all right, boys. The two of ye go on off ahead. I can make my own way home.'

Jimmy looked dubiously at Willie before his expression turned to a leer when he noticed the smile on Dick's face.

'Go on! Get going, will ye.'

They disappeared down the lane.

'I thought it might be you,' he said.

'And were you hoping it was me?' asked Josie as she stepped out from behind the sprawling sycamore.

'Maybe I was.'

'And is that why you came up here?'

'Maybe it was.'

'But that's not the only reason, is it?'

'You should be in bed, shouldn't you?'

'I snuck out, so I did.'

'And what would your father say?'

'There's nothing to worry about. He's over in Rathkeale at a funeral and he won't be back until the morning.'

The banter spilled over the shyness of their first moments together. Yet they had known each other for years. Raised for much of her early childhood in his house, Willie had regarded her more as a younger sister before she went back to the maids and the boarding schools that her father had picked out for her. He had hardly seen her at all after that, just the brief glimpses between school and holidays and staying with relations in the city, and in that time their worlds had grown apart. Josie was on her way to becoming a lady with a different circle of friends and another set of interests and stepping out into a world that extended far beyond the laneways and fields of Shanagolden. But even as their paths diverged, he never could forget the cheeky little madam who alone, through her pout and her puss and her dainty imperiousness, could bend the will of the bould young fella that he had been back then.

So when she came back a month earlier after finishing school and taking up as mistress of the farmhouse in which only her father and brother were living, he had suddenly seen her as a woman, as a companion, as an excitation, as someone he could talk to about his dreams and his frustrations and his hopes and someone whose life he could also listen to. And over the long weeks, he lived off the dream that she might stay on, but still resigned himself to the prospect of her departure. Maybe it would have been better that way. The Josie of thirteen years earlier was only an illusion; the lady who had returned was a different woman entirely.

But she had also remembered. The night before, she'd seen him look at her from across the street at the Volunteers rally and she'd immediately left her friends and come over to his side. In the rare proximity of a public meeting, they'd moved themselves into the crowd so that they could press against each other in the shared familiarity of the moment and they'd hoped that it might go on forever.

Without a word, they had touched, they had felt the warmth of each other's breath, they had joined together under the stars and slowly, shyly, bashfully, they had released their tongues to find each other. He felt the softness of her skin, soaked up the heady scent of her arousal, pressed the contours of her body as close as he could to his chest.

He had ached to take it further and he thought that she did too but, somewhere between them, he could hear the voice of guilt crying out. Shanagolden was a time and a place where conventions were either forgotten or else were submerged under the scruples of faith. And while he had hoped that both of them were willing to challenge prescribed modes of behaviour, he was resigned to the likelihood that neither of them was of the inclination to do battle against the word of God.

So, when he had set out for Reidy's earlier on in the evening, he had already braced himself for disappointment. Maybe she would stay inside the house under the watchful eye of her father or she would recoil from the once-off exuberance of celebration, or from the drink inside him that had caused him to imagine far more than what was the reality.

They held each other for long silent minutes, not letting a word intrude on an intimacy that neither had experienced before. They let their thoughts drift over each other and dreamed that they might be the same before they were woken by the fluttering wings of an owl passing overhead.

'I won't ask you what ye were up to tonight.' Eyes still flaming with emotion, she tidied her hair and straightened her dress as

31

she eased herself from his embrace. 'But be careful with Ned,' she warned. 'There are times when he gets carried away with himself.'

He watched her every step, watched the moonlight shining off her white dress as she stole away into the gloom of the farmyard.

3

JACK NOONAN WAS cleaning out the leftovers when he heard the walking stick tapping on the window. A huge funeral had meant a busy night's drinking and he hadn't had the time to clear it all up before he hit the bed. There were still porter stains on the counter, fragments of broken bottles in the corners and the sour smell of stale ale wafted up from the sawdust.

'You come outside here, Jack Noonan!' Framed against the sunlight was the fearsome red face of Canon Murphy, booming loud enough for the entire town to hear. 'I've something to tell you.'

Expecting yet another lecture on the evils of alcohol and the greed of those selling it to impressionable wretches intent on self-destruction, Jack took his time making his way to the door. He would have preferred to ignore the Canon altogether but, this being Shanagolden and not Chicago where there was serious competition between the various soul-minders, the power of the parish's single pulpit remained unchallenged.

This time, however, His Reverence was brandishing a newspaper. 'Do you see that?'

Jack looked at the headline of the previous day's Freeman's Journal that had been poked in his face. 'Disturbances follow Howth Gun-Running. Deaths in Bachelor's Walk.'

'Death,' intoned the parish priest. 'Tragic and violent death.'

According to eyewitness reports in the newspapers, the Volunteers had landed a consignment of rifles and ammunition at Howth and, even though it was only a small fraction of what the UVF had been allowed to bring into Larne three months earlier, the police followed the fleet of taxis bringing the arms into Dublin. When the locals started to jeer them at Bachelor's Walk in the centre of the city, the British Army was called in and they fired on the crowd, leaving three civilians dead and dozens of others wounded in their wake.

'Sounds bad ...'

'Their souls must be mourned in a fitting manner,' the sermon continued. 'You will not be playing football on Sunday.'

'I heard nothing about a postponement ...'

'I have already informed the county board. I'm expecting their response any moment.' And without waiting for a comment from the club chairman, the Canon strode off to vent his morning thunder on the next sinner to cross his path.

'What was he on about?' Mossy had came in from the yard where he had been stacking the previous night's mountain of empty barrels, bottles and crates.

Jack handed him the newspaper. 'He wants us to call off the county final as a mark of respect to those people killed in Dublin.'

'What's it to do with him? He'd kiss the King of England's arse if he got half a chance.'

'It don't matter a damn. He's only trying to make himself important.' He took the paper back from his son. 'And mind what you say out loud about the Canon.' Along the length of the main street, he could see the pairs of prying eyes squinting through the windows.

The clock chimed to announce opening time. A pair of regulars were already beating on the door, part of the secondary growth that had drifted from Hennessy's bar across the road when the football team began to take off. Those who couldn't play needed to be in the know and where better to start than on the premises belonging to the club's new chairman.

A group of farmers left their asses and carts hitched outside as Jack was filling the first two pints of the day. The morning trade had grown steadily all week as final fever spread through the parish. Everyone was turning into an expert. Opinions, arguments and assessments bounced off the pub's walls as players' abilities were dissected, team selections were proposed, historical precedents were discussed and pisreogs were unearthed.

'You must be coining it,' remarked a patron waiting for his porter.

'Can't complain,' Jack replied as he nodded to Mossy to take the orders at the top end of the bar. Having sensed that another session was about to start and having satisfied themselves that Councillor Hennessy was away for the day, the road gang and its overseer had dropped their tools and sought solace from the rising heat of the morning.

'Cutest thing you ever done, taking over the footballers. If they win on Sunday, you'll clean up entirely.' The customer's eyes dropped down to the pint, masking the sentiment behind the words. It could have been jealousy, respect, begrudgery, admiration or sarcasm; or even a mixture of them all.

Jack had long since given up trying to put motive behind what his neighbours would say to him. Twenty-five years in Chicago after leaving the parish as a lad had removed his familiarity with the hidden language of nods, winks, cryptic comments and words left unsaid that protected those who remained from the attentions of outsiders. Rarely did any native ever come back; the only strangers were those sent to enforce an authority that had never been accepted by a community with its own way of setting rank and settling disputes.

But he remembered enough of the old ways to know that there were many among them who resented his return. When he turned up with a pocket full of dollars and a head full of ideas, he listened to and then promptly ignored the advice on how he should behave. And when a prominent main street publican dropped dead in the throes of ecstasy in a Limerick whorehouse, he immediately approached the widow and bought the business for a fair price instead of leaving first refusal to the dominant merchants of the town.

It wasn't appreciated. A delegation appeared on his doorstep and suggested he might reconsider. He fed them tea and cake and told them he'd think about it.

They and the rest of them with the soft hats and the fob watches, those praying in the front of the church on seats bearing their names, predicted his rapid comeuppance when Noonan's Select Saloon opened its doors. Ever since the land agitation of a previous generation had died down, a new order had established itself and any usurper challenging its position was soon frozen out. But Jack Noonan had seen another world where there was nothing to stop a man making it as long as he stuck at it and, six years down the road, he had not only defied the naysayers but had prospered as well.

Nor did he stick solely to business. When Mossy and his friends came to him one night to do something about the football, he engineered a coup in the club and ousted the entire unsuspecting committee in one fell swoop. They screamed blue murder at the affront to their position but, when the team began to string victories together for the first time ever, the parish stopped listening to the jobsworths whose sole interest in the sport was as a means of reinforcing their standing in the community.

'There isn't a chance of them losing, isn't there, Jack?' Jack shook his head, not to assert confidence in the team but to indicate that no free drink would be forthcoming.

Flint slid away to find a more sympathetic ear. Having held the bag containing the jerseys at one match and at least two training sessions, he could project himself as a man in the know.

By evening, consumption had reduced to a trickle. What was left of the clientele followed Jack, Mossy and Flint down the football field and leaned against the wall to observe the last training session before the big day.

'Keep still, will ye!' shouted the photographer over at the other side of the pitch, his thin voice barely heard over the belly laughs.

And he might as well have been talking to the wall. Never having seen a camera operate before, most of the players were caught up in the novelty of the occasion. Despite the flustered impatience of their trainer Birdie Madden and the pleadings of Jack who was footing the bill, they continued to slag each other and push each other in the back and make silly faces.

John Joe Snaps, as the travelling photographer was known over the length and breadth of West Limerick, had come all the way out from Newcastlewest in his pony and cart laden down with the chemicals, the plates, the tripod, the little tent, the magnesium flashes and the big heavy camera of his profession. He had even left early from the extended wedding breakfast of a

37

strong farmer's daughter in order to reach Shanagolden while the evening light was still bright enough to capture the team. But if they didn't stop clowning around as he tried to pose them against the gable wall of the hall, his journey would have been in vain.

'There's three of them missing,' shouted one of the spectators as John Joe finally prevailed on the players to quieten down.

'Ten ... eleven ... twelve ... Maybe I could do the rest of them as inserts.'

'No. I want them all together,' insisted Jack as he caught sight of Dick Mullane, Jimmy McCarthy and Willie Hartnett bounding over the wall.

'What kept ye?' fussed Birdie, again consulting the big pocket watch that he'd won at a tournament playing for Foynes a few years earlier.

'Come on! Come on!' begged Jack. The messing had started again. 'All this delay is costing the poor man money.'

Willie grabbed a jersey while the photographer was fiddling away under the sheet at the back of his camera. The three late arrivals had to stand in at the back row so that their trousers wouldn't be visible even though Jimmy's shock of scarlet hair could barely be seen over Patie Fitzgibbon kneeling in front of him.

'Will ye stop, boys!' Once in his place, Willie took command. 'Give the man a chance or we'll never get our picture taken.' The voice wasn't loud but the firmness of its insistence had an immediate effect. The fifteen players, their selector, their trainer, their bottleman and their bagman all stood sternly to attention and faced the lens that would record them for posterity with the grim resolve of a tribe going to battle.

John Joe Snaps knew enough about football to realise that he was witnessing champions in the making. After their neighbours in Foynes had captured the Limerick title six years earlier, Shanagolden were attempting to prove that the southern half of the parish could repeat that success in the summer of 1914, even if it was the much-postponed championship of the previous year. And when he saw the intensity burning in their faces after they had settled down for the camera, he reckoned that the bookies' odds of three to one against them were worth a serious flutter.

The first picture snapped, then the second. 'And one for the road,' pleaded the photographer before he emerged from the sanctuary of his sheet. He was immediately surrounded by a mob of curious players gawking at his equipment, poking at the tent of mysteries, asking him questions and sniffing his chemicals. A gang of youngsters jumped over the wall to join them.

'For God's sake, Mr. Noonan,' screamed John Joe. 'Get them away from here or they'll destroy my plates before I get them developed.'

The match went ahead despite the Canon's best efforts. A special train put together by the enterprising stationmaster of Foynes took the entire parish on a roundabout tour of the county, picking up more supporters along the way as it passed through Askeaton, Adare, Limerick City, Pallasgreen, Limerick Junction and Knocklong. Waiting to greet the invasion when it arrived at Kilmallock station were John Joe Snaps and his camera and the side-drummer, the bass drummer, the triangle-player, the cymbals-player and all nine tin-whistlers of the Martyrs of Erin Fife and Drum Band who had adopted Shanagolden for the summer.

They were given the use of a hall across the road from the field to tog out. Players bunched together in groups as they laid their street clothes across two long benches, or hung them up on spikes protruding from the walls.

Studs and hobnails rattled off the floor. Lungs sucked in great draughts of air. Legs were swathed in rolls of bandage. Miraculous medals and scapulars were hung around necks. A line of them waited in turn for Drug Donovan to tap their shoulders and their thighs and rub their muscles down with a brownish-yellow concoction that he scooped from a jam jar.

Alone and already togged out, Willie sat impassively on a bench and stared at some indeterminate point on the ground in an effort to separate his mind from the activity around him.

Birdie Madden paced nervously around the room and consulted his pocket watch every ten seconds as he waited for the preparations to end. 'Keep them out, for God's sake,' the trainer shouted at Jack Noonan who was pressing his shoulder against the door.

'Them all?'

'The whole damn lot of them. They didn't want to know us a few months ago but now since we started winning, they're all full of useless advice.'

'Even the selectors?' Jack jammed a chair under the door handle to prevent it from turning.

'Them especially. The team's picked already.' Birdie's manic steps stopped as he watched Ned being given the final slaps on his hamstrings. 'Are you finished yet?' The watch surfaced again from the fob. 'Sweet Jesus Christ up in Heaven! The match will be over if you don't get a move on.'

Drug ignored him, pulled out a long thin bottle from one of his many pockets, smathered the contents on his hands and rubbed them across Patie Fitzgibbon's shoulders. Behind them, Flint hovered with an armful of yellow and blue jerseys that he had pulled from a jute sack.

'Jaysus, what are you doing here?' Birdie looked across at Jack. 'What did you let him in for?'

'You told me to mind the jerseys, Mr. Madden,' said Flint.

'I didn't, did I? Or if I did, I didn't mean it ...'

An incessant sequence of thumps banged off the door but Jack's shoulder was equal to the challenge. 'I can't let you in!' he shouted out. 'I can't let anyone in! I'm not allowed!'

'Are you denying me the right of entry?' replied a thunderous roar.

'Oh Christ! 'Tis the Canon.'

'What does he want, Jack?' Birdie disengaged himself from Flint's expectant presence.

'We'll have to let him in. He always says a decade of the Rosary before a big game.'

'You're not serious? ...'

'We'll never hear the end of it if we don't.'

'All right, all right, all right,' sighed the trainer as he shrugged his shoulders with distracted resignation. 'Just get it over with.'

Flint slid off to the corner of the room to hand Jimmy McCarthy a bottle that he'd swiped from Drug's collection. 'D'you want a drop?' he whispered. 'This is mighty stuff.'

Jimmy took a slug of the poitín. His spluttering cough woke Willie from his trance.

'Are you out of your mind, Jimmy?' He whipped the bottle from Jimmy's lips and left it aside. 'We want you fit going out on the field. Not drunk.'

Flint retrieved the moonshine and helped himself to a generous slug. 'A drop of the cratur never did anyone any harm ...'

The Canon pushed through the the door, followed by a few stray arms and legs that Jack's shoulder cut off before they could establish a foothold.

'Get out!' he shouted. 'Only the Canon's allowed in.'

'I was secretary the last time we got to the final,' complained one of the excluded.

'We've never been there before. Now, on your way!'

'On yer knees, the lot of ye.' The Canon shoved two players off the bench with an imperious brush of his forearm, pulled his Rosary beads from the pocket of his soutane and knelt down. 'We'll say the five glorious mysteries. Then we'll know for sure that God is on our side.'

'One decade,' insisted Birdie

'Two. It's a county final.'

They reluctantly took to their knees except for Jimmy down in the corner who was beating his fists off the wall.

'The first glorious mystery, the Resurrection of Our Lord Jesus Christ from the dead,' began His Reverence. 'Our Father, who art in Heaven, hallowed be Thy name, Thy kingdom come ...'

'Come on Shanagolden!' roared Jimmy. 'We'll kill the bastards!'

'Jesus Christ!' muttered Birdie, blessing himself as he glanced up towards Heaven.

'Thy will be done ...' continued the Canon after shutting Jimmy up with a ferocious stare.

The referee was banging the door to call them out by the time the Canon had finished. Not content with his two glorious decades, he had added the trimmings of Hail Holy Queen and exhortations to every saint of local, national and worldwide significance to come the side's spiritual aid. Eventually, Birdie picked up the football, slapped it into Ned's hands and all but shoved him through the door into the phalanx of well-wishers gathered outside.

A particularly keen supporter broke from the scrum, grabbed the captain's arm and held it aloft. 'Good boy the Ned!' he shouted.

Willie shook his head in frustration as Ned stopped, the team piled up against his backside and he turned to the crowd. 'Come on, Shanagolden!' he cried. 'We're raring to pull up the spuds!'

'By the hokey, we are!' they cheered.

They hoisted the team up on their shoulders for the short walk to the field across the road. They stopped again for John Joe Snaps to record their entry for posterity. The Martyrs of Erin coalesced in unsteady formation to herald them through the gates with a tune whose origins were lost somewhere between a romantic Moore melody and a rousing chieftain's march.

Ignored by the Ballylanders players, the officials, the hawkers and the thousands of opposing supporters packed at opposite ends of the ground, the referee continued to whistle that the team in yellow and blue was already late for the throw-in.

The euphoria failed to make it across the road where the Canon joined Hennessy, Horgan, Doctor Molyneaux and two other bowler-hatted selectors huddled together against the inside wall of the grounds. Each wave of support piling through the gates added to their sniping indignation.

'Would you look at that fool Flint Barrett following them,' muttered Hennessy. 'Carrying on as if he's part of the backroom, so he is, and the little scut never held down a paid job in his life.'

'I've never been so insulted in all my days,' complained the doctor. 'Who does he think he is, that Birdie Madden? Picking the team himself.'

'A dictator, that's what he is,' agreed Canon Murphy. 'I'm telling you, 'twas a sorry day for Shanagolden when we had to bring a man up from Foynes for to train the team.'

'You can blame Jack Noonan for that,' said the Councillor. 'But we'll soon sort him out. They haven't a God's earthly chance of winning and then we can hunt the lot of them out of the club.'

'And then they'll be back supping in your pub, Thomas Hennessy,' interrupted a voice from behind. 'Instead of going across the road to Jack Noonan's.'

It was only when they took to the field that the enormity of the occasion struck Willie. All through the shenanigans in the dressing-room and the coat-trailing coming through the gates, he'd distanced himself from what was going on around him so that he could concentrate on the game ahead. But when the referee tossed the coin and the heaving crowd of two clubs that had never reached this stage before burst into full voice, he suddenly appreciated what it meant to those who had never got the chance to wear the Shanagolden jersey.

Their opponents Ballylanders felt the same. No longer a contest between players, this had become a duel between tribes as deadly as the clan wars and the faction fights between the generations that had preceded them. And in Shanagolden's case, it was likely to be the only shot at glory that this team would ever get. Win, lose or draw, at least half them were about to follow their brothers and sisters into exile as soon as the championship was over.

Nothing separated them until well after half-time. Each time one side scored, the effort lifted at the other end to squeeze out the equalising point. Then with time ebbing away, goalkeeper Tim Curtin fielded a lob on his goal line and was bundled over by three inrushing Ballylanders forwards.

Half of the Shahagolden team surrounded the referee. 'How can you let that stand?' screamed Ned. 'That has to be a free out.'

But the match official, frantically blowing his whistle and pointing to the 21-yard line, was unmoved. Behind him, Jimmy swung a fist at one of the opposing forwards rising exultantly to his feet.

All hell broke loose as most of the players laid into each other. The police flooded the sidelines to stop the crowd from joining in and whacked their batons off the heads of any spectators trying to scale the fence.

Birdie and Drug rushed over to attend to their goalkeeper who stretched out over his line. 'Is he all right?' asked the trainer.

Drug pulled a bottle from his egg basket, poured some thick brown liquid over his hands and massaged it into Tim's face. The smell alone was enough to set the nose twitching. 'He'll be fine,' nodded the bottleman.

'That was no goal, sure it wasn't, Mr. Madden?'

Before Birdie could vent his frustrations on Flint who was tugging at his sleeve, a Ballylanders player tumbled over him, scattering Drug's bottles as he hit the ground. Flint picked up the nearest one, sniffed it and began to drink it.

Above him, the referee tried to restore order as the venom seeped out of the exchanges. Willie and Dick dragged Jimmy and Ned away.

'D'you see what he done, Willie? Tried to bite me, so he did!' Jimmy was still fighting mad and struggled to get back into the fray. 'I'll kill him! I swear to Jaysus, I'll kill him!'

Drug gathered his bottles, including the one whipped from Flint's lips. Beside him, Tim rose from the ground and flattened a passing opponent with a ferocious uppercut. Another free-for-all broke out, although not with quite the same conviction as the first, and quickly degenerated into a parade of postures backed up by a chorus of jeers and catcalls.

Brandishing his walking stick like a sword, the Canon strode into the middle of the commotion and made straight for the referee. 'I'm abandoning the game. You're unfit to officiate it.'

The match official gaped as if to say that was all he needed to make his day.

'Did you hear me?' repeated His Reverence. 'I'm lodging an official protest with the county board.'

The Ballylanders trainer approached the referee from the othe other side. 'This is a disgrace, ref! You should be hunting the lot of them off the field so as we can get on with the game.'

The Canon grabbed Patie Fitzgibbon, the player nearest to him, and dragged him in the direction of the sideline. 'Come on. We're going back to Shanagolden this instant. This game will have to be refixed for a proper venue and with a proper referee.'

The man in the middle blinked out of his trance to reassert his authority. 'If you leave the field now, I'm awarding the match to Ballylanders.'

'That's fine by us but we'd sooner win the game fair and square.'

Down on the sideline, Birdie thew his hands in the air. 'O Jesus Christ! He can't be serious!'

'He's a fierce stubborn man when he gets a notion into his head,' said someone behind him.

'We haven't been waiting all year for it to end up like this. Will someone stop him!' the trainer seethed. 'You're the chairman, Jack. Will you get him out of the place.'

Jack reluctantly moved in to intervene but Willie beat him to it. 'Off the field, Canon. You've no position in this club.'

Stunned by the first ever public challenge to his authority, the priest stared speechlessly at Willie pulling Patie away to rejoin his teammates. 'Come on, Patie. We're playing on. We'll beat them anyway.'

Taunting his marker into conceding the foul, Ned pointed the free kick in the rising excitement.

'What's left?' asked Jack.

'Less than a minute,' answered Birdie as he watched his players line up for the Ballylanders kickout.

'We need a goal.'

'That's right, Mr. Madden.' Flint stuck his head in between them. 'I think you should be switching Mossy and Jerry Curtin. There's loads of people in the crowd saying you should.'

'Would someone just get him out of here!' Birdie screamed at no one in particular.

The goalie was taking it handy, eating up the last vital seconds as he teed up the football.

'Christ, ref, will you hurry him up!' pleaded Ned.

'Calm down, will you. I'm adding on the time.'

Willie looked the netminder in the eye as he began his run-up. 'Come on, lads!' he roared. 'Charge the kickout! He won't get no distance at all in it!'

And he knew exactly where it was going to drop. Steamed up like an express train, he sprinted, rose to field the ball at full stretch through the forest of swinging fists and soaked up two murderous charges as he passed it to Jimmy. The goalbound shot, however, was hurried and weak, allowing the goalkeeper to smother it and kick it out in the direction of his full-back.

But Willie was still running and he dived like a madman to intercept the clearance. As the entire Ballylanders defence jumped on top of him, the ball dribbled loose for Ned to tap it into the empty net.

'He threw the ball, ref!' screamed the outraged full-back.

'He was in the square!' squealed the incandescent goalie.

'It never crossed the line!' wailed the smouldering corner-back.

'Are you blind as well as crooked, you black bastard?' raved their trainer.

Having already survived one barrage on his authority, the referee had steeled himself to resist a second. 'The goal stands,' he intoned as he brought his whistle solemnly to his lips. 'The game's over.'

Down behind the goalposts, Ned taunted the opposition supporters as the RIC tried to beat back their assault on the fencing.

'Come on, boys!' came a roar from behind him. 'We'll win the fight as well.' Like a herd of buffalo, the Shanagolden crowd charged down the field from the opposite end.

The fencing collapsed and the Ballylanders following poured over the wall to meet them. 'No, make for the peelers!' shouted their leader. 'Make them pay for all the poor people they murdered up in Bachelor's Walk.'

'And the stills they raided on us last week!'

'Come on, Shanagolden!'

'Come on, the Bally boys!'

'Get back to yer barracks, ye cowardly bastards!'

The two sets of supporters merged and wheeled sharply to the left to chase after the policemen now beating a hasty retreat. Some of the Shanagolden faithful made for the goalposts and began to dismantle them as souvenirs. Others surrounded the players and hoisted them up on their shoulders. The Martyrs of Erin assembled for an impromptu rendition of a victory salute.

''Tis a good job you lined them out the way I told you to, Mr. Madden.' Flint wagged his finger at Birdie who was staring at the sky in disbelief as another group of supporters rushed over to congratulate him. Beside him, Drug nodded enigmatically and kept a tight grip on his basket of bottles.

'God damn it!' mouthed Hennessy behind them. 'Oh, I beg your pardon, Canon.'

Horgan, Canon Murphy and Doctor Molyneaux were lost for words but the Councillor quickly recovered his composure.

'A great day for the people of Shanagolden, Madden,' he remarked as he passed by Birdie, still gawking like a lovestruck cow but now with tears streaming from his eyes. 'A lucky win, maybe. But then again, we've always known that we've the best footballers in the county.'

He continued on to slide his way into the cavity in the centre of the crowd where Ned was dismounting to accept the cup from the county board chairman. And before the captain could lay his hands on the trophy, Hennessy grabbed one of the handles, dropped his arm on Ned's shoulders and the pair of them raised it aloft to the cheers and backslaps of the supporters, the flash of John Joe Snaps's camera and the mutilated notes of a wandering fife and drum band.

4

SOMEWHERE ALONG the journey home, the Martyrs of Erin got off the train to take part in the Pattern Day celebrations of the parish that they happened to be passing through and invited the team to follow them. As a result, the cup never made it home at all that night although, by the time the players and supporters staggered into Shanagolden well into the following afternoon, it had already been filled up and drained many times over.

'We've been saving this one till last,' the bandleader intimated to Ned with a conspiratorial wink. 'Although I'm afeared the sound mightn't be quite right. Our triangle was robbed from us last night and bad cess to the low scoundrel that done it.'

He straightened the tunic of his uniform, fingered down the ends of his moustache and steered a stray wisp of hair under his cap. 'But be that as it may, it's my considered opinion that this particular tune is very ... aah, very, very appropriate under the circumstances.'

Newcastlewest's finest whistlers and drummers shuffled themselves into unsteady formation to lead the victorious party and a pair of curious dogs into town along the Foynes road.

'Though my feet are planted in a far-off land,

'There is somewhere they would rather be.

'Sure 'tis planted firmly in the dark brown sand

'Where the Shannon River meets the sea ...' they all sang together and not too badly considering the condition they were in.

The straggle of onlookers joined in; all except Sergeant Stapleton staring stonily at them from his vantage point at the corner of the street. Waving a half-empty bottle of whiskey, Jimmy McCarthy detached himself from the homecoming heroes and stumbled over to the policeman.

'You're looking at men, Stapleton,' he slurred. 'You're looking at real men ...' He paused to belch. 'Not lackeys crawling up the boreen on their hands and knees for the grace and favour of a Saxon king.'

Willie's arm yanked him back into the group before Stapleton could swing his baton into action.

Ahead of them, Jack Noonan's was filled to the rafters as they tumbled through the door. They had to fight their way forward until bleary heads spotted the trophy and the crowd parted like the Red Sea. Ned signalled for quiet before he swaggered up to the counter and planted the big silver cup on top of it.

They waited. He smiled, his eyes darting mischievously to heighten the anticipation.

'Now, fill her up, Jack!' he commanded.

'Come on, Shanagolden!' everyone roared together. 'Now the spuds can be dug up!'

Bottles of whiskey and red lemonade where uncorked with a flourish and poured into the trophy until it was filled to the brim. Before Ned could get his lips around the first sup, Flint had grabbed the handles to tilt a sizeable portion of the contents down his gaping throat.

'Ye took yer time,' remarked Jack. 'Where were ye last night?'

52

'Askeaton … I think,' answered Ned. 'Or was it Cappagh?' He turned to the crowd. 'Can anyone remember?'

The Martyrs of Erin, who might have been able to help him, were too busy trying to detach Flint from the cup.

Jack shouted at Mossy to come behind the bar and give him a hand. 'I suppose ye didn't get a chance to hear the news?' he asked his son as he lifted crates of porter from the floor.

'What news?' Mossy uncorked a dozen bottles and lined them up along the counter.

'They're just after declaring war on Germany.'

More joined in as the celebrations took off, spilling out on the street to lean up against walls with glasses and bottles in their hands. Acquaintances and total strangers hailed each other and slapped each other's backs in congratulation as they drifted in and out of the pubs. Those with less sturdy constitutions slumped to the ground to sleep off the marathon session under the hot summer sun. Like a shoal of piranhas, Flint and the Martyrs of Erin scavenged any drinks left unattended on window ledges. A drunk with a fiddle murdered the air of The Minstrel Boy. Two young fellas amused themselves by firing stones at an empty bottle and daring Sergeant Stapleton to chase them.

While the soil of Europe thumped to the boots of young men marching to war, Shanagolden was toasting its heroes.

Surrounded by well-wishers and descending into the irritable zone between sobriety and tiredness, Willie just wanted to get away from all the gladhanders for a few moments on his own and absently accepted the handshakes, the digs in the shoulder and the arms of embrace. Towering over his retinue, he scanned the crowd and spotted Josie in the distance.

Two of those around him began to argue.

'I'm telling you, Dick Mullane got that last point before half-time,' mumbled one.

'Would you ever you get out of it,' slurred the other. ''Twas Ned Reidy that scored it.'

'Are you saying I'm a liar?'

'At least I got to the match. You never left the pub.'

As the debaters squared unsteadily up to each other, Willie took the opportunity to peel away. But before he could get near Josie, James Horgan had crossed his path.

'Where were you this morning, Hartnett?' demanded the creamery manager.

'I was told I could take the day off if we won.'

'Well, it didn't come through me. And you can tell that to Mullane and McCarthy as well. The three of ye report to my office in the morning.'

Willie balled his fists as he faced off Horgan but his boss, despite conceding six inches in height and years in conditioning, stood his ground with the arrogant certainty of his position. Moments of taunting tension broke only when Josie came between them and edged Willie aside by the arm.

'They're singing your praises today, Willie Hartnett,' she whispered

'Not everyone is,' he replied, his furious gaze still directed over his shoulder.

'Well, they should be. Even my father says you were man of the match. Even better than Ned.'

'Hartnett!' shouted Horgan after them.

'He might tell that to Horgan,' Willie told her.

'Indeed he should,' she answered. 'Isn't he on the co-op committee.'

'We're waiting for you down at the creamery,' repeated the manager.

Willie turned around to face him. 'I don't think the committee will be too pleased with what you're saying, Mr. Horgan ... Sir.'

'Is that what you think?' Horgan leered back. 'Well, let me put you right about a few things ... ah, with your permission of course, Mr. High and Mighty William Hartnett.' He folded his arms as he sucked in the air. 'You might think you're a big hero because of a game of football. Well, I've got news for you, you young pup. You're nothing more than a hired hand. The committee of this co-operative is made up of men of property and standing. You're not one of them and you never will be.'

A small crowd had gathered and pressed in on the confrontation.

'Would you ever go to hell, Horgan!' snarled one belligerent supporter.

'Yeah. Go on off back to your creamery, you sour old bollox, you!' added his companion.

Sensing the mood of the swelling mass of observers, Horgan edged away but still managed a parting smirk just to let Willie know that he'd put him in his place.

'Don't be troubling yourself over Horgan.' Josie restrained Willie's angry arms. 'There's nothing as bitter as an eldest son that's been passed over for the farm.'

Much as it went against the grain, he allowed himself to be led away. If she hadn't been around, he might have swung the fist and smashed the vindictive satisfaction smeared over his manager's jaw. But then he'd be out of a job and he'd be lucky to get another one within twenty miles no matter how much of a hero he might be.

They had it tied up every way he could think of. And they loved nothing better than flaunting in public how much they had everyone under their control. Anyone who didn't have the means to ignore them either toed the line or got out.

But Willie Hartnett was going nowhere. He was damned if he'd let them get the better of him.

Josie got home ahead of her father who had been out all day looking at a holding that had just come on the market and she had the supper prepared just as he arrived in the door. It didn't please him that she'd taken up housework and he'd insisted that he'd more than enough money to employ a maid as well as a housekeeper. But she would hear nothing of it. Since she'd come home after finishing secondary school, she wanted to find out for herself where her practical talents lay. The house and the farm were challenges to be tackled rather than mysteries to be taken care of by hired help and, after six years of listening to the nuns and the teachers going on about every ladylike pursuit from arranging flowers to managing servants, she craved for active participation in something that mattered.

After only two days, Edmund Reidy was won over. Not only could his daughter cook far better than any housekeeper that he'd ever employed but she also had an eye for the appearance and the upkeep of the property that only his late wife had possessed. And the more he watched her turn the rough and ready dwelling into a home of comfort rather than of subsistence, the more he was reminded of the few short years of real happiness in his life.

Land had obsessed him from the moment he was sent out to the fields by his father. Born just before the Great Famine in a mean cottage on a tiny tenant farm, he had survived the devastation that mass starvation, fever and emigration had wreaked on the countryside of the 1840s. And very early on, he got to understand where the problem of rural Ireland lay. Generations of subdivision had reduced most holdings down to a field or two which were exhaustively planted with the rent-paying wheat and oats that settled the gambling debts of wasters living in London. All they had left for themselves was a miniscule plot of potatoes on which to feed an entire family for the year.

But where others saw nothing but despair, he could see opportunity. As families died out, ran out of hope after each subsequent failure of the potato harvest or were hunted out by the new economics of cheap corn flooding in from America, he urged his father to take on any acreage that came on the market. And when he availed of the first land purchase scheme offered by the British Government, he worked night and day to squeeze the last out of what he now possessed as of right and move from precarious subsistence to commercial agriculture.

It was only after the agitiation had quietened down and the emerging class of freeholders had organised themselves into co-operative societies to process their milk and sell them implements and seed at a fair price, that he got a chance to look at the world beyond the daily slog of the farm. For the first time in his life, he had cash to spare, but there was nothing inside the four empty walls on which to spend it.

Hannah was thirty years younger than he when he saw her behind the counter of a drapery in Newcastlewest, her dainty hands fingering the linen shirts he was about to buy with his first dividend from the co-op. Within minutes, she had convinced him to splash out on a wardrobe of clothes and had found a flower to stick into the lapel of his suit.

Within a week she was sure and he was sure and, with the offer of a tidy consideration, so were her father and mother.

He had the cottage extended into a real house by the time Ned arrived inside a year, and built a proper farmyard with decent outbuildings that a son and heir could take over when the time came. He had a lawn planted outside the front door and flowers in beds along its edges and a macadam base put under the

57

avenue and cut stone pillars erected at the gate to await Hannah's return from her mother's house in Newcastlewest after giving birth to Josie.

But she never came home. 'It happens once in a while and we don't always know why,' the doctor had told him when he turned up just a few minutes late. 'Sometimes God comes calling.'

He didn't even get the chance to say goodbye.

The heart that had taken almost fifty years to open up, immediately closed in on itself again. Mrs. Hartnett took in Ned and Josie to mind them during the day while Edmund Reidy lost himself once more in the running of his farm. Pennies that had been lodged in the bank were now poured back into the ditches, the drains and the fertilisers for lush green grass to grow on fields that once had held nothing but bullrushes and memories of the departed. Listening to the advice of the instructors brought in by the co-op, he built up his herd of Shorthorns with selective breeding and took to rearing pigs on the skim coming back from the creamery. And any time time a patch of land became available, he was the first punter into the ring with a bid.

It was only when the years started to catch up on his joints that he paused to take stock. Ned had come home by then, after finishing his education and joined him on the farm. Even though he still was a fit man for his age, Reidy was glad of the help and even more so for the company of another mind that might share his view of what the property was capable of producing if the proper work was put into it. For a man who'd come from the margins of poverty, the forty-three acres of rich dry land were the testament to what his life had achieved.

And loath as he was to admit it, he also welcomed the new softness inside the house. The comfort that Josie's presence brought was seductive. But even so, she should have been doing better; like finding herself a man to improve her station. She had the looks, she had the backgroured, she had the knack with the housework and the guarantee of a serious dowry to reel in any young buck in the county. But she'd want to be quick about it too, now that this war had broken out and would be drawing men away to battle with the prospect of glory.

He closed the minutes book of the Shanagolden Co-operative Society. While the position of secretary was honorary, it was also an indication of standing. The farmers of the parish looked up to Edmund Reidy as an example of what hard work and faith in the co-op could bring.

'If this war goes on for a while, we might get another farthing on the gallon for the milk,' he told his son sitting across the table from him. Having dozed off for a few hours earlier on in a haybarn, Ned was enjoying a second wind of sobriety.

'You wouldn't by any chance be thinking of enlisting?' continued the father as he pushed the book aside. 'I hear they're already looking for recruits.'

'God, no.' Ned sucked in the double strength tea that Josie had brewed for him. 'I've no intention of going off to Belgium to get my head shot off.'

'Good, good. You'll be wanted here on the farm. There'll be no labourers to be got once the troopships start sailing.' Reidy rose from the table, grabbed his coat and his cap and stuck his pipe, knife and plug of tobacco in his pocket. 'I'm off to bed. Clean up after me, Josie.'

As her father left the room, Josie filled a cup for herself and sat down across from her brother. 'You should get on to Father about Horgan. He'd no right to be going on like the way he did today.'

'I'll have a word.' Ned poured himself a refill. 'You'd better be careful yourself, too.'

'What do you mean?'

'People talk.' He brought the cup to his lips and looked away over her shoulder. 'You were seen with your arms around a man in the middle of the street in broad daylight.'

'I don't believe it!' She banged her cup off the table. 'My God, Ned, you're as bad as the rest of them. And Willie your best friend.'

'It's nothing at all to do with me, sister.' He drained what was left of the tea. 'It's what your father is thinking. He wants a good catch for you. And in his mind, that's going to be something more substantial than a labouring man.'

Back in the town, stamina had wilted and the party had finally ground to a halt. The last stragglers reluctantly emptied from the pubs to venture out into the darkness of the night. Some stopped to gather their bearings, some steadied themselves for the journey that lay ahead before decidng that weren't yet quite up to it, some took to engaging in futile half-hearted mumbling but most of them staggered their way home along the glass-strewn street.

A woman opened her window and pleaded in vain to let her children get their night's sleep. Two doors up, another woman screamed as her husband used his fists on her to relieve his frustration. A cat shot out from a laneway.

Separating the comatose from the inanimate, Stapleton tapped his baton off any stray bundle lying on the ground. One groaned, stirred and half-sat up clutching a kneecap. With a swift flourish of the hand, the seargeant whipped the drunk to his feet and marched him in the direction of the barracks.

Dick Mullane and Patie Fitzgibbon had the sense to lean up against the wall of Patie's father's cottage. More tired than drunk as the effects of a sustained day's drinking wore off, they looked up to the stars with their hands in their pockets, each lost in a private tangle of thoughts of his own.

'I'm finished with the creamery,' stated Dick.

'You'll calm down in the morning.'

'No, I'm serious this time.' He kicked a broken bottle out into the middle of the street. 'No one in his right mind should have to put up with Horgan.'

'Don't be stupid, Dick,' answered Patie. 'It's a steady job and there aren't too many of them around here. And it pays way better than labouring on the farms or on the roads.'

'Fair dues to ye, lads.' They acknowledged the slurred praise of the unseen passer-by with a nod of the head. 'Ye're the finest bunch of lads that ever came out of Shanagolden.'

'The finest bunch of lads?' Dick repeated once the drunk had passed by. 'The finest bunch of lads, who get walked on like shite by a hoor like Horgan?' He found another broken bottle to let fly at. 'No. It's time I got out of here. I've won my medal and there's nothing left to keep me hanging around'.

The glass shattered off a door across the road. 'Do you know something, Patie? You'll never be your own man if you stay around in a place like this.' The mother of the squawking infant again demanded silence. 'Anyway, I've been saving up for my passage ever since I started drawing a wage.'

'It won't be much use to you now,' answered Patie. 'There won't be any ships going to America now that there's a war going on.'

'I don't care, Patie. I'm on my way out. And if it isn't to Chicago, it'll be to somewhere else.'

5

THEY WERE left shorthanded. Dick Mullane, who had never missed a day's work in his life up to then, failed to show up at the creamery the following morning and there was no sign either of Patie Fitzgibbon who was the first man they called in for relief. Willie Hartnett was left to unload the carts as well as tip the churns over into the baths while Jimmy McCarthy gave the suppliers back the skim. With many deliveries having been missed the morning before as the victory celebrations had edged into to the dawn, the volume was far higher than normal and they were under pressure from the moment they started.

To make matters worse, the assistant manager had insisted on sampling the deliveries. Some of the milk could have been up to three days old and it had been the hottest weekend of the year. Hungover farmers grumbled as the queue lengthened. A few abandoned their carts in the queue as they walked up the town and banged on Jack Noonan's door in search of a cure.

Horgan ambled in when they were at their busiest, stood at the back of the landing and waited for the most opportune moment to dress Willie down in public. But before he could do so, his smirking assistant told him that a delegation from the committee was looking for him.

'And I hope they keep the ould hoor busy for the rest of the morning,' the assistant muttered as he added a final pound slab to the balance scales and scratched the weight into his book.

Up at the top of the yard, Willie could see the creamery manager leading Edmund Reidy and three others into his office. This wasn't going to be a friendly discussion. Despite the heat already descending, the members of the delegation were all wearing their bowler hats and their Sunday suits.

Much to the assistant's disgust, the committee men re-emerged after only a few minutes. 'Couldn't the meeting have gone on a bit longer?' he complained as he watched them untie their ponies and climb into their traps.

Some time later, Horgan re-appeared and they braced themselves for yet another tirade of petty tyranny. But apart from scowling at Willie, he never came near them and, after a cursory glance over his empire, he locked the door of his office and was gone for the day.

The numbers were winding down when Ned took his turn at the landing.

'Ease back, will you. You're miles off the line.' Willie directed the cart level with the landing. 'Back another few inches ... I saw your father coming in at the head of the committee earlier on. You didn't have a word with him, by any chance?'

'I might have said something last night.' Ned jumped onto the landing to give Willie a hand. 'Horgan was way out of order yesterday.'

'Is that what the delegation was about?' asked the assistant.

'None of your business.' Ned tossed him his delivery book. 'Stick to your figures and make sure you don't leave me short.'

'Nosey hoor!' Jimmy called from the other side of the building.

'Jesus, will ye hurry up!' shouted the next cart in line. 'I haven't all day to be waiting.'

'I'd be a lot faster if you hadn't insisted on filling me with porter all night,' answered Ned.

'A hundred and eighty-six,' called the assistant.

'Check.' Willie lifted the empty churn upright and rolled it back on the cart before taking the next full one from Ned. 'No sign of Dick this morning.'

'I heard he went down to Foynes to enlist.'

'Who?' The assistnant's ears pricked up again.

'Would you ever keep your nose out of what doesn't concern you!' exploded Ned before wheeling off a hot churn of the morning's milking. 'And from what the lads waiting outside Jack's were saying, Patie Fitzgibbon and Johnny O'Brien have gone along with him.'

'A hundred and ninety-three. That one must have been right full.'

'Check ... A few weeks ago, we were all going to die for Ireland.' Willie chalked the weight on the side of the empty. 'Now we can't wait to spill our blood for the British Empire that's supposed to be doing us down.'

The rarely-used packet store beside Foynes railway station had been hastily taken over as a recruitment centre and a squad of Royal Munster Fusiliers regulars had come down on the early train from their depot in Limerick to set it up. Pride of place went to a crudely painted sign over the door of a silhouetted British squaddie swinging his bayonetted rifle at a head wearing a spiked pickelhaube helmet and exhorted those reading it to 'Fight the Kaiser! Fight for the Empire!'

As a steady straggle dribbled into the port from all over West Limerick, an RIC detail directed them into the line snaking back up the main street to wait for their turn to be processed. The numbers surprised District Inspector Sullivan who had expected a few days of wait-and-see before the more enthusiastic would answer the call. But this lot needed no special urging. Mountainy men from the badlands to the west, labouring sons from the big farms to the south and corner boys from the laneways of the towns mixed with a sprinkling of the well-off and of the habitually loyal upholding their allegiance to the Great British Empire.

Indeed, some of those now queueing at the sorting table outside the centre were already well known to the Inspector for their political activity. He spotted one sworn member of Irish Republican Brotherhood taking his place and there were at least two others ahead of him whom he strongly suspected of active involvement. And then there were acquaintances of a more mundane disposition like sheep stealers, poitín distillers, poachers and petty thieves.

If he had followed the rulebook, he should have gone over to the captain and informed him of their pasts. But this was a heaven-sent opportunity. Whatever their motives, many of Sullivan's regular customers had decided to accept the King's shilling and no way was he going to discourage them. As far as the District Inspector was concerned, the more that joined up, the merrier. The appeal for recruits would drain the excess of young males from districts that hadn't the means to support them and, if they were off fighting the Germans in Belgium, they wouldn't be hanging around his patch to cause trouble.

At the sorting table, the captain, an English career officer on secondment to the Munsters after his health had broken down out in India, questioned each arrival to weed out those with no chance of reaching the basic requirments. The sergeant sitting beside him recording the details had recommended engaging Councillor Thomas Hennessy to aid them with his knowledge of the local population.

A tongue-tied recruit approached them.

'Name?' clipped the captain.

'Aah ... aah, Neville, sir.'

Hennessy bent over the officer's ear. 'Teddy Neville, captain,' he whispered. 'That'd be Timothy, sergeant ... He comes from good people, I can vouch for that. His father labours on Lord Kenry's estate.'

The sergeant wrote the name down in the ledger and gave the recruit a slip of paper to bring in with him to the centre.

'Rather rough-looking chap.' The captain glanced over the ragged, rough-hewn bloodshot figure stinking of stale beer and with a three-day stubble on his chin. 'Know him?'

'Yerra, I wouldn't take any notice of that,' muttered Hennessy. 'He's only a bit the worse for the drink. They were celebrating up in Shanagolden last night ... And maybe it's all for the best,' he winked. 'Better you sign him up now before he sobers up and changes his mind.'

He stepped forward to grab the recruit by the hand. 'A wise move, Neilly. Travel and adventure and a chance to stop those pagan Huns from murdering all the poor Catholics in poor little Belgium ... Ah, that'd be Cornelius Woulfe, sergeant. W-O-U-L-F-E.'

'All right, Woulfe,' beamed the captain. 'Step along ... Next!'

Patie had been sitting on a gravestone when Dick came down the main street and turned at the crossroads towards Foynes road instead of continuing straight on to the creamery. He paused for a moment, looked across at the graveyard, blessed himself and followed his mate. Halfway along the road at Robertstown Cross, they heard the hurrying footsteps behind their backs as Johnny O'Brien, just turned seventeen and the youngest player on the football team, caught up with them.

Lost in their own thoughts, hardly a word was spoken during the four-mile walk and it was only when they saw the queue outside the recruitment centre that their tongues loosened.

'Are you sure we're doing the right thing?' asked Johnny.

'You'd be better off going home if you're not sure about it,' Dick advised him.

'I couldn't turn round on my own. Wouldn't the whole town be out watching me?'

Dick took his place in the line, Patie followed him and, after seeing another group approaching along the coast road from the Loughill direction, Johnny joined them as well. 'But I'd go home if you were going home too.'

Dick looked straight ahead to where Hennessy, in a display of his own importance, was flitting between the military men, the RIC District Inspector, the stationmaster and the recruits signing their lives away.

'Are you definitely signing up?' continued Johnny.

'Nothing surer.'

'Why's that?'

'Because I want to get out of this place more than anything else in the world.'

Patie snapped out of his daydream. 'Is that just because of Horgan?'

'It's not just because of Horgan,' answered Dick. 'It's because of the whole bloody lot of them.' He spat on the ground. 'Two days ago, we brought more honour to Shanagolden than anyone ever done before. But to them that'll be boasting about it for the next twenty years ...' He pointed to Hennessy down at the sorting table. '... Like him, like Horgan, like the Canon and the Doctor and all the rest of them, we're only shit to be walked on and we'll never be anything else. I'm getting out of here and I don't care if I've to kill the Kaiser of Germany himself to do so.'

The man behind him tapped him on the back. 'Well said, my friend. That's what has the lot of us here.'

Every time a hand reached out to grasp the slip of paper from the sergeant's fingers, destiny inched closer and Patie's wonder at where he was going increased. But while some like Johnny agonised out loud and others buried their apprehension in their fighting words, he just nodded, smiled, exchanged the odd pleasantry and let nothing away.

It would have been much easier if they had signed themselves away the minute they had arrived; if they had been led away to whatever lay ahead before they had time to think about it. He had decided himself to head down to the port without any premeditation, rising early to be where he was certain Dick would be passing by at the crack of dawn. Having hung around together since childhood, both of them knew that wherever one of them led, the other more than likely would come after him in support.

And as was the case more often than not, it was Patie who had followed. The two of them might have shared similar views on most things but, if it was left to himself, he'd let whatever was bothering him pass him by and, in time, he'd get used to it. But Dick, even if he wasn't big into words, would smoulder with resentment and then burst into action.

'You don't have to come with me,' Dick was telling him. 'You could take Johnny home with you. He shouldn't be here at all.'

'There's nothing to go back to, Dick. Not after you decide to walk out.'

Like most of his generation, Patie had felt the pressures of the Shanagolden that he'd just waved goodbye to. Maybe the schoolmaster was to blame. Stubbornly refusing to accept that education was wasted on those who weren't born to its benefits, the teacher had widened their eyes and, before he had succumbed to the disillusionment of the bottle, had pushed them down a road where they'd developed a respect for the value of knowledge. A generation of youngsters had passed out of his school knowing that they'd been given tools that their parents would never have dreamed of. But if they were ever to make any use of them, they knew that they'd have to leave Shanagolden, leave Limerick and leave Ireland.

For years, most were rearing to go without a moment's thought and all that held them back was the wait for the relation or the friend or the prospective employer to send on the dollars for the passage. And when they got to Chicago or New York, many of them were said to have done well for themselves, making the kind of money that only the gentry could think of at home. Every Christmas, the remittances would come back across the Atlantic, the telegraphed orders that would pay for the clothing and the ware and, if there was anything left over after the necessities were taken care of, might even be invested in a bicycle.

'You're coming home this minute, James Guiney!' The woman burst through the queue to haul the gangly youth off by the ear. Embarrassed by her presence, the rest of them looked the other way.

'He's only fourteen,' she shouted at the table. 'Ye can wait another few years before ye kill him.'

Once she was out earshot, they all began to laugh, warding off any pangs of embarrassment or doubt.

'Dragged away by his mother,' snorted Johnny. 'He'll never live that down, the stupid young fella.'

Mad to get out, though Patie to himself, the same as the rest of them but now he might never get the chance. The young fella's head could have been filled with tales of the wide world beyond

70

the borders of the parish, just like Patie's had been when Jack Noonan had turned up unannounced in Shanagolden twenty-five years after leaving a mud cabin without two pennies to rub together. It wasn't just the wallet full of dollars that had stood out, it was the clothes and the confident swagger and the soul that had been liberated by exile. And the whole gang of young lads were even more impressed when Jack had outbid Thomas Hennessy to buy out the Widow Liston's business, leaving her with enough to purchase a hotel in Ballybunion where she could keep her young stud of a chef in a manner that would keep his eye from wandering.

Spellbound by his cheek, they'd listened to Jack when he said that anyone could make it, even in the emigration-bled hills of West Limerick, if he'd enough faith in himself to keep at it. So when he took over the football club and put his dry cash into the pursuit of a county title, they were more than half-inlclined to go along for the ride. And they'd believed in Jack long enough to deliver the first moments of glory to the town.

But once the cup was drained and the party had ended, they were all back to where they had started from. Maybe Patie would have put up with it knowing that the medal on the mantelpiece was proof of what they had achieved but that never would have been enough for Dick. And when he'd spilled it out in drunken candour at the end of a night of celebration, Patie knew that his best mate had exposed the futility of hoping that the world was about to change.

The muttering around him died away again, as the sun's summer climb beat down on the queue. Sleep was catching up on those who had hardly touched the bed after two days of carousing and they searched for something to lean against, while they waitied for the painstaking processing to run its course.

Suspended by the midday heat between real time and dreamland, Patie watched the heads at the table mutter and nod and exchange glances as each new prospect arrived at the table and imagined what might be passing between them.

He felt like a bullock being sized up at a fair. Hennessy, all action and handshakes, was assuring the two Army men of the pedigree of the beast. The sergeant smirked away to himself as if he was on to something that the rest of them had yet to find out about. The captain squinted over the sergeant's shoulder every few minutes to run his eyes over the ledger and smiled at its lengthening entries. Only the RIC Inspector who'd once been the station sergeant in Shanagolden remained a mystery, his impassive face breaking only for one brief instant when a dart of contempt darkened his features.

'Name?'

Patie jerked awake.

'Name?' repeated the captain.

'Patie Fitzgibbon,' Hennessy answered for him. 'That'd be Patrick Fitzgibbon, sergeant.'

He stepped forward to the Army's embrace, to be grabbed by the Councillor's hungry hand, to be entered by the sergeant's efficient pen, to be totted up by the captain's eager eye.

The evening was drawing in by the time the last arrival at the recruitment centre had been certified as capable of walking unaided, answering his name and identifying his left hand from his right. The captain nodded to the sergeant who, in turn, looked expectantly at Hennessy.

'Ah, Inspector. Would your men be so good as to remove the sign and take the tables back inside the station.'

Sullivan ignored the mixture of arrogance, plámás and cringing wheeled into the Councillor's request. He was damned

72

if he'd clear off so that the three amigos could have a bit of privacy while they shared out their commission.

'Ah, Inspector,' repeated Hennessy, anxious to impress his new friends in the military more than his old ones in the police. 'I think the stationmaster wants his board back. We promised him we'd only need it for the day.'

They waited. The District Inspector stood his ground. The RIC detail hung around to witness the stand-off.

The captain's patience was the first to crack. Taking the book from the sergeant, he moved over to the entrance to the station where the light was better and totted up the names in the columns. Not to be parted from his sacred volume, the penpusher immediately followed him.

'I'll be damned! Over the hundred. HQ will be pleased.'

'One hundred and twelve,' corrected the sergeant.

'West Limerick will never let the Army down in its hour of need,' Hennessy assured them.

'Almost too good,' replied the officer. 'Fact is, if we get the same response in Limerick city and in the other recruitment centres, we may have a problem. The Munsters haven't enough officers and NCOs to whip them into shape.'

The Councillor winced at the prospect of losing some of his recruitment bounty through circumstances beyond his control, especially as he had to give the sergeant his cut.

'I suppose you find it difficult to trust locals as officers?' asked Sullivan. The captain looked blankly at him, the sergeant hid a snigger and Hennessy didn't bother to conceal a scowl. 'It should be much easier up in Ulster. They have a far better understanding of the value of loyalty.'

'Quite, quite,' harrumphed the captain. 'Of course, we could always suggest to a number of them that they might consider enlisting in an English regiment,' he continued, as the interest

73

flickered in Hennessy's small eyes. 'I am led to believe that my old chums in the West Sussex take a rather liberal view regarding the expenses incurred in recruitment.'

The Councillor edged a finger to his lips.

'Mum's the word.' The captain blinked, nodded and allowed Hennessy to guide him into the stationmaster's office.

Left outside on the steps on his own, Sullivan collected the reinforcements that he had brought down with him on the police tender from Newcastlewest. Even the RIC were returning short to barracks. Earlier in the day, two of his own men had transferred their allegiance to the Army on the spur of the moment.

6

SIX WEEKS later, the initial euphoria had passed and the eager had already signed up. As the warm fervour of summer passed the equinox and dissipated into the cool winds of autumn, those remaining held a more cautious view. Discouraged by employers and fathers, the young men stayed on the farms and in the factories and in the creameries as demand grew for the countryside's produce.

Generals on the battlefield screamed for more bodies to stop the German advance. Recruiting agents were pressed to fill the gap but it needed a push from the top to reignite the momentum. While the Unionists of Ulster had enlisted almost en bloc as the UVF was transformed into the newly-created 36th (Ulster) Division together with its own officers and command structure, the response from Nationalist Ireland was slower. All eyes turned on the Volunteers, still assembling and drilling and marching and holding their rallies, but lacking clear direction from above.

John Redmond, leader of the Irish Parliamentary Party and commander of the force, was in no doubt about which way they should turn. Colleagues with an ear closer to the ground like John Dillon, Joe Devlin and TP O'Connor had warned about the ill-feeling generated by the killings in Bachelor's Walk and had advised him to use the situation to lever Home Rule on more favourable terms from the British Government. But Redmond had already been swept away by the drumbeats and pledged the Party's unconditional support on the August Bank Holiday Monday when war was declared in the House of Commons. If Unionism could leap to Britain's defence, he reasoned to his critics, Nationalism's failure to respond in kind might never be forgotten.

Belgium, poor defenceless little Belgium, became the selling point. While most of Redmond's supporters had never even heard of the kingdom until then, they were now bombarded with lurid details of the rape, plunder and pillage inflicted on brave fellow-Catholics by the Kaiser's heathen Huns.

But calls for support, for Nationalist and Unionist to unite in the defence of the homeland and then sort out their differences once the peril had passed, failed to deliver enough troops. Although the founders of the Volunteers had been swamped by the influx of Home Rulers when the Parliamentary Party took over, they still retained positions of influence. So while Redmond and his following were trying to move the force into outright participation in the British Army on the lines of the UVF, others like Patrick Pearse, Seán Mac Diarmada and Eoin Mac Néill fought to keep it focussed on its original aim of defending Irish interests.

As the machinations continued behind the scenes, the first wave of recruits set out on the road to war. In Limerick railway station, the nervous, the swaggering, the bewildered and those just keeping their heads down picked up their kit bags and marched down the platform towards the troop train for Rosslare. With their scalps shorn to the regulation short-back-and-sides, their skin deloused and disinfected and kitted out to a man in the same ill-fitting uniforms, individuality of appearance had been lost as they retreated into the pink scrubbed smoothness of small boys.

The regimental band was there to see them off on the first leg of their journey. So too were the top brass from the barracks, the bewhiskered worthies of the establishment, the recruiting agents making sure that their produce had been delivered, the friends, relations and sweethearts waving goodbye, and the curious drawn in by the razzmatazz of the occasion.

Above the martial music and the cheering commotion, bunting in the imperial colours of red, white and blue hung from the girders of the roof, a banner proclaimed long life to His Majesty and death to the Kaiser, and Union Jacks fluttered in the draughts created by the engine as it built up a head of steam. With the whistles of the train and of the NCOs ringing in their ears, the passengers clambered aboard, loaded their bags on the luggage racks or stuffed them in between the unforgiving pine benches and rushed to the windows for what might be their last look of the only life they'd ever known.

The more fortunate leaned out and, ignoring the wisps of white steam and the sulphur-tinged belches of black coal smoke, reached out to clasp the hands of some that they knew and some that they didn't. The carriage shook, the handshakes became waves, the music grew fainter and the crowd, the platform and then the station itself faded behind them. As they pulled past the laneways backing onto Carey's Road, under the bridge on the Roxborough Road, past the engine shops of the Great Southern Railway, the asylum and the graveyard, and headed out of the city into a countyside on the brink of turning brown, an unscripted moment of silence descended, as they thought about where they were going.

It lasted until the squeal of the brakes halted them at the signals of Killonan Junction. Someone asked where they were, a babble of opinions responded and, as conversation resumed, hands reached into pockets for pipes or cigarettes, knives sliced up plug, palms rolled the flake into balls, thumbs tamped the tobacco into bowls, matches flashed, bowls glowed cherry red to deep draughts of breath and the tight confined air was flooded with smoke.

They mumbled to each other to pass on the matchboxes, recognised acquaintances and tried to figure out strangers. Down in the corner of the carriage, a mouth organ appeared and they all picked up on the tune after the first few notes.

'Daisy, Daisy, give me your answer, do.

'I'm half crazy all for the love of you.

'It won't be a stylish marriage,

'I can't afford a carriage ...,' they sang as arms linked across each other's shoulders and they swayed to the beat.

'We should be seeing a bit of action soon.' A recruit dug Patie Fitzgibbon in the ribs. 'I can't wait to start firing at them Germans.'

'It'll be a change,' he answered.

'It will, to be sure. Anything would be better than waiting for the call down at the docks every morning.'

A deck of cards emerged from a pocket and the aisle cleared to make way for a game. 'Hey, any of you country boys know how to play 45?' asked the owner of the pack as he turned his kitbag over on the floor and smoothed it out to fashion a makeshift table.

'It's like 41 only they get five for the big trump,' Dick Mullane explained to Johnny O'Brien. Pulling pennies from their pockets, they took their places in the nine-hand rubber.

Patie declined the offer and joined a group of observers standing on the vacated seats to get a better view of the cards below them. 'Ye're not regulars, are ye?' asked the man beside him. In their late twenties and early thirties, he and the group of companions around him were up to ten years older than most of the others in the carriage.

'No. We only signed up a few weeks ago.'

'We'd no choice in the matter.' Like the majority of the passengers, the voice carried the flat vowels and the hard consonants of the city. 'We were called up.' Having previously served in the Army, reservists were in immediate demand because they had already been trained. 'Where are they sending ye?'

'Aldershot.' Like everyone else who had been approached in the recruitment centre in Foynes, Patie reckoned that Hennessy was on to some fiddle when he suggested that they might be better off signing up in England. However, not having any strong views on the matter, he allowed himself to be swayed by the promise of a few days leave in Brighton when they landed. 'We're being transferred to an English regiment. The West Sussex Rifles. After that, I think they were talking about shipping us all out to Flanders.'

'We're going to Colchester first. After that, God alone knows.'

Overhearing the discussion, the recruits on Patie's other side turned their heads from the cards and joined in the discussion.

'They're breaking us up,' said one. 'That's what they're doing.'

'The English don't want too many Irish Nationalists in the one division,' added another. 'We might get ideas of our own.'

'Not like the Unionists,' pointed out a third. 'They can have their own officers and do what they like.'

'Would ye ever stop complaining,' challenged a fourth. 'We'll be home by Christmas and 'twill all be forgotten about.'

And Patie withdrew his attentions to watch the sour fields of the Mulkear flood plain speed past the window. They all had their theories about how they were being treated, the Volunteers with their conspiracies, the Unionists with their belief in the rightness of Britain, the radicals with their suspicions of anyone of rank, the part-time Territorials with their enthusiasm to be seen as regular soldiers at last and the reservists with their phlegmatic acceptance of authority. Ever since the moment he had joined up, his ears had been reddened with every side of the argument and he didn't want to hear any more. The first thing the Army had taught him was that thinking was a waste of time. The whens, the wheres and the whys of what they were doing were decided by someone they'd never see nor ever understand and there was nothing in the world that they could do about it.

Just behind the card players, an argument spilled out into the aisle. Insults rang out, threats were issued, fists were raised and, after a moment's hesitation, they were swung at each other. Onlookers jumped down from the benches to join in.

'Fighting mad already,' said the reservist beside Patie. 'They can't even wait until they get to the front.'

'They'll soon see enough of it,' he answered.

'We all will.' Down on the floor, cards were sent flyng as a combatant tumbled over the dealer. 'Are we doing the right thing?'

Patie shook his head. 'I don't want to know.'

'Neither do I.' A sergeant-major looked in from the next carriage, shrugged his shoulders and decided that it might be better to leave them at it. 'But it's too late now to turn back.'

Travelling back to Dublin after gauging the level of support in Munster for the founders' side of the argument, Patrick Pearse stopped for the night in Shanagolden. Ned, Willie and Jimmy were there to greet him in the Reidy cowshed.

'A fair few lads from these parts have enlisted already,' Ned was telling him over the lamplight. 'Even one of our own, Dick Mullane.'

'The damn turncoat.' Jimmy spat on the ground. 'I never though he'd be the one to take the shilling.'

'Easy on, Jimmy.' They had been over the same ground countless times since the war began. 'Dick has his own problems.'

'He let us down. And what's more, he knew Patie Fitzgibbon would follow him.'

'Ah, forget about it.' Pearse sat down on the upturned crate. 'Are there many more likely to join up, Ned?'

'I'm sure there are. It depends on Redmond.'

'And suppose he gets the promise of Home Rule once the war's over in return for bringing the Volunteers into the British Army. How many of the unit are likely to follow him then?'

'A lot,' answered Ned. 'Even more when they keep going on about the Germans murdering nuns in Belgium.'

'What did England ever care about Belgium?' asked Jimmy.

Leaning up against a stall, Willie knew that these were the same questions everyone was asking of themselves. Half of the country was out marching most Sundays but, with every nation in Europe now aiming guns at its neighbours, there didn't seem to be any purpose to what they were doing. The energy, fuelled by an anger demanding respect, was there but it was crying out for direction.

Those who had left for the front could at least point to what they were fighting for. They were real soldiers now, carrying real guns and wearing real uniforms, not like the pretend ones playing around at home with their sticks and their hurleys and only a green sash tied over the shoulder to let the world know who they were. Anyone wanting the genuine article knew where to find it and, even after the first flush of enthusiasm had spent itself, a steady trickle had continued to flow down to the recruiting centre. If it kept up, there was always the chance that taunts of cowardice would turn it into a flood.

'You're very silent there, Willie.' Pearse rose to join him as Ned and Jimmy continued to bicker over Dick. 'What do you think?'

'It won't make much of a difference around here. Hennessy is signing up anyone he can find.'

'And getting well paid for it too,' added Jimmy.

Picking up Pearse's hint, Willie led Jimmy outside as Ned tossed a few forks of hay to make up a bed for the visitor to sleep on.

'You go on ahead, Jimmy,' he told him under the moonlight of the yard. 'I've something else to attend to.'

'You don't have to tell me.' Jimmy winked before disappearing into the lane. 'Best of luck.'

'Is he gone?' Pearse asked Willie on his return. Seeing the nod, he pulled a bible from his bag and held it out in front of Willie and Ned.

'Would ye be willing to go the whole way?'

Ned nodded immediately. Willie gave a moment's thought to the invitation, wondering whether Pearse too was deluding himself with ritual rather than with action. But as he sized up the Dubliner's unwavering gaze, he could find no pomposity nor self-importance nor any agenda hidden beneath the unspoken determination.

'Yes,' he answered. 'All the way.'

'Then place your right hands on the bible and repeat after me ... In the presence of God, I ...'

'Edmund Reidy ...'

'William Hartnett ...'

'... do solemnly swear the I will do my utmost to establish the independence of Ireland, and that I will bear true allegiance to the Supreme Council of the Irish Republican Brotherhood and the Government of the Irish Republic and implicitly obey the constitution of the Irish Republican Brotherhood and all my superior officers and that I will preserve inviolable the secrets of the organisation.'

They were out marching again the following morning. The sixty-odd members of the Shanagolden unit of the West Limerick Volunteers filed down the main street from the church and came to a halt at the crossroads. Although they could now beat a time with their footsteps and could turn smartly on their heels on command, there was little else to remind the curious public hanging around after Sunday Mass that this was the military force pledged to defend Ireland's interests.

Dressed in his green commandant's outfit, Councillor Hennessy alone had the trappings of a soldier although the short, thin, stooped stature of a hungry small-town shopkeeper hardly did justice to the uniform. Nevertheless, he stood in front of his troops and demanded their attention.

'Ye're all to be here again after next Sunday's Mass.'

'When are we getting our uniforms?' asked Jimmy McCarthy.

'Soon. Soon.'

'There was a collection made nearly two months ago,' continued his interrogator. 'They should be here by now.'

'And there's a battalion rally in Foynes on Sunday week,' resumed the commander, his face twitching with irritation. 'We'll be assembling here at two o'clock before we march down to Robertstown to meet up with the units from Askeaton and Kilcornan.'

'Is the money still there?'

'Unit dismissed! Stand easy!'

'Or has it been robbed?'

Most of the unit remained standing where they were, intrigued as to how far the mutiny might spread from the ranks.

'Fair question, Hennessy,' added an observer leaning up against the public house on the corner as he waited for it to open up. 'Why don't you answer the man?'

'Would you give over, Jimmy,' said Dinny Lyons standing beside the thorn in the commandant's side.

'Where's the money?' shouted Jimmy after the departing Hennessy. 'Maybe 'twas spent on British Army uniforms.'

'Now that's a very serious allegation,' continued the street-corner lawyer. 'At the very least, it deserves an answer.'

'Hi!' Batt Mullane, taller, leaner, younger by a year and not half as smart as his brother Dick, pushed Jimmy on the shoulder and spun him round. 'There's no call for that sort of talk.'

'Why, what's it to you, Batt Mullane. Your brother's already after taking the shilling.'

'You take that back, Jimmy McCarthy. You'll say nothing against any member of my family.'

'I'll say what I want. At least I'm not bringing young fellas over to Flanders to die for the King of England.'

The fist caught Jimmy on the point of the chin but he took it without flinching and lashed one back in return. Two belts later and they were grappling each other on the ground as the crowd leaning up against the wall urged them on.

'Jaysus, do something!' Flint grabbed Willie by the arm. 'They're murdering each other.'

A group of them moved in to break up the fight but, as a few more joined in, Mossy Noonan was knocked to the ground. Willie and Ned lifted him to his feet, turned their backs on the commotion and walked away.

'Some things never change, do they?' Willie shook his head in disgust. 'We always end up fighting each other.'

The latecomers quickly lost interest, pulled back from the action and joined the onlookers in taunting the pair still wrestling with each other.

'Kill him, Batt! He's only a tramp!'

'Stick a head in him, Jimmy!'

'Use the boot, Batt!'

'Lay into him, Jimmy! Give him the hiding he should've got at home!'

'Get a move on!' Sergeant Stapleton barged through the crowd to put an end to their entertainment. After dragging Batt out of the way, he proceeded to whack Jimmy repeatedly over the head with his baton.

'I'd say that's enough, Sergeant. You wouldn't want anyone feeling sorry for the pup.'

The policeman paused for a moment as the hand tapped his shoulder. Seeing that it was Hennessy, he dropped the baton back into his belt, pulled the barely-conscious, blood-spattered Jimmy from the ground and gave him a fist into the face for good measure. 'On your feet, McCarthy. You're disturbing the peace.'

'There was two of them at it,' shouted a voice from behind.

'Is that what the shilling buys you these days?'

'King George must be the happy man having servants as loyal as that.'

Ignoring the comments from the chorus leaning up against the street corner, Stapleton locked Jimmy's arm behind his back and marched him towards the barracks. Once he had departed from earshot, the pub opened its side door to lubricate the disappointed onlookers.

Hands stuck in their pockets and eyes glued to the road, Willie and Ned ambled away in the other direction.

Josie hurried up to join them. 'Stapleton had no need to go at Jimmy like that.'

'He'll never be any different,' answered her brother.

'But he nearly killed him. What was the fight over?'

'Nothing much.'

'It's an awful shame to see ye at each other like that.'

'Who?' asked Ned.

'All of ye that played on the team. Ye were always such good friends with each other.'

'Sometimes even friends fall out,' Willie answered. Across the road, he could see Edmund Reidy breaking away from conversation with Hennessy.

'Get the trap, Ned.' Reidy moved in between his daughter and Willie. 'We're going home.'

Maintaining eye contact through the unspoken hostility, Willie stood his ground. The farmer blinked first and turned to his son. 'What's keeping you, Ned? I told you get the trap.'

Caught between two silent forces, Ned tried to look away. His father pounded his stick off the ground. Willie folded his arms.

Family won out. Ned went to untether the pony.

Reidy started to follow, then turned his head to beckon his daughter. She paused, she pouted, she left Willie a last lingering look but she too made her way up the street to the hitching rail in front of the barracks.

7

JOHN REDMOND did get his Home Rule. The rout at Mons had exposed the inadequacies of the small British professional army dwarfed by the huge reservoirs of conscripts that had been mobilised by France and Germany. And when the French crumbled to the east of them before the full might of Von Moltke's divisions pouring in over the Belgian frontier, panic seeped into Asquith's Cabinet and demanded that all possible measures be taken to stem the German advance.

Nationalist Ireland was wooed with the reappearance of the Bill that, only weeks before, had been struck from the agenda when war was declared. But in common with every other initiative during almost four decades since Parnell turned Ireland into a problem that could no longer be ignored by Westminster, Unionist and Conservative objections made sure that the manner and the timing were as begrudging as possible. While the Home Ruler MPs waved the old green flag with the golden harp on the steps of the House of Commons, they knew in their hearts and souls that their victory remained symbolic, as Irish self-government was suspended for the duration of the fighting and, even then, would not come into effect until the position of the Ulster Unionists had been settled.

But whatever private reservations they had, they were not going to show them in public. In a world where gain for one side was immediately interpreted as a setback for the other, the bitter reactions of Tory leader Andrew Bonar Law and of Unionism's Edward Carson meant that Nationalist Ireland was seen to have triumphed. Parties were held all over London that night in the houses of native-born and first-generation Catholics who had climbed onto rungs of respectability in the imperial capital. Finally, they had something to show for half a lifetime of parliamentary struggle.

As for Redmond himself, it was the culmination of a career that had begun at the same time as Parnell's when he'd served as his father's assistant in Westminster. He had been through the heady days of the Land War, of the split following Parnell's disgrace, of the reunification under his own leadership, of the productive years when minority Liberal governments depended on his support and of the lean times when the Conservatives closed their ears to the needs of John Bull's other island. Conciliation rather than confrontation had always been his style and it had eventually brought its reward. Now well into middle age and in poor health following a serious riding accident two years before, his drive had slowed down and election as head of an Irish home rule government in Dublin would provide tangible recognition of what he and his party had achieved.

He returned to Dublin to further celebrations before setting off for the shooting lodge at Aughavanagh on the edge of the Wicklow Mountains that he'd purchased from the Parnell family. A Sunday morning drive down the east coast and then inland from Arklow under golden oak trees, lifted spirits that had flagged under the pressures of London.

'Asquith was true to his word.' As his chauffeur steered the car over the Avoca river into Woodenbridge, the privacy of the moment allowed him to savour the elation of his success. 'There will be no going back on Home Rule now that His Majesty has signed the act.'

'But we must wait until the war has ended,' replied his his wife.

'Then perhaps we should play our part in ensuring that it is over as soon as possible.'

Coming over the humpback bridge, he could see a column of East Wicklow Volunteers marching in the direction of the hotel. And he could recognise the two men on horseback leading the column, their commander Colonel Moore and their chairman Dr. Ryan.

'Isn't that a marvellous sight, my dear?' He tapped on the glass partition and motioned to the driver to stop.

The Volunteers halted as they spotted their leader and saluted him as they stood to attention. Colonel Moore winked at the chauffeur who got out and opened the rear door.

'Dear me, have I been ambushed?' Redmond smiled as he accepted the handshake.

'I'm afraid so, Mr. Redmond' replied the colonel, doffing his hat to Mrs. Redmond. 'Everyone insisted on turning up when the rumour went around that you might be home for the weekend.'

In fact, there were many times more Volunteers, some even from Dublin and from his own native Wexford, gathered in the broad meadow up the road that created a natural amphitheatre as it fell away to the Avoca. Redmond soaked up the cheers as he ascended the platform under the spreading oak boughs that were festooned with green flags, bunting and banners proclaiming the enactment of Home Rule. In the very same place where Parnell had sprung from, he was now fulfilling his mentor's dream. The people were acclaiming their leader because he had delivered.

Dr. Ryan passed him a hip flask of brandy to ward off the chill in the stiff breeze. The colonel bellowed his introductions to the crowd in a voice fortified by the demands of the barracks square. They cheered as their prophet rose to address them; they laughed when he confessed that he had nothing prepared and had to speak off the cuff; they cheered again when he told them that, one hundred and thirteen years after the dissolution of Grattan's Parliament by the Act of Union, Ireland once again would have a government of her own.

And because they had been granted the right to run their own internal affairs, he told them that Ireland would behave like any of Europe's other nations now at war with each other on far foreign fields. They could not stand idly by as sovereignty was violated by those who had pledged to respect neutrality. They would stand up for what was right. They would come to the aid of other small nations that were quaking under the jackboot of the invader.

'These outrages against the defenceless people of Belgium, a nation as true to the Catholic faith as our own, offend every sense of decency of civilized people,' he told them amid loud applause. 'We can never look the other way in the face of such oppression.'

He steeled himself for the moment. No one could now accuse him of putting the interests of Britain before those of Ireland. 'And consequently, I appeal to every Volunteer to serve his country, not only in Ireland itself, but wherever the firing line extends, in defence of right, of freedom and religion. Erin go braugh! May God save Ireland!'

They broke ranks to rush up and congratulate him. John Redmond accepted the adulation with slightly bemused satisfaction.

All over Ireland, Volunteers reacted to Redmond's call. The original executive summoned an immediate meeting and disowned the Woodenbridge speech. But with the backing of his MPs, the Ancient Order of Hibernians, the national and provincial newspapers, leading bishops and the electoral machine of the United Ireland League, the authority of the leader held sway in most places. As units followed him to a man into the National Volunteers, the breakaway organisation attracted over 90% of the membership within weeks of its foundation.

Defection might have been total but for the personal connections established by Mac Néill and the IRB grouping around Pearse, Seán Mac Diarmada and Tom Clarke. In the days following Redmond's appeal, frantic efforts were made to stem the tide and Pearse hurried across Munster in an attempt to counter the authority of local Home Ruler chieftains. One of his first calls led him to Foynes where Ned Reidy picked him up, after leaving his father at the railway station for his monthly visit to Limerick.

'I suppose ye won't be following the uncrowned king of Ireland to the fields of Flanders?' asked Ned as he moved the trap past the string of carters waiting on a shipload of coal to be unloaded.

'Unlikely.' His passenger allowed himself a wry smile.

'So England's difficulty might be Ireland's opportunity?'

'One way of putting it.' Even though they were as far as anyone could get in Europe from where hostilities had commenced, Pearse noticed a military air already descending on the town with the bustle of uniforms, the official notices stuck to the walls of the railway station and the RIC barracks, and the guard mounted at the entrance to the port. 'I suppose you know there's been a split?'

'In the national executive?'

'Yes.'

'We've as good as had one here already.' As Ned rounded the bend leading out the Askeaton road, an Army tender filled with recruits brushed past the trap from the opposite direction and raised a cloud of dust into the crisp autumn air. 'And most of them will be following Redmond.'

'So who's left, then?'

'Willie. Jimmy. Maybe one or two others like Mossy Noonan and Dan Hourigan. But that's the size of it.'

'Four or five is enough.' Ahead up the road at Robertstwon Cross, Pearse could see his next contact waiting for him. 'A few you can depend on are far more valuable. And far easier to control.'

They stopped and shook hands with the man from Askeaton. Another tender passed on its way to the station. 'I wonder do they even know where they're going?' asked Pearse as he mounted the bicycle and waved Ned goodbye.

Dick Mullane, Patie Fitzgibbon and Johnny O'Brien had already ventured into the great unknown. Never having been further than Limerick City in their lives, an entire new world awaited them but they were given little chance to see the England that they had set foot on. All Patie remembered of the boat was the heat and the sweat of soldiers who were too tired to fight and too cramped to play cards as they crammed into the deck between the horses below them and the toffs and the officers in the first-class above. All he saw from the rattling, clattering train after they were offloaded in Fishguard were the dank walls of deserted railway stations occasionally breaking through the darkness of the night and the marshalling yards of a junction where half of the carriages were decoupled and tacked on to another train. And when he finally found an inch of space and a moment of quiet in which to close his eyes, sergeant-majors burst through the carriages, banged sleepy heads with their sticks and roared that they would be arriving at their destination within minutes.

'Frimley?' queried an old hand as the station sign passed by the window.

'The London Line is backed up,' he was told. 'This is as far as we go.'

'God in Heaven!'

'Aldershot is only four miles down the road.'

They fell out onto the desolate platform as the fingers of dawn inched through the mist, gathered their kitbags and stood to attention as the NCOs reeled off name after name. Pay books were produced, examined, noted and returned and and sergeants handed sheets summarising the arrivals over to officers who, after a single disinterested glance, passed them on to the orderlies accompanying them.

'Attention!' roared a fiercely-moustached sergeant-major. 'Prince of Wales' Leinster Regiment! Fall out!'

The column on the platform thinned out as the Leinsters marched off. Once again, their paybooks were checked.

'Says here King's Own West Sussex Rifles,' Patie was told. 'What are you doing with the Munsters?'

'We've been transferred.'

'Bloody cock-up if you ask me,' barked the sergeant-major. 'You can't come with us.'

Almost a hundred orphans who had been assigned to various English regiments were left over when the Munsters and the Royal Irish Regiment departed and they might well have remained forever standing to attention on the Frimley platform had the station-master not telephoned the authorities to protest. Making no attempt to hide their annoyance at being dragged away from whatever they were doing or avoiding doing, a whiskey-nosed officer and a roly-poly sergeant bursting through the seams of his uniform shunted them out onto the street and pointed them in the direction of Aldershot while they tried to requisition bicycles from the local police station.

Bricks were Patie's first impression of the streets around them, hot red brick veiled by a thin black film of coal soot. He'd seen something like it before in Limerick city but here the houses were smaller and cleaner and neater and not broken up into crumbling tenements.

The town might have been a bit bigger than Shanagolden but there wasn't anything like the same number of people around. No children out on the street or men hanging around the pubs and leaning up against the street corner or women gossiping out through open doors. In fact, he had seen only the one public house. There would be a dozen or more in a place of similar size back home. It was quiet too, as if everyone was away working somewhere else, streets with no shops and no animals being driven along them and lined on both sides with nothing but houses all built exactly the same and closed up as if all of their owners had gone away.

But that all changed when they started marching out the Aldershot road in front of the officer on his bicycle and the fat sergeant gasping for breath as he tried to keep up with them. What started as a single column was joined at every crossroad by the footsteps, hoofbeats, motor rumbles and the creaking wheels of field pieces, of other groups making the same journey. Soon, every field around them was filled, flattened and ploughed into muck by horses, tents and fenced-off compounds and Patie was suddenly confronted by the enormity of what was going on around him as an empire converged on the call to war.

The confines of the barracks magnified the effect and, inside the square in which they halted, orders, whistles, footsteps and horses' squeals echoed off the surrounding buildings. Having discharged the most onerous task of his day, the officer pointed to a door and disappeared off to the mess without a further word. The sergeant, meanwhile, found himself a bench to collapse on.

'They said we'd be allowed go to Brighton for a few days,' Patie told the sergeant at the processing counter.

'They what?'

'The captain who signed us up in Foynes had it all fixed up.' He pulled the letter from his pocket.

'Oh, my giddy aunt.' The head shook with disbelief at the document. 'I've never seen anything like this before. 'Ere, Fred, come look at this.'

A second sergeant left his desk to come over. 'West Sussex again,' he laughed. 'What a bunch of scallywags! They've been using that trick for years.'

Patie looked at Dick shrugging his shoulders as if he had expected nothing else, at Johnny's eyes dawning with disappointment, at the spectrum ranging from anger to fatalism in the others.

'And there's no West Sussex arrived here yet,' added the first sergeant as he joined in the joke. 'You'll have to find them yourselves.'

Even though they were weak from hunger and dead on their feet from the lack of sleep, the dozen homeless recruits spent the entire day bouncing from one building to the next as disinterested officers shoved them off onto someone else's plate. Names like Corunna, Gibraltar and Salamanca adorned the various barracks that had dismissed them. Patie had heard of them before when the master introduced them to geography at school. Long words that rolled from the lips and hinted of faraway places where there were pirates and treasure and adventure and opened the imagination of small boys in a far corner of Ireland to the magic of the world.

'We must have must have travelled all over Spain,' he remarked as they retraced their steps past barracks now closing for the night.

'And we'll end up in Flanders where we'll be shot,' replied Dick as they passed through an archway. 'There's a bit of shelter here. We mightn't get a better place to put down for the night.'

Huddled under his greatcoat and resting his head on his kitbag, Patie was surrendering to sleep when he felt a heavy tap on his shoulder. Another trio of sergeant stripes met his reluctant eyes.

'West Sussex?' he was asked.

'Yes,' he nodded wearily.

'Yes. Sir!' he was reminded.

'Yes, sir.'

'Attention!'

The dozen of them got to their feet.

'Can't have you sleeping rough.' Patie thought he detected a hint of sympathy in the sergeant's voice. 'We've just come in from Chichester. Our quarters are just down the road and the cook is still on duty.'

Any gratitude Patie might have felt for Sergeant Roseblade disappeared in the morning. 'You lot! Fall in!' the NCO roared at them as they jumped out for reveille. The dozen recruits that the Munster Fusiliers had deemed surplus to requirements stood to attention as they had their details read out to them before they were delivered to the pen-pushers to record the same details all over again. Life stories were recited, dimensions were measured for a uniform that not only would not arrive but, if it did, wouldn't come remotely near fitting them and hair was shaved down to stubble before they were shunted along to the medical tent.

Underneath the buff canvas sheets embellished with the Red Cross, a selection of bowls, scrapers and chamber pots awaited them as the doctor and his team of orderlies subjected them to the military obsession with lice, bowel movements, venereal diseases and worms.

'Jesus Christ, you can't do this!' screamed Johnny as his trousers were dragged off and a big hairy hand lifted his privates up for closer scrutiny.

'No sign of clap,' muttered the doctor. An orderly scribbled.

'No pox either.' A chamber pot appeared. 'Sample.'

'What?' asked Johnny.

'Piss,' barked the doctor. 'Next.'

Patie shuffled forward for inspection. Thermometers, stetescopes, tongue depressers, purgatives and emetics waited for him in gleeful anticipation.

'Now out to the range,' Roseblade told them the minute they emerged from the medical hut with their orifices smarting and stinking of carbolic. Grabbing their kits, rifles and greatcoats, they fell into line and marched in double time to the long line of fire positions running in parallel with array of similarly spaced target posts.

'I want you to see a Hun every time you take aim,' roared the sergeant as they dropped to the ground. 'I want to see you ripping him open with every shot.'

Patie broke the Lee Enfield but the round slipped from his fingers as he loaded.

'No good!' they shouted over the rattling thunder. 'Move on!'

He rose from his prone position and hurried to the next position.

'Too slow! It's only a few yards. You can roll. Move on!'

The rain was starting to fall. He loaded, aimed and was about to squeeze his finger when a corporal's boot landed on his backside.

'Keep flat! Don't let the enemy see you. Move on!'

Next time he got his shot in.

'Too slow!' The stopwatch was shoved in front of his face. 'Move on!'

The rain thickened, then poured down in buckets, sticking their caps to their heads, filling their boots and their leggings, crawling up the sleeves of their tunics, soaking their hair and their vests, spattering the mud on their faces, obscuring the target from view. A cold breeze from the north doubled the discomfort. Hands shivered as they tried to steady the sights. Chests heaved, forearms cramped, shoulders ached, calves locked and sweat and rainwater dripped from sodden brows.

But there was no let up. Load, shoot, load, shoot and keep going until they were commanded to halt.

'Now I want to see what you can hit,' announced Roseblade. 'See the number of your position. Find the target post with the same number across from you. You have ten rounds, starting now.'

Patie got eight shots in before the whistle blew. A regular ran across to collect the sheets and handed them to the sergeant to examine as he marched past the line of recruits.

'None ... None ... Bloody hell! None ... One ... None ...' Patie waited for his. 'Three ... What's your name?'

'Private Fitzgibbon, sir.'

'You have to do better than that, Fitzgibbon. You have to kill Fritz before he kills you.' Roseblade marched on. 'None ... None ... Hmm! Nine ... And who might you be?'

'Private Mullane, sir.'

'I want a clean sheet the next time, Mullane.'

The cycle started all over again, rolling from position to position before taking their ten rounds at the target.

'Worse even than Horgan on a bad day at the creamery,' Dick mumbled to Patie, his words muffled by the clay caked to his lips.

'Or a heavy training session with Birdie Madden. Homesick already?'

'No. Not yet.'

'... Fitzgibbon, four ... O'Brien, two ... Mullane, eight. We'll do it again.'

Dick did manage to get his perfect score after they completed their sixth circuit and they slumped with exhaustion in the belief that the damp cold earth of the range could hold no more horrors.

'Time for a run,' boomed Roseblade. He pointed to a pile of bricks that had been dropped from a horse cart. 'Pick out a dozen and stuff them into your kit bag.'

The addition of another two stone of mortar to their full issue of kit nearly broke their backs. 'Now take the machine guns,' continued the sergeant. 'One to every four of you. Break it down so that you can carry it. I'll leave it up to yourselves how you go about dividing it up between you.'

Off they set into the driving rain on a roundabout run through the craters, hills, earthworks and bunkers of the camp's perimeter. A corporal with a megaphone followed on a pony to dissuade the backmarkers from keeling over.

They said it was nine miles but it felt at least twice as long. Water poured into them from every direction, from the air, from the puddles they splashed through, from the drips from their caps and down the folds in their sleeves. Mud climbed from the ground and up their legs, shards of stone and masonry scoured their hands as they climbed up banks and dropped into moats and, all the time, the load they were carrying rumbled against their backs.

Shoulders aching, heads pounding, lungs scouring the twilit air for breath, Patie, Dick and Johnny staggered into the square created by the hastily erected tents and sheds and waited for the rest of the straggling column to join them.

'Oy, what about your machine gun?' barked Roseblade.

Their cold, tired fingers fumbled to re-assemble the Vickers, disassemble it and assemble it again, the second time under the scrutiny of the stopwatch. When that was done, they were ordered to clean their rifles, empty their kit and pack it again and then stand to attention as they waited for Roseblade to roll off their names. Only then, when every weary name was accounted for, were they allowed to collapse into their makeshift beds.

'Oy, Paddy!' grunted a Cockney voice from the dark. 'Fold your uniform up proper. Kit inspection at reveille.'

'It can wait ...,' muttered Patie.

'Your funeral, mate. You want another run before breakfast?'

They were spared the run after breakfast. In fact, there wasn't even an inspection, just a bellowed command to get their food down immediately, pack their kit and assemble in the square. The entire battalion stood to attention to be looked over by a colonel assisted by a major, a captain and a line of junior officers and NCOs of various levels of importance.

'Maybe we've won the war,' muttered Private Horatio Tibbs. 'We can collect our money without being shot at.' Known even to everyone as Maggot, the sparrow-shaped Londoner revelled in the attention that his sharp wit could bring. A career soldier who had avoided anything remotely connected with conflict during fifteen year's service in the Army, he was in his element now that he was surrounded by a sizeable proportion of Territorials and volunteers who were drawn from every walk of life and who were largely ignorant of the ways and the workings of His Majesty's Armed Forces.

'Some hope, Maggot,' breathed the man beside him. 'The brass don't turn up with good news.'

On Maggot's other side, Patie shivered in the uniform still damp from the previous day's soaking.

'What about this lot?' The colonel pointed to the newcomers as he passed by Roseblade. 'They're just recruits.'

'They're up to it, sir. Did the full circuit yesterday. Every one of them.'

They were marching within minutes, over a thousand of them heading for a siding up the line from Aldershot station. There they were bundled onto a train waiting underneath a cloud of billowing steam that was already half-full with a battalion of a Welsh regiment.

'Bleeding foreigners, them Taffys,' explained Maggot to his widening circle of admirers. 'Don't even understand the King's English.'

Shunted across branch lines, backed up at signals, jolted over junctions and sidelined on the mainline after Redhill while the expresses passed them by, it took most of the day to reach the sea.

'Well, may God strike me down in anger,' groaned Maggot. 'Newhaven! We'd have been here hours ago if we'd come straight from Chichester.'

Hurried by their NCOs from the platform to the pier, they were the last group to board the steamer bound for Dieppe. Top heavy with a dozen trainloads of soldiers and horses and stinking of vomit provoked by the choppy sea, Patie could hardly wait to disembark on the French side of the Channel. The instant they set foot on the port with its terraces of tall gaunt houses and white cliffs lining its long harbour, megaphoned commands directed them to another train waiting to bring them to Amiens.

The further inland they clattered over the pale earth and the rolling chalk hills, the more obvious the war became. Squeezing himself against the window to catch sight of another strange new land, Patie watched the traffic moving on the roads in the opposite direction grow from a trickle to a steady flow. Coming into Amiens, it had swelled to a flood as women, old men and children loaded their arms and their backs, pushed handcarts and perambulators stacked to the brim with the contents of the house, led dogs, carried cats, drove cows and rolled barrels in a torrent so relentless that even columns of soldiers marching against them were unable to resist. And for once, neither rank nor wealth could buy favour as those with horses or motorcars were slowed to the pace of those on foot in the frantic rush to escape from the fighting.

As the West Sussex alighted from the carriage into the bedlam of strange tongues, strange writing and strange uniforms and stepped through city streets almost bereft of civilians, Patie caught the first direct evidence of a conflict that was raging just a few miles up the road.

'What happened that?' Johnny pointed to a church spire peering through a gap in the rooflines. One side of it was had been blown cleanly away; the other half appeared on the point of toppling down on the rooftop windows below.

'Shell fire,' Roseblade told him.

'And you'll see loads more of it where we're going,' added Maggot.

Yet when they got out of the town on a poplar-lined road running parallel with the slow-moving waters of the Somme, they saw nothing and heard nothing other than a rumble in the distance to remind them of what lay ahead. No animals in the fields, no farmers and labourers saving the hay and the wheat and the barley that should have been harvested weeks earlier, no wagons, no carts, no horses, no life in the villages or on the roads other than the rhythmic clunk of their hobnails off the cobbles. Even the chatter was absent, the aimless banter and grumbles that normally broke up the monotony of a full day's march. It wasn't what they had expected; it had to be an omen of far worse to come.

They halted at the head of an avenue as the adjutant, a major enthroned high on his horse above them, consulted his orders. On a nod from Roseblade and taking their lead from Maggot, the company broke up and pulled from the pockets of their greatcoats their rations and the food that they had foraged from the deserted shops and boulangeries of Amiens.

'First decent stuff I've had to eat since I joined up.' Dick wrapped a long stick of crusty white bread around lumps of soft cheese and cold meat and washed it down with a mouthful of wine.

'Flaming Frog food.' Maggot declined the offer of a piece of the sandwich. 'You never know what they put in it. You could be eating your own grandmother or your dog.'

'Are you sure it's all right?' Johnny looked suspiciously over the food that Maggot had rejected.

'You won't know 'til you try,' answered Dick. 'But it hasn't done me any harm so far.'

Maggot hacked a stubborn lump of bully beef with his bayonet. 'I never trust any meat they give you what doesn't come out of a tin.'

'Damned if I can make out where they are sending us.' The major folded his orders, slid them back into his inside pocket and trained his field glasses down the avenue. Left in charge

103

after the battalion commander had found matters that needed his urgent attention back at brigade HQ, it was slowly dawnig on him that warfare was a sight more complicated than organising golf outings during peacetime. 'Perhaps this is the place. What do you say, chaps?'

The company commanders, their captains and their subalterns, the junior officers straight out of public school with the job of keeping the masses in line, shrugged their shoulders. 'How about you, sergeant?'

'As good a place as any, sir,' Roseblade replied.

A large château, surrounded by beech trees, fountains and an ornamental garden, lay at the end of the avenue. Even though neglect was beginning to show in the overgrown lawns and in the occasional shattered window, its rounded turrets and its striped façade of red bricks and white still spoke of easy and limitless money that had just popped off for the season to Paris.

Much to their surprise, it wasn't deserted. A company from another battalion was already installed and busying itself building defences at the end of a courtyard leading down to the river Somme.

'Company ... Halt!' bellowed Roseblade at the head of the leading group.

A major emerged from a stable. 'Where's your CO? ... Well, 'pon my soul! Blinker Blenkinsop!'

'Why, if isn't Scug Lawford-Stanley!' Their own major slid from his horse and engaged in an arcane handshaking ritual with his host. 'Haven't clapped eyes on you since you bagged that century in Fenner's. '03 was it? Or '04?'

''02 actually. In Parks.'

'Yes, yes, I remember now. Against the Free Foresters.'

'The MCC.'

'Don't remind me. Bosie and his blasted googlies. Never could get a line on the blighter when he twitched the old fingers.' Major Blinker pulled out a hankie and wiped his furrowed brow. 'My word, how time flies.'

The resident sergeant-major stepped into the breach as the officers renewed old acquaintances, recalled long-forgotten cricket matches, shooting expeditions on the Scottish moors and boating on the Thames and filled each other in on the latest gossip emanating from the old school. Leading Roseblade down to a line of tables stacked with shovels, sacks and lengths of timber, he pointed to the line of trenches taking shape along the bank of the river. 'This is the shallowest stretch of the Somme, sergeant. If Fritz presses forward in this sector again, they expect him to cross the river here.'

Pressed on by their NCOs, the battalion queued up at the table. 'What's happening, Sarge?' asked Maggot as he collected his issue.

'You're digging, lad.'

''Ere, I'm a soldier of the King's regiments of foot. I didn't come to France to be no navvy.'

'Suit yourself, Tibbs. If you want to stand out in the open to get shot at, that's all right by me.'

'If we're digging, Sarge, we should be leaving it to the Paddies.' Maggot had hundreds of new faces in his audience and he wasn't going to forego the opportunity. 'But I'd keep an eye on them if I were you. They'd tunnel all the way back to Blighty while your back was turned.'

Sniggers of laughter made his moment. 'Wotcher think, Dick, my old Hibernian flower? Any chance you'd dig me my ticket home if things gets too hot around here?'

'Just point the way, Maggot. I'll even come up outside your front door if you want.' Dick leaned on his shovel and shook his

105

head as he sized up the soil beneath them. 'And then I'll see what your missus is up to while you're away fighting the heathen Huns in the Land of the Frogs.'

Feigning annoyance, Maggot turned to the miserable-looking pair issuing the shovels. "Ey, you lot. You doing any shooting?'

'No.'

'And why not, if I may be so bold as to ask?'

'Yeah, why is it so quiet here?' added Patie.

'There's nothing happening since the Germans stopped advancing. Must be two weeks now. All we've done is dig trenches.'

'Same goes for the Huns, it seems,' continued the other. 'But there's some fighting up the other road, I hear. A big battle going on around Doullens.'

'But nothing here. I think they've forgotten about us ...'

Eyes lit up when the pair realised that someone might be listening to their complaints.

'We're even in the wrong sector. The Frogs control this area ...'

'I don't think the Frogs even want us here ...'

'I can't replace your shovel without proper authorisation. It's against regulations ... The brass shipped us through Dieppe instead of Folkestone ...'

'Think they can beat the Huns on their own ...'

'But they forgot about how to get us up to Béthune ...'

'Would you two ever give over,' roared someone farther down the line. 'We're fed up hearing you moan from one end of the day to the other.'

'Charging us through the nose for everything ...'

'No, you can't have a shorter handle. They're all standard issue ... No-one told them that the trains don't run up the coast ...'

'Twenty francs she was looking for ...'

106

'Of course, I could have told them had they asked me. Spent five years in Clapham Junction, so I did. I'll have you know that I am a senior clerk with the Southern Railways ...'

'Not that it's real money anyway. All them fancy pictures. Looks more like wallpaper to me ...'

'Oy! Oy! Not that one ... Just like back home, you wouldn't go from Folkestone to Rye along the coast. No, you would go inland. Change at Ashford and take the 11:23 for the 9:35 out of Ramsgate via Canterbury ...'

Maggot left the disconnected monologues with just the pile of shovels for an audience. 'Well, well,' he beamed as he returned to his retinue. 'This might just be the holiday I've always fancied. A bit of the vino, some of the ooh-la-la from the mademoiselles, a few naughty can-cans. What more could a red-blooded Englishman ask for?'

7

BACK IN Shanagolden, Canon Murphy did his best to drum up support for the men at the Front. Sunday Mass was the one occasion of the week when he had everyone's attention and, if God, King George, John Redmond and Cardinal Logue were calling for volunteers to deliver Catholic Belgium from the Protestant hordes, it was his duty to pass on the message.

As was his custom, he glanced down from his pulpit before he started on his sermon, sizing up the congregation and reassuring himself of the unchallenged authority of his position. Passive, attentive, obedient, that was how he liked to see them as they waited on his weekly words.

He clutched the crucifix tightly in his right hand as his left sorted out the handwritten notes and his eyes drifted over the front rows ahead of the rail that separated parishioners who could buy their seats from those who couldn't. People of property and standing like Edmund Reidy, sitting there with his son and daughter; like Doctor Molyneaux and his wife; like Sergeant Stapleton presiding over his brood of children; like Thomas Hennessy and James Horgan, both resplendent in the green uniform of an offier of the Volunteers.

He filled his lungs and held his breath to allow the thunder to swell from within. 'We cannot stand idly by,' he began, smashing the silence and jolting the congregation to attention. 'No Christian soul can flinch from action while brave little Belgium is raped, is plundered and is pillaged.'

Hennessy nodded with approval. Had it been any other occasion, Horgan would have leaped on the seat and roared his support.

'It would be against God's will to turn our backs when heathens murder our Catholic brothers and sisters in their beds,' continued the Canon as the puce hue rose in the veins of his face. 'When nuns are violated. When bayonets slash the throats of innocent babies. When churches are burned and holy statues are desecrated. Listen, I tell you, to the words of the King and of our own John Redmond when they ask for volunteers.'

A draught up the aisle quenched the candle and scattered his notes. But he didn't need them any more. The fervour of redemption flowed through his fingers and his trembling arm waved the crucifix over his congregation. 'Mothers, a son in the army is as great a gift as a son to the church. To shed blood for our faith on the fields of Flanders is to follow God's sacrifice of His only Son on the Cross... '

'Form ranks, men!' With Horgan beside him and Stapleton lurking over his shoulder, Hennessy barked the Volunteers into line and led them down the main street from the church. And with the Canon's tirade still ringing in their ears, most of the men in the congregation followed them in the expectation of a repeat of the previous Sunday's excitement.

Willie Hartnett and Ned Reidy stood side by side in the back row. 'I thought we weren't parading until two o'clock,' muttered

Jimmy McCathy, his arm in a sling from the hiding he'd got from the RIC sergeant.

'In accordance with the constitution of the Irish Volunteers, the Shanagolden unit of the West Limerick Brigade will take its vote here and now,' their commandant announced.

'If I remember right, you've to give three days notice ...,' interrupted Willie.

'Do I hear a proposal that we follow the orders of our leader John Redmond and reject those national committee members who repudiated his direction?' continued Hennessy. Behind him, Stapleton removed his baton from his belt and held it in both hands across his waist.

From the middle of the front row, Batt Mullane raised his arm. 'Sir, I'd be honoured to propose the motion.'

'And I'm seconding it,' added Dinny Lyons.

'Hold on a minute,' asked Ned. 'What are we voting on?'

Eyes blazing, Batt turned around to face him. 'The Germans are murdering Belgian babies ...'

'I thought the Volunteers were supposed to be fighting the English,' countered Jimmy. 'Not the Germans ...'

'Nuns are being raped ...'

'We'll take the vote,' Hennessy shouted over the argument. 'If no-one's against it, I deem it to be passed.'

'I'm voting against.' Willie pushed through to the front and raised his arm. Despite being jostled by those around them, Ned, Jimmy and Mossy Noonan also put up their hands.

'I see it's unanimous,' announced Hennessy. 'Volunteers! Attention!'

'Anyone staying loyal to the oath we took, follow me.' Ned moved away to the other side of the road. Willie, Jimmy, Mossy and, after a moment's hesitation, Dan Hourigan joined him. Flint took a step in their direction but then changed his mind and returned to main group.

'By God but ye're some eejits!' roared Jimmy at the overwhelming majority on the far side of the street. 'Do ye all want to be killed fighting in Flanders for an English king that's doing ye down?'

'You're only a coward, McCarthy!' Batt shouted back at him. 'You don't mind if babies are being murdered! You're yellow! That's what you are!'

'You wouldn't let him away with that?' An onlooker jabbed him in the back. 'Would you, Jimmy?'

'At least I'm no traitor crawling up on me hands and knees for the King's shilling, Batt Mullane. Or whatever's left of it after your master Hennessy has robbed you with his cut.'

'Jaysus, I think he has you there, Batt,' added a second shit-stirrer.

'Easy talk, McCarthy!' Dinny Lyons took up the cause while Batt struggled for an answer. 'That's all cowards are good for!'

'Who's a coward?' Jimmy yanked his arm out of the sling and raised his fists in defiance before Willie and Ned pulled him back.

'For God's sake, have ye no shame?' asked one of the clientele waiting for Hennessy's barman to open the back door of the pub. 'Ye're stopping a decent fight from starting up.'

'Sure there's only the five of them,' answered another. 'Wouldn't they be only wasting their time taking on the other sixty?'

'I'd say he's mad enough to try it. You can see the breeding in them funny eyes of his.'

'They're a bit spread apart, all right. I've heard it said that you'd never know where the sheep stop and the McCarthys begin.'

'Take that back, you drunken fool!' Jimmy leapt free of Willie and jumped on the onlooker taunting him but, before he could swing a fist, Stapleton stole up behind him and whacked his baton off his head with practised expertise.

'Eejit,' sneered the tormentor as Willie, Ned and Mossy dived in to drag Jimmy away and prevent the sergeant from inflicting any further punishment on him.

'Attention!' shouted Ned. Ignoring the jeers, he led the five-man column up the main street to Jack Noonan's. A few onlookers followed them, as did Stapleton at a distance.

'Christ, I never thought Mick Fitz would leave us down,' said Jimmy leaning up against the wall of the pub.

'Would you ever shut your mouth, Jimmy!' hissed Ned, pointing his finger over his shoulder to where the sergeant was ostentatiously scribbling in his notebook. 'If the Fenians could fight the way you talk, we'd have run the English out of Ireland years ago.'

Jimmy pouted, but resistance withered under Willie's fierce stare. The spectators pressed in around them as they glanced silently at each other.

'What are we going to do now?' asked Mossy.

'Ye didn't think of that, did ye?' one of their audience pointed out.

'Sure there's only the five of ye?' observed his mate. 'Looks kind of bad, doesn't it?'

'Why don't you join up with us then and make up the numbers?' replied Ned.

'I've better things to be doing with my time than be playing toy soldiers.' The onlooker laughed dismissively. 'Sure no-one at all will take ye seriously.'

Mary Hourigan butted in between him and Ned. 'I think Ned was very brave to stand up to Hennessy.'

'Brave and stupid, girl.'

'Ned's not stupid!'

'Ha?' Drawn by the raised voices, a few more curious souls dawdled up the street to add to the critic's esteem. 'Anyone from around here who crosses Thomas Hennessy and the Canon and James Horgan would want to have his head examined. Am I right, lads?'

Heads nodded.

But not Josie's. 'If you're so worried about not offending Hennessy, why don't you go down to the hall and join up with his lot then?' she asked, eyeballing the star into silence.

'Yeah! Crawl down the street to him, ye bastards!' added Jimmy. 'Aah ... begging your pardon, ladies.'

Much to the disappointment of the onlookers, the fight had melted from the occasion and any potential for conflict had descended to the level of name-calling. As Stapleton resumed his note-taking across the road, they figured out that they were unlikely to be served in Jack's and drifted instead down to Hennessy's for their Sunday morning cure.

The rump of the Volunteers also broke up. Apologising that they weren't going to open for business, Mossy stepped through the door into the pub, Ned walked off with Mary and Jimmy and Dan disappeared in the other direction.

'Here, I'll walk you home,' Willie offered Josie in the sudden calm descending on the main street. 'Aah, that's of course if you'll have me.'

'Are you sure?' All around her, the windows had closed. It was the first time she'd ever felt that she wasn't under the scrutiny of the prying eyes of Shanagolden.

'About your father?'

'Yes.' She didn't demur as Willie eased his arm around her waist.

'Well, if we're taking on Hennessy, Horgan, the Canon, Stapleton, John Redmond and the whole British Empire, what's the harm in adding Edmund Reidy to the list?'

They didn't meet a sinner as they moved through the overgrown hedges flanking the dusty road. Leaves piled along the ditches, still dry and golden before the rains would break them down to pulp. The weather had yet to turn in earnest over an autumn dedicated to death, but the moist tang in the still air reminded them that it would only be a matter of days.

'Is that the end of the football now?' Josie asked as they stopped by a five-bar gate and leaned against the ivy-shrouded pillar.

'It looks like it. There's three of the team already gone off to Flanders and the rest of us is split down the middle.' Above the field of cows chewing the cud, the ruined mass of Shanid Castle punctured the skyline. 'You'll never see Jimmy and Batt togging out for the same side again.'

She squeezed closer to him, glancing her soft cheek against the stubble of his chin. 'Does that make you sad?'

'Ah, 'twould have happened anyway. Time never stands still. People always drift apart.' The rumble of an engine could be heard approaching from the Ardagh direction. He didn't care who saw them. 'Still, we won a championship and no-one can ever take that away from us.'

'Did it mean that much?'

'Oh, it did to be sure.' A few months back and he wouldn't even have considered the question. Kicking around on the field was all he did outside of working in the creamery or at home in the house, a precious few moments of his own choosing where no-one was telling him what to do. 'You know, you dream of it,

115

the glory, the honour it brings ... the way you and your friends and your neighbours and your relations are doing it for the parish. We went and made history and we'll all be remembered for that.'

'That ye did.'

'But now that it's done, you find out that there are other things that matter in your life.' The rumble had materialised into an Army lorry passing them by.

'Like fighting for the cause?' Her eyes turned to his, their softness drawing out the words that he never realised he had in him.

'Maybe. But maybe 'tis yourself, Josie, that matters most of all.'

She'd forgotten about the carrots and the parsnips and they were burned black by the time by the time she'd removed the pot from the range. The joint of beef was overcooked as well, singed to charcoal on the outside and dry on the inside when she removed it from the oven. And the spuds had turned to a watery pulp that that needed daubs of butter and a drop of milk and bits of scallion and plenty of pepper and salt to rescue a trace of flavour.

Her father hadn't said a word and neither had Ned. But both of them glowered through the silent Sunday dinner as they forced themselves through the plates laid in front of them. What should have been the culinary highlight of the week had turned into slops.

Then again, what were they complaining about? Before Josie had come back from school, they were living off rubbish far worse than what she had just served them.

She could blame the hurry she was in after being delayed in the town on her way home from Mass. Or she could tell herself that it was the coal that they were burning in the range instead of the usual turf. Gave out two or three times the heat, so it did, heated the house better, boiled a kettle in no time but it needed watching. Not like before when a pot could be left to boil away for hours in the knowledge that there still would be some water left at the bottom.

But that wasn't the problem and she knew it and so did her father. She was expecting the knock on the kitchen door when, instead of settling for his usual Sunday afternoon nap, Edmund Reidy came to ask questions of his daughter.

'I want a word with you, Josie.'

She loaded the cooking ware into the sink and poured the kettle over them. 'What about, Father?' she eventually replied.

'You know well what it's about. Your mind was somewhere when you were cooking the dinner.'

She scraped the wire brush over the cake of cleaning soap and began scrubbing the charred remains of the carrots from the bottom of the pot.

'He's a fine man, I'll grant you that,' her father continued. 'A great footballer too. With any luck, some day he could be the captain of the county team.'

The clock chimed in the living room.

'A steady worker, from what I hear down at the creamery.'

Reidy pulled up a chair to sit at the table and fished his pipe and his tobacco pouch out of his pocket.

'And he behaves himself well. Doesn't go around getting drunk and getting girls into trouble and starting fights over nothing.'

Josie dropped the pot back into the sink to let it soak.

'And we know his people as being sound. Sure didn't they half raise you when your mother was called away.'

'He has a name.' She hung her apron up on the hook behind the door.

'Under any other circumstances,' he puffed into the empty pipe to make sure that there was no debris left from a previous smoke, 'William Hartnett would be the right match for you.'

'So, what's wrong with him?'

'You're an intelligent girl, Josie, you've been given an education. I don't have to spell it out for you.'

'I want to hear it from you, Father.' She planted the balls of her fists on the table and stared across at him as he sliced the flakes from his plug. 'Because I can't see anything the matter with Willie.'

'It's nothing personal against him, you understand, but he's a man of no property.' He scattered the tobacco on the palm of his hand, added a spit to dampen it, rolled it into a ball and stuffed it into the bowl of his pipe. 'He's a labouring man and he always will be. If you want to get serious about someone, you'll have to do better than that.'

'A better man than Willie?'

Her father struck a match and sucked in the first draught of his smoke.

'It's not me you're worried about, Father. 'Tis yourself and what people might think about you.'

A second and a third match were needed to achieve satisfactory ignition.

'And that's the only thing that matters to you and all the rest of ye farmers.' Her voice rose to a shrill. 'How many acres, how many head of cattle, how much more you've got than the man up the road, so as you can look down on him.'

'Maybe it looks that way to you, Josie.' She thought that her father might explode with anger but he kept puffing on his pipe with an infuriating indifference to whatever thoughts she might have in her head. 'But it isn't as simple as you make it out to be.'

'Why, what's wrong with two people who love each other? Wouldn't I be right in saying that you loved my mother?'

She'd caught him. Neither of them had ever mentioned it before. But aside from the tiniest of grimaces, his composure never faltered. 'You sit down, girl, and listen to me for a few moments.'

She pouted, she knew she should have stood up to him. Instead, she took the other seat as he pointed to the window. 'See that land out there. Forty-three acres and all of it dry. Next year it'll all paid for. No more annuities. So we might be in a position to buy more.'

He tapped the pipe off the table, put it back in his mouth and rose to look out over his holding. 'You see, we're people of substantial property now, us Reidys. We can hold our heads up with the best of them and we've come a long way from the mud cabin your grandfather was born in. But we'll only stay there as long as we make the connections. And much as it pains me to say it, William Hartnett isn't one of them.'

Reidy gathered his pouch and his knife and headed for the door. 'I'll say no more. You just think about it. And, by the way, you've been called to training. You'll get a letter telling you that in the morning.'

9

OWN IN the parish hall, Thomas Hennessy waited at the door to count the Volunteers filing through. Numbers were what mattered. If nine-tenths of the unit followed him, he commanded nine-tenths of the esteem of the parish and he wasn't going to let himself be upstaged by any upstart with notions beyond his station

He'd expected the likes of Willie Hartnett and Jimmy McCarthy to revolt. There were always a few pups from the cottages and the mud cabins who'd entertain notions about themselves before the realities of life descended upon them. In time, most of them would learn the hard way to stick to what they were born to and pay due respect and, if they didn't like it, they could always clear off to the city or to America where they could live out their fantasies without bothering their betters back home.

However, he was surprised by the attitudes of Ned Reidy and Dan Hourigan. Coming from families of substance, they should have known where their interests lay. Give them a few years and they'd be coming into decent properties or, if they decided that farming wasn't the life for them, there was enough money there to set them up nicely in business. And with this war starting up, there were plenty of opportunities. The millions of soldiers signing up for the Army ate their way through a serious amount of butter and bacon and any man farming or trading could take a tidy slice of the action.

Maybe he should put a word in the ears of their fathers, hint that the authorities were keeping an eye on Ned and Dan because of their association with unsavoury elements like Hartnett and McCarthy. Bernard Hourigan might listen all right – or, if he didn't, he wouldn't get his back up at the word of advice – but the other man was a different matter entirely. For all Edmund Reidy's obsession with building up his holding, he still wanted to do everything his own way instead of pulling with those who could help him along.

No, Hennessy figured that he'd best leave him alone. The elder Reidy was the sort of thorny hoor who'd do the dead opposite of what anyone advised him, thinking that there was some other motive behind it all.

Anyway, the two young fellas would soon see sense when all this camaraderie of the football team wore off. And come the winter, Hennessy would have the club sorted out and the right people back in their positions. As long as there was a firm hand at the top, the players would know where they stood and there'd be no more talk about bringing outsiders in to train them and handing over the jerseys and the bottles to drunks and layabouts who were turning the parish into the laughing stock of the county.

Mind you, the episode had taught him a lesson. He'd taken his eye off the ball and Jack Noonan had jumped straight into the gap. And now that the team had gone and won the county, it would be all the more difficult for him to smash that challenge to his authority.

But, by God, he'd do it. Nothing surer. Noonan might have won one particular battle but Councillor Thomas Aquinas

Hennessy knew all there was to be known about long drawn-out wars. Back during the land agitation, everyone was up for the fight and they were all getting involved in the Land League, the United Ireland League, the Gaelic Athletic Association, the Co-operative Movement, the Ancient Order of Hibernians, the Gaelic League, the Confraternity and every other organisation that had sprung up with the Irish renaissance. But only one man had managed to survive every upheaval, crisis, scandal, split and disappointment that had happened during the thirty intervening years and he wasn't going to be pushed aside by a returned Yank who thought money alone could buy an express ticket to the corridors of power.

So, just to make sure that everyone understood how things worked, he needed a show of strength with the Volunteers. They had to be seen to place their faith in him, to follow the line taken by John Redmond and the Parliamentary Party, and enough of them had to answer the call to enlist. And while the farmers wouldn't want to see their sons signing up with the prospect of a good price for the gallon of milk, there was a surplus of labourers already and no one would suffer if a fair few of them cleared off to the Front.

He'd even forked out a few bob of his own to get the uniforms that Jimmy McCarthy had been questioning him about. Sure, there had been a collection but, now that the Army was taking everything that the clothing factories could sew, the price had gone through the roof. Three pounds ten shillings a shot they were asking for the shoddy rejects that they'd dyed an ugly bottle-green over the original khaki. And even though he'd beat them down to two pound eighteen and sixpence, 'twould still eat up the recruitment bounty of at least twenty volunteers before he'd see any of his money back.

'We'll be looking good today, men,' he addressed the gathering once they had all filed in. Sixty-one of them. No more losses. 'The Shanagolden unit will be the talk of the rally.'

'You mean our uniforms have come?'

'That's right.' He pointed the happy faces towards a long table laden with three separate piles of bottle-green bull's wool. 'Now, go over there to Captain Horgan and he'll sort ye out.'

'Lyons, I'd say regular size, that's them in the middle,' began the creamery manager. 'Hi! Hi! Get into line and don't be pushing ... Culhane. Big one, down at the end ... You too, Fitzgerald ... Hi! If ye don't stand properly in line, I'm taking them all back off of ye.'

A pair of them were fighting over a tunic. Horgan cuffed the nearest one across the ear.

'We're a tunic short,' complained the other one.

'Then there should be a spare one in one of the other piles.'

Flint wormed his way in between the belligerents.

'Barrett! What are you doing here?'

'I'm minding the jerseys.'

Hennessy tapped Horgan on the shoulder. 'Yerra, fit him out, James. He's signed up too.'

'The blessings of God on you, Councillor.' Flint's head nodded furiously like an eager pup trying to gain the attentions of his master. 'And you too, Mr. Horgan, sir.'

Horgan pointed to the end of the table. 'Take one of them.'

Flint began rooting through what was left of the pile. An angry hand slapped him across the back of the head.

'Hi! Hi!' barked Horgan. 'The top of the pile. Don't be putting your dirty paws on the rest of them ... Now, go over there and put it on.'

Most of the uniforms didn't fit. Hands hid up sleeves or else sleeves stopped at the forearm. Shoulders tilted to the left or to

124

the right. Waists either bulged or drooped. Legs shot out of trousers like the first shoots of a tree searching for sunlight. The odd seam burst, the odd button popped.

But the Volunteers didn't mind. Now they looked the genuine article, a real fighting force instead of a ragtaggle gang of corner boys. Arms and legs stretched, they tugged under the shoulders and at the waist and whistled as they admired the cut of each other.

'Nothing like a uniform,' said Batt Mullane as he tried to catch a reflection of himself in a window. 'It makes a real man of you.'

'Yeah, I hear it makes the women go wild.' Dinny Lyons adjusted the top button of his tunic. 'What do you think, Flint?'

The others guffawed as Flint struggled to emerge from beneath a tunic that was three or four sizes too big for him.

'Maybe we should mark the occasion.' Hennessy came over with two bottles of whiskey in one hand and a stack of glasses in the other and dropped them on the table. 'Have a drop there, Batt ... and yourself, Dinny ... Go on, have another.' Flint needed no encouragement for his third refill. ''Tisn't every day we make real Volunteers out of the unit.'

'Jesus Christ, I'm not filling drink for that rabble,' protested Horgan as he was summoned to go down to Hennessy's pub and bring back a case.

'Easy now, James,' soothed Hennessy's whisper. 'A bit of kindness can pay for itself many times over.' He pressed his fist against Dinny's stomach, lifted his chin with his finger and straightened him up in military posture. 'There's no doubt about who's the real Volunteers now.'

'Maybe we should find Jimmy McCarthy, sir, and march past him,' suggested Batt.

'Yeah. Make him pure jealous,' added Dinny.

'Show him and all them other cowards what real soldiering is.' Batt pulled in the folds of his trousers. 'And what's stopping us from doing it now?'

'There'll be time enough for that.' Hennessy laid his hand on Batt's shoulder. 'Plenty of time.'

'What's this I see?' Waving his walking stick, Canon Murphy burst through the door ahead of the returning Horgan and headed straight for the Councillor. 'I will not have alcohol in this hall!' he boomed. 'I forbid it!'

Hennessy wrapped his arm around the explosion of anger and edged the Canon aside.

'This is a temperance hall ...'

'I know, Canon, I know. And 'tis a great job the Pioneers are doing in the fight against drink.' He lowered his voice. 'But we want everyone to be of a right disposition.'

'For what?' Curiosity mellowed the outrage.

'Canon, the men gathered in this hall made a very brave decision this morning. In spite of all the pressure that them godless revolutionaries were putting them under, they listened to their consciences and stood by poor little Belgium in its hour of need. And, do you know something?' He lowered his head gravely. 'Some of them may even lay down their lives in the fight against the heathen Hun. Now, under the circumstances, wouldn't you agree that a small drop of whiskey is but small reward for what they are about to do?'

''Tisn't right ...'

'I think God might make an exception in this case.'

'Well, maybe just the one.' The Canon turned his back on the intemperate use of his hall. 'But no drunkenness, mind.'

'You can rest assured that there'll be none of that sort of carry-on happening here. You have my word on it.' Hennessy peered over the parish priest's shoulder to give Horgan the all clear. The creamery manager was mobbed as he stepped in the door with a case of a dozen five-naggin bottles. 'That was a powerful sermon you gave this morning, reminding us of our responsibilities to help our fellow-Catholics in their hour of need. John Redmond himself couldn't have put it better.'

'Well, I did put some thought into it,' admitted the Canon modestly. ''Tis very important that we know where we stand in the eyes of the Lord.'

'Indeed, indeed.' Hennessy nodded to Horgan to clear away the empties as his ear was filled with the finer points of theology. 'Tell me, you wouldn't like to say a few words to the lads? Remind them again of where their duty lies.'

Without waiting for an answer, he raised his hand to the gathering. 'Quiet, everyone. The Canon has something to say.'

Canon Murphy reached into the pocket of his soutane for his beads. 'We'll start with a decade of the Rosary.' He waited until they were all on their knees. 'Our Father ...' he began.

Once into his stride, he made an entire five decades of it and continued on with all the trimmings of Hail Holy Queen and exhortations to every saint up in Heaven before waking them from their mumbling slumbers with a fiery appeal to come to God's aid. As long as it kept them in the hall, Hennessy was happy to let his parish priest at it.

'God will reward you in Heaven for the sacrifice you have made,' thundered the Canon as his sermon clattered to a close. 'May the Good Lord bless you, in the name of the Father, the Son and the Holy Ghost.'

'Amen,' responded Dinny Lyons.

'Them Germans is pure bastards,' slurred Flint.

'Very well said,' complimented Hennessy, rising to his feet and handing the Canon over to Horgan to escort him out of the hall.

'Ye're most welcome, men,' the Councillor greeted the captain and sergeant of the British Army who had turned up at the door. Vigorously shaking their hands, he steered them down to the table that Horgan had already set up. 'Everything fine in the West Sussex, captain?'

'Pleased as Punch in Chichester.' The officer dropped his briefcase and sat down. 'Some damn good material in the last batch you sent over.'

'They're big strong lads, most of them. Plenty of spuds and bacon to make them grow.'

'My word!' beamed the captain, counting the attendance as he raised his eyes from the pipe that he was attempting to light. 'Very keen chaps you have here, Councillor.'

'They still have to be worked on,' whispered Hennessy before turning to address the men. 'Attention!' Most of them straightened up although a few like Flint needed some assistance. 'Our leader John Redmond has asked for Volunteers to aid Belgium in its hour of need. A small Catholic country like ourselves fighting for its life against a foreign invader. Now I know many of ye might be wanted on the farm now that there's a decent price for milk so I'm not telling ye to enlist. But if any of ye wants to, the captain here will be glad to take your details.'

'Put me down.' Batt Mullane stepped forward. 'I'm not afraid to fight.'

'Neither am I,' added Dinny Lyons.

Standing beside Batt as he signed up, Horgan poured him another shot of whiskey and held the bottle up to indicate that there plenty more there for anyone interested in approaching the table.

He needn't have bothered. Once the ice had been broken, others made their way forward. In fact, such was the enthusiasm that Hennessy had to dissuade a few of them by suggesting that they think it over before putting pen to paper. Labourers were one thing but most of the farmers and traders couldn't afford to be without their sons to help them out now that they might be busier than ever. And if anything happened to them, their mothers would never forget who had sent them to the Front in the first place.

After squaring it up with the captain, he marched those not signing up out of the hall. Better to have them out of the way before the rumours did the rounds. The lorry could drop them off at Robertstown Cross where they could meet up with the other units marching to the battalion rally in Foynes. 'Stop a bit up the road where you won't be seen,' he advised the driver. 'Some of the other crowds might get the wrong idea if they see Volunteers coming out of an Army vehicle.'

And just to make sure that they were all out of sight, he sent Horgan off with the lorry to keep an eye on them.

Back inside, the tedious entry of details continued and it needed another couple of bottles to ease the boredom of waiting. A few were on the young side so they had to make up dates of birth for them and coach them on what to say when they reached the barracks. Hennessy reckoned one of them was no more than fourteen but he was a big lad for his age and wisps of hair were already sprouting from his face. Another wheezed with the short coughs of oncoming consumption and hadn't a hope of making it past the doctor.

When the last recruit had been processed, the sergeant marched them outside. The captain remained at the table and, with Hennessy squinting over his shoulder, ran his finger over the entries in the ledger.

'Hmm,' he grunted, totting the numbers up again just to make sure. 'Nineteen. Rather good, I dare say. The CO will be pleased.'

'I make it twenty,' insisted the Councillor.

Without looking up, the captain laid his pen aside and turned over the next page of the ledger. 'Surely you're not including that chap Barrett?'

'Flint signed up same as the rest of them.'

'He's certain to fail the medical.'

'That's not your problem.' Hennessy shrugged his shoulders. 'And 'tisn't mine either.'

'Oh, all right then.' The captain reached into his briefcase, pulled out a cash box and opened it with a dainty key attached to his watch chain. 'Sixty pounds it is.'

'Sixty guineas, I believe. The West Sussex always deal in guineas. Or at least they did the last time' The Councillor had done his own bit of research and had found out that the quartermaster of the Chichester barracks had been claiming money from the War Office for reservists that didn't exist. 'Now that'd be sixty-three pounds if my sums are correct.'

'Five ... ten ... fifteen ...' Big white notes peeled off the plump wad pulled from the box.

'I'd sooner have sovereigns if you have them,' interrupted Hennessy. 'I always like to see the King's head on my money.'

The captain returned the notes, pulled out a bag of gold coins and counted them out.

Hennessy returned the slow smile and handed back a half-sovereign. 'Your luck penny, captain. An old Irish custom. And if I were you, I'd have them loaded up and out of here before any of them change their minds.'

Transport was already on its way. Out on the street, a fair-sized group had left their reading, their darning, their knitting or their

130

Sunday afternoon snoozes to gather outside the hall when they heard the first lorry returning from its third run to Robertstown Cross and a second coming in the opposite direction from Newcastlewest. The town of Shanagolden, through which centuries of rebellion, hunger, agitation and occupation had passed by, was suddenly overtaken by events beyond its control and the flickers of gossip flared into wildfire.

'That was very sudden,' one woman remarked to her husband as she hurried down the main street.

'They don't wait around when there's a war on,' he replied, clamping his cap to his head to prevent the rising wind from blowing it away.

As the lorries pulled up outside the hall, the sergeant called his recruits into line. Batt and Dinny led the way, followed by Mick Culhane, Jerry Curtin, Tim Curtin and Mick Fitzgerald of the football team and over a dozen others, all still clad in their ill-fitting Volunteers uniforms. Bringing up the rear were the unsteady feet of Flint tripping over the legs of his trousers.

The crowd waved to them as they split into two groups and climbed up overt he tailboards. A few of them waved back before the lorries rounded the first corner on the road back to Newcastlewest.

'If they get over there quick, they'll be able to stay together,' said the onlooking woman to her husband. 'Mr. Hennessy says he has it all sorted out.'

Behind them, the Councillor smiled as he fingered the gold in his pocket.

Jack Noonan's pub was quiet that night. Some of the custom had been ghosted away in Army lorries and more of it was trying to figure out how it happened. Not quite sure whether they should be proud, angry or resigned to the day's events, regulars stayed

131

at home in the company of their own thoughts instead of venturing out for the small one, the barstool philosophy and the game of cards.

Downing the dregs of a pint that he'd been nursing silently for the best part of an hour, Willie was the last to take his leave. After letting him out, Jack pulled down the shutters, locked the door and joined his son in the modest task of cleaning up.

'Willie was fierce quiet tonight.' He removed the empty glasses to the counter and wiped down a table with a wet cloth, scattering the pipe ash, matchsticks and an empty matchbox on the floor.

'We all are.'

He turned the chairs over and dropped them on the table. 'I don't suppose we'll win another championship for a while.'

Mossy followed his father with the broom, sweeping the sawdust into the fireplace to rescue the embers from imminent death. 'With most of them gone off to the war, we'll be doing well to field a team.'

Jack straightened his back and tossed the cloth aside. 'It's a crying shame. Ye could have got an awful lot farther. There was a good ten years of football left in that side.' He replaced the chairs on the swept floor. 'Not that it matters a damn any more. We're gone as well.'

'Who?'

'Birdie, Drug, myself. Even Flint but I heard he joined up as well today.' The spittoon had barely been touched. He left it where it was. 'We're all being thrown out. There's a general meeting of the club called for next Saturday night and Hennessy and Horgan and the Doctor and the rest of their gang have it rigged already.'

Apart from a dog lifting its leg against the outside wall of the pub, the street was empty when Willie emerged. Only a single candle flickering in the window of a house opposite broke through the all-enveloping darkness. Shanagolden's youth had departed to a help a foreign power fight a foreign war, all in the misguided notion of standing up for the rights of small nations.

Maybe Pearse had been talking sense when he said that a small committed group was of more value than the mass movement that had joined the Volunteers in an outpouring of euphoria, but nothing could hide the fact they were in a tiny minority. They might have been right but, for all their brave talk, there was a loneliness in what they had done, in how that they had stood out from the rest of the parish.

He'd felt it when the stares of ridicule rained on the pathetic little handful with their hurleys and their ash plants that dared to style itself as an army; when all they had to identify themselves were ragged green sashes tied across the shoulders and waists of their street clothes while the others had trooped down to the hall to be issued with the uniforms of real fighting men. He'd expected the smart comments from the corner boys, but others had jeered them as well, people he'd had more regard for, people he thought might have had minds of their own.

Maybe they did shut up when the lorries had come to take the recruits away. And he could tell that a few were already beginning to have doubts. The minute the tailboards disappeared down the Newcastle road, he could see in the silence of their faces a nagging suspicion that they'd been had, a hidden shame at what they'd let happen in front of their eyes.

But no one was going to admit it. Indeed, they would resent Willie and his group all the more because they would now be a reminder of their own loss of nerve. Instead, they would turn to the Canon's sermons or to Hennessy's promises or to the swing of Stapleton's baton, they'd suppress their reservations under layers of excessive loyalty or piety and they'd curse any disturber who didn't buy into the fiction.

What killed him most of all was losing out to Hennessy. For the first time in as long as anyone could remember, enough of them had stuck together and had done something that the town's gombeen didn't have a hand in. When they brought back the cup in triumph, Willie could feel the wave of liberation sweeping through the entire parish. Old men had told him that it was better than the first time they'd elected their own MP instead of the gentry that had previously been imposed on them or when the authorities had to release Parnell from prison during the land agitation. Shanagolden's triumph on the sportsfield was more immediate, more glorious and more real, a demonstration of the power that lay within a people who had been battered by famine and fever, by emigration and eviction, by poverty and oppression but who still had dared to hope.

And then Hennessy had taken it all away when he broke the back of the team by turning one on another and then selling half of them off to the war. Maybe Dick Mullane was right. No matter how often you rose up, they'd get you in the end and the only solution was to get out.

'Willie!' The whisper broke the quiet, slicing through the darkness of the night.

'Josie!' He turned to see her emerging from a laneway beside the pub. 'What are you doing out this hour of the night?'

'I had to see you.' She edged closer, the soft warmth of her gloved hands spreading over his frozen fingers. 'I'd this terrible argument with my father. He's trying to send me away.'

'Dumping you in a convent?'

'Almost as bad. I'm being called for training.'

'That's great news.' He smiled, puzzled at what all the fuss was about. 'You'll be qualified as a teacher in a year or two. You'll be a fine catch then, my girl.'

'But I won't see you for a long time.'

'Limerick isn't that far away.'

'It's not Mary Immaculate. It's Carysfort in Dublin.'

A full day to get there. A full day to get back. He might see her at Christmas if he was lucky; if her father gave her the price of the train. He put his arm around her shoulders and moved back with her into the lane. 'When are you supposed to be starting?'

'Two weeks time. But I don't want to go.'

'Don't say no straight off.' His hand eased against her chin so that his nose could touch against hers. 'Think about it first,' he breathed.

'I don't want to leave you.'

'And if you stay around here, I'll have to move out. No-one is going to give me any work if your father has a say in the matter.'

10

THEY MANAGED to get only one night in the château. Orders reached their acting commander the following morning just as he was sizing up the office space needed for administering his battalion. The West Sussex and the Surreys were required tout suite to assist in the defence of the British sector as the Germans pushed their armies towards the Channel Ports.

'Oh, bother,' sighed Major Blinker. 'I rather took a fancy to this place.'

'Too damned good,' observed Major Scug. 'Some blasted general had his eye on it, I'll wager. Sent us chaps here to dig the defences before he deposits his stable of mademoiselles.' He steadied his horse, sure that the animal had shared his disappointment. 'Oh, well. Where to now?'

Blinker handed over the instructions.

'Béthune? ... Béthune!' exploded Scug. 'Fifty bloody miles away! And no bloody transport!'

'But them two don't have to walk,' muttered a voice in the crowd watching the mounted majors argue over which was the best route to take.

The road that they finally agreed on ran straight as a die from the crest of one slow rise to the next. Broken only by the occasional stand of trees, village and church spire, stripes of corn and beet and grass stretched as far as the eye could see on either side without a hedge to a draw a line between them. Never in his life had Patie seen such expanse, never had he felt so small in the vastness of the landscape around him, never before had he craved to see a hill or a rock or any vertical feature that might tell him where he was, where he was headed and whether he was getting there.

Filled with lurid rumours of what had happened to those left behind in Belgium after the German advance, the civilians had fled and all that remained was the debris of their passing. Broken carts, items of furniture, bits of clothing, books and houseware were strewn along both sides of the road, the excess baggage of the mass flight that had preceded them. The first time that the column stopped, Maggot and the old hands had swarmed around the abandoned piles of possessions but there was nothing at all left to scavenge. Anything of value had long since been plucked from the vine.

Taking the place of the locals were the men that war had drawn from every corner of the empires of France and Britain, heading south or heading north as their orders commanded. Long lines of stamping infantry with their faces set and their minds switched off as they slowly consumed the cobbles of their journey; long trains of horse-drawn artillery with their retinue of shells and supplies and even longer trains of drays loaded with horse fodder; the occasional troop of cavalry out of place in a world that was passing them by; the odd convoy of lorries, or the staff-car of the brass, or the motorcycle of a dispatch rider, those who had been spared the never-ending footsteps on a journey to the end of the rainbow.

They still hadn't met their war by the end of the day, when they stopped in an abandoned village and found beds that were still dry in houses that were still intact and with larders that hadn't yet been cleaned out. But they knew that it was somewhere to their right where the rumble in the background was amplified by the distant glow that floated over the horizon when darkness descended, and was expanded by the whiff of cordite that hung in the breeze. And even while they were ploughing north on their long steady march, they could notice the hurry of those heading east at the crossroads. Only too soon, Patie knew that they too would be called to plug the line in the face of the enemy's advance.

'Bleeding 'ell!' grumbled Maggot as their stiff legs made it over yet another rolling hill on the second day of their journey. 'My feet are killing me.'

'God, but you're a fierce hard man to satisfy.' Dick shifted the weight of the kit on his shoulders. 'Only the other day, you'd march anywhere to get away from the digging.'

'That was then and this is now. I'd like to see some real action. I came over here to be a hero.'

'Yeah, when are they going to start shooting at us?' asked Johnny.

Any time now, thought Patie. Little signs were telling him that the fighting was getting closer. The rumble was just that bit louder, the traffic was just that bit busier in both directions; they passed by the odd crater of a shell that had gone astray. And they were passing by bigger towns now, ones that had factories as well as markets, that had terraces as well as cottages, that were centres of industry big enough to draw an enemy's attention.

'Sweet Jesus!' gasped Johnny. 'What's that?'

139

Hearing the sudden buzz of an engine, Patie looked around but could see no vehicle in any direction. The he noticed the heads pointing skywards at the cross-shaped object circling above them.

'One of ours,' informed the clerk of the Southern Railways marching alongside. 'Blue, white and red roundels starting from the outside. The Frogs have red, white and blue roundels and the Germans black crosses and I'm not quite certain if the Belgians have any aeroplanes of their own ...'

The pilot of the flying machine banked, turned and swooped low over the column, scattering half of them into the roadside ditches before flying off with an amused wave of his arm.

'Back on your feet!' roared Roseblade.

They laughed it off as they resumed their trek, but it was laced with the tense edge of bravado.

'Do they toss shells down from them things?' asked Dick.

'I don't know if they do now,' answered the sergeant. 'But I expect they will some day.'

'I wouldn't half mind being up in one of those aircraft,' said Maggot. 'Course you'd have to be a gentleman ...'

The war descended without warning. All they heard was a swoosh and the road ahead of them disintegrated.

'Get down!' shouted Roseblade as a second shell immediately followed the first. 'Into the ditches!'

The column broke up and dived into the stagnant drains lining both sides of the road.

'O Lord!' muttered Maggot.

'O Sweet Jesus up in Heaven, have mercy on my soul,' wailed Johnny. 'O my God, I am heartily sorry for having offended Thee ...'

'Shut up!' roared Roseblade.

' ... because they displease Thee, my God, who, in Thy infinite wisdom ...' whispered Johnny, clutching his rosary beads.

'Just a stray.' The sergeant leaped to his feet. 'Get up! Fall in line!'

They emerged from the ditches and took their places under Roseblade's unrelenting stare. Four broken bodies, distinguishable only by their French greatcoats, lay around a crater surrounded by a dozen bleeding wounded.

'Leave them. There's a medical detail just behind us.' He tapped Johnny and two other gawkers into line. 'Ready, Company! Quick march! Left, right, left, right ...'

'There's your action now, Maggot,' mumbled Dick.

' ... Hail holy Queen, Mother of Mercy, our light, our sweetness and our hope ...' Johnny's prayers floated over the flat fields of Picardy as they picked up again on their journey.

With their NCOs bellowing in their ears, they kept moving along as they had been ordered, a stray battalion of the West Sussex and a stray company of the Surreys, volunteers and Territorials from Civvy Street who had never seen battle, mixed in with experienced regulars and reservists. Like Patie, Dick and Johnny, quite a number of their colleagues had signed up together when the notion had taken them and had stayed together through training and deployment.

But they were leaderless now. Afflicted by self-doubt over where they were headed, Major Blinker had called Major Scug, the company commanders and all the support staff with a horse under their backsides to an ad hoc conference while the footsloggers scattered into the fields for a few minutes rest. As the officers gathered on the roadside, a barrage of artillery fire, too concentrated to be dismissed as a pop shot gone wrong, had landed directly on a wagon loaded with shells passing them by and blew them all off to the great Test match in the sky.

Patie hadn't known his officers. He'd never spoken to any of them or being spoken to by them except through the intermediaries of the NCOs but they were faces he could put a name to, people he'd seen in the flesh when their arms moved of their own accord and their lips spoke and their eyes frowned and smiled. When he marched past what was left of them, killing became real.

And even more so when the wounded came at them. Everyone fit and able was moving in one direction, everyone broken and battered in the other. Some walked with their heads bandaged or with their arms dangling from slings, some hobbled on crutches, some were loaded on horse wagons, some hidden in the occasional dull green ambulance painted with the Red Cross, some borne on stretchers.

'Oy, Maggot!' a body swathed in bandages cried out. 'Maggot Tibbs! Is that you?'

'Fred Cockburn, is it?' Maggot cried as they passed. 'We was mates in the Buffs?'

'Yeah, it's me. Fred. I'm going home.'

'You always was a lucky bastard.'

'Yeah. I got out alive.'

And then the stretcher was gone. 'That Fred Cockburn always lands on his feet,' muttered Maggot. 'He must have been born at the end of the rainbow.'

'There's a few up ahead what wasn't so lucky.' In front of them, a detail of German prisoners lifted corpses from a roadside pile and tossed them onto a handcart. A severed head fell from one of them and rolled towards the advancing column.

'O sweet Jesus! ...,' screamed Johnny.

'God's truth!' gasped Maggot. 'George Hawker!'

142

Along with two others, they fled from the sightless eyes leering up from their toes and knelt by the ditch to throw up.

'Company! Halt!' Roseblade strode up behind them. 'Tibbs, O'Brien, Roberts, Fletcher! Get back in line!'

Dick, Patie and few more of them grabbed the vomiters by the arms and dragged them back into the column where they were allowed a moment to regain their composure.

'You'll see much worse than that, so get used to it.' The sergeant took his place at the rear. 'Right! Let's march! Left, right, left, right ...'

'Got it clean enough, so he did,' one of the old hands muttered behind Patie. 'Not like what them Fuzzy-Wuzzies would do to you in the Sudan. You just wouldn't believe some of the things I saw out there ...'

'Poor old George.' Shaking his head, Maggot uncorked his canteen and washed the last remnants of puke from his mouth. 'Him and Fred Cockburn were best mates. If wonder if Fred even knows.'

They stopped at the earthworks on the edge of Béthune where officers pointed and sergeants roared and buck privates went left or went right or halted in their tracks as a retreat from Lille crashed into reinforcements piling forward from the rear. Even those who had seen battle before were unnerved by the bedlam of the shells thundering above them, the horses squealing in terror, the flares and the sulphurous stink of the explosive and the hail of machine-gun fire scything down a company ordered to peer over the defences to catch sight of the enemy.

A group of their mates lost it as the bleeding pulp of the bodies fell back on them and they took to their heels out the road that they had come in. Whistles blew, horses galloped, the last man was felled by a single round of a military policeman's pistol

143

and the would-be deserters were corralled back into line before they even made it to the end of the street.

Orders were bellowed from every direction and the West Sussex were caught in the vortex of conflicting instructions. They were sent to fill sandbags to cover the machine-guns, told that there was no sacking available but to bring shells up to the gun placements, diverted to the medics to haul in the wounded when the ammunition dump couldn't be found, then screamed at to get out of the way.

'Tell us where we're going, sir.' Roseblade collared a colonel standing on his own under the pointed gables of the high narrow houses lining the main square. Not quite sure whether he should be surprised or insulted, the officer jerked his head from the map that he had been examining.

'There's an entire battalion of us. Three full companies.'

'Regulars? Reserves?'

'Mostly reserves and Territorials, sir. Some volunteers that have had the full training. And they haven't run away.'

The colonel took in the steadiness glowing in Roseblade's eyes, then pointed to his map. 'Know where we are, sergeant?' His finger traced around Béthune before following a road to the north. 'Good. Up here is Chalkwood Farm – it has some other blasted name in French but that's what we call it. If I were the enemy, I'd mount my attack there. The town is too well defended.'

The barrage eased up as the West Sussex made their way out of town. Other than the prisoners loading the corpse cart, Patie still hadn't clapped eyes on the enemy. Their bullets whistled, their shells exploded, they sent thousands of banged-up soldiers scampering from the rout of Lille to the safety of Béthune but these men in the grey-blue uniforms with spikes sticking out of their leather helmets still had to transform themselves into the demon Hun pillaging his swathe across Europe. Fritz the German was everywhere around them, picking them off with his rifle, blowing them to bits with his ordnance, mowing them down with his machine-guns but he stubbornly refused to take a shape. All the company could go on were the stories of those in retreat retelling the horrors of the rounds whistling at them in gusts and the dull flat thud from the sky that left no-one living beside them.

They found their Chalkwood Farm nestled in a wooded hole in the landscape and backed up against the river Lys a few miles upstream from where it marked France's border with Belgium. A major emerged from the farmhouse as they marched into a yard centred around a crater that appeared to descend to the far side of the earth. Around them, the outbuildings showed the innards that the shells had exposed and teetered on the verge of collapse.

'Company! Halt!' Roseblade saluted him. The officer perfunctorily returned it and just nodded to the sergeants leading in the other two companies that followed.

'Sergeant Roseblade, C Company, 5th Battalion, The King's Own West Sussex Rifles! Sir!'

'Infantry!' The major shook his head as he made a quick estimate of the reinforcements that had arrived. 'We were promised artillery. Where's your CO, Sergeant?'

'Took a direct hit. Sir!'

Less than fifty yards away from where the last soldier was standing to attention, the yard trembled to the explosion of a shell. Some of the men turned around, a few others broke away and two dived for cover.

'Jesus, Mary and Joseph!' Johnny stood rooted to the spot and blessed himself frantically.

Another shell overshot the yard and blew up on the avenue. More of them jumped for the dubious protection of the outbuildings.

'Sergeant!' the major said quietly but firmly, looking over the scattering formation with resigned irritation. 'Control your men.'

'Company! Attention! You are in the presence of an officer!'

The column reformed. The firing had stopped.

'That's better. No place for cowards!' The officer pointed to a stand of trees beyond the end of the farmyard. 'Sergeant, we're dug in just ahead of those trees. Get your men down there immediately. We're expecting the enemy to attack the minute he finishes up this barrage.' He ran back into the farmhouse.

'You heard the major ...'

The air whistled above and the stables exploded into a cloud of dust and flying masonry.

'... Get moving! Run! You're safer down there than up here!'

They raced through the trees and across the meadow to the hastily-dug trench that ran along the crest of a low ridge overlooking the river valley. A burst of gunfire whizzed over their heads as Patie, Dick, Johnny and Roseblade dived in ahead of the rest of their company. The defence line was already filled with soldiers poking their rifles through the scraggy damp grass above them.

'You came at the right time.' A captain approached Roseblade. 'We took quite a share of casualties trying to break out. Lost some of our machine-guns as well. We didn't think we could hold the counter-attack.' He nodded to the newcomers piling in. 'Spread them out along the trench.'

Patie took his position beside Johnny and Dick and lifted his head slowly to peer out. No trace of movement could be seen on the carpet of grass rolling down the slope, only a sprinkling of inert bodies in British khaki intruding on the green uniformity of the surface.

'Get down!' Roseblade's hand yanked at his shoulder to pull him back into the cover of the trench. 'First thing you learn, lad, is never look out unless you have to.'

On Patie's other side, a soldier scanned his field glasses through the cavity in a shallow dome of stones that had been covered with sods.

'Anything?' asked the captain.

'Nothing yet.' The binoculars shifted their focus. 'No, wait! I see them. Beyond the house on the left.'

'They're coming up the rise on the other side as well,' shouted a second observer down the line.

'We've that covered.'

Patie's curiosity got the better of him again, squinting out through the hole in the dome as the observer beside him wound the handle of the field telephone. Like a field of corn sprouting at lunatic speed, hundreds of spiked helmets rose from the grass and transformed into bodies when the whistles rang out.

'Take their left flank,' the captain roared into the phone that the observer had handed him.

A pair of cross-firing machine-guns raked across the German charge and scattered the guts of a company back down the slope. But the momentum of the offensive continued unabated as the gun posts hadn't enough angle between them to mow down its main thrust.

'If they'd only sent the artillery,' sighed the captain. 'Sergeant, do you have any marksman in your company?'

Roseblade pointed to Dick. 'Mullane was the best of them on the range.'

'Up here, Mullane.'

The observer moved away, edging Dick and Patie up to a position under the dome with Johnny, speechless with terror, clinging on between them.

'See the officer leading the charge from the left.' The captain moved the barrel of Dick's rifle.

'The fella waving the sword?'

'Take him out.'

One shot was all it took. The German bolted upright, quivered and then crumpled to the ground.

'Now, the sergeant just behind him.'

The second target toppled forward over the first. The following soldiers slowed down for an instant before resuming their charge. By then, Dick had already taken out another officer and two NCOs.

'Take over, Sergeant.' The captain moved away up the line.

'Keep picking off their leaders, Mullane. The rest of you, fix bayonets and take position. And then wait for the order.'

The fifth target dropped, then the sixth and conviction seeped from stripes of the main charge as the orders to push on were silenced.

'Just the one shot ...' Johnny's voice recovered, then fell way forever as his head blew off and his blood and bits of his bones and bits of his brains spattered over Patie, Dick and Roseblade.

The sergeant wiped the human debris from his face and stared ahead without flinching. 'Now, men!' he roared. 'Open up! Pick a target and let them have it!'

Patie thought he'd felled one and searched for the next as the momentum of the attack faltered. The surge of action consumed him. He wanted to kill more of them, wipe the bastards off the face of the earth before they got the chance of ending his own life. Killing was no longer a case of taking out men, it was about removing as many threats as possible to his own survival. The

Germans had now become targets as impersonal as the sheets stuck to the posts on the firing range at Aldershot, the only difference being that this lot could shoot back.

His finger stroked the trigger, released, reloaded and shot now with an ease driven into them by the pressure of the range. They kept firing, their Lee Enfields spraying the charge with metronomic calm and cut the attacking wave to ribbons.

'Fire at will!' The blue-grey greatcoats were coming closer, moving too quickly to be picked out as separate targets but the momentum was flagging. Rifles rang out as rapidly as they could be reloaded. Bodies splayed out, near enough to see the jets of blood spurting from the heads, from the necks and from anywhere else that was exposed, near enough to hear the air and the life explode from dying bodies. They kept firing, kept the lumps of lead whistling out from the hot barrels, kept up the frenzy until they knew that the attack was on its knees.

They'd held out. They were safe. They'd mown down so many of the bastards that the enemy turned to retreat. So they fired away at their backs and flattened more corpses over a field that, up to then, had known nothing more than the munching quiet of cows at pasture. And they were disappointed when it was all over, when the frantic eruption of killing had run out of targets.

'You can relax,' Roseblade was reassuring them. 'They won't be back. That was their last throw. They'll try to break through somewhere else now.'

They fell back from the lip of the trench, looked around and noticed that many of their own had dropped from their positions. Blood flowed along the floor of the trench over the corpses and over the twitches and moans of the wounded.

They'd survived only because the bullets were destined for the men standing beside them. They'd drawn the winning tickets in the raffle.

'Well, Mullane, how does it feel to be a killer?'

'I don't know. Maybe I'll know more about it tonight.' Dick pulled away from Roseblade's shoulder pat of approval. 'But it's better than what poor Johnny feels.'

They stood over the body, Dick, Patie and Roseblade, and turned it over on its back. One of their own hadn't made it and Patie felt a moment's anger until he remembered that he had inflicted the same on one or more nameless German bodies lying forever in the meadow in front of them.

The killing was the easy part. It was all so instinctive, like being swept along by a flood tide of activity. Thinking about it was another story entirely.

'He should never have been sent here.' Roseblade lifted the greatcoat over the lump of pulp that once had been the head of Johnny O'Brien. 'I suppose some recruiting agent is drinking his blood money just as we're speaking.'

'No', answered Patie. 'Johnny just followed the two of us when we went down to sign up. He only turned seventeen last June.'

'That's the way it goes.' After getting a summary of the casualties, the captain had rejoined them. 'We lost an entire platoon in Le Cateau last month. All from the same village in Dorset and half of them should never have been sent here. Only joined the Territorials when their mates shamed them into it.'

Part Two

Slaughter

November 1914 – November 1918

Do you remember darling

when we walked the moonlit road?

I held you in my arms, love.

I never let you go ...

11

THE WAR failed to resolve itself quickly. Those expecting it to be over by Christmas transferred their hopes to the big recruitment push of 1915 but the boatloads of reinforcements shipped over to Flanders made no impression whatsoever on the Front. Trenches dug during the first autumn of conflict stayed resolutely where they were. Instead of advancing or retreating, they only got bigger, deeper, damper and dirtier as the landscape around them was pounded to smithereens. Where once there were roads and fields, villages and churches; farmhouses and forests were now covered in a uniform carpet of brown mud with only the endless tangles of barbed wire, the occasional tree stump and the odd pile of masonry to break through the horizontal monotony.

Living bodies came and dead bodies were buried and damaged bodies were shipped home as the frocks made their grand speeches in the House of Commons, the generals consulted their maps, the colonels issued their battle orders and the majors told their captains to lead their chaps over the top. Sometimes a few yards were gained; sometimes none at all as the machine guns ripped through the wave of humanity that had survived the barbed wire and the shrapnel from the artillery bombardment;

and sometimes ground was lost when the enemy counter-attacked and advanced through the holes left in the thinned-out defences. But whether they went forwards, backwards or stayed stuck in the same pit of muck never mattered a damn. What was won today was lost tomorrow, what was surrendered was usually regained within the week.

Every now and then, one side or other would wind itself up for a mother and father of an offensive. Battles they called them, even though they could go on for weeks or months on end, as miles of the Front would move forward together into the curtain of fire and reserves continuously poured in to replenish those who had fallen.

If they were on the receiving end, they'd cower under the cover of the trenches for days at a time, sharing the cramped living space with the rats that chewed them and the lice that sucked them and the mosquitoes that bit them as the sky above them caught fire and the earth around them trembled to the shock of 60 pound shells. Then, usually just before dawn, it would suddenly stop and a deathly silence would descend over the pummelled soil of Flanders before the whistles and shouts from a few hundred yards distant would tell them that the enemy was on his way. They'd shoot as often as they could and as fast as they could and they'd pray that they'd mown the guts out of the advancing wave before their line of resistance was surrendered. And if they hadn't been slashed by the bayonets and the sharpened shovels or passed by the sprinting surge to be rounded up as prisoners, they'd keep scampering back to the next line behind them until the invaders ran out of bodies or the attack ran out of steam.

But at least the defenders had cover. If their side was on the offensive, they'd wait until the artillery had blasted No Man's Land into a canyon of craters and dropped a few short while they were at it to kill off some of their own. Then, when the gunners had run out of shells, the ladders would go up and the subalterns would scream and they'd take their place in the queue to go over the top. Eager to escape the claustrophobia, a few would go willingly but most would close their minds and just follow their orders, figuring that there wasn't much difference between the hell up above and the hell down below. And there were always those who couldn't take it, who'd shriek or cower in refusal until they were forced into motion or plugged on the spot by an officer's pistol.

No one, not even the most gung-ho, wanted to be at the head of the line. Those in the first wave over the top were sitting ducks for the mortars and machine guns that would greet them and had nobody ahead of them to show them the paths through the barbed wire. If the other side caught them cold, they'd fall like ninepins and, besides those in the next group fired up for vengeance, there would be others wishing for more of their mates to drop, so that the attack might be abandoned and they themselves might be spared the slaughter.

Most times, though, the charge would proceed regardless of the casualties. Bodies would be ripped by machine-guns, dropped by rifles, blasted by shells, impaled on barbed wire or even drowned in the fetid pools at the bottom of craters. But once the order was given, there was to be no turning back. Death from the enemy was a possibility; execution by the posse of subalterns, NCOs and military policemen preventing the tail of the column from dissolving into retreat was far more certain.

The quicker they made it across No-Man's-Land, the less time they gave the enemy to pick them off, so they'd run as fast as their legs would carry them. And sometimes the euphoria of thousands of comrades all shouting and racing together would propel them through the hailstorm of murderous lead and into the trenches of the enemy where their flailing bayonets and their swinging shovels would drain them of the fear that had been bursting inside them. But when they'd finally rest amidst the screams of the wounded and the blood and the guts of dismembered bodies on which the rats were already feasting, they'd realise that many of their own were lost in the miserable few yards that they'd conquered.

But their thoughts never filtered back up the line. Back at the base, the brass would be toasting success and issuing more orders for the morrow and hailing the knockout weapon that had been used for the first time in battle. Every major offensive saw a new instrument of slaughter arrive at the Front. More often than not, it was some modification on what already was there like a gun that could fire faster or farther or a mortar that launched bigger shells with more powerful explosive. Occasionally, they'd come up with something entirely different like the gas that wafted silent death from arrays of opened cylinders to burn eyes and skin and to scour lungs until they could no longer take in the air around them.

The big battles, however, were only the showpiece moments. Most of their time up in the front lines was spent squatting in the trenches hoping that their generals and the other side's generals would drift towards a tacit agreement of neither shooting first. But even when the sector remained quiet, the orders would still come down the line to keep the men active and every now and then they'd be sent out on reconnaissance missions, sabotage, raiding parties, night assaults or whatever other jolly jape that the bright sparks back at base could think of. They might get caught, they might get lost or they might hide in a crater for an hour to think up some cock-and-bull story before returning. They might take out a machine-gun nest or they might come back with a new issue of weapons or a few hapless prisoners for interrogation and someone from the base might tell them that their sortie would shorten the war by months. But they'd have heard that story many times before and they didn't believe it any more.

In fact, sometimes even their own line officers would take the initiative and volunteer on behalf of the nameless sods in their company, hoping that the recognition gained might win them a medal or a promotion or, if they managed to come back in one piece, the chance to escape from the madness of the Front to the safety of the base.

And if they weren't sent out, they might spend nights shoring up the trenches, repairing the damage of bombardment and rain, cutting the wire, replacing the wire, manhandling supplies, all physically demanding work that had to performed quickly and silently and in total darkness so as not to arouse the snipers. So when morning came, they'd be dead on their feet and they'd snatch any sleep that they could in between the inspections, the day details, their turns on the observation posts out in No-Man's-Land and the squeaking rats waiting for them to nod off.

All that kept them sane was the prospect of rotation when they'd swap duties with the other battalion in the reserve. And when the brigade had served enough penance in the front lines, they'd get their spell away from the action in the rear as a unit fresh from Blighty took up their slot in the roster. Patie Fitzgibbon was counting the days to his temporary escape from the damp, disease and death of the trenches, when he could look at something more than a few yards away from him and not worry about having his head shot off, when he could straighten his back and walk on dry land and when he could wake up in clothes that weren't always sodden with the rains of the spring, the freezing fog of the winter or the sweat of the summer.

He had already put down sixteen months on a few square miles in the flat fields of Flanders. Ever since the 5th Battalion of The King's Own West Sussex Rifles had dug themselves in by the river Lys north of Béthune, the Front had barely moved more than a couple of hundred yards in either direction. And even though the battalion had immediately been shunted northwards towards Ypres to help head off the German push to the sea, it amounted to nothing more than being lifted from one hole in the ground and being planted in another. The only difference brought by the passage of time was the unrelenting spread of the band of pulverised muck on both sides of the line snaking from Basel to Ostend, that divided the combatants.

A fresh batch of recruits were making themselves known, having come in before dawn to replace a gang of Geordies sent back to their coal mines in Northumberland and a raiding party that had wandered out into the night and had never come back. Even in battalions like 5th West Sussex that had escaped relatively lightly up to then, the volunteers were now in the majority. By the time they had reached their first Christmas, battle, sniping, bombardment, infection and the many diseases that festered in the putrid air of the trenches had already decimated the regulars and another year of war had thinned out the reservists and Territorials sent over to fill up the gaps.

This new lot might have been wet behind the ears and straight off the boat from Blighty, but at least they had willingly entered the war. Soon, even the volunteers would dry up and their replacements would be drawn from the ranks of the disinclined dragged into service by the Conscription Act that had just been introduced in England, Scotland and Wales.

'And where might you lot be from?' Maggot Tibbs welcomed the arrivals. The battalion's first taste of action had established new reputations and the Cockney professional had slipped down the pecking order of attention. But there were always newcomers to impress.

'Chichester, ' answered one.

'Upwaltham,' replied another, a gangly pink-faced youngster who looked as if he'd never stepped outside his village in his life.

'Up where?' repeated Maggot, raising a nervous laugh from the other recruits. 'Up there?'

'Like I said, it be Upwaltham where I be coming from.'

'And no finer place,' the old hand reassured him.

The newcomers looked around for a face that they might recognise. They'd need one. No-one survived at the Front without a small circle of mates, especially in a battalion like the 5th West Sussex which had been around since the early days of the fighting, and it was obvious to Patie that none of this lot had known each other before they joined up.

It was different when he himself had arrived with Dick Mullane and Johnny O'Brien and the rest of the Micks that Hennessy had shipped over from West Limerick and passed off as reservists. Back then, it was all about mates. As well as Patie's own group and the regulars and reservists who had already served with each other, 5th West Sussex had its townies from Chichester and Worthing, its farmhands from villages in the South Downs, its clerks and its shop assistants answering the call of the Empire and its gangs of pals from London or from the mill towns of Lancashire who had all joined up together and who had seen the inside of a train for the first time in their lives when they crossed half of England in order to enlist. After a few weeks of rubbing up against each other, they found it easier to confine themselves to their own little worlds and, while they might have been in the same army, in the same sector, even in the same brigade, they stuck to those they'd known or whose backgrounds they'd known in real life before the war had begun.

The line officers and the NCOs didn't mind. While there'd be the occasional spat between townies and yokels, between the Cockneys and the cloggies or between the Paddies and the English, mates mostly kept to themselves in an uneasy truce of live and let live. They were also easier to command and they would often spur each other to feats braver than those they'd attempt were they cast among a group of strangers. There were even the Pals Battalions, groups of up to a thousand from the same town or same factory or the same football club or university who had all enlisted together when the recruitment drums were beating at their loudest.

The volunteers would have been at the Front months earlier had the War Office stocked up enough uniforms, rifles and kit and many of them had spent the guts of a year drilling in barrack squares and tramping around the south of England, half-kitted out and armed with walking-sticks just like the Volunteers back in Ireland. But when a fresh wave of bodies filled the graveyards after the futile attack on Loos, outsiders with experience in business were drafted in to shake up the timeservers in the Army's support functions. Only then did properly trained and equipped manpower begin to arrive in numbers.

Batt Mullane, Dinny Lyons, Mick Culhane, Jerry Curtin, Tim Curtin, Mick Fitzgerald and Flint had arrived the previous October and swelled the Shanagolden contingent of the 5th West Sussex which had a mystique all of its own due to the presence of Dick Mullane. No-one saw much of the battalion's sniper during the hours of daylight as he departed for his post before dawn, But they'd hear the odd crack of his rifle and the retaliatory ping of from the other side's marksman before he crawled back at nightfall and they'd wonder what he was doing in his lonely vigil hiding behind the lip of a crater or a mound of debris

Dick was cleaning his Canadian-issue Ross Rifle before sneaking out over the top for another day's work when Maggot pointed him out to the newcomer from Upwaltham.

'See that chap?' he whispered into the youth's ear. 'Dead-eye Dick, they calls him. He's a killer.'

'A killer?'

'He's out all day plugging Huns. Every day of the week.' Maggot grabbed the recruit by the arm and brought his finger to his lips. 'I reckon he's killed hundreds of them so far, so he has. Guess how many he plugged yesterday?'

'I've no idea.'

'Then why don't you ask him?'

The recruit glanced around at the others nodding encouragement.

'Go on, ask him,' repeated Maggot. 'He won't bite you.'

'Begging your pardon, sir, but could I ask you a question?' The newcomer tipped Dick gingerly on the shoulder. 'Some of us be wondering like ... aah ... how many Germans you bagged yesterday?'

Dick didn't utter a word in the reply, just turned around with a glare so chilling that it would be months before his questioner would even attempt to look him straight in the eye again. And casting his glance further, he immediately silenced the sniggers of Maggot and his mates at the youngster's discomfort.

Gathering his water bottle, his rations, his field glasses, clips of ammo and an aerial reconnaissance photograph taken two days before into his kit bag, he inched up the ladder and slid out into the first flickers of daylight to a new crater that he'd identified the day before. As the soles of Dick's boots disappeared over the top, the laughter started again. But Patie could see the nervousness in the bravado. While the veterans could take the mickey out of the newcomers, they wouldn't chance the reaction of the battalion's top marksman either. And as Dick refused to confirm or deny their speculation, the legend of the ice-cold killer in their midst grew all the more.

Among his own, however, Dick was still the same young fella that came from the same parish seven hundred miles and the width of two seas away. And if he'd plugged any of the enemy during the day, he'd open up to Patie during the quiet of the night and whisper incessantly away about the place they'd left behind them so that he'd could remove his mind from where they had been landed. Every notch on his gun-barrel increased the conviction that his own time was just around the corner and he was resigned to the fact that the death he'd inflicted on others would surely rebound on himself. He'd survived way beyond the normal lifespan of a sniper, but that was only because he'd always used his bullets sparingly and because he had already marked out his escape every time he pressed the trigger and gave his position away. But somewhere, sometime, in the hidey-holes on the other side of the Front, a marksman as good as himself was bound to appear and, after figuring out what was inside Dick's head, would bag the prize that Germany's army around the Ypres salient had desperately been seeking.

Maybe Dick would make it through this tour as well. Patie knew that they'd only another day before their spell in the front trench was over and they'd rotate with the other battalion in the reserve. A week on, a week off was how it was supposed to be during their time in the Lines, but their roster was at the whim of the brass. If a battle began, if another company had taken a hit, if replacements hadn't arrived, if orders went missing or if a lieutenant-colonel or one of his majors felt the need to impress someone above them, the rotation would be forgotten and they'd have to face another stretch in the hell-hole around them. In a sector as slap-happy as the Ypres salient where they were surrounded on three sides by the Hun, such oversights happened more often than the norm.

Even the practise of alternating companies every few days between the front trench and the support trench was a fiction. Because the combat zone intruded into the German positions, the British positions in the 5th West Sussex's area had been squeezed back on top of each other and the second line of defence was almost as exposed as the first. Stuck in the zig-zag of bays into which the front trench was divided so as to reduce the radius of exploding shrapnel and to prevent attacks from the side or strafing by aircraft from turning them into slaughter alleys, all Patie and his comrades could ever see was ten yards to the left, ten yards to the right and the small patch of sky directly above them.

'What's so funny, Maggot?' The laughter centred around the company's comedian stopped as the sergeant approached and pulled the recruits aside to parcel them out among the bays along the company's quarter-mile section of the line. 'Roberts, you take these two and show them the ropes. Fletcher, tell this pair how to stay alive. And you can take the rest, Maggot. You've survived the Army longer than anyone else in the battalion.'

It took less than a moment's direction for the newcomers to realise that there was an authority in the trench superseding the smart comments of the old hands. He might have put them through hell back in Aldershot and on their first days at the Front, but Roseblade knew how to take care of his men. And unlike the officers that came and went, the company sergeant earned respect the hard way by enduring the same deprivation as those under his command.

Without the NCOs, Patie reckoned that every army he'd come across at the Front – the British, the French, the Belgians, the Portuguese, the Canadians, the Australians, the Newfoundlanders and maybe even the Germans as well – would long since have collapsed into thousands of little cliques all looking out for number one. While Governments declared war, the brass made the plans and the line officers read them out, it was the sergeants who got the squads, the platoons, the companies and the battalions into motion, who dragged the willing and the unwilling along the same direction, who saw where whatever piece of the jigsaw they commanded fitted into the overall picture. They all had their own ways of doing it. Some of them bullied, some cajoled, some shamed, some turned a blind eye to the rough justice beneath them, some made the occasional example and blew a slacker's brains out in full view of everyone, but the most successful just led and their men followed their example.

And it was easy to measure how effective any NCO was. Units that had floggers, cowards or lickspittles over them didn't last very long. They'd run from attack or surrender to the first hint of aggression or dawdle over the top in the hope that some other company would cop it in their place or plug the bastard who was making their life hell when no-one was looking. But C Company, 5th West Sussex had survived better than most, despite the fact that they'd seen action during the early days of mobile warfare and had been through the trench battles of St. Julien and Bellewaarde. And on the odd occasion when the various factions might collectively reflect on it, they would feel a flicker of pride in their longevity and a grudging respect for the sergeant that had led them.

'And the rest of you, start pumping.' The platoons split into work gangs and, under Roseblade's supervision, filed along the duckboards to hold back the tide. Even though their efforts would ultimately prove as futile as those of King Canute, they might get an extra few days of relative dryness before their escape to the rear. Apart from the cold, Flanders wasn't as bad in the depths of winter when the frozen soil held back the flooding but an unexpected thaw over the previous few days had spawned pools of water along the floors of the trenches.

Eager to show what good soldiers they were, Batt Mullane and Dinny Lyons manned the hand-pump that sucked the water out into the drainage dyke they'd uncovered underneath the communication trench. Patie had no idea where that led to. It could end up flooding some other unit's sleeping quarters but, wherever it went, it was no longer 'C' Company's problem.

Keeping their heads down, Patie, Mick Culhane, Mick Fitzgerald and the Curtin brothers filled the jute sacks with clay and piled them on top of each other to shore up the trench's seeping walls. Flint hung about feigning activity but mostly getting in everyone else's way.

Dig, bag, pack and say nothing. The toil settled into a rhythm. If he paced his motion and effort, Patie could lose himself in the task, work up enough of a sweat to keep warm and, for a couple of hours, forget entirely about the war being waged around him.

12

THE STATIONMASTER checked his watch with all the solemnity of his vocation, the guard waved his flag and District Inspector Nicholas Sullivan reached for his copy of The Freeman's Journal. He was glancing through the death notices that had been swelled by casualties at the Front when his eye caught two figures racing down the platform. The slamming carriage door told him that they'd managed to scramble onto the Limerick train as it eased out of Newcastlewest station.

Keeping the newspaper level with his nose, he allowed just a hint of his eyes to edge over the page as the pair bounded breathlessly up the centre aisle in search of a seat. Ned Reidy didn't surprise him as he'd sometimes go up to the city on business to do with the farm or the co-op but Willie Hartnett, decked out for the first time in a tweed jacket and knickerbockers that failed to lend him the air of a gentleman of leisure, was not a man to frequent the railways. Despite the fact that he'd been sacked a month earlier by James Horgan for going missing for two days from his job at the creamery, he now appeared to have more money in his pocket than he ever had before in his life.

Even without his network of informers to confirm it, Sullivan knew that Hartnett and Reidy were involved with the Fenians. Not only had they led the rump of dissidents resisting the Home Ruler takeover of the Volunteers but there had also been sightings of leading members of the Brotherhood like Patrick Pearse, Ned Daly and Con Colbert in the Shanagolden area over the previous year. But the speed at which Hartnett and Reidy had been elevated had taken him aback. The IRB might have muttered revolution over their pints and small ones in the snugs of dingy bars but, when it came to shelling out their limited resources, they could be as stingy as the faceless Civil Servants responsible for the payment of his policemen.

The sudden flush of money raised Sullivan's suspicions and confirmed the fears that he had been harbouring for the best part of a year. The Volunteers hadn't sprung form nowhere and now, with Redmond's Home Rule faction having lost half of their membership to the Front and the rest disappearing into irrelevance, the Sinn Féin element who stayed behind had stepped into the vacuum. While few people expressed it publicly as long as the newspapers continued their support for Our Boys at the Front, resentment against the war was rising slowly and silently in the patchwork of pockets that were forever hidden from British rule.

As the fighting stuttered on to no visible sign of resolution; as victory by Christmas 1914 became victory by Christmas 1915 and then by Christmas 1916, each latest reverse added to the change in the mood. Among the thousands to perish inside a few hours at Aubers Ridge were thirty Limerickmen who were left without a single inch of territory to show for their sacrifice. Loos, the great knockout blow in Northern France, staggered to a halt as both sides sent telegrams home to relatives and shipped back the amputees, the blind, the gas victims and those gone mad

168

from shell shock to the sheds hastily tacked onto the County Asylums. And when the Munster Fusiliers were slaughtered by the heat and disease and by the bullets of Turkish defenders of Gallipoli and the survivors were pulled out in the dead of night not having moved from the beaches in eight months, the trickle of recruits dried up completely, the whispers in the pubs became louder and the District Inspector's policemen were again hearing the faceless taunts as they passed by street corners.

In England, in Scotland and in Wales, they'd introduced conscription to plug the holes left by the dead, the disabled and the demented, but Sullivan and almost the entire middle management of the RIC had warned that they'd be crazy to extend it to Ireland. For once, the authorities in Dublin Castle had listened to their ears on the ground and accepted that disaffection, suffering and resentment carried entirely different meanings on John Bull's other island which, just eighteen months earlier, had been teetering on the brink of civil war.

But they'd dismissed reports from District Inspectors of steady recruitment by secret societies radically opposed to the union with Britain and who they knew had actively sought the support of Germany and its Kaiser. Where was the evidence, asked the complacent officials as they pointed to the continuing health of the Irish Parliamentary Party. Support for the war hadn't dented Redmond's Home Rulers from comfortably winning all eight by-elections called for Nationalist constituencies after the outbreak of hostilities. Unlike some areas in England and Scotland, anti-war candidates had made no impression whatsoever in Ireland.

Keep the lid on, everyone was saying. Home Rule was on the statute book and ready to come into effect once the conflict was over. Both Redmond and Carson had lined up their MPs in support of the new Coalition government. If the belligerent factions of Ireland could come together during war, then surely the goodwill would carry over to peacetime.

However, if those advising the Chief Secretary had come down to Sullivan's stretch of West Limerick, the Inspector could have pointed out to them what was happening in the countryside of Munster. Young men who, in other times, would have emigrated were now staying on farms with their older brothers or were working in the creameries or the bacon factories or as assistants in the shops where comfortable farmers were spending an income boosted by the Front's insatiable demand for food. Given the chance of employment in their own areas for the first time ever, there was no way that this group, who had a better education and higher expectations than their fathers, was going to follow those duped into enlisting during the first flush of enthusiasm. So when the Sinn Féin preachers came around with their message of opposition to the war, they were more than willing to listen.

Sullivan was well aware that Hartnett and Reidy, both sworn members of the Brotherhood, were two of the more effective evangelists hanging around the hurling and football games, the Gaelic League meetings and the music feiseanna in the hope of drumming up support for the cause. But up to then, he had always regarded them more as carriers of the message rather than members of the circle that wrote it. Now that their activity was taking them outside their home area, they had either been promoted from the ranks, or else the IRB was planning activity beyond the mere rhetoric that had sustained it for a generation. Colleagues had told him of the crowd that had turned up the previous summer for the funeral of the old Fenian Jeremiah O'Donovan Rossa, of the display of Volunteer military strength and of Pearse's messianic oration at the graveside.

'Your ticket? ... Sorry, I didn't recognise you, Inspector.'

The policeman handed over his ticket, then winked to the conductor to edge closer. 'Those two men who jumped on while the train was pulling out,' he mentioned softly.

'You mean Edmund Reidy's son and that other fella?'

'You wouldn't know where they're headed?'

'Are they in some trouble?' Sullivan's tensed eyebrows put a stop to the railwayman's curiosity. 'They've through tickets to Kingsbridge. Single ones at that.' A passing landmark caught his attention. 'Next stop Ballingarrane!' boomed his finely-tuned delivery. 'All change for Askeaton and Foynes.'

The Inspector folded his paper and watched the neat fields of the Palatine farmers move past the window. They might have been of German descent and one or two of the old ones still spoke the language, but more of their sons had gone off to fight the Kaiser than those of their Catholic neighbours.

So, Reidy and Hartnett were on their way to Dublin. His suspicions had been strengthened, but was there anyone around who'd believe him?

'You don't mind if I join you?' Without waiting for the invitation, Thomas Hennessy sat down beside him. 'There's a small matter I'd like to pick your brains about.'

Sullivan's shuffle of disinterest failed to deter the Councillor. 'I was wondering about this fall off in recruitment. Is there any reports of lads being discouraged from signing up?'

'Why, have you heard anything?'

'You can rest assured I'd be the first to tell you.' Hennessy's teeth broke into a thin smile. 'Off the record, you understand, but is there any chance that these elements opposed to the war are picking up support?'

'Wouldn't a man in position like yourself be a better judge of what the public thinks than a simple policeman like myself?'

More than the loss of recruiting commission was bothering the Councillor. Sullivan had heard that Hennessy had made a sizeable donation to someone-in-the-know in London in the hope of securing a knighthood and was now debating whether it would be wise to pursue his investment if there was a shift in public sentiment. 'But my own opinion, for what it's worth, is that you can never be sure of what the people will do. They'll swear Parnell is God one day and they'll denounce him as the Devil the next ... Aah, Sir Herbert!' A passenger boarding at Ballingarrane released Sullivan from the unwelcome company.

'I must look a right eejit in this.' Willie Hartnett squirmed in the unaccustomed outfit as they changed trains in Limerick.

'It was all we could find that'd fit you.' Ned Reidy had the dapper confidence to get away with wearing anything. Were he to appear in hand-me-downs from a pawnshop, women would still admire the cut of his clothes and young bucks would ask him who was his tailor. 'And even if you don't look the part, the peelers are slower to take an interest in you if you're wearing the clothes of the gentry.'

Word had come down to them about a gathering in Dublin where their attendance was expected. Not only would it be the first occasion that Willie had travelled beyond Limerick, but it would also be his first chance of meeting others from different parts of the country. Obsessed with secrecy, the IRB kept its membership under a tight chain of command and, for many, the most they would be aware of were one or two local colleagues and their contact from the Supreme Council. While it was the most effective means of guarding against informers, it kept those on the periphery like himself ignorant of where the movement as a whole was headed.

For almost a year and a half, he had busied himself with the Volunteers, keeping their own local unit intact, going on the lookout for new members and building up links with other groups around the county so that they could put up a respectable show whenever they demonstrated in public. It had been a lonely station at the beginning when they were pelted with accusations of treachery against Our Boys at the Front. But they'd stuck at it and, once the war failed to behave in the way that its supporters had predicted, even the uncommitted and the cynical began to entertain a sneaking regard for their persistence. And the longer the fighting dragged on, the more they could point to the emptiness of the Home Rulers' promises. No-one in his right mind believed any longer that those Irishmen who would never make it back from Flanders, Mesopotamia and Gallipoli had died in the defence of small nations.

Yet the activity of the Volunteers had to lead somewhere. It was easy enough to point out where Redmond had gone wrong but, if they hadn't some objective of their own, they too would suffer the fate of those National Volunteers who had stayed behind deluding themselves that they were Ireland's home guard. Once the telegrams began to arrive on the doorsteps and the flow of recruits dried up, the Home Rulers had kept their heads down in case anyone asked them what they stood for and it had been almost a year seen they'd gathered in public. Those same critics were now lying in wait for the followers of Eoin MacNeill and Patrick Pearse.

The introduction of conscription across the water had given the movement breathing space and Willie and Ned had milked it for what it was worth. The people might not have been ready to rise up against England but, if it was to be a choice between death on a far foreign field fighting a war that no longer had any credibility and taking up arms against those who would force

173

them to enlist, the young men of West Limerick would prefer to take their chances on home soil. However, once the immediate threat had passed, the question remained as to what to do next.

Willie hoped that he might get an answer in Dublin from his fellow members of the IRB who, through their invisible network, controlled the national leadership and most of the local units of the Volunteers. Ever since he had first argued the toss with Pearse in Edmund Reidy's cowshed, he had pieced together whatever resources that might be of use and waited for the call to action. It didn't amount to very much, a couple of hundred Volunteers that he could depend on, a handful of rifles, a few hideouts and the details buried inside his head regarding the strength of the military garrison and of the RIC and the weaknesses that could be exploited. But if the same numbers were spread all over the country and they all rose up together, the British would need to bring entire divisions back from the Front to quell them. If they had to introduce conscription to keep their war going in France, they'd be hard pushed to spare them for Ireland.

Ned was winking at two young English ladies in the seat across from them yet effortlessly managing to bury his head in a book every time the dragon of a chaperone turned around.

'Ahem!' she snarled.

It took Willie a few moments to realise that he was the focus of the basilisk gaze. The girls struggled to suppress their giggles.

'Ahem!' repeated their minder.

'Madam?' Ned looked up from his collection of poems. 'May I be of assistance?'

'Indeed ...' The words drained away as the chaperone detected a roguish hint behind the innocent bemusement. 'Humph!'

'Edmund Reidy.' Ned introduced himself over the speechless outrage. 'Of Ballycormick House, Shanagolden. But, pray, do call me Ned. Even my closest friends do.'

'Lady Anna Jermyn,' announced the bolder of the pair. 'And my sister, Lady Charlotte.'

'Daddy must be very important.' The wicked smile provoked another fit of the giggles. 'A grand panjandrum?'

'He's a general,' ventured Lady Anna with mock indignation.

'Forgive me.'

'Forgiven.'

'Next stop Kildare,' chanted the conductor. 'All change for Athy, Carlow, Bagenalstown and all stations to Kilkenny and Waterford.'

'Anna!' The chaperone recovered her spit. 'Do hurry along.'

'Take care of their luggage, Hartnett, like a good chap,' Ned ordered.

Willie grabbed the three cases from the luggage rack and carried them to the door. Lady Charlotte passed him a sidelong glance, unsure of whether to flirt with him, to thank him or to hand him a tip. Lady Anna's handkerchief fluttered to the floor of the carriage as she alighted. Their minder frantically waved for a porter.

Ned picked up the white cloth and held it aloft. Lady Anna waved back as the train moved away.

'None of your scruples in those two.' He folded the handkerchief carefully and placed it in his breast pocket as he returned to his seat. 'We could have had some right fun if they'd stayed on a while longer.'

'Don't you ever talk down to me like that again.'

'What?' Unsure of the tone in Willie's voice, Ned pulled his attentions back from the window. 'I was only having a joke to impress the girls,' he protested. But he got the message in the unsmiling response.

They sat in silence for the remainder of the journey. Willie looked out over the rolling plains of the Curragh where only the occasional furze bush broke up the faded green commonage of grass clipped by the munching teeth of lowland sheep. Far in the distance, the tip of a tower broke through a stand of trees to reveal the centre of the British military presence in Ireland and, more than likely, the senior officers' quarters where the Lady Anna, the Lady Charlotte and their chaperone were headed.

Willie's first sight of Dublin amazed him. On the couple of previous occasions when he'd visited Limerick city, he'd seen the mean soot-stained terraces and the brick chimneys pointing to the sky, he'd drawn the blackened air into his lungs, he'd heard the babble of the carters, of the porters and of the hackneys but the intensity was nothing compared to what hit him when he set foot on the platform of Kingsbridge Station. Every way he looked, he was greeted by marching footsteps, by bellowed commands and by the uniforms of the soldiers, the Dublin Metropolitan Police, the railwaymen, the postmen, the telegraph boys and even those of a herd of Boy Scouts returning from an outing.

'Some smell,' he remarked to Ned as they waited for a tram downwind from the brewery.

'It's only the half of what it usually is,' muttered a man beside him. 'Guinness's are on the short week since they started closing the pubs during the day.'

'Even the best jobs aren't secure any more,' added another. 'Most of the distilleries have closed down altogether.'

Unlike the countryside living off the demand for its food, the war was biting in Dublin. There was real hunger in the faces passing Willie by and a sullen resentment in the groups gathered at the corners, beside the whores touting for business from the uniforms emerging from the station, the beggars rattling their outstretched tin cups, the youngsters peddling their services beyond the trading patch of the established porters and the musicians and buskers murdering the life out rebel songs and music hall numbers with equal efficiency.

A squad of policemen moved through those scrambling to survive and cleared them away with a flourish of their batons, much to the approval of some of those queuing at the tram stop. But the peelers might as well not have bothered. As the tram pulled away within minutes of the law's departure, every one of the hunted had filtered back to their previous positions from the maze of laneways hidden behind the façade of tall buildings that lined the quays of the river.

A group of bowler-hatted passengers in the seats ahead of Willie were loudly complaining about the lack of hackneys as a result of horses being requisitioned by the military, about the rising cost of food, about the difficulties in finding tradesmen or replacing staff who had gone to the Front, about being unable to play tennis any more because all the available rubber had been commandeered for tyre production. Enemies everywhere were causing their discomfort, the submarines that were sinking the merchant ships, the black marketeers, the work-shy slackers left behind while the most industrious had rallied to the flag, the Government regulations interfering in the affairs of honest business.

Neither he nor Ned opened their mouths. Inside the cramped lower saloon ringing with indignation, country accents somehow seemed out of place, as if they too were part of the conspiracy that had soured Dublin into a carping bed of discontent.

They mooched aimlessly around the O'Connell monument at the bottom of Sackville Street until a messenger boy on a bicycle signalled them to follow him on a roundabout journey over Carlisle Bridge that ended outside a pub in a laneway off College Green. Hastily bundled upstairs by the landlord, they found themselves packed into a drawing room with over three dozen others.

Willie recognised Patrick Pearse, Con Colbert and Ned Daly but the others were all strangers and nobody bothered to make introductions. Instead, they were greeted with a frosty silence that was broken by a quiet man with a dark moustache and a limp and an accent from somewhere west of the Shannon.

'What the hell were ye doing on the train?'

Willie showed his surprise but the inquisition was directed at Ned.

'Do you realise who you gave your name and address to?' continued the interrogator. 'The daughters of the head of British military intelligence. Not to mention the woman who was minding them.'

'Lady Anna?'

'Yes. Lady Anna Jermyn. And Lady Charlotte Jermyn. And Agent Emily Colclough. And she told the man working for them who followed ye out to the tram stop.'

'Ye were also spotted by District Inspector Sullivan who tailed ye from Newcastlewest,' added a pale young man with the voice of the gentry and a foppish cravat tied around his neck.

'Sorry about that,' was all Ned could reply.

'Sorry?' asked the young man. 'This isn't a game.'

On a nod from the stooped elderly man in the corner with the thinning hair and the bristly moustache, Pearse intervened. 'We can all make mistakes. But ye'll have to be more careful.'

Willie stayed in the background as discussion was dominated by Pearse and by the young man they called Joe Plunkett. Most of it had to do with details of times and places that passed over his head. Every now and then, they'd ask someone what the state of readiness was in particular areas and a variety of accents would say that they might have enough men to call on but that there wasn't much they could do with only a couple of rifles.

But even if he heard only snatches, Willie could see the bigger picture emerging. The order would be issued in the coming weeks for the Volunteers to parade and manoeuvre in public and all units were expected to take part. However, what would happen next would not be decided by the movement headed by Eoin MacNeill but by those gathered in the room who were not just leading members of the IRB but of a smaller faction within it controlled by those leading the discussion.

They were a motley group, yet their diversity convinced him that whatever they were planning might work. The self-taught like Connolly, the round-faced middle-aged trade unionist with the Scottish accent, and the old man Clarke who had spent decades in English jails for his Fenian activities; those of learning like Pearse, Plunkett and MacDonagh who'd come in from the Gaelic League; the Connachtmen, MacDermott quietly pulling the strings and Ceannt taking everything in; they represented every stripe of the nation's anger.

Nothing was asked of how things were going in West Limerick but, when the meeting broke up and they slipped back down to the pub in ones and twos, Pearse called Willie and Ned aside.

'Ye can't go back, lads. Not for a few weeks anyway. They're on to ye.' He led them down a backstairs into a rarely-used hallway. 'Better ye stay around in Dublin and keep them guessing.' He handed Willie an address in Blackrock. 'Have you ever stood behind a bar?'

'No. But I'm a fast learner.'

'Good. He's a long-time supporter. You'll be fed and found as long as you can help him out when he needs you. And ask him to get you another suit of clothes. You look a right eejit in that outfit.'

The publican was a decent man, a bachelor in his fifties from Tipperary whose brother had once been a leading light in the Fenians, and he didn't pinch on the food or the heating. But the joints were troubling him and he was finding it increasingly difficult to tap the barrels, stock the shelves and clean up after the custom had left. While he did have the services of a widow woman who would come in during the day to cook his meals and clean out the house, that was the extent of her exertions. In her mind, heavy work was a man's work, especially since the man she'd spent years looking after showed no inclinations towards marriage.

So, when she washed up after the dinner and left the sandwiches ready for the tea before departing into whatever occupied her afternoons, the deliveries from the brewery and the mineral water company had to be tackled, the coal scuttles had to be filled for the various fireplaces, the ashes cleared out and, even though the landlord would insist that he was all right, Willie couldn't find it in his heart to leave him struggling away on his own.

Whatever about the city, Blackrock, a seaside town five miles down the Wexford line from the centre of Dublin, appeared to have adapted to the war without major deprivation. Business was brisk after six o'clock as the commuters filed in from the railway station and, after they cleared off for high tea in the boarding house or the family home, another burst would turn up later in the evening. Working for the Government, his landlord had told him, doing nicely out of the new love affair with regulations that told everyone what they could eat and what time they'd to turn the lights out and when they could have a drink and how much fodder could be spared for their horses.

'Of course, it don't seem to apply to themselves,' he had added.

They certainly weren't short of money and the urgency of the war had been accompanied by an urgency to spend. A fair load of them were English, more came from the loyal Protestant middle class of Dublin but, as the publican pointed out, increasing numbers were Catholics intent on gatecrashing the party. And to a man, they saw their future tied to the Empire and Crown.

He'd been on Blackrock's Main Street for almost twenty years, Willie had gathered, he'd been listening in on the drunken conversations of those administering Britain's rule and they'd never once suspected his loyalties. The licensed trade was one of the few occupations left to Catholics from the great sweep of country a train journey beyond the city's limits and, like the domestics they employed in their houses, the customers had relegated their publicans to the status of furniture.

Willie quickly picked up on the nuances that shots of whiskey had allowed to escape from the strictures of confidentiality. Although Dublin Castle had dismissed RIC reports of Sinn Féin and Fenian activity as nothing more than scaremongering, they were coming under increasing pressure from Carson's Unionist presence in the British Cabinet and they deported a handful of prominent IRB members to England. But that only provoked a Home Ruler response of not providing extremists with martyrs that would undermine the position of parliamentary Nationalism and those expelled were almost immediately allowed to return.

It wasn't always easy to place where the sympathies of the clientele lay within the constraints of their loyalty. Some were sympathetic to the no-nonsense approach of the Conservatives

181

and others were affected Liberal concerns. But to a man, they were united in their derision of their superiors dithering between repression and not rocking the boat. Viewed from close at hand, the monolith of the British administration looked far less forbidding.

When Saturday afternoon arrived, the relief barman turned up and Willie got his chance for some time off. His landlord pressed two pound notes into his fist as he headed out the door.

'Treat her right,' he told him with a wink. 'And don't worry about who's following you. It gives you the excuse to be here.'

He made his way up Carysfort Avenue and waited across the road from the stone pillars. She was slow coming out, almost the last of the primly dressed ladies escaping for an hour from the rigid attentions of the nuns and all of them yakking away to each other in their heady moment of freedom.

'Josie,' he whispered as he passed her by. She turned but, as she did so, a tall gaunt academic with a prominent nose passed between them. Willie recognised him from the IRB meeting but there was no response from the other man.

'Willie!' she cried, too late to deny any hint of familiarity. Her classmates blinked, nodded and simpered as they stored up the newfound knowledge for later on that night when they'd returned to the dormitory.

He turned back towards Blackrock and she followed at a respectable distance until she was sure that she was beyond the prying range of the nuns of Carysfort. Only when they reached the anonymity of the Main Street did she deem it safe enough to draw up alongside him.

'How are you, love?' Not having seen her in over a year and then only for a brief moment after Midnight Mass on Christmas

Eve, he was half-afraid of how she'd react to him appearing out of the blue.

She edged her head closer but said nothing. Maybe he should have sent her letters but he'd never been a man for writing.

The publican smiled at them as they passed the open door of his premises.

He sensed the imperceptible touch edging him towards the seafront and then up over the footbridge that straddled the railway. The black wind of March whistled in from the Irish Sea as they stood over the deserted bathing places. He wondered if she was trying to let him down gently.

A sudden gust caused her to huddle in behind him. Then, with one hand clamping her hat to her head and the other snaking into his fingers, she led him down the steps towards the white waves below and around the iron columns of the bridge.

'Oh My God, Willie! I thought you'd forgotten.' They pressed as tightly as they could as other couples passed them by in the sanctuary beyond the squinting windows. She might have known some of them as classmates and he might have recognised others as customers and not necessarily with their wives, but nothing was visible beyond the embrace of their bodies.

The tea shop on the Main Street was filled for the most part by matrons of leisure discussing dress, debuts and the deprivations of war, but a corner was reserved for young ladies and their escorts and was partitioned into booths that allowed for both privacy of conversation and constant surveillance as a guard against any unseemly conduct.

Over her objections that they just share a pot of coffee, he insisted on her sampling the cream pastries.

'Mmm. I always wondered what they'd tasted like.' She wiped the little flecks of icing sugar from the tips of her fingers. He edged his hand closer but the instant cough of disapproval from behind him caused it to retract.

'It's the only place in Blackrock we're allowed into.' She folded up the serviette and laid it aside. 'The nuns have their spies everywhere.' Her eyes twinkled at his surprise.

'But not down beyond the railway.' He signalled for a refill of coffee. 'Not the sort of place that young ladies should know about.'

'My first time down there. But everyone in the class knows about it.' She blushed ever so slightly. He believed her.

'And there's worse,' she whispered. 'Down beyond the next footbridge, there's a place where men go off together with men.'

'You're not serious?'

The coffee pot arrived. He filled up the two cups.

'By the way, you seem to know our maths teacher?'

'Who?' Then he remembered the IRB man that had passed him by at the gate.

'Mr. de Valera. Of course, you probably would have met him. Isn't he from Bruree.' A sudden clearance from the adjoining booths caused her to finish her coffee with unseemly speed. 'We've got to go. Will I see you next Saturday?'

He rushed to hold her coat as she joined the stampede of her classmates.

13

PATIE FITZGIBBON never found the reserve trenches to be a whole lot better than the misery of the front line. Sure, he'd look forward all right to withdrawing from direct exposure to the snipers and the attacks; in fact he'd almost crave it by the time their stretch up front came to an end. And when he was moved back from the damp, death and disease of the war's cockpit, his mind would be obsessed with finding somewhere quiet to drop the head where, for a moment, he could forget about the hell-hole in which he had landed.

But even a mile or two distant from the combat zone, the battalion wasn't given the opportunity to switch off. There was always the chance of a bombardment, of a gas attack or of the occasional stray mortar overshooting its target. And just in case they might become complacent at being two lines removed from the first point of contact with the enemy, orders would ring in their ears to keep them on their toes and they would be badgered into moving supplies up the communication trenches, manhandling the mountains of shells arriving to fill the insatiable appetite of the artillery and endlessly stripping down, cleaning and reassembling rifles, machine guns and mortars.

It wasn't quite as bad when they were sent back to the rear where they hung around the base catching up on their sleep, playing cards, Crown and Anchor and soccer, drinking sweetened white wine in the estaminets, writing letters home or worrying about their wives and their sweethearts. But even there, the brass, the NCOs and the regulations kept intruding on their lives. They could be dragged off to the training grounds where sergeant-majors ran them over circuits, sent them out on full day marches and, when they couldn't think of anything else, had them drilling over any hard surface that reverberated to the beat of their footsteps. They might be dragooned off to rail sidings to empty out the wagonloads of hay and oats for feeding the horses. Or they could be detailed to clean out the quarters at the base where the brass ate and drank, planned and reported, washed and shat, awarded themselves medals, mentioned themselves in dispatches, totted up the casualties, signed telegrams of condolence and gave parties where they could sample the whores who'd been shipped up from Paris or Rouen.

If their superiors were in the right frame of mind and there was transport available, they might get a few days in some place like Dunkirk or Saint-Omer where there were diversions open to the ordinary rank and file. More often than not, a fair load of them would get mad roaring drunk, argue over the girls they'd picked up or the rounds of drink they hadn't paid for, end up in fistfights with local civilians, with French, Belgian or Australian soldiers, with other brigades, with other groups within their own battalion or even among themselves and the MPs would arrive, batter their heads with their batons, slam them into the cells and send them back to their sector throbbing with hangovers.

On this rotation, 5th West Sussex didn't make it out of the base. Nor did they even get their full ration of rest. Someone said that the replacement unit slotting into the roster had been torpedoed in the Channel. Another story claimed that they'd been sent to the wrong sector. Patie didn't believe either explanation. He'd heard them all before and the vagaries of command no longer surprised him.

Eight days was all they were given before they picked up their kit bags, dropped off their memories and faced back into the war. Barely enough time to get drunk, to sleep, to savour a moment of privacy for reading a letter, to cast their eyes over a nurse who probably wouldn't give them a second look in peacetime or even to just listen to sounds that they'd forgotten through all the noise of combat like birdsong or unhurried footsteps or the wind rustling though the trees.

After Roseblade and the other NCOs had located all the footdraggers, ducked the heads of the inebriated into sobering basins of water, broken up a few fights and stuck the barrel of a gun behind the ears of the frightened, the battalion lined itself up at sunset for the trek back.

'And you've to wear these now.' The sergeant issued the company with the new Brodie helmet. Rocketing casualties from head wounds had forced the British to follow the example of the French and the Germans and replace the peaked hat.

'Weighs a ton,' muttered Maggot as he strapped the unfamiliar steel protection to his head.

'It will save you from shrapnel,' replied Roseblade. 'That's assuming you have brains between your ears.'

Going back was the worst part of being at the Front. After a day or two in the forward trenches, the mind would close down and they'd get used to the misery around them. But when it came immediately after a stretch of ease, the contrast was all the more vivid and it felt like stepping once again into Hell.

Sudden changes in deployment were always a bad sign and Patie could feel it in his bones that this was going to be a bitch of a tour. The lengthening days of spring gave the brass ideas about launching their next killer-blow and, with the French taking a pasting in Verdun, there were bound to be a few diversionary attacks on the western end of the Front just to keep the Germans on their toes. Somewhere along the six-hundred mile stripe of slaughter from Switzerland to the sea, a sector had been selected for sacrifice and the others who were to be spared participation in the great battle would be sent out twice as often on night engagements in order to keep the enemy guessing.

He hoped that the weather might save their battalion from direct action. Ypres, with its flat expanses of marshland reclaimed by a network of ditches and canals that had been destroyed by the war, was the wettest sector along the entire Western Front. Now that the earth had thawed from the frosts of winter and they had been battered by a prolonged spell of heavy rain, the land around them had turned into a quagmire where men, animals, ordnance and machinery sank without trace if they strayed from the pathways.

They might be marooned in their trenches, shivering in the damp cold with only their greatcoats to keep them warm as fires brought the instant attentions of the snipers, but at least they could comfort themselves with the thought that neither side was likely to move forward before the warmer breezes had dried out the ground.

'I don't like the look of this cove,' muttered Maggot as they filed into the communication trench to begin their return.

'Attention!' They stood rigid as Roseblade unsteadily marched past them along the semi-floating duckboards ahead of the stiff posture and jerky footsteps of the latest captain to command the company. In the fading light of dusk, the lank blond hair, the weak chin and the haughty blue eyes of the twenty-two-year-old officer exuded all the demeanour of those destined to rule. It was obvious to everybody that he wasn't particularly pleased with the group in which his superiors had placed him.

'All present, sergeant?' he demanded.

'All accounted for, sir. One injury to report.' Unable to face the return, one of the newcomers who had arrived before the last tour had cracked up and, with some help from his mates and a blind eye from above, had shot himself in the foot.

'Coward?'

'No, sir,' insisted Roseblade. 'Accident while cleaning his rifle.'

'Don't believe it, sergeant. Oldest trick in the book.' But there was nothing that the captain could do about it as the victim had already been moved back to the rear. With any luck, he would have been shipped back to England before the paperwork could be raised to have him examined.

'Cor. Worse than ever!' adjudicated Maggot, hitting that precise level of volume that footsloggers could decipher but which was beyond an officer's range of hearing.

The other battalion passed them by. The only contact 5th West Sussex ever had with its alter ego was that fleeting moment every week in the communication trench as they trudged in opposing directions in the dead of a pitch-black night. Never once had they seen each other's faces.

'Must be the dirtiest bastards on the entire Western Front.'

As ever, the front trench greeted the returning battalion with its smell. The sulphur of explosive, the vapours released by decomposing corpses that gurgled up from the wet earth, the stagnant waters of decay in the bomb craters, the rotting food that the rats had spoiled and the traces of chlorinated moisture left over from the last gas attack were all bad enough but worst of all was the choking stink of piss and shit wafting through the

189

trenches, so personal, so immediate and always at its most intense when the battalion being relieved made no attempt whatsoever at hygiene during the last day of their tour.

'Laziest bastards as well.'

They dug over the most obvious stenches, sloshed trench water over the most intense centres of urine vapour and held their noses while they settled back into the grind. Sandbags had leaked, tumbled and burst; duckboards and props had disappeared into the ooze; loopholes had collapsed; parapets, firesteps, parados and even living quarters had crumbled during a day of solid rain and the other lot hadn't bothered their backsides to shore up any of them.

'I wouldn't mind one of those Hun trenches,' mumbled Maggot as he unearthed yet another cesspit. 'I met a mate in Le Touquet before Christmas and he told me about this line they captured near Béthune. Made of concrete it was, with proper floors for quarters and stores and the canteen and proper staircases going up and down between them.'

'Do you want to lead the attack?' Dick sliced the head off a curious rat with the sharp end of his shovel. 'They might have Grand Hotels over on the other side of the wire.'

From the darkness behind the squad, the new commanding officer's voice carried into the bay. 'Sergeant, I want you to make sure we get the most out of that Mullane chap,' he was telling Roseblade. 'Every strike is a feather in our caps.'

'Is that so?' Dick dropped his shovel, found a dry patch of clay inside a shelter and laid himself out under his greatcoat on a makeshift bed. And Patie, Maggot and the rest of the platoon worked through the darkness to squeeze the meanest standard of habitation out of the bays that they'd been condemned to for the next week.

The rains stopped, the sun came out during the day, the moon reappeared during the night and the drenched soil of Flanders began to dry out. The east wind that blew away the moisture also allowed the enemy to launch a gas attack which, mercifully, veered northwards at the last moment towards the unfortunate Portuguese in a neighbouring sector.

The escape made them nervous. Providence worked both ways and most of them believed that what they'd gained from the vagaries of the wind would be balanced by the whims of the brass. They were also convinced that they'd pay for the stand-off between Dick and the captain.

The company's marksman had spent three full days out at his post without firing a single shot in anger before Roseblade got the message. His first replacement lasted another two days, the second was taken out by the opposition within hours of taking up his position in No Man's Land and, after that, they didn't bother looking for a third sacrificial lamb as the rotation was coming to an end.

But there was still time for the captain to make an impression and, robbed of the glory that Dick would bring him, they could see that he was itching for a mission.

Unlike their previous COs who were quite happy to show the face only on the odd occasion and then leave matters in Roseblade's capable hands, Captain de Walcourt couldn't leave well enough alone. No longer a case of making the best of a bad lot, their tour in the front line became a showpiece of how Army regulations could be applied. Dress, equipment and quarters were subjected to endless inspections and every transgression was noted in the little buff-covered notebook that appeared from the breast pocket each time the nose twitched and the icy eyes turned silently to the sergeant beside him to name the culprit. And they were left in no doubt that, the minute they moved back

191

to the reserve, their sins would be totted up and punishment would be meted out accordingly.

Not that they would be told beforehand. The officer never once addressed any of the men, never even engaged eye contact nor allowed any of them to come within a yard of his personal space despite the cramped surroundings of the bays. His only communication was through Roseblade at his side and even the sergeant was discouraged from direct conversation but expected instead to relay his superior's words to the corporal leading the section.

Just in case any of the credit might be diverted elsewhere, this was now to be the de Walcourt show. His first actions were to dismantle the informal network of authority that Roseblade had encouraged to evolve underneath him and he imposed a strict chain of command through those most impressed by the majesty of the rulebook. Within the Shanagolden section, it didn't take him long to recognise the superior loyalty of Batt Mullane and Dinny Lyons and they were awarded the stripes of corporal and lance-corporal.

Yet, if Patie, Dick, Batt or any of the others had known the truth, Captain the Honourable Cedric Arthur FitzStephen ffoliot Mowbray de Walcourt was even more scared of his men than they were of him. Born with the bluest blood of Britain running through his veins, his father had drummed it into him that he was expected to live up to the nobility of his ancestry. Uncles, great-uncles and cousins had served under the flag and many lay buried in far corners of the Empire where they had been felled by rebellious Boers, mutinous sepoys, Zulu spears and the tribesmen of the Northwest Frontier. Only those who had contributed to the roll of honour could be considered worthy successors to the family's titles and estates.

All his life, he had tried to win the respect of his father. Snatched from the cradle and packed off to school, he rose through the bullies and the buggers to excel both in the classroom and on the field. Head boy of the house, opening bat for the cricketing XI, captain of the rugby XV, winner of the founder's prize for Latin grammar and commander of the school's Officer Training Corps, fear of disapproval drove him to win every award and every competition that faced him and the network of gentry, military, old school and university had marked him out as being imbued with the stuff from which rulers were made.

Then the war intervened. Instead of commencing his second year's study of the classics at Oxford, his father transferred him to the Royal Military College in Sandhurst. Many of his old school chums were already there ahead of him and, thanks to the impeccable connections of a de Walcourt, he was fast-tracked along with them to a commission just as the line leadership of the regular army was being wiped out in the opening battles. Not that they had any choice in the matter – the pool of prospective wives from whom they could choose were handing out white feathers to any member of their class who ignored the call to battle.

It should have been his moment of destiny but, underneath the starched uniform and the stiff upper lip, he battled the demons of his fears. And there was no way out. While some of his colleagues buckled under the pressures of leadership and wangled transfers to safe numbers in intelligence, administration or supplies, that was not how a de Walcourt behaved. When England expected, they were not to be found wanting.

And in the Honourable Cedric's case, it was not to be the chummy familiarity of the cavalry or a regiment of the Guards. During the War of Austrian Succession, a great-great-great-granduncle had raised the 136th Regiment of Foot, as the West

193

Sussex were originally known, and, as the various branches of the family were some of the biggest landowners in the county, their menfolk upheld the ancestral colours through five generations.

It wasn't so much the prospect of death that frightened him as being dumped in a situation where he could be killed by forces beyond his influence. The energy that had spurred him on his manic path of achievement was bearable only when he could pull every string, master every extraneous consideration and concentrate his effort on a single goal. But his ordered mind couldn't handle the complexity of the Front with its intrigues, its jealousies, its filth, its resentments and its uncertainties. For the first time in his life, he began to entertain vivid visions of failure.

Most of all, he couldn't understand what made the rank and file tick. Before he crossed the Channel, his only contact with the lower orders had been the servants on the estate and the help at the school whose names, if he remembered them at all, were no more than labels and whose presence in his line of sight was solely to fulfill a function. Inside the trenches, however, there was nowhere to escape them or their suspicious glances or the mask of compliance that hid their contempt. Unlike the Empire that his class was pledged to uphold, their Britain extended no further than the mates in their section or in the village or in the factory they came out of and their loyalties had to be forced into line.

So, if he was to be a successful officer in his first posting after his promotion, an officer worthy of the name of de Walcourt, he couldn't countenance any challenge to his authority. But the sanctity of his writ had already been dented. Roseblade had allowed a slacker to shoot himself in the foot so that he could gain his ticket home to Blighty. The sniper Mullane had stopped doing the job that he'd been detailed to do. And he couldn't

194

touch either of them because both had operated to the letter of the King's Regulations.

Behind his back, he was sure that they were sniggering at their tawdry little victories, provoking a ripple of indiscipline among the rest. He began to dream about them, about the revolt they were leading and, after the string of restless naps in the stinking damp of the forward positions had mangled his grasp on reality, Mullane and Roseblade had replaced the spiked helmets of the Huns as the enemy.

'Message, sir.' The runner handed him an envelope bearing an unbroken seal of red wax. Their eyes lit up with curiosity. He edged back a pace in case anyone might peer into the orders.

They were to go over the top as soon as the command could be sure of the wind.

'Periscope, Sergeant!' He was handed an instrument crudely fashioned from the remnants of a mortar tube and the shards of a shattered shaving mirror. Over the sandbagged breastworks, he could see a green patch of grass emerging from the muck and snaking its way to the barbed wire.

He moved up the bay to get a view from another angle. A rifle popped, the periscope vibrated and it fell from his hand.

'Well, I never ...' sighed Maggot Tibbs.

'Good shot,' murmured Dick Mullane with appreciation.

All eyes were staring at the captain.

'He'll cause us trouble, that sniper,' continued Mullane.

'Bad luck, sir.' Roseblade retrieved the remains of the periscope and examined the damage. 'It must have caught a reflection in the sun.'

Just after dawn, the gunners started their bombardment. Great lumps of metal sprang from puffs of black smoke to whistle over the heads of the infantry and complete their arcs in the positions across from them. Huddled in their shelters, they braced themselves for an entire day of thunder. Yet while the barrage was accompanied with the usual ground-shaking rumble, whiff of cordite, black clouds from the explosive and brown clouds from the clay sprayed into the air, there was something half-hearted about this particular effort. Every now and then, lulls would interrupt its intensity and, when the pounding resumed, it seemed more like going through the motions rather than piling on the pressure.

Left out in the front trench to observe with Mick Culhane, Patie peered through the loophole whenever the dust settled. Whatever their intentions may have been, the artillery had as little effect on the barbed wire as the parties that had been sent out the night before with cutters that too weak to dismantle the thicker German gauge. Many of them hadn't returned; some were caught by the snipers and more had disappeared into the mud.

The soft ground had also negated most of the artillery's efforts. Rather than exploding on impact and blasting all before them along the path of attack, shells skidded gently along the gooey surface of No-Man's-Land and slowly tilted forward to leave their exposed backsides mooning at the rays of the sun.

An hour before sunset, the bombardment stuttered to a halt as one battery after another fell away from the chorus. When the final desultory barrage ended in a full house of duds plopping harmlessly on the muck, they inched their periscopes up again to the lip of the trench. All they could see between them and the wire were swathes of shell-studded mud broken up by occasional stripes of craters.

A hand tapped Patie on the shoulder. Behind him, Batt Mullane, de Walcourt, the colonel commanding the battalion and a selection of officers of various ranks stood in a relay of delegated authority.

'Is it dry from here to wire?' asked Batt, four degrees removed from the original question.

'There's a path there. Except it's nothing but shell craters.'

Heads nodded and shook, lips pursed, noses twitched and snorted. The colonel turned on his heel and, followed by his adjutant, the battalion major, de Walcourt and a straggle of subalterns moved off to inspect the next bay.

'They can't send us out in this.' Dick looked inquisitively at Roseblade.

The sergeant looked away.

'They've run out of shells. We'll have no creeping barrage to protect us.'

The ladders were arriving up from the communications trench.

'The wire has hardly been touched. Isn't that right, Patie?'

A second company, laden down with full kit and with bayonets drawn, filed in from the support trenches to join them.

'Christ up in Heaven!' shouted Tim Curtin. 'We're not even attacking as a line. We're coming out only where the ground is dry.'

'We'll be sitting ducks,' added Dick.

Roseblade pointed to the firestep. The ladders were raised. Lines formed up behind them.

Up in the sky, a reconnaissance plane, protected by a quartet of Fokker Eindeckers, chugged unhindered along the line of the Front. And from across the other side of No-Man's-Land, Patie could have sworn that he'd heard the Germans laughing.

The waited until the last vestiges of twilight had disappeared. For over two hours, they had stood packed liked sardines against each other in the deathly quiet, hoping that reason would descend on someone somewhere back up the line of command.

197

But they knew in their hearts that it wasn't going to happen. Despite every conceivable cockup guaranteeing the failure of the attack, field marshals, ambassadors and Prime Ministers had made deals that couldn't be broken.

De Walcourt returned and studied his wristwatch. The seconds ticked by. He pulled a whistle to his lips and waited again.

Patie was second on his ladder, his shoulder pressed up against the arse of a heavyset farmboy from the Downs, certain of the slaughter that lay over the lip and, like a prisoner stepping onto the gallows, half-wishing that they'd just get it over with. In the last moments of quiet, he could hear the deep breaths sucking a final draught of air from their hole in the ground.

He thought he could isolate the whistle in a neighbouring bay that set everything in motion. De Walcourt blew madly and they started the ascent. Two rungs up and the farmboy toppled back on him and the ladder keeled over but, in just that fleeting glimpse over the top, he'd seen his moment of hell as the machine guns sprayed them with a curtain of lead.

And they kept on spraying as Patie saw the corpses tumbling down, layer after layer of them, spattered, ripped, slashed, headless, legless, armless, trunks twitching furiously even though half the body parts had been shot to bits. He heard the screams of the dying in his ears and the staccato of gunfire and the booms of explosions as he tried to writhe himself free from the mountain of doomed humanity that was threatening to drown him in its blood and entomb him in its entrails. And above the bedlam, he could hear the crazed howls of the lieutenant.

'Keep them moving, Sergeant!' De Walcourt waved his whistle at Roseblade.

'It's no good, sir. They're falling down faster than they're rising.'

'I said keep them moving, Sergeant! We have orders!'

The sergeant aimed his rifle at those next in line to pick up a ladder and start climbing. A shell exploded just beyond the lip of the trench and they all fell back on top of each other.

'I'm making an example!' screamed de Walcourt

Mick Culhane was the first man to get to his feet.

'Name?'

'Private Culhane, sir.'

'You're coming with me!' The captain grabbed Mick by the sleeve and, with his service revolver shoved into the back of Mick's neck, pushed him up the last remaining upright ladder. 'We're going over the top!'

Three steps up and another gust of lead whistled across the lines. Mick dropped back down as a bullet pinged off his helmet. 'What are you doing?' he asked, the puzzlement filling his face as he turned towards the barrel of the gun.

De Walcourt ripped the helmet from his head. Despite the battle raging around them, all activity in the bay suddenly stopped as he pressed his revolver against Mick's temple.

'Private Culhane, you have been found guilty of cowardice in the face of enemy fire,' he recited as if he'd been reading out the dry prose of the King's Regulations. 'There is only one course of action open to me in such circumstances. Have you anything to say before it is carried out?'

Even the Germans had stopped firing for the moment.

The CO pulled the trigger. The circle of bemused onlookers recoiled as bits of Mick's head splattered against the back wall of the trench and his body slid off the duckboard into the pool on the floor of the trench.

'Let that be a lesson to you all!' Eyes on fire, de Walcourt turned his head across the full spectrum of the circle. 'Sergeant! Recommence the attack!'

Roseblade hesitated, as did the rest of the company. Dick moved a step closer and others followed his threatening advance on the commanding officer. They might have made it the whole way had not the bays on either side of them exploded under a double-hit of shells.

Runners rushed down the communications trenches bearing a new packet of orders. Much to de Walcourt's disgust, the attack was rescinded before a single company along the entire length of the sector had managed to make it over the top. Up in the hidden reaches of command, the intended battle was already being written out of the history books, apologies were being made at conferences of the various Allied commanders and a scapegoat or two, senior enough to carry the can but junior enough so as not to make any real difference, were being identified as the over-eager, insufficiently-prepared and badly-advised strategists who had planned the setback.

The Germans pounded them throughout the night and those left standing waited for the counter-attack. But it never came even though the forces of the Kaiser might have eliminated the irritant of the Ypres salient had they the nerve and the conviction to descend on the weakened line of defence.

So, when daylight returned, the West Sussex were left to deal with their dead. Piles of corpses lay spreadeagled across the duckboards and some were already beginning to sink into the ooze at the bottom of the red-stained trench from which the shattered remnants of ladders protruded. Ignoring the soldiers trying to shoo them away with the butts of their rifles, a carpet of rats scurried through their legs to nibble at the dead.

Maggot and Flint searched through the casualties, removing pay books and wallets from uniforms and rings from fingers and pocketing any cigarettes, tobacco or loose change they came across. Turning over another shapeless lump wrapped in tatters of bullswool, a hand reached out and grabbed Maggot's wrist just as he was reaching into the breast pocket.

'Strike me down!' He jumped back from the pile only to turn straight into the wild eyes of a soldier squatting up to his waist in a bloodstained pool and gibbering insanely at the upturned remains of a rifle.

The handcart wheeled in from the communications trench. Roseblade nodded to Dick and Patie to take it. Trying to avert their eyes from anything that might identify the dead, they swung the bodies up for removal.

A second cart appeared as the first wobbled away. The first corpse they lifted parted at the waist and the entrails spilled out around their feet. The gibbering soldier screamed. Patie kicked the guts away and reached for the next lump in the pile.

'Christ, 'tis Mick!' Even though the back of the head had been shot off, the face of Mick Culhane stared back at Patie without a blemish, still bearing the same quizzical expression as it did when de Walcourt had blown the life out of it.

'Not there, Dick.' Roseblade tapped him on the shoulder. 'You can't bury him with the rest.'

'Why not? Mick was braver than any of them.'

'The brass say he was a coward.'

'That's a load of shite, Sarge.' Dick dropped Mick's legs. 'And you know it.'

The sergeant shrugged his shoulders. 'They're running the show.'

'Only for the shells falling on us, we'd have lynched de Walcourt.' Drawn by the anger of Dick's voice, the curious filtered into the bay. Batt pushed forward to intervene but then pulled back when he realised that it was his older brother and the sergeant.

'I wouldn't make an issue of it, Dick. Our captain is too well-connected.' Even though the tirade was coming inches from his face, Roseblade tried to play down the challenge to his authority. 'It won't make any difference. Not now.'

'Then tell that to Mick and all the other poor fools that's been murdered by these public school pups. Only thing is, poor Mick don't have much of a head left to talk to.' He pulled back to again grab the legs and, with Patie holding the arms, they heaved the body up on the cart to join those about to be entered into the Roll of Honour. 'So go on, Mick. Take up your rightful place up there with the rest of them.'

14

THEY'D BEEN called out for parades for Easter Sunday and, unlike Saint Patrick's Day when thousands of Volunteers had taken over the middle of Dublin for their manoeuvres, those in the know were aware that their appearance would be more than a dry run. Following the IRB meeting attended by Ned Reidy and Willie Hartnett, units all over the country were expected to join their colleagues in the capital, taking up arms to force the British to deal with Ireland's demand for self-rule.

Other than a few token deportations which were almost immediately revoked, the authorities had done little to impede the preparations. Volunteers still went out marching on Sundays in their uniforms, still drilled in fields and halls with some of them bearing real rifles loaded with real ammunition. Unionists screamed that they should be disarmed and prevented from assembling in numbers. Businessmen fumed over the disruption to traffic. Clergymen fretted over the encroachment on the sanctity of the Sabbath. A prominent general of impeccable stock demanded that they be forcibly conscripted and immediately dispatched to the Front.

But on an island filled with regular Army, a military-style police force, groups of old soldiers given to parading their medals, a militia run by the British Army, a militia of old fogeys under the impression that they were part of the Army, a very loyal Unionist militia, a loyal Nationalist militia, a suspect Nationalist militia and a very suspect socialist militia, with politicians of every stripe hammering their ears to go harder or to ease up or to drop everything and deal with some pointless local dispute, with intelligence units of the military and the police all presenting their own conspiracy theories, with superiors in London demanding more human fodder for the Front, with merchants with connections pestering them morning, noon and night for contracts to supply the war effort and with the killings in Bachelor's Walk still not erased from popular memory; the regime in Dublin Castle gridlocked with indecision.

So when he snuck off in the small hours to meet with Ned, Con Colbert, Seán Heuston and the other IRB men who'd wedged themselves into leading positions within the Dublin Brigade, it began to dawn on Willie as they moved into Holy Week that the rising might actually succeed, that the great disappointments of 1798, 1803, 1848 and 1867 might finally be reversed.

The optimism lasted only a few days. Word filtered through to Dublin that a shipload of German arms had been intercepted in Tralee Bay on Good Friday. Later that day, they'd heard that Roger Casement, who'd been sent over to Germany to negotiate the support of the Kaiser's government, had been captured after being put ashore from a U-boat.

By Holy Saturday, orders and countermands were flying up and down the organisational structure of the Volunteers. Suspecting that he'd been set up by a clique within the IRB, Chief of Staff Eoin MacNeill furiously tried to contact every unit and warn them off gathering in public the next day. Convinced that the loss of German weaponry had left most of the Volunteers with little more than hurleys for marching into battle, IRB leaders Bulmer Hobson and Denis McCullough gave him every assistance and, just in case there was any confusion, MacNeill's orders cancelling the parades were printed in the Sunday Independent.

Having been summoned, warned off and summoned again, Willie reluctantly donned his Volunteers uniform on the morning of Easter Monday and joined Ned on the train in from Blackrock to Tara Street Station. A few curious boys in sailor suits commented on the colour and asked him which regiment wore the green instead of the khaki but their fathers quickly dragged them away with the unspoken accusation that Willie and Ned weren't real soldiers.

Passing through Sydney Parade and Lansdowne Road, the carriage filled up with Army officers in their pomp accompanied by wives, companions or whatever dressed up in all their finery and taking particular pride in their unfeasibly large hats and by servants bearing wicker hampers bursting with picnic delicacies. On their way to Fairyhouse Racecourse for the holiday meeting they were and all the talk was about fancies for the Irish Grand National and who'd be noticed as the best-dressed lady, so they didn't even pay a second glance to the two Volunteers.

'So we're off marching again?' The throb of Dublin activity was absent as Willie walked across Butt Bridge, almost as if it was a Sunday but without the crowds coming out from Mass. Beyond him, the bright April sun shone down on the porter barges bobbing on the tide in front of the Custom House, on the cattle boats lashed to the quay, on the forest of masts and the white folds of sail, on the belching funnels of troopships, on the silvery surface of the Liffey as it stretched out to the sea.

Ned was as unusually quiet as the city around him.

'Does everyone know what we're letting ourselves in for?' Willie nodded at the young fella ahead of them turning onto Eden Quay in the outfit of Fianna Éireann, the youth wing of the Volunteers. He didn't look a day older than sixteen

'The Army's taking them younger than that,' replied Ned. 'And at least he's making his own choice.'

They took their place among the hundreds gathered outside Liberty Hall. Squeezed in between the trade union headquarters and the quay wall, they looked the genuine article as they fell into line and those who had come unarmed were issued with their weapons. Commandants came out of the hall, assembled their battalions, headed for the tram stop, fiddled in their pockets for the fare and departed for various points around the city.

A Citizen's Army man hurrying for the tram hailed James Connolly as he passed him by. 'What hope have we, Jim?'

'None whatever,' replied his commander, a broad smile filling his face.

Despite the bravado and the gallows humour dominating the chatter, a giddy sense of adventure took over as those remaining marched off, Volunteers in their green shoulder to shoulder with the black of the Citizen Army. But as they moved past the O'Connell Monument and were diluted by the broad expanse of Sackville Street, they suddenly realised that this force taking on the might of the British Empire was a very small one indeed.

The usual straggle of youngsters was following, some of them cheering, some of them jeering.

'Mister, give us a look at your rifle,' one of them begged. Willie kept staring ahead. 'Ah, go on, will you? Please, sir, will you?'

A policeman standing at the Abbey Street junction raised his nose in disapproval but did nothing to stop them. A woman pushing a pram lambasted them for being cowards.

'I swear to God!' The bottle swayed unsteadily in the rag-clad arm. ''Tis the Bould Fenian Men!' The policeman pulled the drunk aside, gave him a kick up the backside and told him to be on his way.

Approaching the Imperial Hotel, Patrick Pearse and Connolly wheeled the column sharply through the soaring granite columns of the General Post Office. A handful of British soldiers stood guard at the entrance. Willie raised his rifle, they dropped theirs and ran off and nobody was playing games any longer.

Ned picked up the weapons. 'Weren't loaded.'

Tom Clarke and Seán MacDermott, one too old and frail, the other too crippled from polio to accompany the march, joined them from the steps as they charged through the door. Staff and customers jolted at the interruption, scratched their heads and returned to their business.

'Come on, you have to get out.' Willie tapped an elderly gentleman on the shoulder.

'Certainly not, young man! Not until I have completed my business.'

'Sir, this is a revolution.'

'Poppycock!'

'A revolution?' asked the saucer-eyed messenger boy at the adjoining hatch. 'Against what?'

'Against British rule.'

'Janey Mac!'

'Come on, sir, for your own safety,' repeated Willie. 'This isn't a joke.'

A pistol shot into the ceiling concentrated minds. Some fuming, some puzzled, some fearful, some slightly thrilled by their presence at a moment of drama, the GPO quickly emptied to let the Rising get on with its business.

A handcart laden with ammunition, boxes of explosive, food and medical supplies and a fat bundle of posters swung in the door. 'Sorry, lads. We got delayed,' panted one of the pair pushing it.

Connolly, Pearse and Joe Plunkett, who was struggling with the terminal stages of tuberculosis, rattled out the orders. Furniture was overturned to barricade windows. A pair was dispatched to the roof to raise the flags of the revolution. Detachments were sent out to occupy neighbouring buildings.

Pearse rolled out one of the posters and led a group to the street outside. Willie crowded against a window to peer out at their commander standing on the steps of the post office. For once, the nerves appeared to have taken over and the force of his presence had left him.

'Irishmen and Irishwomen!' he cried out, voice strained and unsure and stumbling without its natural cadence, to the small crowd standing below him. 'In the name of God and of the dead generations from which she receives the old tradition of nationhood, Ireland, through us, summons her children to her flag and strikes for her freedom....,'

A few ragged cheers rang out as he proclaimed the Irish Republic as a sovereign independent state, traced its legitimacy and guaranteed the rights of its citizens. But the fervour of the words passed over most of the crowd who stood impassively or even sniggered as they waited for the police to turn up.

'... In this supreme hour the Irish nation must, by its valour and discipline and by the readiness of its children to sacrifice themselves for the common good, prove itself worthy of the august destiny to which it is called,' he finished as he read out the names of the signatories. Connolly immediately moved across to shake his hand but his hearty congratulations couldn't hide Pearse's disappointment as the onlookers melted away to read the copies of the Proclamation that had been pasted to the walls of Sackville Street or to gaze up at the strange flags billowing in the sky above them.

'Noble words,' muttered Willie as Pearse returned, absently rolling up the document in his hands. 'But it'll take more than a fine speech to get that crowd out there to take notice.'

'He deserved more than that,' answered Ned. 'He put a fierce amount of work into writing the Proclamation.'

'What was he on about?' asked a voice outside the window.

'I haven't an idea,' replied another. 'Something about a republic, whatever that is.'

Willie broke the glass to allow the barrel of his rifle to point out. The pair outside on the street squinted suspiciously at it before moving across the road to smash the window of a shop. A policeman began to run after them but fled when he crashed into a pair of armed Volunteers emerging from the Imperial Hotel. Within minutes, a crowd pushing handcarts had dribbled in from the lanes and systematically began to loot the entire length of one of the most elegant boulevards in Europe.

'Let me in, will ye,' begged the gangly youth in the piper's kilt banging at the door.

'Will you have a bit of sense, lad, and go home.'

'I know how to fire a gun. I swear to God I do.'

'Leave him in.' A Citizens Army woman tapped Willie on the shoulder. 'We need all the help we can get.'

'I'd have been here sooner only I'd to do the messages for the Ma.' The youngster ogled over the Mauser rifle he'd been handed. 'And then the brother wouldn't give me the loan of his bicycle.'

The mob was making its way across to the GPO's side of the street when they were scattered by the call of the bugle. A troop of cavalry had gathered up by the Parnell Monument, their

209

lances glistening, their sabres drawn, their horses champing, their honour ready and willing to be put on the line.

Volunteers crowded to the windows or rushed upstairs to get a better view. 'Start shooting the minute they come past Cathedral Street,' shouted someone with authority. In the excitement, Willie couldn't make out whether it was Pearse or Connolly or MacDermott or Plunkett. 'And don't be afraid. This isn't an outing any more, lads. It's war.'

He could hear the pounding hooves. He could almost smell the hot breath of the horses as they waited for the signal before opening up. It was the first time Willie had aimed a rifle in his life.

He heard the first crack. He squeezed. He hadn't a clue where his shot had ended up. All he was aware of was that his shoulder had nearly broken from the kick.

Horses and lancers fell on the macadam. Squeals and screams rang out. Those remaining upright galloped straight past the GPO or up the side streets or turned on their heels. A great cheer rang out as the cavalry scattered to the four winds.

'Eejits!' shouted someone. 'What in the name of God were they trying?'

The more excitable were claiming direct hits. Two lancers outside staggered to their feet, one of them after shifting the dead horse that was lying on top of him. They made it to Nelson's Pillar. Willie and Ned were the two closest to them. Neither could bring themselves to press the trigger. They'd seen the eyes of their targets.

A shot rang out from an upper floor of the Imperial Hotel. It missed by a mile. Willie didn't know whether to curse or to cheer.

Runners banged at the door. Reports trickled in from the other locations, some of whom were still in direct telephone contact. Hopes went up as they heard that Boland's Mill,

Stephen's Green, The Town Hall, Jacobs, The Four Courts, The South Dublin Union and The Mendicity Institute had all been captured. And hopes went down when they got news of the failure to take the centre of British rule in Dublin Castle.

'We're not real soldiers at all.' Willie shook his head at the emotional gyrations. 'We haven't a hope of winning this one.'

'We're still here,' answered Ned. 'And that's more than anyone else has achieved in Dublin over the last four hundred years.'

But Dublin didn't rise up like Paris after the fall of the Bastille and an uneasy standoff, punctuated by the occasional engagement, held for a couple of days before the British got their act together. Instead of negotiating as the more optimistic rebels had hoped, the officials were pushed aside and the military took over. One by one, positions were lost as garrison regiments were moved in from Belfast and the Curragh and entire divisions waiting in England to be dispatched to the Front were rerouted to Ireland.

Half of the city came out to play on Sackville Street amid the rotting horse carcasses, the overturned wagons and the abandoned trams. Girls strutted about in looted fur coats, dangling bracelets of gold and fluttering delicate fans. Young fellas wearing bright football jerseys and top hats whacked golf balls down the length of the street with their kid brothers caddying beside them. The hungry feasted on food that they never had seen before and the thirsty toasted their fortune on wines of rare vintage. An enormous pile of fireworks was set alight at the base of the Pillar, just yards from the explosives stored in the GPO.

'Fair play to yiz, boys,' roared the big heavy man dressed in frock coat, a silk hat and a ragged pair of trousers who was tapping the window a half-empty bottle of Cognac. 'Tisn't too often yiz get to live like a lord round these parts.'

The party ended when the shells started dropping from the gunboat moored outside the Customs House. Despite reports of de Valera's battalion inflicting hundreds of casualties on the British at Mount Street Bridge and of Ceannt's men stalling the Army's advance on the South Dublin Union, the noose tightened around Sackville Street. Thousands of regulars picked off the surrounding streets one by one and painstakingly inched forward to the remaining centres of rebellion

From the roof of the GPO, Willie could see flames sprouting all over the city where British artillery had flattened all before it. The civilian population, now taking at least as many hits as the Volunteers, had fled or else had buried themselves in cellars as the heart of Dublin was pounded to rubble.

A shell landed directly on the barricade stretched across the top of Sackville Street and started a fire that quickly spread to every building on the far side. As bottles exploded, fabrics smouldered, chemicals flared and the great plate glass windows of Clery's department store melted and flowed onto the pavement, those manning the Imperial Hotel and Hopkins jewellers fled from the inferno and, dodging the bullets, the shrapnel and the flying debris, sprinted across to the Post Office.

Pearse was trying to rally the defenders when Willie returned from his spell on the roof. Insurgents were making their way from Dundalk, a great battle was won in the village of Lusk in north County Dublin, the RIC were surrendering, some even throwing in their lot with the rebellion. They cheered his words, but everyone from the commander himself down knew that they were unlikely to be true.

Down on the floor in a corner, Connolly was lying on a stretcher with a Cumann na mBan nurse trying to staunch the bleeding in his shattered leg. Just across from them lay two bodies, one totally still, one feebly twitching the tips of his fingers. 'I'll be with you in a minute,' shouted the nurse.

The smoke wafted in from outside where mortars pounded, machine guns raked, marksmen sniped and the Forces of the Crown marched relentlessly towards them. Ping, bang, boom, roared the war machine and they'd only the few rifles and some homemade grenades to stop them.

Yet, into their fourth day they were still resisting. Boys and men; dreamy intellectuals and hard chaws from the back streets; old Fenians who'd done years in English prisons and young fellas just up from the country; women, socialists, Catholic mystics and Gaelic revivalists; those searching for adventure, those for a purpose and those for a focus to their anger; this unlikely collection of amateurs had tied down the second city of the Empire.

Many, especially the leaders, didn't seem too concerned whether or not they came out alive. Any break in the fighting and they'd write letters to wives, sweethearts or family, compose poems or stories or sketch their surroundings as if they were the last records of their lives. Maybe it was a sign of the times when millions were being slaughtered at the Front. At least if you died for Ireland, you did so of your own accord and not because some ruler had forced you to fight.

But Willie didn't want to die. He wanted more out of life than the corpse stretched out across from him had ever tasted. As dusk fell, he caught a moment to catnap behind a long oak table turned on its side and tried to ignore the intermittent gunfire in the distance.

She was in his dreams, her hand waving goodbye as she moved up Carysfort Avenue just like the last time he'd seen her twelve days before. He wanted to run after her, take her away from the nuns, take her where her father would never find her, to some place where the sun was shining and the wind was warm and the grass was green, maybe back to a perfect Shanagolden under the shade of Shanid Castle or looking down on the Estuary from Knockpatrick.

An explosion woke him and he shuddered as his lungs took in the heat and the stink and the smoke. Long shadows filled the great hall from the flickering orange glow outside every window.

'Earl Street's on fire now.' Pearse was hunched down beside him.

'We're sitting ducks.' Ned was on the commandant's other side. 'Once they get the heavy artillery up here, they'll paste the living hell out of us.' He fiddled with the bolt of his rifle. 'We never had a hope, had we?' he asked Pearse. 'Not after the German boat was captured.'

'You'll never find out until you try, Ned. There was always a chance we might get more support; that the British might do a deal instead of taking soldiers away from their war.'

'But you don't really believe that?'

'No, we all knew it was a long shot.' Pearse opened his tunic and fanned his chest with his hat. 'But that's not the point. And if we didn't strike now, what would have happened? Another hundred years of idle talk and doing nothing?' One of the young lads passed him a note. 'Maybe this will inspire others, like Wolfe Tone and Robert Emmett done for us.'

He levered himself along on his backside towards the light. 'And we're not all going to die. Sure, those of us who signed the Proclamation know our fate. But there'll be others like yourselves there to take over. And if you do, then we won't have given up our lives for nothing.' After glancing through the message, he rose to his feet, buttoned up his uniform, straightened his hair and donned his hat.

'A stickler to the last,' muttered Ned as Pearse left them to confer with MacDermott and Clarke.

Willie turned over on his elbows and found a sighthole between the edge of the table and the corner of the window. A shadow was moving between the sandbags across on the far side of Henry Street. His finger tensed around the trigger, then relaxed when he realised that it was only a dog mooching for food.

'I'll never figure out how he got away with pulling the wool over MacNeill's eyes,' continued Ned. 'He must have been doing it for years.'

A hand reached out from the sandbags, fingers twitching to call the dog. Willie aimed again but the animal suddenly took fright and bounded away.

'Seán MacDermott was the main man that planned it.' But they both knew that none of it would have happened without Pearse. The rising had shown his outstanding qualities of leadership, organisation, clarity of thought and writing and the entire movement had been drawn the force of his speaking, yet the man leading it had never been fully accepted by many of his followers. Too smart by half was how the old-style Fenians had seen him, a Home Ruler who'd thrown in his lot with the IRB only after the Volunteers had been founded. Too much of an intellectual for the militarists and one with an English father to boot. A Catholic mystic filled with romantic middle-class notions to some of the socialists.

Even Willie found him strange, the many things going on in his head always creating a distance from which the real character never emerged. The only chink that had ever been exposed was during those moments after he read out the

Proclamation when the dream had foundered on disinterest but, even in the depths of disappointment, he had instantly regained control. Yet, unlike those who always had to find another layer of motive underneath the surface, Willie was prepared to accept that what he saw was what he got. Where others talked, Pearse delivered. When they came up with excuses or the lessons of history, he didn't want to know and he didn't give a damn about how others regarded him.

Old Tom Clarke had recognised his talents and sponsored his rise through the IRB. MacDermott had seen someone who could run the show after he had been sidelined by polio. MacDonagh, Plunkett and Ceannt had been drawn by the force of his personality. And the firebrand Connolly had struck up an instant rapport with a man whose path to the GPO led from the opposite end of the spectrum.

Where he was leading them now was another matter.

The dog came back but no twitching hand emerged to greet him. Henry Street was empty, the quietest Willie had seen it since the start of the rising. Even the looters refused to be tempted out.

'You didn't get the chance to see Josie?' Ned was asking him.

'I might have. How about yourself?'

'No. I couldn't call out. I didn't want it getting back home I was in Dublin.' A flare from somewhere along Moore Street lit up the sky outside. 'You didn't tell her I was here, by any chance?'

'None of my business, brother-in-law.'

'That serious?'

'And none of your business either.'

The ground shook beneath them, the walls trembled around them, the air screamed above them. He was still thinking of her when the heavy artillery rumbled up to pound them.

They lasted another two days, spewing bullets so fast in defence of their positions that their rifles overheated and they had to drain oil from the sardine tins to cool them. They tossed grenades, most of them homemade and more of a danger to themselves than to their enemies. They contested every yard of position, fashioned iron railings into makeshift pikes, dodged the steel hail of the machine guns, came back laughing when the enemy thought that they'd been obliterated by the shells. With their backs to the wall, they drank deep from the well of resistance, obsessed with the dream of dying on their feet rather than bending at the knee.

The incendiaries dropped, starting more fires where none had thought possible. The last positions on Sackville Street fell to the flames of fury, the remnants of the outposts fell back on the GPO and the enemy now had just a single target on which to pound his retribution.

The order to evacuate came as their headquarters caught fire and they scrambled out into the maze of laneways around Henry Street and Moore Street to seek refuge in the shops and the cottages and the tenements. Someone was telling them to make for the Four Courts, that it was still in rebel hands but, by that stage, all chains of command had broken down and it was every man for himself.

Outside on the street, the soldiers were exacting retribution. Civilians trying to escape were singled out and shot. Homes were trashed and then torched as they searched for the rebels. The drunk, the curious and the merely unlucky to be caught up in the conflict were mown down by an Army that could no longer tell the difference between an Irishman with a rifle and one scratching his head.

Just after Saturday midday, a Cumann na mBan nurse with a makeshift Red Cross insignia on her arm and brandishing a

217

white flag walked up the length of Moore Street to Great Britain Street. The officer receiving her ripped off the armband and then had her frogmarched to Tom Clarke's old tobacco shop to spell out how Pearse was to surrender.

Willie was sleeping in the stairway of a tenement when the order came through, the young lad carrying it bursting with tears. After the euphoria of combat, he found it hard to believe that it was all over. Maybe they could have held out longer and tied down the divisions in Dublin; maybe the country was on the verge of coming out in support, maybe help was on its way from Germany or from America or from heaven itself. Stepping out into Sampson's Lane, he found comrades as bewildered as himself, bothered that their survival meant that they hadn't given it their all.

But when he was stripped of his gun and his bandolier and marched down Henry Street in a four abreast column with an unsmiling squaddie shoving a rifle butt into his back, he knew that the dream had ended.

A captain came to ask them their names and, except for the Volunteer standing beside Willie, wrote them all down in his little black notebooks.

'Does that officer know you?' asked Ned once the interrogator had moved a safe distance away.

'He's my brother.'

A sergeant-major turned around on hearing the voices and, rather than identifying who had spoken, expertly tapped the entire row with his swagger stick on the nerves of their kneecaps. A major roared at the detail to get the prisoners moving and they were pummelled into line with fists, boots and butts.

They ended up hunched on a patch of grass outside the Rotunda Hospital surrounded by a phalanx of British bayonets.

Officers marched through the little huddles shouting at them to remain still and nodding to the squaddies to whack anyone who moved an inch out of line. One of them picked out Joe Plunkett for special treatment even though he was bleached with the pallor of terminal consumption.

Another kicked McDermott's withered leg. 'The Sinn Féiners must have very little support,' he chortled to a companion. 'They even take cripples in their army.'

Later in the evening, the detectives arrived. Soldiers shoved their rifle butts under chins so that the spotters could get a better look at the faces.

'Plunkett,' they would pronounce. 'One of the names on their poster.' An officer would consult the notebooks and draw a ring around the name.

'Pearse's brother.'

'Well, well, well. If it isn't Mr. MacDermott. Or Mr. Mac Diarmada as he likes to style himself. There's your criminal that planned this outrage.'

There was a woman among them whose face was vaguely familiar to Willie. 'Evening, Miss Colclough.' A major doffed his hat.

She shook her head at the first three faces before stopping at Ned.

'That's him!' she cried. 'That's Reidy. That's the blackguard who tried to take advantage of Sir Alexander's daughters.'

'General Jermyn will be pleased,' cooed the major.

Her gaze shifted, her eyes locked and her finger pointed at Willie. 'And that's his accomplice.' His name was added to the A-list.

A biting east wind blew the warmth from their bodies as they lay out for the night on the open grass. Around midnight, they were joined by the prisoners from the Four Courts and, because there was no room left on their patch, they were ordered to lie on top of those already on the ground. Two lads he didn't know dropped on Willie but, while he was nearly suffocated by their weight, they at least gave him some shelter from the elements.

One of the officers amused himself by marching past the leaders, drawing his boot on their prone bodies and roundly insulting them to their faces. Seeing a group of nurses looking out from the hospital, he picked out old Tom Clarke, stripped him to the skin and paraded him under the torchlight for their observation.

'See, ladies! It's that dirty old bugger from the tobacco shop across the street,' he cried up at them. 'I'll wager he was peeping at you for years.'

Another prisoner was tossed down on the heap. The moans of agony and the stench of gangrene from his wounds kept Willie awake through the night and he was half-delirious by the time they were forced to their feet in the morning.

A crowd had gathered on the pavements of Sackville Street underneath the smouldering ruins which had been stripped by the looters and shelled by the military. He turned his head for a last look at the GPO and saw the two tattered flags still fluttering on the roof. Across the street from them, the Starry Plough of Connolly's Citizens Army flew above the Imperial Hotel.

'Traitors!' screamed a voice in the crowd.

A man waved the crook of an umbrella in his face.

'Cowards!'

A stone struck the back of his head.

'Murderers!'

A well-dressed matron broke from the pavement to spit at him straight between the eyes. Their escort intervened and shoved her back into the crowd and, for a moment, Willie was almost glad of their presence.

'Where's the inspiration now, Willie?' Ned shook the lump of horseshit from his hair. 'These bastards want to hang us on the spot.'

'Give it time, Ned. The lickspittle is always the first to show his face.' But there was scant sign of hope in the crowd. For a moment, he thought he might have seen Josie in the background but a one-eyed bemedalled war veteran brandishing a Union Jack and screeching obscenities blocked his view. When another stone caught him in the face, he settled for staring resolutely ahead.

Willie wasn't raving from the want of sleep. Josie and three friends had braved the cordon and the searches and made it into the centre of the city. In the leafy suburbs outside the canals, there was hardly a sign of the Rising other than the uniforms, fewer trams running and the absence of bread and milk deliveries. But once she crossed over Baggot Street Bridge, the scale of the devastation astonished her. Some of it was obvious like the fires and the ruins seen down towards Mount Street or around Stephen's Green but even more surprising was the low level damage done to areas where there didn't appear to have been any direct fighting.

The elegant shops of Grafton Street, the financial palaces around College Green, the offices and cafés and pubs running up to the Liffey were all smashed beyond recognition, so casually, so clinically, so totally, as if the people of Dublin had succumbed to a mass frenzy of destruction. From somewhere deep in the city's soul, the angry demons of poverty, disease and despair had escaped and had swept all before them.

And those furies were still out there roaming its streets. Despite the checkpoints and the flood of soldiers demanding passes, most its citizens were out in the open, the curious like herself, the outraged like those waving their flags and flaunting their medals, the hungry begging for money and food, the needy sifting through the ruins, those now homeless who had nowhere else to go.

She followed the crowd crossing Carlisle Bridge for a chance to observe the prisoners in the flesh.

'They're being brung out, so they are, so as we can see them,' a youngster was telling his gang.

'I wonder what they look like?'

'Massive big culchies with massive big feet.'

'Janey!'

'Jemser's brother says he seen them last week up at the Pillar. They'd all gone raving mad, so they had. Chopping off horses' heads with their hatchets.'

'Janey Mac!'

Passing the O'Connell Monument at the foot of Sackville Street, the mood turned sharper. One or two men muttered that they'd a sneaking respect for a bunch of fellas with only a handful of guns who held out against the British Empire for the best part of a week. But in the outpouring of outrage, nobody was prepared to utter such sentiments out loud and, by the time Josie was sucked into the crush outside Hopkins jewellers, the crowd was bordering on the hysterical. Whether out of anger or fear, out of resentment or servility, the city was consumed by an urge to publicly demonstrate its loyalty and, for a brief moment, divisions of class, gender and religion were forgotten as its citizens bayed for retribution.

The jeering picked up volume as they spotted the sunlight flashing off the phalanx of bayonets and reached a crescendo when they caught the first glimpse of the ragged, unshaven, bloodstained prisoners hobbling over the rubble. Waving sticks and flagpoles, handbags and umbrellas, those at the front of the crowd tried to press forward but were held back by the escort of soldiers.

Youngsters pelted the marchers with missiles picked up from the debris and a group of young bucks in straw hats and striped blazers cheered them on before joining in the stoning themselves. 'Isn't that Mr. de Valera, our maths professor?' shouted one of Josie's companions, ignoring the frantic gesticulations of another of the group to keep her voice down.

But Josie was looking elsewhere. She might have been fooled by the film of dirt, the days of stubble on the chin, the matted hair and the blood dripping from a wound in the head but she could never mistake the eyes. 'Oh sweet Jesus!' she cried. 'There's Willie! And Ned!'

She'd half suspected he might have been involved. He'd never really told her what brought him to the capital. She'd never asked what he did on Sundays. But seeing him in the flesh, seeing him being marched to jail and maybe worse at the point of a British bayonet, seeing him being taunted and jeered and stoned by a mob slavering for revenge was a world removed from any romantic dream of patriotic duty.

And she'd never known at all that Ned was in Dublin.

'All them traitors and everyone belonging to them would want to be strung up,' roared the enormous woman in a threadbare dress looking her straight in the eye. 'Our poor boys are out spilling blood over in Flanders and these bleeding culchies are stabbing them in the back.'

'Damn right, Madam,' agreed the small prim man with the bowler, venting an indignation that he never realised he'd in him. 'Frightful damage to property. Hang the lot of them, I say.'

223

'Kill them! Kill them!' The crowd started chanting as it heaved once more to break through the escort and they were carried along by the surge. At the last moment, a rippling wave pushed Josie and her companions away from their accusers to provide them with an escape from a Dublin that they didn't want to know.

15

'**T**IS A SORRY day when the good name of Ireland is dragged into the gutter by traitors promoting the cause of the Kaiser and his heathen hordes ...' Canon Murphy slowly folded his notes, left them aside on the lectern and looked out over the brimming church from his pulpit. Nothing compared with bad news to ensure that everyone turned for Mass. Not that there were any slackers in Shanagolden.

'... And 'tis sorrier still when, among them, are numbered two followers of Judas Iscariot ...,' he continued with the sad thundering glee of someone whose worst prognostications have proven to be correct. ' ... who have brought eternal shame on this parish of ours!' The fist thundered off the lectern.

Prominent in the front row, Councillor Thomas Hennessy and James Horgan nodded with approval. The events in Dublin over the past week couldn't have come at a more opportune time. Ever since the evacuation of Gallipoli at the turn of the year, the war's popularity had fallen off the map and, with it, that of those who had been most outspoken in its support. And while the Councillor had distanced himself from the Army's recruitment drive as soon as credibility would allow him, he had been caught on the hop by the groundswell of resistance against any plan to extend conscription to Ireland.

But now he'd been granted more time to extricate himself from the possibility of backing the wrong horse. Men from Shanagolden, like Johnny O'Brien and Mick Culhane, had died at the Front. So for some, the attack on the same Army that was fighting out in France had diminished the claims of Sinn Féin and the Volunteers to be acting in the name of the people of Ireland. Hennessy and Redmond and the rest of the Home Rulers could claim with justification that the patience of their methods and their acceptance of the rule of law didn't set brother against brother and family against family.

It would have been better still if Horgan had learned to hold his tongue but the creamery manager had nailed his colours so tightly to the mast of the Empire that he couldn't resist the opportunity to trail the coat. Taking his usual position just outside the church gates and affecting an expression of familiarity laced with concern as the bulk of the congregation shuffled out, Hennessy accepted the handshakes of his followers and of a few of those who had recently strayed from the path. Understated but effortlessly visible, his presence let those passing by know that Shanagolden had its guardian who cared about them but who could also turn on them if they upset the hierarchy of standing. And just in case anyone didn't get the message, Doctor Molyneaux stood a few yards away from his left shoulder and Sergeant Stapleton, caressing the top of his baton against the sleeve of his tunic like a barber stropping a razor, hovered directly behind him.

The formation had been perfected by years of convention. But this time, the best chance they'd ever get to reel in the waverers and silence the smart Alecs muttering over their small ones in the corner of Jack Noonan's bar, Horgan departed from the script to push himself into the faces of those coming out.

'Do you see what your son done?' he blasted into the ear of Joe Hartnett, limping off home on long legs bent out of shape by years of hard labour. 'He'll get what's coming to him, so he will, the traitor.'

Willie's father lifted his sad silent eyes to Horgan and let them roll on to Hennessy, to Molyneaux and to Stapleton before continuing on his way. Keeping up the tirade, Horgan walked after him but, failing to provoke a response, he turned back to face the church and the clusters of gossip gathering in front of it.

'Nothing good ever came out of them cottages,' he roared after the departing figure. 'Thieving treacherous blackguards. That's all them Sinn Féin rebels are! And you'll never change them!'

Out at the Front, the mood was no different. The rain bucketed down on the walls of the reserve trenches, washing off the mud and pouring it down on the channel flowing along its bottom. Hiding under their waterproof capes, the Shanagolden section huddled together, each of them conscious that events in Dublin had separated them from the rest of their battalion.

Even within the group, the fault lines had surfaced. While Dick Mullane, Patie Fitzgibbon, Tim Curtin and Mick Fitzgerald kept their heads down and said nothing, Dinny Lyons, Batt Mullane and Jerry Curtin proclaimed their disgust with varying levels of animation at the treachery of the Sinn Féin Volunteers. Flint sat between them, his head darting in both directions as he tried to make up his mind about which side to agree with.

'Worse than the Germans, I tell you.' Batt's trenchant denunciation carried over the spatter of the rain, loud enough for anyone to hear. Always needing someone to please, thought Patie. Back home it was older brother Dick and it was the same when he had first landed at the Front. But soon there were others to impress like Roseblade who didn't particularly care because he treated everyone the same, and de Walcourt who had instantly spotted the need within him.

The Army loved fellas like that, lads who might be coming from places like orphanages or institutions, or where the father was dead or hadn't hung around and who'd spent their life searching for a figure of authority. Once they had been shown that the world outside the gates of the barracks no longer mattered, they'd do anything they were told.

'We're over here putting our lives on the line and a crowd of traitors are murdering our comrades back home.' Batt squeezed the rain from the ends of the moustache clipped to the dimensions that officers liked to affect. 'Makes you sick, doesn't it?'

'Even the English lads won't be seen talking to us now.' Dinny nodded in agreement. 'And I wouldn't blame them either. These so-called patriots are killing their mates.'

'At least in the trenches, you know where you stand,' added Jerry. 'Out here, it's one soldier against another. You don't have to worry about some renegade stabbing you in the back.'

District Inspector Nicholas Sullivan waited in his office in Newcastlewest for the latest set of instructions. In the days following the rebellion, orders from RIC headquarters had floundered from one sea-change to the next. First they demanded that he come to Dublin to identify any prisoners from his district. Then he was told to stay put and complete a report on why rebel elements in West Limerick hadn't been picked up. No sooner had he begun to put pen to paper than he was ordered to prepare a list of suspects for the Army to arrest.

He could have pointed to the mountain of unanswered correspondence that he had passed on to his superiors over the years. He could have told them of the many occasions that they'd been warned of the activities of Willie Hartnett, Ned Reidy and the local leadership of the Sinn Féin Volunteers, of repeated visits by leading IRB men like Pearse, Con Colbert and Ned Daly to the area, of the slow leakage of members from Redmond's Volunteers after Aubers Ridge and Gallipoli. He could have reminded them of the information he'd gathered that had led to Casement's arrest in Tralee Bay on Good Friday as he waited for a German submarine.

But in the frenzy to avoid blame and exact retribution, reason no longer mattered. Officialdom had been discredited all the way up to Dublin Castle where Chief Secretary Augustine Birrell and Under Secretary Sir Matthew Nathan had been forced to resign from their positions, where the Army had taken over command and ambitious officers could make names for themselves without ever having to expose themselves to the perils of the Western Front; where enterprising officials could refashion the record of history.

An Army major that Sullivan had never seen before barged through the door without bothering to knock and plonked a sheet of paper on the desk. 'Add anyone else you can think of.'

The Inspector looked down through the names. 'Where did you come across these?' he asked.

'You don't need to know.'

'Then I suggest you tell whoever it was that he doesn't know what he's talking about.' Sullivan pointed his finger at the list. 'That fella is one of my informants and those two as well ... This fella shoots his mouth off when he has a few drinks in him but he'd run a mile from you if you asked him to do anything ... Who came up with this lot of names?'

'They're Germans. Secret agents, I expect.'

'No, they're Palatines and they've been here for the last two hundred years. In fact, they were brought over here by one of your German kings because he thought they'd be more loyal than the feckless Catholics around them.'

Sullivan crossed out over half of those destined for the roundup but he resigned himself to the fact that many of them were likely to return. It was too good an opportunity for anyone in the police or the military with a score to settle. And once the likes of this major who didn't know the first thing about the area or its people had cleared off back to wherever he came from, the inspector would be left to keep an even more resentful population in check, as well as having to build up a new network of informants from scratch.

Unlike his superior, Sergeant Laurence Stapleton had no qualms about taking advantage of the imposition of martial law.

'That's the place there,' he pointed out the captain as they swung up the main street of Shanagolden. While he waited in the lorry, the squad of soldiers dismounted and swung their sledgehammers to batter down the door of Jack Noonan's pub. Once inside, they brushed past the proprietor and his wife standing at the bottom of the stairs in their nightclothes and forced their way into the bedrooms.

Mossy had climbed out the window when they entered and had slid down the roof of the scullery to the top of the rain barrel but two of the squaddies had detached form the main group and closed off the exit from the yard. Hands raised, Mossy was marched back into the house, past his mother and father held down by the arms so that the barrels of rifles could be pressed to their chins, and shoved in front of the captain.

'Looks guilty to me,' sneered the officer. 'Take him out.'

As the prisoner was led away, the captain grabbed a bottle from behind the counter and tossed it to his men. 'Help yourself, chaps. Can't waste good whiskey on these bloody Sinn Féin rebels.'

Outside on the street, a second lorry roared in from the Rathkeale road. Jimmy McCarthy and Dan Hourigan were tossed out over the tailboard and, along with Mossy, they were manhandled up against the outside wall of Jack Noonan's to be handcuffed. Before they could be loaded into the first lorry, Stapleton pulled Jimmy aside and dragged him in front its headlights. Anyone looking out the window could see the sergeant mechanically kicking and beating his prisoner into an unconscious lump of pulp.

Sullivan watched the stream of prisoners, almost two hundred in all, being led into the dimly lit courtyard of the barracks. The early arrivals were stuffed into the cells and, when these were bursting at the seams, the remainder were shackled to railings, hitching posts, window boxes, gates and any other bar of anchored metal that could be found inside the compound.

About half of those he'd known to be active in the IRB were picked up, but others, including the most influential still at large in West Limerick after the capture of Reidy and Hartnett in Dublin, had slipped the net. The great majority, however, were either attached to the harmless end of nationalism like Sinn Féiners organising resistance to conscription or Gaelic Leaguers, or Irish dancers, or those involved in the Gaelic Athletic Association, or who had no connection whatsoever to political activity.

And much to his disgust, many of them had been bashed about for no apparent reason. The military had failed to understand that most of those pulled in had never been in any trouble with the law in their lives and, while they might not have been favourably disposed to British rule, were unlikely to get involved to the extent of active resistance. But after the hidings they had received, their viewpoints might change and, with many of them being teachers, journalists, shop assistants, barmen, travelling salesmen and agricultural instructors, they were in a position to convince others as well.

'What happened him?' he asked as a badly beaten prisoner was dumped on the floor of a cell. It took a few moments to identify him as Jimmy McCarthy.

'Nothing to do with us,' answered a captain. 'One of your chaps did the damage. That mad sergeant in Shanagolden.'

A teacher from Rathkeale who, unlike McCarthy, had no record of any public activity other than collecting folk songs that were in danger of being lost, had suffered similar treatment. A well-known and well-respected hurley-maker whom some eejit in a uniform had decided was a manufacturer of sinister weapons, had to be carried in strapped to a stretcher. A blood-covered figure hauled in his nightclothes turned out to be a priest.

Anyone with an ounce of sense would have immediately realised that these weren't rebels. In fact, they were the very people who had the most to lose from rebellion and unrest. They and their families were the main beneficiaries from a generation of progress that had allowed the mass of the population to gain entry into positions and professions which had previously been reserved for the Protestant gentry.

Sullivan swore under his breath as the lorries continued to arrive. The rebellion in Dublin had unexpectedly granted the high moral ground to the authorities but the arrogant stupidity of the military was throwing it all away.

16

T HE PRISONERS weren't quite sure of what lay in store. Leaders like Pearse, MacDermott and MacDonagh had few illusions as to their fate but the rest thought that they might be treated as prisoners of war. Germans captured at the Front weren't shot but were transferred to POW camps in England or the Isle of Man and Volunteers fighting in uniform and adhering to the conventions of war fully expected similar treatment.

The relative leniency of their confinement reinforced their hopes. Unlike the naked hatred that they'd experienced from their captors, their jailors had treated them with respect. Even though they were deprived of normal human comforts, they weren't consciously humiliated and the one soldier that Willie had seen physically ill-treating a prisoner was quickly removed.

But suspicion returned when the courts martial started. Locked up in cells along the stack of landings, they saw comrades being whipped away without a moment's warning and the measured quartets of footsteps would continue to echo through the bars long after they were marched to the drumhead tribunal set up by the military.

Those pulled out at the beginning had never returned but were transferred instead to the disused jail in Kilmainham. When the shots fired out at daybreak on the Wednesday in its Stonebreakers Yard, they knew that Patrick Pearse, Tom Clarke and Thomas MacDonagh had been executed. The following dawn, Joe Plunkett, Ned Daly, Michael O'Hanrahan and Willie Pearse fell before the firing squad and their bullet-torn bodies were flung into the quicklime.

They needn't have bothered with Plunkett as he had only days to live before the consumption finally finished him off, but no way were the dispensers of justice to be denied their trophies. As a sop to compassion, they allowed him to marry his fiancée Grace Gifford on the eve of his execution but then hauled her out of his arms before they had a chance to embrace.

As those left in their cells awaited their sentence, word would come through of others who had been spared from the ultimate penalty but most of them were youngsters or had very peripheral involvement. One pair who'd done little more than deliver a few messages found themselves facing eight years of penal servitude; another man following MacNeill's instructions and who had tried to stop the Rising was handed down ten years of porridge for his efforts. Even two drunks who had tagged along behind the column of prisoners being marched out Power's distillery were given their stretch for being enemies of the Empire.

Along with four others, Willie and Ned waited inside the cold damp walls of their cell in Arbour Hill prison with its peeling paint and its rashes of mildew under the light that was never turned off. They'd take their turns on the two mattresses and try to grab any sleep that they could. It was better than the uncertainty of waiting or the loneliness of thinking.

Sometimes when the silence got the better of them, they'd break into conversation. They'd talk about where they came from, or what they'd been doing before they got involved, or places they'd like to see if they got a chance. They'd ask Willie and Ned about football or the city lads about how they put up with all the noise and the smoke and the crowds of people around them. One night they broke into song, belting out rebel tunes like Boolavogue, The Rising of the Moon, The Bold Fenian Men and A Nation Once Again and the entire landing joined in over the protests of their jailors.

But most times, Willie would have preferred to have been left to himself. Every mind inside the prison was battling its own doubts over its fate. Some had accepted the inevitable and would almost feel left out had they escaped after the initial batch had been executed; some were bewildered; some, like himself, were certain that they didn't want to die. But nobody wanted to expose their innermost thoughts lest they might be seen as being cowardly, or as letting the side down, or as putting undue pressure on others over what was a very private decision.

And then they came to take another four away. Con Colbert, commander of the garrison in Jameson's Distillery and originally from Athea, a town fifteen miles west of Shanagolden, was in Willie's cell and he was hauled out to join Michael Mallin, Éamonn Ceannt and Seán Heuston on the lonely walk down the landing.

'If you ever get the chance, can you call in on my father and mother?' he asked as he walked through the door for the last time. 'They'd like to hear it from someone from our own part of the world.'

'I'll do that, Con,' Willie replied. 'That's a promise.'

They said nothing as the lock was turned. Being one of the signatories, Ceannt's fate was already decided and, if three others on the next level of command were being taken away with him, it was obvious their death warrants had also been signed.

When the light of dawn stole in through the window, those squatting on the floors of their cells didn't have to be told that the firing squad had now filled a dozen graves.

Three days later, they came calling for Willie and Ned and marched them down into a converted staff room where a lieutenant-colonel presided over a bench of three officers.

'We might be in luck,' muttered Ned. 'If they were going to shoot us, we'd surely deserve a full colonel.'

'The prisoner must be kept quiet at all times,' hissed the frosty-eyed lieutenant acting as Crown Prosecutor before reading out a list of charges so immersed in legal jargon that neither of them had any idea what they meant.

A captain tried to intervene but was immediately silenced. The denunciations continued. 'Have the prisoners anything to say?' concluded the presiding officer.

'Does it matter?' answered Willie.

'The prisoners plead not guilty,' interjected the captain. He tugged Willie's sleeve. 'We must abide by procedures,' he whispered.

Miss Emily Colclough was called, was asked to identify them and was instantly marched out before she could be questioned.

'Oh, rotten luck, I'm afraid,' sighed the captain. 'How did you manage to upset one of General Jermyn's most trusted agents?'

'William Hartnett and Edmund Reidy,' announced the lieutenant-colonel. 'This Field-General Court Martial has found you guilty of occasioning casualties on His Majesty's troops and of conspiring with His Majesty's enemies. You are hereby sentenced to death by firing squad.'

'I fought for my country against yours same as your people are fighting the Germans ...'

The gavel banged, drowning out Willie's response. 'Take them away,' shouted the lieutenant.

They were marched outside to the tender waiting to take them to Kilmainham. 'There must be some avenue of appeal.' The captain followed the escort to the gate. 'Legal procedures were not followed correctly.'

'A waste of time, captain,' Willie told him. 'It doesn't matter a damn what you do. They'd already decided to kill us. The trial was only an excuse to justify it.' The Kilmainham detail took them from their Arbour Hill colleagues and bundled them into the tender. 'But thanks all the same. You tried your best.'

They saw more evidence of the fighting on the short journey across the Liffey. Kingsbridge station was barely visible beneath a layer of uniforms and gun emplacements and, further up Steven's Lane, shell holes pockmarked the ruins of the Mendicity Institute and the scorched walls of Power's distillery. All along the way, there were streetlights hanging from buckled standards, tram-wires dangling on the cobbles and the debris of wagons, carts, trams, barrels and lumps of masonry piled against the pavements. It must have taken entire divisions of the British Army, maybe 20,000 troops or more, to put them down.

'Well, at least we put it up to them.' The soldier beside him motioned Willie to shut up. 'They won't forget this fight in a hurry.'

'I told you to keep quiet.'

'What are you going to do? Kill me? Rob your General Maxwell of his pleasure?'

The guard thought about it for a moment.

'Christ in Heaven, Ned. I always told you your wandering eye would get us into trouble.'

'The ould bitch. She couldn't even take a bit of fun.' Ned asserted his right to the limited space on the bench and elbowed

237

the soldier beside him to make room for him. 'Still, I can go to my grave with an enhanced reputation.'

It was only when he was banged up on his own in his cell that the implications of his sentence came home to Willie. Not only did Kilmainham Gaol stink of disuse, decay and damp but the stench of death hung over the rows of cells where over seventy prisoners waited for the firing squad.

Back in Arbour Hill, he might have seen them being dragged away to have a list of charges pressed against them but that was still a step removed from despair. There was always an even money chance that the court martial wouldn't impose the ultimate sanction.

Kilmainham was the end of the journey. The only way out was in a box.

A sniper's bullet or a gunner's shell could have done for him in the GPO. He could have gone down in glory trying to shoot his way out of Sampson's Lane. He might have died of wounds or have burned to death or have been blown to bits holding a homemade grenade. But there was nothing heroic in being executed by a bench of British officers pretending to administer justice.

He could hear the chaplain's steps making their way to a cell up the landing from him. He counted them, twelve in all and a wheel to the left. Seán MacDermott's time had come.

They were so insistent on their procedures. If they decided to wipe out an entire village or even an entire nation, they'd have the gallows and the firing squads ready, their magazines filled, their guns loaded and their mass grave filled with quicklime to take the corpses. But first, they'd have to compose the ritual. We're administering justice, old chap, British justice, they'd sigh and they'd don their wigs and adjust their black caps and

238

appoint their prosecutors and their defence counsels and send everyone who came before them to their instruments of judicial death.

Another chaplain trod on the floor outside. They were making for Connolly this time, even though the wound in his leg was now consumed with gangrene. It would take a hell of a job to stand him up so that he could be shot according to the guidelines laid down in the rulebook.

They'd agonise themselves to distraction over the method. They wouldn't give a curse about whom it was to be inflicted upon.

Coming up to dawn, he heard the cell doors open again, he heard the tattoo of footsteps precisely in time and the muffled shuffle in between them, he counted the minutes to the Stonebreakers Yard, he heard the garbled directives to the squad, he heard the curt prose of the death warrant from the officer's crisp lips and, after an agonising delay, he heard the fusillade of shots ring out.

Minutes later, the ritual was repeated. British fair play had claimed another brace of trophies.

And they all bought into it. The captain defending them at the court martial might have been shocked by the arbitrary sentence of death, might have been appalled by the blatant breaches in judicial procedure, might have felt genuinely sorry for Willie and Ned but he still didn't question. Their jailors might have wished them good luck as they embarked on their final journey, might have paid them the respect due to soldiers who had fought the good fight but they too, would continue to carry out their orders.

Regardless of its shortcomings, they all had to believe in the superiority of British rule over all other forms; otherwise, they could not justify painting a third of the globe with the red of the Empire.

And even some of their own had fallen for the spiel. There were prisoners who'd remark how civilised the whole process had been, how it had been peppered with acts of human kindness. They almost sounded grateful that they were to be executed by upstanding Britons rather than by those barbaric Huns who shoved their bayonets through the hearts of Belgian babies.

It fell to District Inspector Sullivan to deliver the messages. He could have passed them on to the local RIC presence but, having served as the station sergeant in Shanagolden before his promotion, he felt it his duty to bear the bad tidings in person.

Anyway, there was already enough bad feeling in the town without giving an ignorant thug like Stapleton the excuse to gloat over other people's misfortune. The executions, carried out in the dead of night after courts martial that nobody was ever aware of and then casually dripped into public knowledge through a curt one-line statement, had already become personalised in West Limerick in the form of Con Colbert from Athea. But when two well-known footballers from the one parish who were only minor figures in the rebellion were added to the list, a whole swathe of the population would blame a distant government in London to their graves.

Joe Hartnett was turning up from the road towards his cottage when the Inspector hailed him from the police car.

'Mr. Hartnett!' he called out but Willie's father kept on walking, the bad leg trailing behind the good. Sullivan jumped out and followed him up the lane. 'Joe! Can I've a word with you a minute?'

'You don't have to,' Joe called back without turning around.

'I'm sorry to have to tell you.' The row of small houses came into view at the end of the hawthorn and briars lining the lane. 'Is there anything I can do?'

'So you're going to kill my boy and you want me to feel sorry for you?'

Unnerved by the open contempt, Sullivan bit his lip. People like Joe Hartnett mightn't have had much time for the police but, if they held a different opinion, they'd always have kept it to themselves. 'No, Joe,' he sighed. 'It's just if you want to see him. Or anyone else in the family. I can get you to Dublin by tomorrow.'

'I'll think about it.' Joe kept on walking home without breaking his step. 'And if I feel like it, I'll let you know.'

Edmund Reidy wouldn't come to the door but his daughter did. She didn't ask him in as was custom but left him standing awkwardly in the yard with the hens clucking around him. Nary a trace of emotion marked her face, just the absent stare through him as if he didn't exist.

'I'm sorry,' he stammered. 'I've been asked to inform you that Ned is to be ... executed on Saturday morning.'

He'd done his job. The thick skin that he'd grown over thirty years of policing had taken its fill for the day. 'Again, I'm very sorry, Josephine,' he repeated.

'Inspector!' He was turning to the car when she broke her silence. 'And Willie Hartnett? ...'

'I'm afraid so.' He held out his hand. She grabbed it for a moment, then cast it aside once she'd steadied herself. 'I can arrange for you to visit him ... Both of them, if you want.' The offer floated past her as she stepped back through the half-door and hid herself in the house.

They knew all about it in the town as well when he drove through up the main street. Nobody had to tell them. The sight of a police car was enough.

Eyes avoided him as he passed them by on his way to the barracks. A few of the pubs had closed and the normal evening

241

bustle was absent. The corner boys were nowhere to be seen. There was no sign of Councillor Hennessy emerging from his premises to welcome the District Inspector to town.

He'd expected the silence. He'd known that somewhere beneath all the public denunciation of the rebellion, another voice was waiting to be heard, one needing just the merest touch of guilt to spark it off. Whether they agreed or disagreed with the actions of Ned Reidy and Willie Hartnett, they were still kith and kin and, like any parish in Ireland, they wouldn't lightly turn their backs on their own.

With his son shipped off to an internment camp in Wales, he'd expected Jack Noonan to have a black ribbon tied to his door knocker. He'd expected the McCarthys to show their usual bitterness towards the law. He was aware of the views of the schoolmaster.

But he hadn't expected to see the cloth of mourning hanging from the window of Jim Fitzgibbon's cottage. Young Patie was over in Flanders with the Army and his father was publicly siding with the rebels. Further down the street, the Fitzgeralds, also with a son at the Front, were letting their sympathys be known, as were Tossie Curtin with two boys joined up and the Widow Mullane who had given her only two children to the Army. Shanagolden had been scarred with resentment and it was beyond the powers of Nicholas Sullivan and his policemen to heal it.

Josie stared at the photograph of the Shanagolden footballers taken a few days before they won the county championship. Hidden under the mattress from the eyes of her father, it was her only picture of Willie. There he was, trying to look inconspicuous in the back row so as to cover his street trousers but failing to diminish his presence. Without ever seeing them play, anyone

242

looking at John Joe Snaps's photo would have instantly realised that he was the engine of the team.

She put names to the entire lineup of players. Young Johnny O'Brien and Mick Culhane buried somewhere in France. Jimmy Mc, Dan Hourigan and Mossy Noonan banged up in Wales. The two Mullanes, the two Curtins, Patie Gibbons, Mick Fitz, Dinny Lyons and Flint at the Front. Connie Greaney back in the seminary in Maynooth. And Ned and Willie waiting to meet their death in Kilmainham.

She put the picture away as she heard her father returning from the fields. He'd be wanting his supper just as usual. And she'd make it just like usual, glad of a routine that would keep her occupied.

They all wanted to spare her any contact with what had happened. After getting on to her father, the nuns had immediately dispatched her home and told her that she'd completed her training. She would have been finished anyway in a matter of weeks.

Once back in Shanagolden, no one wanted to talk. They'd cast glances in her direction, some laced with sympathy, some with hostility, some with curiosity but none of them sure enough of their thoughts to put them into words. She'd overhear them at times when they'd be whispering to each other but they'd turn away with embarrassment when they'd realise she was there.

In fact, the only person to say anything to her face was the police inspector who had told her an hour back that Willie and Ned were to be executed. She'd spent most of the time crying in her room while her father went out to look over his stock. But they were only shallow tears. The real ones would come that night when the full realisation of their sentence would hit her.

The kettle was boiling on the range. She made the tea and piled the sandwiches on a plate. He began to eat in silence.

243

The clock chimed.

'They won't execute them all, Father. There's too many of them.'

He reached for the mustard and spread it over the slices of hairy bacon.

'They'll be back,' she continued. 'You wait and see.'

He poured another cup from the pot.

'The people are changing, Father. Some of them are saying now that Ned is a hero.'

He finally raised his head from his plate. 'Did you talk to Canon Murphy about the position?'

'After what he said about Ned from the altar last Sunday?'

'Makes no difference. I put a window and a seat into his church and I'm one of the biggest contributors in the parish. So if the school needs a new teacher, then my daughter is getting the job.'

Even though he hadn't finished the sandwich, she pulled the plate and the knife from under him. 'Your son is sentenced to death and that's all that's bothering you?' Gathering her own dishes as well, she tossed them into the sink.

'I'm going down to Hartnetts to see if any of them is going to Dublin. At least they might give a damn!'

He caught her eye as she hung up her apron and stormed out of the kitchen, primed himself to shout at her but then turned away to drop his chin on his upturned hand.
Even in her anger, she thought she saw the tiny glisten of a teardrop hanging from his eyelash.

Once the dust from the rising had settled, Dubliners grated under the imposition of martial law. As the grisly details of the executions leaked out and tens of thousands of them turned up for Requiem Masses without any coffins, stories grew legs in the only public gatherings that were allowed by the military. Priests, they were saying, were being prevented from administering Holy Communion to the condemned. Joe Plunkett had been snatched from his deathbed before he could even touch his bride's hands. James Connolly had been propped up by stakes so that the firing squad could rip the rest of his body to shreds.

And it being just after Easter, the image of the blood sacrifice was all the more vivid to a devoutly Catholic population. Pearse's jail cell poem to his mother hit the streets and his execution was immediately likened to Christ's death on the Cross. Street singers composed ballads that soon rang out every laneway as the city was corralled under the heavy hand of General Maxwell. Those Irish Parliamentary Party MPs who had returned home for the recess witnessed at first hand the sea change in public opinion. When the House of Commons resumed its sitting, they brushed aside Redmond's outrage at the Rising and denounced the executions and the secret courts martial held in the dead of the night. Some went so far as to recognise the insurgents for having fought the good fight, however misguided, and claimed that if the British Army were any bit as good as they were, the war would have been over long ago. The most vocal of them all, John Dillon, exposed the murder of leading pacifist Francis Sheehy-Skeffington and two other journalists while they were held in military custody.

Having given Maxwell carte blanche to put down the rebellion by whatever means he saw fit, the British Government began to have second thoughts when reports of the executions and the summary justice inflicted on uninvolved civilians crossed the Atlantic. Irish-Americans, a key component of the coalition that had voted President Wilson into office, were demonstrating outside British consular offices in New York, Boston,

Philadelphia and San Francisco. Hopes of enticing the United States into the war were evaporating.

Prime Minister Herbert Asquith took matters into his own hands and paid a personal visit to Ireland. Despite the efforts of the military and of the officials covering their backsides to prevent any unmanageable news from reaching his ears, he managed to meet some leading RIC officers and read the ferocious open letter from the Bishop of Limerick denouncing the executions. Realising that Maxwell had to be reined in before the entire powder keg of resentment exploded, the firing squads were ordered to stand down.

Word took its time filtering through to Kilmainham. The priest failed to arrive in the cells of the next pair scheduled for the Stonebreakers Yard. A rumour floated between the iron bars that Éamon de Valera had been reprieved because he'd been born in New York and could claim American citizenship. Another of those waiting in line was said to have escaped as a result of his birth in Argentina. Countess Markievicz wasn't going to get it because she was a woman.

More stays of execution made their way to the landing. Relatives stopped arriving at the doors of the condemned.

'Willie!' shouted Ned from the cell opposite. 'I think we're in luck. They've filled their quota.'

Willie stared out on the yard. Soldiers were dismantling the posts where fourteen of his comrades had been gunned to their deaths. He could be facing years of hard labour but, no matter how long the stretch was, it was better than being tossed in the quicklime. Not yet twenty-two years of age, he had a lifetime ahead of him that he still wanted to enjoy.

17

AFTER THE FIASCO in March, 5th the West Sussex enjoyed the quietest few months of their war. Most of it was spent at the rear although, in the case of C Company, it would have been infinitely more bearaable if anyone other than Captain de Walcourt had been over them. Away from the tension of the forward trenches, their commanding officer's manic mind had to find something to occupy itself and nothing pleased him better than to send his men out on endless fatigues, marches and training exercises. Even if it meant running his entire complement into the ground, he became obsessed with breaking Dick Mullane as punishment for his refusal to snipe any more Germans. And following the treacherous rebellion in Dublin, the list of enemies expanded to include the entire Irish contingent under his command, with the exception of those like Batt Mullane whom he'd promoted for good behaviour.

However, the colonel commanding the battalion eventually decided that the captain had lost the run of himself, sent him off on a hush-hush training course back at regimental headquarters in Chichester and gave the company an extra week's leave in Le Touquet in order to defuse the situation. He'd even tried to get them passes back to England but, because of the buildup that had been going on for months, he couldn't find any room for them on the troopships for their return.

When they reported back to duty in mid-June, C Company and the rest of 5th West Sussex along with an assortment of other battalions from the sector that they had been manning since the early months of the war, were bundled together to create a new division of regulars and then ordered to pack up and march. It took them a full three days to cover the sixty miles to their new position near Maricourt where they were to plug a gap left by the French Army, which was now haemorrhaging by the tens of thousands in its defence of Verdun.

The battalion was already aware that something was in the air. They'd seen entire divisions of Kitchener's New Army landing off the troopships in Boulogne and Calais and they'd been told that these all-volunteer brigades were being sent off to pack along a twenty-five-mile stretch of Picardy straddling the River Somme

Along their journey south over the cobbles, there was further evidence of preparations for the mother of all battles. Trains of up to fifty wagons long pulled into stations to feed the insatiable appetite of the war and, at every crossroads they passed, great columns of men, munitions, machinery, supplies and fodder were pouring off to the Front. Enormous guns and howitzers, bigger than anything they'd seen since they'd landed in France, were unloaded from the flat cars, together with their gargantuan shells and their crews of gunners, observers and officers, and wheeled with glacial speed to their destinations by road tractors or by teams of up to a dozen horses. They even came across one howitzer so heavy that it had been left on the tracks and had a railway siding all of its own built to hold it.

Filled to the brim, the lorries and wagons crawled eastwards. Emptied of their loads, they moved back west. The roads were as clogged as they'd been during the early days of the war when the civilians were fleeing from the advancing Huns but, this time, the manpower moved to the steady step of the planners rather than to the frenzied confusion of retreat.

Still, the clear summer skies above them no longer carried danger. Germany's supremacy of the air had ended when the French Nieuwpoort 11 and the British Sopwith Pup had caught up with the Fokker Eindecker's advances in technology and they didn't have to worry about being strafed or being spotted for the artillery as they moved along the rear. For the first time since he had walked off the troopship in Dieppe almost two years back, Patie Fitzgibbon suspected that the brass might actually know what it was up to.

Maricourt was a definite improvement on Ypres. Instead of packing the surface with sandbags to create breastworks that would defend them from the snipers and the machine-gun posts, they could dig into the soft chalk soil that remained dry throughout the summer and most of the winter. Rather than staggering over duckboards floating on the water table just feet below the surface, they could walk or run over floors that were solid and could be cleared of debris.

Neither did the walls of the trenches collapse like the crumbling clay of Flanders. They only needed the occasional shoring to keep them in shape. The permanence of the defences had also allowed the previous tenants to build vestiges of relative comfort like decent sleeping quarters, separated latrines, gas curtains that didn't fall down, food stores that could be secured against the rats and deeper levels that were accessed by real honest-to-God stairways where they could retreat during heavy bombardments.

Best of all, Picardy didn't stink of rotten vegetation and submerged corpses like the flat sodden fields of Belgium.

Around them, the preparations continued. Wagonloads of ammunition wheeled up the communication trenches to stock up the machine guns. Teams of sappers tunneled beneath them to link up abandoned mine shafts and pack them with explosive. Parties disappeared into the night with heavy-duty wire cutters to hack paths through the barbed wire. Gas helmets were distributed even though the few who had previous experience of wearing the model they'd been issued with had found them to be of no practical benefit whatsoever during a serious attack.

Up in the forward trenches, the infantry was having it handy. Although the Germans occupied the higher ground, there was little activity from the other side of the wire. Even the snipers confined themselves to a few desultory warning shots before dozing off for the day under the heat of the sun.

'But it won't last.' Maggot Tibbs sat on the firestep and spread the Crown and Anchor cloth over an upturned Mills bomb crate. 'You mark my words, Jerry Curtin. The only time the brass makes life comfortable for Tommy Atkins is when they're planning to visit the horrors of Hell on him.' He pulled the dice from his pocket. 'Now, who wants to make his fortune?'

Jerry advanced a penny on the heart and a second on the anchor. No fortunes were ever going to be made when most of them were skint after returning from leave. And anyone who did come back with money in his pocket was smart enough not to shoot dice with the Cockeny croupier.

'Go on, lay 'em and play 'em.' The banker looked expectantly for another punter. Flint never had a penny to his name. Nobody in his right mind would chance Dick Mullane. Patie Fitzgibbon refused the invitation. Tim Curtin found some urgent reason to disappear around the traverse. ''Ere, Batt. You didn't get to pop your pickle in Tookey. You must have a bob or two left.'

'You're not supposed to be gambling up here.' Ever since his patron had parted from the company, no one paid a blind bit of notice to the stripes on Corporal Batt Mullane's sleeve.

'How about you, Mick?'

Mick Fitzgerald shrugged his shoulders and found a threepenny bit. After laying it on the anchor, he took back a penny in change.

'Why did I have to end up in a company full of skinflint Paddies?' Maggot held out the three dice in his fingers. 'Now, who'll do me the honour? Good on you, Mick. May you be lucky.'

Mick rolled them out on the cloth.

'Inky, pinky, parley voo. Spade, diamond and crown for you. Bad luck this time, better luck next time.' The arm reached out to rake in the stakes but another hand grabbed it by the wrist.

'Not allowed, Maggot. Not allowed.'

'We's only having a bit of fun, Sarge,' pleaded Maggot. 'It never bothered you before, did it?'

'Not me.' Roseblade pointed over his shoulder where de Walcourt was coming around the traverse. Within the blink of an eye, the oilcloth, dice and money were stuffed inside Maggot's pack.

'What did I tell you, Jerry Curtin?' muttered the banker. 'The horrors of Hell have returned.'

Supplies kept coming forward. Every dug-out in the trench was loaded with ladders, ammunition, empty sandbags, flares, grenades, spades, wooden stakes, lengths of angle iron, rolls of barbed wire and all the other paraphernalia of attack. Saps, extensions to the front lines that ran to a dead-end in No-Man's Land, were excavated to hold the overspill and provide staging posts for attacks.

There was some purpose to the activity in the sector occupied by 5th West Sussex and the battle-hardened French unit to the right side of them knew what they were doing. But their left flank was nothing short of chaotic as a division made up entirely of Pals Battalions and led by inexperienced officers struggled to cope with the intricate demands of an army at war.

Back in the support trench, Patie watched these volunteer soldiers fuss and fluster over every command and wondered were he and his comrades as naïve when they had first arrived at the Front. Always on edge, they hadn't yet learned how to switch off, how to grab whatever kip they could and how to resign themselves to the fact that there was nothing they could do about the cock-ups caused by the brass back at base.

He felt the superiority of the old dog, the cute hoor who'd survived almost two years at the Front, the hard chaw who'd seen mass action in two major battles, the worldwise veteran who'd learned how to keep himself alive through bitter experience. But he envied them as well. The newcomers still remembered something about life beyond the trenches and they hadn't yet been forced to accept that filth, fire and slaughter were the new reality.

Le Touquet had shown him how far his own group had descended. They'd been waiting on leave for almost six months and, when they were given the extra week, they thought that their dreams had come true. All that pay had been collecting in their pockets when it couldn't be spent at the Front, so they'd enough to do it right this time, the best of wine, women and whatever else took their fancy.

The first night, they started off by getting drunk, by getting laid and by getting stuck in a fight with a gang of locals. They were sozzled again by the second afternoon, most of them weren't up to getting laid but they'd still enough in them to have it out with a company of Jocks before the gendarmes split every head within swinging distance of their batons. By the third day, they were scrapping among themselves, Paddies against Cockneys, townies against yokels, cloggies against anyone, arguments starting over the slightest excuses, fellas so far gone from the gutrot that they'd even take sides against their own.

After three heavy hangovers, Patie was longing for escape and wandered off to find out what the rest of Le Touquet was up to. Rambling beyond the informal division separating the squaddies from the genteel part of the resort, he walked past restaurants, shops and hotels catering for those for whom pleasure was a serious part of their lives. Passing by the station, he'd tried to chat up a waiting girl who wasn't in the business, practicing the bit of French he'd been learning from a book that a chaplain had given him, but she didn't want to know him any more after a group of local railwaymen warned her off. Later on, he'd gone off with Dick and Mick Fitz to have a swim but the MPs told them that the beach was off limits to anyone in a uniform. The three of them then looked for a café away from the action but every proprietor they visited had had his fill of feuding Tommies and wouldn't serve any Rosbif unless he was an officer.

So they left the paradise reserved for spick and span officers, for the daring young ladies who'd popped over for a few days from London to experience the thrill of being less than fifty miles from the Front, and for the black marketers spending the profits they'd made from the poisonous rations issued to the troops. Instead, they ended up with the rest of the company back in the camp at the top end of the town where they settled into the daily cycle of drink, sex and fistfights. By the end of the fortnight, their leave had reduced to a pointless ritual punctuated by occasional doses of the MPs' discipline when things got out of hand. Most of them were relieved when they made their way back to the ordered regime of the line.

Those that thought about it suddenly realised that they could no longer handle life without combat.

And those still capable of handling civilisation might never return to enjoy it. The newcomers coming up the communication trenches wandered about awkwardly, heads gawking with curiosity rather than crouching with caution, making noise and smoke where they didn't have to. Without old hands above them or around them to show them the ropes, rich pickings awaited the Kaiser's snipers whenever they woke from their summer torpor.

But the marksmen were forced to wait. Just before dawn the following morning, the orders came down from on high. As their summer turned from sunshine to rain, a half-million soldiers packed into the trenches along the twenty-five miles of the Somme Front and looked on as the artillery indulged itself in the most stupendous bombardment ever seen over the war-scarred fields of Northern France.

Ears throbbed to the never-ending whistles of the whizz-bangs and the Jack Johnsons screaming overhead and the flat booms as they flopped back to earth over on the far side of the wire, unleashing throbs of earth-shaking vibration sometimes so intense that they'd coalesce into a continuous roar. Noses recoiled at the acrid tang of the cordite and ammonal and clogged with grains of sand and clay. Black puffs and white puffs and grey puffs and flashes of bright orange tarnished the air through which tangles of flying wire and the splintered remains of wooden posts rose and fell and expired in the wastes of No-Man's-Land. Great clouds of dust jumped up from the vapourised ground to cover every exposed pore in their bodies with a fine grey-brown film whenever the wind blew the wrong way.

It carried on through the nights. It carried on through the days. It carried on through good weather and bad weather, through sunshine, through rain and through mist. They wondered whether any living thing could survive.

Between the war and those banged up in the internment camp in Wales, there weren't too many able-bodied men left in Shanagolden. Wives, daughters and hired help were now doing much of the work previously reserved for their husbands, fathers and brothers. Even the morning's milk queue at the creamery hadn't escaped.

Josie Reidy waited for her turn behind Mary Hourigan. Her father had twinged his back loading the cart after milking and she'd insisted that he take to the bed before there was no one left to do the heavy work on the farm.

Not fit work for a lady, he'd protested. No indeed, she'd agreed, but she wasn't prepared to watch the farm fall apart around her when other families were making do the best they could in the circumstances.

Especially when there had never been a better opportunity to make money. With U-boats sinking supply ships and their own food producers handicapped by conscription, the bellies of England and its army cried out for whatever could be sent over from Ireland. And they were willing to pay the going rate for anything that could be forced down the throat. Quantity was all that mattered and every farmer was exhorted to produce as much meat, milk and grain as was humanly possible.

But they'd pay for it, warned her father in the first serious conversation he'd ever had with his daughter over the business of the farm. People were getting used to producing any kind of rubbish and were forgetting about the standards of quality and hygiene that the dairy co-operatives had prided themselves on when they were originally set up. Some day, the boot would be on the other foot and they'd all suffer for their greed.

'My God, but they're as slow as ever.' Six carts ahead of Josie, the new man on the landing laboriously wheeled a churn over to the separator bath and then gaped open-mouthed at the assistant manager calling out the weight.

'They didn't pick him for his brains,' answered Mary. 'Do they think we've all day to be waiting?'

The farmer behind them eyed them with the suspicion of someone not fully comfortable at this intrusion on the world of the male.

'What's bothering you, my good man?' Mary asked him. 'Is it that we've finally found what ye do be up to when ye're claiming to be working yer backsides off?'

He looked around for moral support but there was none to be found. Standing up on the cart and holding the reins in her well-developed forearms as if there were a team of wild horses rather than a single donkey pulling them, Mary Hourigan looked every inch the warrior queen on her way to battle.

'In fact, I'm wondering what they do be doing when they go off to the fair,' she continued, her raucous laugh carrying down the full length of the queue. 'Or where they're off to when they're having us believe that they're out counting the cattle or walking the land.'

A pony and trap passed her by.

'Do you hear that, James Horgan?' The creamery manager tapped the animal to keep moving but curiosity got the best of it and it decided to stop and listen to the harangue from above. 'In fact, any man with a decent bit of self-respect would be up there lending a hand at the separator so as we could get home to attend to our domestic duties.'

Maybe it was just to shut Mary up, but the man on the landing picked up a gear and Josie got away just as she was about to give up hope. The ass never made it back to the farmyard as quickly during his previously unhurried life and, without even pausing to tidy up her hair, she changed into her good clothes, hopped on her bicycle and pedalled back into town.

A drover was herding cattle against her and the milk queue had barely moved in her absence but, after checking the dainty little wristwatch that her father had given her to mark the completion of her training, she realised that she'd enough time to spare to compose herself. Cycling up the main street at a pace more befitting the new teacher on her first day at work, passing by shopkeepers pulling down the shutters, publicans sweeping the sawdust out onto the street, a pair of policemen leaving the barracks to begin their morning patrol and women bringing buckets of water back from the pump, she was hailed down by Canon Murphy furiously waving his walking stick at the school gate.

'Miss Reidy. A word with you before you go inside.'

She dismounted from the bicycle.

'Aah ...' He looked in both directions before bowing his head. 'As a rule, I do not approve of women working in close proximity to men, especially where it may influence the formation of impressionable young minds. But mindful as I am of your father's standing, I'm prepared to make an exception in this case.'

Although not quite sure of where the conversation was heading, Josie nodded gravely. 'I understand, Canon.'

'Good. Excellent. Aah ... As you may be aware, the principal has yet to choose a wife. It may be in everyone's best interests were

257

you to favourably consider any approaches Mr. Hurley might make to you ... aah, that is, towards a permanent understanding ... if you know what I mean?'

'I fully understand, Canon.'

Canon Murphy sighed with relief, tucked in the folds of his soutane and shuffled away as if a great load had been lifted from his shoulders.

After leaving her bicycle beside another leaning against the side wall, Josie poked her head into the silent school. The first classroom was empty but, poring over the roll book behind a desk in the other, sat a lanky, slightly dishevelled man of about thirty with a Gaelic League fáinne pinned in his lapel.

'Yes?' he muttered absently as if he'd been interrupted in the middle of an abstruse mathematical conundrum.

'Mr. Hurley ...,' she began.

He immediately jumped to his feet and held out his hand. 'Céad míle fáilte, Miss Reidy. Still a few minutes before the mob arrives.' The other hand flicked a straggly lock of light brown hair back over his forehead. 'It'll be bedlam this morning. A dozen or more starting junior infants. Their first steps in life's great adventure.'

She accepted the handshake with hesitation.

'Aah!' His eyes lit up with absent-minded energy as he broke into a broad grin. 'The Canon must be marrying you off already. Yerra, don't take a blind bit of notice of him.'

He sat back on the top of the desk and pointed to her to take his chair. 'Anyway, I've been seeing a girl in Foynes this past year, but he doesn't approve of her.' The hand cupped around his mouth. 'She has a business of her own, you understand,' he whispered.

'Oh.'

'Not that he approves of me either.'

'Why's that?'

'Oh, politics, politics.' He reached back and slammed the roll book shut. 'Not that that should bother you. I hear you're quite friendly with a man of my way of thinking.'

She tried to contain it, but she knew that she was blushing.

'Willie Hartnett is the soundest man I know. And I hope for everybody's sake that he gets back here soon.' He hopped to his feet as the footsteps pounded the corridor outside. 'Now, let's get down to educating the willing and the unwilling.'

An army of children of various ages flooded in the door.

'Ciúnas!' barked the school principal with a surprisingly authoritative delivery that froze them in mid-movement. 'This is your new teacher, Miss Reidy.'

Their saucered eyes transfixed on Josie, they meekly filed to their desks. She waited until they'd all settled into their places before rewarding them with the hint of a smile.

18

THE BOMBARDMENT along the Somme lasted a full eight days. On the morning of the seventh, they added the gas to the mix and released clouds of chlorine from the oojah cylinders that floated northwards in the breeze over No-Man's-Land and onward to the German positions. A barrage of canisters followed, plopping into the enemy trenches to release the colourless phosgene vapour that boffins had recently developed as a more effective means of delivering death to its victims.

As night fell, the brass themselves came to visit, officers so high up the chain that rows of pips and crowns and crossed swords wreathed with laurel were dripping from their shoulder boards, and told them that they were on the eve of the great push which would bring the war finally to an end. The volunteer battalions cheered lustily as the general and his high colonels and their retinue of adjutants moved on to their next batch of customers and listened to their line officers explain that the ferocious firestorm of the preceding week had wiped out the German defences.

'Just a stroll in the park when you go over the top,' they heard one major utter. 'You won't meet a single living Hun between here and your objective.'

His Pals Battalion, almost a thousand young men all drawn from the same terraced town in Lancashire and most of them employed in his family's cotton mill where he himself had been the manager of the weaving shop, hung on every word that was said. Almost two years since they'd put down their names during the frenzy of enthusiasm at the outbreak of war, this would be their first taste of battle.

But the regulars of 5th West Sussex had heard it all before. The Big Push had already arrived at the Front when it was announced at Neuve Chapelle and, when that fizzled out after a few hundred yards of slaughter, the message was repeated at Aubers Ridge, at Ypres, at Loos and at a whole string of other setbacks so ignominious that they no longer rated a title. Having bled most of the comrades that had started the war with them, they no longer believed in the success of any grand plan cooked up by the desk officers back at the base. The most that they hoped for was a modest few miles, maybe gaining a stretch of elevated landscape that was easier to defend or the bulwark of a river bank or perhaps showing the enemy that the reinforcements of Kitchener's volunteers were also capable of fighting.

'Our initial target for today is the enemy reserve line. Then we move on to capture Montauban village.' Captain de Walcourt gave C Company his tuppence worth but few of them were listening. 'Zero hour is 7:30 ack emma. I expect nothing less than total success.'

Patie Fitzgibbon watched the ladders being raised against the wall of the front trench as it filled with those earmarked for the first line of attack. Ten thousand of them were going over the top together along the entire twenty-five-mile stretch of the Front. Every few minutes, they were going to be followed by successive waves of equal numbers before the artillery wheeled their light guns forward to protect them with creeping barrages of shellfire.

He shuffled the 70lbs of kit strapped to his back. They'd been given the full issue of tools, ammunition, hand grenades and rations and had been loaded with stakes, rolls of wire, lengths of angle iron and bits of machine guns so that the entire paraphernalia of the trench could be shifted forward at one go. In the clammy heat of pressed bodies and a thin warm mist drizzling down from above, the sweat seeped out of their pores and stuck their skin to their underclothes like glue.

'I'm getting out of here,' muttered Dick Mullane beside him. 'If there's any Germans left over beyond, they'll know exactly when we're going to attack.'

'You can't move back ...'

'No, over the top. Now.' He inched his way up the ladder. 'We've a better chance if we sneak out while it's still dark.'

Figuring out that anyone in the first wave had nothing to lose, Patie followed him up to the lip. A hand grabbed him by the ankle.

'Where are you going?' asked Roseblade.

'To find a crater to hide in out in No-Man's-Land.'

'Then lead the way.'

Patie slithered forward along the path that Dick had flattened through the long damp grass. The occasional starburst lit up the sky for the gunners but the bombardment had eased up in their own sector. Behind him, he could hear the soft rustle of the rest of the platoon as they emerged from the trench.

They edged from one crater to the next, stepping carefully over puddles left by the rains so as their splashes might not alert German sentries at their listening posts, and moved as closely as they dared to the British wire.

'Still intact,' whispered Roseblade.

263

'If we can't even cut our own wire, then I doubt if we've done much damage to the Jerry positions,' answered Dick.

Patie rooted in his kit for his cutters. Dick, Mick Fitz and Tim Curtin followed him as he crawled out of the safety of the hole. They found a stretch hidden from German observation by a huge mound of earth between the two lines, hacked a path through the barrier and marked it with strips of white rags.

An incendiary flared above the German lines, the flash of white light diffused by the mist into a sheet of illumination that provided a momentary silhouette of what lay before them. 'There. Ten o'clock.' Patie pointed to a crater that had punctured the line of enemy wire and left a length of angle iron pointing in its direction beside the white rags.

Not trusting the accuracy of their gunners, they retreated back to their hideout to wait for the signal to attack.

Just after sunrise, the artillery began its final fling and tossed everything bar the kitchen sink at the German positions, the barbed wire, No-Man's-Land and anything else that caught its fancy. Two shells, one on either side, landed dangerously close to the platoon's crater but, like much of the barrage that preceded them, they turned out to be duds.

Patie inched his periscope over the lip and edged it sideways until he found a gap in the grass. The dawn mist was beginning to clear but, in its place, the cloud of smoke and dust left the visibility much as it had been during the night.

'Three minutes,' Roseblade told them as the bombardment signed off with a hail of shrapnel whizzing over their heads.

They fixed their bayonets and crouched against the face of the crater, hips, thighs and knees coiled like a spring.

'Two minutes.' The ground trembled beneath them like it had been pounded by a giant's footstep, then flashed like fire and roared like the Apocalypse and a great gust of wind momentarily cleared the air before it was filled by a storm of dust. Three miles to the west, 10 tons of high explosive blew one side of the village of Fricourt apart, lifted it into the sky like an enormous column of clay and held it there for a few glorious moments blotting out the light of the sun before scattering it to the earth in a carpet of debris.

Three miles further on, 25 tons of ammonal exploded in another set of mines dug under La Boisselle and heaved the landscape even higher above the clouds in order to rain it back down over miles of trenches.

They heard the whistles. They heard the shouts. 'For King and country, West Sussex!'

Now or never, thought Patie.

They shot over the lip and made straight for the gap in the wire. Immediately, the German guns and mortars rang out, the shells looping over their heads and centering unerringly on the scramble of men behind them as they emerged from the trenches. A dense cloud of white smoke blew over them, camouflaging their advance as they followed Patie, running towards the hole that he'd spotted in the German barrier during the night.

Patta-patta-patta went the machine guns spraying from the mist. Ignoring general orders to advance at walking pace so as not to get ahead of the creeping barrage that was supposed to be covering them, they jumped, they ran, they stumbled and they staggered over the pit as fast as their legs would carry them and passed by the rattle of the Huns with the guns. But the waves behind them weren't so lucky and, even in the midst of the artillery's roar, Patie could hear their screams as they were mowed down by a solid hail of lead.

The moment they caught sight of the German line, they hurled their Mills grenades and waited for the bangs before jumping into the front trench with one hand cocked on the rifle and the other ready to clutch their short-handled spades. Crouching on the floor and waiting for the numbers to back them up, they steeled themselves for the response.

Not a scream was to be heard. The enemy had already deserted his first line of defence.

But the German 8/15s were still hammering away. Patie, Tim Curtin and Mick Fitz followed Dick as he peeled away to sneak up on the machine gunners from the rear and Rosbelade took another group with him to deal with the second post.

Dick flicked his fingernail across his throat as they crept over the sandbags. Unaware of what was behind them, the Germans were tapping the barrel and adjusting the ammo roll to clear out a jam and never got the chance to react as they were jumped on and slashed across the throat with bayonets.

He'd shot from a distance; he'd blown bodies to bits with a Mills bomb; but Patie had never before stabbed a man to death, had never physically touched someone while he was taking his life. As he wiped the warm blood from his weapon, he felt the relief of not having seen his victim's face.

Back in the trench, they waited with the rest for the second and third waves to catch up. Roseblade had lost a man slashed in the guts and, rather than revealing their position to any Huns further back, they had to leave him writhing in agony in the little sandbag-shrouded outpost as the mist burned off into a bright summer's morning. Two more of the platoon hadn't made it, dead, wounded or lost somewhere in the cockpit that they'd crossed.

'Anyone seen Flint?' asked Dick.

'He was just behind me going through the German wire,' said Jerry Curtin. But there wasn't a sign of him in the trench.

'He'll turn up.' Patie tried to ignore the foreboding. Apart from relieving the dead of their valuables, Flint mightn't have learned the first thing about soldiering during nine months at the Front, but his survival alone had acted as a good luck charm for the rest of the lads from Shanagolden.

De Walcourt was one of the first of the next group to arrive, his anger at Roseblade going off on his own only partially assuaged by the capture of the trench. Within minutes, they were followed by the rest of the company that hadn't been blown to bits coming over the top or impaled on the wire or cut to ribbons by the machine guns in the mad dash across No-Man's-Land.

'I'll deal with you later,' the captain told his sergeant. A series of shells exploded behind them. Not for the first time, their own gunners had completely miscalculated the speed of the advance and their only consolation was that the friendly barrage had also confused the enemy artillery as to who was in control of the German front positions.

Roseblade stood his ground. A 15-inch howitzer shell, big enough to blow the entire company to Kingdom Come, plonked into the trench floor between them. They dived into the dugouts but it didn't go off.

'Cor blimey,' gawked Maggot Tibbs as soon as they realised that their number wasn't up. 'Johnny Hun knows how to take care of himself.' They'd sought cover in a spotless canteen propped up by wooden columns and complete with tables, benches, pots, pans, utensils, crockery and a rudimentary kitchen. Circles of cheese and cylinders of sausage hung from the roof, jars of pickled vegetables and loaves of black bread filled up the shelves. 'Out!' roared de Walcourt before they could sample the fare.

The artillery had adjusted their gunsights and were now raining their explosive on positions at least a half-mile further on.

De Walcourt was again arguing with Roseblade. Dick removed his helmet, placed it on the butt of his rifle and held it aloft above the lip of the trench. A hail of small arms fire erupted from close by. 'We're in right trouble now,' he sighed.

'Get them moving,' the captain was bellowing at his sergeant. The company, now reinforced with the surviving straggle of a Pals Battalion from Norfolk, pulled itself together. Heads inched up over the top, one body exploding with blood was flung back into the trench but, suddenly from their right flank, a concentrated shower of light shells peppered the German resistance.

They took advantage of the mayhem created by the battery of rapid-fire French 75mm field guns and by teams of Hotchkiss machine guns, leaping over the top and rushing up the communication trench to capture the enemy support line. Most of the surviving Germans had fled ahead of their bayonets and grenades but one jumped on Dick only to be beheaded by his flailing trench spade. The handful of survivors raised their arms in surrender.

Panting with exhaustion and shot of nervous energy, they sagged to the floor. Roseblade grabbed a water canteen from a dead German and passed it around. Patie peered around the traverse into the communication trench leading back to the reserve line but couldn't see anything beyond the first bend.

'Vot behind?' asked Dick in an attempt at broken German.

'Is no trouble,' answered the prisoner who didn't appear overly downhearted by his capture. ' I speak English. I Polish and I spit on Nemançki.'

Just like ourselves, though Patie. Sucked into a war that, when all was said and done, didn't really concern them.

Footsteps clattered into the next bay, broad East Anglian accents telling him that they were friendly. The line began to fill with British to their left and French to their right. He turned back to his own group and sat down.

'Clear, Sergeant?' de Walcourt demanded.

Roseblade got to his feet. 'No resistance here, sir.'

'Then let's move on, shall we. We haven't met our first objective.'

Nobody moved.

'Lead the way, Sergeant.'

Most of them were still slumped on the ground.

De Walcourt fired his pistol in the air. 'I said move on!'

'Give them a few minutes to recover, sir,' pleaded Roseblade.

The colour rose for a moment in the captain's face before the stiff upper lip regained control. 'Are you questioning my authority?'

The sergeant picked up his rifle. Patie, Dick, Maggot, Mick Fitz, Dinny Lyons, Jerry Curtin and three others reluctantly stood up, slung their packs on their backs and pointed their rifles forward to cover each other as they entered the zigzag length of the communication trench. Movement stopped around the second bend where they ran into the wall of an enormous crater.

'Why have we stopped, Sergeant?' shouted de Walcourt from the rear of the group.

'The Germans have dynamited the trench,' replied Roseblade. 'We'll have to go over the top to advance.'

'Then give the order.'

The sergeant's face sagged with resignation. 'We've no ladders, sir.'

'You don't need ladders.' The captain barged his way up the line. 'Run your men up the slope of that crater.'

'Are you crazy?' Roseblade turned around to face him. 'We'll all be coming out one by one at the same point. We'll be sitting ducks for any German sniper.'

De Walcourt's eyes lit up with distant fury. His open hand slapped across Roseblade's cheek. 'You're relieved, Sergeant.'

The ground shook as a shell exploded in the support trench behind them. Everyone except their officer dived for cover as they were showered with clay and chips of masonry.

'Get up!' screamed de Walcourt. 'Get moving!'

Nobody budged. He fired his pistol in the air. They got to their feet.

'Climb up that crater!'

Dinny Lyons and Jerry Curtin led a group up the steep slope. A machine-gun chattered and their blood-spattered bodies tumbled back to knock over those following behind them.

Still trembling with rage, de Walcourt turned to Dick. 'You lead them, Mullane! I'll deal with Roseblade!' He cocked his pistol and pressed it against Roseblade's temple.

Dick turned around and, with a single fluid swing of his bayonet, slashed the officer's neck from ear to shoulder.

They leaned up against the wall of the trench. Dinny and Jerry were barely identifiable, the other pair were shot beyond all recognition. One of the farmboys from the Downs shivered with shock as he rose from beneath the pile of corpses and cleared bits of hair, bone and brain from his face.

But everyone else was looking at the other body sprawled on the floor. Captain de Walcourt's gaping lifeless head was skewed at an impossible angle as a weak spurt of blood pumped from his severed jugular. Dick stood over him and calmly wiped his bloodstained bayonet on the officer's tunic.

Patie, Roseblade, Maggot and Mick Fitz edged closer to form a circle around them.

Maggot sneaked a look over his shoulder before shaking his head. 'Cor, Dick. You've gone and done it this time.'

'Done what, Maggot?' Patie loomed a full ten inches over the Cockney. 'I didn't see nothing.'

'Neither did I,' added Mick Fitz.

'There must have been another Jerry hiding here when the Captain led us around the traverse,' continued Patie, staring intently down on Maggot.

'And the bastard got away before we could catch him.'

Maggot looked for backing from his sergeant but Roseblade was still gaping with shock.

'Am I right, Maggot?'

'If you say so, Patie.'

A rush of footsteps from behind broke up the circle. 'Where's the captain?' asked the lieutenant leading the group.

'Dead, sir,' answered Patie.

'What happened?'

'Slashed by a Hun, sir. You're in charge of us now.'

The officer, not yet out of his teens, blinked as he looked around and self-consciously reached for his pipe. Mick Fitz passed him a cigarette and lit it for him. 'Any other casualties?'

Patie pointed to the four bodies lying at the foot of the crater.

'Oh, bad luck ...' The lieutenant sucked on his smoke. 'At least we know who they are. Not like the chaps who caught the blast behind us. Nothing left of most of them. And one of our own shells too, I'm afraid.'

Patie hung back at the end of the group returning to the main trench. Dick stood his rifle on its butt, removed the bayonet and slipped it back into his pack.

'I wouldn't have done it myself, Dick,' Roseblade was telling him. 'But thanks all the same. I thought I was a goner.'

'It wasn't for you, Sarge. That was for Mick Culhane.' But Dick's calm resolve was stumbling. 'Jesus Christ, Patie, that's the God's honest truth. I done it for Mick Cul, so I did.'

'No one's saying anything, Dick.'

'I saw nothing either,' added Roseblade.

Patie guided the pair of them back to the support line where a detail of prisoners was removing bits of shattered bodies from the huge hole where the firebay had been. The company had survived better than most over almost two years of war. Now maybe half of their number had perished within a matter of minutes.

He tapped the lead prisoner on the shoulder and pointed back up the communication trench. 'There's another five of them up there.'

The German gazed quizzically at him. Patie spread out his five fingers and pointed again. 'Five. Funf.' The prisoner nodded and took another two with him.

At least the remains of Dinny, Jerry, de Walcourt and the two pals from Chichester were all in one piece. Unlike the jumbled-up fragments in the firebay, they'd get a grave of their own where someone who loved them could grieve when this war was all over. And Patie and a man he'd never known and would never again meet, who had marched off to a far foreign field to kill each other, were still driven by instinct to respect each other's dead bodies.

Nor did he even know who the enemy was any more. He'd shot at the Jerries, he'd tossed grenades at them, he'd sliced through their necks and they'd shot at him and ripped through at least four of the platoon with their machine guns and maybe a few others with their rifles and shells. But his group had also taken out their own officer and most of their casualties came from a gunner who either didn't know how to aim his howitzer, or where to aim it, or who was told to aim it at the wrong place.

Orders kept them going, an opposing uniform gave them focus; while surrender to the unthinking certainties of military discipline helped to keep them alive. But when they started to take out their own, the fragile convoluted logic that had sent them to the Front began lose all sense and meaning.

Over on the other side, there might well have been German soldiers wondering the exact same as himself. Patie looked up to the blue sky above him, to where he knew there were no answers. Then a small slight soldier in an oversized uniform returned from the dead.

'I'm telling ye straight, lads.' Flint dropped down into the trench right beside him and wiped the sweat from his brow with relief. 'There's some right quare things going on back there.'

19

NO PLACE ESCAPED the slaughter. The great industrial cities of the Midlands, remote Scottish parishes, West Country villages and mining communities in Northumberland and Durham were all visited by the horror of the Somme. As the Pals Battalions were led to their death, the batches of telegrams arrived to tell mothers and fathers, sisters and brothers, wives and sweethearts that a generation of their menfolk was now pushing up poppies. War descended like never before on the schools and the factories and the clubs that had sent bands of their youth off to the Front.

Like hundreds of towns all over Ireland, Shanagolden also got to hear of the carnage. Two of their own had fallen and even the most ardent supporters of the conflict began to wonder why. The great campaign that was supposed to be over by Christmas, then by the following Christmas and, after that, by the following summer, looked as if it would end only when there wasn't a single man left standing who could carry a gun.

And the loyal were part of an ever-shrinking minority. While Britain's army pressed for conscription so that more could be forced off against their will to the killing fields, they were also banging up men of the parish, two for fighting them and another three just for opposing them. The house searches, the curfews, the road blocks and the arbitrary arrests continued unabated as General Maxwell, his garrison and the authority they'd gained under martial law wrested the initiative back from the ineffectual political control.

Even a minimalist effort to shore up Redmond's position came to nothing. A proposal to bring forward Home Rule in the twenty-six overwhelmingly Nationalist counties was blocked by the Southern Unionists. Dismissing the plan as a sop to terrorists, they and their Conservative colleagues exposed how low the Irish Parliamentary Party's standing had sunk in Westminster.

On a national level, those favouring the gradualist approach had been put in their box. On a local level, the excesses of the military rekindled an underlying hostility that had been hidden for a generation but which had never disappeared.

Josie Reidy felt the anger that was swelling in the community every time the lorry called around to the farm to rip up the floorboards, scatter the hay, dig up the vegetable garden and tap through the roof with petty regularity.
Jack Noonan stared impassively at the squads tumbling into his bar to rough up customers, smash glasses, spill drinks on the floor and taunt anyone whose caution had been eroded by alcohol into resisting arrest.

Mary Hourigan didn't bother to contain her feelings as she rained curses of blood-curdling vividness on those implementing the edicts of Maxwell.

Councillor Hennessy figured out that the Army was on a loser and conspicuously allied himself to the anti-conscription movement, much to the disgust of James Horgan. Left without an ally to confide in, even the creamery manager began to distance himself from the agents of the King's rule, as did

Sergeant Stapleton who left it with the military to soak up the resentment towards martial law.

And District Inspector Sullivan watched the administration that he'd pledged to uphold unravel through pig-headed stupidity.

Willie Hartnett looked up at the bogs and the snipegrass covering the slopes of Arenig Fawr, Foel Goch and Carnedd y Filiast and they reminded him of home. But everything beyond the barbed wire fence and the watchtowers was a world forbidden to those held inside the perimeter.

Frongoch, a misbegotten internment camp stuck in the mountainous wilds of North Wales, where two valleys came together and another one left to empty into Lake Bala, had been his home for months. A thousand German prisoners-of-war had been cleared out to make room for almost half of the 3,500 Irishmen rounded up by General Maxwell and his soldiers after the Rising. Such were the numbers when they first arrived that a second camp of wooden huts had to be built further up the valley.

Along with Ned Reidy, Jimmy McCarthy, Dan Hourigan and Mossy Noonan, he was among those banged up in the original version, an abandoned distillery whose damp stone walls roasted in the heat and shivered in the cold and which still hosted a plague of rats nosing for grains of barley that the long-departed whiskey makers had left behind them.

But he knew that it could have been worse. He could have ended up in a regular prison like Lincoln or Dartmoor or Wormwood Scrubs, under the thumb of hardened screws with little interest and even less sympathy for revolutionaries attacking British troops while the nation was at war. Instead, he and his comrades were guarded by a military regime hastily

277

cobbled together out of those too old or too young to go to the Front, or else who had been out there and were in no fit condition to return.

When they arrived from their initial detention centre in the Cheshire town of Knutsford, control of the camp had quickly become the subject of competition. The authorities were mostly quite willing to leave it to the prisoners' own command structure to keep order but, every now and then, directives from above would result in the petty enforcement of regulations. Exercise would be limited to specified periods, assembly would be restricted, cells would be searched, guards were expected to snoop on conversations, and tempers would rise before the edict was forgotten and sanity was restored.

They were in one of the bad spells when outdoor life consisted mostly of dragging their feet along the muddy path inside the perimeter, gathering each morning and afternoon for the only physical activity that could soak up their energy. Hands in pockets, heads bowed and muttering to each other out of the sides of their mouths, they'd coalesce in small groups along the straggling column until their guards tried to make them march in single file as prescribed by the rulebook.

Willie didn't really mind the occasional rows. There was nothing like resentment to keep the spirits up and breaking the prisoners up when they gathered in groups only made them all the more determined to get to know each other. Under normal circumstances, a generation of revolutionaries, supporters, barstool philosophers and the unfortunates who'd been pulled in by mistake from all over Ireland would never have met but, in the hothouse of a British internment camp, convention, suspicion and shyness had disappeared. And liberated from the narrow parochial horizons of their previous involvement, a greater picture of nationality and how independence might be achieved began to take shape among those who had cheated the firing squads.

They had done everything they could during the months of imposed idleness to broaden their minds. Academics who'd followed Pearse's vision taught mathematics, literature, Irish, French, Latin, science and history to those who'd never got the chance of a formal education. The heir to a profitable retail business with a string of shops in the major towns of Munster unlocked the mysteries of accounting and finance. An electrical engineer explained how the new source of power might be harnessed for everyday applications and showed them the generating potential of Ireland's major rivers. A dairy scientist told them how a growing international market for cheap food of guaranteed quality could be supplied by the country's co-operatives.

But most of all, they wanted to know how they could learn from the weaknesses of the Rising to make sure of a better result the next time out. They talked of taking on the British on their own terms, of fighting them in the hills and the glens and the bogs rather than in the set-piece conflicts of conventional warfare. They talked of setting up an entire government of their own to raise money, levy taxes, hold elections, pass legislation and administer justice, education and public health that would simply ignore the British presence. They argued endlessly about the best way of striking out on their own and, in the rarefied air of a prison where dreams hadn't been broken, a cohort of impatient young men in their twenties and thirties began to convince themselves that they were capable of carrying off not just their war, but also the peace that lay beyond it.

And when reports filtered in through a sympathetic local lad about that other war over in France, they knew that they couldn't do any worse.

'I hear the British lost sixty thousand at the Somme last Monday week.' Willie kicked a stone from the path and pinged it off the steel column supporting the perimeter fence.

'A hundred times as many as we had in the GPO.' Ned rooted in his pockets for a cigarette. 'And all in the one day.'

'Not enough of them,' muttered Jimmy.

'And I also heard that Dinny Lyons and Jerry Curtin were among the dead,' added Ned as he struck a match off the stone wall of the distillery.

They waited for Mossy and Dan in the group behind them to catch up. All five of them shuffled forward together in silence.

'Oy, you lot! Break it up!'

They ignored the elderly corporal fulminating behind the bristles of his angry moustache.

'I said break it up!'

'We just heard that two of our friends have been killed.' Ned stopped to glare at their jailor. 'Fighting for your bloody king over in France.'

Other groups who'd known each other from earlier days began to coalesce along the circuit as news of the casualties spread around. Their guards didn't bother to interfere.

'That's four of us gone now.' Mossy took a drag of the cigarette that Dan passed on to him.

'They took the shilling. They knew what they were doing.'

'Maybe they did, Jimmy.' Willie shook his head. 'But they were our mates too. Don't you ever forget that.'

Back in the base camp, an old clothing factory on the outskirts of Amiens that had been bombarded by the Germans and then commandeered by whichever Allied army happened to be passing through at the time, Patie Fitzgibbon found a fortnight-old copy of The Times and searched it for coverage of the battle he'd come through.

It wasn't immediately apparent that his experiences and the reports in the newspaper referred to the same war. Field Marshal Haig, the man who'd ordered the mass attack on the German front lines, had announced substantial progress on the first day of the Somme and was confident of the Big Push's success. Another writer hailed the wonderful open-air life of those on the Front with their regular and substantial meals, their healthy exercise and their freedom from care and responsibility which kept them extremely fit and content.

Patie could have got angry as he read through the blatant rubbish peddled by liars who had never left the comfort of their clubs in the West End of London and who regurgitated whatever the politicians, the brass and their minions had fed them. Instead, he took it as the inevitable reaction of those who could send wave after wave of gullible volunteers to their death in the expectation that, if enough of them spilled their guts soaking up German bullets, the sheer weight of numbers might finally succeed.

But it hadn't worked out that way. Away from the abattoir of the front line, he'd met others who'd survived the horrors of the first days. Entire battalions had been shot to bits in the futile march over the top, not once, not twice, but many times over, as the eejits who'd ordained their slaughter sent another batch of glum heroes to repeat their sacrifice. Carpets of bodies piled up along the entire British sector as each failure of attack provoked nothing more than a craving to reproduce it in all its bloody futility. Before they eventually retreated back to where they had started out from, those stranded between the artillery bombardments of friend and foe heard death's chorus wail out from their comrades as they perished on the killing fields of No-Man's-Land.

5th West Sussex had been lucky. Sent to the eastern extremity of the British sector, they'd been faced by the weakest German defences along the entire line of attack and they'd also been covered for most of their offensive by the seasoned French gunners on their right flank. When they'd taken stock of their position at the end of their first day after capturing Montauban, they found that they were one of the very few British units to have met their objective.

A photographer was sent out to snap them advancing into the village's shattered square grimly holding their rifles and then of their smiling dusty faces in the sunshine, helmets askew, standing in a group over the bodies and the rubble. But it was all put on just for show. The last German had retreated from Montauban more than two days before the camera had arrived.

Someone said that a picture of C Company had ended up in one of the London dailies, a salute to Britain's heroes of the Somme. And the Army did need its heroes. Having committed entire divisions of amateur soldiers, commanded by amateur officers and covered by amateur gunners, to the bloodiest day's action of the war, success, no matter how insignificant, had to be found somewhere. Otherwise, the cheer squads back home might question why the bombardment to end all bombardments had barely scratched the German defences, why the promised walk in the park had been met by a lethal hail of gunfire, why the French Army had succeeded where their own had ignominiously failed.

Newspaper proprietors cast C Company, 5th West Sussex into the role of Britain's finest, as did the thrusting senior officers and the frock politicians jostling for position in the War Cabinet. And just to please those championing their exploits from the safety of London, the seventy-odd survivors of their own and of the

Germans' artillery were scrubbed down, kitted out and marched out into the makeshift parade ground surrounded by the gaunt, shell-pocked redbrick buildings of the abandoned factory.

Patie stood in line as the regimental sergeant-major, his stick ramrod straight under the crook of his elbow and his moustache waxed to mathematical perfection, barked out the commands. They liked spit and polish and drills and the rulebook back at the base. Ritual was far easier to understand than warfare.

Flanked by his two aides and followed by the battalion's own officers and a gang of pressmen and photographers, the lieutenant-general, an old West Sussex man himself before his wife's connections with the hunting set won him promotion to the Army's upper echelons, emerged through a gap in the buildings. A cine camera set up on a tripod followed his brisk progress to the top of the yard where he wheeled around sharply to face them.

'Sir!' The NCO raised his hand in salute. The company followed him.

The general returned the compliment and, like a judge sizing up prize cattle at an agricultural show, he strutted down the line to inspect his soldiers.

The first aide coughed. His superior and the retinue of followers shuddered to a halt. 'Sergeant Alfred Roseblade, sir. Military Medal,' whispered the cue.

The second aide opened a presentation case. The medal was whipped off and pinned to Roseblade's tunic. Nudged by his first aide, the general grabbed the recipient's hand and shook it firmly for the cameras before moving a few steps on to his next assignment.

'Private Horatio Tibbs, sir. Military Medal.'

Maggot beamed as he accepted his award. The sergeant-major scowled at the levity.

Informed that he need have no further direct contact with rank and file, the general swivelled around and moved back a few paces to address the column. The sergeant-major scanned the faces and uniforms for any last-minute transgressions and searched for Flint in particular, before his fearsome expression met its match in Dick Mullane.

'Damned good show,' began the commander, his eyes directed over their heads. Behind him, the battalion's colonel and the company's major were making no great effort to hide their embarrassment. Patie wondered how much they knew of what had actually happened in the German communication trench on the 1st of July.

'First company to reach enemy lines,' continued the clipped delivery spattering like a machine gun. 'Fine feather in our caps ... Glorious day for the West Sussex ... Will go down in our annals with Vimiero and Ulundi ... As will the name of Captain Cedric de Walcourt ... Only the regiment's second ever VC ... Shame he didn't make it ... Brave soldier ... Splendid West Sussex family, de Walcourt ... Example to us all ... Dismissed.'

And with his duty complete, he turned smartly on his heel. The aides, the cameras and the reporters followed him out of the yard.

20

MOSSY NOONAN, Jimmy McCarthy and Dan Hourigan were home by Christmas. Along with over half of the detainees, they had been beneficiaries of incoming Prime Minister David Lloyd George's attempt to take some of the heat from Britain's problems with Ireland. Frongoch was closed down, Reading Jail was cleared out and General Maxwell was recalled to garrison duty in England.

But as active participants in the GPO and having originally been condemned to death, Willie Hartnett and Ned Reidy were transferred to Lewes Gaol in Sussex. Unlike the ad hoc regime of an internment camp with its pragmatic tolerance of the inmates' own command structure, their new home was part of the regular prison system and run under established channels of authority. Discipline was far more rigorously imposed, disputes were common and conflict between the jailors and the jailed culminated in a mass hunger strike that was only resolved when the British government capitulated to its new American war allies and released all the remaining prisoners the following June.

If Frongoch had been the University of the Revolution, then Lewes was the school for post-graduate studies and among its students were the senior military figures to survive the Rising like Éamon de Valera and Thomas Ashe. As most of them had been active in the IRB since before the outbreak of war, discussion was less about the blue-skies prospects of the New Jerusalem after the struggle and concentrated more on the nuts and bolts of getting there. While a minority saw mass political participation as the road forward, the majority had little time for engaging in a parliamentary system that produced those like John Redmond whom they dismissed as pliable puppets of British rule.

Even though they'd heard that one of their own, Joe McGuinness, had won a narrow victory in the South Longford by-election despite having been nominated against his wishes, Willie and Ned had no idea of what to expect when they collected their meagre bags of belongings and joined the rest of the group on the platform. Out of circulation for fourteen months, this was their first sight of a different world from that which they'd left.

There was khaki everywhere, on uniforms, on vehicles and on huts. Posters exhorting greater effort were pasted over every flat surface available. The station and the train itself were full of soldiers, either coming home on leave or being shipped off to war underneath pictures of women proudly waving goodbye to their brave husbands and of dastardly foreigners listening in on innocent conversation. The enthusiasm of 1914 was a distant memory and had been replaced with the sullen resignation of carrying out orders.

They quickly became conscious of the staring faces, not just of the soldiers but also of the businessmen, the women and the railway employees. Stepping into the carriage, they were faced with an unconcealed rudeness that left them standing along the aisles even though there were the odd free seats dotted here and there among the benches. Not having advertised the fact that they were Irish revolutionaries, they were puzzled by the

286

hostility, as it was very much out of character with middle-class England's reluctance to display its emotions in public.

'What's the problem?' Not wanting his accent to raise the temperature, Willie kept his voice to a whisper.

'Look around you,' answered Ashe. Other than themselves, not a single man in his twenties or thirties was dressed in civilian clothing or else wore a Government-issue armband to show that his work was essential to the war effort. Nor had they seen anyone of their age out of uniform in the town itself or in the station. Even those sent home from the battlefields minus an arm or a leg or a pair of eyes had dressed to remind everyone that they too had once been soldiers.

The story was the same in every town they passed through. Village greens and public parks had been commandeered by sandbags, sentries and billowing rows of bivouacs. The entire country had been roped into the war effort and there was little sign of an end coming in sight. The streets around London's Victoria Station had none of the big city bustle that Willie had expected. Traffic was muted and pedestrian movement was thin and hurried. Even though it was a bright summer's day, the people had withdrawn into themselves as if they were sheltering from a cold wind, pausing only to gaze into shop windows that looked stripped of their normal display of products.

Muted snatches of conversation caught their attention as they passed by queues at the bus stops or outside food shops. Hun submarines had sunk ships bringing staples of wheat, meat and butter from America, Argentina and the colonies. Hun Zeppelins were bombing London's docks, its factories and entire streets of the East End. Black market spivs had cornered anything that was going and were ripping starving families off with their exorbitant prices.

The distant chimes of Big Ben told the time. 'We'd better be moving.' Ashe led the group back to Victoria to take the underground to Euston for the boat train to Holyhead and Dublin.

'You wouldn't fancy staying on for another few days?' asked Ned. 'I've a cousin living in Camberwell who's married to a manager in the GWR. She'd put us up if we turned up on the doorstep.'

Ned's cousin wasn't overly pleased and her husband even less so, but blood was thicker than water even if it flowed through the veins of a convicted enemy of Britain. The two sons, one nine and the other eleven, kept staring at Ned and Willie as they sat down for high tea.

'Admiralty has to do something about these U-boats,' snorted the husband as he took his share from the single can of sardines. War shortages had shorn the evening meal of its usual delicacies. Ravenous factories had stripped the household of its maid. 'Otherwise we'll bloody well starve to death.'

'Language, George,' chided his wife. 'Not in front of the children.'

George scraped off a minimal coating of margarine from the little cube resting in the butter dish. 'Nothing again today, Eleanor?'

'Not in the shops. But I did hear of a warehouse in Peckham ...'

'No black market, dear.' He leaned back in his chair and thumbhooked his braces. 'I'd rather do without than line the pockets of these criminals. Damned unpatriotic.'

The younger of the boys raised a devious eyebrow. Ned matched it with a conspiratorial wink. 'Are you a spy, Uncle Edmund?' asked the youngster.

Eleanor instinctively reached for the pot. 'More tea, anybody?'

'Shh.' Ned brought his finger to his lips. The boy nodded. He understood. His brother looked over the two visitors, not quite sure whether to be impressed or to be dismissive of George Junior's gullibility.

George Senior fixed them up with the next passage home, so they had only the following day to walk around London.

'At least there's something we can thank John Bull for.' Willie let his eyes follow the elegant arc of Regent Street as it looped down to Piccadilly Circus. 'Otherwise, I'd never have got the chance to see the place.'

They were getting used to the looks from passers-by and one woman left her place in a bus queue to call them cowards to their faces. But the mood changed once they moved through Trafalgar Square and on to Whitehall where generals, admirals, serious men in bowler hats and one-armed soldiers carrying messages moved from building to building.

One or two nodded at Ned as if they knew him. He deftly acknowledged the recognition. 'Our reputation has preceded us, it seems. The daredevil agents returning to base with the secret German blueprints.'

A group bearing placards demanding an end to the war had gathered outside the Downing Street home of the Prime Minister but were corralled by a detail of policemen into a harmless circle almost invisible from the main street outside.

Looking at them from outside the cordon, Willie finally realised that he was free. Unlike those publicly expressing their opinions under the suspicious eye of the law, he could walk past all the uniforms and none of them could stop him or harangue him as long as he kept his mouth shut. He could get up when he wanted, go where he wanted and talk to who he wanted about what he wanted, for the first time since he had been frogmarched down Henry Street over a year before.

Before him, the yellow-brown towers of the Houses of Parliament loomed over the Thames and cast their shadow over half the world. Like many of London's great buildings, they stood as a monument to the power and money of an Empire which stretched its fingers over land and sea and which, even in the depths of wartime, looked in no way diminished.

The sights had satisfied his curiosity and had given him an understanding of what they were up against. But now he wanted to go home to where there were hills and fields and villages and people that he knew.

Paddington Station was filled with soldiers returning from the Front. Most of them would never make it back. Willie and Ned found the last pair of empty seats in a carriage filled with the wounded.

They'd seen enough of the maimed over the previous two days and they were no longer shocked by the sight of hundreds of young men who'd never stand up again unaided or hold a child in their arms or cast their eyes over the world around them. But they weren't prepared for those damaged inside the head. As the train trundled through the night up the Thames Valley and under the Severn into Wales, they saw the shivering and felt the vacant stares and heard the ranting of souls shattered beyond sanity.

Many of them had also suffered physically. Some coughed with a retch so deep that they waited for their entrails to throw up. Gas, they were told by a briskly-efficient middle-aged nurse; victims of the silent plague that came with the wind and left a mark that none of them would ever forget.

Others had been burned, dismembered or scarred beyond recognition. The war had developed new ways of killing even more effectively and more horrifyingly than anything that had been unleashed on mankind before. Mustard gas clung to the legs and the arms and any exposed surface where it dissolved in the skin's moisture to burn and to blister and to blind and left effects so agonisingly painful that they couldn't be bandaged or touched. Incendiary grenades splashed sparks of white-hot phosphorous that caused the body to feed its own fires. Flame throwers blasted great gusts of fire into trenches. Shrapnel became ever more lethal as the shape of the missiles was refined.

But for all of their soldiers' suffering, Willie felt none of the hostility towards a fit man in civvies that he'd experienced on the streets of London. Most of them had retreated into a world of their own and those still capable of understanding their emotions looked as if they were either glad to have picked up a wound that would remove them from the horrors of the Front, or else glumly contemplating what the future could offer them.

'Take cover! Take cover!'

Willie turned around to the source of the screams and saw the soldier's legs banging off the seat behind them in an intense tattoo of uncomprehending frustration. The nurse rose to soothe her delirious bandage-shrouded patient, her demeanour suggesting that she wouldn't mind if the only two able-bodied men in the carriage would lend her a hand.

'An incendiary,' she whispered as they grabbed what was left of the man's arms. 'Burned half of his body. He would have been better off dead.'

'Take cover!' the soldier screamed again, his entire deformed body trembling uncontrollably as she extracted a syringe from a case and filled it from a small phial. They held him down as best they could, keeping him steady so that she could find a vein in which to administer the morphine.

The body sagged as the painkiller took effect. The air whistled out through the holes in the bandages left for the mouth and the nostrils. A nametag fell to the floor as Willie released him. 'Pte. M. Fitzgerald, King's Own West Sussex Rifles, Shanagolden, Co. Limerick,' it read.

'Oh Christ!' He showed it to Ned. 'Mick Fitz.'

'Do you know him?' The nurse eased Mick into a more comfortable position.

'We come from the same place. He's known the two of us since we were children.'

'I'm afraid he doesn't know you any more, poor soul. He'll never know anyone again.'

Many of the wounded were taken off at Swansea and were replaced by a battalion on its way to replenish the garrison in Ireland. The remaining shell shock cases were all moved into Willie's carriage and, although he and Ned were surrounded by the wails, the screams and the stares, it was preferable to the uncomfortable company of serving British soldiers.

They said goodbye to Mick Fitz as they got off in Limerick and, while they hoped that there might have been a spark of recognition, they knew in their hearts that all that was left of him was the shell. The Foynes train was waiting on the opposite platform and, having hardly slept a wink on the boat or on the journey from Rosslare, they slumped on an empty seat and dozed off.

'Hi! Willie!' He felt a kick on the soles of his feet and rubbed the sleep from his eyes. Dusk was falling, but he recognised the glint of twilight shining off Robertstown Creek as it flowed past Aughinish Island and into the mud flats of the Estuary.

'Will you leave me alone, Ned.' He curled up again to grab a last few winks.

A second tap woke him up. Mossy Noonan was standing above him. 'We were waiting for ye last night. So we're damned if we're going to make it a second wasted journey.'

Ned tossed him his bag as they pulled into Foynes station. He stretched the stiffness out of his limbs and stumbled towards the door as the train shuddered to a halt.

A huge cheer rang out as Willie stepped onto the platform. Hands grabbed his legs, hoisted him up on shoulders and carried him to the street outside, whose whole length was lit up by flaming tar barrels. He'd been dreaming about the county final on the train; now it appeared to be happening all over again.

'Good boy there, Ned! Good boy there, Willie!' roared the crowd. 'Come on, Shanagolden!'

They carried them up to a brewery dray festooned with green and white bunting. More hands reached out to shake him. A band, the very same Martyrs of Erin Fife and Drum Band although with two changes in personnel, struck up a passable rendition of Let Erin Remember.

Ned stepped forward towards the adulation. 'It'll take more than an English prison to keep a Shanagolden man down!' he bawled out to another wave of applause. 'It'll take more than an army of British soldiers to force the people of Ireland to their knees!'

Willie retreated to back of the dray as Ned worked up the crowd. Dan Hourigan slapped him across the shoulders. Jimmy McCarthy punched him in the chest.

'Good to have you back.' Mossy handed him a naggin bottle of whiskey. 'Go on. Take a sup. I'd say you've earned it.'

'It's another world, lads.' He felt the flush of heat rippling down his gullet. 'This can't be the same place I left.'

'Everyone's behind us now. At least in public.'

'Even the Canon and Horgan and Hennessy and all the rest of that crowd?'

'Well, not quite ...,' began Dan.

'The Canon banned tonight's reception,' interrupted Mossy, shouting to be heard over the cheers. 'But nobody's taking any notice of him any more. Not since the Bishop backed the Rising. And as for Horgan, well, there's some people you'll never change.'

'What about Hennessy?'

'No flies on our councillor. He's leading the campaign against conscription now. No more money to be got from finding recruits.'

They wobbled on their feet as a heave rippled through the crowd and bounced off the dray.

'You heard Mick Fitz was badly injured a few months ago?' continued Mossy. 'They say he'll never be right.'

'We saw him on the train.' Willie grabbed the sideboard for support. 'They were bringing him to St. Joseph's.'

'Then we should go in and visit him.'

'I wouldn't do it, Mossy, if I were you. Anyway, he wouldn't even know who you are.'

Another surge sent Ned tumbling back between Dan and Mossy. He grabbed the two of them by the shoulders and forced his way back to the front of the makeshift platform.

'They tried to beat us down.' Arms raised, Ned stoked the resentment of his audience and found expression for their anger. 'But we wouldn't bend. West Limerick will never bend. Ireland will never bend until she is recognised by the nations of the earth as an equal!'

'Come on, Shanagolden!' boomed the crowd.

'Come on, Shanagolden!' Ned's fist shot forward into the night's sky. ''Tis time the spuds were dug up!'

Over on the far side of Foynes's wide street, Nicholas Sullivan kept his policemen in line. Some were itching for a fight but more were looking for an excuse to withdraw from a standoff where they hadn't a hope of imposing their authority.

Much as he would have wished to, the District Inspector couldn't afford to remove the RIC presence from the celebrations. He had put himself and his force out on a limb in order to keep the Army away from what was certain to be a powder keg. Even though the worst excesses of martial law had been curbed following General Maxwell's replacement by General Mahon who had a far better understanding of his fellow Irishmen living outside the walls of the Big House, fourteen months of the military's heavy hand had left the area thirsting to show that it still hadn't been subdued. The only way of handling it was to let them get it out of their system. The police might have to eat some humble pie in the process but at least they were willing to take it on the chin rather than jump in bald-headed to make a bad situation even worse.

'Wait 'til they break up,' Laurence Stapleton was muttering to another sergeant beside him. 'Get your lot to take out Hourigan, Noonan and that schoolteacher if he's around. We'll deal with McCarthy, Reidy and Hartnett.'

Sullivan shoved his hands between them and yanked them apart. 'You do that, Sergeant, and you're on your own.'

The man from Glin shrank back in disavowal but Stapleton's lip curled with defiance.

'In fact, if anyone has notions of moving in on the crowd without authorisation, he'll face a hearing,' continued the Inspector. Ears pricked to overhear the showdown. 'And I don't care how many pals he's got in the military, they won't be of any use to him in an internal inquiry.'

Up on the platform, Reidy was firing up the crowd for all he was worth. Sullivan could have pulled him in on any number of charges and even the least confrontational hobnob of the RIC would applaud him for doing so. Anywhere else in the kingdom, this tirade would be considered sedition in peacetime and outright treason when the state was at war.

The inspector watched the mood change from triumph to confrontation and saw the shackles of compliance corrode in the rhetoric. The rebels had learned more than defiance from their incarceration; they now had the confidence within themselves to challenge every vestige of authority and the capacity to provoke an entire aggrieved people to follow them.

Ned Reidy knew how talk from a platform, knew how to play their emotions and was making a far better fist of it than the generation of representatives who'd grown comfortable within the system that they were pledged to oppose. If the military raised the temperature with another round of needless provocation, maybe he might lead his followers to battle. And having learned from the mistakes of his previous outing, this time he would rouse them with greater effect.

However, if it came to shooting, Nicholas Sullivan was even more fearful of what Willie Hartnett might achieve. He'd seen his steely determination on the football field, his capacity to inspire not by words but by silent example. But there was no sign of him up on the dray, no sign of him in the front rows of the crowd. For a fleeting moment, the Inspector felt a tingle of panic, of having lost the threads of surveillance of the tableau before him.

Then he spotted his quarry hidden under the porch of a shop, his arms embraced around Josie Reidy as they pressed against each other with a passion fired by long separation. And the policeman remembered that Hartnett was still only a lad of twenty-two, young enough to be his own son and strangely and vulnerably human as he faded out of the tumult of public emotion into a corner where he could pick up the strings of his private life.

Realisation of what such ordinary young men like Willie Hartnett might do filled Sullivan's heart with trepidation.

Ned was ranting from his podium, the crowd was whooping and Foynes and all the other towns along the Estuary were savouring a rare moment of victory over the forces of law and order. Soon the cavalcade would begin its four-mile march of triumph to Shanagolden where they'd celebrate through the night and dare the peelers to challenge them.

But Willie and Josie didn't care. They desired nothing more than just to hold each other, feel each other's warmth, breathe in each other's scent, feel each other's heartbeat pounding against their own, rustle each other's hair against their cheeks, melt lips and tongues together so that realisation of return would flood upon them and leave them in no doubt that it was real.

'Oh, Willie, my love,' she finally said. 'It has been so long.'

'Four hundred and nineteen days.'

'You counted?'

'Every one of them.'

The street had thinned out, the tar barrels were being doused. They stepped back out into the warm summer's night.

Footsteps followed behind them, not the light rapid dance of a people celebrating but the dead heavy pounding of duty. Five paces back, a peeler matched their movement and was shadowed by a colleague a further ten yards behind. From across the road shone the deadpan attention of the District Inspector.

She puckered with annoyance, he sighed with resignation. 'They were never going to lose sight of me the first night.'

Knowing that they weren't going to get any more privacy, they tagged along at the back of the crowd.

21

THE BATTALION commanders were waiting at the pier head in Folkestone, ticking off the names as the rank and file of 5th West Sussex reassembled after a month's leave in England. Most had headed back to homes where they hoped that wives or sweethearts would be waiting but, going by the downbeat demeanour of some of the returnees, not all had found matters as they had left them.

A sizeable group of them had gathered around a promenade bench where Maggot Tibbs was hosting a Crown and Anchor session as the officers pointedly looked the other way.

'Taken up with the grocer, she has, the trollop.' The lanky thatcher from Arundel hovered his fingers over the oilskin board before dropping his sixpence on the club. 'Not even his proper woman, mind. The bugger has a wife and five nippers back in the big house and my Violet put up in an apartment in Worthing.'

'You was too slow off the mark, Bert.' His colleague plumped for threepence on the crown. 'You should have married her before we was shipped out.'

'Dunno about that, Reg.' The thatcher picked up the dice. 'Harry Baldwin got a right land when he found his wife is expecting and he being out at the Front for over a year.'

'Give over your moaning, Bert,' said Maggot 'The war will be over before you throw.'

'Making a mint on the black market, he is, the bugger.' Bert rotated his wrist in a slow lazy arc. 'While we's out dying for King and country.'

'Club ... Club ...'

'Thinks he can buy her ...'

'... And a club. The stick to beat her with. Your luck's changing, mate.' Maggot covered the sixpenny piece with three more. 'Do you want to let it ride?'

'He might be making all that dodgy money, that bleeding grocer.' Bert scooped up his winnings. 'But it ain't half as dodgy as what you's got stuffed in your pockets, Maggot Tibbs.'

Unlike their English colleagues, Patie Fitzgibbon and the other four survivors never made it home to Shanagolden. Having officially been recorded as enlisting in Chichester, that was as far as their ticket went and, between the U-boats disrupting the Irish Sea sailings and the monumental incompetence of those left minding the shop at regimental headquarters, passage across the channel could not be arranged for love or for money. Instead, they were given an allowance to cover their lodgings in Brighton and a rail warrant for one return trip to London. They'd finally collected the sweetener that had lured them into signing for the West Sussex in the first place.

Away from camp, they got the chance to experience a modicum of normality. Instead of the extended sessions of drinking, whoring and fighting that filled their entire days in the restricted rest areas in France, they got the craving for immediate pleasure quickly out of the system before relaxing into a summer holiday on the coast. The only connection with the day job was having to dress in uniform when venturing out. Any time they wore civvies, they were sure to be stopped by the police or reported by vigilantes as spies or as conscription dodgers or as black marketeers and having a strange accent in a strange country didn't help.

On the other hand, there were those who liked nothing more than to be seen in the company of serving soldiers. Batt Mullane made the most of walking around in his best outfit complete with gleaming medals, picking up the free drinks from publicans eager to impress their customers and regaling them with his stories of life at the Front. But a military bearing was a necessity, something Flint clearly lacked when he also tried to cash in on the loyalty card.

Patie might have enjoyed the break more had he not carried his last memories of Mick Fitzgerald. In fact, Mick should have been with them as they hadn't seen much action after the early days of the Somme. Back in the rear at the time, they'd missed the next push in their sector and had survived the winter's cold and the coming of spring in that twilight zone between tension and boredom when nothing was happening on the line.

Then just as life in the bullring was about to settle into comfortable inactivity, the Germans moved ahead in the air race with their Albatros D-III and exploited improved artillery observation by peppering the British forward positions. On an ordinary morning along a quiet stretch of the Front, Mick was caught by a spatter of incendiary that set him on fire and would have killed him had he not tumbled over into a pool of muck. When Patie and Tim Curtin pulled him out, all that remained were the charred remains of the front of his body and a wail that begged Heaven for mercy.

That scream stayed inside Patie's head longer than the punctured gasp of any man that he'd stabbed, longer than the incomprehension of shell victims as they watched the life gush from the half of their body that was left, longer than the wheezing agony of those corroded by chlorine, longer indeed than any other horror that he'd come across at the Front. And it burned such a stamp in his mind that he woke every morning throughout his leave with his ears ringing, his head throbbing, his hands shaking and his body all covered in sweat.

The pain was eased somewhat by swims in the sea, lazing out in the sun and walks in the South Downs, up along ancient chalkhill pathways between Brighton and Lewes where they were holding the leaders of the Rising. When they learned that Ned Reidy and Willie Hartnett were among those banged up inside, Patie and Dick Mullane set out about paying them a visit. It took days of persistence to pierce the barriers of red tape and the astonished official hostility only to be told when they finally wangled a pass that all the Irish prisoners had been released.

The sergeant-major was roaring. The Crown and Anchor school broke up. Kit bags were picked up and slung over shoulders and they fell into line as they were called to embark. Patie looked back over his shoulder from the gangway to the white cliffs in the distance as he faced into another indefinite stretch at the Front. After three years of soldiering, it pained him to return.

They were being moved again. In fact, it wouldn't even be the same 5th West Sussex, as they were transformed for the second time inside a year. Having already absorbed the survivors of a Pals Battalion that had been wiped out on the first day of the Somme, they now took in the remnants of a Territorial Army unit decimated during the attack on Arras and would also be picking up a batch of the conscripted to bring them back up to full strength when they returned to the forward positions.

'Wipers,' they groaned when they realised that they were returning to the most notorious sector of the entire Front.

Sticking out like a sore thumb in the Teutonic order of the enemy's lines, the sodden trenches of the Ypres salient had survived almost unchanged despite being flattened every few months. Just after they went on leave, the sappers had stuffed 500 tons of high explosive in mines under one of the few ridges of elevated ground in the area and had blown 10,000 Germans into the next world in the process and it still failed to make any difference.

The train took them as far as Saint-Omer where they were stuck for over a day on a siding. At least they were far enough back from the forward positions to escape the German aerial bombardment and it was summer outside rather than the depths of winter. They'd heard of battalions arriving at the Front or returning from leave losing men to frostbite and exposure as they waited for days for the war-induced gridlock on France's rail system to sort itself out.

'Out!' barked the sergeant-major as a second night in the stranded carriages loomed. They scrambled up the cutting to a bridge crossing over the line with the full weight of their kit laden across their shoulders.

Tired, hot, thirsty, cranky and stiff from dozing in the carriage, Patie set out on a thirty-five-mile march that would take them through the night and much of the following day. Although they'd travelled further by foot a number of times before, they'd been getting used to the increased usage of trains and lorries for troop transport as the war progressed. Striding out to the commands of a drill sergeant who'd managed to avoid active service was like turning their backs on all the technical progress that the conflict had brought with it.

He'd even got used to the cleanliness of leave. Scrubbed, deloused and disinfected before being released to Brighton, the opportunity of a daily wash was a luxury denied to him at the front. But between the sweat of the train and of the march that followed and the close proximity of an entire battalion, Patie knew that his skin would be crawling again by the time he reached the Front.

'Flaming night marches,' moaned Maggot. 'Oh Lord, why do they punish us so?'

'For getting the clap in London,' answered Dick. 'Too much of that hanky panky down in Whitechapel Road. The brass got wind of the feckacting you were up to.'

'Bleeding blabbermouths. I'll stick to mademoiselles from now on. More discreet, if you ask me.' Ignoring orders not to expose naked flame at night, he lit up a packet of cigarettes and passed them round to his Crown and Anchor patrons. 'God bless the ladies of Tookey. They know the way to a man's heart.'

The night exploded to the east of the column, flares lighting up the sky and the dull sharp thuds rending the air.

''Oo, lad, 'ee put out cigarette!' rang the Yorkshire tones of the sergeant-major.

'Wot's the geezer saying?' Maggot lapsed into a denser layer of Cockeny.

'He's telling you that the light from your smoke will inform the enemy of our positions in the middle of an incendiary storm.'

'Well, I'm glad you told me, Private Fitzgibbon. Cor, they do breed them stupid up North.'

'Wat 'ee saying, lad?'

'Nothing, sarge. Like yourself, I'm just happy to march and I was sharing my joy with the rest of the lads. Everyone should do at least fifty miles a day just to stay healthy.'

The forward positions were quiet when the battalion returned but the steady accumulation of new arrivals told them that they were gearing up for yet another Big Push. Following the mutinies in the French sector after the April offensive in Champagne degenerated into slaughter on a monumental scale, pressure had been mounting on the British brass to provide some relief. The prospect of another mass waste of life like the Somme filled every infantryman between Nieuwpoort and Péronne with dread.

5th West Sussex prayed that Ypres wouldn't once again be plucked from the map by the strategists back at base. The salient protecting the handkerchief-sized patch of their territory still free of the Hun provided the Belgian government with a fig leaf of legitimacy but it had come at the cost of hundreds of thousands of corpses. Unless they committed their entire forces to the attack, neither side was likely to advance more than few hundred yards over the swamp that separated them. The foot soldiers waiting for the next attack already had four inconclusive battles to demonstrate the pointlessness of any campaign in the sector.

Sergeant Roseblade was waiting in the support trench when the company trudged its way up the communication line. Gathered around him was a group of middle-aged newcomers, stooped with age, paunched from civilian life and showing none of the hungry sharpness of soldiers hardened by the demands of active service.

'C Company reporting for duty, sir!' Exuding the bravado of experience, Maggot's salute was an example to those framing its regulations. 'Recuperation successfully accomplished on the Home Front, sir! Where's the enemy, sir, so that I might shoot his black arse back to Hunland?'

'All right, Maggot, I'm impressed. Now take this lot up to the front trench and show them how to stay alive.'

'Keep your heads down.' The new arrivals followed Maggot up along the duckboards. 'First thing to remember, chaps, is never look up.' He pointed to the step cut into the point of the bay. 'You

305

stand on this firestep here if you want to take a shot. Or you can use this periscope here if you want to see what's happening in the world outside.'

'Er, sir?' The veteran of the trenches acknowledged the politely-raised hand. 'What happens if we don't?'

'A sniper blows your head off.' To emphasise the point, Maggot removed his helmet, placed it on the butt of his rifle and lifted it over the lip. A bullet pinged off it immediately.

Patie watched the newcomers glancing silently at each other as they were faced with the reality of warfare. 'Where did they get this lot? There isn't one of them younger than forty. They're too old to make soldiers out of them now.'

'That's what they're sending us now.' Roseblade poked through the dugouts to see what state the company they were relieving had left them in. Even in the height of summer, the trench was still as damp as ever.

'Is there no one else left?' Dick picked off a couple of rats scurrying out of their hidey-hole. The new arrivals jumped when they heard the shots. 'The brass must be scraping the bottom of the barrel.'

The following morning, Dick was back in No-Man's-Land. Sniping was the only privacy a man could get up in the forward lines and the only place where he could escape the claustrophobia of the trench. Some of them, particularly the townies, could adapt to the security of the defensive cage built around them, but he found it difficult to take more than a few days of having his horizons limited to the suffocating walls of mud and the thin blue line of the sky directly above him.

Ypres hadn't changed much in his absence. If anything, the mutilated landscape had flattened out any remaining landmark that had survived the previous three years. Farmhouses that had dotted the rich fields when they first arrived back in the early days were reduced to shattered humps of rubble. Where once there were trees, barely visible stumps merged into the earth around them. Only the remnants of the Cloth Hall behind him, the snaking lines of barbed wire and the rusting carcasses of machinery broke the monotony of the light-brown carpet of caked mud, the darker patches where there was still water on the surface and the stripes of raggedy green flecked with red poppies sprouting between craters that were slowly sinking back to ground level.

Artillery rumbled in the background and engines were hauling more men, machinery and munitions forward but the immediate vicinity was silent. Even though the sky was clear, the airmen had yet to stir from their huts.

Dick checked his fallback positions once again before he settled down behind an enormous mound of earth. He'd be at a disadvantage during the morning when the sun reflected off the British lines but he'd have the upper hand in the afternoon. Somewhere across from him, a German sniper was also planning his day. They'd never clap eyes on each other but both would consider it a personal contest to determine which of them was the better marksman. The impersonal statistics of competition kept his mind from dwelling on the consequences of his work.

A distant movement caught his eye. He squeezed the trigger, then silently sprinted twenty yards along the wall of the crater to his next position. Even though he didn't wait to check, he would have been surprised if his round hadn't found the mark. Careless, very careless, he wondered if the easy target who'd needlessly exposed himself was a raw arrival dragged to the Front as the recruiting sergeants scoured Germany for its last remaining stocks of manpower.

Maybe the Huns had reached the same position as the British and the French. The pick of their manhood was either dead, maimed or mad and all that remained were the old, the very young and the useless.

Another shot rang out from not more than twenty yards distant on the other side of the mound. Dick looked back to see one of the newcomers, who had turned up the day before, fall back bleeding into the trench. Another victim to carelessness.

'Hey, Tommy! Good shot!'

He tensed, scanned cautiously over both shoulders, slipped his hand inside his tunic for the short dagger he always carried with him just in case he might be surprised.

'Is no danger, Tommy,' continued the heavily-accented English. 'We not see each other. We not shoot each other.'

He was surrounded on three sides by the disturbed clay of Flanders. 'Yeah, I suppose you've got a point there, Fritz. No grenades.'

'No grenades,' agreed the German. It would have been the height of bad form to refuse. 'Hey, you Irish?'

'How can you tell?' Dick retuned the dagger to its sheath.

'I work two years making the sausage. For my uncle in Dublin. Damn good sausage too, everyone wants to buy him.' He heard a matchstick strike. 'You want a cigar?'

'I never smoke on the job. But thanks all the same.'

'You better off. We only get very terrible tobacco now in Germany. So, Paddy, you tell me now why you fight for the King of goddam England?'

'I don't even think about it.'

'Ja. Maybe you have right, you smart Irish son of a dog. I too stop thinking when I come to this shit hole.'

22

THE LAST of the schoolchildren were straggling back down the main street. Willie Hartnett leaned up against a wall on the other side of the road and waited under the warmth of the afternoon sun. A fortnight with time on his hands had worn the shine off freedom. While Ned had his work on the farm and could fling himself into burgeoning political activity as the graduates of Frongoch University took over Sinn Féin, he felt like a fish out of water in the strange world of talk, meetings, pulling strokes and soft-soaping voters.

The morning after his return, he'd gone along with Ned to Clare to help out in a by-election caused by the death of John Redmond's brother Captain William, killed at the Front during the assault on Messines. Sinn Féin had put Éamon de Valera up and, just in case anyone was in any doubt about who was now running the show, the candidate turned up at every rally in his Volunteer uniform. But Willie had been little more than an ornament as the campaign moved along from one village to the next with the local organisation deeply suspicious of any outside help coming from the southern bank of the Shannon. After a fortnight of listening to them tracing relations and in-laws, recalling wrongs inflicted on teams by hurling referees, warning

309

of superstitions associated with blue bottles, magic fiddles and trees cursed by the fairies, and dredging up memories of boycotts, cattle drives and feuds with their neighbouring parishes, he retreated back home a week ahead of the voting to a county that wasn't beyond his powers of comprehension.

More than a year of enforced idleness had left him craving for something to occupy himself, something that would remind him that there was a real world there outside the dreams of his prison cell. Everyone might have cheered him to the rafters when he came back from Lewes but, with the peelers snooping around and the Army still maintaining a presence, nobody was keen to draw the attention of authorities on themselves by giving him a job. And even though the creamery and many of the farms were crying out for working men, James Horgan would roast in hell before he'd have anything again to do with Willie and Edmund Reidy would move heaven and earth to keep the returned hero away from his daughter.

The school door opened. Josie and Philip Hurley came out, wheeling their bicycles ahead of them.

'Welcome home, Willie.' The school principal shuffled his books awkwardly under the crook of his left arm and extended his right hand in greeting. The bicycle wobbled, the books teetered and the tousle of hair dripped over his eyes before Josie steadied him up.

'And it's good to be back, Philip.'

'Now, I wanted to speak to you about something.' Hurley regained control of the handlebars. 'Work needs to be done on this building. Urgent maintenance, to correct years of neglect.'

'Like what?'

'Oh, I … I don't know. You could paint the place. Fix the roof; I believe it's leaking. There's a draught coming under the doors. Maybe you could see to that while you're at it.'

'You're leaving it to my better judgement?'

'Precisely.' The teacher strung the books together with a length of twine pulled from his pocket and tied them to the crossbar. 'And don't worry about getting paid. That's all been sorted out. Miss Reidy will supervise you.'

He pulled a pair of bicycle clips from another pocket and popped them over the legs of his trousers. 'You can start next Monday after we send our little angels home for their summer holidays.'

Whistling a merry tune, Hurley mounted his steed and cycled off into the dust that a gust of warm air had raised from the road.

'May I carry your books, Miss Reidy?' Willie grabbed the satchel from the basket on Josie's bike.

'Oh, I don't know about that, Mr. Hartnett,' she answered primly, ignoring the face peeking out from under the veil of a squinting window.

The outbuildings were freshly whitewashed. The cart was new, its wheels firm and gleaming with the vivid scarlet of the red lead coating. The well had been bricked up and covered with a canopy to ward off the deposits of bird and beast. Dung that had collected over the years, sticking, drying and caking itself to every nook and cranny, had been washed out and cleared away. Even the weeds had been pulled from the cracks in the stones.

Never had the farmyard looked so prosperous. Not only had spare money been spent on it but also time and effort. Ned Reidy could scarcely believe that this was the place he'd grown up in.

He'd returned home in the small hours from Ennis, where half the population of Clare had been celebrating de Valera's stunning victory. Although Sinn Féin had won two by-elections in the preceding months, nothing compared with the latest success where Redmond's Irish Parliamentary Party had put up a popular local candidate with connections in every parish and where they played the sympathy factor of Willie Redmond's gallant death in battle for all it was worth. Most of the leading Volunteers had involved themselves in the campaign and a result giving them over 70% of the vote surpassed their own wildest estimates of popular support. The inroads made into traditional bedrocks of the Redmondite following, like the clergy, the shopkeepers and the farmers, had convinced even the most military-minded among them that there was a future in political activity.

Ned had also carved out a name for himself. Called on to stoke up the crowd at a public meeting in Sixmilebridge, he'd filled the packed square with the fire of defiance and sent them home happy, even though Dev was unable to turn up after he'd been delayed on his way there by the military. The following night, they asked him to speak in Kilkishen and, after that, they queued up to secure his services for every possible engagement right up to polling day.

The momentum was intoxicating as he sensed how just a mere turn of phrase or a pause or a change in the pitch in his voice could fashion the mood of hundreds. Wild ideas that they'd talked over in the exercise yards of Frongoch and Lewes suddenly came flooding back and, as his speeches flowed from his lips, he found the context in which to put them into words. By the time the votes had been cast, he was receiving the effusive congratulations of Dev, Arthur Griffith, Thomas Ashe, Michael Collins and the other leading lights of Sinn Féin.

After the adulation of the election, it hadn't been easy to adjust to the early morning quiet of Shanagolden. He'd waited a few minutes at the crossroads, soaking up the emptiness and the absence of activity before cutting across the fields to his home.

The cock was crowing. The farm stirred itself into life. As dawn broke over the fields, Ned could see the herd of cows coming together to be driven in for the milking. A candle flickered in a bedroom window as his father rose from his sleep. The back door opened and a swish of the broom cleaned the dust from the kitchen.

Jimmy McCarthy came up the lane, a small red terrier at his heel doing its best to imitate all the contrariness of its owner.

'You took your time, Ned.' Jimmy twirled an ash plant in his hand. 'He's been waiting for you for weeks.'

'Is he bulling at me?'

'Hard to tell.' The terrier sniffed the ends of Ned's trousers before figuring out that their owner needed to be treated with respect. 'How did the election go?'

'Dev walked it. Nearly three to one over Lynch.' Ned swivelled his head around the yard. 'Not your work. More of a woman's touch, I'd say.'

'Your sister's been driving him mad ever since she came back from Dublin. If you ask me, she learned too much of that domestic science while she was away training up to be a teacher.'

Edmund Reidy limped out into the yard. The hip that had been bothering him had yet to warm up for the day. He nodded to Jimmy who immediately made for the fields to herd in the cattle.

'Fine time for you to be returning, Ned.' But there wasn't the expected gruffness in his father's voice. 'We could have done with you last week when the cattle broke out into the field I'd been saving for the hay.'

'I'd a job to do in Clare.'

'I heard that.' His father picked one from a selection of sticks leaning against the wall beside the back door. 'Well, will you be staying this time?'

'I might be.'

'Then you'd want to be making up your mind. Dairying isn't something you can do only when you feel like it.' His gait steadied, Reidy reached into his pocket for his pipe. He didn't bother to light it, just hung it from his lip as part of his apparel. 'Mind you, if you are planning on staying around, you couldn't have picked a better time. There's great money in milk, pigs and oats at the moment.'

'So I see.'

'Looks a different place, doesn't it?' Reidy opened the door of the milking shed. 'I didn't see the point of it at first. But when 'tis all cleaned down, it doesn't take that much work to keep it that way. She's a clever girl, that sister of yours.'

Ned went down to open the gate. The cows lumbered into the yard and obediently made for the shed apart from one wild-eyed rogue who needed the lash of Jimmy's ash plant across the hinquarters and the angry rebuke of the terrier to keep her in line. The herd looked in good shape, far better than those he'd noticed in Clare or in England, bulging udders, nicely-toned bodies and hides and no sign of any ailment or disease. Unlike many other farmers who'd been dazzled by the easy money of feeding the war, his father hadn't compromised on his stock.

Ned went inside to change out of his suit and found working clothes that had been hanging untouched in the closet for almost a year and a half.

'About time,' Josie told him as he buttered a slab of bread and gulped down the cup of tea that had been waiting on the kitchen table. 'Your father's not getting any younger. Now get up off your backside and give him a hand.'

Grabbing a three-legged stool, he sat under the tits of a cow mooning absently into the near distance while she waited to be emptied. Easing and squeezing with the knack that he'd learned

314

as a child, he listened to the tattoo of the hot milk drilling against the side of the bucket before it fanned out to sink under the blanket of froth. He kept up the rhythm until the animal whipped her tail to lash out at a non-existent fly or maybe until she was telling him that she was done.

Jimmy had an empty bucket ready at the next cow, took Ned's full one, moved the milked cow out to the yard and replaced her with another at the stall. Josie again, Ned guessed, as the operation moved like clockwork and they were ready to wheel the churns onto the cart from the new landing that had been tacked on to the side of the milking shed in half the time that it used to take.

It was slick, it was clean and it was the way of the future. He remembered a creamery manager explaining to him in Frongoch how an independent Ireland could be training its farmers to produce the best milk and the best meat in the world if they only thought about what they were doing instead of lashing in to bag the quick profit. And now he'd seen it in action on the holding that he was in line to inherit, if he had the urge to do so.

'Wash your hands,' his father told him before they entered the kitchen. 'And leave your boots outside the door.' Josie had gone off to the school and Jimmy had taken the cart to the creamery where he'd be at the head of the queue and wasting less time that could be used back on the farm.

'I'm finding it hard to do all the work myself.' Reidy poured out the tea and started on the hairy bacon sandwiches that Josie had left out for them.

'You've Jimmy.'

'He's a good worker, I'll grant you that. But he's got no understanding. You still have to tell him everything and sometimes it goes against the grain of what he's used to. No, I'd want someone like yourself around.' His father spread a dollop of mustard over the meat. 'This is our big chance to make something serious out of the place.'

'Well, I'm back, amn't I?'

'Yes. But for how long?'

'As long as it needs me.' Ned realised that his mouth was already moving ahead of his brains but there was nothing he could do to stop it. He hadn't made up his mind about where he wanted to go, but he was afraid that, if he disappointed his father now that the question was put to him, one of his options would be closed off. 'I want this holding just as much as you do.'

'Well, then, maybe 'tis time we expanded.' Reidy took his pouch from his pocket and shaved off a few slices of plug. 'I hear there's seventeen acres after coming on the market. Decent land too if a bit of work was done on it.' He rolled the scrapings of the bowl into the fresh tobacco. 'Morty Hayes's old place out the Foynes road. I might just have the cash put away if the price happened to be right.'

'Do you want me to have a look at it?'

'Do that.' The pipe lit up to puffs of blue smoke. 'And you could talk to the auctioneer while you're at it. See what number is inside in his head. Let on that you're half-thinking of setting out on your own.'

Ned followed his father back to the milking shed and threw buckets of water over the floor to dislodge the dung that the cattle had left after them.

'You could also have a word with Josie,' he was being told. 'She's seeing Willie Hartnett again. She won't listen to me at all.'

'That's none of my business, Father,' he replied as he picked up the yard brush. 'If that's what they want, then far be it from me to come between them.'

23

THEY WERE moving with a speed not seen since the early days of the war. Instead of killing off entire waves of attack to grind out a few yards, the Allied armies now advanced in groups with a mechanical monster ahead of them to smash open a path through the defences. After four years of stalemate, the conflict was finally drawing to a conclusion.

When the push started in August, it was merely a case of recovering lost ground. After Russia pulled out of the conflict following the Bolshevik Revolution, hundreds of thousands of battle-hardened Germans were released from the Eastern Front to reinforce their positions in the West and their commanders threw them into action in a last throw of the dice.

New offensive tactics yielded spectacular results. Small groups of crack troops isolated weaknesses in the Allied positions before the main advance mopped up the rest. Instead of splattering massive bombardments across No-Man's-Land, the artillery pinpointed specific targets for short sharp barrages that retained the element of surprise. Soon, the Kaiser's forces were pushing to within forty miles of Paris as they gained more territory in three months than they had in the previous three years.

But like the British at the Somme and the French at Chemin des Dames, they bled a swathe of their manpower in the process. Once the offensive paused for breath, Germany was as exhausted of capable soldiers as its enemies and failed to find its second wind. The three great powers had slugged themselves to a standstill and, like the stranger entering the bar at the end of the brawl, only America, with its troops arriving at the Front in ever-increasing numbers, had enough fighting men left to tip the balance.

Now under the overall command of the French General Foch, the Allied armies of France, the British Empire, Belgium and Portugal and the forty-two divisions of fresh American manpower counter-attacked at Soissons and Amiens. Turning the German battlefield tactics back on their creators and using tanks in concentrations big enough to make a difference, they met surprisingly little resistance and quickly regained what had been lost. And while further progress wasn't quite as effective where the enemy had regrouped behind defence lines of canals, rivers and railways that criss-crossed Flanders, they now had the momentum to pick off towns like Lille, St. Quentin and Bruges that had been under occupation since the beginning of the war.

As part of the relentless machine moving east, 5th West Sussex were within sight of Ghent. Two days before, they had been cheered into a small Belgian town on its southern outskirts and toasted with the last few priceless bottles that had been saved for the occasion. The liberators had come, the enemy had gone, old scores were being settled before civil law returned and everyone wanted to be best friends of the British and Portuguese soldiers – at least for the night.

Yet while the Germans were pulling back and their Central Power allies Bulgaria, Austria-Hungary and Turkey were surrendering like ninepins, they hadn't disintegrated into a rout.

Territory was still being contested long enough to ensure an orderly retreat and they were firing every shell left in their arsenal rather than let them fall into enemy hands.

Just as they were finally beginning to believe that the fighting could be over by Christmas, Patie Fitzgibbon, Dick Mullane, Tim Curtin, Batt Mullane, Flint Barrett and the rest of C Company were roused from their quarters in a schoolroom for yet another strike, this time on enemy positions guarding the road east as it crossed over a canal.

'Pack in behind the tanks,' Sergeant Roseblade was telling them while they waited for the ironclad behemoths to arrive. Rumours had been circulating for days that the Hun was on the point of surrender

'The locals are saying the Kaiser's been overthrown.' Maggot Tibbs finished off the last of the egg and chips bought from an entrepreneurial Belgian in his makeshift estaminet that had sprung up overnight. 'Ran off to Holland with his missus and his money, the thieving bastard.'

The tanks roared up through the town square, bobbing up and down like ships in the harbour as their caterpillar tracks rolled over the waves of rubble.

'Might even be over today.' The Cockney veteran washed down the last of his breakfast with a swig of sweetened white wine and joined his comrades in the shadow of the monster.

'Everyone knows the war's over. The Huns signed the surrender during the night.' Unimpressed by the willingness of his colleagues to fall into line, a recent arrival counted out his Belgian francs for his œuf et frites. 'Dunno why we're being called out again. Waste of bloody time if you ask me.'

'Blame that new CO.' Maggot whipped a chip from the newcomer's paper twist. 'Spent the bleeding war behind a desk and now he wants some action before it's all over.'

'And get us killed so he wins his medal.' The chest puffed out with indignant defiance.

But it didn't argue with the barrel of Roseblade's rifle pressed to his back. 'Did they ever teach you, son? Orders is orders.'

Patie caught the captain's furtive glance at his wristwatch as he nodded to his sergeant. The officers had been told. The rank and file hadn't.

'I'm telling you it's eleven o'clock,' insisted Maggot. 'Has to be. The eleventh day of the eleventh month.'

The Germans hadn't been informed either of their impending defeat. Dug in on the far side of the canal, they blew up the bridge as the first tank crossed it. The next in line tried to use its fallen comrade as a stepping-stone but the angle was too steep and it toppled back to the safety of its own side.

Roseblade frantically waved his finger. Those left exposed by the first two machines scrambled back behind the cover of the remaining tanks which formed in a line along the bank and began their bombardment. Three recent arrivals failed to react quickly enough and were instantly cut down.

'Keep plugging them!' roared the sergeant.

Dick found shelter behind the toppled machine and began to pick off positions revealed by the little bursts of orange return fire. Crawling into the gaps between the tanks, the machine gun teams assembled their Vickers and added to the storm of metal whizzing back and forth across the canal. Behind them, Patie set up his Stokes mortar and collared Flint into passing him the rounds.

They pasted away to no great effect, going through the motions of a war that was on its last legs. Reinforced by concrete, the defences withstood the best that could be thrown at them and there was no sign of the artillery arriving in support.

Then a shell landed on one of the remaining tanks and blew it to bits. The defensive circle contracted further.

'Fall back!' Roseblade was shouting. A runner dodged through the rubble to tap the sergeant on the shoulder and then rap on the door of the nearest tank. A captain waved his arms in a flat circle from the pivot of his elbows and a Very light shot into the sky.

A second flare lit up in response and the fury of battle drained from both sides of the canal. White flags inched their way up makeshift poles over the German and British positions.

'Cease fire!' barked Roseblade into the sudden silence.

Patie rose to his feet, stretched his shoulders, arched his back and picked up the stench of burnt flesh amid the smouldering plates of hot metal. The cessation had come too late for the tank crew.

Then he noticed the great emptiness that had descended on Flanders. It wasn't just the obvious that had stopped – the boom of the shells and the rattle of gunfire and the cloying stink of explosive – but the entire backdrop as well. Gone were the smoke, the aircraft, the flashes, the horse screeches and the dull throb of distant action that had rumbled without pause for over four years.

The sky had cleared itself of its past week of drizzle, mist and fog. It was turning into a lovely late autumn day.

Twenty minutes later, the colonel arrived accompanied by the major, the bugler and the battalion commander's batman carrying a flagon under his arm.

'Stand to for inspection!'

Out in the middle of a battlefield, they threw away their cigarettes and stood to attention. The colonel sniffed as he passed by the rows, his breath wheezing from the flu but still managing to keep a stiff upper lip.

'C Company, all correct, sir,' reported Roseblade. 'Except for three dead.'

'Very good, sergeant. You may stand down.'

The bugler blasted off his tune.

'Company! At ease.'

A church bell rang in the distance. The batman passed out the ration of rum. Their war had come to an end.

As long as they left their heavy weapons after them, the Germans were given three days' freedom to march back home without being followed by the victors. C Company heard the guttural commands from across the canal signalling the beginning of the exodus before wheeling around to return to their billets.

'They should have let us finish them off,' complained an eighteen-year-old whose time at the Front had lasted less than a week. 'We'd have killed them all and we'd never have to worry about the Huns again.'

'Three days to run off home!' spat another recent arrival who had spent over a year contesting his call-up on medical grounds. 'A flaming liberty, I call it. They was beat, so they was, but now they can let on they wasn't because they won't let us frogmarch them off to the prison camp.'

'More bleeding marching? I've had my share, thank you very much.'

'Ooh, the mademoiselles are happy.' Girls showered them with kisses and planted flowers in their tunics as they marched through the centre of the town.

'We won't have to pay for our van blong tonight.' An aged café owner was bellowing something in Flemish.

'God's happy too.' The priest blessed them as they passed by his church.

'And so is Rover.' A dog ran alongside the column, gasping with excitement and wagging his rapturous tail.

But they kept moving until they found sanctuary in the schoolroom. Unlike the cheering locals outside, few of them were in much of a mood to celebrate. They sank on the chairs and the benches, let their muscles sag with relief and tried not to think about an uncertain world that lay ahead.

Removing a set of beads from his tunic, Tim knelt on the floor and prayed. Dick cleared the remaining rounds from his rifle and stuffed them in his pocket. Roseblade studied his pay-book and Batt his appearance in his shaving mirror. Even Maggot and Flint were overcome by the solemnity of the moment.

Patie felt as if a part of his life had been wrenched from him as the tension of combat deflated. The Brodie helmet no longer weighed on his head nor the dead load of his pack on his shoulders. Instead of reaching for weapons, his hands could do what they liked. Instinctive motions like crouching and peering over the shoulder were now redundant and he could straighten his back or look around or walk at whatever pace he wanted.

Yet his mind screamed against the new freedoms that had suddenly been thrust upon it. For over four years, officers, NCOs and Germans had limited his powers of decision but now he would have to adjust. He wanted to be somewhere, anywhere, away from his comrades in the billets and from the crowding revellers in the town where he could collect his thoughts in private.

But they kept pressing in on top of him. The battalion sergeant-major barged in the door to issue a list of petty instructions about not fraternising with the locals, engaging with the enemy, exposing themselves to infectious diseases, trading in goods that could be subject to rationing or engaging in conduct conducive to the dissemination of military secrets. A pen-pusher of indeterminate rank passed around sheets of paper listing items of uniform, weaponry and equipment required to be presented at their next inspection. A Church of England chaplain rambled on about thanking God for their glorious victory.

And from outside, the mayor, resplendent in his tricolour sash of black, yellow and red, was knocking on the window and waving an enormous bottle of brandy. Maggot let him in but Flint beat him to the first glass. The round of drink softened the mood, the Belgian cracked a joke that no-one understood and the entire billet fell around laughing.

More locals arrived. The butcher sliced up lengths of sausage, the baker brought hot sticks of bread straight from the oven, the café owner hauled crates of golden beer, the grocer had retrieved jars of meat paste and fat discs of wax-covered cheese from his cellars.

They tumbled out into the square to join the party. A brass band set itself up on the steps of the courthouse and, after starting off with La Brabançonne, The Flemish Lion, La Marsellaise, God Save the King and the national anthem of Portugal, blasted out strains of can-can and ragtime. Girls and women rose to dance and were immediately joined by the Portuguese soldiers. Still short of available men, they then turned to the British squaddies and dragged them to their feet. Some of the waltzing couples fell instantly in love.

Military policemen tried to break up the embraces of international friendship but an angry coalition of Belgians and their guests banished them to the fringes. Excluded from the celebrations, the Red Caps gathered in a group for self-protection and skinned their eyes for any signs of desertion ahead of demobilisation.

As the momentous Monday wore on, entire families poured in from the surrounding villages. Quarters of smoked ham, thick slices of brawn, baskets of fruit tarts, pastries and pies were passed around. An effigy of the Kaiser was burned outside the town hall to tumultuous applause. Fireworks, Very lights and star shells flared up the sky. The band took to its feet and led long processions of dancers up and down the main street.

Showered with every known alcoholic concoction and some that had just been discovered, C Company slid towards terminal inebriation.

'We won!' Maggot threw his arms around Patie. 'We won! Sent the bleeding Huns back to Hunland.'

Patie looked back at the rubble and at the burnt-out tank beyond it. Won what, he asked himself, won what?

They were due for home leave ten days after the signing of the Armistice and no trifling event like the end of a world war was allowed to disrupt the rotation schedule. By then, the mood of the occupied had turned from relief to revenge. In Aalst, a town fifteen miles west of Brussels that was to be 5th West Sussex's last stop in Belgium, locals spat fire over the departing anarchy of the Germans. Not a morsel of food could be found, anything of value had been looted, anything that couldn't be carried off had been smashed and tempers rose further when their menfolk returned from four years of forced labour in the munitions factories of the Ruhr or from exile in an army that had been stranded on the other side of the Front.

They took it out on any target they could find. Women who had fraternised with the occupiers, traders who had supplied them and officials who had co-operated with them all felt the years of pent-up wrath.

Yet from the train taking them back to Dunkirk, Patie was amazed at how localised the impact of the war had been. Passing through Dixmunde, he could see the stripe of devastation where shell, shot and fire had reduced the land to its primeval origins and had buried an entire generation of Europe. But less than ten miles away in either direction, the farms and the towns bore only the occasional scars of conflict and were already returning to something approaching normality.

They waited less than a day on the quayside before they were packed onto an ageing mailboat along with another five battalions. Left with standing room only on the decks for the five-hour crossing, haggling colonels in a hurry to get home had seen to it that maritime regulations were ignored.

Drink that had been bought, stolen or cadged poured down thirsty throats.

'We are Fred Karno's Army, the ragtime infantry,' they sang,

'We cannot fight, we cannot shoot, what bleeding use are we?

And when we get to Berlin, the Kaiser he will shout,

'Hoch, hoch, mein Gott, what a bloody rotten lot

Are the ragtime infantry."

Out came the Crown and Anchor boards, on oilskin, felt or cardboard. After hearing that they couldn't be changed back in Blighty, anyone left with coins, Belgian francs and French local-issue currency bet the lot on the last hurrah of the dice game that had sustained an entire army through its war. Even the military police joined in and one of the Red Cap sergeant-majors offered to buy up the lot from the eventual winner, albeit at a 30% discount.

A mighty cheer rang out when the white cliffs broke through the haze to reveal the castle perched upon them. Beacons, lighthouses and breakwaters passed by as the overloaded ship, its foghorns blaring and its decks barely clearing the water, staggered into the harbour.

Dover was festooned in red, white and blue. Bands lined up in wait on the quayside as they walked down the gangways and pumped out marches to the thousands of boots pounding ashore. The outrageously-costumed holder of a medieval office popped a ceremonial cannon, garlands were tossed and showers of confetti descended from the sky. Glistening in the brass and braid of their ranks, generals, colonels and admirals took their textbook salutes. Every available dignitary of church, state and Mammon dressed out in his finest to lead the welcome for the first batch of returning heroes.

Batt soaked up the adulation, his eyes transfixed with rapture as loyalty to King, Country and Empire was endlessly proclaimed. Betraying a pride in their regiment that Patie had never suspected, old soldiers Maggot and Roseblade were moved to private tears. Flint agreed with one and all that it was a marvellous occasion. Tim Curtin was racked with the cough and the fever that had been at him since Dunkirk but wouldn't report in sick if it meant spending even one more day in Flanders. Dick took it all in his stride and nobody plucked up the courage to ask him how he felt.

And Patie just wanted to get home.

24

THEY WEREN'T the deliberate footsteps of the warder doing his round. Too brisk and too purposeful, they broke the quiet of the night as they tapped off the landing. Willie Hartnett had heard them two years before in Kilmainham when they came just before dawn to take the condemned away to the Stonebreakers Yard. He could tell from the pace and the weight where they were headed and he knew that they would stop outside the door of his cell.

It wasn't that they were going to execute him. If they had wanted to get rid of him permanently, they would have shot him while trying to escape when he was coming out of the Sinn Féin meeting in Limerick City. Or they might have called a drumhead tribunal to deal with him before they tossed into Strangeways Jail in Manchester. But that was all of six months back and, if the British didn't feel like stretching Willie's neck when the Viceroy claimed that he'd unearthed evidence of a Sinn Féin plot to join forces with the Kaiser, then they were unlikely to do so when the heat had long since gone out of the situation.

But the warders might be indulging in unofficial activity of their own. Ever since the Germans had surrendered, some of those who had never seen military action were experiencing an overwhelming urge to demonstrate their patriotic fervour. Beating the living tar out of a seditious Irish rebel might prove to be an acceptable substitute for spending an entire war sitting on their backsides with a key in their hands from one end of the shift to the other.

Prison was a different place for Willie this time around. Unlike his previous visits when he'd been held along with hundreds of Volunteer comrades in Knutsford immediately after the Rising while they were waiting for Frongoch to be cleared out or when he and Ned Reidy were moved to Lewes when the Welsh internement camp was closed down, he was now banged up in a wing with only hardened English criminals for company.

He had never felt so alone in his life. Most nights, the four walls would get to him and he'd curse his stupidity for allowing himself to be goaded into retaliation. When the seventy-three Sinn Féin leaders who had been picked up were being shipped across to Liverpool, he'd smashed the jaw of a jailer fondling his privates while he was sleeping on the boat. So instead of being held as a political under a reasonably relaxed regime like those in Gloucester or Lincoln, he was handed a three-year criminal sentence for assault and left to face the full rigours of penal servitude in one of the toughest prisons in England.

The footsteps stopped. Against the thin light of a bare bulb down the landing, he could make out three silhouettes. The key dug into the lock and Willie was dragged out into the corridor separating the two lines of cells. A swinging baton reminded him to shut up and he was handcuffed as they deposited him before the wing's head screw waiting for him in the central hall.

'I'll deal with him myself.' Willie watched the dead eyes sizing him up as the subordinates were dismissed. Finnegan had never been known to lay a hand on a prisoner. The rank and file staff did the manual labour for him.

'That way, Hartnett. Move.' The jailer tapped on the door leading to the stairs. Down they went to the ground floor, their brisk footsteps echoing off brick and iron. Behind his back, Willie could feel the fumbling of a key.

'Keep quiet,' whispered Finnegan as the cuffs sprang open. 'And keep holding your hands as they are.'

Another three doors opened and closed. One warden looked quizically for a moment at his superior before obediently turning his key. But at the exit to the world outside, recognition was instant.

'Everything ready, Rafferty?'

The gatekeeper nodded. Before he knew it, Willie was bundled into the back of a waiting lorry, covered with lengths of timber and suddenly realising that he was in the midst of the unlikeliest of allies.

'I hope he's worth it,' the driver was saying in the cab. Like those of the two screws, the accent was unmistakeably Liverpool.

'You'd better be, Willie Hartnett,' Finnegan shouted back. 'We've blown our cover to get you out.'

Bumping along the road for what seemed forever, Willie tried to figure out why the IRB had sacrificed three of its deeply-hidden members for his escape. During the previous six months, the Brotherhood had made no effort to contact him and there were times when he feared that he had been completely forgotten about. Maybe he was just an afterthought in the minds of those now running the Volunteers and Sinn Féin. Unlike Éamon De Valera, Arthur Griffith, Countess Markievicz or even Ned Reidy, he was hardly known outside West Limerick and his arrest would never have the same impact. And if they were trying to raise the hackles against the British in the area, the movement would have been better served by having a public figure like Ned languishing in an English jail on charges so ludicrous that even the rabble-rousers of Fleet Street took them with a pinch of salt.

'Get into these quick.' Rafferty handed him a bundle of clothes as the lorry stopped by a quayside. As the first flickers of dawn made themselves known, Willie could make out the shapes of the Liver birds looking down on the Mersey from their clock towers. Puffing gentle clouds into the still sky, a steamer waited beneath them.

He tugged at the tightness of the breeches and the dog collar barely made it around his neck. Heightwise, he was on the same dimensions as the previous owner of the uniform but he and the chaplain diverged seriously when it came to the horizontal axis.

'There mustn't be a pick on him,' he gasped as they squeezed the last trouser button shut.

'A Jesuit,' muttered Finnegan. 'Used to self-denial, I'd say.'

Captain Father Professor Sir Roderick Dermod O'Morchoe More, The O'Morchoe of the Stacks and the Glens, Bt, SJ, DSO, DD, PhD, Roman Catholic chaplain to the King's Own West Sussex Rifles, proclaimed the paybook.

'Yes, he's one of us,' confirmed the driver of the lorry. 'You'd be surprised by the amount of members we have on this side of the pond.'

'I'm impressed,' answered Willie.

'Well, you'd better be. If anyone starts up a conversation with you, you'll have to speak like a toff.'

Micheal Collins was waiting in a motorcar outside the terminal as the troopship tied up at Dublin's North Wall to disgorge its complement of Dublin Fusiliers and Royal Irish Regiment into a crowd of waiting relatives. With the entire leadership of the Volunteers, the IRB and Sinn Féin filling cells of English jails, the big Corkman had taken effective control of every arm of Republican resistance.

'Good to have you back, boy.' He whacked his fist into Willie's upper arm. If they'd been standing out in the open, the greeting might have been a bear hug followed by a half-Nelson. 'Sorry about the delay. It took us a few months to get Rafferty transferred into Strangeways.' He tapped a fingernail against the dog collar. 'You didn't get a vocation on the way over?'

'One or two of them wanted me to hear their confession.' In fact, once he had stared through them as if they weren't there, Willie had been left alone for the rest of the voyage.

'You didn't, did you?'

'No.'

'Maybe you should have. There's no knowing what sort of information you might pick up when a man is telling you his sins.' The fist dug into his ribs this time. 'Yerra, I'm only having you on, Willie boy.' But nobody ever quite knew whether Collins was serious or joking, not even when it came to suggestions of sacrilege.

'The uniform will get you back as far as Limerick. They won't challenge an officer or a priest or a toff with a title suffering from shell shock. But you'd be better get out of it after that.' Willie took the first-class rail ticket as he got out at Kingsbridge Station. 'Now off with you. And make sure you get everyone pulling together behind Ned Reidy.'

'I don't care what your own views are, Jimmy. The Volunteers are backing Ned and that means every one of us is doing everything we can to get him elected.' It was the same story everywhere Willie went. Leaders in Dublin might have developed grand visions of strategy but they weren't shared by foot soldiers who remained deeply suspicious of anything to do with elections organised by the British government. And without the guiding hand of the Volunteers, the Sinn Féin clubs of Limerick Northwest had descended into inter-parish rivaly, more interested in pulling one over their neighbours than in joining together to win the seat.

'Then they should have put you up as the candidate, Willie. We'd have all backed you. No problem there.' Even Mossy Noonan, who could see the value of political activity, remained to be convinced. 'But Ned's a different matter. He's not the reason most of us around here took the Oath. You're the man we followed.'

'Ye might want me but there's another 15,000 voters we have to convince. Outside of Shanagolden, they know Ned way better than they know me. And he has a way of speaking about him that you need for winning elections.'

'I still don't like it, Willie,' argued Jimmy McCarthy. 'They're only using for their own ends, I'm telling you. They only sprung you from jail so as you'd order us to row in behind Ned.'

'And that's exactly what I'm doing, Jimmy. I'm ordering ye.'

'Officially?'

'Yes. Officially. And whatever other way you want.' He sat back on the chair. The fire in Drug Donovan's cottage was flickering towards death. 'For God's sake, lads, do ye want to have that gombeen Thomas Hennessy representing us to the rest of the world?'

Once they got it off their chests, they'd fall into line, just like they would in Glin and Ballyhahill, in Askeaton, Athea, Foynes and in all the other places where the Volunteers were active. The only difficulty would be in getting around to them all. Willie had been given little more than a week to rescue the Sinn Féin campaign from the shambles that it had fallen into. While Ned might have had the gift of the gab, he didn't understand the first thing about battering a score of feuding parishes into an election machine.

5th West Sussex received an even more spirited reception in Chichester as they marched up the length of the town to the barracks. Those lining the streets waving their Union Jacks were the sisters, the fathers, the wives, the mothers, the children, the sweethearts and the neighbours of their own triumphant regiment, the survivors of a war that had seemed without end.

Everywhere they went, the talk was of a land fit for heroes. Posters screamed about punishing the Huns, about pushing them back behind the Rhine, about hanging the Kaiser, about squeezing Germany down to its last penny to pay for the war. A general election, the Khaki Election as the newspapers immediately dubbed it, had been called and candidates of every stripe flocked to the company of men in uniform so that they could bask in the glory of their victory.

'No better than animals, those Huns.' A well-wisher slapped Patie on the back. The soft hands and plump waistline had never been near the Front and the fine clothes hinted that their wearer had done very well for himself out of the war.

'Damn good job we won.' Another hero of the Home Front threw his arm over Patie's shoulders. 'Otherwise, it would be the end of civilisation.'

'If it hadn't been for Britain, those blasted Frogs would have run away. No backbone, I tell you.'

'And will they thank us for saving them? I think not.'

But once inside the barracks, the only talk was of demobilisation. Peace wasn't peace until they saw the back of their uniforms and were wearing their Civvy Street clobber.

'Dunno what they still want us for. We've stuffed Johnny Hun's arse and he won't come back looking for more.' The thatcher from Arundel had whipped out a deck of cards and was dealing out a hand of whist. Unlike Crown and Anchor, they could keep tabs on what was owed without ever breaking regulations by putting money on the table. 'Meanwhile, all the dodgers are taking our women.'

'We'll be home soon, Bert,' said his mate, the one-time road ganger from Midhurst. 'Maybe your Violet will take you back.'

'I don't think so, Reg. And who's saying I'd have her?'

'Forgive and forget. That's what everyone does at the end of a war.' Reg sorted his cards by suit. 'Spades, is it? I heard Harry Baldwin took his missus back even though the whole village knows the child is another man's bastard.'

'Lay them and play them.' Reg's partner led the ace of trumps and followed it with the king, queen and knave. 'Everything will be like it was, Bert. You'll see.' But even as he was raking in the tricks, the doubts were already beginning to sprout.

Demobilisation wasn't the only matter to occupy the Army. Peace brought new tasks in its wake and units were moving from France and Belgium into Germany to ensure that the terms of the Armistice were being upheld. Those back in Britain were told that they could be shipped out to support the occupying forces or sent off to Russia to help the Whites take on the Reds in the emerging civil war.

There was also the Empire itself to uphold. Territorials who had replaced regulars in the garrisons of India and Africa for the duration of the war now had to be relieved. Numbers were being beefed up in trouble spots like Ireland. Territory and colonies captured from the Central Powers in Palestine, Mesopotamia and East Africa needed to be policed.

After days of rumours, many feared the worst. 'I don't fancy the Fuzzy-Wuzzies. I was told they eat their young when they gets hungry.'

'What's India like, Maggot?' asked Batt Mullane

'Bleeding hot. Full of flies and beggars and dodgy food.'

'It can't be that bad.'

'Of course, you do have all these natives to wipe your arse. Even a squaddie can afford a servant out there.'

'I wouldn't mind that. Better than Russia anyway. I hear they freeze to death out there.'

But 5th West Sussex struck it lucky and they were granted an early reprieve from life in the home depot with its spit and polish inspections, its endless square-bashing and its re-imposition of petty regulations that had been ignored during wartime. Regulars whose terms of colour service were up, reservists who had been recalled and those who had volunteered when war was declared were summoned to the regimental office and told that they were on their way back to Civvy Street.

Patie Fitzgibbon, Dick Mullane, Flint Barrett, Batt, Tim Curtin and a dozen others from C Company were sent down for their medical and then given their back-pay, their Z22, their Z44, their Z18, their Z11 and all the other forms that the Army's pen-pushers had invented while real soldiers were away fighting the war. All told, there were only six able-bodied survivors of the hundred who had landed in Dieppe in 1914 and just eighteen of those who had fought at the Somme.

'Anyone out first gets the best jobs,' Reg the road ganger reminded them.

'And the best women as well,' added Bert the thatcher.

Maggot Tibbs was the only one of them not to share the relief of discharge. 'Fifteen years of service, Sarge,' he told Roseblade. 'I'm a soldier of the regular Army. What am I going to do now? I never known any other life.' But despite his protestations, he was also handed his comics.

And then it was all over. Equipment was ticked off and anything missing was docked from their pay. An Out-of-work Donation policy covered them for up to six months unemployment and they were given an allowance of £2/12/6 to buy civilian clothing, a rail ticket to get them home and instructions on where to hand in their greatcoats when they arrived.

But Tim failed to make it out of the barracks. The day he reported back in Chichester, the medics took one look at him and sent him to the infirmary. They were too late. By the end of the week, he had become another victim of a flu epidemic that was claiming more lives than the war.

The entire company dug into their pockets to give him a proper send-off. A London newspaper picked up the story, the War Office telegrammed its regrets and the regimental commander spoke at the graveside of a volunteer soldier who'd survived the Somme and Passchendaele only to be struck down by sickness when he was within sight of home.

After a last drink in honour of the departed, Patie, Dick, Batt and Flint left for the railway station and made their final goodbyes to mates whose lives they had shared for over four years. As some talked of reunions and others about seeing their old comrades fixed up in decent jobs, Patie handed Roseblade the money left over from the whiparound to erect a proper headstone over Tim Curtin's grave.

'Make sure it's one that stands out. He deserves more than just a cross in the ground.'

Part Three

Freedom

December 1918 – July 1921

Then came the call to arms, my love,

and the hills they were aflame.

Down from the silent mountain, the

Saxon stranger came …

25

UNLIKE IN Chichester and Dover, Patie's return to Foynes was unannounced. Apart from the scatty-looking man with the wild hair reading a book written in Irish, the dozen passengers in the carriage glanced curiously at their uniforms and then found other sights to occupy their attention.

'Some welcome.' Batt shook his head in disgust as he alighted from the train. Catching his reflection in the window, he straightened his forage cap and made sure that the campaign medals dangling from his chest were in line. 'They were mobbing us back in England but there's no one at all here to greet us.'

Patie picked up his kitbag and slung it over his shoulder. Other than the discharge money in his pocket, he had nothing to show other than a few meagre belongings for his time spent in hell. Not even a souvenir. Unlike the majority of his colleagues, he couldn't bring himself to stuff a Mills bomb or a bayonet into his pack to remind him of the trenches.

Some were already talking wistfully of their time at the Front, brushing memories of the rats, the lice, the damp and the disease as well as the slaughter from their minds. On the boat between Holyhead and Kingstown, demobbed Dubs, Leinsters and Inniskillings launched into the hopeful It's a long Way to Tipperary of 1914 as often as the real songs of the trenches like Fred Karno's Army or Hanging on the Old Barbed Wire and toasted the camaraderie of the world that they were leaving behind. Maybe war would give them a recognition that they might never have otherwise earned but, if that was what they wanted out of life, Patie thought that there had to be a better way than taking millions of young lads away to get killed so that a handful of survivors could go on bragging about their exploits.

Or it could have been that they hadn't seen any action at all. War experiences were turning into a matter of distance. Those furthest from the fighting had the best stories to tell and they got better with each passing day.

The wild-haired passenger, who introduced himself as Philip Hurley, approached them as they set off down the platform together. 'Pardon me for asking ye, lads, but were ye over in France?'

'Flanders most of the time,' answered Patie. 'That's in Belgium. We were only a year in France.'

'Was it as bad as they say?'

'That depends on who you're listening to.'

'It was tough.' Batt preened with pride as he filled out his chest. 'But it made men of us.'

Other than the motorcar touting for business outside the station, the town didn't look a whole lot different from the Foynes that Patie had left on a Tuesday evening in the middle of a forgotten summer. And after the bustle that he'd seen in Dublin and Limerick, it was quieter than he'd expected, with only a handful of people venturing out under the slate-grey sky.

But while the buildings and appearance were the same, the air of the town had changed. There was resentment in the eyes lifting momentarily to look him over, the same sullen suspicion

342

that he'd met in French villagers or in captured German soldiers. Although he was stepping back into his home parish, Patie felt a complete stranger, a ghost returning after life had moved on.

'It's the uniform,' muttered Dick. 'It's not theirs. It belongs to an occupying army.'

Not that Batt picked up on the unspoken hostility. Walking with an even more exaggerated military gait than usual, he led them up the main street in the hope that a band might materialise from around the corner to surprise the homecoming heroes. But no one, not even the young boys who'd gasp with awe at the sight of a real soldier over in England, took a blind bit of notice of his gleaming boots, his corporal's stripes and the line of campaign medals hanging from their ribbons.

A crack of uncomprehending hurt lined his face as the expectation of triumph melted in the sea of indifference and their march stopped outside the post office where Dick collared a sidecar and haggled with the driver over the fare home. For a moment, Patie thought that Batt would burst into tears but he'd picked up enough of the stiff upper lip to hide his disappointment.

'I thought there'd be more happening here,' Patie remarked to Hurley who'd tagged along with them when he'd heard that they were heading for Shanagolden. 'What's going on at all?'

'All the excitement's up in Shanagolden. There's a big rally this evening over next Saturday's election.'

There was no sign of anything resembling the banners and posters lining Chichester's streets that extolled Britain's victory in the war and how much each politician had contributed to it. Foynes's only visible concession to electoral activity was the few wind-battered signs erected by various political interests and all of them opposing the extension of conscription to Ireland.

'Who's standing?' Patie climbed up on the sidecar and squeezed his pack in between his legs.

'They've split the constituency and PJ O'Shaughnessy isn't going forward again so there's two seats up for grabs. This part is in Limerick Northwest and the Home Rulers are putting up Thomas Hennessy.' Hurley took the blanket from the driver and spread it over their legs to shield them from the raw edge of the wind. 'He's being challenged by Ned Reidy for Sinn Féin.'

A platform had been fashioned out of a hay float and was parked at the bottom of the main street where it widened out into the crossroads. Despite the sharp cold of the night, a crowd from all over West Limerick had turned up to witness the torchlit debate in the most keenly contested constituency in Munster.

District Inspector Sullivan kept his column of policemen out of harm's way. Ignoring pressure from above, he wasn't going to drag the RIC into the political arena. The conscription crisis had sunk the force's stock to a new low with the public and they were reduced to ridicule when a newly-appointed gung-ho Viceroy had rounded up almost the entire Sinn Féin leadership on the unsubstantiated claim that they were engaged in a dastardly plot with the Kaiser. In such circumstances, any intervention was bound to be counter-productive.

But that didn't stop his men from getting involved in a more indirect way. Up on the platform, Hennessy was pointing out the Sinn Féin hecklers in the crowd and, with the help of the creamery manager Horgan, Sergeant Stapleton and some of his colleagues were busily establishing their identities. No doubt the information would find its way to the military in the fullness of time and the soldiers might make a better fist of their next roundup than they did on the previous occasion when they failed to pick up Ned Reidy, despite having been provided with a comprehensive account of their target's movements.

Since he was still technically on the run, Sullivan could have arrested Reidy on the spot, but even the local military commander could see the folly of pulling in a candidate in the middle of an election. Sinn Féin had already claimed twenty-five constituencies without a contest and over half of the winners were languishing in English jails.

He could also have detained Willie Hartnett whom he'd spotted mingling with the hecklers at the back of the float and not making any great effort to hide himself. Stapleton had made a tentative approach but the numbers were against him. Any attempt at plucking the escaped prisoner from the ring of supporters surrounding him was sure to provoke a riot and, in the hostile environment of a small West Limerick town, the police would be on a hiding to nothing.

Reduced to the role of powerless spectators, Shanagolden showed up the increasing irrelevance of the RIC's authority. Gains slowly ground out over the thirty years since the end of the Land War were melting away as entire communities geared themselves up for confrontation with their rulers. With tempers rising and moods souring, Dublin Castle was banking on opportunists like Hennessy to save its bacon. Quite apart from his personal distaste for the Home Rulers' candidate, the Inspector knew in his heart and soul that they were backing the wrong horse.

But what was the alternative? The gulf between the police and Sinn Féin was now too great to be bridged. Nicholas Sullivan might have faced an unsatisfactory future under Thomas Hennessy and his ilk but he faced none at all should those forces led by Ned Reidy prevail.

Listening to the comments on his way to the meeting, Patie gathered that the momentum was clearly on the Sinn Féin side. The Irish Parliamentary Party's credibility had been shattered by the failure of yet another British Government convention on Home Rule, Sinn Féin had made all the running in the campaign against conscription and its prestige had been further boosted by the ludicrous German plot unearthed by Lord French to make up for his failures while commanding the Army in France.

Despite all the setbacks, however, the smart money was still piling on Hennessy. Unlike many of his party colleagues, the councillor had kept the local organisation intact and years of delivering the vote by fair means or foul gave him a serious edge before the campaign started in earnest. Now with the chance of landing the seat for himself instead of beavering away in the background for the sitting MP, he had loosened the purse strings of his fortune to shower drink, favours and introductions on anyone between Askeaton and Athea that was willing to take them.

'Fair dues to Ned Reidy for standing against him,' the man beside Patie was saying. 'But it's better to be safe than to be sorry. Hennessy has a wealth of information on everyone in West Limerick and he won't be slow to use it if he don't get elected.'

'The women will make sure of that,' agreed another. The extension of the franchise to all men over 21 regardless of property and the granting of the vote to all women over 30 had more than trebled the electorate and added a further level of uncertainty. 'The man of the house might have a sneaking regard for a rebel like Ned but his missus is sure to look at it different. Bread on the table, that's what she wants, and she knows Thomas Hennessy is the man to deliver it.'

The flustered chairman, a solicitor from Newcastlewest who had built up a sizeable practise out of representing both rebel and businessman alike, tried to bring order to the proceedings but was drowned out by the shouts of those closest to the platform. Although he'd been provided with a chair like the two candidates on either side of him, all three were up on their feet as the clamour and the cat-calls reached a crescendo.

The chairman eventually managed to restore order and the candidates agreed to speak alternately.

' … And who's been making representations on behalf of every one of ye for the past thirty years, I ask ye?' Hennessy pulled at the lapels of his coat. 'And all for no reward.'

'So where did you get all the money for that big house of yours?' demanded a voice in the crowd to the cheers of one group of supporters. 'From sending young fellas over to be killed in the war?'

'Well, 'twasn't from robbing honest citizens at gunpoint …,' shouted someone on the other side of the platform.

'Who are you calling a robber, you thieving sleeveen?'

'It's time for Ireland to stand up for itself,' shouted Ned over the bedlam of the hecklers. 'We've no need to be sending messenger boys over to Westminster to become more English than the English themselves …'

'How dare you insult Thomas Hennessy, as true an Irishman as you'll ever find in West Limerick …'

'And a thieving one at that …'

A fist was raised on one side of Patie. An opposing partisan squared up behind his other shoulder. He pulled back to let them at it although the would-be combatants seemed more intent on posturing than action and would have left it at exchanging cat-calls had their supporters stopped egging them on. In the end, they settled for two ceremonial punches before Stapleton and his peelers whacked their heads and hauled them aside without a whimper of protest.

'Howya, Patie?' The recognition startled him. 'Welcome home.' Mossy Noonan slapped his arm across his shoulders.

'Howya, Moss? I'm glad someone remembers me.'

'Not the reception you expected?'

A huge roar interrupted them. Ned had scored with some major rhetorical point. 'Not quite.'

'The army uniform isn't the draw that it used to be.'

'So I gather.'

'Come on. We won't learn nothing new here.' Mossy nodded in the direction of his father's pub. 'It's all been said a hundred times before.'

There were only two customers inside and neither showed any awareness of life around them.

'It's a long time since we welcomed a man wearing a unifrom into these premises.' Jack Noonan slapped a pint of porter and a large glass of whiskey on the counter. 'But it's good to see you, Patie. And 'tis an awful pity that only the four of ye made it back.'

Patie brought the large one to his lips.

'To Johnny O'Brien, Mick Culhane, Dinny Lyons and Jerry Curtin.' Jack raised a glass of his own to the photograph of the football team hanging over the bar. 'To Mick Fitz and Tim Curtin.'

'Mick Fitz?'

'He threw himself off the roof of the asylum. No one had the heart to stop him.'

'To the boys,' toasted Mossy.

'To our comrades.' He had never cried once through four years at the Front but now the tears welled up in Patie's eyes as he was confronted with the visual reminder of an age that had passed. They were only young fellas back then and the half of them that had survived were still young fellas in body but had aged to old men in their minds.

'We might have taken different sides over the past few years.' In an attempt to suppress his emotions, Jack threw back his measure of whiskey and slammed the glass off the counter with such force that it roused one of the comatose regulars. 'But we were all bred from the one stock.'

'And we never forgot that when we were out there.' Patie accepted the refill and again raised his whiskey. 'Come on Shanagolden!'

'Come on Shanagolden!' answered Mossy and Jack. 'Now the spuds can be dug up!'

The public meeting was over and the crowd was streaming up the main street to grab a few pints before turning for home. 'So who's going to win this one?' asked Patie before the pub was overwhelmed.'

'Everyone says Hennessy can't be beaten,' answered Mossy.

'But that's not what you're hearing from behind the counter?'

'No.' Jack poured out another three measures of whiskey. 'There's a big shift to Sinn Féin. A lot of people are thinking that the Home Rulers are nothing more than puppets of John Bull.'

Although he knew that they weren't going to take him, Willie Hartnett kept himself inside the cordon provided by Jimmy McCarthy, Dan Hourigan and the two dozen other Volunteers protecting him. With such an obvious RIC presence around Shanagolden, he could have skipped the occasion but, because the contest was so delicately poised between Ned and Hennessy, cocking a snook at the authorities through his attendance at the meeting could be worth a few vital votes.

Even if they were only a handful, they'd still matter. Limerick Northwest was one of Sinn Féin's prime targets in Munster, not only because of its traditional sympathies but also because

Thomas Hennessy represented exactly the type of shameless gombeen that its leaders wanted to supplant.

'You're marked, Hartnett.' Snarling like a caged animal, Stapleton brushed past the group around Willie. 'We've a circle drawn over your heart back at the barracks.'

Jimmy McCarthy turned to confront the sergeant but Willie tapped him on the shoulder. 'It's not the time nor the place.'

Across the street, he could see Inspector Sullivan coming to the same conclusion and signalling to Stapleton to pull back. For a moment, the eyes of the police commander met those of his quarry, locking more in curiosity than in competition, before Willie's gaze strayed to seek out Josie. He hadn't been able to see her since he had returned. She'd been under continuous police surveillance ever since news of his escape reached Shanagolden.

A cluster of over a dozen uniformed peelers and a pair of plainclothes detectives caught his attention and there she was, right in the middle of them. She waved, he waved back but that was as close as they could get. The rules of the game had been set. The RIC were touting her as bait, daring him to break from his circle of protection so that they could send him back to prison.

'I'll see you soon,' he shouted out.

'I'll be waiting,' she called back.

'You'll be waiting a while,' snorted Stapleton.

'Hey, Stapleton! Will you be singing the same tune after Saturday?' asked Jimmy. 'You might find out that you've got a new master to serve.'

The crowd that had been dispersing drifted back towards the focus of the impending confrontation. Willie searched again for Sullivan and the Inspector nodded in response.

'Come on, lads.' He grabbed Dan Hourigan by the arm. 'Don't forget we've an election to win.'

'Come on Shanagolden!' one of them shouted out.

'Come on Shanagolden!' they answered. 'Now the spuds can be dug up!'

She waited until the last of the stragglers had disappeared. Apart from the man coming to retrieve his hay float, only Josie and her escort remained at the crossroads. Most of the peelers were grumbling under the breaths about the wind coming down from the hills but she was thinking of too many other things to feel the cold and, even if she did, she wasn't in the mood to please them.

At least she had caught sight of him. It gave her some measure of reassurance. Another long separation had filled her with doubts that she knew were irrational but which she couldn't dispel. She'd received just the one letter from Willie during the six months but most of it had been blanked out by the prison censors. And even though she wrote to him three or four times a week, she doubted whether he had heard much from her either.

Ned had told her of the difficulties in getting anything in or out of Strangeways, particularly out of the wings where the long-sentence prisoners were being held, and she didn't know whether to believe him or not. Not only was it difficult to track down her brother while he was on the run but any time she came across him, he was always rushing off on secret business with a new generation of leaders who were taking over the Volunteers and Sinn Féin. If he never had the time to talk to her, maybe he never had the time to do something about Willie. Sometimes she even took to wondering whether Ned had wanted him out of the way altogether because he'd been ordered to do so by her father.

Then just over a week earlier, Philip Hurley had told her of Willie's escape as they locked up the school for the day. But her joy was over in an instant. A detail of peelers waited for her outside the gate and never once had they left her out of their

351

sight from that moment. Even when she retired to her bed for the night, she could hear their boots shuffling in the yard outside.

The wind gathered strength and suddenly she felt the chill piercing through her coat. One of the detectives kept staring at her, daring her to get a move on home, and she realised how childish it had all become. But she still wasn't going to give in.

The impasse continued until a motorcar pulled up at the crossroads. 'I'll drop you home if you like, Miss Reidy,' offered Inspector Sullivan over the protests of the detective. 'There's no point in you freezing yourself to death. And there's no point either in having this many men following you around.'

26

B Y THE SATURDAY, Limerick Northwest had taken to the election with the same enthusiasm as the seven hundred other contested constituencies across Britain and Ireland. Eight years had passed since the last time that voters had been granted an opportunity to cast their ballots and, with a greatly expanded electorate and victory in the war to end all wars in between, it had captured public participation like no other contest before.

The Union Jack waved all over Britain as the parties paraded their patriotic credentials and engaged in a Dutch auction of policies designed to bring the Huns, their Kaiser, their goose-stepping generals, their factories, their colonies and their sausage dogs to their knees. In some of the industrialised cities, returning soldiers had seen enough of the idiots commanding them in the trenches to believe that they could make a better fist of running the country themselves but, by and large, the outgoing Coalition had the whip hand. It was they, after all, who had held firm when weasels in the pacifist wing of the Liberals lost their nerve and talked about reaching a settlement with Germany while the fighting was still at its height.

Such considerations cut little ice in Ireland. The individual contests were either a straight fight between Unionists and Nationalists or, as was the case in a majority of the constituencies, between those Nationalists who saw the way forward through engaging with the House of Commons over Home Rule and those who considered no future other than outright independence like that declared by Poland and Czechoslovakia during the preceding weeks.

Nowhere was the competition more intense than in Shanagolden, the home place of the two candidates that mattered in the Northwest division of County Limerick. Even before the polling station opened in the school, the main street was packed with voters defying the cold and the dark of the morning. Both sides had postered the parish with a vengeance, by nailing them to the line of telegraph poles leading to the post office and, in an exercise of proclaiming rights of territory, by pasting them on every exposed surface that could be seen.

Outside Thomas Hennessy's bar, the councillor and James Horgan waited in the back of a motorcar, glancing at their watches as a steady stream passed them on their way up the street. Holding his hand on his hat to prevent it from blowing away, Batt Mullane tapped on the window.

'What's that you're wearing?' the candidate barked out the door.

'My uniform. And I've got all my medals pinned to my tunic underneath the greatcoat.'

'For God's sake, would you ever run home and find yourself a decent suit of clothes.'

Batt blinked with surprise. 'But I thought it would impress the voters.'

'You've been away too long, sonny.' Hennessy got out of the car and saluted the voters on their way to the polls. 'Not that I've anything against it myself but that happens to be the same uniform they wear when they drag the Sinn Féiners from their beds to arrest them.'

'Yeah, but ...'

'Some people don't trust it any more, do you understand?'

As Batt headed back home, Hennessy leaned back into his car. 'We'd be better off walking until young Mullane comes back.' He shook his head as he looked back down the main street. 'I don't like the look of this. There's a fierce load of them out already and they wouldn't all be on our side.'

Those already up at the schoolhouse had to run the gauntlet of supporters from both sides canvassing them as they made their way through the gate.

'Reidy. You won't forget Ned.'

'Hennessy. For Limerick and Shanagolden.'

The door opened and those at the head of the queue were allowed in. 'Will ye take it handy,' pleaded the Presiding Officer Philip Hurley. 'Ye'll all get to vote but we can't fit everyone inside at the same time.'

'I'm going in now,' demanded a big strapping labourer barging his way through those ahead of him. 'I want to be back drinking in Hennessy's before the crowd comes in.'

'Take your turn like the rest of them.' Despite giving away a few inches in height and a few stone in muscle, Hurley stood his ground.

The labourer turned his back and brushed past Hennessy who had just arrived at the polling station. 'Hi! You didn't tell me I'd have to spend half the day waiting around.'

'Easy on, Neilus. Calm down. You'll be done in a few minutes.'

'Yerra, go stuff it.' He pulled his arm from the councillor's restraining tug, tossed his pollimg card aside and barged through the crowded doorway. 'I couldn't be bothered.' An unseen hand immediately darted to the floor to pick up the discarded slip of paper.

An hour later, Willie Hartnett was waiting outside the school in a pony and trap. Beside him, a tone-deaf fiddler wandered from one half-remembered tune to the next and looked hopefully at the upturned cap in front of his boots every time someone emerged through the gate.

Their people were coming out but the Sinn Féiners weren't getting them to the polling stations fast enough to keep up with the Home Rulers. Hennessy's supporters had a fleet of motorcars at their disposal and could move from one district to the next far quicker than their opponents. Entire squads of impersonators were criss-crossing the constituency of Limerick Northwest to clean up every loose vote that hadn't been claimed, while Ned's campaign team were relying on horsepower just to hold on to their own.

Taidhgín Connors, an elderly smallholder, came out accompanied by his wife and his two sons.

'You have the vote now, Mrs. Connors,' Willie assured her as he helped her into the trap. 'They passed an Act of Parliament a few years back giving it to women.'

'Are you sure it's not against the law?' Mrs. Connors shook her head dubiously. 'And what about the two boys?'

'There's no property requirement either now. As long as you're of age, you can vote.'

'Are you certain?'

'You have my word on it.' Willie leaped up between his passengers and grabbed the reins. 'You voted right, didn't you? The X in the bottom box?'

'Of course I did. Sure haven't I known Ned Reidy since he was a gossoon.'

'She did all right,' confirmed her husband.

'And tell me, did you enjoy voting?' asked Willie.

'Of course I did. Can I go voting again?'

'Well, now that you mention it, you could help us out. I just happen to be on my way to Kilcolman after I drop you home. But maybe we might go straight out there because it turns out that I've a few spare polling cards in pocket.'

The pony jumped as an enormous motorcar bounced around the bend in the road and missed the trap by inches before it screeched to a halt. Waiting voters left the queue to gape at Flint and Jimmy McCarthy sitting in the front seat.

'Christ Almighty, where did you get that?' asked Willie.

'Some rich American staying in Adare hired it for the week. But he has... aah ...' Jimmy winked suggestively. '... other things on his mind at the moment. And don't worry about it being reported. His chauffeur was quite happy to be locked up for the day as long as we left him with a bottle of whiskey.'

Willie sized up the dimensions. Manna from heaven as long as they had someone who could run it. 'Are you sure you know how to drive?'

Flint stiffened with offended dignity. 'I'll have you know that I learned under shell, shot and fire on the Western Front.'

They could fit at least ten into the limousine. 'Jimmy, grab the next ten of our voters as they're coming out.' And as long as the driver didn't go off the road, they'd make it to Glin inside half an hour. 'Then go down to Jack Noonan's and pick up ten polling cards each for Ballyhahill, Glin, Loughill, Foynes, Askeaton, Cappagh and anywhere else in between. Just make sure you've the right number of men and women for each polling station.'

Thomas Hennessy felt the first pangs of doubt in Ardagh. The homework had been done, the transport had been arranged, the voters had been lined up, their supporters running the post offices controlled all the public telephones, the spare polling cards had been distributed over two dozen transfer points across the constituency and the undecided had been left with a half-crown in the pocket and filled with enough drink to keep them honest.

But somewhere along the line, the meticulously planned operation was falling down. By mid-morning, they should have been finished with their own definites and well into mopping up the dodgy votes. Instead, they were still scrambling to get out their supporters while the Shinners had moved on to cashing in their stolen polling cards.

He ignored the elderly couple and two young men descending from a pony and trap. Waiting impatiently outside his car for another couple walking up the road, he tried not to listen to the incessant chatter of his driver.

'By my count, that crowd has voted four times already. Hartnett's been bringing them around all morning.' Batt Mullane loosened the button of his collar. The clothes were a bit tight on him. He'd filled out during his time at the Front. 'I seen them in Kilcolman and in Reens and in at least two different places in Rathkeale.'

'And you missed them in four others.' Hennessy took a swig from his hip flask to ward off the cold.

'I think we should object to them this time, sir.'

'And they'll challenge the six people we've inside at the moment. Will you ever get it into your thick head that we've got loads more impersonators on the road than they have.'

'I don't know about that.' Batt pointed back to another car coming in from the Carrigkerry side. 'That's not one of ours, sure it's not, sir?'

'And how are the Mulcahys this fine morning?' In one deft movement, Hennessy shook one hand and threw the other arm around a pair of shoulders as he guided the pedestrians through the school gate. 'Sure ye won't forget me, will ye?'

'Oh God no, God no, Mr. Hennessy, sir.' stammered the husband. 'We ... we wouldn't dream of anyone else. Would we, Mary Ellen?'

'Oh God no.' She clutched her Rosary beads even tighter. 'And that's the God's honest truth, Mr. Hennessy, sir.'

The motorcar pulled in and disgorged four passengers. Willie Hartnett left his trap to approach the driver.

Hennessy tapped the window of his own vehicle. Batt jumped out to open the door.

'Head back to Shanagolden.' They were in danger of being outflanked. He had to get a handle on the numbers from Horgan who was organising the operation from the post office in Shanagolden. They might need to get another few cars on the road.

'Maybe we should tell the polis where Hartnett is, sir,' suggested his chauffeur. 'I mean to say, what kind of an election is it when an escaped convict is allowed to get away with carrying a gang of vote-stealers all over the county? And in broad daylight, at that.'

'And how did it go this time, Mrs. Connors?'

'I didn't like the man giving out the papers. He'd a fierce bad manner about him. No understanding at all. Not like our own Mr. Hurley.'

'The oul hoor called Nancy a liar, so he did,' added he husband. 'And straight to her face.'

'He said I wasn't Mary Ita Leahy at all, God rest her.' Mrs. Connors tightened the hold on her shawl. 'And poor Mary Ita barely dead in her grave from the flu.'

'God rest her soul.' Willie bowed his head with equal solemnity. 'So ye didn't get to vote after all?'

'Of course we voted. I wouldn't let anyone get away with insulting my character like that. I did say a quick Act of Contrition on my way out. Just in case, you understand.'

'You can't be too careful.' He led his travelling vote show up to the waiting motorcar.

'No you can't,' she agreed. 'Aah, you are certain it was Mary Ita's dying wish that her vote be used to elect Ned?'

'I heard her say it with my own ears.' He turned to the driver of the car. 'Which ones are you covering, Seán?'

'We're doing Limerick West for Con Collins. Newcastle, Monagea, Tour, then over to Drom and back through Castlemahon before I hand them over to Jim Colbert back in yer constituency.'

The Connors family were admiring the Model T Ford. 'Ye wouldn't like a tour of the county?' Willie asked them. 'Mr. Finn here can bring ye around.'

Hennessy stormed out of his car and burst into the classroom where Philip Hurley was accepting a polling card and crossing a name from the electoral register.

'That man has voted already!' The candidate barged past the line of voters and thumped his fist off the desk.

Hurley ignored him, stamped the ballot paper and handed it out.

'I'm telling you he's voted already!'

'Excuse me, Councillor.' The Presiding Officer took the next polling card offered to him and threaded his finger down the register. 'You know as well as I do that this man is Maurice Noonan. He's entitled to vote here.'

'Then he was impersonating someone else earlier on.' Hennessy stood between Mossy and the black metal box resting on a chair beside the desk.

'That's a very serious allegation, Councillor. I hope you can back it up.' Hurley drew a line over Mossy's name with his pencil. 'And what's more, may I remind you that ...' He picked up a booklet and flicked through the pages. '... Paragraph 3 ... aah .. section (d) of my instructions expressly forbids any candidate from interfering in the act of voting.'

'Young man, don't you be telling me the regulations ...'

'You may carry on, Mr. Noonan.' Mossy took the ballot handed to him. 'Put the paper in the box here beside me when you've made up your mind.'

'Would you ever get the hell out of here, Hennessy,' shouted someone in the queue. The councillor turned around to the line of hostile stares. He was still sure of winning but it was looking increasingly like Reidy was going to beat him in his home parish.

'Where's Stapleton?' he demanded when he came out. 'Get him!'

Batt was standing rigidly to attention as if he was still in the army. 'I don't hink he's around, sir.'

'Why not?'

'I seen a lorry load of polis heading up into the hills about an hour ago. If you ask me, sir, I'd say they're raiding a still.'

'Oh, Mother of God!' Hennessy clasped the two hands to his forehead. His big day was falling apart.

'I still think we should have Hartnett arrested, sir.'

'And hand another thousand sympathy votes to Ned Reidy? Just shut your mouth and drive me out of here!'

He could have told them that it was a wild goose chase. But County Sub-Inspector Peter Callaghan, Nicholas Sullivan's superior, owed the Excise commander a few favours and the capture of the leading poitín maker in the area had shot to the top of the agenda. With all the soldiers coming back from France and the increased tax on whiskey to pay for the war, demand had shot through the roof and stills across the length and breadth of the county were said to be working around the clock to supply the Christmas trade.

Or so the official story went. District Inspector Sullivan no longer knew what to believe as the various elements inside the apparatus of officialdom tried to grapple with the civil and political unrest, while furthering the ambitions of their own organisations. As the Army garrison, the RIC, military intelligence and the various departments in Dublin Castle all pulled in different directions, and with each being supported by its own champion in the Cabinet, policy changed like partners at a set dance and without any concession to consistency.

So if those above him wanted a raid on the day of election, then that's what they got. Or, as Sullivan suspected, maybe that was what they had wanted in the first place. If the force was off chasing the moonshiners of West Limerick, Thomas Hennessy and his cronies could steal whatever votes they liked without fear of police intervention.

Keeping himself hidden behind the hedges, Sergeant Stapleton led a mixed force of a dozen constables and Excise men as they crept up to the ruins of Shanid Castle. Further down the slope, Sullivan, Sub-Inspector Callaghan and the Excise commander waited for their men to wipe a long-running criminal enterprise from the map of the county.

'Drug's getting careless. It's very rare for him to be boiling during the day.' The Sub-Inspector sniffed the cloying scent of fermentation and watched the grey plume of smoke billow up into the cold still air. Silhouetted against the low winter's sun, the telltale sign could be seen for miles. 'Maybe it's the pressure he's under.'

'I hear they're getting a shilling a bottle.' Sullivan blew into his hands to keep them warm. 'He'll be clearing over two pound a day after he's paid for everything.'

'I've been waiting all of thirty years to catch Donovan.' The Excise commander screwed his eyes in anguish at the mere mention of his mortal adversary. 'That man has caused me more heartbreak than anyone else in the entire province of Munster. I want to get him before I retire. Just the once. Then I'll be able to draw my pension in peace.'

Up the hill from them, Stapleton emerged from his cover behind an outcrop of rock and peered into the ruins. Slowly he brought himself to his full height and waved his arm for his superiors to join him.

'What is it, Stapleton?' wheezed Callaghan, panting from the exertions of his climb.

'I think you'd want to see this for yourself, sir.' The sergeant pointed through the gap into the castle. Beyond the barrel of spent wash bubbling over the smouldering sods of turf, Ned Reidy's election posters were plastered across the width of the far wall.

Willie pressed himself against the barrier of tables and metal grilles dividing the hall of Rathkeale Courthouse in two. Over on the other side, clerks were collecting bundles of ballot papers, tying them together with string and loading them back into the empty black metal boxes. Behind them, the Returning Officer, a solicitor very much given to the propriety of his appearance, was fussing to himself as he ran his eyes up and down the large sheet of paper in his hands.

After the tumult of the afternoon as the numbers began to take shape, the crowd had quietened down and were now waiting on the final pronouncement. Hope mixed with fear, expectation with resignation and overnight experts on the intricacies of elections argued over their predictions with decreasing conviction.

They said it was going to be close and so it turned out. Early returns had gone the Home Rulers' way and their supporters cheered as a number of boxes from around Adare gave them an opening lead which widened considerably when the votes of serving soldiers were added. Not having previous exposure to the electoral landscape of West Limerick, gloom immediately descended on Ned's supporters and blame was heaped on the local organisation in the offending district for its failure to get the vote out.

'I'm telling you, we're done for,' Flint was telling him after the figures were totted but Willie had been more interested in the reaction of Hennessy who didn't appear to share the rapture of his followers. By his own reckoning, Sinn Féin had managed to collect a respectable vote, certainly more than he had expected in an area where they had few people on the ground.

Optimism increased as the count wore on. A good showing in the hill country beyond Newcastlewest had narrowed the gap but every advance was whittled back by results from polling booths where Hennessy's machine had beaten them to the voting cards of the dead, the missing and the insane. There was still a stubborn deficit to be overcome when they opened the last boxes.

'It'll be tight but I think we've made it,' a Home Ruler was saying behind him.

'Hell will have frozen over before Thomas Hennessy ever loses in Shanagolden.'

'Do you hear them bastards?' Jimmy McCarthy tugged Willie's sleeve. 'Crowing already and the count not yet over.'

'We're done for, we're done for,' repeated Flint.

Hennessy pushed forward to catch sight of the first papers being turned over. Ned waited back by the wall with Mary Hourigan. Philip Hurley was scribbling numbers in a hardback copybook. Mossy squinted over the shoulders of a Home Ruler, trying to read what the man was writing down. Flint hopped up and down to get a look at what was going on.

'Hennnessy ... Hennessy ... Reidy ...,' droned a tallyman. 'Hennessy ... Hennessy ... Hennessy ....'

'Aaah!' Jimmy turned away in disgust. A Home Ruler jumped into the gap left at the barrier.

'Hennessy ... Reidy ... Reidy ... Reidy ... Reidy ...'

'Are we winning?' Flint's head poked through the scrum.

'Hennessy's still ahead.'

But Willie could sense the mood chaging. Ahead of him, Henessy's shoulders were stiffening.

'Reidy ... Reidy ... Reidy ... Reidy ... Hennessy ... Reidy ... Reidy ...'

'The tide's coming back.'

'Reidy ... Reidy ... Hennessy ... Reidy ... Fowler ...'

'Who's that?'

'That Unionist fella from Askeaton. He'd a bake with Hennessy over some land he wanted to lease out.'

'Reidy ... Reidy ... Hennessy ... Hennessy ... Reidy ...'

'Do you think Fowler will cost Hennessy?'

'Well, he won't help him by standing against him.'

'Reidy ... Reidy ... Reidy ... aaaand Reidy ... That's the lot.'

Hennessy barged away from the barrier followed by a clutch of his supporters. Willie searched around for Hurley in the disintegrating huddle.

'What do you make of it, Philip?'

'We walked away with Shanagolden. Almost three to one.'

'Will it be enough?'

'I don't know. Either way, it's sure to go to a recount.'

Hurley took his leave of the damned to join the elect on the far side of the barricade. The crowd looked on curiously from a distance as the officials and the candidate agents argued the toss over every minute detail. Further speculation ensued as the experts dissected the body language. Willie left them at it to join Ned, Josie and Mary.

'We're winning everywhere.' Ned pulled on his cigarette. 'A newspaper man was telling me we've taken every other seat in Munster outside of Captain Redmond in Waterford. We can't let this one go.'

'Ye did the best ye could,' said Josie. 'And even if we don't take Limerick Northwest, we've beaten Hennessy out the gate in Shanagolden.'

'He wasn't expecting that.' Mary turned her face towards the opposing candidate. 'Would you just look at the pus on him, the mean old devil.'

Activity picked up again at the barricade. Ned, Hennessy and a big red-faced man in a tweed suit were summoned to the Holy of Holies.

'Ahem,' began the Returning Officer from the podium where he was joined by the three candidates. 'Ahem ... ahem!' he continued in a vain attempt to surpass the murmurs of expectation.

'Would ye ever shut up!' shouted Mossy Noonan.

'Ahem ... thank you.' The official unrolled the sheet of paper with all the solemnity of his position. 'I, Aubrey St. John Vereker, by the authority vested in me by His Majesty King George the Fifth, by the grace of God King of the United Kingdom of Great Britain and Ireland, Defender of the Faith, Emperor of India, do hereby ...'

'Will you get on with it, you ould bag of wind!'

'Shhh!'

'... Do hereby declare that the votes cast on the fourteenth day of December in the year of Our Lord 1918 for the parliamentary election in the Northwest division of ...'

'Did you ever hear such rubbish?'

'Will you leave the man speak!'

'Ahem ... the Northwest division of the County of Limerick to be as follows: Electorate, 15, 906. Valid votes cast, 15,254 ...'

'Jaysus, we missed a few ...'

'Shhh!'

'Fowler, Henry Spencer, 126 ... Hennessy, Thomas Aquinas, 7,510 ... Reidy, Edmund Stephen, 7,618. I hereby ...'

The remainder of the Returning Officer's declaration was drowned out by the pandemonium as Ned was chaired by his supporters, and the Martyrs of Erin Fife and Drum Band led the triumphant march out into the square.

'A nation once again,' they sang.

'A nation once again,

And Ireland long a province be

A nation once again.'

'Come on Shanagolden!' they roared into the black night. 'Come on Shanagolden! Now the spuds can be dug up!'

Willie passed by Hennessy on the way out, his face darkened by defeat. Some of Ned's more jubilant supporters jeered the defeated candidate as he hurried off into the night and a scatter of isolated fistfights broke out at the fringes of the celebrations. Across the road, the police looked on, unwilling to intervene too early just in case both factions found common cause and attacked them.

For as long as it would take them to parade from the courthouse down to the centre of the town, Rathkeale would belong to the people. But that would be as far as it would go.

While Sinn Féin might have captured almost three-quarters of the parliamentary seats in Ireland, most of their MPs were either in jail or on the run.

The real power in the land was lined up across from the cheering crowd and itching for a fight. Willie and Ned would get no more than a moment to savour their victory before being forced to make their escape.

27

NEW STATES had sprung up all over Europe in the aftermath of the war. The disintegration of Russia spawned Finland and the Baltic republics of Lithuania, Latvia and Estonia, Poland rose from the ashes of three separate empires, Czechoslovakia hived itself off Austria-Hungary and a collection of disparate countries and colonial provinces had joined themselves together to form the Kingdom of the Serbs, Croats and Slovenes. All of them made their way to the Peace Conference of Versailles in the January of 1919 and all of them got a hearing as the victors shared out the spoils, repaid old debts and carved up the map of the world.

There was one exception. Despite meeting as a democratically elected parliament in Dublin's Mansion House, despite adopting a programme of government and despite putting together the structure of an administration, the delegation from the newly-proclaimed Irish Republic was told to go to hell. Unlike the other new nations, they had sought to separate themselves from one of the victorious Allies and learned the hard way that the high-faluting rhetoric of President Wilson's Fourteen Points applied only to dismantling the vanquished.

Left with a parliament that wasn't recognised and a leadership unavailable to the people for a variety of reasons, the euphoria of Sinn Féin's victory was followed by a vacuum. Over the previous eighteen months, Volunteer numbers had more than doubled as prisoners were released from Frongoch and from the jails of England but, without any clear direction from above, many of them, like the Fourth Limerick Brigade, were now champing at the bit.

'What use was that election?' asked Dan Hourigan. The Shanagolden unit had gathered in the ruins of an old mud cabin on a hillside overlooking the town. Directly below them lay the Reidy farm bordering on the road from Newcastlewest to Foynes. 'The people went out and voted and then they get punished by the authorities for electing the wrong man.'

They had spent the evening scampering over the fields in short bursts from one cover to the next. Divided into two groups, they alternated between hunter and prey with one side attempting to surprise the other before they were seen. It was a strategy that Ned and Willie had fleshed out with other Volunteer leaders in Frongoch as an alternative to the drilling and manoeuvres of regular armies. The military disaster of the Easter Rising had convinced them that massed attack and defence formations hadn't a hope of succeeding against the overwhelming numerical advantage of the British.

At first, the unit was sceptical as their heads were filled with romantic notions of rushing into battle to wipe out entire squads of the enemy and it took some time for Willie and Ned to explain the realities of fighting to them. But once they got used to the idea, they quickly learned the fundamentals of how to move over the countryside without being seen, how to cover comrades, how to encircle enemy positions and how to disperse and regroup once the objective had been achieved.

370

The Shanagolden experience had been replicated over the entire brigade. With Willie and Ned supervising them, units in other parishes along the Estuary trained along similar lines, worked out where the enemy could be successfully ambushed and identified hiding places and safe houses. But they were still only playing games. While the Mansion House parliament, now known as Dáil Éireann, put together the civil structures of the Irish Republic, those on the ground tried to figure out how it could be defended without guns, direction or money. Their weekly training was no more than a means of keeping the men occupied after the euphoria had wound down.

'The only thing the British notice comes out of the barrel of a gun.' Jimmy McCarthy caressed the Mauser rifle, the only weapon that the score of them making up the unit had between them. And if they ever did get the opportunity to use it, they would have to make it count with just five remaining rounds of ammuniton. Not even the fill of a magazine.

Willie watched the Army lorry threading its way northwards from Newcastlewest, its headlights flickering in the twilight to announce yet another raid. This time it passed straight through Shanid Cross without turning right. For once, his parents' house wasn't going to feel the thick edge of the military. A Crosley tender loaded with police rattled down the main street of the town and approached from the other direction. 'It looks like your place is getting it tonight, Ned.'

The unit could only watch as the two vehicles met on the road and turned up the laneway towards Ballycormick House. Since the district had been proclaimed a Special Military Area by a British Government now dominated by red meat Conservatives and subject to the whims of martial law, the authorities had concentrated on goading the Volunteers to come out and fight. Ned and Willie, both officially on the run, were particular targets

371

and their families had been subjected to constant harrassment. Not even Edmund Reidy's standing as one of the leading farmers in the area saved him from the petty vindictiveness of searches, damage to crops and interference with stock.

Jimmy loaded a round into the rifle. 'Worth one shot at least.'

'You haven't a hope of hitting anyone from here.' Willie whipped out his arm, grabbed the weapon, pulled back the bolt and removed the bullet. 'What do you want to do? Tell them we're here? Give them the chance to slaughter us?'

Jimmy wasn't going to argue with him, neither were Dan nor Mossy and, apart from Ned, none of the rest of them had been involved long enough to challenge Willie's leadership. But he recognised the grumblings and, having heard reports of units in Tipperary and Clare already engaging directly with the RIC, they would soon lose patience with his cautious approach.

It had taken a huge effort on his part to batter the brigade back into shape when he returned for the election, and the heavyhanded response of the Crown Forces was bringing even the most indifferent elements of the population to their side. Within the Volunteers, however, were many whose natural inclination would be to lash out first and worry about the consequences later. Unless they found some outlet for their resentment, those under Willie's command were likely either to fade away into disillusioned inactivity or else disintegrate into quarrelling factions.

'What are they at now?' asked Ned. The joint patrol had fanned out around the farmyard but hadn't moved for over an hour. Night had fallen and the only visible signs of life were the dim flickers of candlelight in the bedrooms of his father and sister.

However, the animals were aware of the activity around them. The cattle lowed, the pigs grunted and the dog barked without pause. Once, the door opened and Josie stuck her head out for an extended moment before retreating indoors again.

'They know we're here.' Willie caught the glimpse of faint shadow movement in the yard as the curtains on Josie's window opened and closed again. 'They want us to come out and play.'

When the tender and the lorry first arrived in the yard, Josie had wanted to confront them but her father had held her back.

'Let them come in,' he'd warned her. 'There's no knowing what they might do if you go outside on your own.'

They waited for the knock on the door, for the boots to stamp over the yard, for the outhouses to be slammed open, the hay to be strewn, the floorboards to be ripped up, the barrels to be smashed. But the military were playing a new game and, once she realised what they were up to, she was determined not to humour them. So she made the supper for herself and her father, cleaned up the kitchen, corrected the copybooks containing the sixth class's essays, banked up the fire for the night and went upstairs to her bedroom as if nothing out of the ordinary was going on.

She tried to will herself to sleep but the dog refused to let up. It was going to be a long night and, if Jimmy McCarthy was unable to turn up for work, an even longer morning. With Ned on the run and her father stretched to keep the farm ticking over, she'd have to take the milk down to the creamery herself before she set off for school.

The house shook to the dull thumps of boots banging off the door. They'd lost their patience. Even though their frustration would cause them to inflict even more damage on the property, the small victory filled her with a meaningless satisfaction.

Pulling a shawl over her nightdress, she made her way down the stairs. Her father was in the kitchen ahead of her, leaning belligerently on his stick and standing between her and the squad of soldiers. An officer stepped through the broken door, looked her over with forced indifference. The squaddies lifted their rifles and one of them tried to poke his barrel in her back but he wilted in her glacial stare as she turned around to face him.

Sergeant Stapleton was waiting for them in the yard, a whiff of whiskey off his breath, a sod of turf in his hand and a bucket of paraffin by his foot. Beside him, the dog's blood flowed over the cobbles. She hadn't noticed that he was no longer barking.

'If the stupid thing had learned to shut up, it'd still be alive.' The sergeant kicked the animal's limp body in her direction. 'Now, where is he?'

Neither of them answered.

'Where is he?' He dipped the end of the sod in the oil. 'And is your fancy boy here as well?'

A constable lit the turf. Stapleton waved it in a fiery arc.

'You know very well that Ned isn't here.' The flame came within a foot of her face. 'He isn't that stupid.'

The sod zoomed into the air and landed in the haybarn. Her father spat on the ground as the sour smell wafted in their direction and the whoosh of flame climbed up the wooden columns supporting the roof. The chickens squawked frantically in the adjoining henhouse.

They climbed back into their vehicles when the fire had taken hold. 'We'll be back,' sneered Stapleton. 'We'll keep coming back until we've captured that treacherous son of yours.'

Her father turned back into the house without a word.

'Or maybe we'll find his dead body rotting in a ditch on the side of the road,' the sergeant shouted after him as the tender moved off.

Ignoring the heat, the smoke, the crackling spatter of embers and the dying shrieks of the poultry, Josie remained outside in the yard, transfixed by the bright orange pyre until it was spent.

They watched it all with the powerless anger of the bullied welling inside them. Once the tender and the lorry parted ways at the head of the road, Willie told the unit to disperse.

'They won't be back for a few days, so it gives us a bit of time to think of what to do next. So go on home, lads, and keep quiet until we get on to ye again.'

Only Ned remained with him on the hillside as the embers faded into the night. The haybarn, the milking shed and the henhouse had been burned to the ground, the cart had been reduced to charcoal and the well had doubtlessly been soured with what remained of the paraffin.

'It'll take us a long time to recover from that. There's very little profit in the business at the moment.'

Quite apart from the simmering unrest, the war's end had hit Shanagolden heavily in the pocket. Without an army to feed, the price paid for the gallon of milk and the hundredweight of pigmeat had dropped steeply and, having been supplied with barely-eddible rubbish over the previous four years, the English market had turned its back on produce from Ireland.

'We're wasting our time going through parliament.' Willie slung the rifle over his shoulder and followed Ned down the slope. 'We'll only end up like the Home Rulers, adopting the ways of the British and doing everything to please them.'

'I know.'

'And we can't take tonight lying down. The people will expect us now to hit back.' The cattle were still agitated, galloping up and down the field in groups as the stench of burning lingered in the air. 'The only way to take them on is with the gun.'

'But we haven't got any. And if we had, we don't know how to use them against regular soldiers. We learned that the hard way in the GPO.'

'There's a load of rifles in the barracks in Foynes. Machine guns and Mills bombs as well. Stuff they collected that never made it to the Front.' A fox darted across their path, drawn to the few chickens that had escaped being roasted. 'And I know the man who can show us how to get them.'

'Who?'

'Dick Mullane.'

'Are you sure?' The herd was in a mood to do anything. Ned reinforced the gate with rocks just in case they took it into their heads to charge through it. 'He spent over four years in a British uniform.'

'Mossy's been talking to him. He wasn't too happy with what he saw over in Flanders.'

They heard the commotion in the town as well. The people had turned in for the night but no one had been sleeping. They'd watched the Crosley depart from the RIC barracks, they'd seen the faces of Stapleton and his constables staring down the road ahead of them rather than running their eyes over their surroundings, they'd sensed the tension that was powering the police out on a mission of retribution.

At some point in the night, a curious door opened. Others heard it and they too ventured out of their beds to gaze west towards the hills. First there was a flicker, then there was a flare and soon the slopes above them were lit up.

'Edmund Reidy's place,' mumbled Jack Noonan. 'They must be looking for Ned.'

'They won't find him there,' said Drug Donovan.

376

They looked at each other, each sizing up the line of observers in their nightclothes and overcoats filling up their doorways as the smoke wafted back towards the town. Jack and Molly Noonan, Drug Donovan, Flint Barrett, Dick Mullane, James Horgan, Patie Fitzgibbon, Thomas Hennessy, Doctor Molyneaux, Canon Murphy and his new curate Fr. Connie Greaney, all were wondering where their neighbours stood and how they'd react when resentment began its inexorable slide towards confrontation. But none of them was in the mood for talking. Some had relations in the Volunteers, some in the police and the army, some even in both and it was still too early to let their own sympathies be known.

Despite the cold, they kept to their vigil until they saw the headlights of the tender piercing the darkness of the Newcastlewest road. As it clattered up the main street, Stapleton banged its panels in drunken triumph and his constables kept their eyes from engaging with the shivering people of Shanagolden.

28

L IKE MILLIONS of returned servicemen all over Europe, Patie Fitzgibbon hadn't found it easy to wind his life down to the reduced emotional demands of peacetime. Four years of trying to keep himself alive had given an immediate purpose to his existence, but now that he no longer had to worry about charging over the top or a sniper picking him off or a stray shell blowing him to bits, he was found it hard to care about anything happening around him.

Sometimes he wasn't quite sure whether he had come back at all. Every time he slept, the demons would return and fill his head with visions of the hell that he'd escaped from. De Walcourt's mad eyes as he blew Mick Culhane's head to bits in front of the entire company. The gurgled scream of the German machine gunner whose neck he'd slashed at the Somme. Major Blinker and Major Scug exploding to the heavens on their first march to war. The first time he'd seen the white cloud of chlorine slide over the lip of the trench.

And the nightmare would always end with the white flames leaping from Mick Fitz as they burned his skin, blackened his bones and sucked the soul from his body.

Most nights, Patie would wake up screaming and shaking, bedclothes soaking from his sweat and tossed to the floor by his flailing legs and only when the flashing colours of death were replaced by the dark of the bedroom would he realise that it was all in the past. Unlike the majority of his comrades, he'd made it home in one piece.

Sure, there was the guilt of having survived when others were pushing up poppies but, once he was awake and in his senses, he was glad to be rid of the rats, the lice, the stench, the filth and all the other aspects of the trenches that had reduced an entire generation to a life of barbarity. He was equally happy to have left behind him the crushing boredom of months of inaction when they'd either rot in the muck, hang aimlessly around the estaminet or flatten their feet to ridiculous drills. And between his discharge money and the job that had been found for him at the Co-op along with Dick Mullane, he was better off than most people in Shangolden.

But he no longer knew where he fitted into the town. Some, friends he'd known since childhood among them, remembered the uniform that he'd been wearing when he'd returned from the Front and now saw it as a reason for keeping their distance. Others of a more loyal nature viewed him as an awkward reminder of a war that they had profited from but in which they had taken no part. And a few that were used to exercising authority were suspicious of anyone who might have seen too much of the world for their own good.

Apart from Mossy Noonan, everyone had formed their opinions of the returned soldiers. No one had canvassed Patie during the election. Hennessy's crowd were sure of him sticking to the form expected of veterans and the candidate himself was slow to approach him just in case it might revive awkward memories of who had recruited the youth of Shanagolden during the early days of the war. Neither had the local Sinn Féin organisation bothered to seek his vote. It might have been difficult for Ned Reidy or Willie Hartnett but he'd expected more from others who weren't on the run.

It was only a small issue but it confirmed Patie's suspicions that everybody saw him as a freak. On the odd occasion, he'd feel like talking about his experiences so that those who stayed at home might learn some of the truth about what went on over in Flanders rather than the rubbish printed in the newspapers or flogged on the newsreels of the cinema. But no one ever asked him; they just nodded politely and distantly when he entered the pub and left him to sit down in the corner where he could sup his bottle of porter and his small whiskey on his own and not bother them with tales that might contradict their preconceived ideas.

He'd met others who'd felt the same way. There was a bar in Newcastlewest and another one in Rathkeale where war verterans met to find ways of helping each other out in getting jobs and entitlements and lodging claims for injuries sustained during their service. But one visit had been enough for Patie. All they talked about were the good old times when they were fighting the war that had made men of them and, when they weren't reminiscing, they spent their days complaining about an ungrateful population which had refused to acknowledge their sacrifices.

Content to wallow in their golden memories, they remained locked in a time that had passed them by. None of them wanted to return to the world that they had left. But Patie, Dick, Batt and Flint had come back to a Shanagolden that might have looked the same on the surface but which had been changed irrevocably underneath.

Of the four of them, nobody took Flint seriously and he'd managed without any difficulty to make it back into the society that he'd left. Within a matter of weeks, they'd forgotten that he'd ever served at the Front and were quite surprised when he'd occasionally lapse into reminiscing about military life after his glass had run dry.

Batt couldn't adjust to life outside of uniform and joined the RIC at the first opportunity. The same recruiters had also approached Patie and Dick, dangling way more money than they'd ever get at the Co-op, but both of them had had enough experience of taking orders from regulation-obsessed superiors to last them a lifetime. Bad and all as Horgan was, they were free of his petty tyranny once they left the creamery at the end of day.

He was half-thinking of following Dick to America. The two of them were fish out of water, distrusted by every side in a country that was seething with the same strain of bad blood as that which had just devastated Europe. But they might have to wait the best part of a year to find a ship that would take them. The U-boats had sunk many of the vessels crossing the Atlantic and those remaining were being filled with over a million doughboys waiting to be shipped home from the war.

'What did you make of last night?' Dick sat down beside him in the corner of Jack Noonan's. There was no one else inside the bar other than Mossy, who had the good sense to find some work to occupy himself while they talked away in peace.

'Why are you asking?'

'Because nobody's talking about it. Everyone is nodding and winking and waiting for you to express your opinion without revealing theirs.' Dick topped up his small one with an equal measure of water. 'This place hasn't changed one bit.'

No it hasn't, Patie thought, but then he was as defensive as the rest of them. Soldiering had made him very reluctant to air any comments that ran against the majority opinion. Every time anyone opened his mouth in the estaminet, in the billet or in the trenches, he was aware that someone else might be listening in on him and that same someone could well be the superior that might send him out first over the top or the mate that would turn his back on him when he was in trouble.

And the Shanagolden that he'd returned to was no different. There were figures of authority like Stapleton, Canon Murphy, Horgan and Hennessy, old mates like Dan Hourigan, Jimmy McCarthy, Ned Reidy and Willie Hartnett, acquaintances that would pass him by on the street and he didn't know where he stood with any of them. So he kept the head down and said nothing to anybody, not even to Dick, his closest friend who was marooned in the same boat of mistrust as himself.

'Christ, Patie, you're no different from all the other cute hoors in this town. Haven't you any opinion of your own? Or are you waiting for someone to tell you the right thing to say?'

'I don't know what to say, Dick. I'm just sick of the lot of it.'

'And I am too. But I'm hopping mad over it as well.' Dick sank his small one, chased it with the bottle and called for another round. 'Let me put it another way. I didn't come home to have the likes of Stapleton and Hennessy putting me back in my box as if the four years I spent fighting at the Front never mattered a curse. I had one Captain de Walcourt in my life and I'm damned if I'm going to put up with another.'

'So what are you going to do about it?'

'Willie Hartnett wants us to join up with the Volunteers.'

'And you'd like me to come along with you?' From the corner of his eye, Patie noticed Mossy edging ever closer to them.

'Yes.' Dick took the round from Mossy, who refused all offers of payment. 'They need soldiers. Real soldiers who've been through battle and who understand the ways of the British

383

Army. And if I'm going to stick my neck on the line again, I'd prefer to have someone I can trust covering my back.'

'Remember, it's all about creating confusion.' Faces blackened with grease and soot to avoid recognition, Willie, Mossy, Dan, Patie and Jimmy gathered around Dick in the laneway. Foynes was quiet in the dead of night with just a slight rustle of a breeze, the distant lapping of soft lazy waves in the harbour and the slow rhythmic creak of boat timbers. Across the road from them, a faint flickering glow marked the outline of the RIC barracks.

'Noise, light, fire, smoke, anything at all you can think of and the more the better. Then hit them hard before they have the time to react.'

It was like a night raid all over again to Patie but, instead of being stuck between two imperial armies on the strange flattened fields of Flanders, he was now seeing action in his home parish. Without even thinking about it, he slipped into the taut disciplines of speed, silence and cover until he noticed how far off the mark his colleagues were.

'But you have to keep absolute quiet yourselves until the very last moment,' Dick was warning them. 'We're dealing with seconds here. Confusion gives them to us. Noise loses them and, if we make too much of it, we'll be sitting ducks.'

They soaked the sods in the paraffin and rushed across the street in two groups, each stealing up one side of the barracks. Three ... four ... five ... Patie counted the pants of his breath, lit up the turf, waited another three breaths for Dick's whistle; then smashed the window with a hurley and tossed in the flaming sod.

With smoke and fire leaping in from four different points, the five constables and two sergeants inside rushed out the door where they were immediately felled by the hurleys of the waiting Volunteers. Mossy, Jimmy and Dan tied them up while Patie, Dick and Willie burst into the smouldering barracks.

Making immediately for the iron door at the back of the stairway, Dick shot the lock off with their only rifle. Willie and Patie followed him into the armoury, pulled the rifles from the racks and shouted for Mossy and Jimmy to relay the weapons outside.

The fire was taking hold, the smoke gathering with increasing blackness, the heat radiating off the gloss-painted walls. Patie rammed his crowbar into a padlocked cage and levered the door off its hinges. Outside, he could hear Ned roaring up in the lorry that he'd taken from outside the station.

'Just what we need.' The cage opened up to reveal a treasure trove of machine guns, ammunition, grenades and explosive.

'Grab the ammo and gelignite first,' shouted Dick. 'Guns don't blow up.'

The relay behind them dropped the rifles and, under Dick's direction, whipped out the less stable contents. 'Keep it moving, keep it moving,' he urged them. 'We'll pick up whatever's dropped afterwards.'

They were back outside within minutes, loading the lorry with four dozen Lee Enfield rifles, a Vickers machine-gun, three Lewis light machine-guns, crates of gelignite, boxes of Mills bombs, a Stokes mortar and enough ammunition to take on a small army. Behind them, townspeople left their beds to witness the barracks burning with increasing intensity. A few cheered but most looked on in stupified awe and, because the unit had already cut the telegraph wires, none of them were alerting the authorities to send out reinforcements.

'I'll see ye in hell!' grunted one of the trussed policemen propped up against the wall of the adjoining building. A sudden burst of flame lit up his features.

'You'll be there before us!' Grabbing a rifle, Jimmy jumped from the lorry. Without batting an eyelid and in full view of half of the population of Foynes, he plugged Sergeant Stapleton in the head.

'Jesus Christ, Jimmy!' Willie leaped from the box of grenades that he was sitting on. 'There's no need for that.'

'Ye can argue about it later.' Dick grabbed him by the arm as Jimmy climbed back into the lorry. 'Let's get the hell out of here first.' He banged the back of the cab. 'Everyone's here, Ned. Get moving!'

'You don't shoot prisoners, Jimmy.' Willie bounced up and down off his box as the lorry barrelled between the hedges along the narrow road running towards Creeves Cross. 'It's wrong.'

'It's personal, Willie.'

'And it's stupid as well.'

'He'd it coming to him.'

'I don't care how many scores you had to settle with Stapleton.' A crate of gelignite sild across the floor between them. 'Shooting him in front of half the the town will only turn everyone against us.'

'You saw what he'd been doing for years. Well, he sure won't try it again in a hurry.'

Willie slumped back as the vehicle found a stretch of level road that hadn't been scoured with potholes. The raid couldn't have gone better. Dick and Patie had filled their heads with what real fighting was about, about planning and details and timing instead of the half-cocked attacks that they'd thought might work. Within minutes, they'd have enough arms dumped to keep a decent campaign going until the end of the year and they'd have covered all traces of themselves, the weapons and the lorry long before the authorities would have put a search party together to chase after them.

But then Jimmy had to mess it all up on them. Instead of making the peelers look like fools and having the whole county marvel at their daring, all the talk would now be about killing Stapleton in cold blood. If they were to hold the support of the people, they had to show that they were better than those they were fighting against

'Forget about it, Willie. It's done.' Dick opened the breech of a rifle and peered down the barrel. 'Anyway, soon you won't even think twice about it.'

'Is that the way it was over in France?' Dan asked him.

'People kept dying all the time. You got used to it.'

'Like Stapleton?'

'Yes. Like Stapleton. Like Johnny O'Brien and Mick Culhane and Dinny Lyons and Jerry Curtin ...' Dick picked up another rifle and examined it. '... Like all the rest of the misfortunes who never made it back. Like all the Germans we killed ...'

He snapped the breech shut and pointed the barrel between Jimmy's eyes in one lightning move. 'We killed them just like that, Jimmy.'

The target turned as white as a sheet.

'Of course, our guns were loaded at the time.' Dick pulled the rifle away. 'Death. He's one persistent bastard. He even followed us home.' The lorry almost overturned taking a corrner. 'For God's sake, Ned, will you take it handy! Do you want to ruin a good night's work?'

He loaded a magazine in the gun, removed it and reloaded it twice more and shook his head at the rustiness of his movements. 'Look at poor Tim Curtin. He came through the

Somme and Passchendaele without a scratch only to be done by the flu when he landed back in England.'

The lorry screeched to a halt. It was as close as it could get to the ruins of the cottage lying a hundred yards up the lane. Dick and Willie tossed the load to Dan, Mossy, Patie and Jimmy waiting outside. 'It's your show now, Willie.'

'Are you pulling out?' Willie had been avoiding the question ever since he'd first approached Dick. It had been more of a roundabout suggestion than a direct invitation to join the Volunteers and Dick had responded by telling them the way they should go about it, adding that he might just tag along to point out what they were doing wrong.

'I thought you knew me better than that.' Dick lifted the last box of gelignitie and passed it out over the tailboard to Mossy. 'I joined the Volunteers nearly five years ago and, while other things might have happened in the meantime, I don't remember me ever resigning my membership.' He gathered up the remaining rifles. 'No, it's just that I'm better suited to being a foot soldier. I need someone like yourself or Ned to be leading me.'

They clambered down to join the others as Ned drove off to abandon the lorry on some other back road in the middle of nowhere.

'I told Willie I was in for the long haul. How about yourself?'

Balancing a box of Mills bombs on his shoulder, Patie followed Dick up the barely discenable track towards the ruined cottage. 'I'm still thinking about it,' he answered.

'I bet it got the blood flowing again?'

He couldn't deny it. The raid had been his first taste of raw excitement since he'd come back. Much as he was loath to admit it, he'd missed the thrill of battle.

'Nothing like action to keep the nightmares away.' Dick flattened the rusting gate with his boot. 'It's when you've time on your hands they start bothering you.'

But Patie still wasn't sure whether he wanted to go back to putting his life on the line. Once was enough.

'If you want to pull out, Patie, no one will hold it against you. You did your bit tonight and it wouldn't have succeeded without you.' They stopped to hack through a clump of briars blocking their path. 'But 'twould be best if you told them now. Otherwise you'd never know when someone might turn sour on you.'

Even though the roof of the cottage was gone, the big fireplace sunk deep into the gable wall was still intact and could be covered over with sods and flagstones to provide a dry store for their cache. Apart from a rifle and a hundred rounds of ammunition each and the three pistols taken by Ned, Willie and Dick, they dumped the night's entire haul until they had an idea of how best to use it.

Home was five miles over the fields, two hours if they pushed it. They split up with only Dick and Patie returning together.

'Our cover will be blown if we don't turn up at the creamery.' Dick climbed on Patie's shoulder to scale an overgrown Mass path that separated two townlands. 'Horgan would be sure to get on to the peelers.'

Patie wobbled on an unsteady foot wedged between two big tree roots as he hauled himself up. 'Too early for that. There's an awful lot still to be done.'

'So you're staying on?' Dick pulled him up the final step onto the elevated path inside the double ditch.

It was never going to be any other way. He had followed Dick down to the recruitment centre and across the killing fields of Europe. 'Of course I am. At least I know who I'm fighting for this time.'

29

'WHAT WAS he doing in Foynes?' asked County Sub-Inspector Callaghan. 'That wasn't his area.'

'I had him moved out of Shanagolden for a few weeks until the place settled down.' District Inspector Sullivan waited in the Rathkeale office of his superior as Callaghan digested his report on the attack on Foynes barracks. 'Tempers were getting high in the town after the raid on Ned Reidy's father's farm. I thought it might be the wisest course of action.'

'Well, it didn't do him much good.' The Sub-Inspector stamped the document, added his initials and handed it back to its author without giving any indication that he had taken a word of it in.

On a personal level, Sullivan hadn't grieved too long for Laurence Stapleton. The late sergeant was the main reason why the force was facing more difficulties in Shanagolden than in any other parish in his district. And even though his death was denounced from the pulpit, in the newspapers and in the council chambers as the vilest possible affront that could be inflicted on humanity, there weren't too many visible signs of sorrow in a town that had endured his abritrary enforcement of the law for almost a decade.

In fact, apart from the Canon, the doctor, Councillor Hennessy and the creamery manager, no one was expressing outrage over the incident. Even a majority of the constables in the barrracks seemed more relieved than angry at the demise of their superior.

There were the usual calls for action when news of the attack became public. The Army cranked itself up to wreak revenge on the entire population, only to find that its authority within the Special Military Area had been rescinded. Following yet another gyration in the corridors of power, the Chief Secretary, one of Llyod George's Liberal colleagues, had wrested back control of Irish affairs from the Viceroy and his uniformed chums, when the Prime Minister returned temporarily from the peace conference in Paris. Inspired no doubt by reservations expressed by the Americans, he had resisted the automatic renewal of the order re-imposing martial law until he had fully evaluated the situation on the ground.

Not that the RIC's period of ascendancy would last very long but, while they still had the political upper hand, the District Inspector moved quickly to ensure that no provocative action be taken while they hunted down Stapleton's killers. In one of his first actions, he had ensured that Callaghan appointed Jarlath Flaherty, an experienced and conciliatory sergeant, to take over the running of the Shanagolden barracks instead of some gung-ho sycophant who'd follow without question every order handed down to him by the military.

'So where do we go from here?' asked Callaghan.

'I need to find out who else is in the Volunteer unit.' Despite his ambivalence over the victim himself, Sullivan was deeply angered by the fact that a member of his force had been murdered in the line of duty. 'I'm sure Reidy and Hartnett were involved and more than likely that Jimmy McCarthy. But there were at least another four of them there.'

'What did the witnesses say?'

'All struck by blindness, deafness and loss of memory.'

'Life is full of surprises.' Callaghan rose from his chair to look out the window. 'We need to show something, Nicholas, before our soldier friends return.' He laid his hand on Sullivan's shoulder as he accompanied him to the door. 'Very important people are demanding a breakthrough. It's the price we have to pay for their support.'

The driver was waiting in the yard to bring him back to Newcastlewest. A detective sent down from the County Inspector's staff in Limerick joined him in the back of the police car to confirm his worst fears.

'They had military training,' he was told. 'Only experienced soldiers could have planned this operation and pulled it off as quickly as that.'

Not only had the rebels access to weapons, but they had picked up the expertise to use them. And if men who had volunteered for the war were now turning on the army that they had served in, Sullivan could no longer take traditional loyalties for granted. 'So it could have been anyone? There must be hundreds of war veterans in the area.'

'Not as many as you'd think.' The detective handed him a list. 'I've removed all of the wounded, those who arrived too late for active service or who were posted to the support units, anyone who's taken to the drink since he came back or who suffers from bad dreams at night or anything else that might turn him into a military liability.'

'Did you find anyone who served with the Americans or with the French Foreign Legion?'

'No one at all. Every known veteran in the area signed up for King George.'

The District Inspector ran his eyes through the names. Less than thirty possibilities living within ten miles of Foynes. 'Only two in Shanagolden?'

'There were four I looked at, but one of them has joined the force and the other one is only a harmless nuisance.'

'Should we pull them in?'

'I don't think it was them. They're still at their jobs and they turned up for work at the usual time the morning after the raid. They'd more than likely have gone missing for the day if they'd been involved.'

A herd of cows being driven back from the milking slowed the car down as it passed through Reens Pike. The farmer and the labourer with him kept their distance from the policemen. Even in previously loyal areas, the population was receding from direct contact with the civil authorities.

Dick Mullane and Patie Fitzgibbon? Their military records were exemplary and there had never been any reports of them acting out of the ordinary. And if there were any suspicions about their allegiances, their manager at the creamery would be the first to inform the police. Dismissing them as suspects, Sullivan brought his attention to bear on the other names on the list. He might follow up on these three brothers from Askeaton who had served with the Munsters in Mesopotamia. Two of them had been decorated for gallantry and the third had been disciplined for insubordination.

But at the back of his mind, he realised that he was denying an awful possibility. If disaffection among the population had reached the hearts of an army of men who had won a war for Britain, then he and his force were facing far more than the sporadic actions of isolated bands of rebels.

Out of the corner of his eye, Jack Noonan caught sight through the window of Batt Mullane walking across the street with a bucket in one hand, a brush in the other and a bag draped across his shoulder. Curious to find out what the new constable might up to, he abandoned his solitary task of polishing glasses and stepped outside. The removal of Stapleton from their lives had improved the general mood of most people in Shanagolden, but the turn for the better was rapidly being undone by the latest recruit to the police barracks.

Being a local man sent to enforce the law on his reluctant neighbours was only part of the problem. Batt had always been on the periphery of the group, the last fella that the rest of them would hang around with, the weakest player on the football team, who would have been dropped had there been anyone else around to take his place. Whenever they had taken to the field, he was always the first one that Jack, Birdie, his team-mates and the supporters would single out for criticism.

'Will you hold on to it!' half of them would shout.

'Will you get rid of the ball!' the other half would scream.

'Will you go out and tackle him, for God's sake!'

'Would you ever stay back and mark your own man!'

And Batt would be listening to them. Instead of playing his own game, his head would be filled with contradictory advice and the more he heard, the more confused he'd get. Jack knew that they'd been unfair with him but, in the hothouse atmosphere of the football field, someone had to be the butt of everyone else's frustrations. Always trying too hard to please whoever was over him, gawky, awkward, innocent Batt Mullane fitted the bill to perfection.

He might have expected more respect when he came back from the war with the stripes on his sleeve and the campaign medals on his chest but the time was wrong and the place was wrong for marching around a small Irish town with the stride and airs of a sawn-off general. And when there was no one in Shanagolden of a mind to listen to his stories and he had to put on civilian clothing so as to get some work like the rest of the population, he was back to being the same anonymous young fella that he'd been before he left for Flanders.

But now that he'd been given a new uniform to wear, he had his chance to get his own back on those who had laughed at him and given out to him and put him down. Barely a week on the job and he had already pulled Jack for serving after hours, two drunks for disturbing the peace when they'd done nothing more than lean up against each other in mutual support, and old Morty Hayes for possession of poitín when all he'd been doing was rubbing down his greyhound.

Jack went so far as to have a word with the new man in charge of the barracks, even though fraternising with the peelers was now looked down upon by most people in the parish. Sergeant Flaherty had been understanding and had accepted that, regardless whatever other problems lay between them, an over-zealous implementation of petty legislation was in nobody's interests. But as he explained, his hands were tied once the official report had been logged and the law had to take its course. However, he did hint that he might have a quiet word with the keenest constable under his command.

If Flaherty had spoken to him, the results weren't evident. Dropping his bucket, Batt filled out his chest for a pose of authority that the late Sergeant Stapleton would have been proud of. Pulling a poster from his bag, he slowly unfurled it, brushed the back of it with paste and stuck it to the wall.

'£3,000 REWARD,' announced the big bold type. 'For information leading to the capture of the murderers of Sergeant Laurence

Stapleton. All approaches will be treated in the strictest confidence.'

Tempting, thought Jack, enough to set a man up for life. He had a fair idea that his son was one of those involved and he was even surer of the identity of four others.

Full of fussy importance, Hennessy ventured out of his premises to view the message plastered on the wall next to him. Batt touched his cap in deference as the Councillor passed by.

'A terrible deed, Constable. A terrible deed indeed.'

'Murdering scum. That's all they are, Mr. Hennessy.' Batt dropped his brush back into the bucket of paste. 'Nothing more than common criminals.'

Sucking his pipe with slow easy draughts, Drug Donovan leaned against the drainpipe running down the front of Jack's pub. 'I'll bet you a pound to a penny, Jack Noonan,' he muttered between puffs. 'That money won't ever be claimed.'

Batt's eagerness in the face of general unwillingness was mainly due to the military reclaiming their dominance within the Crown Forces. Sinn Féin's call in Dáil Éireann for a boycott of the RIC in every walk of life had weakened the position of the police, dried up recruitment and led to a serious lowering of morale, and the Viceroy Lord French had made the most of the opportunity to bring the Army back into the frame. An entire stripe of West Limerick from Askeaton to Glin was once again declared a Special Military Area and subjected to the arbitrary whims of martial law.

Back on the wrong side of the musical chairs, District Inspector Sullivan found himself reporting to a Major Forrester who had been sent down to West Limerick to speed up the apprehension of the murderers of Sergeant Stapleton.

'Damned case is becoming an embarrassment.' The Army man had spent most of the war stationed in India and a promising career had ground to a halt. While he had marked time keeping an eye on Pathan tribesmen on the Afghan border, classmates at Sandhurst had passed him out on the back of their war experiences in France, Gallipoli and Palestine. 'Bloody natives must think we're blithering idiots.'

Even though he was a native himself, Sullivan didn't bother to argue. Still in his mid-thirties, Forrester had plenty of ambition left in him and the opportunities provided by a far-flung outpost of the United Kingdom might rekindle the momentum of his early climb through the ranks. And that being the case, listening to local advice would be a long way down his agenda.

The inspector had suggested that it might be a waste of time to search those attending the fair in Newcastlewest but the points that he'd made were beyond the major's comprehension. Fixated with tribal warriors swooping down from the hills and dastardly double-dealing traders in the bazaar, Forrester had come to the conclusion that Willie Hartnett, Ned Reidy and all the other brigands involved in the Foynes raid would gather for the monthly market.

'And why would they do that?' Sullivan had asked him as they looked out on the square from the steps of Desmond Castle.

'Every bandit is the same. Bravado for the sake of bravado. Saw enough of the blighters in the Northwest Frontier.'

'I see.'

'Bloody fools if you ask me. Scuttled off when we attacked them in numbers. A short, sharp campaign and Bob's your uncle.'

Even though there was at least another hour before they'd see the dawn, the drovers had arrived with their stock and the hawkers were already setting up their stalls. Dealers, tanglers, three-card-tricksters and beggars dribbled in along the three streets and a laneway leading into the Square. Straddling the boundary between sweet land and sour, Newcastlewest could draw people from every walk of life and from every sector of the economy.

By mid-morning, the Square was bursting at the seams. After a Special Military Area order had proscribed every open fair in the county in the interests of security, a backlog had built up over the previous two months. Now finally given the chance to do business, dairy men with an excess of sucklers on their hands, hill farmers looking for animals to graze over the summer, fatteners searching for stores and every merchant and dealer who lived off the pyramid of the cattle trade, piled into the town to make up for lost time.

Thankful that the soldiers were remaining out of sight for the moment, Sullivan threaded through the confusion of humans, animals and carts, stamping over the carpet of animal dung and the streams of piss and ignoring the attentions of the beggars and buskers as he checked out where his men were stationed. In front of him, a prosperous-looking merchant was sizing up the boys and girls waiting to be hired out as help for the year.

'She's very well behaved,' pointed out the father of a sad-faced girl of no more than fourteen. 'Does what she's told.'

The merchant ran his hand over her breasts and her backside.

'She's in good health. Never been a day sick in her life.'

The chin was lifted to get a better look at her face.

'If you're not happy, maybe her sister might interest you. She's a year younger but she doesn't look it.'

'No. This one will do.' He reached into his pocket for his wallet. 'Three pounds down and six more at the end of the year.'

The inspector nodded to a detective on the lookout for stolen goods as he passed down a line of traders' stalls and examined the clothes, implements, quack cures, religious goods and knick-knacks on display. An Excise man mooched through the barrows laden with vegetables, eggs, country butter, cheese and game just in case anyone was slipping bottles of poitín to his more discerning customers.

The uniforms were left to deal with the hardy annuals. One pair of constables patrolled the Square, following the three-card-tricksters with their tiny portable tables, the trick-of-the-loop men, the Crown and Anchor croupiers and the beggarwomen holding babies under their shawls and prodded them with their batons to keep them on the move. A second detail made sure that the whores servicing the needs of bachelor farmers confined themselves to a particular laneway and also kept an eye out for pickpockets. A third kept tabs on the accordionists with their little collection bags hanging from coils of wire tied to their instrument, the fiddlers with their caps upturned for donations at their feet and the off-key singers waving their cups before passers-by. The playlist had changed over the winter with rebel songs of the Fenians and of 1798 now supplanting Moore's melodies and Percy French favourites. Even more pointedly, the street entertainers weren't bothering to tone down the aggressively political content of their tunes when policemen passed them by.

Sullivan would have been within his rights to have the lot of them arrested for vagrancy and, if it had been left to the military, half the town would have been rounded up and taken away before the morning was out. But the law and its implementation were two separate animals entirely in rural Irealnd and it wasn't until the RIC had realised this truth that the force had made any headway in gaining a reluctant tolerance of its existence. And now, even that toehold in the population had all but disappeared.

'Peeler, peeler, dirty rotten peeler,' chanted a gang of young boys, daring the District Inspector to chase them through the maze of stalls, animals and barrows. One stuck out his tongue, another pointed his index fingers from the corners of his forehead and a third pulled his lips open to make a face. Deflated by Sullivan's indifference, they turned to mocking other strange-looking invaders who had descended on their town but, in the back of their eight-year-old minds, they glowed with the satisfaction of knowing that they'd dented the majesty of the law.

The main business of the day was conducted a hundred yards up Bishop's Street from the Square. Sellers stood by their stock in the Market Yard waiting for approaches. Buyers and dealers moved around with practised disinterest until something on offer caught their eye. Trying to give the impression of stopping at random, they'd talk about the weather, the political situation, the prospects for various football and hurling teams or whether there was a dog worth backing for the coursing, before they'd pass an off-chance remark regarding the beast that happened to be looking them in the eye.

Both sides knew that it was all for show but the ritual of the deal had to be observed. A cow that had been kept for a year couldn't be sold in an instant. It just wasn't right.

So, as a hint of interest cranked the mechanics of the bargain into motion, a support cast would emerge from the crowd and make itself known to both buyer and seller. Tanglers liked to think of themselves as the vital cog which bridged the gap between the two parties and there may indeed have been such facilitators plying their expertise on that particular day in

Newcastlewest. But most of those hanging around incipient deals were redundant chancers in search of a drink.

Flint fulfilled the role as Edmund Reidy haggled with another farmer of indeterminate age with a red, whiskey-shot face, wild shaggy hair and a bristling straw-coloured beard flecked with silver and wearing an ancient coat held together with lengths of plaited straw. The cow whose merits they were discussing hung its head in an expression of absolute boredom as if to say that it had experienced all the charms that Newcastlewest could offer and would now prefer to be led back to its field.

'Eight pound, one shilling and sixpence,' offered Reidy. 'Not a penny more.'

'A fair price! A fair price!' Oblivious to the two negotiating parties, Flint danced between them.

'Eight pound two and six.' The farmer shook his head vehemently as if his honour had been impugned. 'I'll not go any lower.'

'I'd settle for that!' advised the mediator.

'Are you trying to rob me?' The buyer turned his back in disgust but it was no more than a half-hearted gesture that stopped in mid-motion. 'All right, then. Eight pound two shillings. And that's my final offer.'

'He's come half way, so he has!'

The farmer pursed his lips as he leaned on his stick.

'Tis good money, so it is.' Flint winked at Reidy in an unappreciated display of knowledgeability. 'You won't get better today.'

'I'd take that as an insult, only 'tis getting on in the day.' The vendor sucked in a deep draught of air to help him come to his momentous decision. 'I'll accept it only on condition you pay for the drink.'

'There, now! Will the two of ye shake on it!'

Rediy spat on the palm of his hand and held it out. The farmer grasped it and the deal was done before Flint could reach out his own arm to seal it.

'Ye'll be heading over to Lee's then, I suppose?' he suggested.

Buyer and seller finally noticed the presence of the intermediary, pointedly ignored him and headed for the nearest pub down in the Square. An anticipatory smile draping his face, Flint followed them past the barricacaded shopfronts surrounding the square.

Earlier in the day, the bar had been filled with parties striking bargains, vendors who'd paid tanglers or young fellas to report on expressions of interest in their stock, old acquaintances catching up on the news in neighbouring parishes and drovers quenching their thirst. But as the fair wore on and the more sensible put away what money they had left, the clinetele had been reduced to comatose supping of slowly declining glasses and the conversation to unintelligible argument or rambling monologue.

The barman's eyes lit up at the sight of three reasonably sober customers breaking into his dark premises through the cloud of tobacco smoke. Reidy signalled to him with a twitch of his eyebrows.

'Powers, isn't it?'

The farmer nodded.

'Two large ones then, Billy.'

Flint tapped the purchaser's elbow. 'Didn't I bring ye together on the price, didn't I?'

'Yerra, get him one too,' conceded the vendor. 'Or else we'll never get rid of him.'

'Aaah ... Billy, make that two large and one small.'

Before the barman could lay out the glasses, gunfire rang out in the Square outside. One or two of the other customers shook to attention before reverting to their trance as Reidy and the farmer moved over to the door to look out.

Two pickpockets, one assault, one vagrancy, one larceny, one immoral conduct, one wilful damage to public property and two drunk and disorderly.' The Newcastlewest sergeant read out the list to his superior. 'Under the circumstances, a quiet enough day so far.'

'No sign of the feud?' Inspector Sullivan had been hearing rumours all week to the effect that a long-standing dispute between the parishes of Athea and Ballyhahill might erupt at the fair.

'Keeping their powder dry. I heard the Shinners made some attempt at a truce and called in the two parish priests to witness the agreement.'

'Should we be thankful?'

The sergeant thought about it for a moment. 'I don't think so. More than likely, they'll combine their grievances and turn them on us instead.'

The crush in the Square was thinning out as drovers collected their charges and began to move them out by the spokes of roads leading from the town.

'It's a pity they don't take the shit with them,' observed the sergeant. 'It'll take us days to wash the smell out of the Square.'

But while the animals were heading off to pastures new, the number of humans hadn't diminished appreciably and many of them were in a less sociable mood as a day's heavy drinking took its toll. However, they hadn't got out of hand and Sullivan was breathing relief that the force had got through the day without resorting to their batons when he saw a scatter of people of people and animals up at the Bishop's Street corner of the Square.

The panic slammed him into action. 'Tell your men to advance up towards the Market Yard!' he shouted at the sergeant. 'And tell them to cover themselves. This could be a raid by the rebels.'

Further disturbances erupted behind him. He turned to see people running from the other two entrances to the Square ahead of the Army lorries screeching to a halt to block the exit roads. Soldiers dismounted to form a cordon around the fair and the remainder of the battalion moved into the pubs and shops to order customers and staff out at gunpoint. Just in case anyone was hiding underneath them, barrows and stalls were knocked over and their contents were smashed off the ground. When the military was satisifed that they'd located everyone, the entire attendance was corralled into the crush in the middle of the Square.

Taking umbrage at being forced back against her will, a cow that had galloped down from the Market Yard lowered her head to charge at the nearest soldier who immediately felled it to the ground. Hearing the gunfire, the crowd squashed back on itself in panic, heaving one way and then another as a volley was released over their heads.

Caught in the middle of the commotion, Sullivan, the sergeant and over a dozen constables forced their way to the front of the corral. A soldier raised his rifle to him but the inspector whipped it from his grasp and made a beeline for Major Forrester.

'What the hell are ye doing?'

The major was too busy detailing his NCOs to organise the search through the crowd to answer the policeman.

Sullivan's voice raised in anger. 'What in the name of God are you doing, you stupid fool?' Caught by the novelty of Crown Force commanders arguing in public, the crowd quietened to a murmur. Forrester raised his head from the huddle and turned it around with contemptuous indifference. Resigned to the futility of confrontation, the inspector and his men walked away to leave the military free to do whatever took their fancy.

By the time the soldiers had finished their business, the Square had all but emptied. Covered in blood, dust and dung, those injured in the crush were lifted to their feet and staggered away through the debris strewn from the overturned barrows and stalls, from the smashed shopfronts and windows, from the broken carts and wagons. Looters sifted through the wreckage and Sullivan was of a mind to regroup his men to stop them but, when the soldiers joined in on the ransack, he let them at it.

'Seems the birds have flown the coop.' Forrester didn't seem unduly worried about his operation's lack of success.

'What did you expect?' Sullivan was only half-listening. His attention had been caught by the two men crouching around the remains of the cow that had started the panic. 'Reidy and Hartnett were never going to be here. It's the last place on earth you'd find them.'

'A valuable exercise nevertheless.' The major opened a note passed to him by his batman. 'Puts down a marker. The natives will know better the next time than to shelter these criminal elements.'

'And I hope you feel the same way when they start picking off your soldiers.' Sullivan drifted away, passing by the conference over the cow.

Buyer and seller were prodding the cow with their sticks. Despite their best efforts, the animal remained resolutely dead.

'The deal was done,' insisted the farmer. 'We shook hands on it.'

Reidy straightened up and shook his head. 'The goods weren't delivered in saleable condition. Under such circumstances, all obligations entered into become null and void.'

'There was a witness to it!' shouted the first party after the departing second party. 'I'll find him. You mark my words, sir, I'll find him even if I've to travel to the ends of the earth.'

He wasn't the only disappointed party to the transaction. Across the Square, the would-be tangler stood among the zombies in the only pub that had managed to escape the turmoil of the day.

'Hard luck, Flint,' maintained the barman, his arms crossed in defiant refusal and his head shaking at the sole conscious figure on the other side of the counter. 'I'm afraid the round was never paid for.'

'Aah, come on, Billy.' Flint's jaw sagged with thwarted thirst. 'Just the one. Come on. Be decent about it.'

30

SATURDAY WAS always the quietest morning of the week. With their energy drained from five days of toil, labourers, farmers, merchants and shop assistants kept the head down to husband what was left for that evening and for the day of rest that followed. In normal times, Sergeant Flaherty and his constables in the RIC barracks would look forward to a handy few hours when they could catch up on paperwork, go out on a leisurely patrol, issue the occasional word of caution, and rest up before Shanagolden and the countryside surrounding it took to drinking for the night.

But the age of equillibrium had passed. Those stationed at the coalface of law and order no longer had any latitude to mete out justice as they saw fit. Military men with no idea of policing and even less of the sensitivities of rural Ireland demanded immediate results. And if that meant locking up entire towns and subjecting their inhabitants to every form of humiliation, then so be it. But they didn't have to live among the consequences of their operations. When the raid was over and half the homes in the parish were smashed to bits, the soldiers could retire to their guarded fortresses while RIC men and their families still lived among the taunts of resentment and the boycott campaign that had been organised by Sinn Féin.

Flaherty could have handled the excesses of the military but for their recruitment of supporters among those under his own command. In Shanagolden, they'd wound up Batt Mullane to treat the apprehension of Sergeant Stapleton's killers as a personal crusade. As the early shift eased down from its gentle exertions, the keenest constable in the whole of County Limerick was still out pounding his beat and getting up everyone's nose.

According to the regulations preventing policemen from serving within two counties of their home, Batt should never have been posted in the town in the first place, but someone up the line had had him foisted on Shanagolden. It could have been the military, the intelligence gatherers in Dublin Castle or Councillor Hennessy looking for a channel of information to replace Stapleton, but whoever it was, he'd made the Sergeant Flaherty's task of keeping a lid on the situation immeasuably more difficult.

Whereas his colleagues were merely ignored and greeted with silence, the people of the town went out of their way to shun Batt. The moment he stepped out of the barracks, the main street would empty, recalcitrant children would be hauled inside and the doors would slam shut as he passed. Even the dogs and the cats had picked up on the public mood and disappeared up laneways whenever Constable Mullane came into view.

By midday, he had Shanagolden all to himself as he bore down on Jack Noonan's pub. A torn poster, one of those offering a reward for Stapleton's killers, fluttered in the breeze. Every morning, he pasted them up on the wall across from the bar, even though it'd be ripped down as soon as he was out of sight. But Batt would not be deterred. If he kept replacing them, someone would eventually crack. The £3,000 bounty was too big to ignore.

From an upstairs room over Jack Noonan's pub, Willie Hartnett saw Batt march down the street with the stiff gait of a soldier. Coming into town was dangerous but, if it meant getting the occasional wash, a proper meal and a decent night's sleep, it was worth it. On the run for over five months, he'd crack up if didn't get to touch the odd moment of reality.

Mossy had set up the room which could only be accessed from inside the building through the closet of his own bedroom. And if the occupant happened to be disturbed by a raid, he could be out within seconds by sliding down the roof and into a hayshed that had an unnoticed side entrance leading straight out into the lane. The five of them who had dropped out of public view took it in turns to occupy the outpost which gave them the most effective means of gauging the level of the authorities' response to their activities.

Ever since the raid on Foynes, the Fourth Limerick Brigade had mainly concerned itself with building up a network of companies that could operate on their own, setting up hideouts and safe houses, distributing arms into local dumps, enforcing the boycott of the Crown Forces and holding up banks and post offices to finance their operations and to support the families of Volunteers. But even though they'd set up a tidy operation on the ground, they were still waiting for direction from above. For all the flowery talk coming out of Dáil Éireann, there was no real leadership in the Volunteers, now renamed the Irish Republican Army or the IRA, and the recently-established General Headquarters did little more than react to whatever initiatives were taken at local level.

So they didn't know whether they were an army, a band of raparees swooping down from the hills to snipe at the Crown Forces or a local milita raised to defend their supporters. Nor did it help that three different command structures were trying to pull the strings. Apart from Richard Mulcahy's Volunteer GHQ, there was the Dáil's own authority through Minister for Defence Cathal Brugha and the shadowy presence of the IRB continuing to lurk in the background.

Wille had rejoined the Brotherhood when it was reconstituted in Frongoch after the executions of its leaders. But unlike Ned who had become deeply involved in the new Supreme Council, he no longer believed in the necessity of the obsessively secret organisation. Now that the struggle was involving the population at large through the boycott and the alternative system of courts, taxation and policing being set up by the Dáil, everyone knew who the leaders were at both local and national levels.

He watched the reward poster blow up the street past Batt. Maybe someone in the town might crack some night in a fit of jealousy or greed or spite, but the litmus test of their resistance to the British had yet to be claimed after two months. Thanks to the provocative stupidity of the military authorities, the Dáil was winning the political battle hands down and even sworn enemies of Sinn Féin like Doctor Molyneaux were willing to call in Shanagolden's Republican court set up by Philip Hurley and Josie Reidy to settle disputes.

It might have been more difficult to build up support had the area been left to the RIC. The new sergeant knew that there were better ways of getting on with the people than beating them into submission and, if he'd been given the time to run his own show without interference, the IRA wouldn't have found it as easy to fan the flames of resentment.

Batt lifted his head and Willie moved back from the window, cursing himself for being careless. But before his curiosity got the better of him, the policeman's attentions were diverted to a horse galloping up from the crossroads bearing a big, angry, dishevelled figure waving a stick.

Never a talkative man at the best of times, Drug Donovan sat in his customary spot at the corner of the bar and faced into a slow pint. On the other side of the counter, Jack Noonan held a glass up to the shaft of sunlight entering through the crack over the door and meticuluosly polished it to sparkling splendour. Long years of practice during quiet mornings had fostered the mastery of silence in both and they used such moments to gather their thoughts, reflect on the great questions of life or think of absolutely nothing at all.

They would have been enjoying their mutual solitude again but for the presence of Flint. Perched on a stool beside the sole paying customer, he resisted every effort to ignore him.

'The best football team ever in the county, weren't they Drug?' He pointed to the photograph behind the bar.

Drug stared morosely into the middle distance. Jack put down the polished glass and picked up another whose sparkle was infintismally inferior.

'We're good enough to win again this year, I'm telling you.'

A damp sod hissed in the fire.

'They're still only young fellas. Plenty of years left in them. Amn't I right, Mr. Noonan?'

'Half of them are dead.' Drug scraped the bowl of his pipe with a penknife.

'And the other half are on the run,' added Jack.

Silence returned but only for a moment. Glasses trembled as the door crashed open.

413

''Tis him!' exclaimed the hairy apparition framed in the sunlight. ''Tis the man himself!'

Jack tried to put a name to the big straw-haired figure with the red face but none came to mind. 'Can I help you?' he asked.

The stranger bore straight down on Flint. 'You were there in Newcastle! You saw it!'

'The commotion?' Flint glanced around in search of an escape. 'Right in the middle of it, I was.'

'Feck that! You saw the deal.' The fat calloused finger jabbed into the smaller man's chest. 'You were witness to it.'

'The deal?

The farmer beat his stick on the ground with blazing impatience. 'The cow!'

'Aaah, the one over the cow.' A glimmer of opportunity flickered across Flint's narrowing eyes. 'I might have been.'

The stick beckoned to Jack. 'What's the man having?'

'Powers,' insisted Flint. 'A large one.'

The farmer nodded and left a ten-shillings note on the counter. Jack poured out the whiskey, which disappeared in a single gulp.

'A pint there as well.' The stranger tilted his head in Drug's direction. 'And whatever you're having yourself.'

'If it's about the cow you sold to Edmund Reidy,' Flint fiddled with the empty glass. 'If you don't mind, I might just have another.' The second measure disappeared as quickly as the first.

'And would you swear before a court of law that you witnessed the transaction?'

'The law? ... I don't know ...' The sharp intake of breath was rewarded by another shot of Powers. '... But then again I might.'

'Halt!' The door swung open again.

'Michael Barrett!' Batt Mullane pounded into the bar and dropped his hand on Flint's shoulder. 'I'm arresting you in connection with the murder of Sergeant Laurence Stapleton.'

The farmer shoved himself between the law and its quarry. 'Will he get jail for that?'

'That and more, if there's any justice in this world.'

'Then it appears I've been took in by the lowest form of scoundrel. Constable. You give him the full rigours of the law.' He whipped the ten-shilling note from the counter and bounded out the door ahead of Batt and Flint.

'A free drink from Flint?' snorted Drug once quiet had returned. 'Nah. Too good to be true.'

Inside the day room of the barracks, ConstablesReilly, Walsh and McKenna waited for Sergeant Flaherty to detail the shift. In normal times, they would have been out already as the daily patrol of the Shanagolden area had been set in stone for over thirty years but, with ill-feeling exacerbated by the disturbances at the Newcastlewest fair, parts of the route were considered unsafe without a military escort.

And even if they did know where they were going, they'd still stick to the rulebook and drag out their departure as long as possible. The boycott, now in its second month, was beginning to wear them down and they were loath to leave the safety of their building. Even previous supporters like Councillor Hennessy or Doctor Molyneaux no longer wanted to be seen talking in public to members of the force.

So, as had been their custom since the turn of the year, they took their time about changing into uniform.

'Eejits!' McKenna raised his head from the newspaper. 'As if we hadn't enough trouble in Newcastle without them opening up on the crowd.' Always reading, he was, looking for the going price for pigs and cattle and searching for announcements of auctions. 'I can put up with it myself. But it's getting tough on the missus and the young ones.'

He rolled up the paper, stuffed it inside his civilian coat and reached for his boots. 'No, I've my mind made up. 'Tisn't worth it any more.'

'I was thinking of resigning myself but I can't afford it.' Old enough to be McKenna's father, Reilly pulled up his braces and took his tunic from the rack. 'Only another three years and I'll have the full pension.'

'Where's the polish gone?' Walsh rooted through the assortment of brushes and tins. 'You won't get another job that pays anything like this one.' The youngest of the trio, he had joined up eighteen months earlier when it looked as if conscription was about to be extended to Ireland. 'We're doing very well now since they gave us that big rise.'

'It still hasn't stopped the resignations.' McKenna straightened his back and caught his reflection in the window. 'I was thinking of Palestine. They're setting up a new police force out there.'

'That's even worse.' Reilly shaved enough thin slices of tobacco from his ounce plug to last him through the day and packed them into a leather pouch. 'You'll be got at from both sides.'

'At least it won't be your own crowd that's shooting at you.'

'What's the money like?' asked Walsh.

'As good as here after all the rises we got.' Hearing the footsteps in the hallway, McKenna closed the top button of his tunic. 'And it'll cost you nothing at all to live over there. It's all provided for.'

'Well, I wouldn't fancy it. I knew a few lads who were over in Mesopotamia with the Munsters and they were saying that the heat out in them parts would kill any white man no matter how healthy he was.' Dropping his voice, Reilly nodded towards the doorway. 'Watch it. Here comes Batt the Thresher.

'Christ, I thought he was on nights,' muttered McKenna.

Preceded by the handcuffed Flint, Batt marched into the room.

'Well, Batt, what have you Flint up for this time? Hold on, let me guess. Would he have sunk the Titanic?' McKenna turned to the suspect. 'You didn't, did you? By God but you're the dark one, Flint Barrett.'

Batt stared at his colleague with barely concealed disapproval. 'He'll be charged with murdering Sergeant Stapleton.'

Hannon and Walsh burst out laughing.

'Would you get out of it!' mocked McKenna.

'Go show him to the Sergeant, Batt.' suggested Reilly. 'We're too busy to deal with it ourselves at the moment.'

'Where in the name of God did they get him?' McKenna shut the door after the departing Batt and sat back on his chair. They'd get another few minutes before Flaherty got around to detailing the shift. And if Batt was being especially awkward with the sergeant, they might even stretch it out long enough not to have to go outside at all for the day.

'And then there's the fever out there as well, Martin.' Reilly figured out he'd get at least enough time to have a smoke. 'I heard it killed more of the Munsters than all the shots them Turks fired at them.'

'Aah, that's only talk, Francis. Palestine is nothing like Mesopotamia. Wasn't Our Lord born out there ...?'

Sergeant Flaherty was laboriously writing up his daybook when heard the knock on the door of his office. Everything had to be recorded for the military, or at least for this Major Forrester who now had overall authority over the district. Dates, times, places,

417

suspects, informers, expenses incurred and reasons why. All just to cover themselves, Inspector Sullivan had told him.

Well, if they wanted details, then details were what they were going to get. He started on his account of a side of bacon reported to have been stolen from Councillor Hennessy's shop, when the door rattled again. On the off-chance that it might be a superior, he hurriedly closed his tunic over the ample folds of his stomach.

'Yes?'

'Sir?' Constable Mullane's voice wafted through the keyhole.

'Just a minute.' One strap of the sergeant's braces had wormed its way out through the lower folds of his tunic. Just the sort of detail his visitor would immediately report to Forrester. He had to take the tunic off again in order to realign the suspension of his trousers. 'All right, Mullane. Come on in.'

His eyes clouded over with resignation when he saw Batt marching Flint into the office. 'What's it this time?'

'I've it on good authority that Barrett here was part of the gang who committed the atrocity.'

'Which one?'

'Which one? Why, killing Sergeant Stapleton, of course.'

'I see. Murder of a policeman in the course of his duty. Hmm. That is the most serious charge in the book. Death penalty and no questions about it.' The sergeant shook his head gravely. 'Well, Flint, what have you to say for yourself?'

'I never done no atrocity, sir.' Without being asked, Flint stepped forward and leaned with his cuffed hands against the desk. 'I never done no murdering Sergeant Stapleton, sir. I never done no sinking the Titanic either, sir.'

Flaherty waved his hand in dismissal. 'Oh, go on off with yourself.'

'The blessings of God on you, sir.' The suspect's head bobbed with furious gratitude. 'I done nothing, I swear before God ...'

'Just go, will you.'

Flint disappeared out the door past a furious Batt. 'And get someone to take those cuffs off you! They cost money!' Flaherty shouted after him.

'I'd good information, Sergeant ...'

'And I've better information, Mullane.' The sergeant closed the daybook in order to keep its contents away from Mullane's prying eyes. 'If you want to pull in Stapleton's killer, you can chase after Ned Reidy and Willie Hartnett ...'

'We're aware of them, sir ...'

'Jimmy McCarthy, Mossy Noonan, Dan Hourigan ...'

'We're on to them too, sir ...'

'And while you're at it, you might have a word with Patie Fitzgibbon and your brother Dick.'

'Dick?' Flaherty quite enjoyed the shock of his constable's reaction. 'That's not possible, Sergeant! He fought for his King and country.'

'Yes. And so did Flint, if you remember.'

Josie Reidy had spent most of the day inside the school with Philip Hurley going over documents and evidence submitted to them by parties to various disputes over land, payments, damages and inheritance. The schoolmaster had insisted that anyone using the Republican court should put down the main points of their argument on paper so that when the case came to an open hearing, the presiding officer could cut through the theatrics, the traded insults and the appeals to the gallery and go straight to the core of the argument.

It might have reduced the entertainment value but those availing of the system run by Dáil Éireann found it to be simpler, quicker and, on the whole, fairer than the courts of the British administration. Acceptance of the justice it meted out had contributed hugely to the credibility of the Irish Republic and many of those who had doubted whether the people of the country could run their own affairs without the guiding hand of the Empire were now changing their tune.

'There's no case at all here.' Josie rolled up the submission with the rest of the documents. 'He hasn't a leg to stand on.'

'Maybe he didn't put it down right.' Hurley pored over an Ordnance Survey map and traced the boundary between the townlands of Rathfarra and Dunmoylan. 'We could call him in and give him a hand to put it into words.'

'His problem isn't with his writing. It's just that he's chancing his arm. The will left the farm to his brother.' She tied the bundle of papers together with a string. 'And he doesn't deserve anything either. The brother ran the farm with his father while he was set up in business in Rathkeale.'

'Some people mightn't like it. He passed on a good few bob to the movement when we asked him.'

'And he's looking for ten times as much with this claim.'

The light was beginning to fade. 'We'd better finish up.' Hurley packed all the documents into a cupboard fitted into his desk. 'You might have some chance of getting through the curfew but I've got none at all.'

Once night fell, the military took over the town and, while the patrols mightn't turn up at all for a week or more, there was always the chance of being surprised in the dark. So far, they hadn't pulled in any woman for breaking the curfew although Josie wasn't sure whether that was a result of etiquette or that the authorities couldn't bring themselves to believing that the other half of the population was also actively involved in the Volunteers.

Twilight was usually the safest time of the day. Particularly on a Saturday, the peelers would be winding down and the military wouldn't be seen for at least another hour. As long as Batt Mullane wasn't still on the prowl, she might get a chance to see Willie. It had been more than two weeks since he'd last been in the town.

Her heart dropped when she saw the lantern bobbing on the other side of the street and then come across the road to cross her path. But even though she could pick out the helmet in the gathering gloom, the gait was slower, heavier and more deliberate than that of the terror of the town.

'A grand evening, Miss Reidy, thanks be to God.'

She ignored the approaching ConstableReilly.

Undeterred, he continued to look her straight in the eye. 'Tell Willie we've the names of seven suspects who raided the barracks in Foynes,' he whispered as he passed by. 'And make sure Dick Mullane and Patie Fitzgibbon get out of Shanagolden fast.'

31

WEEKS OF honest police work had gone into nailing Dick Mullane and Patie Fitzgibbon. District Inspector Sullivan made sure that all the pieces were in place before moving in on the two former soldiers and a unit of detectives was tailing them in the hope of leading the RIC to the leaders of the Fourth Limerick Brigade. But just as they were about to strike, the pair had disappeared into the night and not a trace of them had been seen ever since.

He'd gathered enough evidence to stand up in any court but now it was all useless. The force had leaked and fingers pointed to the Shanagolden barracks. Jarlath Flaherty put his hand up immediately, admitting that he'd inadvertently revealed their suspicions to one of his constables. And while Batt Mullane might not have tipped off his brother, any one of a dozen others could have put two and two together. McKenna was looking to get out, Walsh had only joined up for the money and to escape being sent off to France,Reilly might have been getting it in the ear from his missus who was a relation of Fitzgibbon, two of the others were known to be involved in the poitín trade in their spare time, a third was big into the horses and rumoured to be up to his ears in debt and a fourth was tipping around with a woman who wasn't his wife. Sullivan could have launched his own investigation but it would have taken up weeks of his time without any certainty of a result and might have well have the effect of driving more of them into contacting the rebels in an attempt to cover their backsides.

Anyway, it was only going to be a matter of time before confidentiality broke down. Months of social ostracism were having their effect, absenteeism had shot through the roof and entire barracks had resigned after their families had been contacted by the rebels. It wasn't beyond the bounds of possibility that some of those remaining had agreed to pass on information in return for protection and money and that a few were actively involved with the enemy.

Morale might have held had the RIC been in control of events. Local knowledge gained over years of patrols could have been used to separate hostile intent from harmless activity, to identify possible informants, to keep informal lines of contact open in case matters got out of hand but, when the Army couldn't be bothered to listen to those on the ground, even the most conscientous constable lost interest in his work.

Regardless of who the mole was, the force's credibility had been seriously damaged in West Limerick and even County Sub-Inspector Callaghan had distanced himself from the debacle. Although Sullivan had kept quiet about the extent of Flaherty's involvement, his insistence on the sergeant's appointment had left him tarred with the same brush of blame.

Major Forrester wasn't slow to remind him. 'Bad show you chaps failed to net Mullane and Fitzgibbon. Some of your men may have gone native, Inspector.'

'They were born native, Major. Just like myself and everyone else in the force.'

As midnight approached, activity in Newcstlewest was confined to the backrooms of pubs where only the most hardened drinkers were defying the curfew. A detail of soldiers waited at the bridge and a second at the Maiden Street entrance to the Square. Just a handful of lights, none more than pinpricks, broke the dark silence of Bridge Street.

Sullivan didn't particularly want to be around. This was a military operation carried out to whatever procedures the Army felt like using. It was also a chance for Forrester to rub the RIC's nose in the mud. And maybe that was the way to go about it. By adhering to the letter of the law, standard policing procedure had made little headway in the inspector's district against an opposition that had divorced itself completely from allegiance to the Crown. The rebels didn't even have to threaten retaliation against anyone in the community who might inform on them. Their very existence was enough to rekindle centuries of resistance to any form of civil authority.

But the military's effectiveness grated with Sullivan. If information could be squeezed out of detainees only by torture or by intimidation, then there was no difference between the authority that he stood for and that of the rebels. It was easy for soldiers who could accept an order without question, but policemen had to live with the consequences of their actions long after the army barracks had emptied. And judging by the rash of resignations, many of his colleagues could no longer see the point of upholding an increasingly resented regime.

'We are reliably informed that one of the criminals involved in the Foynes murder is in the town tonight,' he was being told.

'Who?'

'Need to know, Inspector, I regret to say.' Forrester touched his finger off the tip of his nose. 'Secrecy is a major issue.'

But it didn't stop the major calling a police constable up to the observation post behind the lorry. Batt Mullane smirked at Sullivan with the favoured arrogance of a rent boy as Forrester whispered into his ear.

'Are you sure won't you have a few crubeens before you go?' The landlord's wife lifted the lid off the pot hanging on a crane over the open fire, pulled the cured pigs' toes from the simmering water and dropped them in a bowl. Dan Hourigan let them cool for a minute while she went back into the kitchen to find some mustard.

'You don't have to come back from now on,' the landlord was telling him. 'They only needed to see you the once just to be sure that the money was going where it was intended.'

He wiped the first crubeen in the little plate of mustard and brought it to his lips.

'Herself has a great way of cooking them.' His host turned proudly to his wife. 'Isn't that right, Bridie?'

He'd never tasted anything like it. Just the right anount of give in the rind, plenty of chew without being tough; little strings of meat stretched between the bones to give substance to the grease and tenderness to the gristle; and a flavour salty enough to draw out a thirst but not so overpowering that it drowned out the herbs.

'I throws a few juniper berries into the pot,' she explained. 'A bacon curer in Limerick told me about it.'

He washed the saltiness down with the porter and bit into a warm slice of brown soda bread with the butter melting through it. After a week up in the hills with nothing to eat but hard tack, he would have settled for a lot less.

'But we'll need some way of getting it to ye,' the landlord continued. Dan had slipped through the cordon in order to

426

collect from the businessmen of Newcastlewest. Despite attempts at counter-persuasion by an active group of British ex-servicemen in the town, the majority gave willingly, some even enthusiastically and only a handful had refused. Maybe they were backing a winner but the IRA weren't complaining. Anyway, it made no difference to the contributors, as the amount handed over was equal to that saved by refusing to pay income tax to the British Government and most of it went into a loan scheme set up by Dáil Éireann to fund the Irish Republic.

'We could send someone down every month. Someone the authorities wouldn't be suspicious of.'

'Then I'd suggest ye get a woman to do it. They can hide things in places that the Crown Forces might be too shy to search. Would I be right, Bridie?'

'Indeed you would, Mikey.' The wife collected the discarded crubeen bones and tossed them into the fire. 'But you'd want a bould woman to do it. One with a look on her face that'd stop a peeler stone dead, if he ever had notions of laying his hands on her.'

She lifted the corner of the curtain and looked out into the lane. 'Anything stirring up your end, Mikey?'

'Divil a bit, Bridie.' Her husband peered out into the street through a crack in the shutters. 'But it might be better to avoid Maiden Street and Brewery Lane. Too many places for them to hide.'

She sprinkled the fingertips of Holy Water on Dan and insisted he bless himself for luck. 'May Saint Ita and Saint Senan bring God to your side, Dan Hourigan, and Saint Munchin as well. Now, you'd best be on your way before the man with the hooves catches up with you.'

He snuck out the back door, climbed over a wall into the backyard of the next house and edged out into an alley that led down to the quay of the river. If the military were still on patrol, they'd more than likely be around the Square and on the streets leading off it. He thought he caught a distant glimpse of movement to his right and visualised the outline of two sentries guarding the bridge but he couldn't be sure in the darkness.

Over on the other bank lay the main highway from Limerick to Killarney and its junction at the church with the Yellow Road, his safest route out of town. Still clinging to the shadow of the lane, he glanced once again up and down the length of the North Quay, not quite believing the stillness of the night. The bridge was as quiet as ever but the lightness in his belly was telling him not to chance it. Nor was it worth considering the footbridge down to his left.

The river plopped with the regular beat of footfall too light to be human and too heavy for a bird or a rat. He strained his ears to pick up a response but there was no reaction to the noise. Another sequence of plops was accompanied by a barely audible screech. An otter was patrolling his stretch of water.

Dan darted across the street and hid under a coal dray while he gave a last look before he vaulted over the quay wall. The Arra River, a tributary of the Deel that had been channelled into an ornamental feature of the town, was shallow from a dry spell and he landed on the slabs of a weir without disturbing the water. The silhouette against the flickering light from the castle confirmed his suspicions about the sentries.

All that separated him from safety were the ten paces across the river, the climb up the far bank and another twenty paces up to the Yellow Road. He forced himself to calm down, to soften his breathing from the harsh pants of anxiety and to listen again to what was around him.

The otter had gone. Still, languid and spent from the drought, the river made nary a sound. He eased one leg forward, dropped it a couple of feet into the water and swivelled the other silently ahead of the first. Another two silent paces and he was nearly halfway across but suddenly conscious of his exposure. Fighting the urge to dash into a rash splash, he moved his sodden feet forward with excruciating deliberation to the South Quay, pressed himself up against the wall and slowed his breath.

The current rippled against his thighs, too slow and too soft to break the meniscus of the surface. His hand spread out to unearth a fingerhold that might raise him from the water and found a crack in the masonry. Down at river level beneath it, a protrunding stone felt solid enough to take his weight.

He still couldn't hear another movement around him but the back of his mind refused to believe it. Another life force was intersecting his own, tickling his hopes of safety. Somebody somewhere was looking down on him, daring him to clamber up the bank and over the quay wall and present himself for arrest. And they had him cold. It was too late to turn around and go back.

Fingers found grips, one leg stepped on the stony outcrop, the other found a hole above big enough to accomodate his toes. His hands stretched out again, pulled his torso up to the steep grassy slope, grappled the curved outline of the top of the wall and held the tug of his body as he pivoted over it on the fulcrum of his groin. Landing soundlessly on his knees, he hid himself under the lee of a tree, let the river drip from his trousers and boots and and counted the seconds as he waited for them to come.

Twenty, thirty, forty. After a minute, he dared to hope that he might be safe, that the inexplicable fears within him were the result of being too long on the run. He wouldn't mind sitting the next visit out and leaving it to Jimmy or Mossy or Patie.

Just yards down the road lay the church and the turn-off leading from Newcastlewest to Monagea and Tournafulla. There might still be an army post on the road but it was on the edge of the town and surrounded by fields offering alternative routes. Crouching like a sprinter, he shot across the road to the beckoning welcome of safety.

Lights shone. Whistles sounded. Lorries screeched into position from both ends of the road and turned on their headlights. Rifles raised with lethal intent, a company of soldiers closed in on him from three sides. A British officer forced himself forward between them. 'Is this Hourigan?' he asked.

'That's him,' confirmed Batt Mullane, illuminated with the triumph of capture. 'That's the murdering bastard who done for Sergeant Stapleton.'

'Informing on your own,' Dan hissed back at the policeman. 'You'll pay for that some day, Batt Mullane.'

The officer lifted his pistol. Barely a foot separated he tip of the barrel from his face. Dan braced himself for the worst. He hadn't come armed, figuring out that if he was spotted, he hadn't a hope anyway.

'What the hell are you doing?' shouted a voice behind him. 'We might get something out of him if we get a chance to interrogate him.'

The tension eased on the gun. The officer's lip curled into a smile. 'Perhaps you're right, Inspector.'

Dan exhaled. Then the arm stiffened again, the barrel trembling slightly as the finger itched against the trigger. He closed his eyes. But the shot never came. Instead, hands grabbed his, slid under his coat, down his sleeves, around his waist, along the legs of his trousers.

'Got something here!' exclaimed an English accent. 'Coo ... must be over a hundred pounds here.'

430

'That's evdence. That's government property,' pointed out the voice of the inspector.

'Like hell it is. Share it out amongst yourselves, chaps.' With Dan now handcuffed, the officer returned the pistol to its holster. 'Hourigan. You're about to sing like a canary.'

'It's your choice, Dan. Everybody is behind you.' Guarded by two soldiers, Mary Hourigan sat by her brother in the infirmary of Limerick Jail. Strapped to the bed, Dan's drawn face looked blankly up at her. Into the fifth week of his hunger strike, she couldn't tell whether he was listening to her or whether he had lapsed into delirium.

'And if you come off the strike, no one will think the worse of you.' She reached out her hand to touch her brother's face but one of the guards grabbed it. 'Lay your hand off me, you hireling!' she snarled at him. He jumped back at the ferocity of her voice and, somewhere buried beneath his weapons and uniform, she could see twitches of the soldier's discomfort.

'Ned and Willie told me they'd understand', she whispered. 'There's no honour lost if you want to save yourself.' She fancied that she'd seen a flicker of recognition. The other soldier was edging closer to overhear but she froze him with the venom of her glance.

But what would he save himself for? Once they'd given up on trying to extract information from him, a court-martial had sentenced Dan to death but a series of appeals, intervention by the American Government during negotiations regarding the rescheduling of Britain's war debts and a wobble between the various factions in the administration had delayed execution of the warrant. While they continued to argue, Dan had upped the ante and refused to take food, insisting that, if the British occupiers of his country were going to execute him, he be shot like a soldier rather than hanged like a criminal.

As Dáil Éireann organised candle-lit vigils outside the jail and priests denounced from the pulpit the barbarity of sending a man starving to death to the scaffold, the military authorities grappled with the conundrum of how to bring their prisoner back to full health so that they could then hang him in a manner that befitted his crime.

'I won't give in,' he wheezed to his sister. 'Better to die from the hunger than to swing from an Englishman's gallows.'

A military hand came down on her shoulder, apologetic rather than demanding, and she allowed herself to be turned away and out of the cell. There was still the chance that his sentence might be commuted, that Éamon de Valera might mobilise Irish-American outrage to bring pressure on the American Government which would in turn open the splits in Lloyd George's coalition, that prisoners might be released in another attempt at brokering peace in Ireland. But argument was wasted on Dan. He was hell-bent on becoming a martyr.

Respectful silence greeted Mary as she stepped out the gate. Mulgrave Street was dappled with flickering candles. A newspaper reporter attempted to approach her but withered away when he felt the silent disapproval of the crowd. Detectives lurking at the entrance to Shaw's bacon factory thought about following her but changed their minds when they realised how prominent their exposure might be.

'Hail Mary, full of grace, the Lord is with thee ...' The priest resumed the Rosary. Thousands of mostly female voices in the kneeling vigil murmured the responses in a low-pitched rumble that sounded as if it had come from the bowels of the earth.

Waiting at the corner with Cathedral Place, Josie Reidy took Mary by the hand and they walked past the shuttered shops and pubs of William Street, Cornwallis Street and Nelson Street until they reached the sanctuary of the railway station.

Yielding to pressure from Dublin Castle, the Army summoned County Sub-Inspector Callaghan to the jail. Fearful of a repeat of the disturbances that followed two years previously when Thomas Ashe died from a ruptured gullet after an attempt at force-feeding, the authorities insisted on the presence of a senior policeman to prevent the military from making another pig's ear of a delicate situation.

'The eyes of the world are watching us,' the Inspector-General himself had told him. 'There are dozens of American reporters in Europe waiting to return home after the Peace Conference. We cannot give them the wrong story.'

'And what do you suggest we do? Hang him now? Let him starve? Force-feed him and then hang him?'

'I will leave that to your better judgement,' replied the IG from the safety of the force's headquarters in Dublin's Phoenix Park. 'Just make sure that we are not faced with another mass funeral and the wrath of the public upon us.'

The car was waiting for him at the station as he arrived back from the capital to the unfamiliar silence of Limerick. Black ribbons adorned poles and lamp posts and hung behind windows. A large banner ran down the facade of a grain store at the top of William Street proclaiming support for Dan Hourigan. The numbers attending the vigil outside the jail were increasing by the day.

Although many had been coerced into showing defiance, majority sentiment in a city that had declared its own soviet just months before, was clearly lined up against an authority which had appointed the sub-inspector as its visible representative. Watching the stony faces greet his arrival outside the jail,

433

Callaghan was painfully aware that he was on his own. If the civilian arm of the administration had any conviction about imposing themselves on the military, they would have sent down one of the heavy hitters instead of a policeman of a rank four rungs below the head of the force. The most a representative of his standing could achieve was a fig leaf of protest to which his superiors might point in case any awkward questions were asked in Westminster.

One of the press pack intercepted him as he stepped from his police car through the decades of the Rosary. 'Are we looking at a resolution, Commissioner?' The accent was distinctly transatlantic.

Callaghan brushed the question aside but the reporter was blessed with a persistence unknown in Irish newspaper circles. 'This is a big story Stateside, Commissioner. What can I say to the folks back home?'

'Nothing.'

The gate rescued him. Inside the prison walls, the brightest lights shone from the infirmary.

'Why wasn't Hourgian moved across the road?' he asked the governor leading him up the stairs and past a series of doors guarded by warders with big iron keys.

'The soldiers were afraid that the IRA might try to spring him from the City Hospital. So they brought the doctors and nurses across at gunpoint. I don't think they're enjoying their experience in our humble home.'

Down at the end of the long gloomy corridor, a colonel was having little luck as he tried to impose his will on the medical staff. Regardless of what rank he might hold, no soldier was going to tell them what to do and they all but pushed him out of the isolation ward in which the starving prisoner lay.

'Forrester!' shouted the exasperated officer. 'Inform them that this is a military situation. Impress upon them that security outweighs all other considerations.'

The major pulled out his pistol and waved it at the dissenters. A channel opened up and the colonel re-entered the ward. Forrester stood guard at the door to discourage others, and especially Callaghan, from following.

'If you chaps hadn't interfered, this problem would have been dealt with weeks ago.'

'With a drumhead execution?' The policeman sighed with frustration. 'We saw where those got us after the Rising.'

'Oh, poppycock! The niceties of the courtroom are wasted on bandits.'

'Why not?' Callaghan recognised the futility of being drawn into argument but the sneering, half-demented arrogance had provoked him. 'A grieving widow, six orphaned children, a good Irish Catholic who always remained true to his faith. There was plenty of sympathy to be got out of Sergeant Stapleton if his murder had been worked right.'

A flurry of movement behind him distracted Forrester, who turned to glance inside the ward. 'Rather a moot point now, Inspector. This Hourigan chap appears quite intent on death by starvation.'

Callaghan followed the major up to a bed upon which Dan Hourigan was strapped. Eyes closed behind protruding lids, features gaunt and stretched, skin sallow and breathing laboured and shallow, the prisoner appeared marooned between life and death and oblivious to the presence of Forrester, the colonel, the doctor, the nurse and the orderly surrounding him.

'He's been like that for the past week,' the doctor told Callaghan. 'And he could stay that way for another month. You never can tell how long they'll last when their bodies start to eat up their organs.'

'I'll be damned if we wait that long,' spluttered the colonel.

'And we shan't.' Forrester clicked his fingers. Shoving the medical staff out of the way, a trolley wheeled up beside the bed. One soldier clamped the prisoner's lips with bulldog clips, the second rammed a rubber tube up each of his nostrils.

'What are you doing?' The doctor tried to regain his bedside position but was physically restrained by Forrester. 'I cannot recommend this course of action,' he appealed to the colonel. 'Anything could happen.'

'Spare your concerns, Doctor.' The major produced his pistol and waved it. 'Just make sure that this criminal is in a fit state for his hanging.'

'I must insist ...' The doctor's feeble show of defiance ended when the barrel of the gun was pressed to his temple.

'Force the food into him!' shouted Forrester. 'Do you hear me? That's an order!'

The doctor and the orderly jumped to it, one depressing the food pump, the other spasmodically removing and replacing the tubes to give the prisoner a chance to draw breath. But the nurse was made of sterner stuff and resolutely refused to co-operate. Pistol drawn, Forrester advanced towards her but Callaghan placed his body between them.

The stand-off was interrupted by a retching cough. The major turned around to see the liquid mush explode out the corners of Dan Hourigan's mouth. His face reddened with fury.

'Keep it up!' he roared at the orderly. 'Give him a bellyfull!'

Blood spurted from the prisoner's lips.

'Doctor! He's choking,' screamed the nurse. 'We have to turn him over!' She jumped forward to remove the tube. The doctor unbuckled the straps.

'Leave him!' Forrester pushed them aside. 'Leave him, I tell you!'

'Colonel!' The doctor found a second wind of resistance. 'This ...'

'He's playing silly buggers, you fool!'

'I think he's dead,' said the nurse behind the major.

All eight of them inside the ward swooped over the prisoner. Blood and vomit covered his face and his neck. The chest was no longer moving. The nurse grabbed his wrist and tried to find a pulse. The doctor unwound his stethoscope and tapped it over the heart.

'He's gone.'

Turning smartly on his heel, Forrester followed his colonel out of the ward. 'Stupid bastard,' he sneered as he closed the door on the corpse behind him.

Dan had heard the voices around him, had felt the frenzy of activity, had gagged on the slurry of mush pouring through his nasal cavities, down his gullet and into his stomach. The pain didn't matter any more. He was long past it.

Something had switched on his lungs. They were coughing like never before. And up the length of his windpipe, a viscous heat erupted to close off the last remnants of air to reach him.

Death was tapping his shoulder before they could get the chance to hang him. He'd seen them to the showdown and he had them beat. John Bull and his agents had killed him and they'd have to live with the consequences.

But the moment of triumph disappeared in the instant of its realisation. Down the long white tunnel he saw every moment of his twenty-five years pass by. And when he came to its end where he was beckoned to cross the great divide, the final memory of his time on earth was the last morsel of food to pass his lips, the best crubeens he'd ever tasted in his short life.

32

THE LIGHTS of the infirmary dimmed. The crowd outside on Mulgrave Street immediately took to their knees and the wailing decades of Hail Marys floated over the wall and up the flight of stairs to where the body lay. Within the hour, the undertaker arrived and brought his hearse to the gate.

'I have been instructed by the deceased's next-of-kin to receive the body,' he informed the sentry. The hatch shut without an answer. The curious rose from their prayers and crowded around the glass-panelled carriage drawn by a pair of black-plumed horses.

The governor himself delivered the request.

'You can take him away. I've completed my post-mortem.' The doctor handed Sub-Inspector Callaghan a sheet of paper. 'Death due to asphyxiation from internal bleeding caused by force-feeding through an externally applied rubber tube.'

'He starved himself to death.' Major Forrester tried to grab the death certificate but the policeman refused to release it. 'Write out a new certificate!'

'Get yourself another doctor.' The medic packed his instruments into his bag.

'About the body ...' interrupted the governor.

'They can't have it.' Forrester signalled to a soldier standing in the corridor. 'It's the property of His Majesty. The prisoner was under sentence of death. He will be buried in an unmarked grave inside the walls of this prison.'

'They'll get fair sour outside if they hear that,' muttered the orderly.

'Take it away!' barked the major.

'Where, sir?' asked the soldier.

'Anywhere. Just find some place and dig a hole.'

Nobody lifted a finger as the sentry laboriously unbuckled the straps.

'Get one of your chaps to help him.'

'Not our job,' answered the governor. 'And we don't have any shovels in the jail either.'

Forrester approached the body, then shrank back when he saw Dan Hourigan's dead mouth flop open and heard a trapped wheeze of air laugh back at him. The soldier dropped the buckle and fled from the room.

'By Jesus, I'd say he's cursed you.' The orderly leaned back against the wall and lit up a cigarette. The doctor and nurse walked out into the corridor unhindered. The colonel froze with indecision.

'And he'd curse anyone else that'd try to bury him as a common criminal,' continued the orderly. 'I've heard quare stories in my time of dead bodies haunting those that would interfere with them. They never let up. Never. Not till your dying days.'

'Superstitious rubbish!' But there was no one at hand to share the major's conviction.

Then the pounding began. The thousands gathered outside stamped their feet in time and Callaghan, the colonel, the governor, Forrester and everyone else inside the jail shook to the seismic rumble of anger.

The row over Dan Hourigan's remains took centre stage when American newspapers carried graphic accounts of the scenes outside the jail and a monster gathering filled Chicago's Soldiers' Field to hear President of the Irish Republic Éamon de Valera rail against the British occupation of his country. Incensed by the hostile reaction just as Britain's image in the land of its paymasters was recovering from the Amritsar massacre in India, Lloyd George and Chief Secretary Ian Macpherson over-rode Conservative objections and wrested control of Irish affairs back from the Army. Forrester was identified as the scapegoat, although his punishment amounted to no more than removal from direct military command to an advisory post on secondment to the RIC.

So when the body was handed over to the Hourigan family, crowds lined every step of its journey along the Coast Road. Thousands gathered in the town of Askeaton and in the villages of Kildimo and Mungret and even more at Robertstown Cross as the hearse crawled its way through prayer and lamentation to Shanagolden. They arrived from all over West Limerick to pay their respects as Dan was laid out in the parlour of the family farmhouse and waked through two nights and two days. And when the sons of the parish carried him on a relay of shoulders over the entire mile and a half of the removal, every leading figure in Nationalist Ireland who wasn't on the run was waiting in the church to greet him.

Down the road from the funeral Mass, almost every policemen in the district had been called up and instructed to keep a respectable distance between themselves and the mourners.

'We've too many here.' Sergeant Flaherty ran his eye over the hundred-odd constables lined up in military formation. 'Too big a chance of somone losing his head.'

'We had to turn up in strength.' District Inspector Sullivan was aware that their presence was likely to inflame an already volatile situation. But he had his orders. 'Otherwise the military would have intervened.'

He was even less certain of the mood of the men under his command as they watched the killers of Sergeant Stapleton gather openly around the church in broad daylight. Emotions ran from those seeking revenge, to discomfort at being got at from every side, to sneaking regard for the enemy. Even though the rash of resignations had removed most of those whose loyalty or whose resolve was open to question, it still had to run its course as the unending boycott wore them down. Reduced to holding up shopkeepers at gunpoint to buy the basic necessities for themselves and their families, their alienation from the nation around them was almost total.

If he had been an optimist by nature, Sullivan might have hoped that the show of strength would bolster morale, but three years of wildly fluctuating policy had robbed him of any confidence in the future. All the RIC could do was to grin and bear it while those above them argued the toss; then do their best to pick up the pieces.

Thirty masked IRA Volunteers formed a guard of honour as the tricolour-draped coffin came out of the church on the shoulders of Willie Hartnett, Ned Reidy, Mossy Noonan, Jimmy McCarthy, Dick Mullane and Patie Fitzgibbon. Marching down the hill towards the bridge behind a lone piper's lament, they turned their eyes and their raised rifles at the RIC massed on the bank and faced them down.

Dan's passing had removed all remaining ambiguities. Cheated out of carrying out the death sentence imposed on him, the Crown Forces were certain to execute any of the six surviving members of the Foynes raiding party they might come across, without bothering with the formalities of the law. Nor was there any point in hiding their faces as their names were known and photographs of them taken from the John Joe Snaps's picture of the Shanagolden football team had been plastered all over the county on Wanted posters.

On this one occasion when they were protected from capture by the sheer force of numbers, Willie wanted the peelers to see them in the flesh as their living, breathing enemy leading an armed and uniformed IRA column, to see a procession of tens of thousands following them, to see the momentum of rule pass from their hands. He wanted those in the service of the King of England to understand that they no longer carried any authority in Shanagolden, or in any other part of County Limerick. He wanted them to know that they were an alien force in a land that had cast off its shackles to pledge its allegiance to the Irish Republic.

And he needed the public display of defiance. For all the activity of the Republican courts, the boycott and the collection of revenue to fund the parallel administration of the Republic, the IRA had yet to show an ability to impose their physical authority on the territory they claimed as their own. But so far, the military campaign had consisted of little more than occasional and disjointed attacks on unoccupied barracks and courthouses and, while it had resulted in the agents of British rule abandoning their most remote outposts, the Fourth Limerick Brigade needed to keep piling on the pressure in order to maintain the faith of their supporters.

The silent standoff lasted over a minute. Down at the end of the front line, a constable cracked, removed his helmet, threw it on the ground and melted into the crowd of cheering mourners. Satisfied with the token victory, Willie turned his eyes on the Inspector who held him firmly in his gaze. They nodded imperceptibly at one another, like boxers acknowledging that the fight was on, before the coffin-bearers continued their march over the bridge and up over the hump halfway down the main street. Behind them, mourners turned stony stares on Batt Mullane. Some dragged an outstretched finger across their throats as they passed him.

Down the slope they went past Jack Noonan's, past Hennessy's, past shop and bar, past terrace and cottage, past slate roof and tin roof and thatch. The same six shoulders bore Dan on his last journey through Shanagolden, the wailing pipes filling the wide street of closed doors and leading the rhythmic time of the gigantic funeral party through the crossroads, past the creamery and up to the cemetry around the Protestant church. In through the gates, they stepped up to a freshly dug grave between the headstones of countless generations of families that had peopled the town since it had been founded by the sixteenth-century Elizabethan Plantation after the Desmond Rebellion had been crushed.

Mourners followed them into the graveyard and, after they had covered every square inch inside the walls, those that couldn't be accomodated gathered on the road outside, spilling up the hill along the Demesne road and the Ballyhahill road and down the slope to the crossroads. When they had settled to join in on the last prayers and to listen to the graveside orations, the RIC took the opportunity to edge closer but couldn't get any nearer than the foot of the main street.

Still restlessly looking around for any sign of trouble, Willie heard Ned pledging that Dan's sacrifice would never be forgotten and that the fight for which he gave his life would not cease until the last invader's boot had left Irish soil. He caught the booming message of Micheal Collins, Minister for Finance and leader of the IRB as it carried beyond the crowd to taunt the RIC constables to resign and return to the nation of Ireland. All for show, but the stirring words of resistance had impressed the crowd.

As the gravediggers lowered the coffin down by the ropes, Willie called the guard of honour to position. Twenty-one guns fired into the air. The crowd remained standing to attention while he handed the tricolour and Dan's beret and gloves to his mother.

The constable's desertion pierced the RIC command like a hot arrow. Inspector Sullivan, Sergeant Flaherty and the eight other sergeants of the district kept their emotions under control but each of them knew that the force had been humiliated. Any chance of playing the incident down disappeared when a cinecamera rolled as the helmet bounced off the ground.

Sullivan watched Collins, the three dozen in the colour party and other leading Limerick IRA leaders Seán Finn, Dinny Hannigan, Seán Wall, Michael Colivet, Jim Colbert and Garrett McAuliffe disappear into the crowd once the coffin had been swallowed up by the grave. Without their uniforms and with their heads covered against the thickening drizzle, they'd be next to impossible to identify among the tens of thousands of mourners. And even if his policemen did pick one of them out, they'd be on a hiding to nothing.

The crowd rubbed it in as they spilled out through the gates of the graveyard and flowed back across the crossroads towards the main street. Taunts of 'coward!', 'traitor!', 'hireling!' and 'runner!' were flung at them with a venom fired up by the rituals of death and by the incendiary eulogy of Ned Reidy. Standing firm at the end of the line like the last defender of the Empire, Batt Mullane bore the brunt of the abuse. Behind him, a second constable gave up the ghost, removed his tunic and drifted in his vest through the drizzle like a sleepwalker towards the rapturous tide of mourners.

'Come back!' shouted Batt but his words were drowned out by the jeers.

'Count your days, you turncoat.' The mourner aimed his finger between the constable's eyes. 'You don't have too many of them left.'

Batt was about to swat the outstretched hand away when he caught sight of Willie Hartnett, Mossy Noonan and Jimmy McCarthy darting among the crowd.

'There's three of them over there!' he shouted to his colleagues. 'We could take them out now!'

'What do you want? Start a bloodbath?' whispered Constable Walsh beside him. 'We'd have to kill hundreds of mourners before we'd even get near them.'

'Even your pals in the military aren't that stupid,' muttered ConstableReilly.

'They murdered Sergeant Stapleton.'

Footsteps stopped to hear Batt's shouting.

'And now you're after seeing how many of them want to murder us, you stupid fool.' Walsh stared straight ahead over the gathering hostility.

'By Jesus, I'm wondering which side you're on, Walsh.'

'I'm covering my arse, that's what I'm doing.'

'And 'twould be an awful lot easier if toadies like you weren't running off and telling tales to British Army officers who haven't a notion about what's going on over here,' addedReilly.

Seeing Jimmy McCarthy drift away from the others and pass within twenty yeards of the RIC column, Batt moved forward and raised his carbine. 'McCarthy! Give yourself up!'

The crowd parted ahead of the gunsights. Jimmy turned to flee.

A single shot rang out.

'Oh Holy Mother of God!' shrieked the woman standing beside Batt as he fell to the ground, blood spurting from the hole in the corner of his forehead and dripping down over the surprise locked onto his face.

Like a giant concertina, the mass of mourners swayed away in fright and swayed back in curiosity. But the body rated no more than a fleeting glance. Once the onward movement restarted, they filed past the dying constable as if he had never existed. Only the cinematographer took any notice, scurrying around his subject to find the most graphic angle from which to capture his passing.

Not a word was uttered to break up the monotonous pounding of boots on road. A third constable detached from his colleagues and melted into the crowd. The Inspector turned to the sergeants who swivelled their silent heads towards the men under their command. The entire ranks of the police stood impassively to attention as their colleague breathed his last.

'We'll have to abandon Shanagolden,' Sullivan told Flaherty once the last straggling mourner had moved on and the cameraman had folded up his tripod. 'Tell your men they're being transferred to Newcastle.'

Dick Mullane rose from his knee, Patie Fitzgibbon took the rifle from him, passed it to the relay of Volunteers who would hide it from capture and the pair of them had already slipped into the moving crowd before any prying police eye had turned to seek out the source of the shot. Passing within yards of the peelers, Patie watched the frustration smoulder under the rigid faces, many of whom recognised him but knew that there was absolutely nothing they could do except grin and bear the humiliation.

During four years at the Front, he'd never felt any personal animosity towards the Germans. Sure, he'd be as fired up as the rest of them when they went over the top to shoot and slash any living body that got in their way but, when the fury in his belly had been quenched, he'd understand that it had been either himself or the enemy in a straight contest for survival.

But the hunger strike had changed his perspective. The bullying pettiness about the attempt to grind Dan Hourigan into humiliation filled Patie with a rage that he had never experienced during the war. No matter how bad things got in Flanders, the sides always afforded each other a grudging respect, but there was none of that present on his home patch. As far as the authorities were concerned, any Irishman who lifted a gun in defence of his own was a lesser breed who could never be considered a soldier.

So he cheered Dan's refusal to bend, even to the point of his death. He saw his escape from the hangman as a victory, as a trophy that had been whipped away from the British. As far as Patie was concerned, the other side had made this war into a personalised struggle where point scoring was as important as the casualty count, where the level of defiance rather than the expanse of territory held was the true measure of success.

And the RIC were the first line of opposition. Unlike the millions whom the tides of emotion, of conformity or of regulation had washed up in the trenches, the peelers had been given the choice. They could either throw their lot in with their own people or they could continue to beat them down them in the name of a foreign power. So when Batt dropped from Dick's single shot, Patie felt not a moment of remorse over the death of a former team-mate and a comrade-in-arms with whom he'd shared the horrors of the trenches.

A policeman parted from the ranks, threw his helmet away and fell in with the marching mourners. Another small triumph, a further chink in the enemy armour. Patie stared at the twitching faces, daring more of the peelers to follow their colleague.

Although wilting under the weight of the naked hostility, the rest of the line held firm. A few eyes drifted towards Patie, seeing the real soldier in him, one who had come through the bloodiest battles ever fought on God's earth, rather than a drunken lout bragging of his exploits in an ex-servicemens' bar who'd never been within miles of the action. He should have been on their side, they were thinking, and now they realised that he was not.

Away from the immediate vicinity of the enemy, the surge of his emotions sagged and he suddenly felt the clammy heat of the day. Squeezed out by the tension, the mist and the overcoat covering his Volunteer uniform, the sweat gushed from his pores as he followed the crowd up the main street to Jack Noonan's.

As cool as a cucumber, Dick opened the door ahead of Patie into the crowded bar. Conversation died instantly as the customers realised who had entered and a pathway opened up immediately to the counter.

'Knock it back, Dick.' Jack had two glasses ready and filled them with whiskey. 'I'd say you need it.'

A stool emptied in front of him. Dick slumped down and dropped half of his jorum down his throat. Patie leaned up against the bar beside him. The heads turned slowly away from the man who had just killed his brother and the babble cautiously resumed.

Neither Dick nor Patie was in the mood for conversation. Instead, they stared straight ahead over the harried heads of Jack, Mossy and Molly at the enamelled signs and the bevelled mirrors advertising various brands of beer, tobacco and whiskey, at the yellowing labels of the empty bottles on the top shelf, at the ponderous pendulum of the clock swinging the afternoon towards evening.

'I'll have to break it to my mother myself.' Dick downed the rest of his glasss. 'But I doubt if she'll understand.' He rose from his stool, shoved his hands deep into the pockets of his coat and trudged out the door on his own.

33

THE NEWSREEL of death and defection turned up in cinemas all over the world and denunciation was swift and varied. On the floor of the House of Commons, MPs thundered about this new low in Fenian barbarity and, on Fleet Street, press barons screamed for immediate retribution. But in the neighbourhoods of Irish-America, the drama was viewed as the fruits of Saxon oppression and in Germany as proof of British double standards. Like Fiume, Teschen, Amritsar and other unknown towns on the faultlines of empires, Shanagolden flickered for a few weeks on the troubled map of 1919.

Even though the British government had more serious issues on its plate, not least the systematic assassination of its most effective detectives, Shanagolden was its most public problem and earned itself the biggest diversion of resources. Martial law was slapped on every police district west of the River Deel and an entire brigade of the Army, complete with armoured cars, tenders, two reconaissance aircraft and a quartet of tanks, was dispatched from Dublin to restore law and order and bring the bandits to book.

Faced with universal hostility, the all-military response got nowhere. After a month of ineffective patrols, even the signed-on-for-life squaddies were muttering mutiny as they were thrown into a conflict that they neither understood nor were trained for. Fighting rebels was one thing but endlessly trashing houses, searching women and children and torching farmyards, creameries and businesses in a futile search for arms and fugitives had corroded morale and left many of them wondering why they'd ever enlisted in the first place. The enemy that they'd been ordered to root out remained hidden in the shadows of the sour damp landscape broken only by bleak unforgiving villages and their squinting windows.

So the Army wound down its campaign and, despite lurid newspaper headlines claiming the mission to be a major victory over the peddlers of terror, they retreated to the garrison of Limerick under the same cloud of failure as the police before them. The order proclaiming the Special Military District was allowed to lapse for a third time and the RIC was again ordered out to clean up the mess. Unlike their earlier interventions, however, they had far less success on this occasion. Stretched in numbers and shattered in morale, the best they could achieve was to send out the rare mass patrol on bicycles before retiring to a few selected barracks, where they kept their contact with the public to a minimum.

Weekly reports made their way up to the rarified rooms of Dublin Castle and the absence of any sensational activity swept everything under the carpet until an independent inspection demanded by the Inland Revenue, the Post Office and the Department of Local Government shattered the complacency. Accounts of a total breakdown of British civil administration found their way across to London, questions were asked in the House and decisive action was demanded against the illegal Sinn Féin state operating under the noses of the authorities.

Another conference was called and the various tentacles of His Majesty's rule apportioned blame for the fiasco in equal measure to the rifle of the soldier and to the baton of the policeman. It was then tacitly agreed not to bring the matter up again until the next bureaucratic war. Once the proceedings were duly recorded, the civilians retired to the privacy of their offices and left the security forces in peace to come up with their own unofficial solution.

Down in the trenches of Newcastlewest's Desmond Castle, the exchanges were less cordial. The amiable military commander, a decorated veteran of two wars who made every effort to co-operate with the RIC and tried not to antagonise the locals, was replaced by a choleric senior officer from the Miltary Foot Police.

Colonel Guthrie-Shaw rested his chin on his clasped hands as he read an open file in front of him. 'Murdered one of your men right in front of your eyes ...' He raised his head in disapproval. 'And you did absolutely nothing about it.'

County Sub-Inspector Callaghan and District Inspector Sullivan were pointedly not asked to sit down. Such comforts were reserved for the colonel's sidekick flanking him behind the desk. The unsinkable Major Forrester had returned from rebuke and clucked over the damning details of the document. 'Extraordinary,' he sighed. 'Most extraordinary.'

Breaking the discipline of a lifetime, Callaghan folded his arms to signal his independence from military command until the appearance of the next order proclaiming martial law. 'There was nothing Inspector Sullivan could have done without his entire force being lynched by the mob.'

'So now the rabble is running the show?' Unaccustomed to hearing his statements answered, the colour rose in Guthrie-Shaw's face. 'Spineless, that's what I call it. You people have surrendered to mayhem.'

Other than a clumsy attempt to demonstrate who was in charge, Sullivan failed to see the point of raking over a three-month-old report. The force's difficulties on the ground had moved on in the meantime. Brute military force had driven the population into the arms of the opposition and, when they had the problem dumped back on their laps, the RIC hadn't been given the manpower to isolate the rebels from their supporters.

But try to explain that to an MP Provost-Marshal whose wartime experience consisted of rounding up stragglers at the tail of the advance and executing them to dissuade others from deserting.

'If you please, sir.' Forrester coughed to gain the attention of his superior. 'The Constablulary cannot be trusted to impose order. There are Sinn Féin sympathisers at every level.'

'Damn right there are!' The colonel reached into his briefcase. Still folding his arms, Callaghan yawned at the futile theatrics. Sullivan cupped his hand over his chin as he watched the sidekick quiver with anticipation.

'But we'll soon see about that, eh.' Guthrie-Shaw waved the document in triumph. 'Fact is, martial law has been reimposed over all of County Limerick west of the Maigue. Inspector Callaghan, your entire force is now under our command.'

'And your policemen will be reinforced by special reserve units who will report directly to us,' added Forrester.

'You're welcome to them, Colonel.' Callaghan waved his hand as if he was tossing a beaten docket aside at a racecourse. 'But I might as well tell you, we've already pulled out of every station between here and the Kerry border.' He headed for the door. 'Come on, Nicholas, let's not detain these war heroes of the rear any longer. They have to plan the conquest of West Limerick.'

454

Sullivan followed him, then turned around for a parting shot. 'And you won't get much use out of the barracks either. Most of them have been blown up.'

Although they were still visited by the occasional patrol, both the RIC and the Army had withdrawn their active presence from most of the area covered by the IRA's Fourth Limerick Brigade. But Willie Hartnett was certain that it was only a temporary retreat. Once the Crown Forces sorted themselves out, they'd be back in greater numbers than ever. Dan Hourigan's funeral was a setback too public for the Dublin Castle authorities to ignore and, while forces loyal to Dáil Éireann had taken over the civil administration of the area, they needed a credible military force to back them up.

Able to move about freely for the first time in over a year, he set about reorganising the brigade. While they had more than enough Volunteers, they were short of firepower, as the ammunition captured in Foynes ran down and a steady trickle of arms was either captured, lost or damaged beyond use. Whenever they pulled back, the peelers had been cute enough not to leave a single weapon behind and, without a functioning barracks to attack, the IRA had been left without any means of replenishing their arsenal.

So they were better off using what they had to the maximum effect. Their comrades in the east of the county had shown them the way. Rather than calling out local Volunteers on haphazard missions whenever someone got it into his head to attack the barracks in the town, the First Limerick Brigade had set up a full-time unit of over twenty members, which would plan its missions in advance in order to tie down as many of the Crown Forces as possible. Living off the land, sheltered in a network of safe houses and avoiding towns and crossroads wherever possible, the flying column could move up to twenty-five miles a day and draw the enemy into the futile chase of a quarry that never stood still.

The Fourth Brigade had the bones of a column in the six survivors of the Foynes raid who had been on the run for the best part of a year, and Willie had identified another two dozen who had the toughness and the personal discipline to take to life in the hills. Putting them all together with Dick Mullane and Patie Fitzgibbon training them in the real arts of soldiering, they had the resources to plan at least one major operation a month, as well as engaging in minor attacks whenever the opportunity arose.

'It won't be as easy here,' Ned Reidy was telling him as they looked over an abandoned cottage up a secluded laneway off the road between Shanagolden and Ballyhahill. 'We don't have the same places to hide in.'

It was the best base that they could find for the moment. Their area didn't offer the mountains of East Limerick to retreat to or the laneways of Limerick City to get lost in. Bare uplands, rolling meadows and small towns where everyone stood out like a sore thumb weren't the natural terrain of guerrilla fighters. But they knew the land better than any soldier or policeman and, well removed from any road access, the wide spaces scoured by streams, and covered by bullrushes and scrub could be turned to their advantage.

'You can't see this place from the road,' Willie pointed out. Shrouded in ivy and briars, hidden behind a grove of bushes and its roof under a carpet of sods, the house had merged back into the landscape that surrounded it. But it was dry inside with its own supply of water, a working fireplace and a cellar with enough space for half the column to sleep in relative comfort. The only giveaway was the lingering aroma of malt and turf

456

smoke that met anyone coming within twenty yards. 'The Excise spent years looking for it and never found it.'

'Where's he operating from now?'

'God only knows.' Without even being asked, Drug Donovan had handed the poitín distillery over to the brigade together with instructions on how to disappear should they be disturbed by uninvited visitors. 'I'm sure he has a few other stills to fall back on. Come on, let's have a look at the next place.'

It took them over two hours to tramp through the dark across fields, bogs, woods and hillside, crossing ditches, streams, the Owvane River and tracks that had been forgotten since the Famine, before they found the ruined cabin hidden in the slopes above the high road between Loughill and Glin. They'd have done it quicker if it had been daylight, and quicker again during the summer and when they got to know the route better.

'You'd go off your head if you were stuck here for a stretch.' Ned sized up the crumbling walls and what remained of the roof thatch. 'None of the comforts of Drug's place.'

'But easier to defend.' A steep path, invisible through the furze from below but exposed to those hiding above, snaked its way up from the river. 'And easy to get to if we've to move in a hurry.' Their trek had crossed just four roads and only the last, running from Loughill to Ballyhahill, carried any traffic.

Finding some shelter in the corner, Willie dropped his bag on the floor and stretched himself out.

'You're not sleeping here, are you?' asked Ned. Their coats were damp from the winter rain, their boots were covered in muck and a wind was whistling in from the Estuary. 'You'll get your death from pneumonia.'

'There's only one way to find out. If I survive the night, then this'll do as a hideout.'

Josie was milking in the shed when she heard steps in the yard. She stopped for a moment to let her ears decide how many and what type they were. Friends ambled or waddled or hurried with eclectic stride; foes arrived to a harsh measured beat.

Only the one, she figured out, and not of a military disposition. She relaxed, conscious of how even the most innocuous sounds could make her worry. She had lost count of the number of patrols that had passed through the gate over the past year and, while she never let her mask drop when the Crown Forces were around, she'd shake with supressed anger the minute they had gone.

Her father took the visits in his stride but not the damage to the farm. Ever since the peelers had burned down the barn and the hen house, he had taken to lying on in the bed whenever the slightest ailment hit him and the upkeep of the property, which he'd religiously maintained up to then, had been allowed to slip. She accepted that he was getting on, that a man well into his seventies was going to slow down at some stage, but she could also detect that his spirit had cracked. When the project of a lifetime had been smashed by a wilful act of the authorities, there wasn't the same will to start all over again.

She did her best to keep the place going. With Ned and Jimmy on the run, there was no one else to turn to when her father was in one of those moods and failed to rise out of bed for the milking. By the time she'd come back from the creamery, she had to rush down to the school and there were mornings she when didn't even have the chance to clean herself properly. By lunchtime, her mind might be wandering from exhaustion, the children would pick it up and the boldest of them would test the limits of her authority.

It wasn't too bad in the winter when most of the cows were dry, but she dreaded the spring that was coming with its calving

458

in the middle of the night and the likelihood of her father's absences increasing. She was half of a mind to sell the herd and go into dry stock. Although it wasn't anywhere near as profitable, it needed far less work than dairying. Anyway, money wasn't the issue. She was making enough out of teaching to keep the two of them alive and her father had more than enough put away to see out the rest of his days in comfort.

But they'd need every penny of it. Neighbours who hadn't a nest egg or an income to fall back on were suffering from the downturn. Not only had prices dropped after the war, but the continual disruption by the military was making it next to impossible to scrape a living. A dairy industry that had been the envy of Europe only a few years back was now reeling from irregular delivery, reduced attention to quality and frequent punitive raids on creameries.

Half expecting that it might be Mary Hourigan offering to deliver the milk for her, she rose from the stool and peered out into the yard. Instead, she was greeted with her first sight of Ned in weeks. Without a care in the world, he passed into the shed, looked over the cows, tapped the churn to see how much milk was in it and stretched back on a pile of hay as if it was his favourite armchair in the parlour.

She emptied the bucket into the churn.

'Where's Father?' he asked.

She picked up the stool and moved on to the next cow.

'Is he still in bed?'

The animal was anxious for some reason, frantically swishing its tail the moment she grabbed its tits. Maybe it had picked up a disease.

'He's usually up by now, isn't he?'

There was a small scratch on the udder, nothing more than a minor irritation. Her taut fingers relaxed. The cow sensed her relief and calmed down.

'He's not sick, is he?'

'No. He just got fed up of working.' She squeezed out the last of the milk.

Ned took the bucket and emptied it. 'Here, I'll finish them,' he said.

She felt like refusing the offer out of spite. Turning up every now and then when it suited him and behaving as if he was squire of the manor while she worked day and night to ensure that his inhertiance didn't fall to rack and ruin. She would have been better off leasing it out like Ned had done with the holding that he'd bought up the road.

But her brother wasn't the real source of her anger. She'd seen even less of Willie. When the peelers and the military had pulled back, she'd thought they might get some chance to be together, but he'd disappear for weeks on end, tramping over half of the county and never saying much about where he'd been.

His absences wouldn't have been as bad if he'd confided in her. After all, she was as active in the movement as he was, running the court, managing the money and collecting every bit of information about what went on in the town and passing it on to the brigade. But when it came to active service, Willie Hartnett was the same as the rest of them. He couldn't recognise the Volunteer inside the skirt.

So when he went off on his travels, she never knew whether he was still alive or whether the peelers had caught up with him or, when she was tired and irritable like she was at that moment, whether he was seeing some fancy woman stashed away in a far-off town. But any thoughts of jealousy were immediately followed by pangs of guilt that she would ever suspect such behaviour of him. Secretive as he might be, Willie wasn't of the type like Ned who could never keep his hands in his pockets and his eyes pointed straight ahead.

'Go on up and get your father out of bed,' her brother was telling her. 'I'll have everything ready for him when he comes down.'

Out beyond on the road, she could hear the growl of the lorries. The Army had returned in strength and there was talk of another curfew.

'Is that why you're back?' she asked him. He was safe as long as they didn't come up the lane and she didn't hear any indication of the convoy stopping before it turned up the main street at the crossroads.

'We need to know what they're up to this time. They look as if they're planning on staying for a while.' He opened the stalls to release the milked cows. 'If you're not rushing to make it in time for school, you might get a chance to see what's going on.'

A big scatter of soldiers surrounded the burned-out shell of the RIC barracks as Josie passed by on her way home from school. In the middle of those standing guard, an officer looked through a telescope set up on a tripod and barked instructions at a private holding up a long stick marked out like a giant ruler. Another pair stretched out a surveyor's chain between them.

Across the road, the corner boys were passing their usual smart comments but without the customary bravado. Curiosity had blunted the cutting edge of their cynicism. They'd have to see what the military was at before they could tell everyone that they were going the wrong way about it.

In the middle of the street, a gang of boys from her fifth and sixth classes were kicking a rag ball which skidded into the middle of the soldiers. One of them picked it up but, when he

461

attempted to return it, the young lads all turned their backs and walked away.

'Funny,' she heard the squaddie remark as she dismounted her bicycle and left it up against the wall of the Post Office. 'It's like as if I'd the plague.'

'That's Ireland for you, son,' answered his sergeant.

The engineer folded up his tripod and placed it in the back of a lorry. Unrolling a chart, he checked off the dimensiuons against numbers entered in his notebook. A gang of carpenters arrived, hauling planks and lengths of hoarding. Civilians, but they weren't local. From the accent, Josie thought that they might be from Ulster.

Posters were pasted to the other side of the wooden screen proclaiming the latest regulations for the defence of the realm. Curfew from sunset to sunrise or from six in the evening to eight in the morning once the days began to lengthen. Gatherings of more than five people in public were no longer permitted without police authorisation. All fairs, meetings and sporting events banned until further notice. It would henceforth be considered a crime to promote or act in the name of Dáil Éireann and the illegal Irish Republic. Anyone harbouring a criminal and not surrendering immediately rendered himself liable to summary justice.

'Sore losers,' muttered the man beside her. Sinn Féin's sweeping successes in the recent elections had seen most of the local councils switch their allegiance to the Republican government of Dáil Éireann. The last fig leaf of consent had been cast aside and the British mandate in three-quarters of the country could only be upheld now at the point of a gun.

And maybe that was what they had intended. She caught a peek of the drawing as the engineer, unaware of the curious squints behind him, flattened it out against the hoarding to stop it from ruffling in the wind. The new barracks looked bigger than the one it would replace, more like a fort than a building for conducting police business.

'Oy, you lot! Move on.'

The engineer jumped when he heard the sergeant's command and awkwardly gathered in his drawing. The small crowd stood where it was, arms folded across chests and looking vacantly ahead until the sergeant returned to his business.

She had to pass a checkpoint at the crossroads and she could see a second down the road at the entrance to their laneway. They probably had one outside Willie's place and Dick's place and Jimmy's place as well.

Flanked by machine gun posts in the adjoining fields, the armoured car blocked the Ballyhahill road as it climbed up the hill from Shanagolden. The rain had returned, rolling over the uplands and sliding down to the plains below, its thick cloying damp seeping into the bullswool of the soldiers manning the checkpoint, climbing up their puttees to touch on their breeches and dripping down from the brims of their helmets. Buffeted by the wind and set against the slate-grey sky, the wet soaking browns of the bracken and bullrushes and the bare dark twigs of the trees, West Limerick was showing its least hospitable face.

'Bloody rain,' complained a private. 'Bloody wind. Bloody natives. This place is worse than bleeding Flanders.'

'You've said it, mate.' His colleague shook himself to dislodge the ring of droplets on the point of descending on his face. 'And over there, the bullets only came from one direction.'

'I won't be half glad when this tour is over.' The first man cupped himself into his greatcoat to light up a cigarette. They weren't supposed to smoke on duty but no one would spot him. The corporal had disappeared off into a field to answer the call of nature and, with them stuck on a road with no traffic, he wouldn't be in any hurry to return. As for the tin box on wheels behind them, he'd heard the clinking of the dice as the crew whiled away the time at a cramped session of Crown and Anchor.

His partner was of a more nervous disposition, but plucked up the courage to light up himself and then immediately threw his smoke away when he caught a glimpse of movement in the corner of his eye. 'What the hell?' he cried before the approaching cyclist took shape. 'Hello, our day is brightening up.'

'Ooh, a tasty piece of crumpet indeed ...'

Josie's High Nelly wasn't made for cycling up hills and she dismounted just after she caught sight of the roadblock. All week, she'd thought of going up the road but, what with her father's erratic behaviour, a couple of court cases landed on her desk and a weary reluctance to approach yet another checkpoint that would be well away from her normal travels, opportunity and conviction had to wait to come together.

She could see them eyeing her up, their hungry gazes starting at her face and moving slowly down the line of her body. Squaddies, young enough to still harbour impressions, old enough to be able to restrain them. It couldn't have been easy on them to be stationed in the naked hostility of Shanagolden.

Raising her head and fluttering her eyelashes with inaccessible seduction over the prim distance of a schoolteacher, she convinced herself that she could handle two lost souls looking for any possible diversion from the boredom.

'I'm afraid you must turn back, ma'am,' said the bolder of them with surprising politeness. 'We have our orders. No one is allowed through.'

'Begging your pardon, ma'am,' asked the other. 'Are you the schoolteacher?'

'Indeed I am, sir.' She dressed him down as if she was pointing out the obvious to her classroom and then allowed a slight hint of kindness to shine through. 'And I'm looking in on some of my pupils. They haven't been to school in over a week.'

'That's because of the blockade, ma'am.'

'We've checkpoints on every road leading out of the village.' The pair of them were vying for attention.

'My good man, Troubles or no Troubles, our children must be educated.' The second soldier seemed more impressed by her firmness. 'It is my duty to ensure that the Attendance Act is enforced no matter what the circumstances.'

'Oh, go on, Harry. Let her pass. You can see she's a lady.'

'Oh, all right then. But you must be back within the hour. There's a curfew in force, you realise.'

Giving them the merest of smiles, she remounted the bicycle, pressed the pedals up the incline and through the gauntlet between the barrel of the armoured car and the machine guns set in the fields. Only when she was well out of sight did she dismount, panting from the effort and shaking from the nerves. There was no one around where the hill flattened out and a narrow sideroad forked off to the right but she couldn't shake off the suspicion. Another quarter of a mile on, Ned had told her, and then across an abandoned path that lost itself in the bushes to the right. She was certain that she knew the place, she'd been up there many times before but, when she looked out over the bleak expanse of bullrushes, bracken and briars, she wasn't so sure.

Hidden under a mound of ivy, the remains of a stone gatepost marked out the entrance to the path and she rested the bicycle against it.

'Back here,' whispered a voice. Patie Fitzgibbon's head emerged from the bracken, a rifle draped across his arms and field glasses hanging from his neck. 'Hide your bicycle.'

She counted the paces down the path and turned into a small clump of bushes. He was waiting for her in the hollow, four day's stubble on his chin, his coat damp and ragged and a broad brimmer on his head.

She flung herself into his arms just to feel the reassurance of his presence and stayed there to soak up his warmth. She'd have stayed longer if she could, feeling the thump of his heart and the tickle of his jaw across her neck and the locks of his hair through her fingers and the pressure of his arms across her back and sucking in the scent of his body, but he knew and she knew that they only had the few moments.

'I haven't much time, Willie,' she panted between kisses. 'There's big squad of Royal Engineers in the town working around the clock rebuilding the polis barracks ...'

'They've no one to man it.' The knuckle of his forefinger traced up her backone.

'No, you're wrong there.' Her hands cupped the back of his head and pressed his face into the angle of her neck so that her lips brushed against his ear. 'ConstableReilly's sister-in-law told me that they're going to re-occupy it with these new recruits they're bringing in from England and Belfast.'

Relaxing his grip on her, he rolled over. 'We'd better burn it down again before they arrive.'

'Not a chance. You won't get near it.' They both sat up, her head resting on his shoulder. 'Shanagolden is completely surounded. They've a line of sight on everything that moves. There's a blockade on every road leading into the town and they've set up observation posts and machine guns in the fields in between.'

'Are you sure?'

'I've seen them all with my own eyes.' She planted a last kiss, rose to her feet, smoothed out her coat and brushed off the clay and dried leaves. 'Look, I have to go or I'll be caught in the curfew.'

The light was already beginning to fade. Not daring to look back but confident that his eyes were following her, she moved back quickly down the path to retrieve her bicycle.

34

'**I**T'S TOO GOOD of an offer, Nicholas. I won't get one like it again.' District Inspector Sullivan had seen many of his constables and a few of his sergeants hand in their resignations, disappear into the night or, as had happened at Dan Hourigan's funeral, walk off the job in front of half the county. But he had never expected his superior to throw in the the towel. After more than thirty years of upholding the law over one of the least compliant beats in His Majesty's empire, County Sub-Inspector Callaghan would be leaving at the end of the week to take up his appointment as Deputy Inspector-General of the Newfoundland Constabulary.

'A relation of the wife called in on us last year on his way back from the war,' he explained. 'He's since been elected a member of their House of Assembly and he wrote to me saying they were looking for an outsider to sort out a few problems.'

Sullivan accepted the brandy from the cabinet behind the Sub-Inspector's desk that was opened only on the rarest of occasions. 'I'll be sorry to see you go, Peter.'

'I shouldn't be telling you this, but I'll be glad to see the back of the place.' Callaghan opened a bottle of port and topped up their glasses. 'No matter who wins out in the end, there's no life

469

here for me here anymore. I'll be condemned either as a British collaborator or as a Sinn Féin sympathiser.'

'Who's taking your place?'

'I don't know. Some Army man, I suppose.' The Sub-Inspector unbuttoned the collar of his tunic, an unheard-of departure from a dress code that he had previously enforced to the letter. 'He's welcome to it. He can run a force I'm no longer proud to be part of.'

Sullivan declined the top-up.

'God damn it, Nicholas. I'm out of order. You should stay on and make the best of it. I don't have the fight inside me anymore.' Callaghan found a humidor in the cabinet and offered a Havana to his District Inspector. 'A present from the wife's cousin. Don't bother inhaling. Just let the smoke drift over your tongue and let the scent rise up your nose.' He flicked the match off the side of the box. 'I suppose you think I'm giving up, don't you? Leaving you in the shit? Well, you're damn right.'

The blue wisps hung in the sunlight.

'A year ago, I'd have charged the lot of them. But now I'm not allowed to. So what, in the name of God, am I doing here?'

The discipline of the RIC, which had held despite eighteen of their members being killed during the previous year, was now breaking down. The dribble of new recruits, attracted by another sizeable increase in pay and conditions, sang to a tune other than the unwritten code of conduct that had shaped the careers of Nicholas Sullivan and Peter Callaghan. Intelligence groups, at a loose end since the Germans had surrendered, had found an outlet for their energies in Ireland and had infiltrated the police, the civil administration and the Army in pursuit of their own agendas.

A few weeks earlier, a gang of off-duty policemen out on the batter had murdered two innocent civilians in reprisal for the shooting of a constable. Callaghan's attempt to investigate the circumstances had been stymied by military intervention and the two victims, despite one of them being a fifteen-year-old girl and the other a seventy-year-old invalid, were branded as rebel sympathisers aiding and abetting an ambush. And whatever remaining authority the force had wielded in his half of the county disappeared when a riot in Newcastlewest between the IRA and a gang of ex-British soldiers ended in the rebels taking over the second biggest town in County Limerick for a few days and then escaping from the Army in a blackout.

'And now we'll have these thugs descending on us.' Outside in the yard, the first batch of the RIC's Reserve Force were climbing out of a lorry. Having failed to entice enough replacements for the resignations through normal recruiting procedures, the authorities had spread the net beyond Ireland and had lowered the standards of entry. 'Keep away from them, Nicholas, I'm warning you. They'll drive the last nail in our coffin and everything we've spent years working for will all go up in smoke.'

Sullivan surrendered to the repeated attempts to fill up his glass. Holding the amber liquid up to the sunlight, he joined his departing superior in toasting the health of the Newfoundland Constabulary. Like a wake, he thought, like the passing of an entire way of life.

Their first planned operation was a fiasco. The entire Fourth Limerick Brigade's flying column had spent the night waiting in the fields around a bend on the coast road near Barrigone, getting soaked, tired and irritable. But the Army failed to oblige them and the lorry making the daily run to Foynes never arrived. All fired up with nothing to shoot at, the grumbling began as they set out on their ten-mile circuitous march across the fields. By the time they were skirting Shanagolden, Jimmy McCarthy

471

and a recent arrival from the Askeaton battalion were trading insults loud enough for any snooping ears in the vicinity to hear and the mood only lightened when someone realised it was Saturday and not Friday and the supply lorry ran only five days of the week.

But they had better luck on their second outing. An RIC cycle patrol sent out from Newcastlewest turned up exactly when expected on the road into Ardagh and they pinned them down for over three hours before the peelers decided to retreat to their base. The column might not have inflicted any casualties, but they'd kept the enemy at bay, used their ammunition sparingly and picked up more than they had fired from the belts of bullets abandoned by the fleeing police.

The brigade had also picked up much-needed credibility from the ambush. Tongues started to wag when word of the Barrigone job had leaked out and the ex-servicemen of Newcastlewest taunted suspected Republican sympathisers on the incompetence of their so-called army. But when Newcastlewest and the area beyond it was temporarily declared off-limits to the forces of Dublin Castle, the next confrontation between the factions developed into a full-scale riot and the RIC and the returned soldiers were driven from the town before an entire British Army battalion came to their rescue.

Some of the more hotheaded Volunteers were itching for a follow-up after the triumph of Newcastlewest, but Willie Hartnett kept the flying column out of it. There was nothing he could do about local members acting on their own initiative, but he wasn't going to waste the Brigade's meagre firepower on any unplanned operation. The Crown Forces had hundreds of times as many weapons at their disposal and the column's only hope of success lay in engagements of their own choosing where the time, the location and the circumstances were to their advantage.

For the thirty Volunteers who had taken permanently to the hills, the biggest enemy was boredom. Having survived months in the trenches when nothing at all happened, Patie Fitzgibbon and Dick Mullane were used to the tedium between bursts of action and they used up the time to batter the rudiments of cover, surveillance and movement into young fellas who were mad to take on the enemy without ever thinking of how to go about it. Some days, they'd take a few with them on a scouting expedition and get them to note the movements of army columns or police patrols. When they got back to their base, they'd get them to discuss the best way of taking on the Crown Forces and then run a training exercise based on what they had learned.

As the weeks wore on and calculation replaced blind passion, their confidence in each other as a unit increased. The next operation went like clockwork, an attack on a big house overlooking Askeaton that the Army had commandeered as a base. After capturing over two dozen rifles as well as two officers, the column released their prisoners after interrogation a few nights later to walk buck-naked down the main street of Rathkeale.

But the most tempting target lay beyond the Brigade's reach. Down below the shoulder of rock from where Patie was training his field glasses, the RIC barracks rose from the ashes as the Royal Engineers and the builders brought in from Belfast worked around the clock to cement the British presence in Shanagolden. The Union Jack fluttered in the breeze above the homes of good share of the column, daring the IRA to come down from the hills.

The convoy roared in, four Army lorries, two Crossley tenders and an armoured car at each end. Law and order was being restored with all the pomp that the British Empire could muster in the restive outpost of West Limerick. But it failed to impress

473

the townspeople who, almost to a man, turned their backs on the squad of civilians dismounting from the vehicles and filing in line into the reconstructed RIC barracks.

'I'm glad to see the rule of law being restored.' Creamery manager James Horgan provided the sole voice of welcome. 'It's high time them bandits were brought to book.'

'We'll do our best, sir,' Major Forrester assured him. 'And we do appreciate local support.'

Inside the day room, the recruits gathered around a long table where an Army orderly was taking measurements. Behind them, they heard a window shattering and those with a view outside saw a gang of stone-throwing boys being chased up the street by Horgan.

'Won't make no difference, I tell you.' Constable Maggot Tibbs waited in line beside Constable Warren, a fellow-Cockney veteran of the trenches and Sergeant Fry, another former career soldier discharged after twenty years service with a twisted leer on his face and a cigarette hanging permanently from his lower lip. Unlike his two colleagues whose time in the colours had run out, Fry's demobiliastion came after serving fifteen months in military custody for the rape and attempted murder of a woman in Belgium.

'His Majesty's Government has never yet issued a uniform what fits.' Maggot looked disdainfully at the clothing that he'd been provided with. 'Hello, what's this? A police tunic, Army breeches, a Glengarry cap! We'll look like bleeding monkeys!'

'You won't need a uniform for that, Maggot,' suggested Warren.

Forrester marched past. 'Problem, Tibbs?'

'Begging your pardon, sir, but I don't think we look quite the part.'

'Shortage of uniforms.' The major jerked up a tunic with the tip of his stick. 'Have to make do.'

''Ere, Maggot.' Warren's arm got lost in the sleeve of the outsize tunic. 'I hear you fought with the Micks in Flanders. What was they like?'

'Bleeding barmy, if you ask me.' He'd even ended up in the place where most of them came from. Or maybe there were loads of other Shanagoldens in Ireland. Everywhere sounded the same. Ballythis, Castlethat, Kill-something-else. Not that he would have wanted to tangle with them, but this new police reserve division was the only work he could get. He'd spent a year living off his wits after his discharge and, when the money ran out after drinking most of it and gambling what was left, there was nowhere else he could turn to.

That was the bloody Army for you. He'd given them most of his life and stood by them through thick and thin even before the uniform became popular. And what was their gratitude? Threw him out on the street at the first opportunity and he a decorated hero of the war. Fat lot of good his Military Medal did him on Civvy Street.

So when he'd seen the poster outside Whitechapel tube station seeking experienced men 'willing to face the rough and dangerous task of assisting the Royal Irish Constabulary', he jumped at the opportunity. Ten shillings a day and full board and lodging was a far cry from sleeping in the kips or under the arches of railway bridges and robbing the bottles of meths from the unconscious beside him. He'd never seen money like that in the West Sussex, not even if he added in all his winnings at Crown and Anchor, and they weren't too particular about who they recruited. So if they wanted to send him to the jungles of Africa or to the North Pole to earn it, Horatio Tibbs MM wouldn't complain.

'Barmy barmy or barmy peculiar?'

'Stone bleeding barmy. I had this mate Dick what slashed the captain's throat right in front of everyone.' The breeches were causing serious discomfort to his meat and two veg. 'Just like that. Killed him stone dead, would you believe?'

The conversation died as Forrester banged the bench with his swagger stick. 'Name is Major Forrester, King's Own West Sussex Rifles. I have been seconded to the Royal Irish Constabulary.' The stick tapped like punctuation off the surface. 'Know why? Native police hadn't the stomach for the fight. One of their chaps shot before their eyes .'

'I don't know about this geezer,' muttered Warren.

'Seen his type myself at the Front.' Same regiment too. Maggot could see another Captain de Walcourt behind the bench and this time there was no Sergeant Roseblade or Dick Mullane to take him on.

'And what did they do?' continued the major. 'Nothing ... Absolutely nothing.' The stick balanced between the fingers like the conductor of an orchestra priming himself up for the overture. 'Result? Anarchy. Gangs of murderers inflicting their savagery on His Majesty's subjects.' He sucked in a majestic draught of air. 'Our mission, chaps, is to restore order. Take whatever steps are necessary. Any questions that may arise will be dealt with after the event. Is that clear?'

A hand shot up.

'Yes, Constable Warren?'

'Pardon me, sir, but why isn't the Army replacing the RIC?'

'Matter of procedure, Constable. We have been afforded the opportunity to decide for ourselves what is to be the appropriate level of response to any given situation. You will not, and I repeat this, you will not be hamstrung by Army regulations.'

'You mean we can do what we like, sir?' asked Fry.

'I did not say that, Sergeant. However, you may interpret anything I have said in whatever manner you wish.'

'I quite understand, sir.' Fry's upper lip curled into a smile and was met by the blank assent of his commander.

The mesage came in a roundabout manner and with the belated imprimatur of the IRA's General Headquarters. The RIC detective who had planned the execution of the Lord Mayor of Cork Tomás Mac Curtain in his bed had been spotted in Foynes by a deckhand on a visiting coaster.

'He's posing as a representative for a Dublin shipping agency,' explained Willie.
'The Cork City Brigade have asked us to take him out,' added Ned. 'They're fairly certain he led the operation as well.'
'It's a one-off job,' Willie's eyes rested on Dick's. 'I need three volunteers.'

'I'm game for it,' Patie offered. They'd been stuck for over a week in their hideout while army and police vehicles criss-crossed the roads around the clock and they were all beginning to suffer from cabin fever. Minor disagreements were turning into arguments, their food rations were running down, they could have done with a change of clothing and a decent wash and, while they had the consolation of tying up an entire battalion of soldiers in a wild goose chase, patience was wearing thin. Even at the Front, there had always been the prospect of relief but, up in the hills of West Limerick, they'd have to wait until the fine clear spell of weather broke and the focus of intense military activity moved elsewhere.

'I'd like Mossy with me as well.' Dick smathered the remains of the bacon grease over a stump of stale bread. 'Any idea how to snare him, Willie?'

'I'm told he's a hoor for the women. The bigger and the bolder, the better.'

'Like Mary Hourigan?

'You've taken the words out of my mouth.'

'Would she help us out if we asked her?'

'She might.' Ned drained the last of the cold tea. 'I'll go and ask her myself.'

In spite of the danger and the tiny margin for error, Mary needed no persuasion at all to take part in what Patie considered to be a suicidal operation. Up on the steep rise overlooking the main street of Foynes, he watched her coming out of the railway station and passing by the telegraph office. Pulling his eyes away from the field glasses, he glanced at his watch. Half-past twelve on the button but there was till no sign of the target.

'He's late.' Over the three previous days of observation, the detective had been punctual to the minute. Mary continued her walk, then turned around at the end of the street and retraced her steps as if she'd left something after her. 'I see him coming out now.'

'I have him,' whispered Dick, lining up the sights of the Ross Rifle that they'd captured in the Askeaton raid.

The RIC man's head bobbed between those of the other pedestrians as he made his way back to his office. A lorry hid him from view but, when it passed, Patie saw him slow down as Mary approached him with a saucy flounce to her gait. He lifted his hat and the two of them stopped.

'Move back a small bit,' Dick was urging her from afar. 'Just another few inches.'

The street traffic thinned out. There was no one else visible in the sweep of the binoculars. Mary moved sideways as she'd been told.

Patie was already on the back of the pony when the shot rang out and held the reins for Dick as he mounted his steed. Within minutes, they had cleared the woods and were galloping over the fields to where Mossy was waiting by the lane behind Knockpatrick with three bicycles.

'I take it you got him,' Patie asked as they hurried back on foot over the last leg of their flight.

'Do you doubt me?' Dick dived into the ditch and peered out on the road. 'And thank God Mary didn't doubt me either. It was a matter of inches.' He edged his way through the hedge and scampered across. 'Mind you, I couldn't tell you whether that faint of hers was genuine or put on.'

'Desperate, that murder in Foynes.' James Horgan topped himself up with another measure of whiskey. Back in the privacy of his parlour, he could tipple away to his heart's content without any frowning disapproval from his social equals. 'But at least this lot will restore order. They've that military cut about them. All business and none of the nonsense.'

'Maybe.' His guest Councillor Thomas Hennessy lifted the lace curtain on the window and looked across the main street towards the RIC barracks. The Black and Tans, as the Reserve Force had quickly been christened, had got off to an ignominious start and the killing of the detective-inspector, most likely at the hands of Shanagolden locals, had left them thirsting for revenge.

Such uncertainty led to people staying indoors, buying poitín off Drug Donovan rather than real whiskey in the bars and stashing their money away instead of spending it; nothing but bad news for Hennessy's many businesses.

'They'll put Hartnett and Noonan and that little pup McCarthy back in their boxes.' The host lifted his glass to the picture of King George over the fireplace. 'Not likeReilly and Flaherty and

McKenna and all those other yellow-bellied cowards who ran away when the going got tough.'

Not getting a response, he drifted over to Hennessy and dropped his arm over his shoulder. 'Only Lar Stapleton and Batt Mullane had the right idea. I was proud of them, Thomas Hennessy, I'm telling you. Damn proud of them. Weren't afraid to stick to their principles.'

'Yes, but look where it got them.' A pair of farmers were entering Jack Noonan's. There must have been up to a dozen customers in there while the Councillor's own premises was doing very little trade. If it wasn't for the shop, he'd be better off closing it down and selling the license.

'Heroes. Both of them. Stood up to those murderers.' Horgan moved back from the window. 'Tell you what. I'm going to point out who these Sinn Féin terrorists are to the new commander.'

'I'd be careful, James, if I were you.' That interfering eejit of a schoolmaster descended from his bicycle and went into Noonan's. Hennessy wondered what he was up to. Not only had Philip Hurley never been seen inside a pub before, but he was also the local organiser of the total abstinence movement. 'If you're going to be talking to the Black and Tans, you'd want to be discreet about it.'

'Discreet? Discreet?' Horgan dropped the glass on the mantelpiece where it wobbled on a stud before settling on the safe side of the equilibrium. 'Yes, maybe you're right. I won't make it obvious.'

'But if you are talking to the commander, you might just mention to him that Jack Noonan is the ringleader.'

35

THE LAST TWO customers had left, although not without a prolonged and mutually unintelligible argument on the doorstep. Even the curfew and the presence of a trigger-happy Black and Tan squad in the town was not enough to instil a respect for closing time and it took the heave of Jack Noonan's shoulder on the door to ease the pair out into the street.

Trade was slowly picking up again after the initial reluctance to venture out and many of the regulars were defiantly holding the view that no half-dressed English mercenary was going to interfere with the habits of a lifetime. But fewer had turned up that night and on the previous night, after the news came through of the detective being shot in Foynes. The menace of retribution hung over Shanagolden.

Jack put it out of his mind as he swept the dirt and the droppings from the floor and wiped down the tables and the counter. Another long day was drawing to a close and, with Mossy on the run and help next to impossible to hire, he was on his feet from morning to midnight. The custom mightn't have been frightened off but, with the Tans around, nobody was willing to be seen working in the most obviously Republican pub in the town.

He was emptying the spitoon when the door smashed open. The sergeant, a real evil-looking bastard with a pencil-thin moustache emphasising the sneer of his mouth, made straight for him and he barely saw the butt of the rifle before it smashed across his jaw. When he lifted his head from the floor, the barrel of the gun was aimed at the bridge of his nose.

'Fucking murderer!' the sergeant screamed.

Jack wiped the blood from his face. The slightest touch of his fingers on his chin racked him with pain.

'Don't you fucking move, you Irish pig!'

He knew it was the end. Spitting a broken tooth from his mouth, he forced his lips into a smile before the bullet smashed through his forehead.

The shot stopped Maggot in his tracks. Even during the war, they'd make some effort to capture the collaborators before handing them over to their own police.

'Christ!' stammered Warren, the only member of the squad capable of opening his mouth.

Fry stamped the heel of his boot into the bleeding head just to make sure. Or maybe it was to remove all traces of the smile of death. 'What are you looking at, mates?' he shouted at the rest of them. 'Drink up!'

They were still too shocked to move.

'I said drink up!' The sergeant grabbed the bottle nearest him and raised it to his lips.

Reserve evaporated when another hand shot to the shelf behind the bar and they all joined in grabbing the whiskey and slugging from the neck as they set about smashing the pub. The blast of alcohol removed their inhibitions and fired up their frenzy as the clock, the glasses, the windows and the stoneware pitchers were reduced to shards.

'Keep it up!' roared Fry. 'Break everything you see!'

A picture fell from the wall, the frame shattering and the photograph of a football team falling out. Maggot picked it up and was about to throw it into the fireplace when he noticed the names. He recognised most of them. Jerry Curtin, Dinny Lyons, Mick Culhane, all of them buried at the Front. The young lad Johnny O'Brien, killed on their first day of action. Mick Fitz who'd gone mad from the white phosphor. Tim Curtin who had died of the flu. Batt Mullane, Patie Fitzgibbon, Dick Mullane, Flint Barrett. He wondered where they were now.

'You're slacking, Tibbs!' Fry drew another boot at the body of the landlord. 'What's the matter with you?'

'Nothing, Sarge.' Maggot hid the photo inside his tunic and rammed the butt of his rifle into a mirror advertising a brand of plug tobacco. All around him, his colleagues were downing the whiskey by the neck and frantically reducing every stick of furniture to firewood.

A grey-haired woman's head peered over the bannister at the top of the stairs and she wordlessly descended as the orgy of wrecking lost steam. By the time she was standing over her husband's unrecognisable body, all other activity had stopped and Maggot watched her in awe as she wiped the blood from the brow and flicked back the fringe of hair.

'What's happening, Jack?' she whispered. 'I heard a shot.'

Her other hand eased under the back of the head and lifted up the sightless eyes and the mess where the mouth and the nose had been. 'Oh, sweet Jesus,' she wailed, the whine uncoiling from the depths of her heart, carrying beyond them to the night sky and, even though they couldn't understand the words of the lament, they reckoned she was damning them all to Hell and beyond.

'Shut up, you bitch!' screamed Fry.

483

'A Thiarna, déan trócaire. A Chríost, déan trócaire ...'

'Bleeding witch is praying to the Devil,' said Warren. 'I told you she was a banshee.'

Fry grabbed a rifle and shot into the ceiling. 'Shut fucking up, I told you!'

'Déan trócaire ar a anam dhílis ...'

'Right! That's done it!' The sergeant whacked her across the head but she kept wailing away as if nothing had happened. 'Grab her, men.'

Two of them picked her up and dumped her in the only chair left intact. More of them grabbed lengths of plaited straw and tied her down.

Fry stuffed a towel in her mouth, removed his tunic, pulled off his braces and dropped his trousers. 'Right, chaps. Let's have a bit of fun.'

She was still alive when Maggot's turn came around. But her clothes were in shreds, blood was streaming from the scratches and bites and he had to take another swig of whiskey before he was pushed on top of her. She didn't bother to resist, just looked through him as if he was dirt while the cheers and the grunts rang around him. He pulled away without ever making contact.

Fry pushed him aside, kicked the chair over and unrinated on top of her as she lay on the ground. Pulling up his trousers, buttoning up his fly and looping his braces over his shoulders, he turned tiumphantly around to the half-naked squad.

'Is everybody happy?' he boomed.

'You bet your life we are!' they all shouted together.

'Ach saor sinn ó olc ...' mumbled the voice on the ground.

'Then fuck her!' Fry pulled the bottle from Maggot's hand, poured it over her head and flicked a lighting match. She was still wailing the same lament as the flames set fire to her hair and consumed the rest of her whiskey-drenched body.

Josie had heard the details at third hand from the sister of the woman who'd been forced at gunpoint to clean out the barracks. After setting fire to the pub and wrecking a few cottages just for the fun of it on their way back, the Tans had stayed up all night finishing off the rest of Jack Noonan's whiskey and complimenting each other on their bravery. Their drunken words of bravado had been pieced together into a coherent account by the time the town woke up to see the charred gap on one side of the street and smell the stink of burned-out flesh.

A vigil of women were kneeling outside the ruins as she passed by on her way to the school, their anger chanelled into prayer that a detail of Tans tried to disrupt but were repelled by the rhythmic fury of their keening. Philip Hurley met her at the gate, his hair wilder than ever, the colour drained from his face.

'I'm sending them home,' he told her. A brother and a sister were walking back down the main street, their little lost eyes looking for an answer. Another group met them and turned back.

'Do they know?' she asked. 'I mean, all of what happened.'

'Of course they do. You can't hide something like that from them.' He held his hand to his brow and leaned back against the pillar. 'Oh my God! What do you teach them now?'

'Is it true what they're saying, Miss?' A small hand tapped her hip. 'What the Tans done to Jack and Molly?'

'I'm afraid so, Eddie,' Hurley answered for her. 'Sometimes terrible things happen. And maybe the best thing we can do is to say our prayers to God to make sure nothing like it ever happens again.' He took the boy and his sister by the hand and led them inside the gate. 'It's all right, Josie. You go on off home for yourself.'

She protested but he insisted and she could see that he just wanted to be left alone. She was feeling the same way herself, needing a bit of space to put her emotions into words the way adults liked to hear them.

The checkpoint was no more than half-hearted down at the crossroads. Some of the Tans were hung over, others not quite sure where they fitted into the infamy of the night before as they were buffeted by the silence of hatred. She gave them the look as well and no one stopped her climb up the Ballyhahill road.

She knew they'd be worse later on in the day when self-justification overtook the shame that any of them might be feeling. Having passed the threshold of mercy, they'd realise that their only chance of survival in Shanagolden would be to keep kicking any thoughts of resistance from the minds of the locals.

Mossy was on lookout. Josie was incapable of looking him straight in the face but he didn't seem to pick it up as she hurried down the path to the abandoned cottage. Willie, Ned and Dick were leaning up against the outside wall.

'We saw the fire. Patie thought it was Jack's place.'

Trying to be as factual as her anger would let her, she told them what had happened during the night. Even Dick showed surprise.

Willie broke the lingering silence. 'Oh, Jesus Christ! We can't tell him that.'

'He'll find out anyway.' Just like her class who'd had the vision of Hell visited upon them that morning. 'It must have been Horgan who fingered them. He's been spotted once or twice sneaking out of the barracks. No one else in the town is talking to the Tans.'

'We'll have to take him out,' Ned was saying.

'No, warn him off first,' Willie countered.

486

'You might regret it,' said Dick.

She didn't know how she felt herself about it.

'Everyone gets the one chance, even Horgan ...'

'The Tans didn't give Jack and Molly any chance ...'

'I don't care ...'

'We can't be seen to take this lying down ...'

'He won't listen to us anyway. Then we can deal with him ...'

She stepped between Willie and her brother. 'We give him a warning,' she decided. 'But let Philip or myself do it. Better if the rest of ye kept away from the town.'

The letterbox clanged in the hall. James Horgan woke from his slumber and sat upright in his armchair. The glass had fallen from his hand and a dribble of whiskey had stained the carpet. A half-empty bottle rested on the table.

He looked at the clock. Just after midnight. Too late to be his wife. Nor did he expect her to return as long as the Tans were stationed in the town. Telling him that she'd no intention of putting herself in the line of fire, she'd left to stay with her sister in Ballingarry the day the squad had arrived in Shanagolden.

The letterbox rattled again, followed by slight clunk of something small banging off the floor. It wasn't a visitor either. Even Thomas Hennessy and Doctor Molyneaux had refused to saltue him after the incident in Jack Noonan's. All talk they were but, when the heat came on, they were no different from the rest of the Shinner supporters in Shanagolden.

Horgan rose unsteadily to his feet, the back of his head throbbing from the sudden movement. The smell had been the problem. It had been hanging in the air over the remains of the pub for two whole days and he could feel it tickling his nose every time he woke. That and the whining prayers of the vigil that had only ended up a few hours earlier at nightfall when the

Tans drove their lorries up outside the ruins and forced the wailing old hags out of the way.

He picked up the envelope from the hall floor. A spent bullet fell out into his hand as he unolded the sheet of paper. 'This is your only warning, you traitor,' read the neat, perfectly-formed handwriting. 'Leave Shanagolden immediately. Do not ever again set foot in County Limerick.'

He opened the door. Not a sinner could be seen in the pitch darkness of the curfew. Cowards. None of them had the guts to say it to his face. Well, James Horgan would show them.

Halfway up the street to the barracks, he heard a door open behind him. He ignored it but, when he heard a second, his step faltered.

'Traitor,' whispered an unseen voice. He quickened his walk.

'Traitor, traitor,' chanted the hoarse chorus, barely audible but he knew what they were saying. 'Traitor, traitor, traitor.'

He broke into a trot and pounded on the door of the barracks. A suspicious eye poked out. 'Who is it?'

'It's me. James Horgan. Let me in. I have to see Major Forrester.' The peephole slammed shut. The whispers continued behind him. He pounded again.

'All right! All right!' He could hear the lock turning.

A stone caught him behind the ear. 'Judas, Judas,' they hissed but he could see nothing when he turned around.

'What's the matter, Mr. Horgan?' a sharp voice asked from inside.

He stumbled in the door as it opened. Hands grabbed him and he was hauled inside as the entrance was instantly shut behind him. A constable fired a shot through the peephole.

'They're out to kill me,' wailed Horgan. 'And me the only law-abiding citizen of this town.'

'Hmm.' Forrester sat behind his desk as he spent over a minute poring over the three-sentence note.

'I need protection ...'

'Standard ploy used by these thugs.' The major folded up the letter and handed it to the dodgy-looking sergeant standing by his shoulder. 'But don't you worry, Mr. Horgan. Your safety is assured. The village has been secured.'

'The bastards got Batt Mullane. They got Lar Stapleton ...'

Forrester brought his forefinger to the tip of his nose. 'Not for general consumption, you understand.' He lowered his head conspiratorially. 'We may decide to conduct a little sortie in the very near future. And when we do, Mr. Horgan, it will be the last you'll ever hear of Hartnett, Reidy and Mullane.'

He snapped his fingers. 'Sergeant Fry. Organise an escort party to ensure Mr. Horgan returns safely home.'

Maggot looked out the upstairs window before venturing to the door. He couldn't be too careful after the night's disturbance and, although he never saw a single face, he could feel the daggers of their hatred all around him as the eight-man detail escorted the slobbering shit-scared creamery manager along the few hundred yards back to his house. Fry had suggested that half of them stay outside on guard for the night but there were no takers and the sergeant didn't press it.

Whether they had willingly or unwillingly participated in killing the publican and his wife, they were all bound together now and it wouldn't pay anyone to raise a colleague's hackles if he was depending on him for protection. Know your mates and cover your back was the first lesson he'd learned in the Army and he needed it more than ever in this hellhole where everyone from the new-born baby to the old crone on her last legs was their sworn enemy.

He should have listened to the voice telling him that the terms of service were too good to be true. Demobbed soldiers couldn't get their old jobs back when they returned from the Front or, if they did, they found their wages reduced and here was HMG offering more than twice they'd ever earned in the service for putting the Paddies back in their box. You'll be all right, they'd told him at the recruiting depot, usual spot of danger as in every military operation, but the Irishman was white, he was baptised a Christian and he was not at all like the the heathen tribesmen in the Northwest Frontier or the black savages of the Sudan.

Was he hell? Maggot had heard what they'd done to Batt Mullane. Shot him dead right in front of an entire company of policemen and they were saying that his brother, his old mate Dick Mullane, had done it. Not even the most vicious Paddy gangs in the East End had ever stooped so low as to kill one of their own family but, here in Shanagolden, no one seemed to see anything wrong with it.

Ireland was different to anywhere else he had served. Out in India, they could play one lot against the other and the tribes in Africa might see Mother England as an ally against their enemies, but everyone here was out to get them. No one would talk to them or salute them or serve them or sell anything to them or clean out the barracks or cook their dinners, except at the point of a gun.

It wasn't real soldiering either. They were supposed to be policemen, mercenaries taken on because the local Bill weren't up to the job, and it had none of the traditions of a regiment. A man could be proud of serving in the West Sussex but there was nothing but lunatics in the company he had been landed in. Even if he had been conscripted, a man could enjoy the Army after a while. He'd find mates and they'd have a bit of a laugh and they'd stand by each other, not like in this RIC Reserve

Division where he wouldn't trust the next man as far as he could throw him.

Not one of the bastards laughed at his jokes. They were all afraid of that madman Fry and what he might do when his mood changed without warning. Not one of them would even play Crown and Anchor.

'Too quiet,' muttered Warren as they stepped out into the dawn with their rifles cocked and looked up and down the deserted main street. 'I don't like it. I don't like it, not one bit.'

Even in the early sunrise of midsummer, there'd be some sign of life, maybe a drunk staggering home who'd never made the curfew, or a farmer wandering in early to the creamery and catching up on his sleep while he waited in his cart. And if they didn't see anything moving, they'd hear a sound in the backgound of a window being opened or the clop of horseshoes or the iron rims of cartwheels creaking over stones.

A gust of wind blew in from a laneway, lifting a torn-down Wanted poster of Willie Hartnett and Ned Reidy into the air, and Maggot watched it billow across the street past the post office. 'Cor blimey!' he shouted. 'Look at that, Sarge.'

Fry followed his pointed finger up to where a body swung from the top of a telegraph pole with a placard hanging from its neck.

Maggot cursed himself for opening his mouth. He and Warren were sent up the ladder. 'SPIES BEWARE. NO MORE WARNINGS,' read the placard under the sightless eyes and the stretched neck of James Horgan. Down below them, the entire town had come out to fill their upturned faces with unspoken approval of the creamery manager's fate.

'Just like rats, that's what they are. Hiding behind their shutters and peering out their keyholes.' Warren's agitated hands began to untie the noose as Maggot held the body. 'Course they seen nothing. Never do, the filthy savages.'

491

Way up in the hills above them, Willie caught sight of the two Tans hauling Horgan's body down from the pole. Halfway down, it slipped from their grasp and the ladder wobbled precariously but they held on.

'Have a look.' He handed the field glasses to Ned.

'It's brought out the crowd. The Tans won't like that.'

'Nor will they like losing their only informer.' The column had wrought its revenge as publicly as possible but, rather than satisfaction at levelling the score, Willie had felt the whole cycle was running beyond their control. Maybe it was a reaction to the first killing that he had consciously taken part in, where he had seen the victim die right in front of his eyes and had heard his last plea for mercy.

They'd sneaked out across the fields in the middle of the night, Ned, Dick and himself, and had descended the steep slope from Mount David to break through the cordon. Hidden in the backyard of Horgan's house, they'd seen him scuttle off to the barracks after Josie had slipped the warning through the letterbox and they'd waited the best part of an hour for his return. Dick had sized up the escort and figured out that eight was too many to take on but, when the Tans left despite Horgan's pleadings, they knew that they had their informer in the bag.

Willie had closed his ears to the sobs as he and Ned held the creamery manager by the arms in the parlour of his house and stuffed a cloth in his mouth while Dick shot him in the head through a cushion. He couldn't remember whether Dick or Ned suggested hanging Horgan from the telegraph pole but both of them had agreed over his opposition when they'd found the ladder and the rope at the back of the dead man's house and he'd hefted the body up on his shoulders while the other two hoisted it from the rope.

As they made their escape back across the fields, Willie tried to figure who the real losers of the night before were. Had the Tans provoked them into a foolhardy operation that could so easily have gone wrong? Had they been diverted from their war into the pursuit of vengeance? And while the enemy could disappear when the fighting and the killing was all over, they and their people would have to live with its consequences.

The years on the run were driving him crazy. Sometimes it was the boredom, sometimes it was the tension, sometimes it was the fear, sometimes it was the weight of having to think everything out, and they all came together to corrode his hold on reality. He could barely remember the last time he'd slept two nights running in the same bed or had walked down a street without having to look over his shoulder. Instead of worrying over a dead body that they'd strung up as a trophy for the entire town to gawk at, he should have been making his way that morning to work where he'd earn the few bob to bring home to his woman and they'd be thinking of their life together and the children they'd be raising and the hopes that they'd have for their futures.

'It'll scare the life out of them,' Ned was saying. 'The Tans don't have a single friend anymore.'

'I know,' he agreed. 'But they're still there and we haven't touched any of them. We have to do something to draw them out. They haven't moved from Shanagolden since they arrived.'

36

'**M**ISS, IS Mr. Horgan gone to Hell?'

'That's not for us to know, Eddie. Only God can decide.'

'Maybe he said an Act of Contrition before he was hung.'

'Maybe he did, Martin.'

Josie didn't know what to tell a classroom whose previous week had been interrupted by two days of savagery. But then again, the children had recovered far more quickly than their parents. Young minds saw events and moved on. Adults dwelt on the whys and the wherefores and nurtured their grudges and shrank from their fears and worried about saying the right thing in the right place.

Not a word of regret was expressed over James Horgan's death, or at least not in public. The horror inflicted on Jack and Molly Noonan was too deep to ignore and that one of their own should have partaken in it, however indirectly, had magnified their anger. Even former friends like Councillor Hennessy and Doctor Molyneaux agreed that the creamery manager had been given a fair warning and that, in the circumstances, he'd got no more than what was coming to him.

But as the immediate tension wound down and Shanagolden settled into an ominous wait for the next move, doubts were expressed in private conversation. Philip Hurley had been badly shaken and Josie herself was in two minds about the necessity to swing the dead body in public. While the brazen defiance of the act had scared the life out of the Tans, she knew that the decency lost in its barbarity would be hard to recover.

In the end, they let the pulpit rationalise their emotions. With the Canon spending most days talking directly to God, the curate had taken over the running of the parish and Father Conny had told them at Sunday Mass that, rather than dwelling on the sins of the past, everyone should look to the future in order to prevent the recurrence of evil.

But children had no time for such generalities. There was right, there was wrong and there was nothing in between. Eddie Costelloe and Martin Sheehan and little Hannah Enright could sense her confusion and kept bringing up the execution of James Horgan every time she moved on to handwriting, spelling or the multiplication tables. She could have got cross and told them that they were too young to be talking about subjects like death and betrayal but, even if she'd wantd to shut them up, her voice lacked the firmness that morning to impose her authority.

Anyway, she could do nothing to stop them thinking. Most of them were smart boys and girls, willing and curious and grounded in decency. If they enjoyed school, they'd develop a love of knowledge and a respect for the disciplines of learning and they might get chances that their parents never dreamed of. There was a new country that Willie and Philip and herself believed in and it would need a generation who could think and act for themselves and not feel beholden to any foreign king or government to run its affairs.

But they were looking for guidance. They could ask Josie questions that they were too shy to bring up at home and, before she'd say anything herself, she'd let them talk about whatever it was among themselves. Sometimes, they'd come up with their own answers and they'd amaze themselves at their powers of reasoning and she'd watch their faces glow as she smiled in approval.

They'd landed her with the big question that morning and she could see their disappointment. She was even less sure of the answer than they were.

They'd put on the brave face, moved squads out on the street and mounted their checkpoints but it took the best part of a week to lift the spirits in the barracks. Sergeant Fry was all for exacting immediate revenge but the major wasn't quite as keen. Instead of excoriating the IRA's savage execution of Horgan, more attention had been given to the deaths of the Shinner publican and his wife and, when Opposition MPs raised the issue in the Commons, Forrester got it in the neck from Dublin Castle for not containing the controversy.

But once Shanagolden was shoved off the headlines by other engagements, word came down from the office of the newly-appointed RIC Inspector-General Hugh Tudor that local commanders were free to carry out whatever reprisals they liked. If it meant holding an entire town responsible for the IRA activity in its area, then so be it.

'Only way to discourage the murder gangs,' explained Forrester. 'Short, sharp punishment. The locals will soon get enough of it and they'll turn their backs on these criminals.' He turned his back to look out the window of the day room as the entire complement of the RIC Reserve Force tooled up for their mission of pacification. Hatchets, batons, sledgehammers, pickaxes and bayonets were distributed from the pile on the table and tied to kitbags. With the weight of hardware pressing on his shoulders, Maggot felt as if he was emerging from the dugout in readiness to go over the top once again.

They had another half hour to wait for nightfall and the bottles of whiskey, taken at gunpoint that morning from one of the pubs, were passed around. 'Drink up, men!' Fry was shouting, the mad glint of violence igniting in his eyes. 'It's more fun when you're pissed.'

And pissed they were when they marched out the door in a passable imitation of military formation, making as much noise as they could as they swaggered up the street. 'Fucking Irish pigs! Fucking Irish pigs!' they all roared together, smashing the butts of their rifles through every window they passed by.

'Now, let's do it properly, men. Let's do it the Army way.' Fry split them into groups of eight and they spread along both sides of the street until they each reached a doorway. When his whistle blew, the sledges swung and they charged into the houses.

The sergeant himself led Maggot's group and took the pickaxe to the door of the bedroom. They piled in after him, grabbed the man and the woman, flung them from the bed and kicked them crawling back out into the main room. Shoved on by a colleague, Maggot climbed up the loft, dragged the three children down and lined them up against the wall beside their parents.

The eldest of them bit his fingers and he would have ignored it only Fry spotted his grimace of surprise. 'Tibbs, are you going to let the little fucker do that to you?' So Maggot swung his other hand and slapped the child hard across the face and sent the blood spattering from his nose.

'Come on, you lot!' roared the Sergeant. 'We haven't even started.' He picked up a hatchet and drove it into the dresser, cleaving a big crack and scattering the china to shatter off the floor. 'Make these pigs understand what happens to anyone harbouring criminals.'

They all joined in on the demolition, Maggot as heartily as the rest of them. He never wanted to be in this God-forsaken place and now he was stuck to a madman like Fry who was going to get them all killed. Fortified by another few swigs of whiskey, he swung his pickaxe with a frenzy that he hadn't felt since jumping into the enemy's trenches during the war. Furniture, crockery, floorboards, bedclothes, wall plaster, anything at all that could be smashed or ripped or slashed or thrown into the fire was destroyed in front of the occupants.

'Keep it up, men!' As they flailed at the last few sticks of furniture, Fry shoved the tip of hatchet under the father's nose but failed to provoke a response. All five of them stood there with the same blank look on their faces until one of the men found a rag doll, waved it in front of the young girl and tossed it into the fire.

'Baba! Baba!' she wailed as the flames consumed the toy.

'Shut up, you little bitch!' The burning straw illuminated the sergeant's demented gleam as he whacked the child as hard as he could across the face. The father moved to protect her but was instantly set upon and Fry kicked him repeatedly in the head, ribs, belly and balls until his screams and those of his bawling family could no longer be heard.

With nobody left to beat and nothing left to smash, they speared turf sods from the fire with their bayonets, tossed them on the pile of broken and furniture and left the house blazing before moving on.

They piled into the day room, dropped their weapons and tools, flopped on the benches and opened their tunics to cool down. It wouldn't have been like that at the Front where the NCOs would have them running and marching whenever they were back in the rear but all they did in the RIC was drink and gamble in their time off and any physical effort at all left most of them exhausted.

But they weren't too tired to brag about their night. Bravado buried any other emotions that they might have been feeling.

'Little bastard was cringing, so he was. Afraid I was going to kill him.'

'Kept saying her prayers, the fucking old hag. Well, she won't say them again. Knocked her fucking teeth out, I did.'

'You should've seen his face when I let his wife have it. Best of all, he knew he could do nothing about it.'

'Don't know nothing better, the fucking savages.'

'You said it, mate. Fucking savages!'

'Fucking Irish savages!'

'Won't try anything funny now.'

The major popped his head in and sniffed with disgust at the pounding bootsteps of a young constable still racing on adrenalin. But there was no trace of disapproval in the condesenceding sneer while he closed the door behind him to leave them at it.

''Ere, Sarge, I got two suspects outside.'

Fry followed Constable Warren out and signalled to the others to follow. The street was clouded in smoke, lit up by at least a dozen separate fires and they cheered on some of their colleagues as they fired over the heads of bloodstained townspeople staggering out of their blazing homes.

'All I've got, Sarge.' Warren jerked the barrel of his rifle in the direction of two prisoners in their nightshirts. 'No one else we can pin it on.'

Fry inspected them with sadistic satisfaction. 'Not very convincing, Constable.' He shoved his baton into the smaller man's breadbasket as if he was prodding cattle.

'We've heard reports that they were regulars in Noonan's pub.'

'Consorting with known terrorists. Good enough for me.' The sergeant rammed his baton again, this time with more force, and the prisoner doubled up in pain. 'Tibbs! Over here!'

Maggot jumped at the mention of his name and jumped again when he recognised the small slight man in the nightshirt. 'Flint! What are you doing here?'

'Do you know him, Tibbs?'

'Do I know him, Sarge? We was in Flanders together, so we was. Three years at the Front. 'Ere, what's he done?'

'Strung Horgan up.'

'Give over, Sarge. Flint wouldn't know how to tie his own shoe lace.'

'That's right, Maggot,' wheezed Flint. 'You tell him.'

'Shut up, you murderer!' Fry's baton swung again. 'Has to be him, Tibbs. Or else that other creature.' He turned to the tall, stooped prisoner with the long droopy face. 'Hey, boy, what's your name?'

Warren belted the butt of his rifle off the second man's ribs when he refused to answer. It made no impression on the impassive face.

'Another dummy. There all dummies here.' Fry spat into his eyes. 'Tibbs, you and Warren take them into the yard and dispose of them.'

Flint's eyes widened with disbelief. The other man continued to focus on the middle distance.

'Sorry, Flint.' Maggot shrugged his shoulders. 'I did my best.'

'What are you lot looking at?' Fry pulled a Thompson sub-machine gun from one of the constables and fired a burst over the crowd that had gravitated towards the barracks.

'Who are that lot?' The major intercepted them as they frogmarched the prisoners to the front door.

'Them that done for Horgan, sir,' answered the sergeant. 'We'll deal with them in the yard.'

'No, we'll follow procedure this time. Send them to Newcastlewest in the morning. Let a military court take the flak.'

When the lookout came back to the cottage to tell of the flames coming from the town, it took all of Willie's powers of persuasion to prevent most of the column from rushing down to take potshots at the barracks.

'We don't have enough weapons to take attack a fortified building,' he insisted over their objections. 'We can only take them on when they come out.'

'And will ye shut up,' added Ned. 'There could be a night patrol around waiting to take us.'

Willie felt the discipline that had held them for months ebbing away. Not knowing what had happened, all the Shanagolden lads feared the worst for their families and neighbours. Jimmy McCarthy had to be threatened with Dick's gun before he calmed down. Mossy Noonan said he didn't care if they shot him and was only dissuaded when he was told that, if he went, he'd be giving the rest of them away.

Once the arguments faded out, Willie left Dick and Patie to keep the others in line and went out himself with Ned to their observation post to view the extent of the destruction. One side of the main street around the ruins of Jack Noonan's was mostly ablaze, although the fire appeareded to have passed its peak. It looked as if the creamery had also been set alight.

502

'Oh my God!' sighed Ned as he took the field glasses. 'If we don't hit them back, we're done for.'

Willie tapped him on the shoulder to keep quiet. There was something moving in the distance, the faint tap of what he took to be footsteps hurrying up the road. He tried to make out where they were coming from before the wind rustled through the leaves in the hedge below them and he lost track of the sound.

He couldn't argue with Ned. The stakes were rising and they were caught between a rock and a hard place as the Tans drew them towards retaliation. If it had been anywhere else, they could have struck at another location so as to draw the enemy away but Shanagolden had become a matter of honour and their credibility depended on being seen as capable of defending their own. Being outgunned, however, their only realistic tactic was the ambush in a place where they could melt into the landscape. Maybe they might get a chance when the Tans moved out of the town but that could take anything up to a month and the morale of the column might wither away.

He heard the noise again, louder this time and definitely the steps of a civilian moving quickly up the Ballyhahill road. Training the binoculars through the gaps in the ditch, he caught the figure moving through the moonlight and reached out his hand to get Ned's attention.

'Who?' he mouthed with his lips. It was definitely the shape of a man and he looked as if he was seeking them out but only Josie knew of their hideout.

Ned shrugged his shoulders, pointed to the fork in the road where the rise flattened out and sprinted back up towards it across the field. Willie edged through the bushes and aimed his rifle up the road should the man try to run back down in escape. When there was no sign of him returning, he crept slowly along the ditch until he saw the intruder in conversation with Ned.

'It's all right,' Ned whispered. 'It's Philip.'

Although agitated, the schoolmaster was able to give them a detailed account of what happened in the town. 'I don't think they killed anyone. But they're trying to pin Horgan's death on Flint and Drug Donovan.'

'They can't be serious,' said Ned.

'They are. They're taking them to Newcastle in the morning to a military tribunal.'

'When?'

'They didn't say. But I could get Father Conny to ring the chuch bell when they set out. Three rings, a pause and then another three.'

They left Hurley and hurried back to the cottage. All except Patie were asleep. 'I think everyone got tired of arguing.'

'Then we'll wake them up.' Willie prodded Jimmy and Mossy but he wasn't going to take a chance on Dick. Nobody ever did.

'Right, lads,' he told them when all twenty were awake. 'We're going to war. So bring everything down to Shanid Cross.'

The sour stench of burning thatch hung over the town and blackened rafters smouldered as the escort detail emerged from the barracks with their two handcuffed prisoners still wearing their nightshirts. Not a single local was there to see them although Maggot was sure that they were all peering out through the lace curtains of those houses still standing. Nor were there any carts on the street as there was nowhere for the farmers to take their milk. Before they'd finished up for the night, Fry had led a group of them out to torch the creamery now that its immunity had disappeared with the death of its manager.

The major wasn't taking any chances and called the two lorries right up to the door. Ten of them piled into the first, all fully tooled up for the journey. Maggot and Warren sat either side

504

of the two prisoners in the back of the second with Fry and three others on a bench opposite.

'And come straight back once you've picked up supplies,' Forrester instructed his sergeant. 'It's a straight handover. I've telephoned ahead.'

The church bell rang as they set off. 'Announcing your funeral already.' Fry poked his stick on Flint's Adam's apple and lifted up his chin. 'Look, the little bastard is shitting himself all over our nice clean lorry.' He pressed the stick further into the prisoner's throat. 'Do you know how many hours it took to clean it out for a fucking savage like you?'

Maggot edged his boots away from the brown scuttery mess on the floor to which Flint added a layer of vomit. Even though the air whistled through the truck as they turned at the crossroads, the stink rose to his nose.

'Fucking pigs!' spat Fry. 'Can't hold their arses together.'

Flint's eyes shut in terror as his insides were jolted by every pothole in the road. The other prisoner continued to stare into the distance with the same haunting expression that had stayed on his face since his arrest.

Warren banged him on the knee with the butt of his rifle. 'Do you ever say anything, Paddy?'

The prisoner turned his head slowly and wiped the constable down with his sad lingering eyes. Warren cracked first and turned to his sergeant. 'Gives me the creeps, this bastard,' he complained. 'He reminds me of the Grim Reaper.'

But before Fry could reply, the lorry rocked to the crack of an explosion.

Before the sun had risen, every single item in the arsenal had been carried down to the crossroads below Shanid Castle including the last remnants of the Foynes booty that they'd never got the chance to use. The Vickers machine gun, too heavy to be carted around by the column, was set up in a field rising above the road with a full sweep of fire to aim at. A convenient pothole was stuffed with what was left of the gelignite with a trip wire stretched between the two ditches.

They were all in place as the first red fingers of dawn crept over the horizon, all dotted around both sides of the highway with a line on every square inch below them and such was their thirst for revenge that there was no argument over the danger that the ambush posed for the two prisoners. Flint and Drug Donovan had some chance if the operation was successful; they'd none at all should the convoy reach Newcastlewest.

Patie levelled the Vickers in line with the plane of the road and swivelled it left and right along its horzontal axis. The movement was fluid and steady. It had survived seventeen months of storage in the roof thatch and he hoped that the ammunition was in the same condition. They'd only the few belts rolled across Jimmy's shoulders and chest but just two five-second bursts of fire would be enough.

All their training had gone into the ambush; all the knowledge that Patie and Dick had picked up during four years at the Front. They were betting the lot on this pot and all they had to do was wait and try not to think of anything going wrong. Patie had seen more than his share of plans collapse in the reality of battle but he willed himself up to a level of certainty that he'd never once felt during his time in Flanders. Seeing his confidence and that of Dick, the rest of column fell into their positions without a word and remembered every detail of their instructions.

The distant sound of the bell woke him from his nap. Down the road, he could see the dust rising into the still morning air and soon he could hear the rumble of engines. He eased his finger on

506

the trigger of the machine gun and nodded to Jimmy to keep the belt steady. They were still angry from the night before but now it was sheathed with the cold purposeful sense of anticipation as the convoy drew ever closer.

Two lorries, just as they had anticipated, and they assumed that Drug and Flint would be in the second. The lead vehicle bobbed over a slight rise and Patie could see the driver looking straight ahead and the Tan beside him fondling his weapon.

The passenger jerked suddenly to attention. He must have caught sight of the Vickers, his hand leaped up to warn the driver and Patie edged the machine gun into line. But before the lorry could stop, its front end shot up and what was left from the explosion spat bodies, chassis and coachwork into the air before cartwheeling into the ditch and toppling back head over heels into the crater.

Patie was raking the vehicle before the debris hit the ground, the hailstorm of lead drilling through man and machine, piercing the fuel tank and setting it on fire, smashing any thoughts of resistance before the Tans had time to recognise the trap that they'd fallen into. The burst spent itself without warning but Jimmy had the next belt tacked on like clockwork and Patie blew what was left of their ammo in a lethal spray of the second lorry's cab.

Dick was already in motion as Patie released the machine gun and picked up his rifle and the pair of them jumped into the second cab and clambered over the perforated bodies into the back. A Tan swivelled around with his weapon but he wasn't quick enough for the slash of Dick's hand-held bayonet that severed his throat. The remaining Tans rushed over the tailboard only to be mown down by a volley of rifles waiting below them and all that was left in the lorry was Flint frozen in terror, Drug looking on as if nothing had happened and the quivering sergeant with his hands clutching his rifle.

'Take it easy,' he stammered. 'I surrender.' The weapon dropped to the floor and he raised his hands. 'I expect to be treated according to the terms of the Hague Convention.'

'Don't tell me about it. Explain it to our legal expert.' Dick picked the sergeant up by the shoulders of his tunic and flung him out over the tailboard. 'You might also explain to him why you murdered his father and raped his mother.' He hopped down from the lorry and stuck his boot on the prisoner's neck. 'Mossy,' he shouted. 'It's Sergeant Fry. We've saved you the pleasure.'

'Ye took yer time,' Drug muttered as Patie shot his handcuffs open. Behind him, a single shot rang out on the road.

They tipped over the Tans, checking to see if there was any sign of life in bodies blown apart by gelignite or ripped apart by lead. Only Sergeant Fry looked relatively unscathed, as a slight trickle dropped from just over his ear.

'Eighteen, I make it,' countd Patie.

'That'd be the lot.' Dick pressed his boot against a prone backside. Fingers clenched slightly and then relaxed. 'I think this one's still alive.' He grabbed the hands and turned the body over. 'Hey, Patie! Have a look at this.'

'Well, well, well. It's a small world.' The eyes opened and blinked at Patie. 'Maggot Tibbs.'

'Patie ... Dick ...,' the Tan wheezed.

'Come on. We'd better be going,' Willie was saying behind them.

'We knew this fella over in Flanders,' Dick told him.

'It's up to ye, lads.' Willie pulled Jimmy away from Fry's body and sent him to show two of the others how to disassemble the Vickers.

Patie raised his rifle. 'I suppose we have to.' Maggot's sag of relief faded into taut lines of dread.

'No, leave him go, Patie.' Dick was shaking his head. 'Better they hear it from the horse's mouth.'

'For God's sake, come on!' Ned was shouting.

'On your feet, Maggot.' Dick grabbed his former comrade by the tunic and lifted him upright. 'Now clear off that way and don't you dare look back.'

They gathered their own weapons and those that they'd captured as Maggot stumbled back down the road towards Shanagolden. The ambush had passed off to perfection and the Tans hadn't managed to fire a single shot in retaliation. Leaving the bodies where they lay on the road, the column melted back into the fields that hid them.

He'd felt relief, he'd felt satisfaction, he'd felt vindication in six years of fighting but never before had Patie felt elation after battle. They'd wiped the bastards out, every last one of them except for the messenger they'd let go to instil the fear of God in the rest of them. They'd avenged the killing of Jack and Molly Noonan, the destruction of the town and the wanton brutality that had been inflicted on their people. Maybe John Bull would try to come back but, after this humiliation at the hands of a band of rebels armed with little more than a rifle and few bullets, he'd think twice about who and how many of his hirelings he'd send to re-occupy this small West Limerick town that didn't want to have anything to do with him.

And by God, the column had been good. Disciplined, patient and deadly, the Fourth Limerick Brigade had hit the enemy with a ruthlessness that he'd never forget. The generals in Dublin Castle and the politicians in Whitehall now knew that, if they kept raising the stakes of terror, there were warriors in the hills more than capable of striking back.

Yet somewhere beyond the pride and the satisfaction, Patie also felt the inconvenient tug of emptiness. What they'd done that morning had to lead somewhere. They couldn't go on fighting as if nothing else mattered. Otherwise, killing would consume them like it had Fry and the rest of the Tans. And unlike their enemy, they had nowhere else to retreat to.

'Was it like this at the Front?' Willie asked him as they waited behind the hawthorn for a horse and cart to disappear around the bend at the end of the road.

'Sometimes,' he answered. 'And the odd time, 'twas far worse.' He thought back to times when tens of thousands had been slaughtered in a single day, when there were thousands of machine guns raking across the line of advance from every angle, when tons of high explosive dropped from the sky, when gas crept up on them and mortars rained down on them and bodies were impaled on the barbed wire. And he asked himself why the horrors of the Somme and Passchendaele had been outshone by a trifling engagement in a remote corner of Europe that had left just seventeen dead.

'How did ye live through it?'

'We managed. We even got used to it.' Patie slid the stand of the Vickers through the ditch. 'But none of it was as personal as this.'

The heat was rising, the road was empty and Constable Maggot Tibbs had no idea of where he was headed. All he wanted to do was to put as much distance between himself and the IRA men who'd killed every one of his mates. After that, it was six of one and a half-dozen of the other. Everyone in Shanagolden wanted to string him up but at least he knew the place and there was a barracks there with Major Forrester and the other half of his RIC company. Anywhere else was a step into the unknown with no chance at all of assistance.

The first sign of life was at the crossroads where a boy scurried across the road to hide in the burned-out shell of the creamery and, as he walked up the rise of the main street, he could sense every eye in the town watching him. The faces appeared at its crest where the road twisted to its left and they slowly formed a gauntlet to direct him back to the barracks. Not knowing whether or not they were going to lynch him on the spot, he allowed the force of their hatred to press him along the path that they'd marked out for him.

But nobody laid a hand on him. As he knocked on the door of the barracks, the murmurs stirred and they grew in volume while he waited.

'Oh, come out ye Black and Tans,' they sang.

'Come and fight us like a man.

Show us how ye won yer medals out in Flanders ...'

Feet started pounding to the time. He banged again, the dread rising through his guts that his colleagues inside had also been taken out.

'... Then tell them how the IRA

Made ye run like hell away

From the green and grassy fields of Shanagolden.'

The peephole slid open. 'Let me in!' he croaked at the fear-filled eye. The slot closed again. He could hear no rumble of the bar being lifted.

'Ah, the day is coming fast

And the time is here at last

When every tout and traitor will run before us ...'

'Let me in! Let me in!' he screamed, banging more furiously than ever. 'It's me! Constable Tibbs!'

'And if there is a need ...'

The door opened a crack but closed again so quickly that it caught his leg as he stumbled through.

'Trapped in his own snare!' shouted a voice among the singing and the jeers.

'Get in!' Hands hauled him through and dropped him in the hallway as if he was more of a bother than a comrade. He lay on the rough tiles of the floor, gasping with nervous reaction, as his two colleagues clambered over the upturned furniture into the relative sanctuary of the day room.

Even though most of them were ex-servicemen, the RIC was nothing like the Army, where mates stood by each other and never left anyone behind if they could help it. But here in this sodden shithole in the middle of nowhere where the police had to be paid way over the odds to stop them from deserting, it was every man for himself. The constable beside him could turn on him just as easily as the silent locals waiting for their chance behind their half-doors and the lace curtains drawn across their windows.

All he could hear was the banging outside, the knocks on the door and the taps on the windows. Nothing vigorous, just a soft incessant tattoo rumbling into his ears from every corner as the savages outside celebrated their seventeen trophies. He'd heard the old soldiers back in the barracks in Chichester talking about fighting the Zulus and the Fuzzy-Wuzzies and the Pathan tribesmen and how the war cries and the drum beats would float over the night air in an attempt to scare off the King's regiments, but he'd dismissed it as the usual old claptrap of the mess when they had nothing better to do with their time than put the wind up new recruits who didn't know their arses from their elbows.

But now he was hearing it for himself and not in any dusty corner of the Empire separated by oceans, jungles and deserts.

Shanagolden was only a day's travel away from London and its natives had fought alongside him during the war. Dick Mullane and Patie Fitzgibbon could have killed him that morning but instead, they'd consigned him to eternal shame like the lone doctor who'd returned from the First Afghan War with the news that a British expeditionary force of 16,000 had been slaughtered.

'Do you want to get killed?'

Maggot followed the voice into the barricaded room where the remnants of the company cowered behind walls, tables and desks and pointed their rifles in the general direction of the exterior. A heavy cloud of tobacco hung just below the ceiling and the intensity of the fumes made his eyes smart. Even Major Forrester had deigned to mix with the other ranks and sat right in the centre of the room behind a shield of wooden crates looking at nothing in particular. Every few minutes, his hand shot out in an involuntary spasm to reach for the dead telephone.

'Bleeding nightfall before the relief comes,' he heard someone mutter.

Cooped up like animals in a zoo, they suffered the dead heat of the steamy summer's day as sweat seeped through pores to paste raw skin to tunics and leggings and boots, as muscles contracted with the lethargy of fear, as heads shrank ever lower into their boltholes, as they confined their movements to lighting cigarettes and their conversation to the occasional whisper of complaint. The pounding continued outside, the same, unceasing, low-level instrument of terror that barricaded every mind into thoughts of his own personal survival. No one had asked Maggot what had happened to their seventeen mates. They might have known, but none of them cared.

Nicholas Sullivan wasn't overly concerned either, or at least not to the point of putting his own men in danger. When news got back to Newcastlewest that the convoy had been blown up two miles out of Shanagolden, the District Inspector sat back at his desk while, further down the hall, the RIC's parallel management structure tied itself up in knots over what to do next. Without Major Forrester at his side, Colonel Guthrie-Shaw flapped about like a drowning rat as he blared out instructions to Sub-Inspector Callaghan's replacement, but the newly-arrived former quartermaster of the Gibraltar garrison wasn't going to put his head on the block until he had picked up some knowledge of the area and of the men under his command.

Various other military and police commanders were summoned and each found every conceivable excuse to pass the buck. Even among those on their own side of the conflict, there was little sympathy for the indisciplined squad of thugs holed up in Shanagolden.

'Might be difficult to organise transport at such short notice,' Sullivan could hear. 'Most of our vehicles are currently out of service.'

'Damn it, Captain! Get them back!'

''Fraid it's not quite as simple as that, sir. Regulations insist that we do not send vehicles out on patrol in an unserviceworthy condition.'

'To hell with the regulations! We have a company under siege!'

'With respect, sir, are you asking me to countermand the specific written order which you issued last week?'

The building shook as the colonel slammed the door on the departing Army captain and the District Inspector waited for the tremors to subside before the anticipated call bellowed down the corridor. Given carte blanche to take whatever he needed, Sullivan put together a convoy of four Army lorries, two

514

Crossleys, an armoured car and a staff car for himself and set off on the voyage of rescue through the gloating faces of contempt lining both sides of Church Street and the Ardagh Road. Sentiment had changed in the town since the IRA had temporarily taken it over following the February riot and ex-servicemen displaying their loyalty to the Crown had disappeared from public view.

Stopping before every turn to check for mines and possible ambushes, it was well into the afternoon by the time Sullivan's circus reached the huge crater at Shanid Cross where flocks of crows were descending on the broken bodies and the lumps of twisted metal were soaking up the rays of the sun. He climbed out to survey the devastation. All of the dead wore what was left of their Black and Tan uniforms. Half had been blown apart in the explosion, others shot by rifle, ripped by machine gun or slashed by bayonet; every one of them falling in action except for the sergeant who looked as if he'd been executed after he'd surrendered.

Sergeant Flaherty opened the door of the Crossley but Sullivan waved him back in. 'There's nothing we can do here now, Jarlath. We're better off leaving the bodies here and dealing with them on the way back.'

Mesmerised by the ferocity of the attack, he kept looking back at the crater and the pile of bodies as the staff car drove off on the final leg of the journey. Past the burned out buildings at the bottom of the main street, the entire population of Shanagolden was gathered outside the barracks and greeted the convoy with an icy indifference far more menacing than the taunts and jeers that had sent them on their way from Newcastlewest. Seventeen bodies lay roasting in the sun and not a single one of them displayed any emotion other than the primeval triumph of vengeance.

The crowd made way for Sullivan and Flaherty to approach the door.

'They even got their prisoners out alive.' Flaherty pointed to Drug Donovan and Flint Barrett, washed and scrubbed like never before in their lives, standing at the head of the gauntlet. 'It's the end of the road for us here in this part of the county. No one will fear us any more.'

'Bad cess to you, Maggot Tibbs,' shouted Flint at the catatonic Tan in the ragged uniform sleepwalking his way to the waiting lorry. 'You're no friend of mine now.' The audience broke out in applause.

The major was the last to appear but his sprint from the door banged straight into Drug. 'Keep him away, keep him away!' he screamed. 'That creature is possessed by the Devil!'

Sullivan stepped forward to claim the last of his passengers. 'Lost nearly half of your men, Forrester. And the rest of them are running off like rabbits.' Grabbing him by the locks over his temple, he flung Forrester through the open door of the staff car with all the venom that had collected on him during that day of slaughter. 'So tell me, my brave Mr. Black and Tan Major. Who are the cowards now?'

37

A FTER THE Shanid Cross ambush, Shanagolden settled down into the stalemate that was slowly enveloping the country. Bit by bit, little chunks fell off the edges of His Majesty's United Kingdom as the authorities in Dublin Castle abandoned all pretences of civilian administration in the areas proscribed by martial law. Instead of maintaining a continuous presence in a barracks, the RIC, the Black and Tans and the new Auxilliary Division, recruited from demobbed British officers who had been finding it hard to adjust the less glamorous demands of peacetime, retreated to the bigger towns from where they launched reprisal raids into the surrounding villages and countryside.

Shanid was only one in a series of engagements that ratcheted up the tempo of the conflict. After the IRA had assassinated eleven British secret agents in their beds in the early hours of a Dublin Sunday morning, the Auxies invaded a football match that same afternoon and killed eleven spectators and a player when they turned their guns on the crowd. A week later, an entire column of Auxies was wiped out in West Cork and the Crown Forces exacted their revenge by burning down the centre of Cork City.

In between expressing outrage at IRA atrocities and promising a firm but even-handed response, the politicians of London talked about devolving Home Rule and introduced legislation giving the Unionists their own six-county slice of Ulster where they were guaranteed a permanent majority. But as far as the rest of the country was concerned, debating the fine points of revenue-generating powers and the allocation of responsibility for national debt had long since fallen below the bottom line of relevance. As activity in Westminster was reduced to futile gestures, the Crown's authority in Ireland passed from the deal-makers to the hardline militarists like General Sir Hugh Tudor who had set up the Black and Tans, General Crozier, one of the founders of the Ulster Volunteer Force and now commander of the Auxies, and incoming Chief Secretary Sir Hamar Greenwood. The rest of Lloyd George's Cabinet either cheered them on from the sidelines, looked the other way, or wrestled ineffectually with what was left of their Liberal scruples.

While the fighting spread relentlessly eastwards, a normality of sorts began to return in the south and west of the country as the British presence receded and Sinn Féin's alternative government solidified its grip on the everyday administration. Republican police enforced the law in the absence of the RIC, Republican courts settled disputes, Republican county councils ran the public hospitals and patched up the roads and regulated markets and fairs and, despite the financial and organisational obstacles placed in their way, they made a better fist of their responsibilities than the inefficient and sometimes corrupt agencies that they had replaced. In most of Munster and parts of Connacht, the roles had reversed, as Dáil Éireann now became the functioning authority and the Crown Forces the promoters of anarchy.

With the return of some semblance of order, trade in the basics slowly re-emerged in the smaller towns. But even though the creamery had reopened and most of the low-level daily harassment had disappeared, the edge of conflict still hung over Shanagolden. Josie Reidy and her classroom of children could pass weeks on end without ever catching sight of a uniform but, whenever they began to grow comfortable with the promise of peace, the Crosleys would roar into town and the Tans or the Auxies would jump out to arrest the first few people they came across, smash up a few houses and disappear in a cloud of dust.

They had just left as she cycled home from the school, the shattered glass and the broken furniture strewn across the main street a souvenir of their visit, and she wondered who they'd taken away this time. There hadn't been any IRA activity in the immediate vicinity for over a month so maybe the prisoners would escape with merely getting kicked about and then being locked up by a drumhead tribunal. But the Auxies contained even more war-damaged psychopaths than the Tans and, if they just happened to be in a mean mood, they'd toss the bodies into some ditch out the road and claim that the criminals had been shot while trying to escape.

'We don't know who he was,' old Mrs. Sheehan told her. 'He might have been a traveller for the brewery after coming down for the day from the city.'

'Faith, but he kicked up a right commotion when they arrested him,' added Mrs. Costelloe leaning out over the half-door of the next cottage. 'All airs and graces he was and him telling them that he'd come here on business.'

'And he showed them his credentials as well, just in case they didn't believe him.' Mrs. Sheehan straightened out her shawl in a display of indignant disapproval. 'But they thrown the poor man into the tender all the same.'

The unfortunate stranger might have been the only credible suspect they could find. Most of the men of the parish under the age of forty were rarely seen during the day, either gone on the run or else working away out in the furthest field, or back in the deepest recess, or up in the highest loft. Even Philip Hurley who wouldn't know one end of a gun from the other had been forced to disappear and Josie had been left to run the entire school on her own.

Without the menfolk around, raids would sometimes launch the town into frenzies of speculation. When there was no visible protection from the random imposition of punishment, casual words could turn into suspicions in an instant and suspicions into accustations of collusion and Josie might have to root out Philip and Fr. Connie to help her cool down tempers before they fermented into demands for retribution.

Out beyond the crossroads, she spotted a young man being assisted into a cottage by an elderly couple. Battered, bruised and with his only good suit in tatters, he would never forget his visit to Shanagolden but at least he had escaped with his life. Many another man hadn't been as lucky.

Solid information was harder to come by as the old hands of the RIC were sidelined by the incoming Tans and Auxies. Most of those sympathetic to the cause had resigned or had disappeared in the middle of the night. But the Fourth Brigade still got the odd tip-off and the flying column made its way under the moonlight through the fields and the lanes to where the road from Askeaton snaked into Foynes.

Almost a year had passed since the ambush at Shanid Cross and the war had changed from the occasional spectacular to the solid grind of minor engagements that tightened the Brigade's hold on its territory. But while they were slowly gaining the upper hand, Willie Hartnett knew that they were still as far as ever from claiming victory. The Crown Forces had now adpated to the IRA's game of providing a moving rather than a static target and the two sides played cat-and-mouse with each other along the twenty-five-mile strip of land on the south shore of the Shannon Estuary. Every ambush was met by reprisal, every raid by selective retribution and, even though each tit-for-tat exchange saw the flying column inch its way further towards outright control, it lacked the firepower to land the knockout blow.

Manpower and organisation were no longer a problem and, with a squad of part-time Volunteers to call on in every parish and a farmyard at every crossroads willing to provide shelter, they could mount attacks wherever and whenever they pleased. All that held them back was the shortage of weapons. General Headquarters had been promising for over a year, but they were still waiting for rifles to replace those captured by the Crown Forces, and ammunition was in such short supply that most missions were limited to just two or three bullets a man.

Unless their weaponry demands fell from the sky or, even more unlikely, GHQ's solemn undertakings turned into reality, there would be no more spectaculars like Shanid Cross. Progress lay in the relentless sequence of minor successes that chipped away at the enemy's resistance and squeezed him further back along the road from which he had come. The full-time soldiers of the column would often grumble at the reduced pace of conquest, but their day-to-day involvement led them to understand that the struggle for independence had now become a war of attrition.

The part-timers, those still working their days on the farm or on the roads and called out only when an operation was planned for their immediate vicinity, were another matter entirely. Faced with the constant fear of arrest or of random execution by tanked-up Auxies, isolated from their comrades and distanced from the overall campaign happening outside their own parish, the failure to land another crushing victory on the lines of Shanid had led some of them to see enemies under every blade of grass and to conclude that every British raid was the result of an informer's tip-off. Girls suspected of fraternising with the Tans, domestic staff in the big houses, businessmen trading with the Crown Forces and those of a landlord background became the focus of speculation and, even though doubts were based on fact more often than not, attempts to root out collusion resulted in at least one execution of an innocent and the forced exile of one or two more.

Any time the IRA campaign slowed down, suspicions festered and the only way to prevent communities under siege from turning in on themselves was for a successful operation to divert their attentions. Now into their third year of open conflict the summer of 1921, the Fourth Limerick Brigade was forced to bet the house on an ambush that they hoped would mirror the success of Shanid.

They still had an hour of darkness when they reached the gap on the eastern approach into Foynes and the thirty of them took up their positions in the long grass and the rock ledges overlooking the path that the convoy was expected to take. Every available weapon and bullet had been pressed into service. Even the Vickers machine gun had been brought out for only its second outing of the war and waited to be fed with the belt of ammunition that the Limerick City Brigade had bought from an alcoholic Quartermaster Sergeant.

The waiting was the worst part, trying to keep the mind on an even keel until the target moved into sight. A relay of spotters had been set up all the way down to Robertstown Church and Willie and Ned lay at the end of the chain, scanning for signals and listening for any sounds from the sky. Ever since the British began to use surveillance aircraft, movement had been confined wherever possible to night, and operations, no matter how well-planned, were abandoned if the escape route could be followed from above.

'I've a bad feeling about this one.' Ned handed over the field glasses. 'There's something not right about it.'

'Aah, we'll be all right, Ned. No need to worry.' Not a sign of movement could be seen down the length of the road, but one of the new lads on the ledge below Willie was fidgeting with his rifle and another kept shifting the weight of his body in order to find the perfect angle of repose. They were all getting nervous, all except Patie Fitzgibbon and Dick Mullane who never betrayed a flicker of emotion once an operation swung into action.

Willie passed the field glasses back. The shuffling around him was upsetting his concentration, an irritant distracting him from picking up the faint mechanical drones that might signal the enemy's approach. Much as he tried to conceal it from the others, the strain was getting to him as well. Instead of the cold anger that drove them a year ago and smothered all thoughts of personal danger, they fretted over what might go wrong.

Surprise worked both ways now. The Crown Forces could flush the IRA out of their hiding places by drawing them into mounting ambushes and then cutting them off before they could make their escape. And the Auxies, most of whom had been decorated for bravery at the Front, were far more likely than the Tans to stand and fight rather than crack under the pressure of attack. Maybe they had no choice in the matter. Commissioned out of the ranks during the Great War, killing Fenian rebels for their King was the only way left open for them to retain the trappings of an officer and a gentleman.

'We have them.' Ned pointed to the white and red handkerchief waving in the distance and then blew a single blast through his whistle. 'Two ... three Crosleys ... Damn it! They're using hostages.'

Willie grabbed the binoculars. Two civilians were strapped to the front of the lead tender slowly making its way towards them. Behind the prisoners, he could see the tam o'shanter bobbing on the Auxie driver's head, scanning left and right for any sign of danger.

'Do you think you can take out the last Crosley?' he whispered to Dick above him.

'I should. Although I can't promise.'

'Jesus, Willie!' protested Ned. 'We can't take the chance. If this goes wrong, we'll never hear the end of it.'

'And we can't let an opportunity like this pass us by.' And no damn way was Willie going to let the Auxies get away with terrorising the people he sprang from.

He counted the seconds until the second tender was level with the whitethorn bush on the side of the road before raising his thumb and then pressing the detonator with a sudden surge of fury. As he was doing so, Dick's single shot took out the third driver whose vehicle crashed into the exploding wreck ahead of it and the Vickers raked the second and third Crosleys while the lead one sped away towards Foynes.

'Christ, no! Wait!' Their heads filled with glory, the two fidegety lads never heard Willie's scream and were cut down by the machine gun in the back of the first tender the moment they jumped down onto the road. A further blast of lead ricocheted off the rocks, catching another Volunteer just above the ear, before the vehicle disappeared around the bend.

Mossy Noonan's Mills bomb finished off what was left of the last Crosley and Willie shouted at them to get the hell out of the place, leaving their dead and the Vickers behind before the Auxies returned.

They covered the five miles inside an hour and found shelter in the straggly necklace of woodland along the little river flowing down from Creeves to Barrigone. Exhausted and bedraggled, they rested against the butts of trees, took off their sweaty boots, cleaned their rifles and retrieved the stash of food that they'd left there the night before.

'Twelve-three.' Jimmy McCarthy hacked off a lump from the leg of hairy bacon and wiped the blade of the knife off the arse of his trousers. 'I'd say we won that round.'

'Does that include the civilians?' Ned washed down the slice of brown soda bread with a slug of milk.

'They'll be all right.'

'They're certain to be shot, Jimmy.'

'So that makes it twelve-five.' Dick was relieving himself against the other side of a tree that was backing onto the river. 'More than likely, the Auxies would have shot them anyway.'

Ned had had his fill of the numbers. The column had lost three of their own yet everyone seemed more concerned with how many of the enemy they'd taken out. Two of the young fellas had been with them less than a month, cousins from back behind Glin whose fathers had been taken from their beds and executed in front of their families by the Auxies.

They'd got their result all right but it would be their last engagement for the foreseeable future. The Vickers was gone as was the last of their gelignite and their only grenade and the twenty-seven survivors had barely a bullet each left between them. If the Auxies and the Tans only knew how depleted they were, they could tighten the cordon and pick them off without a whimper of resistance.

Edging away from the others, he dropped his swollen feet into the cool embrace of the river and lit up a cigarette. Moves were being made to find a solution and Michael Collins had called him away to Dublin the month before to hear his opinions on the Fourth Brigade's strength on the ground and on the conditions for a truce.

Willie joined him on the bank.

'This war is poisoning us, Willie.'

'I know.'

'It's turning us into savages.'

'I know.' Willie rolled up the legs of his trousers. 'And the worst of it is that, even if we stopped now, the damage has already been done.'

'We've lost our discipline.' Ned picked up a flat stone and tried to skim it over the water. It sank on its first contact. 'We don't care any more about who we kill. Look at those two misfortunes tied to the front of the Crosley. They might have survived if we'd called off the attack.'

'No, they wouldn't have.'

'How do you know?'

'All right then. I don't know.' Willie peeled off his shirt and threw it aside. 'I didn't know before we started that we'd lose three men and that we'd have to leave them dying on the road. And I didn't know that I'd feel sad and sorry about them getting killed and that I'd feel guilty and sad more for myself because I'd led them to their deaths. And I didn't think that, when we were escaping, I'd forget all about them because all I wanted to do was to save my own skin.'

'So now we're as bad as the Auxies?'

'No, we're not. Or at least I can't let myself believe that we are. I like to think, Ned, that we still have some sense of decency.'

'What do you mean? Like Jimmy? Like Mossy ever since the Tans done for his father and mother?' Ned tossed the butt aside and rose to his feet, wobbling unsteadily on the loose stones on the bed of the river. 'Like Dick? Jesus Christ, he's nothing more than a killing machine?'

'Dick killed way more in Flanders than he ever did here. And he never glories in it. He just does the job that needs to be done.'

'Yeah. It's just a job to him.'

'Do you think so?' Willie rooted through the pockets of his coat. 'Did you ever hear him crying to himself in the middle of the night?'

'We all cry during the night, Willie … Oh my God! Where did you get the soap?'

'Out of your house, Ned.' Willie stepped into the river and washed himself before passing on the disfigured bar. 'You're not the only dandy around here.'

Ned stripped off his clothes and left them on the bank. 'Aaah, a moment of civilisation.' Layers of sweat and grime rolled into the river. He could put up with the damp, the cold, the lack of sleep, the occasional pangs of hunger, the constant need to be on his guard. The one part of being on the run that he'd never got used to was the dirt clinging to his skin for sometimes weeks on end. If they couldn't keep themselves clean, there was nothing at all to separate them from animals.

Even though it was the height of summer, the sudden splash of water was still cold where it touched his torso and groin but he didn't mind in the slightest. The momentary sting on his skin lifted the fatigue, forced him to think rather than to complain. 'We still have to find a way out of it, Willie.'

'I agree with you. But it has to be on our terms.'

'I'm not sure we're strong enough for that anymore. The people are exhausted. They want peace. We've no weapons left and the Crown Forces are learning how to take us on.'

'Maybe. Or maybe you're listening too much to what they're saying in Dublin.' Willie immersed himself in a pool deep enough to cover most of his body. 'Down here in Munster is where the real war is being fought, not up there. We've taken everything the British have thrown at us and we're still in control.'

'But for how long more?'

'Longer than the British.' He joined Ned on the bank and began to dry himself with his coat. 'Do you think we're war weary? They're in an even worse situation than we are. They've corrupted their entire culture with this war. Opening up the jails and arming lunatics to make up the Tans. Signing up gentlemen murderers and calling them the Auxillaries. They've let the worst elements of their military kill, rape and burn their Empire into infamy.' He picked up his shirt. 'And they still haven't beat us. They can't sink any lower and even their own people are turning against them now.'

Ned heard the aircraft overhead, then saw the metallic lump whistle to the ground a few hundred yards downstream. 'Want to bet?' he shouted over the thump of the explosion.

'Incendiaries!' screamed Patie as the plume of acrid smoke rose from the trees. 'Into the river, lads! They're trying to smoke us out.'

The trees were too damp for the fire to take hold and they managed to avoid contact with the smouldering fragments of phosphor that reacted with everything they touched. And there was just enough air trapped below the banks of the river to stop them from inhaling the carpet of smoke wafting across the floor of the wood.

They waited for over an hour before they dragged their shivering bodies out of the water and stayed put until nightfall as the aircraft continued to drone across the sky. Crossing the fields in the darkness, they could hear the tenders and the armoured cars patrolling along the roads in the distance and, when morning came, they decided that it would be safer to spend the day sleeping in the ditches rather than trying to break through the mobile cordon around Shanagolden and their path to safety in the hills beyond.

When he woke later in the evening with his joints creaking from the time in the water, Patie strained his ears for any sound other than birdsong, grasshoppers, animal rustle and the snores of his comrades. Nothing out of the ordinary could be heard, not a motor engine, not an aircraft, not a footstep, not a voice anywhere around them.

'Strange, isn't it?' he asked.

Willie rubbed his eyes and sat up. 'What's happening?'

'Nothing. Nothing at all.'

'What are you on about?'

'No, listen. It sounds as if they've gone away.'

Patie scanned across the fields in every direction as the rest of the column roused themselves from their sleep. The area hadn't looked as quiet since the morning he had walked down to Foynes to sign up for the Great War. Just over two miles across the fields and he'd be home.

'Looks tempting, doesn't it?' He handed the field glasses to Willie.

'Too tempting, I'd say.'

A few of them were willing to give it a try but caution prevailed and the column hung on through the night. They'd nothing to lose by waiting on when they had almost no arms to protect them.

Taking what was left of the ammunition, Patie and Dick went on ahead at sunrise, moving under the shadow of hedges that they'd known since childhood and signalling the rest of them on when they were sure of the path ahead. One field at a time, they edged ever closer and still Patie heard no sound. Dread crept into his mind that the Auxies had shot up the entire town in reprisal for the ambush.

The newer lads were getting impatient as they stopped within sight of the church. Just a field separated them from the cross at the top of the town but, if there was any military presence in the area, they would surely see it pass by. An hour had gone by before Patie caught the first sign of movement, an ass and cart making its way to the creamery. When it was followed soon after by a handful of people walking into the town, he could tell from the brisk confident pace that there were no Crown Forces around.

Keeping to the line of the hedge, they stole across in single file to the gap opening onto the road. There was no one to be seen in either direction, nobody around the school or around the church. But neither was there any sense of danger in the air.

'What do you think?' asked Patie as they hid behind the wall of the church, keeping three escape routes open in case they were surprised.

'It's worth a chance.' Willie peered out through the gate under the laurel tree. 'God damn it! This is our home town and it's been a year since we appeared here in public.'

Never had Patie's feet trodden with such care on a road that he'd been down a thousand times before. Never had he looked at the house as a strange feature on the deserted main street rather than the home in which he'd spent most of his life. For a moment, he was transported back to a ghost town that he'd seen in Flanders after the German retreat had left nothing living nor habitable in its wake.

Over the bridge and around the twist in the street, Dick covering him on one side and Mossy on the other, he heard the first sounds. Someone was singing to the tune of a fiddle. There were cheers and there were shouts in the background. But he still approached the rise in the road with caution.

He raised his hand for the others to follow. Together, the flying column of the Fourth Limerick Brigade looked down Shanagolden's main street to the crossroads. The entire parish was out, spilling out of the pubs, slapping each other on the backs, yelling and singing, men and women embracing each other in public. Not yet nine o'clock in the morning and they were already celebrating like the time they won the county final or when Ned had beaten Hennessy in the 1918 election or like that Belgian town that Patie had been in when the Armisitice had been called.

They weren't noticed for a few moments as they strolled down the hill. Then one woman turned her head, tapped another beside her, embraces were dropped, drinks were left aside and the whole lot of them ran up to mob their tired, unshaven and ragged band of rebels. Patie felt the arms grabbing his legs, the shoulders pressing under his buttocks, the strange sense of elevation as hands reached up to shake his, the triumphant procession wobbling back down the crossroads.

'The truce!' Philip Hurley was shouting at him. 'Haven't you heard?'

Patie thought of a victory in Belgium three years back that he'd never really felt part of.

'It comes into effect at noon today,' the schoolmaster continued. 'Dev is going over to London on Wednesday to begin the negotaitions with Lloyd George.'

He'd relish this one. 'Twould make up for the detachment he'd felt on Armistice Day when everyone else around him was celebrating like mad.

'Isn't it unbelievable, Patie?' Mary Hourigan planted a big wet kiss on his lips. 'Just the couple of thousand of ye and ye've brought the entire British Empire to its knees.'

He didn't want to be the centre of attention. He'd have preferred it if Ned had accepted the accolades on behalf of the column and roused everyone with one of his speeches. But they kept crowding in on top of Willie and he didn't know how to answer their questions that they kept firing at him and the congratulations that they kept showering on him and the cheers and the small talk and the instant insincere friendships of two-faced chancers like Hennessy who would have collected the ransom on his head off the British had he been given half a chance.

He just wanted to be left to soak it all in for himself. He wanted privacy for the moment. He'd spent the last seven years fighting under one guise or another. He wanted to reassure himself, really and truly, that every sacrifice that they'd made and every life that they'd taken and every life that they'd lost had been worthwhile.

He wanted to be alone.

The rains came to his rescue. Down came the thunder shower in buckets, scattering the crowd and sending everyone, even the children, the infirm and the total abstainers, scurrying for the shelter of the pubs. Maybe God was signalling His approval.

Only Josie remained out in the open. Drenched to the skin, they approached each other and held each other under the torrent falling from the skies and felt each other's warmth as they pressed their lips and circled their tongues and squeezed their fingers and panted their breaths in the momentary solitude of the crossroads.

They were still there when the downpour passed as quickly as it had arrived. An Army lorry screamed up from the Newcastlewst direction and he toppled her over into the cover of the landlord's memorial as the Auxies unleashed a hail of gunfire up both sides of the main street.

Mossy, Dick and Patie were the first out of the pubs and Jimmy followed to release his last remaing bullet in the direction of the speeding vehicle.

'The murdering bastards!' he shouted after them.

'They couldn't stop killing even when the war is over.' Mossy jumped into Doctor Molyneaux's car parked on the other side of the street. 'We could catch up with them if we wanted.'

'What's the point?' Willie dropped the unloaded rifle that he'd instinctively raised to his shoulder and watched the lorry disappear over the rise in the main street as it sped off in the direction of Rathkeale. 'They're gone ... After nearly eight hundred years, the hoors are gone forever.'

Part Four

Brother against brother

July 1921 – February 1923

You fought them, darling Willie,

all through the summer days.

I heard the rifles firing in the

mountains far away ...

38

PEACE DROPPED like an explosion. Freed from the burden of searches and checkpoints and worries about their own safety, the country emerged from hiding into the bright sunlight of the summer to talk and to play, to drink and to sing, to buy and to sell, to travel, to eat and to make merry. Years of repressed energy found their release in those magic few days of in the middle of July 1921.

The euphoria lasted most of the week. Then the digestion began.

For those who had the most to lose, the future held nothing but fear. District Inspector Sullivan faced a steady stream of informants looking for protection as the rebels descended from the hills and their supporters came out of the woodwork. But what assurances could he give them? Even in those towns where they had maintained a presence throughout the Troubles, the RIC's authority had disappeared.

Not that he had anything other than contempt for the supplicants arriving at the barracks. Their only motivation had been greed or spite or snobbery, or a combination of all three and their only problem was that they hadn't switched sides as quickly as the most vociferous of those condemning them. If he had been of a mischievous bent, Sullivan could have passed on information about some of the stalwarts now loudly proclaiming their patriotism that would have catalogued their record of squealing, but that had never been his way and anyway, enough blood had been spilled.

'They were banging the windows of the house again last night,' complained the merchant who'd made a fortune out of supplying the force with rotten food that no one else would buy. 'I demand that something be done about it.'

'We'll look into it,' was all that came out of the inspector's mouth. Run off after the Black and Tans, his mind was telling him. Only the regular RIC remained in Newcastlewest as the Tans and the Auxies had hightailed it back to Dublin and England the moment the Truce came into effect. And even then, they left as much bitterness as they could after them, ransacking bars and houses and dumping two corpses along the road with the backs of their heads blown away.

Less than half of Sullivan's depleted numbers had shown up that morning. Most of the missing would never be seen again. Without military protection, their uniforms were now a liability in an area where memories and grievances stretched back through centuries of time. And the inspector thought about what was in store for himself. Despite all the rubbish talked by Colonel Guthrie-Shaw and his superiors about bringing the rebels to their knees and reducing them to little more than surrender, everyone on the Crown's side of the fence knew that they had lost to a ragtag collection of farmers and labourers and shop assistants with hardly a weapon between them.

Regardless of what way the negotiations worked out, a new order would descend on West Limerick, one in which Nicholas Sullivan would play no part. But until they told him otherwise, he would remain at his post in spite of whatever threats might be laid against his personal safety. His only concern was for his family but, apart from his wife, they were scattered over Ireland, England and America and were far enough away from anyone who could trace them. He'd suggested to Bessie that it might be better if she went to stay with her sister who was the matron of a nursing home in Worthing, but she'd hear nothing of it and wasn't going to desert the man she'd been married to for thirty-four years.

He buried his head in his hands as ConstableReilly guided the last of the supplicants out. 'And those are the people we're defending,' he sighed.

'You'll be all right, sir.'Reilly closed the door behind him. 'They've been told you acted honorably and they believe it.'

He looked up at the constable's impassive features. 'So you were their contact all the time?'

'Yes, sir. I followed my beliefs to the best of my abilities. And if I might add, sir, you did the same yourself.'

'And I always suspected it was Walsh.' Sullivan could have felt betrayed by a colleague who had served almost thirty years in the police, butReilly's actions were no different from the hundreds of others who were snitching to the military or the intelligence services, or to faceless civil servants in Dublin Castle. And at least he'd acted out of conviction rather than for personal gain.

'No. He's too busy making money, sir.'Reilly folded his hands behind his back in contravention of the Force's most cherished regulation. 'I suppose you'll be wanting my resignation?'

'Don't be silly,Reilly. You can't do any damage to us now. In fact, you're more valuable to us inside the barracks than outside. And anyway, I believe you're only a few months from retirement.'

'Thanks, sir. I was hoping you'd say that.'

District Inspector Sullivan watched the constable depart back to the day room, disappointment and relief mixing with professional annoyance that he'd been outwitted for the past three years. Caught out by a timeserver likeReilly! If word of it ever got out, he'd never live it down.

Councillor Thomas Hennessy figured that it was time to convert everything into cash. The Truce had resuscitated a market that had been dormant for the best part of a decade and which had missed out on the immediate postwar boom experienced by most countries of Europe. Land-hungry farmers, their second sons and gentleman investors were looking around at what to do with the money accumulated during the fat days of the war, and enquiries were coming into his auctioneering business for holdings that had been for sale for years. Values were still a far cry from what they had been during the last period of normality, but at least property was moving, rather than losing money through taxation, and through tenants and lessees who could no longer be evicted when they refused to come up with the rent.

Others would have said that he was getting out at precisely the wrong time, but the councillor had little faith in the immediate future. For all the rosy talk on the other side of his bar counter, he knew that the ceasefire could break down at any moment and another bout of conflict would cause an even greater collapse. And even if the negotiations did lead to an independent republic or dominion, the new state might have its own currency which would soon lose its value against real money. He'd read about the troubles that the Germans, French and Italians were having in keeping their marks and their francs and their liras afloat and he didn't want a similar fate to befall his own hard-earned fortune.

Only the Bank of England could be trusted. The British Government might have been experiencing its own economic woes as a result of its war debts, but hell would freeze over before the pound sterling, backed by the gold-filled vaults of London, would be allowed to turn into fancy wallpaper.

And unlike those selling under pressure or those now coming back to the market, Hennessy's profits were already guaranteed. Tipped off by Constable Walsh, he knew in advance when and which properties would be ransacked by the Tans and the Auxies and he'd bought up a fair few of them at knockdown prices when their owners had run out of the energy needed to start up all over again. And in return for a small slice of the action, he'd let the policeman front for him, so that there were no records tracing his fingers through the transactions.

Even after all the deductions like keeping the land registrar and the other parties' solicitors sweet so that deals were completed with the minimum of red tape and the minimum of inspection, there would be enough left over to deposit in the City of London where a man could always be sure of his money. Maybe when things settled down and his political stature was restored, he could bring some of it back, but he'd have to wait until those with revolutionary ideas were sidelined and sensible men were given the chance to lead Ireland back on the road to recovery.

The school was open again after the summer holidays, but Josie Reidy's mornings were no longer the frantic juggle of trying to keep the farm from falling apart and running the Republican court while, at the same time, educating the entire youth of the parish. Philip Hurley had come out of hiding to take the nine-year-olds and upwards off her hands as well as opening the building before they arrived, while Jimmy McCarthy's return meant that she no longer had to worry about the milking and delivering to the creamery. The Truce had also breathed a new lease of life into her father. Dipping into his savings, Edmund Reidy splashed out on thirty choice acres that had come on the market and was looking at another property which would propel him into the exalted circle of hundred-acre men.

So she was in an unusually carefree mood as she cycled up to the crossroads, passing out the line of asses and carts on her way. 'Any sign of Ned coming back?' roared Mary Hourigan standing behind the reins like a cowboy trying to bring a galloping stage coach under control.

'Maybe next week.' Josie had seen little of Ned since the ceasefire and even Willie was away for weeks on end as the second Dáil Éireann debated the terms unfolding from direct negotiations with Lloyd George's British Government. Both of them had been on the Sinn Féin list of candidates that had been elected without opposition four months earlier. 'But you never can tell.'

'You might tell him I can't wait around forever.' The other farmers laughed at Mary's raucous response but, beneath all the bluster, Josie knew that she still held a candle for her brother. And left on her own on the farm with a widowed mother who'd never pulled herself together after Dan's death, she faced all the loneliness of a young woman of marriageable age working it away on her own.

Mary could have taken on a labourer or two who would have given her more time for herself but, having taken on the responsibilities when her father died and Dan was jailed the first time, she wasn't willing to go back to being at the beck and call of any man. With one brother a priest out in Africa on the missions, another a doctor in England, a third settled on his own property in Australia and her two sisters married well, the farm would be hers when her mother passed on and she was making sure that it was going to be run the way she wanted.

At least Mary was hanging on to what she had gained. For all the hardships brought on by the Great War and the Troubles, women had gained unprecedented opportunities to live a life outside the kitchen. But now that the men had returned from the fighting, they were being pushed aside once again regardless how good a job they'd done filling in. Josie had been running a school, a farm and a courthouse and, while she'd welcomed the reduction in her workload, she also felt a pang of regret at being sidelined. Maybe when they got their new state, the men might realise the contribution that she and all the other women had made in their absence.

She wondered most of all whether Willie would remember. He mightn't have been cut out for the life of a politician and he'd unsuccessfully tried to get Philip Hurley nominated for the Dáil in his place, but at least he'd retained an innocent belief in what the fight for freedom was all about. And she wondered what he'd do when it was all over. Willie had gone from being a labourer at the creamery to an army commander, but she knew that he'd throw away his uniform at the first chance he'd get. Maybe he might try to get an education, build on the avenues of interest that had been aroused when he was interned in Frongoch. She was painfully aware of how self-conscious he felt about his own lack of schooling compared to hers.

Meanwhile, she'd have to inspire another generation about the value of learning. A new nation was being built and it was their chance to turn it into a fairer place than the one she'd been brought up in.

The new manager had graduated at the top of his dairy science class in the Queen's College in Cork but had been out of a job since his previous place of work had been blown up by the Auxies. With half the plants in Munster out of commission, he jumped at the first opportunity he got and, even though it meant moving seventy miles from where he'd been living and almost a hundred miles from his home town, he'd been taken on because he'd take the drop in pay and because, without wife or child to think about, he was immediately available.

But then again, maybe they were desperate to get anyone at all. After he'd accepted their terms and conditions, they told him that the rebels had strung up his predecessor in the main street as an informer.

Like most creameries emerging from two years of mayhem, Shanagolden was a challenge, but at least its committee was aware of the problems facing them. Volumes had dropped below the level of profitability and standards had fallen during the years of producing any sort of rubbish for the voracious appetite of the Great War. But he was mad keen to shake off the frustration that had gripped him over a summer of enforced idleness and he descended like a whirlwind on a co-operative society that was trying to pull itself together on a supplier base whose herds and savings had been savaged by the Crown Forces' vindictive policy of reprisal.

It had taken him just an instant to realise that the creamery was in serious trouble, and less than a day to work out that the weights and the books and the fat contents were being fiddled and that no notice at all was being taken of even the basic rules of quality and hygiene. If the plant was to keep going after all the wanton destruction by the Tans, his farmer employers had to get as fair a price as possible and their milk had to be turned into the best butter that the machinery could make. And if they got that far, they could then think of making cheese and canning condensed milk so as to provide a source of income less dependent on the whims of the market market and on the seasonality of supply.

But it wasn't going to happen with the staff that he'd inherited. Despite the most strenuous representations made on their behalf by Councillor Hennessy, the assistant manager and the cutest but laziest of the three labourers were shown the door and, after sweet-talking the butter-maker out of his year-long depression, he'd spent two weeks himself shifting milk on the landing before the tough-as-nails young woman who was always at the head of the morning queue told him that he was working his way to an early grave. So he'd taken her advice and taken on two former employees who'd just come down from the hills after wiping out a sizeable proportion of the Crown Forces in West Limerick.

That night in the pub, a raggedy little man called Flint bummed a drink or two off him and told him about the legendary Dick Mullane, who not only had been the most lethal sniper along the whole length of the Western Front, but who had shot his policeman brother right under the noses of the entire RIC division. He'd taken the story with a pinch of salt, especially after Flint claimed that he'd served four years at the Front himself and that he'd twice escaped execution by the Crown Forces by the skin of his teeth during the Troubles. Still, he was intrigued by the pair starting up the following morning.

They turned out to be ordinary, unremarkable men in their mid-twenties who looked no different from those around them, although he did catch a momentary glint in the stocky fella's eyes that suggested something more serious beneath the exterior. They were damn good workers as well, getting stuck in without a word of complaint and never needing to be told what to do. The big easygoing fella, Patie they called him, was a lot smarter than he looked and had taught himself how to keep books and tot up strings of numbers in his head without having to write them down.

By the end of the week, the manager had found himself a new assistant who could run the collection and the records, leaving him free to sort out the quality, the money and the machinery.

Seeing that her advice had been taken also made the big girl happy. She'd warned him that anyone recommended by Councillor Hennessy was only a waster and that he'd be better off ignoring what all the half-baked experts in the town and on the committee were telling him and trusting his own judgement instead. She was some woman, that Mary, afraid of no one and running a good-sized farm all on her own after her brother, the rebel hero Dan Hourigan, had died on huger strike. He wouldn't mind getting to know her better.

The new man was a big improvement on James Horgan. Patie Fitzgibbon's memories of his last time working at the creamery were dominated by the petty tyranny of the late and unlamented manager. But now, instead of being constantly pulled up and made to work back for no reason other than to show who was boss, they were allowed to get on with their work. Maybe it was a sign of what the future laid in store. Never before would someone of Patie's background have been given the chance to work as an assistant manager.

But unlike most of those who hadn't been directly involved in the fighting, he didn't hold the same optimism about the negotiations that were to resume within the next few weeks. The Truce might have made everyone's life easier, but it wasn't an end in itself. The fighting had only been suspended and he wouldn't put it past the British to drag out the talks so that everyone got used to the peace before they went back on the offensive again. So while he worked away during the day at the creamery, he joined up at night with Dick, Mossy, Jimmy and the rest of the column to collect whatever arms and ammuniton they could lay their hands on and dump them in case they were ever needed. Until a treaty was signed and he was formally discharged by the government to whom he had sworn allegiance, Volunteer Patie Fitzgibbon was still a soldier on active service in the army of the Irish Republic.

'You're part of the staff now, Patie.' Dick grabbed the first churn from Mary Hourigan's cart and wheeled it over to the separator bath. 'You don't have to help me out on the landing.'

Although old habits died hard, Patie went back to his desk and waited for the scales to settle. 'Check. One hundred and seventy one!' he shouted as he entered the weight in the ledger. 'Chalk it down!'

'That's right.' Mary was telling Dick. 'Chalk down what Mr. Fitzgibbon says is the weight, like a good man. And look lively about it. I haven't all day.'

'He's keeping a right good eye on you, Mary,' Dick scratched the number on the empty churn.

'Who? Patie?'

'Mr. Harrington. The manager.'

'Would you go on off with yourself, Dick Mullane.' She rolled the empties back onto the cart.

'He's not married either. A single man with a good job living on his own in a strange town.'

'I'd say he might be entertaining serious intentions about you, Mary,' added Patie. 'You could do an awful lot worse in these hard times.'

'Easy known what your fine new job has done to your brains, Patie Fitzgibbon.' The farmers behind her cheered her on. 'Adding up them figures has you seeing the strangest of things.'

But underneath the bravado, he thought he saw the faintest trace of a blush on Mary Hourigan's cheeks.

She jangled the reins and the ass, unimpressed as ever by the urgings of his warrior queen, plodded the cart around the building at his own untroubled pace to wait for her skim while Patie totted up her weights. No one, not even those with far bigger herds than hers, would beat her again that day and he might even point the numbers out to Mr. Harrington. Behind him, his boss interrupted his conversation with the fitter and found some reason to place himself beside the skim tank.

Unsure of how long it would last, everyone was trying to grasp their piece of normality in this land fought over by two governments and paused between two doors of history. Even Patie himself was thinking of what he might do with the pay packet that he'd be getting at the end of the week.

The talking was over for the moment. After much discussion, Dáil Éireann had agreed on the delegation and had sent the five of them and their secretary off to London to strike a deal with Lloyd George. While they were locked in conclave, all the other members could do was to wait for the occasional despatches to make their way back across the Irish Sea.

For some, it was the chance to indulge in speculation and they were already thinking of what jobs they might land in a government that had yet to be negotiatied, let alone agreed on by the Dáil. For others, the inactivity led to fears of whether the British would shaft them or their own crowd would shaft them or of who was going to sell out whom. For a few, it meant time to reactivate the administration of the Irish Republic, which had lost its way during the weeks of euphoria that followed the Truce.

Little cliques were developing. The IRB insiders kept close to Michael Collins. The original Sinn Féiners, those who were already members of the party before the Volunteers took it over after the Easter Rising, took their lead from Arthur Griffith. The fighting commanders of the Munster flying columns found common cause. The men from Ulster looked for reassurance from each other as their people were being hunted from their homes by murder gangs tolerated by the new Unionist government of Northern Ireland.

Each day of uncertainty chipped away at the unity of purpose that had forced Britain to the negotiating table. And outside the debating chamber of the Mansion House, the army that had got them that far waited for directions.

After weeks of uncertainty, Willie Hartnett had had his fill of Dublin. They could call him back when they had something definite to talk about but, in the meantime, he'd be better off staying amongst his own. There were already Dáil deputies saying that the fighting was over, claiming that the IRA was so short of weapons as to make it impossible to resume the campaign. But if that was the case, then the Truce was nothing more than a surrender and the British could impose any solution they liked.

The Fourth Limerick Brigade didn't see it that way and, to the best of his knowledge, neither did the First nor the Second nor the Third nor any other unit in the neighbouring counties. Regardless of what the armchair generals in the General Headquarters might say, they'd driven the Crown Forces out of Munster and Connacht and John Bull would need to call up his entire army, navy and air force if he ever wanted to return.

'And how might the negotiations be going, Colonel Hartnett?' asked the passenger beside him as the train chugged out into the open country after stopping in Maryborough. It took Willie a few moments to place him as he shrugged a non-commital answer.

'Is it true that we'll be offered Dominion status? Something like what they have in Australia and Canada?' continued the journalist working for a Limerick-based local newspaper.

'Your guess is as good as mine, Alphonsus.' A few other heads turned in the carriage. 'In fact, I'd go so far as to say you'd have a better idea of what's going on than I have.'

'Isn't that Colonel Willie Hartnett?' whispered a lady in the seat behind him to her companion. He winced at the mention of rank. In their efforts to create the appearance of a functioning state, Erskine Childers's propaganda unit had gone mad granting everyone titles and every IRA commander was now referred to as a general or a colonel or a commandant even if his only contribution to the campaign had been to appear by mistake on a Wanted poster.

He looked out the window at a landscape pausing for breath during a moment of peace. He couldn't wait to get home.

Patie had met Josie on the train up from Foynes and kept her company while she waited on the platform as the arrivals from Dublin spilled out of the carriages. Now that the railways were offering a full service again without the threat of disruption, anyone with the time and the money was availing of their first chance in years to travel the network. Inside the crowded temple of transport, ladies of means coming back from the capital summoned porters to carry their purchases, a retreat of nuns mingled with a squadron of touring cyclists in their knickerbockers and tweeds, commercial travellers were arrriving, British soldiers were departing and a noisy class of uniformed schoolboys on an excursion waited in line for a harried pair of Jesuit priests to tick them off their list.

He hadn't been to Limerick himself since he'd come home from the Front and the bustle of activity around the station failed to hide the scars of the Troubles. The shops, the pubs and the commercial hotels all looked run down, as if money had stopped passing over the counter, and many of them bore the marks of bullets, the scars of destruction or the erosion of disuse. Nelson Street, Queen Street and Roches Street were pocked with buildings that had burned down, closed down or had just fallen down from neglect and nobody had bothered to reconstruct them. Three years on, the city looked a far cry from what it had been in 1918 and further again from that September Monday when he, Dick Mullane and Johnny O'Brien had been sent off to war.

'Spare us a copper. Spare us a copper, sir, and may God bless you.' Squatting on the floor with his back propped up against an enamelled hoarding advertising a brand of plug tobacco, a blind man rattled his tin cup. Even though he was wearing uniform of the enemy, Patie searched in his pocket for a coin and wondered what lay in store for the wreckage of the Empire's wars should the Britian of his allegiance leave Ireland completely. A few more of the ex-serviceman's comrades were working the platforms with their empty sleeves, their disfigured faces, their white canes or their pinned-up trousers legs, hobbling on their crutches or pulling what was left of their bodies around in metal bowls. Maybe this was their last hurrah, their final chance to extract pennies of sympathy from the departing garrison.

'There he is!' Casting aside the propriety of the schoolteacher, Josie was waving beside him like an excited schoolgirl and then surrendered to a surge of welcome that swept her up the length of the stationary train.

He left her at it and allowed himself to be drawn to the newsboy roaring the title of his paper with a streetcall from which the decades of repitition had robbed all vestiges of intelligibility. In between the advertisements for the gentlemen's outfitters of William Street and the doctors of Pery Square, the death notices, announcements by the grocers of Brusnwick Street that they had reopened for business and a single sentence informing that the negotiations in London were continuing, the Chronicle mentioned that the eldest son of one of Limerick's finest families had won a prestigious annual prize at Cambridge University. Most likely, it would be the last the city would ever hear of him. Smart lads like this budding mathematician never came back.

'Patie Fitzgibbon!' He felt the tap on his upper arm and turned around. 'I thought it was you!' Sergeant Rosebalde slapped him around the shoulders.

'Alf! Long time no see.' Patie returned the embrace and nodded at the British Army kit bag on the ground. 'Going home?'

'Yes. We've finished our tour. And we're damn glad to be out of here.' Hands shook with the unexpected resumption of a familiarity that had survived four years in the trenches. 'No offence.'

'None taken.' The newsboy tapped Patie's elbow for his penny. 'And I'd be a liar if I said we weren't glad to see the back of ye.'

'You made quite a name for yourself, Patie. I thought you might.'

'We all did our bit.'

'A bit?' Roseblade shook off the attentions of a porter. 'You mightn't realise it, but you and Dick Mullane were the number one targets of the Limerick garrison.'

'Should I feel proud?' Patie edged them away from surrounding ears that were pricking with interest. Suspicion of the unfamiliar had kept him alive during two years on the run and he still felt uncomfortable at opening his mouth where a stranger might overhear him.

'You can thank Maggot Tibbs for it. He turned the pair of you into legends.'

'All over and done with now, I hope,' he shouted over the blast of escaping steam. 'Do you want to go to somewhere quieter where we can talk?'

'I'd love to but our train is leaving in a few minutes.'

'Then maybe some other time.' They'd been mates, they'd been foes and Patie would have liked to pick up on their friendship again. His former sergeant was one of the few decent memories he had of the Front.

A second lieutenant barely half his age was trying to attract Roseblade's attention. Josie was waving at Patie through a swarm of khaki on the move. The stationmaster was consulting his watch with all the solemnity of his calling. The guard stood primed with his flag.

They shook hands under a blast of sulphur-flavoured smoke blowing back up the platform. 'Before you go, Alf, do you want to meet a real legend?'

He was surrounded by a group of well-wishers as he emerged from the carriage but broke away the minute he saw her. Josie ran the length of the platform to make sure that no one else intercepted her Willie, all but crashing into a disapproving Reverend Mother in her disrespect of decorum, all but toppling over a stack of mailbags in her haste. She was away from all the prying eyes of Shanagolden and she didn't give a damn.

He dropped his suitcase with a clatter and lifted her off her feet as they touched. He crooked his arm under her bottom and twirled her around and panted against the angle of her neck and she nestled in the power of his embrace as he held her aloft as his queen and they laughed into each other's faces when they heard the polite coughs harumphing around them.

'Alphonsus Sexton. Miss Agnes Mulqueen. Miss Kathleen Mulqueen. Father Andrew Shinnors. May I introduce Miss Josephine Reidy.'

They sized her up with suspicion. She gave them the best smile she'd got. One by one, they melted. 'You're a very lucky man, Colonel Hartnett.' The elder and more severe-looking of the Misses Mulqueen gave her the stamp of approval with the faintest suggestion of a titter. 'Come along, Kathleen. Father Shinnors will find a cab to share with us.'

Underneath the joy of return, Josie could feel the tiredness in his bones as they slid away from the main current of movement and rested in the eddy of a pillar. 'Now tell me, Colonel Hartnett, is this politics even harder than fighting a war?'

'Oh, give me fighting any time. I'm just not cut out for the Dáil. Arguing the toss about absolutely nothing from one end of the day to another.'

'And Ned?'

'He's taken to it like a duck to water. I don't know how he does it with all these little feuds going on on the side.' He stepped back to retrieve his suitcase. 'There's Brugha and Collins. Childers and Griffith. Stack and O'Higgins. Rory O'Connor with just about everyone else.'

'And your own are selling you out.' She pointed to Patie in conversation with a British soldier.

Patie returned the wave. 'Willie Hartnett, Josie Reidy,' he introduced to his companion. 'Alf Roseblade. He was my sergeant over in Flanders.'

'A pleasure, Miss Reidy.' Roseblade extended his hand. 'An honour to have met you, Colonel.' The whistle sounded with impatience. He hurriedly picked up his kit bag and slapped Patie on the shoulder. 'Give my best wishes to Dick and Flint, Patie. And maybe we'll meet again some day.'

'I hope we do, Alf. Maybe some day we will.'

Intrigued by the crack opening on a part of his life that he'd never talked about, Josie watched Patie's lingering wave of goodbye.

'So what's it likely to be?' asked Patie.

'I've no idea.' Willie shrugged his shoulders. 'To tell you the truth, I'd be the last to find out. The story keeps changing the whole time.'

'Maybe you should have Patie up there with you,' she said. 'He's well connected with everyone.'

'You wouldn't catch me at that game, Josie. I'm just a simple foot soldier. Always was and always will be.'

'You know more than you're letting on,' she continued after Patie had left them.

'We just keep getting these reports that this has been conceded and that is being investigated and they're working towards a compromise on something else. But it's all rumour. Nothing definite to go on.'

'And you don't seem too happy either.' A flock of starlings fluttered above them before coming back to roost on the roof girders.

'I don't know. I just have a bad feeling about it. There's this big row about Dev not going on the delegation to London and even the dogs in the street know that it's split down the middle.' She felt the tremor of his doubts as he pressed his arm tighter across her shoulders. 'The British must be laughing their heads off, not that they ever took us seriously anyway. It never seems to have entered their heads that we've the same right to independence as Finland and Poland and Czechoslovakia and all these other new states that got their freedom a few years back.'

But his mood lightened as they stepped out into the autumn sunshine of a Saturday afternoon. Up on the high steps of the station they stood, watching the pedestrians snake along the footpaths, the carts laden with sacks of flour, bags of coal and barrels of beer teeter by ahead of the occasional lorry, car and bus and the herds of cattle and pigs being driven to the slaughterhouses, to the freightyard or back out the country. Apart from that couple of Saturdays in Blackrock during the weeks before the Easter Rising, this was their first time together away from the attentions of family and neighbour.

'Well then, Miss Reidy, let's enjoy a bit of this Truce.' He took her properly by the hand and they melted into the crowd below.

39

ICHAEL COLLINS should have been in attendance at the meeting of the IRB's Supreme Council but the mailboat carrying him back from London had been delayed after colliding with a fishing boat outside Holyhead. Instead, he'd sent on a copy of the Treaty ahead of him to the central Dublin hotel so that the Brotherhood's position could be determined ahead of the lunchtime meeting of the Dáil's cabinet.

'It's the best we could get under the circumstances,' Assistant Minister for Defence and IRA Chief-of-Staff Richard Mulcahy was saying, as Ned Reidy pored through the turgid prose of the document.

'Give me a minute, Dick. I want to read it for myself.' Conversations were mumbling around him as those outside the cabinet who hadn't been kept abreast of the negotiations tried to interpret the results of two months of discussions. The detail covered many more areas than the simple demand for independence that had fuelled their war, some of them highly symbolic but ultimately meaningless, others seemingly innocuous but with far more serious implications under the surface.

The deeper Ned examined it, the more concerned he became. If they accepted what was in front of them, the Unionist government of Northern Ireland could opt out of the new Irish Free State, they would still have to swear an Oath of Allegiance to the British King, the Royal Navy held on to their bases in Cork Harbour, Castletownbere and Lough Swilly, the British government retained a veto over the constitution and Ireland would be lumped with its share of the debt run up by a war which they'd opposed.

'There'll be a fair bit of disappointment,' he answered at length.

'It gives us independence in all but name,' argued Collins's leading supporter in the cabinet. 'We've financial autonomy, our own Foreign Minister, our own army, our own police force, every instrument of power of a functioning state. This goes much further than anything the British have offered us before.'

And if Mulcahy was in favour, then the Supreme Council was going to side with the Treaty. Ned looked around the room at the impatient and the puzzled, at the angry and the disappointed. Liam Lynch, Liam Deasy, Harry Boland and some other long-standing members were expressing their opposition, but they were always going to be in the minority. The leadership of the Brotherhood was dominated by Collins's supporters, filled with handpicked allies who had been swayed by his energy and vision in Frongoch and whose faith had been reinforced by his dazzling leadership during the campaign. Their loyalty would overcome any doubting Thomas who had fallen by the wayside during the Big Fellow's absence in London at the negotiations.

Yet even if Ned was one of Collins's inner circle of confidantes, he was still going to make up his own mind rather than having it bent for him by the zealots. Having spent two or three years on the run fighting for the Irish Republic, he knew that most of his colleagues in the Fourth Limerick Brigade would consider swearing an Oath of Allegiance to the King of England as a sellout. And some of those with a wider view of what the struggle was about would view the partition of the country and abandoning half a million Ulster Catholics to a Unionist state as nothing short of treachery.

But there was also the reality to consider. To the best of his knowledge, many of the IRA units were in no position to carry on the fight. If the British called their bluff, they wouldn't last jig time before they ran out of bullets or places to hide. The offer of a real sovereign state was far more than a continuation of the war was likely to deliver.

Power was what mattered, not the appearance. For the first time in over seven hundred years, Ireland could run its own affairs. Seven years earlier, the entire country would have settled for a glorified county council and it still couldn't get it.

Searching for an overlooked comma or a paragraph that might sway his intentions one way or the other, Ned looked over the document one last time. Mulcahy was forcing the issue as the numbers added up. Three had voted against and four in favour before they asked him for his opinion. Boland's eyes pleaded with him from across the room. Deasy drummed his fingers on the table. Lynch had resigned himself to the worst.

No to preserve unity.

Yes to make the best of what was on offer.

'I don't think we have any alternative,' he answered with a heavy heart. There were still a few more of them to put their views on the record, but everyone knew that the last chance of an upset had passed.

Five months of the ceasefire had allowed farming to settle down. Those with ambition could see a future ahead of them and none showed more than Edmund Reidy. Despite being only a few years short of his eightieth birthday, he was back in the saddle, fitter than ever and raring to take on the world. Even the arthritis wasn't bothering his hips during the first winter for as long as he could remember.

Josie marvelled at her father's vigour, yet was repelled by the narrowness of his vision. Nothing mattered to him but land and the status that it brought. Now that the last vestiges of the Anglo-Irish gentry were on their way out, he was seeing the final barrier to the highest rungs of respectability disappear. All that was bothering him at the moment was Mary Hourigan taking a shine to the new manager of the creamery.

'Ned missed his chance there with Mary. She spent years waiting for him but he was too busy getting himself thrown into jail and running off into the hills.' He piled another few spuds on his plate. 'Jesus, they were made for each other. Thirty-five acres of adjoining property. You wouldn't get a match like that if it was made up in Heaven.'

At least he kept off the subject of Willie Hartnett. If Lloyd George and Éamon de Valera could sign a truce, then so could Edmund Reidy and his daughter.

He was reaching for the pipe. Without giving him a moment to contemplate the last spud in the pot or the last slice of boiled bacon on the long serving plate with willow pattern, she cleared the table and dropped him his mug of tea with its two spoons of sugar and enough milk to take the scald out of it. She even left the Freeman's Journal beside his elbow, although his eyes weren't what they used to be and he was finding it difficult to read the newspaper in the candlelight.

Once the little blue puffs rose from the bowl at regular intervals and the tea descended in satisfied slurps, she was able to make her escape. It wasn't a night for cycling, but she forced herself down the lane, out beyond the crossroads and up the hill to Philip Hurley's house on the Demesne road. Willie, Patie Fitzgibbon, Dick Mullane and Mossy Noonan were there in the front room ahead of her, waiting on Philip to finish reading the document.

The clock ticked away in the background as the schoolmaster pencilled notes into a copybook and fingered his way back through the type.

'Hmmm.' He shook his head, then flicked the lank fringe out of his eyes.

They raised their heads in expectation. He aimed his pencil at the document, allowed it to hover over the middle of the page before dropping it again and turning the leaves back to the start.

Willie lay back in the rocking chair with his arms folded and eyes closed. Mossy picked up a dog-eared book and glanced through the opening pages. Patie was examining a pre-war map of Europe hanging on the wall, trying to figure out where all these newly-independent countries had sprung from. Dick kept his eyes trained on the door.

She threw another sod into the fire and stoked the ashes through the grate.

Philip was shaking his head again, this time demanding their attention. 'It's way short of what the Dáil was looking for ...'

Willie raised his eyebrows.

'... We're still in the Empire and the Unionists have the six counties to themselves.'

Patie and Mossy pursed their lips with rejection.

'What about this Boundary Commission they're talking about?' Josie asked. 'Aren't there Nationalist majorities in Fermanagh, Tyrone and Derry City?'

'A waste of time, Josie. Once the Border is drawn, the British aren't going to concede any more territory. Will the Dáil wear it, Willie?'

'I don't know, Philip. We certainly won't like it. There's a feeling abroad that the British coaxed us into a ceasefire, let us get used to it and then tricked the delegation into conceding on the Oath and Partition.' Willie rose to his feet and stood with his backside to the fire. 'But there's those who'll take a deal at any price.'

'Would Ned be one of them?' asked Patie.

'Most likely. I hear the Supreme Council of the Brotherhood is in favour and Ned is very close to Collins. The Big Fellow doesn't believe we can continue the fight.'

'I'd say nearly every one of the lads would see this treaty as a sellout.' Dick turned his attentions away from the door and back on the gathering. 'And despite what all them GHQ generals are saying up in Dublin, we can always pick the war up again. In Limerick alone, they'd nearly ten thousand between the Army, the polis, the Tans and the Auxies against just a few hundred of us and we still ran them out of the place.'

'It won't be as easy time, Dick.' Unlike those who'd spent the war up in the hills, Josie had been in daily contact with the mood of the town. There was no better barometer than children who'd blurt out in the schoolyard what their parents were afraid to say in public. 'I don't think the people have the same stomach for another five years of fighting.'

But she was only playing the devil's advocate. She was as disappointed as the rest of them that the Republic they'd created and all that it stood for could be cast aside in favour of a parliament that still touched its forelock to an English king.

Three years of fighting had suppressed disagreement. But now that it had ended, every forgotten rivalry bubbled to the surface. They might have been held in check by a firm hand from the top, but the cabinet itself was split down the middle. And in the corridors of Dublin's Mansion House, Dáil deputies gravitated around its two leading figues as the Sinn Féin monolith split into factions.

Willie Hartnett had no doubts about where he stood, but he was surprised by the flux of associations and alliances coming into being. Some of those he'd thought might have shared his views were now expressing doubts. Others whom he'd dismissed as outright opponents were voicing contrary opinions.

Those who'd been behind the IRA, those who'd been against it and those who had stayed on the fence, were all applying pressure of one kind or another on any deputy suspected of wavering convictions. Local supporters had forcibly given vent to their views one way or the other other as the deputies returned home for the Christmas break. The Church heirarchy, business interests, farmers groups, the press and many trade unions had come out strongly in support of the Treaty.

When the Dáil reassembled in the first week of January 1922, most of the persuaders left Willie alone. Along with a group of other brigade commandants from where the fighting had been fiercest, he watched from the sidelines while those of a less military background were singled out. First their principles were appealed to and then their common sense. And if that didn't work, as was almost always the case, they'd play on any rivalry they could think of. One's enemy's enemy suddenly became one's friend.

So while great lofty speeches were made in the chamber, and procedural compromises were unveiled to give the appearance of trying to preserve unity, the real business went on in the alcoves of the corridors. One side would denounce de Valera's cowardice for not leading the delegation to London and leaving Collins to carry the can. The others would badmouth Collins's treachery for signing a document without the prior approval of the cabinet. Dev should have gone; Dev had to stay behind to keep everyone else in line. Collins and Griffith were intent on doing their own deal with Lloyd George; the British had the delegation over a barrel and they had to take the best deal they could get.

Personality had taken over from principle, politics had supplanted the gun and exchanges became ever more bitter as they scrambled for the few remaining uncommitted votes. As the formal oratory wound down after anyone who felt like it had said his piece for the record, the deputies paused for a recess before the vote.

Hoping to get a few minutes of peace and quiet, Willie found an upturned crate to sit on behind a stairway a respectable distance away from the last-minute horse-trading. Closing his eyes and leaning his shoulders back against the wall, he shut his mind to the animated babble and the occasional insult passing over his head.

'I thought I might find you here.' Ned's tap on the kneecap roused him from his doze. 'All over now bar the shouting.'

They hadn't spoken in weeks. The tensions of the negotiations had driven a wedge through the bond that had shared almost a decade of combat and prison and, before that, another two decades of sport and growing up. 'You're not trying to win me over at this late stage? Are you, Ned?'

'No. I'd say your mind was made up from day one. And I've known you too long to waste my time trying to change it.' Ned propped himself up on the crate beside him. 'Still, I think this is a great opportunity. We'll finally have a real government of our own.'

Willie'd had his fill of plámás and he didn't want to hear any more, least of all from Ned.

'For once, Willie, Ireland will count for something. What was it Robert Emmett said before the English hanged him? *And when Ireland takes its place among the nations of the Earth, then and not till then shall my epitaph be written.* We won't be forgiven if we throw it away when we have it in our grasp.'

He hadn't been in the mood for an argument. He hadn't even contributed to the debate inside the chamber, instead leaving his record in the hills to speak for itself. Willie knew that he'd never been a man of words. Others were better at lifting the crowd or at putting their point of view across and, if that raised them to a position of influence, then the best of luck to them. He never begrudged anyone making the best out of what they'd got.

But he didn't like to be talked down to. Nor did he take to the half-learned rubbish that Ned was spouting out to him as if he was an eejit. Some fancy pen-pusher in Collins's entourage had come up with a line of justification and every one of the Big Fellow's admirers was spouting it off word for word.

'Maybe it's worth thinking over,' Ned continued.

'Yes, maybe it is,' he answered. 'But maybe ye should have told us that this was what ye'd settle for before we marched on the GPO. Do you think Patrick Pearse and Tom Clarke and Con Colbert gave up their lives for an Oath of Allegiance?'

'Then what do we do? Start fighting again? We've nothing left to fight with, Willie. You know that as well as I do.'

'We'd nothing to start with either.'

The conversations up the corridor were winding down as if everything that needed saying had been said. 'For God's sake,

Willie! Can't you understand we're in no position to press for any more? ...'

'What do you mean we aren't? We're after hunting the English from most of the country. If we hadn't them on the run, do you think they'd be talking to us? For the first time in our history, we have them by the balls. We can't lose our nerve now.'

The division bells rang, knocking Willie from his train of thought. He stared for a moment at Ned before returning on his own to the chamber.

'There's no need for us to fall out over this!' If Willie had heard the call down the corridor, he wasn't answering.

Not yet ready to face the passions of the chamber, Ned flopped back on the crate. He hadn't wanted to meet Willie but, because the numbers were so tight, he'd provoked a discussion that was always going to lead nowhere.

Most of the Dáil was in the same boat. The rancour over the Treaty had spilled over into every aspect of their lives. Families had split down the middle as fathers and sons and brothers and sisters took opposite sides. Friendships that had gone back years had fractured, neighbours set upon neighbours, comrades that had surivived years on the run no longer trusted each other.

'Ned!' someone was calling. 'Jesus Christ! Where are you, Ned?'

He waited for the voice to come closer.

'They're voting! You've only a minute before they close the doors!'

He slid off the crate and onto his feet.

'Aah, there you are!' panted Richard Mulcahy. 'We still don't know which way it'll go.'

He wandered into the chamber and through the division doors where the tellers were jotting down numbers. And then he followed the rest of the deputies back towards their seats. Even though Sinn Féin remained united on paper, the split had already occurred as the opposing factions gathered on opposite sides of the room.

Ned took his place in the second row behind Collins, Mulcahy, Arthur Griffith, Kevin O'Higgins and WT Cosgrave who'd surprised everybody by opposing De Valera. Willie was huddled in the far corner with the warlords of Munster.

To nobody's great surprise, the Treaty passed on a vote of 64 to 57. The real contest lay in the Presidency. Dev had resigned after the first division and immediately offered himself for re-election. If he was successful, he would appoint a new cabinet without Collins, Griffith and Cosgrave which would revoke the agreement with Britain.

Ceann Comhairle Eoin Mac Néill, the speaker of the Dáil, signalled to the tellers who nodded at each other in agreement. He tapped his gavel in a call for order. Ned couldn't make out from the tellers' demeanour which way it had gone. Promoting peace and a new state was one thing, overcoming Dev's personal prestige was a far greater challenge.

A thin voice questioned whether all procedures had been followed correctly. Another asked if everyone had got the chance to vote. A third raised some abstruse point of order before the impatient gathering intimidated the nitpickers into silence.

'On the vote to elect the President of Dáil Éireann,' intoned the Ceann Comhairle with all the drama he could muster. 'Éamon de Valera, 58 votes … Arthur Griffith, 60 votes …'

The remainder of Mac Néill's statement was drowned out by wild cheers on the Pro-Treaty side of the house. Walls thumped, floors were stamped in the chamber and up in the gallery and deputies clambered over benches to shake Collins's hand or clap him on the back. A stout quartet of backbenchers hoisted a bemused Griffith on their shoulders.

Ned remained where he had been seated. They'd stuck it out, they'd won, they'd held their nerve and their faith in a new state that was about to be born. And yet there was no satisfaction in the victory. The anger and sense of betrayal radiating across the floor was enough to remind them that only half of the country would be pulling with the new government.

'Have you a moment?' Collins had detached himself from the celebrations and steered Ned into the corridor outside. 'I know it's not everything we wanted. If the British had been in any way generous with us, we wouldn't have had half the bitterness.'

'We could have done without that bloody oath.' Ned tapped the ends of his unlit cigareette off the cardboard packet. 'What does it matter except to make it look like we haven't real independence? Not like Poland and all those other new countries who got theirs.'

'The difference is, the British were on the winning side during the War.' Muttering with his customary impatience, the Big Fellow rooted through his pockets for the matches. 'They can't let it be seen that their empire has lost anything. If we'd been ruled by the Austrians or the Germans, we would've got the lot.' Blue curls of smoke floated to the ceiling through a low shaft of sunlight. 'Look, I need another Munster man with me in the Provisional Government. That's where this Treaty will be won or lost.'

Willie slumped back into his seat when the result was announced. He hadn't been very confident about the outcome on the Treaty and, in a way, it hardly mattered as those who'd carried the fight had been outmanoeuvred by the sweet-talking lawyers, the haggling merchants, the teachers who could tell him how to put legs under hens and Collins's government-within-a-government inside the IRB's Supreme Council. They could vote through all the agreements they wanted. Making them stick in a country bred on rebellion was another matter entirely.

But he had been taken aback by Dev losing out to Griffith. For all the Jesuitical contortions he could perform on any point of principle, the Long Fellow alone had the vision to pull everyone along in the same direction. And he was even more surprised by the glee with which Dev's downfall had been greeted. They'd followed their leader when he was winning, they were now catcalling him in his defeat.

One by one, they left the chamber. Liam Mellowes and Countess Markiewicz, Frank Aiken and Cathal Brugha, Austin Stack and Seán McEntee and finally the Long Fellow himself. Only Con Collins, stunned into silence, remained beside Willie until the noise across the floor had died down.

'A bad day for Ireland, Willie.' The lesser-known Collins tossed his copy of the agenda on top of the paper piled on the floor.

'A bad day indeed, Con. The British have beat us out the gate without firing a shot.' Willie joined his fellow Limerick deputy in his trek towards the door. 'Give us another few months and we'll be tearing each other apart.'

The morning after the Treaty was passed, District Inspector Nicholas Sullivan sat at the back of Shanagolden church listening to the sermon at the Sunday Mass. As he had for much of the previous four years, the curate was filling in on the pulpit for his parish priest. Although Canon Murphy's nerves had staged a recovery of sorts around the time the Truce was signed, he'd gone off the rails again in the meantime and had to be packed off to a nursing home after he took to leading squadrons of angels down the main street in hot pursuit of the demons of the IRA.

Conscious of the various views held in the parish, Father Greaney produced a masterpiece of balance, urging everyone to look into his own heart to find what was right and to respect the opinions of others. As well he might. Just like the upright ConstableReilly, the young priest had managed to conceal years of active involvement in the rebellion from everyone except Sullivan.

There were others who had come out of the most surprising corners of the woodwork once the fighting had ended. Doctors, magistrates, landlords and businessmen, of impeccable reputation and whose well-being had been tied to the fortunes of the British administration, admitted to helping out the 'cause'. The Inspector didn't quite believe many of the protestations but some of them were genuine rather than chancers finding a new master to please.

Then again, what did it matter to him? With the signing of the Treaty, the RIC no longer had any official status and would be disbanded by the end of the month. Many of his colleagues, particularly those with visible Unionist sympathies, were heading north to join the Royal Ulster Constabulary. Others were finding work in Britain or in Palestine or in the colonial service and a few likeReilly who had done their bit for the IRA would be taken on by the new police force, the Civic Guards, that the Irish Free State was setting up. More than likely, he would take the pension himself. He had only another few years to go anyway and it was too late in life to transfer what remaining loyalties he possessed.

And he certainly wanted no part of the bitterness that was about to unfold. The embers were being fanned as he stepped out of the church and he lingered out of curiosity to observe the effects on the after-Mass gathering while his wife caught up on years of gossip with former neighbours that they had been unable to visit during the Troubles. Not unexpectedly, conversation was more animated than usual but, rather than the usual seamless exchange of civilities, those streaming out gathered into well-defined groups and consciously avoided any contact with others.

Perhaps Nicholas Sullivan was the only person in Shanagolden that morning who could look on with a sense of detachment. Not only had he not lived there for over ten years but his dispute was over and done with and, having accepted defeat with good grace, he was allowed to abstain from holding any opinion on its successor.

As he wandered back into the town on his own, his professional eye picked out the alliances, his trained ear gathered fragments of conversation and his prodigious memory, undimmed by the passage of time, fitted names and origins to every face he passed by. Putting everything he saw and heard together, he watched the cracks undermine the unity of a community that, despite every pressure put on them, had held together during the worst of the Troubles. It would be the same story in towns and villages all over the country that morning. There were both sweet sides and bitter sides to victory.

Those who already had the most felt the happiest and particularly those who hadn't latched on to the Sinn Féin steamroller when they had the chance. Councillor Hennessy's proprietorial air had returned for the first time since Ned Reidy had robbed him of the seat that was destined for him in the House of Commons. Doctor Molyneaux accepted the tipped hat brims expected of his standing in the town.

But satisfaction wasn't just confined to the Johnny Come Latelys. Farmers who had put up rebels on the run and who had suffered the reprisals of the Tans for their efforts, shopkeepers who had never turned their backs on the appeals for provisions and tradesmen who had hidden and repaired weapons were expressing relief that something real had come from their contributions.

'Thank God it's all over,' the wife of a blacksmith was saying.

'Maybe now we can settle down to a normal life again,' agreed a dairy man. 'No Tans or Auxies to worry about any more.'

Those who had taken a more active part weren't quite as elated. Sullivan edged past a gathering of his former prime targets. He'd spent two years trying to nail Dick Mullane and Patie Fitzgibbon, two of the two most lethal IRA men in the entire country, and now he could walk nonchalantly past them as they vented their anger with Jimmy McCarthy and Mossy Noonan. Fitzgibbon even passed him a glance as if to say that they'd drawn a line under their past dispute and their real enemy now were those across the street strutting their newly-acquired status.

'They're all coming out now,' McCarthy was complaining. He hardly looked a day older than sixteen. 'The Castle Catholics, the recruiting agents, the informers, everyone who hid under the bed while we done the fighting.'

Mullane just nodded. Sullivan saw only the shell of anonymity but, when he looked for meaning below, he was touched by the menace of hidden anger. And when all four pairs of eyes flickered in his direction, he moved away.

The thundering hooves would have shifted him anyway. Standing like a charioteer in his pony and trap, Edmund Reidy careered down the main street and all but knocked down Flint Barrett in his charge.

'Get out of the way, Barrett!' the old farmer roared. 'We're the gentry now!'

40

THE TREATY had been passed and the British were on their way back across the Irish Sea, but it wasn't at all clear who was taking their place. Both Michael Collins's Provisional Government that was to oversee the transition and Arthur Griffith's new Dáil cabinet had set themselves up as the legitimate authority within the twenty-six county Irish Free State; de Valera's old cabinet continued its allegiance to the thirty-two county Irish Republic and James Craig's Unionist administration cemented its hold on its six Ulster counties by unleashing the sectarian persecution of its Special Constabularies.

South of a Border that was already assuming a semblance of permanence despite the promise of a Boundary Commission, Collins was quickest off the mark. Dressed in his stately new uniform of Commander-in-Chief of an army yet to be defined, he presided over the formal transfer of Dublin Castle to the Provisional Government. Within days, newsreels of the British Army's ceremonial departure from the seat of seven and a half centuries of colonial rule flickered in every cinema in the country and the Free State of a paper document became a reality in the popular mind.

With a visible presence to hang their hats on, most of the County Councils transferred their allegiance to the Provisional Government and the Irish personnel in the former British administration who hadn't moved north to Belfast or back to London set up the new state's civil service. And to copperfasten the trappings of independence, postboxes, post offices, telephone kiosks and buses were all painted green over the imperial red and stamps were issued with the overmark of Rialtas Sealdach na h-Éireann.

However, the Army remained as it was, pledged to the Irish Republic even though the majority of the General Headquarters Staff were on the pro-Treaty side while most of the brigades were in the opposing camp. Although some of the political hawks in the Provisional Government and in Griffith's cabinet wanted to purge it immediately of anti-Treaty sentiment, Collins and and his Defence Minister Richard Mulcahy realised their regime's military limitations and were reluctanct to provoke a split. With no direction from the top, local units acted on their own initiative and occupied the army barracks being vacated by the British. As the phased withdrawal gathered pace, effective control of the country had passed to a collection of semi-autonomous brigades who were lining up either for or against the Treaty.

Ned Reidy, newly-appointed Minister for Public Health in the Provisional Government, joined the Volunteers for a convention of the four Limerick Brigades in one of the city's theatres. They'd been streaming in all day from all over the county and also from parts of East Clare. Not all of them had taken an active part in the war but, since nobody was quite sure which side most of the strangers were on, the faction leaders reckoned that they'd cancel each other out and refrained from unduly questioning their credentials. Anyway, apart from the flying columns, the notion of participation had a certain flexibility and could range from gun-running, gathering intelligence and sheltering men on the run to tearing down an RIC recruitment poster after a night on the sauce.

His green colonel's uniform straight from the tailor's rack and his Sam Browne belt and cavalry boots wafting of freshly-tanned leather added an aura to Ned's presence and he was guided up to the stage where he was seated beside Willie Hartnett, Paddy Ryan Lacken, Jim Colbert, Michael Colivet, Ernie O'Malley and other local commanders. A few cheers rang out from the gathering below, less than he'd hoped for but more than he'd expected, as he raised his hand in military salute. Maybe enough of them would see sense and row in behind the new state rather than hanker after the unattainable.

He shook hands with his colleagues on the platform and the response, while not warm, was at least civil. The discipline of the hills had instilled a sense of public unity among those leading the campaign. Regardless of how deeply they might have differed in private, they never let it show.

Despite his own misgivings, Collins and Mulcahy had insisted that Ned make a play to coax the Limerick brigades to the pro-Treaty side. Guarding the last river crossing that separated the West of Ireland from the rest of the country and standing on the gateway to the heart of Munster, the city's strategic importance could not be ignored by the Provisional Government, particularly since its four barracks would be vacated within a matter of days by the Royal Welsh Fusiliers. But Limerick was also the centre of some of the war's fiercest combat. Those who had triumphed there over the British had done so on their own with little or no help from the IRA's General Headquarters. Now that the fighting was over, they weren't likely to pay attention to any orders coming down from Dublin.

As the auditorium heaved to order, the other commanders gave him the floor. Ned had always been at ease speaking in public, knowing instinctively what his audience wanted to hear and how they wanted it said. Once his first dart hit the mark, he could tug the heartstrings and draw them into feeling that his message was theirs. But he couldn't put his finger on what would inspire this particular gathering of Volunteers. Maybe they didn't know themselves, because they were as divided and as confused as the rest of the people of Ireland.

One of the others, he couldn't quite identify the voice behind him, congratulated him on his appointment as a Government Minister. A polite applause greeted him as he settled into his pose of oration, easing the unaccustomed twitch of nervousness in his stomach.

They listened as he saluted their courage, their convictions and their stubborn refusal to be cowed by an infinitely superior military force that had stooped to the depths of depravity to defeat them. He reminded them that they had succeeded where the combined forces of Germany, Austria-Hungary and Turkey had failed and had brought Britain and its Empire to its knees.

Finding his spit, he piled on the imagery of their heroics. A few cheers rang out but they were too sparse to ignite the tumult. He'd expected a better response. So he told them that, man for man, there was no better fighting force in the world than the army of the Irish Republican and he was proud to be counted among them.

The volume inched higher, maybe as high as he could lift them.

'No other nation in Europe took on the mightiest of all of the empires,' he continued. 'No other nation in Europe fought for its freedom all on its own. And today, in this year of 1922, seven hundred and fifty-three years since the invader first stepped on our shores, Ireland takes its place among the free nations of the earth and can do so with pride at our unparalleled achievement.' He paused for a moment to let every spark of passion gather in his eyes and fill out his voice. 'We have our state now. Like every country recognised on God's earth, we have a civilian authority that binds every one of our citizens to the common good. And now is the time that we, the fighting men who made it all happen, will pledge our allegiance to the Provisional Government of Saorsát Éireann.'

He willed the roar to erupt but only a tinkle of cheers broke the silence of the theatre and then quickly faded, out of embarrassment.

'Go to hell, Ned! And take your Provisional Government with you,' shouted Dick Mullane after the last apologetic gesture of support had withered away. 'I'm backing Willie.'

The gathering opened up to let the men of his own flying column be seen. 'I won't be supporting you either, Ned,' said Patie Fitzgibbon. 'I take my orders from the Supreme Council of the Army of the Irish Republic. They're calling a national convention in a few weeks and you can put your case there if you want to. But until they tell me otherwise, I'm going along with whatever my commander Willie Hartnett says.'

They didn't cheer Patie, they just clapped, but the effect was the same and maybe even more so because of its cold formality. Those behind Ned joined in and it suddenly struck him that he didn't even resemble them any more as he stood alone facing the crowd in his spanking new uniform with its sparkling brass buttons and its bright shiny leather. Everyone else looked like a fighter just down from the hills, even those on the platform in their tattered trench coats, their broad black brimmers and their frayed breeches, with a few days stubble on their chins and smelling of the sweat of combat and of the heather of the slopes.

The footstamping joined in as the handclaps rose to a crescendo.

'Willie! Willie! Willie!' they chanted.

Knowing he had been beaten and more disappointed than surprised at the outcome, Ned descended from the stage and walked back up through the throbbing hostility of the aisles, wondering whether he'd been set up from the start. Both he and Willie avoided each other's eyes as they passed.

Mr. Harrington was waiting for them on the landing when Patie and Dick turned up at the creamery on the following Monday morning. Even though the other two labourers said they'd work back to cover them, the manager looked none too pleased about hearing of their early departure the previous Saturday, when Willie had come calling in a lorry carrying a dozen other colleagues in the brigade.

'For God's sake, Fitzgibbon, I thought you'd grown out of it.' He was standing above them but the landing's three feet of elevation failed to reinforce Harrington's presence against Patie's size and the hardness of Dick's demeanour. 'I'd great hopes for you but I can see now they were misplaced.'

'I'm sorry about it, sir, but we'd no choice,' Patie explained, suppressing his annoyance. 'We were called away.' And why should he have to explain? He hadn't missed a minute's work since he'd started six months earlier and most weeks he put in far more than that what was expected of him. What was more, he'd organised it so that everything was done right in his absence and he'd come back to check everything out after he returned on Saturday night just to be sure.

'A creamery is a business, not a charity. And I expect everyone appointed to a position of responsibility to treat it that way.' The manager sat himself down at the desk beside the scales and opened the collection ledger. 'I'm sorry to have to do this but you're back on the floor.'

'You'll do no such thing, Flor Harrington!' Arriving unnoticed, Mary Hourigan leaped straight from her cart to the landing. 'Patie Fitzgibbon was putting his neck on the line like a true Irish patriot while you were off enjoying yourself at the pictures. In the company of a lady, I might add, who might well be disappointed if you turned out not to be the man she'd thought you were. So if you cause Mr. Fitzgibbon any disquiet whatsoever, I'll ...'

Harrington shrank back in his chair as she rolled up her sleeves.

'... I'll never look at you again as long as I live.' Hands pressed to her hips, she towered over the desk. 'Now, get your backside off that chair and go back to your office and let a man who knows how to work the scales and write up the weights do the job he's being paid to do.' Much to his embarrassment, the manager was rewarded with a peck on the cheek and a playful tap on the backside to guide him back to his little room up at the other end of the building.

'And what are you waiting for, Patie Fitzgibbon, you with that look of a slow sheep on your face?' she roared as she manhandled the first churn onto the landing. Her chorus had arrived to take their places in the queue behind her and were enjoying a bravura performance from their grande dame.

Patie resumed his position, called out Mary's weights with a flourish and signed them off in the book and Dick chalked them onto her churns with a theatricality that befitted the occasion. And everyone had a good laugh as if nothing had happened.

But there would be no reprieve the next time. Although he'd grown used to the increase in his wages which gave him a few bob extra to spend on himself on top of what he gave to his mother and father, Patie knew that it was only a matter of time before he'd be called away again.

Despite successfully facing down Ned's efforts to take over the Fourth Brigade, Willie had left Limerick fuming at the ramshackle organisation in the city. While the Provisional Government busied itself with setting up the trappings of state, those opposing the Treaty were more interested in parading around with their weapons than making sure that normal services were resumed. For all Dev's prestige and the organisational skills of the likes of Harry Boland, they were left with no headquarters, no reliable means of communication, no money and no way of enforcing their authority other than through those on the ground who were too used to doing things their own way than to listen to orders from above.

Even in the Fourth Brigade's home patch, which was solidly under anti-Treaty control, it had taken an enormous effort to impose some semblance of order. After the British and the RIC departed from Newcastlewest, the flying column had been forced to reassemble in order to dissuade some part-timers, including a few opportunists who had joined up after the fighting was over, from holding up banks and commandeering supplies. That still left them with the problem of paying and feeding Volunteers who had no work and no income while others who had contributed nothing to the campaign or who had even collaborated with the British were doing nicely for themselves now that peace had returned. In the end, Willie, Mossy and Jimmy had marched into a bank in Askeaton waving their rifles, given the manager an official receipt, accepted a cup of tea from him and left with enough money to keep their more needy members from starvation.

And with the immediate threat of conflict having disappeared, much of the momentum faded from the parallel administration

580

that had held everyone together during the fighting. Some of the Republican police had taken the pro-Treaty side and the split had reduced the universal acceptance that they had previously enjoyed. Even though they did their best to remain impartial, the courts were undermined by taunts of favouritism by their political opponents. The welfare sytem collapsed as the County Council, caught in a limbo between two competing authorities, was unable to collect property rates and its other sources of income.

So while Patie and Dick still put in a day's work at the creamery, they were being called out most nights to settle disputes. The collapse of the old order sprouted new arguments over land, watercourses and rights to hunt, graze and cut turf; the decline of authority prompted the settling of old scores; the hope of the ceasefire had degenrated into envy, bitterness and greed.

'You'll see to it that that hoor of a neighbour of mine don't get his way?' the farmer was telling him as he totted up the weights. They looked a bit on the high side. 'Won't you, Patie?'

'We'll be up to you tonight, Taidhgín, to try and sort things things out.' He flicked back over the previous week's figures. They were up by over a fifth. Once the supplier had moved on around the back to the skim tank, Patie took the hydrometer from the drawer underneath the desk and dropped it into the separator bath. It sank well below the mark.

'Watering the milk, was our Taidhgín?' Mr. Harrington had sneaked up behind his back. 'We can't have anyone pulling the wool over our eyes.'

'Better off we say nothing this time, sir.' Taidhgín Connors had only the few acres, the money was tight and his neighbour was trying to squeeze him into a position of selling out. 'But tomorrow morning, I'll make it my business to check everyone's churns before we take them in. Taidhgín'll get the message and it's up to himself after that.'

'I don't ...'

'Maybe I might tip off Mary Hourigan on what I intend doing.' Patie cut in before the manager made an issue of it. 'She'll make sure the rest of them will understand.'

'Are you sure?'

'In fact, sir, I think it might be better if you called around to her yourself tonight. She'd listen to a man of real authority like yourself more than she'd listen to me.'

'Hmm.' Harrington gave an unconvincing impression of deep consideration. 'Do you think so?'

'And while you're at it, sir, you might bring a bunch of flowers with you as well.'

They met in Limerick Junction, not as the friends they had been since childhood, nor as the teammates who'd led Shanagolden's footballers to glory, nor as the comrades who'd commanded one of the most successful IRA units during the war. Two months of the Treaty had done for whatever their previous lives had shared and now Willie Hartnett and Ned Reidy faced up to each other as two angry chieftains on the bare platform of a railway station so far out of the way that it didn't even have a village around it. They'd been sent by their respective commanders, Liam Lynch and Richard Mulcahy, to try to find a way out of a gathering crisis.

'We'd an agreement, Ned, and ye broke it.' Within days of the Limerick Brigades rejecting Ned's plea for support of the Provisional Government, the pro-Treaty 1st Western Division came in from Clare in the middle of the night and were handed over the Castle Barracks by the departing Royal Welsh Fusiliers. Although Ernie O'Malley's 2nd Southern Division occupied the other three barracks the minute they got wind of the British evacuation, both sides immediately flooded in as many men as they could muster from neighbouring counties in order to reinforce their positions and only the reluctance of former colleagues to open fire on each other prevented the city of Limerick from being engulfed in all-out conflict.

'I'm sure it's just a misunderstanding.' Complete with his bowler and winged collar, Ned had shed his military manifestation in favour of the political.

'Misunderstanding my arse!' Further down the long platform, curious heads rose from their newspapers and forced Willie to contain his anger at the anodyne reply. 'Ye done a deal with the British and I'm just wondering what else ye might be doing with them behind our backs.'

'Look, Willie, I'm sure we can sort it out ...'

'There's only one way of sorting this out. You get Collins and Mulcahy to order Brennan to withdraw his men from the Castle and get the hell back to Clare with themselves.'

'And what if we don't? What do I tell Mulcahy?'

'There'll be no army convention and any chance of sorting matters out peacefully will be gone. That's straight from Liam Lynch, by the way. The choice is up to yerselves.' An express whistled by on its way from Dublin to Cork, almost knocking them over in its draught. 'But remember if you want to start a fight, ye haven't a hope of holding Limerick as things stand.'

'I'll pass on the message.'

'Don't just pass it on. Tell them what they should be doing. You're one of their top men now so maybe it's time you acted like one.' He immediately regretted the personal swipe. It might have revealed the weakness of the anti-Treaty side. 'Look, Ned. If ye pull Brennan's men out, there's a chance that tempers might cool. I'll make sure that they don't come to any harm and I'll also give you my personal guarantee that none of our lot move into Clare.'

'I've no reason to doubt you.' Looking for a flicker in the eyes or a bit lip or a clasping of hands, Willie searched for the key to Ned's thoughts. Before, Willie could read them like a book but now that Ned had taken to the sweet talk of politics, he'd learned to separate what went on inside the head from what appeared on the outside. 'We might have our differences, Willie, but there's nothing to be gained by us killing each other over them.'

They shook hands but the warmth wasn't there. They could have talked about Shanagolden, about Josie, about football, about the first fingers of spring and they could have rediscovered a spark that allowed trust to burn off the suspicion between them. Instead, they waited without words, looking up one track and another for their trains, his back to Limerick and Ned's to Dublin and they were both relieved to be rid of each other's presence.

His carriage shuddered to halt at Pallasgreen and a squad of rifle-toting youths made a big play out of asking every passenger who they were, where they were coming from and where they were going in a manner suggesting that they had spent their entire lives studying the phraseology of the RIC. It was if a second border had been drawn through the country.

'What business have you going to Limerick?' The boy soldier's chin sported just the few straggly hairs and he looked lost inside the trench coat. 'Have you any documents in your possession that might identify you?'

A colleague was digging the inquisitor in the ribs. 'Do you know who that is, you fool?' he whispered.

The first youth gave him a second glance before shrinking back in embarrassment. 'I'm ... Christ, I'm sorry ... Jesus, I made a mistake, Colonel Hartnett.'

'Dress you up like a fighting man and you're still the same eejit, Pakie Ryan,' roared someone at the back of the carriage.

'Would ye ever get sense, boys,' added another. 'Don't ye know who the lot of us are?'

The squad looked to Willie for guidance. 'It's all right, lads. Carry on.'

A few of the passengers came up to him with their complaints. Could he do something about a roadblock on the back road to Nicker? Could he find a place for an aged uncle in the County Home? Could he get the bridge on the way into Cappamore fixed up? It had been blown up by the Tans two years back and, despite all the promises they'd got, nothing had been done about it in the meantime.

Willie had enough problems on his plate in his own part of the county and he should have told them that they'd be better off getting on to the East Limerick Brigade but they'd probably tried them already. Instead, he wrote down their names and their details in a notebook and, maybe if he'd the time and he remembered it, he'd pass their complaints on to whoever dealt with them. And even if he did get that far, there wasn't much chance of anything happening. The money had dried up and the mechanics of government had all but broken down.

But someone would want to start listening. The people had put up with over three years of hardship in the hope of something better coming out of it and, no matter how deep their views were on the Oath, the Republic and Partition, sooner or later they'd get fed up with the two factions playing soldiers while all around them fell apart from neglect.

The city was bustling with activity but it all came from groups of young men armed with rifles or revolvers standing guard outside the great buildings lining George's Street, now rechristened O'Connell Street, and along Mulgrave Street and the quays. Other than troops of boys marching around with sticks against their shoulders in imitation of the real soldiers around them, few civilians were venturing out and most of the shops were boarded up.

'Will you be calling in the rest of the lads?' Jimmy McCarthy asked Willie as he stopped at Matthew Bridge where the other side had blocked off the road. After the inital frenzy of activity had died down, the patchwork of occupied buildings rationalised themselves into two mostly-contiguous zones. Brennan's Claremen were holding King's Island and part of Thomondgate while the rest of the city was under anti-Treaty control.

While the reorganisation had reduced the possible points of friction, it had also reduced day-to-day contact and the good-humoured slagging of the first few days had been replaced by mutual suspicion. New arrivals not brought up in the live-and-let-live rivalries of the city were also adding to the tension.

Willie turned back towards the city centre. 'There's enough here already. Too many if you ask me.' He'd left anyone with a job back in the Fourth Brigade's own area together with a few full-timers to prevent matters from getting out of hand. A lorry filled with poorly armed soldiers tootled past them as it came down William Street towards Sarsfield Bridge. 'Where did that lot come from?'

'They've been piling in all day,' Mossy Noonan told him. 'And there's those who've never been involved joining up on both sides. Hurling clubs, football clubs, rugby clubs, they're all lining up against each other. Even the fighting factions are coming in from the country to settle old scores.'

'No sign of an answer, Willie.' Ernie O'Malley had left his command post in the Glentworth Hotel and sat by the telegraph as Willie entered the Post Office.

'It'll be at least another hour before Ned gets back to Dublin.'

They waited as the sun began to set and the guards retreated into the buildings they were occupying. 'I also gave my word that Brennan's men could slip off without being seen.' Loud words were being exchanged outside a pub on the opposite side of Lower Cecil Street. 'We'd be better off telling the hangers-on to go home.'

'Maybe.' O'Malley loosened the front of his tunic. 'Although we'd have no control at all over them then.'

'No. They're more trouble than they're worth. Some of them will get notions that they own the place and they'll start robbing all before them.'

The teleprinter rattled to life. The clerk ripped off the sheet and handed it to O'Malley. 'Time to go, Willie. Walk up the town and have a word with Mr. Brennan.'

Only the occasional streetlight was working. Most of O'Connell Street and Patrick Street cowered in the shadows and any sounds that could be heard were the muffled tones of conversations escaping from under closed doors. Three times Willie and Mossy were stopped before they reached Matthew Bridge. Fumes of whiskey wafted over one of the checkpoints.

They were on their own as they climbed over the upturned carts that separated the two factions. 'Halt!' cried a voice from the dark. 'Who goes there?'

Hands raised, they continued on to the barricade on other side of the Abbey River. 'Colonel Willie Hartnett,' he answered. 'I have a message for General Michael Brennan.'

Rifles converged on their backs. He handed over a note to a uniformed major who shone his torch over both of its sides before peering repeatedly at the signatures, the stamps and the watermark. 'Just yourself. Your colleague stays here.'

Leaving Mossy behind as a hostage, he marched with his escort up Nicholas Street towards the barracks. A light shone over the massive turrets of King John's Castle guarding the city's original crossing over the Shannon. Even if the wrong side had captured it, he was still moved by the sight of the Tricolour fluttering in the breeze for the first time in the fort's seven-hundred-year history.

Brennan looked none too pleased but he too had received his orders.

'Have ye a train train ready?' Willie asked him.

'It's leaving Athenry about now. It should be here inside two hours.'

'Then stop it at Longpavement. We'll spread the rumour later on that ye'll be leaving from the main station in the morning. Ye should be well gone by then.'

The pro-Treaty commander left him in the room on his own while he went out to talk to his staff. Willie looked out on the river. The Shannon was as placid and as still as a mirror on both sides of Thomond Bridge, its current and the Curragower Falls buried under the high point of the tide. From far beyond any street he could see, a lone set of hooves clopped through the silence of the night.

'We could have held out,' Brennan insisted in his return.

'Maybe ye could have. But was it worth killing a few hundred to find out?'

41

NED REIDY was never quite sure what was going through the mind of Michael Collins at any given moment. The President of the Provisional Government who also happened to be Minister for Finance in Arthur Griffith's Cabinet, leader of the Irish Republican Brotherhood and the effective Chief of Staff of one half of the Irish Republican Army, was a man of action, whose immense vision, drive and astuteness had energised the War of Independence. He also had an extremely low boredom threshold and, when one part of his many functions stalled for an instant, the rest of his high-revving machinery could slip out of gear.

As a result, there were times when Ned thought Collins's main motivation was variously to enforce the Treaty, to shaft Éamon de Valera, to comply with whatever the British wanted, to establish himself as the undisputed leader of Ireland, to unilaterally rewrite the Treaty, to patch over differences with Dev, to invade Northern Ireland, to walk away from it all once he had reunited Ireland as an independent republic and to woo every woman in the country. There were even occasions when he believed that every one of these conflicting ambitions was simultaneously filling the Big Fellow's head.

A few weeks earlier, Collins had been cock-a-hoop over getting a tip-off about the British withdrawal from Limerick that allowed Michael Brennan to occupy the Castle Barracks before the local IRA units knew what was happening. Although everyone knew that the action was like waving a red rag before a bull, he'd justified it on the basis of the city's unique strategic importance and on the humiliation dished out to Ned at a rigged convention of the Limerick brigades. But when the anti-Treaty elements grabbed the other three bases and flooded the city with reinforcements, the Big Fellow jumped at the offer of an intact withdrawal of Brennan and his followers.

Circumstances had changed, Collins explained to anyone who asked him. It no longer mattered that the retreat from Limerick looked like an abject climbdown and that it had incensed the British and Griffith, both of whom were demanding an all-out military assault. The big issue now was to facilitate the upcoming IRA convention and it wasn't the time to set brother against brother when the unity of the movement was at stake.

Days later as delegates were being elected all over the country, there was another change of tack. The numbers weren't stacking up, the British were screaming for decisive action, Griffith was wailing about the affront to the democratic vote of Dáil Éireann and even Mulcahy was nervous. So rather than risk the possibility of the military setting up their own executive independent of the Dáil's authority, the Provisional Government banned the meeting from taking place under legislation introduced to legitimise the actions of the Black and Tans.

However, it didn't stop the convention from going ahead, although the absence of most pro-Treaty elements had robbed it of its claim to speak for an undivided army. The more militant voices insisted that the forces which had liberated the country could not hand it over to the politicians, and pressed for the immediate installation of a military junta.

'They could be fighting among themselves now. Easier for us to pick them off if we have to.' Collins grabbed Ned around the shoulders and almost crushed the life out of him as he dragged him to the window.

'And even if they all stick together, they won't be a match for this lot.' Down below in the barracks square, over two hundred recruits were marching to the bellowed commands of a sergeant-major. 'We've a few thousand signed up already. Enough of them there to justify those colonel's pips of yours.'

They looked like an army as well, uniformed and responding to commands with the ease of experience. 'Where did you get them?' Ned asked the Big Fellow as they descended the stairs.

'War veterans. Our former masters left the paperwork behind them, so we knew where to find them. Most of them were out of work so they jumped at the prospect of a steady wage at the end of the week.' The corridor had yet to be cleaned out and was littered with mementos of the departed Dublin garrison. 'Even a few officers came out of retirement to lend us a hand. Not that we could put them in positions they were used to, you understand? But they sure know their stuff, these boyos.'

The door at the end of the building looked as if it hadn't been opened in years and, when its rusty handle refused to turn, Collins's shoulder lifted it off its hinges. 'Now, what do you think of this lot, Ned Reidy?' He bounded like a pup over to the three Rolls-Royce Whippet armoured cars, complete with their rotating turrets, parked in the courtyard. 'Little beauties, aren't they?'

'Did the British give them to us? Or did they forget to take them home with them?'

'Who cares, boy? We got them, that's all that matters. And there's a whole arsenal of weapons and ammunition in that building over beyond.' The Big Fellow slapped the nearest vehicle across the bonnet with his open palm. 'The machine of the future. Wheels instead of tracks. Goes five times as fast as a tank and every bit as lethal.'

Ned rubbed his finger along the bulbous pimpling of rivets. It felt like handling stolen property.

'I've even found names for these noble vehicles. This one's Ballinalee, made of iron like Seán Mac Eoin ... This'll be Danny Boy. That should get Dan Breen's dander up ... And this is going to be my own favourite, Slievenamon.

'Alone, all alone,' boomed Collins's rich baritone.

'By the wave-washed shore,

All alone in the crowded hall ...'

'Are the British are paying us to take on the Republicans?' asked Ned.

'I don't know who's paying for our new army. There's money in the kitty and that's all that matters. So we're using up what we've got and you know as well as I do that we're wasting our time claiming to be a government if we don't have the soldiers to back us up.' Collins opened the hatch and jumped behind the wheel of Slievenamon. 'And anyway, who's saying we'll be turning on our own, Neddy boy?' he whispered through the armour as he searched for the controls of the turret. 'We can just as easily drive this machine in the direction of Belfast. What better way to unite us than to take on a common enemy?'

Philip Hurley had left her the key while he went off to a Gaelic League meeting in Rathkeale and Josie Reidy had the schoolmaster's house to herself while she waited for Willie Hartnett to return. Instinctively, she began to tidy the place up, although she made sure not to disturb the chaotic pile of books, pamphlets, sketches, pencils and notepaper strewn across the table in the front room. But she did allow herself a glance over the open page of handwriting, the first chapter of a history of Shanid Castle.

Maybe he might get around to finishing it. Philip had a habit of starting learned works on topics such as variations in the style of the thatched roofs in West Limerick, the habitats of birds of prey, the manufacture of traditional musical instruments and a biography of local nineteenth-century faction fighter Kennedy O'Brien, but they tended to lose momentum as soon as the initial enthusiasm waned and they might hibernate on his desk for a few years before they came to his notice again. His efforts at writing lingered in the same limbo as that half-made violin waiting forever on the wall to be varnished and strung.

She'd been waiting around almost as long herself. Twenty-six years old in a month's time with a well-paid job of her own, a small legacy from her mother that she had recently come of age to inherit and a position of trust in the community, and she still had to sneak out to meet her man away from the sight of her father. Of course she should have stood up to him and dared him to throw her out if he objected to her seeing Willie, but somehow the two of them had settled into a routine where argument was avoided as long as she didn't mention his name.

If she'd been living in the city, she would have got away with finding a place of her own but, in a rural parish like Shanagolden, a woman had to live in the house of her father until another man took her away to get married. She'd hoped that the new Republic they'd fought for would have changed all that deference to the old ways, but whatever dreams she'd held had long since been by dashed the Treaty.

Politics was another taboo subject in the house, at least from her point of view. Edmund Reidy had got over Ned letting Mary Hourigan slip from his grasp and now basked in the reflected

593

glory of a son in the Cabinet. People looked up to the Reidys now, he was fond of telling her, and even those with their hoity-toity old money might divert themselves up the lane to supplicate a request to the Minister for Public Health. She'd watch her father's delight in making them wait while he changed out of his rags into his Sunday suit and there were times when she'd feel a slight twinge of satisfaction herself, but mostly she would have preferred to hunt them back out onto the road. A year back, they were willing to come to her Republican court to have their cases heard but, now that they'd got the sniff of a new treasure chest of favours, they wouldn't give her the time of day.

Even though Philip, herself, Father Conny and few others were still the only functioning authority in the area, the smart money was betting against them. Although Ned hadn't been seen for months in Shanagolden, the aura of his appointment had drawn out feelers from the likes of Doctor Molyneaux and his circle. Even Councillor Hennessy, who had moved his business interests elsewhere during this time of uncertainty, was said to be on the point of reinvesting in Shanagolden and had made roundabout inquiries regarding how mutual interests could be pursued.

The inevitability hurt her most of all. The Fourth Brigade might have sent the enemy packing from northwest Limerick but she knew in her heart and soul that everything they'd achieved would be snatched from them. It would only be a matter of time.

The growling engine broke the silence of the night. Not yet over the legacy of the Tans, she approached the window with trepidation, but it was only Willie climbing out of an open-top Rolls-Royce with a woman trailing an unimaginably long scarf at the wheel.

'Should I be jealous?' she asked.

'Her father owns of the biggest machine-tool companys in Pennsylvania. Of course you should.' He tossed his coat and hat aside on the sofa before clasping her with those long gangly arms. 'She jumped off a liner in Cobh and came all the way up to Limerick to meet a real Irish rebel boy.'

'And did she find what she was looking for?'

'More than she ever dreamed of.' His fingers were rough and cold and tingled the backs of her ears. 'She's a journalist as well with one of the biggest newspapers in America. Covered most of the Great War from the Front and not from the safety of a fancy hotel in the middle of Paris.'

The passion that she'd half-hoped for and then half-feared faded as he slumped back on the armchair. 'Josie, things is not looking good. Dublin is sliding out of control.' After a reconvened Army Convention, a splinter group had seized the Four Courts and other prominent buildings in the captial in a replay of the Easter Rising, proclaimed a new military authority to run the country and invited all IRA men opposed to the Treaty to join them. 'The British have been pumping weapons into the Free State Army on condition they take out the Four Courts. It's only a matter of time.'

'And it's worth starting another war for all that?' She should have changed the subject. It wasn't often they got the chance to be together and now he'd start off on another rant. But then she was stuck in it as deep as he was himself.

'Oh, I don't know any more.' His voice softened as his arm snaked around her shoulders again. 'I just thought it was worth fighting for something more than what we got in this Treaty. A place where everyone is born equal instead of doffing the cap to those who think they're bred better than you. Like not handing it all over to the likes of Hennessy and those other weasels now swarming to the Free State side with their top hats and their wing collars ...'

'Like Ned?'

'Yes, like Ned, like a lot of other fellas I fought alongside. They know we could've carried on and built a real nation but they couldn't say no when Lloyd George dangled the trappings of power in front of their noses.' He tightened his grip and spun her around to face him. 'Will you marry me, Josie?'

She burst out laughing. He shrank back, puzzled, maybe even embarrassed. 'Oh, for God's sake, Willie! I thought you'd never ask.'

The continuous tooting woke Willie just after sunrise. Out in the front garden and quite oblivious to Miss Abigail Schleppenhauser waiting impatiently in her Rolls-Royce, Philip Hurley continued his morning's exercises with his India clubs, his concentration breaking only when his guest for the night almost knocked him over as he hurried out the door.

'I was asked to get you to Dublin by this afternoon.' The special correspondent of the Boston Globe barely gave him time to sit down before throwing the car into gear. Willie wondered which one of the Anti-Treaty leaders was the subject of her attentions. Or perhaps she had been rebuffed by Michael Collins and Ned Reidy.

They were at Robertstown Cross before he had finished buttoning his shirt, past Barrigone Church before he had belted his coat and covered his head and most of the way to Askeaton before he had time to draw breath. Miss Schleppenhauser approached driving with the same military efficiency as her reporting and no distractions were allowed to interfere with her pursuit of the objective. While her eyes were glued to the road, it suited Willie fine to be spared her relentless probing for answers he couldn't or didn't want to supply.

However, the sole heiress to the Lehigh Consolidated Tool & Die Corporation fortune of Allentown, Pennsylvania, met her match in the cows of County Limerick who, for reasons best known to themselves, refused to be intimidated by her lordly limousine as they meandered along the road to be milked. Each time they waited for the highway to clear itself of disinterested livestock, she was too overcome by the futility of her impatience to tell him what all the rush was about. But she began to calm down when the Gothic spire of the city's St. John's Cathedral broke through the horizon and, once they passed the saluting guard outside the military headquarters in the Glentworth Hotel and saw on Tait's Clock that they had twenty minutes to spare for the early train, she was sufficiently composed for conversation.

'Big pow-wow in Dublin. Every chief expected to turn up.'

'I see,' he responded as neutrally as possible.

'Keep me informed, Colonel Hartnett.' Commands came more naturally to her than requests, as a taxi trying to move in ahead of her at the station found out. 'The Globe is always first with the news on Ireland.'

Most of the Limerick anti-Treaty leaders were gathered beside the waiting train, all in civilian clothing. 'This gets you into a special Sinn Féin Ardfheis on Sunday. Make sure you turn up.' Jim Colbert handed Willie a little green and white card allowing him to vote at a national convention of the party's delegates. 'By the way, I hope Abigail wasn't the cause of any embarrassment.'

'Who is she best friends with?'

'My lips are sealed, Willie. But aah ... you'd be surprised.'

A second group stood further up the platform. Colbert, Michael Colivet, Ralph Slattery and Con Collins tipped their hats to them as they passed by and William Hayes, Dr. Richard Hayes, Michael Brennan and George Bennett acknowledged the greeting with equal civility.

'Are we all friends again?' asked Willie once they were out of earshot of the pro-Treaty representatives.

'Events have moved swiftly over the past few days.' As they settled into their compartment, Colbert filled him in on the deal reached between Éamon de Valera and Michael Collins. In an attempt to preserve the unity of Sinn Féin during an election made necessary by the terms of the Treaty and in a last ditch effort to head off a civil war, the two leaders had agreed on a joint list of candidates based on their respective strengths in the outgoing Dáil. Once they gained their expected majority, the factions would then split the government between them. 'But we need an Ardfheis to ratify it.'

'Trouble in the Four Courts?' The occupation of the centre of the country's judiciary and other prominent Dublin buildings by Rory O'Connor's Army executive had now entered its second month.

'Possibly. Rory and Liam Mellowes are none too happy, but Liam Lynch might talk them around. The other lot might be an even bigger problem. Arthur Griffith and his supporters are supposed to be spitting fire with Collins for selling them out.' Colbert passed Willie a document detailing the division of power once the new cabinet took over. 'And don't worry about your own seat. Yourself and Ned Reidy will be dividing up yer area between ye.'

He'd seen similar chances of a resolution before. The Truce, the Treaty, the resolution of the stand-off with Brennan in Limerick were all supposed to unite everyone under one banner

598

until all the outstanding issues had been settled. But none of them had worked and Willie was reluctant to put his faith in the pact cobbled together by Collins and Dev. Still, the leaders had gone much further this time and had also agreed procedures for sorting out disputes before they got out of hand.

Maybe the time had come for everyone to put some trust in the future. No matter who was in charge, they couldn't run the country without hope. And until the night before, he'd never realised how much he wanted it for his own life as well. He'd spent years meaning to ask her, but there was also something getting in the way like being thrown in jail or going on the run and sometimes he wondered whether he was just looking for excuses for not entering into a commitment for life.

Was the entire population was doing the same? Was everyone looking for an ancient grudge or a matter of principle to divide them so that they could relieve themselves of their responsibility to run the country? They'd lived through seven centuries of oppression and maybe they'd be lost without it.

His colleagues were arguing the toss over whether too many concessions had been made to the other side and were asking him for his opinion, but he'd lost the thread of the discussion and, anyway, he couldn't have cared less as he settled himself into his own private thoughts.

His mind watched her showing the promise of life to a room full of children sitting in the same desks that they themselves had occupied twenty years before. His mind watched her cycling in the road towards him, each feature becoming clearer with each turn of the wheel. His mind felt the softness of her skin rubbing against his face and the softness of her voice caressing his ear. His mind felt the share and care of his worries and hers. His mind filled with every part of his Josie.

Not quite believing that they were all back together inside the same building, the maelstrom of delegates heaved and ebbed as numbers were totted up, passes were checked out and last minute searches were launched for those who had yet to turn up.

Their reserve melting in the general thaw around them, they sought each other out in the foyer.

'Enjoying the good life?' Willie poked his finger at Ned's waistcoat. A few inches had been added to the waistline of the Minister for Public Health.

'Better than the tack we'd to eat in the hills.'

'Sure.' He dropped his arm across Ned's shoulders. 'Good to see you again, Ned. Maybe we might sort it all out this time.'

'I hope so. Although not everyone on our side is happy. We have complaints about giving in to criminals.'

'And we have a few wanting to provoke a civil war just to clear the air.' Stewards were calling them to take their seats in the hall. 'By the way, we might even be seeing more of each other ... brother.'

'You didn't, did you?'

'Thursday night.'

'Took yer time. Eight years, was it?' Ned returned the embrace. 'Well, ye have my best wishes. Does my father know yet?'

'No. We haven't told anyone so far. She wants to wait until he's in the right mood before she breaks it to him.'

'Ye could be waiting forever, Willie.' A big ignorant school bell rang the final call before the doors were to be shut. 'He's from another age and I don't think he'll ever accept you. Ye'd be better off telling him ye're going ahead whether he likes it or not.'

They moved inside, parting to their respective sides to take their place among the gathering. 'Hey, don't forget I expect to be best man!' Ned shouted across to him as Michael Collins stepped up to speak.

They gave the Big Fellow a rousing reception. Not just his personal following on the pro-Treaty side, but the entire hall of the Mansion House burst into applause when he promised hope of a new start and an end to the split that had set brother against brother. 'Unity at home is more important than any Treaty with the foreigner,' he pledged the packed Sinn Féin conference. 'If unity at home can only be got at the expense of the Treaty, then the Treaty will have to go.'

It was just like old times when they all stood together. Even Willie began to believe that the President of the Provisional Government had once again beaten the British at their own game, that he had hoodwinked them into supplying an army on the pretext of taking out dissidents, that he had now put together a force capable of coming to the aid of the beleaguered Nationalist population of the Six Northern Counties and of standing up to the common enemy should they decide to resume hostilities.

Dev was just as warmly received as he spoke of the shared ideal that had seen Ireland through its struggle with the mightiest colonial power in the world, of how they had fought shoulder to shoulder for the cause of Erin and would gladly do so again if called to action, of how everybody had risen above personal considerations for the greater good.

And both the Big Fellow and the Long Fellow agreed that the constitution to be written would reflect the wishes of the people of Ireland rather than the dictates of any foreign power.

Apart from a small scattering of sour faces, delegates left for home filled with a hope that they hadn't felt since that wonderful week of the Truce ten months before. Some stopped in hotels to have a drink with comrades to whom they hadn't spoken since the vote on the Treaty. Rivalries were forgotten as they shared compartments on the train and caught up on old times. And as they clattered across the Midlands to Limerick, Willie and Michael Brennan joked about the bluff and counter-bluff of their stand-off in the Castle Barracks.

Nicholas Sullivan wasn't interested in offers. A generous pension had freed him of any financial worries and, for the first time in his life, he could pursue what interested him rather than what he was ordered to do. And he had enough to occupy himself for the time being. Ever since he had walked out of the barracks in Newcastlewest for the last time, he had spent his days leisurely doing up the cottage in Shanagolden that an unmarried cousin had left to Bessie in his will.

But they'd come back again asking for the third time and he'd relented and he'd made the journey to Dublin at the expense of the new Provisional Government of the Irish Free State. A car was waiting to pick him up at Kingsbridge Station and it stopped for a moment on the quays to give him a view further down the Liffey to the Four Courts where nothing out of the ordinary appeared to be happening.

Were the newspapers making another mountain out of a molehill? In his strangely detached state as a retired member of the now-defunct Royal Irish Constabulary, he'd taken to reading every available account of the unfolding drama of Truce, Treaty and stand-off and, once he'd got past the headlines, he reckoned that most of what was written was either inspired speculation or a version of the truth adapted to suit a particular point of view. His interest was driven by nothing more than curiosity, or perhaps something to pass the time now that he had plenty of it on his hands. For all of his transferred allegiances that the pro-Treaty side might presume, he really didn't care who might prevail in this internecine dispute. The government that he'd defended had departed and that was the end of his contribution as far as he was concerned.

'We're building a new state, Inspector Sullivan.' General Eoin O'Duffy had taken over the Inspector-General's office in the former RIC headquarters in the Phoenix Park. 'We're looking to the future rather than dwelling on the past. Men of experience are needed to help us in our task.'

An orderly in a soldier's uniform left a tray on the desk and poured the tea from a silver pot into fine bone china cups. As pukka as the military, who had left their crockery after them.

'I accept we were on different sides in recent years. Our members took up arms against your force. Men under my command shot and killed members of your police. Perhaps some of these actions were beyond what was necessary and, if they were, I apologise for that.'

It wasn't even a proper brew of Assam and Ceylon that woke a man up in the morning and invigorated him after a long journey. Instead, his cup had been filled with some effete blend like Earl Grey which was fit only for the salons of hostesses of a delicate disposition.

'It's time to let bygones be bygones. And from every report I have heard about you, Inspector, you behaved with honour no matter what the circumstances. Ireland needs men of your calibre, your probity and your experience.'

Some symbols of the old regime remained on the wall. Crests embossed into the plaster had been brushed over but the outlines survived. After years of fighting, was the change of regime no deeper than the coat of paint that transformed red postboxes to green?

'And I see you have chosen to remain here rather than move north or to England. That tells me I might be addressing a man who has faith in the future of his country.' O'Duffy paused for a moment but, before Sullivan could get a word in, decided that his monologue still had a few chapters to run. 'The Civic Guard will need a commander for its Limerick Division when it begins operations at the end of the year. A decisive hand at the helm with detailed knowledge of the area. Rank of Chief Superintendent, equivalent of a County Inspector, leading an unarmed force of four hundred Guards. We're recruiting them already.'

Drill calls could be heard from outside in the yard.

'Of course, there will be access to weapons where members' lives may be at risk. And I do have to advise you that we expect subversive elements to do everything in their power to derail the establishment of law and order. Especially in Limerick and the other divisions in Munster.'

The fist slammed down on the desk. 'But we'll be ready for them. Don't you worry, Inspector Sullivan. The extremists are in the process of being isolated and soon there won't be enough of them to put up a fight. Meanwhile, however, we have to put a proper police force in place. Get a firm grip on the lawlessness that has taken over since the Truce. Larceny, assault, poitín-making, offensive public behaviour, all the petty crime that makes everyone's life a misery. The people are crying out for the restoration of order and this State is pledged to provide it ... Milk and sugar?'

'Aah, yes, please ...'

'Blackguards taking the law into their own hands up and down the country.' O'Duffy gave his cup a spirited stir. 'Some of them even claim to have been freedom fighters. But you know as well as I do that they were never anything more than street-corner buckos. They weren't on our side and they weren't on your side.' The tea drained in a single mouthful. 'So, what do you say?'

The offer was more than he had expected. Command of an entire city and county was two steps higher than Sullivan had achieved in the RIC and, if the new force was unarmed, it might stand a better chance of acceptance than its predecessor. Maybe the country was settling down following the election pact between Collins and de Valera.

And the house was nearly ready to move into. Within a few weeks, time might weigh heavily on his hands

But something in O'Duffy's tone unsettled him, a willingness to blame everything on criminal elements, just like the British military leaders before him. Pleading that he had a long train journey ahead of him to think it over, he promised to telegraph his answer the following morning. And by the time he had left the station in Newcastlewest after a man-in-the-know told him that Collins had agreed a new constitution with Lloyd George, which was certain to shatter any understanding he had reached with de Valera, Nicholas Sullivan had already decided to decline.

42

ESPITE THE best efforts of its authors, the de Valera-
Collins pact began to unravel within a fortnight. By
polling day, it was in tatters as the two halves of Sinn
Féin campaigned actively against each other in an election that
the Provisional Government had turned into a referendum on the
Treaty. In north-west part of the new multi-seat Limerick
constituency, it translated into a straight fight between the two
outgoing deputies and, despite the anti-Treaty forces controlling
the area, Willie Hartnett knew that the odds were stacked against
his side of the argument.

Overnight, every telegraph pole in an and around
Shanagolden had been plastered with Vote for REIDY posters
and, as the polling station opened in the school, a fleet of motorcars disgorged voters to perform their public duty. There to greet
them on their way in were Ned Reidy and Councillor Thomas
Hennessy.

Willie nodded to his opponent but their eyes never met. By his
side, Philip Hurley was incandescent with rage, his stray locks
even more dishevelled than usual and almost on the point of
spontaneous combustion.

'See this!' The teacher shoved a copy of the local newspaper into his hand.

'Reidy Leads Limerick Sinn Féin Ticket in West,' blared the headline. 'Voters Urged To Continue Preference For Dr. Hayes and then for Pro-Treaty Candidates of Other Parties,' continued the next heading.

'They've double-crossed us!'

Not being a military man, Hurley had taken the breakdown more deeply than most, but even Willie, who had initially been sceptical, had been shocked by how quickly events had turned. One visit by Michael Collins to London and all the brave talk of standing up to Lloyd George and Churchill over the Oath of Allegiance was quickly forgotten. And when the Big Fellow and Arthur Griffith came back with a Free State constitution that was subservient to the Treaty and subject to a British veto, not a word was mentioned of the joint IRA force coming to the aid of their Nationalist brothers who were feeling the brunt of an escalated campaign to drive them out of the six Ulster counties.

'And look who's paying for it all.' Hurley's hands trembled with rage as he pointed at Hennessy gladhanding the arrivals. 'That ... that ... pardon my language, Willie ... that dirty treacherous scoundrel of an informer is trying to steal this election by fair means or foul.'

Money was only part of the problem. The pro-Treaty side had the Church, the farmers, those businessmen who hadn't pulled all their money out of the country to the safety of London, the ex-servicemen's associations, the Unionists, the newspapers and the trade unions lined up behind them. Between the press and the pulpit, they controlled the main channels of information, they had a functioning government to back them up and they had a leadership that knew what it wanted.

Patie Fitzgibbon brought along a few supporters in a pony and trap and said Mossy Noonan was on his way with a couple more, but that was the extent of Willie's election machine in Shanagolden. Like most places in the country, the majority of those of a political bent had taken the pro-Treaty side, while those of a more military disposition were opposed and were at a severe disadvantage when it came down to the mechanics of getting out the vote.

After an hour standing out on the road shaking hands, Willie had had enough. The committed would come out to support him and he'd get enough scratches to hold his seat but there was nothing he could do about the less enthusiastic against the combined might of Ned's and Hennessy's organisations. And when the only anti-Treaty car in the area arrived to tell him that a row had broken out in Kilcolman after Jimmy McCarthy and two colleagues had shot the tyres off a lorry carrying pro-Treaty voters, he just didn't want to know any more.

'We should never have trusted them in the first place,' Dick Mullane was telling Willie as they drove into Adare after leaving Hurley and Mossy to keep an eye on Shanagolden. 'Collins and his supporters were only buying time to build up their own forces. They'll turn on us the minute they're ready.'

'And can we take them on?'

'I wouldn't bet on it ... Christ! Even the gentry are backing Ned.' A liveried chauffeur waited at the wheel of a limousine to collect a half-dozen voters and return them to their homes. 'A lot of our lads know nothing about fighting for territory and then holding onto it. Even worse, they don't want to know. They still think that the raid on the barracks is all that matters.'

Willie stepped out for a few words with his supporters who were facing the same difficulties in getting out the faithful as those at all the other polling stations they had visited. 'And there's a fair few people who just want some peace and quiet,' the local organiser told him. 'They've had their fill of fighting and arguing to last them a lifetime.'

On the road out towards the city, a squad of Collins's new Free State Army covered both sides of the bridge across the Maigue. Patie and Dick lifted their rifles from their knees. The driver kept the car moving as the Freestater sergeant acknowledged Willie with a frosty nod.

The guns remained cocked. They weren't shooting each other yet but it was only a matter of time. Unlike the standoff at the Castle Barracks in March, this wasn't a case of old comrades who, despite falling out, were still reluctant to turn on each other. The men guarding the bridge in their bottle-green uniforms were part of a new military force that owed no sentimental allegiance to the shared experiences of the War of Independence.

'This crowd are more willing to learn what it takes to win a regular war.' Dick kept his eyes fixed on the soldiers fading behind them. 'They know the right places to occupy if they want to control the town. It's not the barracks and the public buildings. It's the bridges and the high ground and the roads in and out. But try explaining that to some of our leaders and see how far you'll get.'

And like Henessy coming back to reclaim his possessions, the Freestaters knew that the country was there to be taken. Willie, Dick, Patie and their brothers-in-arms might have run the British out of Ireland but the prize that they had won was now set to be stolen from their grasp by a force that was far better equipped, far better trained, earning a guaranteed weekly wage and organised like a professional army.

Despite every attempt to convince himself that it would never happen, Ned Reidy knew all along that confrontation was inevitable. When the call came in the darkness of night and he hurried down to Dublin's quays before the midsummer dawn had a chance to break, Michael Collins was already barking out instructions to the hundreds of soldiers gathered along Winetavern Street and in the maze of the lanes behind Merchants Quay.

Under the despairing eye of an artillery veteran, a pair of 18-pounder field guns was manhandled into position with a stack of 200 shells divided between them. 'Would yiz ever wait until they're registered,' he shouted at the eager recruits mesmerised by the sight of the exotic weaponry. 'Yiz'll blow yerselves up the way yiz are going at it.' It took the crack of an officer's pistol to calm everyone down.

'Not enough training,' Collins muttered. 'We've been forcing them along but there's only so much you can do with young lads who've never held a gun in their hands.'

'What about the war veterans?' Ned asked.

'Better we don't show too many of them in public for the time being. It could give the wrong impression.' They wandered down to Richmond Bridge and waited at its southern end. Across the Liffey, rifle barrels poked out of the windows of the Four Courts. 'No sign of them surrendering but we'll give them another twenty minutes.'

Not that anyone expected Rory O'Connor and his comrades to vacate the building, especially after the election of a fortnight earlier had demolished any remaining pretences of Sinn Féin unity and turned the occupation of the courts complex into a three-sided game of poker. Ignoring their political leader de Valera and their chief-of-staff Liam Lynch, the Republicans taunted the British to attack them in a move that they hoped

611

would reunite the country against the common enemy. Meanwhile, a majority of the Provisional Government insisted that the Free State Army take out the rebels so as to establish the democratic legitimacy that the election had conferred on them. And the British, who still had over 5,000 soldiers remaining in the country, put every conceivable pressure on Collins and his cabinet to spare them being sucked back into a conflict that they thought had ended.

Behind the scenes, Collins and de Valera exchanged notes that might have allowed the standoff to continue in the peculiarly Irish tradition of ignoring the obvious, but events on the ground were forcing the momentum. British demands for action against the Four Courts occupation increased when General Henry Wilson, security advisor to the Unionist government in Northern Ireland and the man many held responsible for planning the attacks on the Nationalist population, was assassinated in London. And when the Free State Army arrested one of the leading members of the First Dublin Brigade, the Republicans retaliated by kidnapping General JJ O'Connell. Arthur Griffith, Kevin O'Higgins, Eoin O'Duffy and every senior officer of the Army then threatened to depose Collins if he didn't come to the rescue of O'Connell, one of the most popular figures on the Free State side.

So the Big Fellow called Ned and his other closest confidantes from the Brotherhood to his side and delivered his ultimatum to Rory O'Connor. As they stood by the quay wall, a red sun edged over the horizon above Dublin Bay and its rays shone on the numbers of Ned's wristwatch. Eight minutes past four.

Behind them, the artillery commander waited for the signal beside the field pieces delivered by the British under the cover of darkness. An English accent broke through the silence. "Ere, mate. Better you leave it to us.'

612

'Register's all wrong, Percy,' added another voice from the far side of the Irish Sea. 'Same as with the other pieces. These Saturday soldiers ... May God give me patience.'

'Where did this pair come from?' Collins turned his head away from Ned's question. 'Another one of your presents from Winston Churchill? What else is going on that we don't know about?'

Everything was in place, everybody had their excuses to parade before history and Ned wondered how long the operation had been in the planning. Even though the British blamed Wilson's killing on the anti-Treaty elements, he himself knew that Collins had ordered the action. And that being the case, had the whole pact with de Valera been nothing more than a bluff?

'You know where this is leading us?' he asked the man whose judgment he'd implicitly trusted since their shared captivity in Frongoch.

'I do.' Collins took a step back and folded his arms. 'But we have to take action if we're to establish our authority. If we don't, the British will come back to do the job for us.' He looked over Ned's shoulder to where the seconds ticked by on the watch. 'And maybe it's best to take the other side on now while they're split into factions.'

Ned scanned Gandon's landmark across the river for a last-minute climbdown. But there was no sign of movement other than a flock of starlings roosting among the columns that held up the dome.

'Time?' whispered Collins beside him.

They were the elected rulers of the country, he reminded himself. At some point they had to make a stand against those defying the wishes of the majority. And if they had to leave it to the British to do the job for them, they'd be showing that the people of Ireland lacked the courage to govern themselves.

'Time,' he confirmed. Time to forget friendships of a lifetime. Time to set brother against brother.

They walked back from the bridge to the cover of Winetavern Street. The Big Fellow waved to the artillery commander and the bombardment of the Four Courts began.

Adare was taken without a fight. Surrounded on three sides by a joint Republican force drawn from the First, Third and Fourth Limerick Brigades, the company of Free State soldiers decided on retreat. With vehicles already waiting for them, they withdrew to Castleconnell, the town on the road out from the city to Dublin that was the Provisional Government's last remaining position in County Limerick.

But even though they were retreating, Patie Fitzgibbon could see that the opposition had retired in good order; everything done with a minimum of fuss, no weapons or ammunition mislaid, and on the road within minutes. It was more than could be said for his own Fourth Brigade, which was lucky even to have made it to Adare in the first place.

He was just finishing up for the weekend in the creamery when Mossy Noonan arrived with news of the surrender of the Four Courts and of the remaining Republican positions in Dublin. They were all meeting down at the crossroads where Willie was calling a dozen or so each from Shanagolden, Foynes and Kilcolman into line. Only half of them were armed with rifles, a few more with shotguns and he'd split them into two groups because they'd only a single battered lorry for transport.

To make matters worse, they didn't have a driver. Earlier on in the day, Flint had come across a bottle of Drug Donovan's best and no amount of effort could revive him. Jimmy McCarthy claimed he'd learned how to drive from watching their comatose chauffeur but, after failing to get the vehicle out of gear, he gave up the ghost. By this stage, the corner boys had gathered to have a good laugh at their expense and they were almost on the point of marching on foot down to Foynes when Jimmy burst into Doctor Molyneaux's house and forced him at gunpoint to drive them to the station in Newcastlewest.

All that kept them going was a shared anger at the events in Dublin. Even though the pact had fallen apart in mutual recrimination, nobody believed that they'd end up taking shots at each other. And certainly no one expected the Freestaters to accept arms from the British in order to turn on their own. The East and West Brigades were moved by the same sense of betrayal and local rivalries were put aside as Free State Army posts were run out of the towns and every available man in the county answered the IRA's call to converge on Limerick city.

'We've been ordered to hold a line from Waterford to Limerick and then up the length of the Shannon.' Willie told Patie as they watched the last traces of dust settle on the road east from Adare. 'Lynch is supposed to have escaped from Dublin and he'll be setting up his headquarters in the city.'

'We should hold a few back just in case. Cover the bridges over the Maigue, like here, Ferrybridge, Croom and the one down the back road from here.' Patie unfolded the tattered Ordnance Survey map and pointed to the positions that had been abandoned by the Freestaters. 'We only need five or six on each. I can organise it myself if you want.'

'No. I want yourself and Dick with me. I've been told the setup in the city is a complete shambles.'

Willie hadn't been exaggerating. Patie could hardly believe the disorganisation that greeted the column's entry along the Cork Road over the unguarded Ballinacurra Bridge. The only Volunteers visible as they marched down O'Connell Street were

615

small groups leaning up against the entrances of hotels and chatting and smoking among themselves. Up a side street, he could hear windows being smashed and see looters disappearing into the lanes with their laden handcarts.

The same groups were occupying the four bases that had been vacated by the British Army, the Strand Barracks on the north bank of the Shannon, the Castle Barracks commanding King's Island and Thomond Bridge, the Ordnance Barracks at the head of the route east to Tipperary and Waterford, and the New Barracks overlooking O'Connell Avenue and the Cork Road. But unlike the last time Patie had been in the city, there seemed to be no overall control. Back then, they had the likes of Ernie O'Malley who had some understanding of leadership; now everyone was running his own little kingdom.

'We've more generals here than soldiers,' an old acquaintance told him when they arrived outside King John's Castle only to be informed that they'd be better off marching back across the city to the New Barracks. 'There's a load of Holy Joes wanting to rid the city of sin and they're driving everyone mad with their clampdown on drinking, gambling, keeping company and every other sort of enjoyment. At the same time, another crowd are living it up in the hotels they've taken over. And then we've got these chancers claiming to be Volunteers when they're nothing of the sort. All they're doing is commandeering supplies and issuing receipts that don't mean nothing.'

He offered Patie a cigarette, then changed his mind and gave him the entire packet. 'But we've no problem with the gaspers. Two tobacco factories here and we can take all we like. There's no order at all here since Lynch and O'Malley and the rest of them went up to Dublin to occupy the Four Courts.' They watched Willie through their smoke rings, having it out with an officious self-appointed commander. 'And I think the local people are getting fed up. Most of them were behind us a month ago and we could have really inflamed them over the attack on the Four Courts but now they think we're only a load of eejits who don't know how to run the city.' He flicked the butt of his cigarette into the sky and watched it drop to the ground. 'Still, we can always go up in smoke.'

Liam Lynch's arrival the following day restored some sanity to the situation and the freeloaders claiming to be Republican Volunteers were cleared from the streets by the new arrivals from the county. But the defence of the city was as chaotic as ever, while the IRA leadership who had escaped from the surrender of Dublin settled into their new headquarters in the Glentworth Hotel.

'Can you explain to them in simple terms what we should be doing?' Willie asked as he waited late in the evening at the end of the corridor.

Patie had spent the day tracing out maps of what should be defended and listing out how many men were needed at each post, what equipment they should have, who was to be their next line of communication, where they should fall back to if they had to retreat and how the chain of command should operate. He'd already tried out his plan of defence on one of the barracks commanders but, after only a few minutes of explanation, he could see that he might as well be talking to the wall. They couldn't get it into their heads that military bases on their own were nothing more than mere trophies. What mattered most in securing the territory was controlling access in and out along the roads, across the rivers, along the rail tracks and canals.

They'd been hanging around the best part of an hour when another general with a fistful of papers butted in ahead of them claiming urgent attention. Willie finally lost patience, stuck his revolver under the intruder's chin and barged into the bedroom that the Chief-of-Staff was using as his office.

'Leave them on the table beside the door. I'll get to them as soon as I can.' Head bowed, Lynch was busily signing scraps of paper.

'This isn't about requisitions, Liam.' Willie slammed his fist off the desk. 'This is about how to fight a war.'

'Sorry, Willie. I'm just snowed under with all these orders I'm supposed to authorise.'

Given his moment, Patie showed his plans and Lynch looked over them with interest. 'I can see what you're getting at, Patie.' But within minutes, his eyes started to glaze over. 'Look, could you leave it until the morning? We'll have a better chance of organising it properly.'

'That's if we still have the chance, sir. Anyone can walk into the city at the moment and take it over.'

'Don't get me wrong. I understand the gravity of the situation.' Lynch clasped his hands behind his head and yawned the stiffness from his shoulders. 'Be down here first thing in the morning. I'll make sure everyone is here and they know what needs to be done.'

Willie nodded to Patie that that was as much as they'd get for the time being. Darkness had descended and the warm summer's air was still and quiet as they walked past the People's Park to the New Barracks.

'I think he was listening, Patie. And he should be in better form in the morning.'

But they never got the opportunity to find out. As the meeting with Lynch and his commanders got underway, over a thousand Freestaters marched into the city from Castleconnell and occupied the Jail, the Customs House, the Courthouse, two of the police barracks and four of the city's five bridges without meeting a whimper of opposition.

43

SHE WASN'T intending to tell him just yet and she mightn't even have told him at all but another tirade from her father tipped her over the edge. It all started innocently enough as Edmund Reidy studied his copy of the Irish Independent and rambled his approval of the Free State Army finally blasting the Republican rabble out of their last remaining positions in Dublin.

Josie would have ignored him if he had left it at that. She was used to the ranting monologues that always ran out of steam when he realised that she was taking no notice. They'd taken opposite sides on the Treaty and nothing that could be said was going to change either point of view, now that divisions had descended into open warfare. But this time he was gunning for an argument, insisting on an answer, demanding that she justify why anyone holding an opinion other than his own could live under his roof.

'Your bloody roof?' she'd exploded. If she hadn't lifted the farmhouse out of the kip it had become and if she hadn't kept it maintained for the past six years, the roof would have long ago caved in on her father. And on her turncoat of a brother as well.

He was appalled by her use of bad language and demanded an apology. She told him he could go to Hell.

He rose from the table. She thought he was going to strike her and her fingers wrapped around the handle of the frying pan. He might have been in his late seventies but there was still power in the frame and anger in the movement. But he settled for words instead, telling her that she'd have nowhere to go if he threw her out on the road. He'd make sure she lost her job and that no other school would take her on. He had connections now, real connections that could make trouble for anyone who dared cross his path.

She knew that they'd hit dangerous territory. Words that might never be forgiven nor forgotten were on the point of being exchanged. But restraint wasn't so easy when she was saddled with the helpless worry of watching everything around her slide back into war.

'You'll be walking the streets, my girl,' he taunted. 'Just you remember that.'

'No. I'm getting married,' she answered, her hand trembling as it clung to the pan behind her back.

'And who'd have you other than that tramp Willie Hartnett?'

'Willie proposed to me a few weeks ago and I accepted.'

'He didn't?' He shook his head with disbelief.

'He did!'

'He's no good, I'm telling you.'

'Oh, for God's sake!' She dropped the pan into the sink. 'The entire parish knows we've been walking out together for years and you still can't accept it.'

'Willie Hartnett,' he sneered. 'Member of Parliament and head of a ragtaggle army of layabouts. I'll tell you something about your precious Colonel Willie Hartnett. Colonel, my arse! He comes from nothing and he always will be nothing. And now him and that gang of his have started a civil war.'

'And what about your own son strutting around with his airs and graces in his shiny new uniform paid for by the British ...?'

'You'll take that back, my girl!' The blood rose in his cheeks. The eyes fired with mad anger. 'Ned is a minister of government now. One of the most powerful men in this country, he is. He's brought respect to this family ...'

'How? By selling out his comrades ...?'

'What comrades? Only bandits and corner boys and he's well rid of them.' The vein was lifting in the middle of his forehead. 'Thanks to Ned, us Reidys are people of substance now and no one will ever look down on us again ...'

'I'm not listening to this any longer.' She whipped off her apron, threw it at his feet and turned for the door.

'If you ever step outside that door, you'll never come back!' He hobbled to catch up with her. 'Do you hear me, girl? I'll make sure you'll never work again! I'll make sure that Hartnett is run into the ground! I'll never let you marry beneath yourself ...'

She slammed the door and crossed the yard.

'And if it wasn't for that Willie Hartnett of yours, we'd never have been burned by the Tans or by the Peelers,' he kept on shouting. 'We'd have another fifty acres by now. We'd have an estate fit for a lord. It took Ned long enough to see through that bastard's scheming ... Uuoogh! Christ! ...'

When she thought about it later, she knew that she'd heard the wheezes. She knew that she'd heard him hit the ground. She knew that the dog had risen from his slumber to whine over him. She knew that she'd left him to die all on his own in his farmyard. But at the time, she was too filled with anger to look back.

They were down almost to their last line of defence. Just the three military barracks were left in Republican hands after the Strand had been battered into submission by the 18-pounder field gun sent down from Dublin. A week of intermittent fighting had left Patie Fitzgibbon, Dick Mullane, Willie Hartnett and another thirty Volunteers manning the barricade across the Roxborough Road that protected the one remaining link between the Ordnance and the New Barracks and the routes out of Limerick to the south.

Once the Freestaters had been allowed to gain a foothold inside the city, their vastly superior arsenal quickly began to tell. Despite Patie and Dick leading groups out to dynamite the bridges over the Mulcair and the Groody in order to cut off the supply lines from the capital, armoured cars, field pieces, mortars, machine guns and another 1,500 Free State fully-armed soldiers under Eoin O'Duffy's command flooded in along the road from Killaloe, along the railway line from Ennis and by ship around the entire southern coastline. All they had to face them were rifles and a few machine guns hijacked from a departing British consignment sailing out of Cork, and a single clapped-out armoured car that was no match for the Freestaters' Rolls-Royces.

Patie knew that they could have held out indefinitely had Limerick been properly defended before the Freestaters' entry. And with more motivated troops fired up by bitterness against the treachery of the broken pact and of the bombardment of the Four Courts, he was certain that they'd have held on to their part of the city had they set up a series of barriers before the enemy could pile in their reinforcements. But a shambolic leadership had blundered from one crisis to the next and, as possession of the most strategically-important position in the country slipped street by street out of their hands, Lynch and his staff abandoned the short-lived capital of the Munster Republic and moved their headquarters to Fermoy.

'What good is Fermoy to us?' he asked Willie. 'If they take Limerick, they'll have opened up half of Munster as well as giving them control of both sides of the Shannon.'

A hundred yards down the road on the city side, Freestaters had restricted themselves to the odd pop from their Vickers gun and an occasional volley to raise the dust on the street. And as if to emphasise their patience, they'd allowed curious groups of locals to wander about their positions, climb over the sandbags and view the opposing Republicans through the field glasses supplied by their commander.

'We can still hold out if we want to,' added Dick. 'The back roads are covered and we've enough food to keep us going. All we need are some reinforcements and maybe we could even regain some of the ground we've lost.'

'I've asked for them, Dick. I can't do any more.' Willie was scanning his periscope across the Free State positions lining the top of William Street. For the first time in Patie's memory, he seemed reluctant to take responsibility.

A sniper's bullet pinged off the building behind them. Dick took the periscope and tried to locate the marksman. Civilians on the other side cheered, then fled for cover as Dick scattered the dust within inches of a Free State officer's toes.

Clouds were building up, adding a threat of thunder, and most of the curious disappeared. Both lines of combatants settled into waiting and Patie was filled with a deadening sense of low-level danger that hadn't touched him since the dog days of the Great War when nothing much happened for months on end and yet a sniper could always blow a head off without warning. And just like when they went over the top in a mass attack for a few miserable yards of ground, he'd once again lost track of what exactly he was fighting for at the moment. If the generals who had departed for Fermoy couldn't say whether they were attacking, defending or just harrying the enemy, what chances had the buck Volunteers beneath them?

'Like waiting for the Somme to kick off, isn't it, Dick?' He lit a cigarette for both of them. They still had hundreds of packets of Craven A, taken from Spillanes before the Freestaters grabbed the tobacco factory guarding Sarsfield Bridge on the morning they'd entered the city.

'It might be starting now.'

Through a crack in the barricade, Patie saw three armoured cars pass into Mulgrave Street to unleash a sustained burst of machine gun fire at the Ordnance Barracks.

'Wasting their time,' muttered Dick. 'They need shells to have any effect.'

'They're just frightening the lads inside.'

'Of course, we could always try to take one of the Rolls-Royces out.' A single rifle round echoed in the distance. 'Are you on, Patie?'

'How would you do that, Dick?' asked Willie.

'Sneak up on it like the way the Germans done against the tanks. Toss a grenade under the wheels or under the turret. Or else pour petrol around the turret and flick a cigarette in after it. They might think they're invincible under all that armour but there's nothing they can do when you're up real close to them.'

The cars withdrew back down William Street only to reappear after ten minutes. Patie thought he'd figured out a way of getting out on Mulgrave Street close to where the vehicles would pass by on their way back. Dick had scavenged two Mills bombs from the Ordnance Barracks. A day of soul-destroying inactivity while the noose slowly tightened had left them itching for retaliation.

'Come to me, my little baby,' Dick cooed through the barrier. The lead car stopped at the junction of Old Windmill Lane, rotating its turret like a fly checking out its surroundings before laying its eggs. Maybe it was deciding to turn up Roxborough Road instead and attack their barricade.

A runner tapped Willie on the shoulder. 'Message, Colonel Hartnett.'

Willie ripped open the envelope.

'Is there any message you want to send back, sir?' On seeing the shaking head, he scurried back in the direction of the New Barracks.

The armoured cars had changed their minds and returned to the Free State line without opening up again.

'We've been ordered to evacuate the city and withdraw to Kilmallock.' Willie tore up the slip of paper and threw it away. 'And now they're telling us to set fire to the barracks and blow up the bridges on our way out. Christ Almighty! What a crowd of eejits we've got over us!'

For the life of him, Willie couldn't figure out why Kilmallock rated a full-scale defence operation while Limerick, of far greater military and economic importance, had been abandoned without a decent fight. But at least a proper effort had been put into holding the line over a fifteen mile stretch in the geographic centre of Munster. By occupying the approaches and the river crossings, the Republicans had seen off repeated assaults on the town twenty miles south of Limerick and, denied their expected easy follow-up to their success in the city, the Free State advance collapsed in confusion. On facing their first real taste of combat, quite a few of their new recruits switched sides and the weapons they brought with them left the two sides facing each other at roughly equal strength for the first time since hostilities broke out.

The Republicans could even have turned the tide had they struck back before the enemy was reinforced from Dublin and one or two of their leaders had the wit to consolidate their position by capturing the smaller neighbouring towns of Bruff and Bruree. But these were little more than isolated attacks by individual companies and, when nobody else joined in support, they were retaken by Free State forces that had been swelled by another 2,500 men backed by a fleet of armoured cars and batteries of heavy artillery.

One of the 18-pounders could be heard beginning its bombardment from the Bulgaden direction, as Willie joined his fellow-commanders inside a cowshed at the edge of the town. Without anyone capable of bringing a focus to their discussions, the arguments flew back and forth. Éamon de Valera might have managed it had it not been dominated by military matters; Liam Lynch if he had a clear idea about what their objectives were; Liam Deasy if he'd been in command instead of being Lynch's deputy, and any of the rest of them if they'd stop for a moment to listen to what someone else was saying. But, as with all matters on the anti-Treaty side, everyone was his own expert.

'Maybe it'd be best if we pull back to the hills,' said Lynch. 'Hit them with flying columns like we did with the Tans.'

'We have to hold the Bruff Line,' countered Deasy. 'If we don't, they can advance on West Limerick and Kerry.'

'And how do we keep ourselves going if we don't establish an alternative administration?' asked Dev.

Unable to get a word in and doubting whether it would have any impact even he did, Willie slipped outside into the farmyard. More shells could be heard landing in the distance. The Freestaters were still too far out of range to inflict anything other than accidental damage but they were moving closer as the momentum of their advance picked up steam. Their troops mightn't have had the same motivation or experience, but at least they knew how to move under a single chain of command.

They'd take Kilmallock the same way they took everywhere else. Their own side would be split between a dozen different units all fighting their own private wars rather than joining together into a unified force. Willie had brought over a hundred Volunteers from the Fourth Limerick Brigade but they'd only follow his commands and nobody else's. It might have been different if they'd seen a clear leader pulling everyone in the same direction.

'We're wasting our time here.' One of the Tipperary brigade commandants joined him in the yard and leaned back against a rusting hay rake. 'They'll never come to a decision. I'm heading back to the Glen.'

Other groups were already melting away. Seaborne landings by Free State troops in Cork and Fenit had sent them rushing back to defend their home patches. One by one, the various commanders drifted out of the cowshed to consult with their own followers. Willie sought out Patie Fitzgibbon and Dick Mullane gathered under the arch of the Blossom Gate with the rest of the Fourth Limerick Brigade and told them to get ready for the journey back west.

Not every Republican made it out of Kilmallock. Coming in the back way from Bulgaden across the railway line, Ned Reidy's column surprised a squad waiting under the bridge who had yet to be told of the order to retreat. With the Knocklong road now clear ahead of them, Ned's men were then able to advance unopposed behind the Rolls-Royce armoured car that Michael Collins had christened Danny Boy. Using its cover to protect them from the expected resistance and hoping that the artillery bombardment from Ash Hill on the other side of the town would distract its defenders, they edged cautiously into the main street

Not a sinner could be seen. The townspeople had either fled or were buried in the safety of their houses. Bars and shops that had been occupied by the Republicans bore all the hallmarks of a hasty retreat with their open doors, carts upturned outside them, half-eaten sandwiches on the counters and tea still warm in the cups. Into the midday sunshine framed by the Blossom Gate, dust could be seen rising in the distance along the road out to Charleville.

The temptation was to follow but Ned had only two lorries as well as the armoured car. And even if he could put wheels under his entire troops, they'd still be outnumbered. Instead, he sent his men around from one house to the next just in case any straggling snipers remained and kept a close eye on them to prevent any needless damage. A few faces nervously peered through the curtains as the search parties passed up both sides of the street and then slowly filtered out of their homes as a second Free State column moved down to meet them from the main Limerick road.

As over 3,000 soldiers converged from three directions on the abandoned stronghold, Collins, Eoin O'Duffy and Bill Murphy joined Ned at the entrance to the football field beside the Blossom Gate where Shanagolden had won the county championship eight years earlier almost to the day. Although O'Duffy was technically the leader of the operation and Murphy the officer commanding the division, everyone deferred to the Big Fellow whose mood alternated between triumph and suspicion of how easily they had captured Kilmallock in the end.

'What do you think, Ned?' he asked. After having been held at bay for over a fortnight by the best-organised resistance they'd met since the shooting began, they had geared themselves up for a bloody final assault where they could exploit their superiority in men, artillery and armoured cars.

'It's not a trap.' Along with the rest of them, Ned felt the anti-climax of being denied a conventional military success. 'They're heading for the hills.'

'Eejits! They won't find it so easy to hide if they're seen to be attacking their own.' Collins opened the collar of his tunic and nodded acknowledgement to a stream of curious passers-by. 'This is your part of the country. Do you think we should strike while the iron is hot? Open the road to Kerry?'

'It's too good an opportunity ...'

'You're damn right it is! Do you hear that, O'Duffy? Saddle up the posse, like the man says!' The Big Fellow bounded into his Leyland open tourer staff-car and directed the driver past cheering soldiers out the Charleville road. All for show, of course, as they wouldn't be chasing the Republican retreat into Cork but it looked great for the photographers of the propaganda office who had followed their advance. Instead, they would be heading west through Bruree and along the Bruff Line to Newcastlewest and Kerry.

Bearing a silver trophy and surrounded by an entire parish united in triumph, Ned had gone back the same road the day before the final piece fell into place for Europe's Great War. They'd still be young enough to play football at their peak but most of them had died out in Flanders or else in the struggle for freedom. And most of those still alive had taken up the arms of his enemy.

'Are you having regrets?' Collins asked him as he returned from his poses for the cameras.

'I was just thinking of the time we won the county on this field. Playing with Willie Hartnett and Dick Mullane and Patie Fitzgibbon. We did some celebrating on the way home.'

'And now ye're at each others' throats.' The Big Fellow looked up at the sky as if trying to avert a painful memory. 'I know the feeling only too well. But we have to believe we're in the right.'

Republican prisoners were already clearing the streets of debris. A medical detail tended to the wounded and townspeople queued for their first sight of a doctor in weeks. A cart distributed water to the waiting buckets of housewives. Whatever their detractors might say, Ned believed that only the Free State could provide a realistic basis for the future.

'The sooner we get this over with, maybe the less of us will get killed. And maybe the easier it'll be for us all to make up.' A woman broke from the crowd to plant a kiss on Collins's cheek. 'Look at it another way, Neddy Boy. You're going home!'

He hadn't seen Shanagolden in almost six months. Heeding those concerned for his safety, he never made it to his father's funeral and it was only now, as a clear road opened in front of him, that he was struck by his sense of loss and by the guilt of his absence. He should have ignored them and turned up for the final goodbye.

'Go on, General Reidy, you're leading the advance.' Collins nodded to his driver restart the engine. 'This is your division now.'

The column was forming. Soldiers clambered up into their lorries. A trio of armoured cars waited impatiently to lead the way. Reports were coming in that they were unlikely to meet any resistance on the road, at least not as far as Newcastlewest.

Ned sat in beside the driver of his staff car. Returning a month late at the head of an army, he wondered what sort of welcome his hometown would give him.

44

ALWAYS A MAN who prided himself on his ability to anticipate events, Thomas Hennessy reopened for business on Shanagolden's main street on the very day that the Free State Army captured Kilmallock. And with Jack Noonan now no more than a distant memory, his premises immediately regained its prime position among the hostelries of the town. Enticed by rumours of drinks on the house, the bar filled up within minutes of opening its doors and, when word filtered through later in the evening of the Free State breakthrough, the Councillor availed of the opportunity to toast the restoration of law and order.

But at least he had the good sense not to overdo it. Conscious of the reputation enjoyed by Republican leaders who came from the area, he saluted the gallant fight that they'd put up and then urged everyone to bury past differences, accept the democratic authority of the state and face up to the challenges now facing a newly-independent country. It wasn't that such all-embracing sentiments needed to be expressed, as nobody active on the other side of the divide would be seen dead in his establishment, but there was always the chance that some two-faced freeloader would go off telling tales at the first opportunity.

The customers nodded in agreement. What was done was best forgotten. Looking ahead was the mood of the day.

'Jaysus, what were you saying there, man?' Doctor Molyneaux's was the sole voice of dissent. 'Making up with these blackguards? Sure they nearly killed me the time I was forced to drive them to Newcastle.'

'There'll be time enough to show them who's boss.' More pressing matters occupied Hennessy's mind. During his absence, positions of influence had slipped from his grasp. Maybe he should have stayed around instead of selling off his entire interests in Shanagolden after the Truce and buying them back at a fraction of the price, as the peace dividend failed to materialise and gloom over the Civil War hit rock bottom.

'Are you sure?' Now that Canon Murphy was permanently confined in a retirement home for priests who'd strayed off the rails, the Doctor was the only other survivor of the old coalition of interests. 'We are living in changed times, Thomas Hennessy, you mark my words.'

'And maybe for the better.'

'I wouldn't know about that, now. Gramophones, telephones and saxophones. Moving pictures. This new dance they call the Charleston. Women getting the vote and smoking cigarettes.' Molyneaux accepted another top-up of his glass. 'Yerra, I'm not so sure I want to be part of it any more.'

Even with the support of his man in the Government, it would take time to rebuild the edifice of Hennessy's connections. A new parish priest had yet to be appointed and was urgently needed to rein in the suspect sentiments of the curate, Father Greaney. And without the backing of the parish priest, he wasn't in any position to take on that troublemaker of a schoolmaster Hurley. Nor was the creamery manager any help. Florence Harrington might have been all right if he'd been left alone but, once he'd got himself romantically attached to Mary Hourigan, whatever views he might have held would never be heard again.

'I hears the Staters is in Newcastle.' A breathless herald planted himself in front of the counter in the expectation of a reward for his message. 'I hears the Irregulars is run off into the hills.'

'Have you now?' asked Hennessy. 'And who might have told you?'

'Everyone's saying it. Sure isn't the whole county saying it?'

'Then it can hardly be news.' He shook his head to tell the barman not to pour out a drink for the latest arrival who lingered at the bar with the decreasing optimism of a dog outside a butcher's closed door. Generosity was wasted on the impotent.

He'd need to be more careful this time. The path to influence was still being carved out and he couldn't afford to be associated with those like the late James Horgan who never knew when to keep the trap shut. It might be better to spread his bets. A few contacts on the Republican side could turn out to be useful.

'Yes, changed times indeed, Doctor,' he agreed.

Josie Reidy was turning in for the night when she heard the banging on the door. Thump, thump, thump went the brass knocker, too frantic for any soldier or policeman or anyone else that she'd rather not meet. Despite her exhaustion after yet another day of trying to run a big dairy farm on her own, she rose from her bed to find Mary Hourigan filling the porch.

'Kilmallock's fallen,' she told Josie. 'There's an entire division of the Free State Army spreading out over West Limerick.'

'Led by Ned?'

'Led by Ned. They're already in Newcastlewest. They should be here in Shanagolden in the morning.' Filled with helpless anger, Mary wanted someone to talk to, but Josie just wasn't in the mood. Even though her hopes had risen with the more organised resistance in the east of the county, she knew that defeat was inevitable once the anti-Treaty forces had withdrawn from the city. Only she wasn't yet ready to confront its reality.

She put the kettle on the range and waited for it to boil, through the heavy ticking of the grandfather clock that floated in from the hall. Faced with her neighbour's lack of comment, Mary hadn't an answer inside her.

'It's all over.' Josie broke the long silence as the water began to whistle. 'There's nothing to stop the Staters now.'

'The lads can still hold the high ground. Block off the Barna Gap, Carrigkerry and the Coast Road.'

'For what, Mary?' She spooned the tea into the pot and dropped it over the kettle's spout to let it steam.

'To hold out. We can't just let them walk all over us. Not after they going behind our backs to get help from the British.'

They'd nothing more to add as they supped their cups and they almost fought each other to be the first to wash up. 'Call around sometime tomorrow, will you?' she called as Mary climbed into the trap. 'Please. If you get the chance. I'm just too tired to think about anything at the moment.'

She lay awake for hours in the close heat of the night, thinking of another day ahead of milking forty cows and waiting in line at the creamery among neighbours, some of whom would now be cock-a-hoop at the Free State victory and wouldn't be slow to show it. Herself and Mary and a few more of them who'd been involved since it started would have to watch in silence as the Freestaters marched into town and the fruits of their struggle would be snatched from their grasp.

And when she'd get home, she'd have to take the pitchfork out into the back meadow and turn more of the hay that had been cut a few days before until it was time to round up the herd again for the evening's milking. Neighbours had given her a hand in the weeks after her father's death, even those on the other side of the fence who might gladly have shot her for being a Republican but who would still drop tools to help another farmer in distress. But not any longer. They had their own troubles too with the shortage of labour at the busiest time of the year.

She didn't know why she was doing it. The farm had been willed to Ned, the house as well, and all she'd been left were the few pounds hidden inside the chimney breast and the money in the bank that had been drawn down almost to nothing over the past few years as Edmund Reidy bought up whatever land he could lay his hands on. She could have felt aggrieved by the unequal division of an estate to which she had contributed far more than her brother. But she really didn't care about property after seeing how an obsession with statute acres had poisoned the goodness that had once lain inside her father.

Josie could easily have dumped it all on Ned's lap. If her brother wanted the farm, then he could run it himself, but she hadn't heard a word from him, not even when she told the solicitor to post on the contents of the will. And maybe she might have walked out on the place if Willie had been around.

Her mind had almost been made up when she got home from the funeral. But then, the dog got over its mourning and shyly loped over to greet her and the cattle lowed out in the field and a scatter of neighbours drove them in to be milked and a meitheal went up to cut the turf in her piece of bog up in the hills and she realised that he couldn't simply abandon the best herd and the best farm in the parish. So she stayed on another few days; it stretched into weeks when stories appeared in the Dublin newspapers, first of her father being murdered by the Republicans and subsequently of him dying of a heart attack in the process of being kidnapped, and she was damned if she was going to let herself be driven out by Free State lies and propaganda.

But what use was it now that they'd lost their war? The school would be starting back in a few weeks, the farm was dragging her down and the future she'd fought for had gone up in smoke. All alone on a hot August's night, Josie Reidy wept over memories of her father that pierced the bitterness of their final confrontation, and cried out for her man who was back on the run.

The night he and Bessie moved into the cottage out on the Foynes Road, there had been a glorious sunset. Nicholas Sullivan decided there and then that he wanted to paint. So, with the unrestrained enthusiasm of a late vocation, he found an artist in Adare to teach him the basics and, armed with the rudiments of sketching, brush strokes and mixing paint, he set forth to capture sights that he remembered from his days on patrol around Shanagolden.

Above all, he was filled with a mission to transfer the majesty of Shanid Castle to canvas. The centuries hadn't left much standing of the 12th century fortification, but the three-foot-thick walls of one of its towers still perched proudly on an outcrop overlooking the plains of Limerick and reminded every passer-by of its former grandeur. And out of those stones screamed the soul of the first Geraldines to enter the county with the Norman invasion. 'Seanaid abú!' cried generations of Fitzgeralds as they launched into battle to build the most powerful dynasty of Ireland's Middle Ages.

Rulers might come and go but Shanid was a permanent reminder of the land that it stood on. Nicholas Sullivan felt it his duty to record it, as it witnessed one of the more momentous moments of its long history.

It was still dark when he loaded his bicycle that morning with his canvas and his brushes, with his paints and his palette and his easel. And it was still quiet when he passed by the crossroads in the hope of catching the colours of the dawn reflecting off the ruined walls and off the hillside that pushed them against the sky. Wisps of mist hung over the flat land to his left but they were already being eased from the stage by a gentle breeze sucking the sultriness from the air and allowing a red line of half-light to edge over the eastern horizon.

He might be in luck. He might witness the sunrise in all of its clarity as it belted the spectrum of its rays westwards and scoured the landscape they fell on with blaze, hue and shadow. He might capture the mood of a single moment against a backdrop that had seen armies and nations and whole tribes of people pass beneath it for as long as the landmass of Ireland could remember.

'Aah ... The top of the morning, Inspector.' Flint Barrett almost toppled Sullivan from his bicycle as he sprang from a ditch, carrying a coil of copper pipe and a five-gallon bucket.

'Good morning to yourself, Flint.' They were standing on the exact spot of the Shanid Cross ambush. Faint lines in the macadam still marked out the crater that had blown an entire squad of Black and Tans to their maker. 'By the way, there's no need to bother with titles. It's just plain Mr. Sullivan now.'

'And a good job too.' Drug Donovan rolled a pair of forty-gallon drums onto the road. After more than a year of unimpeded production in the comfort of the master craftsman's own home, the poitín still was back on the move as the rule of law was on the point of return.

'Moving back to the castle, Drug? Or maybe back to the hills?'

'No offence, Mr. Sullivan, but that'd be telling.'

Nor were Flint and Drug the only souls stealing across the countryside in those early morning hours. No sooner had they disappeared back into the fields than another group scampered from one side of the road to the other. Seeing the outline of rifles slung over their shoulders, Sullivan dismounted from his bicycle at a safe distance and watched the entire complement of at least forty cover each other under the command of voices that he recalled from another time in his life. Dick Mullane, Patie Fitzgibbon, Willie Hartnett, Mossy Noonan and Jimmy McCarthy, run out of Kilmallock, were now on their way home.

He willed them to hurry up. The sky was brightening and the opportunity to witness was receding. Sullivan knew that this was going to be a spectacular sunrise but he couldn't take a chance on moving while the Republicans were still within earshot. They mightn't intend shooting him but, in those edgy minutes around dawn, nervous minds could see danger where it wasn't and nervous fingers could stroke triggers without warning.

Its bindings either frayed from overuse or else rotten from neglect, a bag fell apart and the old policeman watched the entire squad fall on their knees to collect what had scattered on the road. Single bullets, a firing pin and a few sticks of explosive were recovered, each handled like gold dust and greeted with a whispered triumph of discovery. If that was all the arms in their possession other than what was slung across their chests in makeshift bandoliers stitched together out of rough lengths of fabric, then the forces opposed to the Treaty hadn't a prayer.

Within minutes of the Republicans vanishing up the slopes of the hillside, the other side made its appearance. With the armour to protect them and the engines to move them and the ammunition to repel any attack, some were so certain of their safety from ambush that they sat on the bonnet of the lead armoured car. Engine noise drowned out the words of the song they were singing as the lorries, propelled by the fuel of success, ate up the yards of the road. It was their highway now, reclaimed from the enemy, another secured line of communication, another link in the broadside of the Free State's advance.

But then, he'd seen Black and Tan convoys exude the same bravado on the same stretch of road just two years before. And the castle had seen many more armies on the move beneath its walls.

The blaze was fading. The sun had already climbed through its shades of red and orange, its shadows shortening as it moved from dawn to morning. He'd have to come back some other time. Nicholas Sullivan turned his bicycle around and followed the trail of dust stretching back to his home.

The speed of the Free State advance caught them unawares and the IRA's Fourth Limerick Brigade was hard pushed to keep ahead of the soldiers fanning out over the county as they retreated from Kilmallock. With thousands of troops at his disposal, enough transport to carry them and enough firepower to protect them, Ned Reidy had taken over every town of significance right up to where the land suddenly rose from the plains, before the Republicans could regroup.

Lacking the arms and the numbers to hold onto fixed positions, the Fourth Brigade took to the hills as they'd been ordered by their Army Council but, even in their old familiar territory, they could no longer be sure of their surroundings. Some houses that had sheltered them during their war with the Tans had taken the side of the Free State, others had had their fill of the fighting and didn't want to know any more and, of the remainder, there was always the chance of being turned in by an opportunist trying to kick ball at both ends of the pitch. Everywhere they looked, they were filled by doubt and suspicion.

Even their home place was off limits. Cast out to the high ground overlooking the town and exhausted from a thirty-mile march through day and night, Patie watched the Free State advance on Shanagolden. Led by two armoured cars, five lorryloads of soldiers poured in from Newcastlewest to advance unchallenged past the queue of carts waiting at the creamery and up the main street to meet a delegation of welcome.

'Can you see who's in it?'

'They're too far away.' He passed the field glasses to Willie. 'But I could tell you who some of them is anyway. Hennessy, Doctor Molyneaux, that young fella Hennessy brought back with him from Dublin.' Not to mention the other new faces in the chorus to replace James Horgan, Sergeant Stapleton and the Canon. Eight years back, their hold on the football club had been broken, but now, three wars later, the old guard was back running the place as if nothing had happened. 'Don't it make you wonder why we ever bothered?'

'I see Ned has arrived,' muttered Willie. A staff car drove down the street to the crossroads, having come into the town from the direction of Rathkeale. Dick Mullane lined up the figure rising from the passenger seat with the sights on his rifle.

'Go on, Dick,' urged Jimmy McCarthy. 'Plug the bastard.'

'No. Leave him. We haven't gone that far yet.'

'He's out of range anyway, Willie. I couldn't guarantee you what I'd hit from this distance.'

Even if Ned had been within range, no one would have sniped him. Despite the ever-increasing bitterness between the factions, fighting between Freestater and Republican hadn't descended to the level of cold conflict like that against the Tans or out in the trenches where the enemy wasn't clouded by any shade of ambiguity. For someone like Patie or Dick who'd been through some of the worst fighting that the world had ever seen, there

642

was a quaint chivalry regarding the courtesies both sides were forced to extend, brought about by the fact that they'd still have to live with each other once the shooting was over. So, while it was all right to fire at an advancing enemy or to take out a protected weapon like an armoured car, it was considered bad form to attack an unarmed opponent or one engaged in non-threatening activity like sentry duty without first giving him the chance to surrender.

Not that it was likely to last. Back in the early days of the Great War, there was a similar resistance to all-out conflict. Patie had heard stories of ceasefires during the Christmas of 1914 when opposing armies climbed out of the trenches to exchange greetings and drinks and play games of soccer. By the time the following winter had arrived, the generals had made sure that such fraternal activity would never be repeated.

'They might be looking for you, Willie.' Dick pointed to the squad of soldiers that had left the crossroads to advance up the laneway of the Reidy's farm. Some were no more than a few hundred yards below Patie as they entered the yard but, instead of going into the house, they made for the outbuildings. 'Jesus, has Ned got so high and mighty that he still thinks you're nothing more than a hired hand?'

Five of the Freestaters emerged with pitchforks, one with a dung fork and, with a detail to guard them, they began turning the hay in the back meadow. The remainder of the squad took their scythes to the field beyond it.

'Easy run a farm when you're a Free State general,' cracked Jimmy McCarthy. 'You can take all the free labour you want.' A head turned below them to run a suspicious gaze along the length of the hillside. They'd have to move on, to edge further back into the sour brown fields of the high land and find a new hideout that Ned wouldn't know about. And from there in a last stand of resistance, they and the Third Brigade and remnants from the city and from the centre of the county would have to work out how they could block the Free State's advance into Kerry.

As the soldiers below them turned their attentions to the hay, Patie and his colleagues collected their meagre packs of belongings. For the first time since they'd sent the Black and Tans packing, they were leaving their town in the hands of the enemy.

It wasn't as bad as Ned Reidy had feared. Towns had been abandoned by the Republicans over most of the county and Shanagolden was no exception. Just as with Newcastlewest, Rathkeale, Ballingarry and Askeaton, they experienced that strange empty echo as the lorries ground to a halt, as the orders were barked out and as the bootsteps banged off the road. Faces would peer out, then doors would open and they'd round a corner where the enthusiastic would be waiting to greet them and everyone would breathe a sigh of relief that there hadn't been any act of resistance.

But no matter how easy their entry might be, they could never shake off the sense of occupation. Like anywhere else in rural Ireland, authority had always been imposed from outside and, even if a son of their parish was leading its return, it was still regarded as an invasion. Ned might have seen the happiness in those welcoming an end to the anarchy and might have observed the acceptance in others of the reimposition of order but, even among the most enthusiastic, the reception was little more than grudging. A parallel structure for settling scores and for recognising standing had grown up through the centuries of foreign rule and it mattered not a damn whether rulers who tried to superimpose their claims to govern came from London or

Dublin or Limerick, because they were still seen as interfering strangers.

He could see it in the line at the creamery. Many of the farmers cheered him as one of their own, a lad younger than themselves who had risen to become a general in the army and a minister in the government, but they too were reserving their judgment. The authority represented by the division of soldiers under his command would have to earn their respect before it could entertain any hope of acceptance.

And those were his supporters. Others, including his sister and Mary Hourigan and a few more who'd sheltered him and fed him during their fight against the Tans, turned their faces away the minute they saw him climb out of his staff car. Not a word was uttered in their silent rejection but he could spell the accusations of traitor in their minds.

They looked beaten, they looked bitter, they looked as if they were filled with the helpless anger of those who'd realised that the system was loaded against them and he knew exactly how they felt, because the very same sentiments had driven him to take up arms against the British. And neither would they ever forgive him for accepting half of what they willing to settle for because that was the best deal that was on offer.

He would have liked to have argued the toss so that the whole parish could make its own judgment, but he knew that debate was beyond those who had taken the other side. Logic, reason and the pragmatic arts of politics and diplomacy didn't matter. Opinions had already been moulded by the romantic attachments to unattainable ideals like a republic or an end to the Oath, which had looked important on paper but which made absolutely no difference in practise. All that mattered to them was the language of the settlement.

But words never brought food to the table. Nor did they rebuild the roads and the railways and the creameries and all the other tools of the economy that had been blown up or had crumbled from neglect during the years of conflict. Nor did they provide the means whereby a man could get paid, or borrow money, or lend it out, or sell property, or buy goods, or engage in any activity that might create employment and spread wealth around, and pay a government to teach his children so that they might start out in life with a better chance than their parents.

'It's time we got back to business,' Councillor Hennessy was telling him.

'A bit of order around these parts wouldn't go astray,' added another of the reception committee.

'There's some right blackguards in them Irregulars,' muttered Doctor Molyneaux between puffs of his pipe. 'I hope we've seen the back of them now.'

A few more heads nodded as they converged on the crossroads, but they weren't the ones Ned wanted to see. The new State had to reach out further if it were to put down roots, if it were to convince the people he came from that there was a time to stop being against everything, if it were to cajole them into supporting a government of their own for a change.

He looked again at Josie, waiting her turn to be unloaded with her face resolutely staring at some point in the middle distance. The rejection was total. He couldn't even tell her how sorry he'd been that he wasn't able to make it to the funeral and share with her the last memories of their father and talk to her about the estate, about her taking the house and maybe a few fields of the farm and the pick of the herd.

Nor could he wish Mary well on her upcoming wedding and confess what a fool he had been to let her slip from his attentions. The cart brushed past as if Ned and his soldiers weren't there. In her mind, in those of Drug Donovan, Philip Hurley, Father Connie and even of Flint Barrett and in those of the other stony faces he could see speckled among supporters and neutrals, another army ruled Shanagolden.

He knew that they were still around. He could feel the presence of Willie Hartnett hanging on the breeze that edged around corners and spread up the lanes and wafted under the doors of the houses, whispering that the Republicans hadn't gone away. Ned could be vested with the authority of government and with command of the military, he could have been the captain who brought the county championship home to Shanagolden, he could have been the victor in the election of 1918, he could have been the public face of his parish and his county, yet here among his own, they would always look to Willie for inspiration.

General Ned Reidy, Minister for Public Health, would never be regarded as anything other than his sidekick.

45

PATIE FITZGIBBON wouldn't have bothered them but for the fact that he hadn't eaten for days. They'd helped out the Brigade in good times and bad but they were also on their uppers. Anyone entering the yard could see from the rotting thatch, the flaking whitewash and the crumbling shed that there was no money at all coming into the farm. While the dairymen down on the lowlands were suffering from the destruction of the creameries and from the disruption of the markets, their difficulties were nothing compared to those of the smallholders eking out a subsistence up in the hills from grazing store cattle that could no longer be sold.

When nothing was offered, Patie was forced to wave his gun and he settled for half of what they could find even though Jimmy McCarthy wanted to take away the whole lot. A shoulder of bacon, a bag of flour, a mixed sack of carrots, parsnips and potatoes, a can of milk and a creel of turf wouldn't go far among fifty hungry men constantly on the move as the Free State patrols edged ever closer. And this was the end of August, the most plentiful time of the year.

'That's all we have.' The woman watched Patie, Dick Mullane and Jimmy load the booty on their backs. She wouldn't turn them in but she'd make damn sure everything was hidden should they ever return. 'What are we going to do for the winter?'

'Ye'll find something,' said Jimmy.

'We gave ye all we had to spare when ye were fighting the Tans,' the husband called after them as they headed out into the night. 'Now ye're coming back wanting more.'

The next place had even less to spare. Even if they'd ransacked it at gunpoint, they'd have got nothing more than a few scraps from the old farmer living on his own. In the end, he took pity on them and brought them most of the way back in his ass and cart. Maybe it was a hint that no one else in the area had anything for them either and, after accepting the offer of a lift, they couldn't very well pound the doors of his neighbours.

None of the other parties fared any better as they trickled back to the abandoned cottage from an evening spent scouring the countryside for anything that would keep starvation at bay. Some could muster up nothing better than berries and crab apples that hadn't yet ripened. One of the lads had snared a rabbit and was roasting it on a spit over the fire in the grate.

'We won't last long on this.' Willie bent over the sorry little pile of commandeered provisions and sorted the dry foods into daily rations. 'How did it go, Patie?'

'Like drawing blood from a stone.' Most of the lads were catching up on their sleep. Nights were still dry and warm in these dying days of summer. It would be a different story within a few weeks, when the autumn damp would slowly begin its rise up the masonry and up the legs of their trousers. 'Everyone's either fed up or else they've nothing left to give us.'

'Not worth going back to?'

'No. Not even at the point of a gun.'

Led by Mossy Noonan, the last group arrived back with nothing more than a quarter-filled sack of turnips. The entire column had returned; not a single desertion despite miserable weeks on the run in a countryside where allegiances were still sorting themselves out. It might have been a different story if the Freestaters had been less vindictive. As hastily-recruited troops flooded into the county and a Dublin Guard that appeared to operate independently of any command set about mopping up resistance outside the towns, families of suspected Republicans were driven from their homes on little more than the say-so of an anonymous neighbour with an axe to grind. And rather than accepting their opponents shutting their mouths, keeping the head down and burying the rifle in the thatch, the newcomers from the capital demanded outright surrender and were hell bent on locking up anyone they could lay their hands on.

'A bit of news, lads,' announced Mossy. 'I just heard Collins was killed outside Cork the other day.'

'Mighty!' Jimmy shook his fist. 'Only pity it wasn't sooner.' But he was alone in his response. Everyone else still awake realised that their conflict had tumbled down past the last step of bitterness. Although Collins was on the other side and Patie suspected that he'd set them up with the Pact election, he was still the most charismatic military figure during the Tan War. His death somehow diminished everyone's fight for freedom.

'They'll find it hard to replace him,' Dick muttered eventually. 'This could be our chance to turn things around.'

'No, they'll find someone else. And even if he isn't another Michael Collins, he'll still be better than anything we've got.' Willie gave the fire another poke. 'What's more, they'll take the gloves off now. At least Collins might make the effort to find a settlement whenever the mood took him. Now we'll have the likes of O'Duffy and Blythe calling the shots.'

Collins's death while touring Free State outposts in the middle of Republican territory had unnerved the Provisional Government of the Free State. Control of troops, whose discipline was already groaning under rapid expansion, slipped another notch and broke the momentum of the advance into the enemy's rural strongholds. If they'd been better armed and better organised, the IRA might have rolled the tide back enough to spark off a rash of defections, but the complete absence of any military strategy limited their gains to the temporary occupation of a handful of towns and the capture of enough Free State arms and ammunition to reduce the conflict to stalemate.

Summoned to a Cabinet meeting in Dublin, Ned Reidy kept his silence while his colleagues argued over the progress of the war. Although the room sizzled with heated discussion, there was none of the inspiration of the Big Fellow's personality nor of the organisational drive of Arthur Griffith who had died of a brain haemorrhage just ten days before Collins. They were losing the unity of purpose that had led them to the brink of victory.

Spurred by personal ambition and by animosities that had been buried but not yet forgotten, factions coalesced around those favouring an immediate military response and those who preferred to cloak any reaction in a legal framework. It was easy to tell them apart. One side of the table dazzled to the spit and polish of Army uniforms, the other was laden with the formality of wing collars, waistcoats and fob watches. Argument rained back and forth between them.

'Anarchy! Must be stamped out by whatever means possible!'

'It's our responsibility to save the country.'

'But it won't look right. It has to look legal.'

'Oh, for God's sake! The Army can do whatever it wants. They can always plead self-defence ...'

'... And who'll thank us for it ...?'

'... The Church is behind us. I'm reliably reformed that the bishops will condemn the Irregulars as an unjust and immoral force. So it's time for us to set an example ...'

'... Instead of meeting with the enemy behind our backs.'

Richard Mulcahy was roundly condemned for his secret talks with Éamon de Valera and they turned on Ned as well when they realised that he had also been party to the discussions. Not that the meetings had led anywhere, as Dev appeared to be acting independently of the IRA's Army Council, while Mulcahy seemed more interested in driving a wedge between the Republicans' political and military leaderships than in securing a ceasefire.

Tempers were rising as they broke for lunch. Seeing Mulcahy and Kevin O'Higgins making a beeline for him from opposite directions, Ned ducked out of the building for a few moments on his own. Without Collins around to smother any doubts with his infectious enthusiasm, he was no longer quite sure where he stood. It was all very fine for the lawyers and the academics to spout on about imposing the rule of law by whatever means necessary but, now that Dublin had quietened down, most of them were insulated from what was happening on the ground. What had started out as a campaign to establish the legitimacy of the Free State, was now degenerating into a series of vendettas and, with freebooter units like the Dublin Guard operating in the shadows, he was finding it increasingly difficult to restrain the troops under his command.

'We've gone too far down the road to pull back.' Mulcahy caught up with Ned as he strolled along Saint Stephen's Green.

'Are you talking about your soldiers or mine?'

'Ned, if we'd been worried about what people thought of us, we'd never have run the British out. It's the same in this fight. We won't win it if we're not prepared to go the whole way.'

A column of soldiers passed by. They acknowledged the salute. 'Those are our boots marching in Dublin now. Did you ever think you'd live to see the day?'

The city had come out for the sunshine. Crowds moved up and down Grafton Street, walking, talking and peering into shops that had reopened for business. The scent of roasting coffee hung over Bewley's. Newsboys blared from their boxes. Normality of a kind had returned.

'This is our city, our capital, a place that will soon have its own parliament buildings and embassies and government ministries,' continued Mulcahy. 'It's ours, it's all ours for the first time in over seven hundred years. But we have to finish the job that the Big Fellow began. We'd never be forgiven if we threw it all away.'

Ladies fluttered admiring glances at their uniforms. Gentlemen tipped their hats out of respect.

'So the time for half-measures is over.' Mulcahy turned back towards Kildare Street.

A wedding party passed by Ned on its way to the breakfast, a couple placing their hopes on the future of a city that was again finding its feet. Having led them this far, who was he now to deny them?

Anyway, they didn't need his assent. An inner circle was already forming to replace Collins and Griffith and everything had been sorted out in Ned's absence. Discussions behind the scenes led to a tacit understanding that WT Cosgrave and Kevin O'Higgins could run the government while Mulcahy was given his head with the military. A Public Safety Bill would allow the Army to execute anyone found looting, possessing arms, commandeering property or acting in any other manner that might endanger the Free State.

'Extreme situations require extreme measures,' the Cabinet was told as the meeting resumed. And such was the collective determination to uphold their authority that the proposal, granting the Army powers far in excess of anything the Black and Tans ever enjoyed, went through on the nod.

Pressure from brigade commandants at a loss as to where the campaign was heading led to Republican leaders being summoned to a gathering in the Galtee Mountains. With most of Limerick now in enemy hands, it had taken Willie two days to cross the county to attend. He might as well not have bothered. The meeting lived up to his worst expectations and, instead of agreeing on what they were looking for and on how best they could they could continue the fight, most of the talk had centred on finding someone to blame. The Freestaters were being bankrolled by the British and had to be made to pay for their treachery. De Valera had gone behind the Army Council's back in his negotiations with Mulcahy. The people had allowed themselves to be duped by an election. Politicians couldn't be trusted. Units that had been expected to support them were sitting on the fence.

Liam Lynch, in particular, appeared to be obsessed with Richard Mulcahy. Former colleagues on the IRB Supreme Council, they'd developed a deep respect for each other during the War of Independence and had worked night and day to head off the Civil War just a few months previously. But that ended abruptly with the bombardment of the Four Courts and, with each publicly accusing the other of bad faith, the growing feud between them was fuelled by the bitterness of broken friendship.

Others had similar tales to tell. Willie could have added his tuppence-worth about Ned Reidy but he'd heard his fill of personal disappointment. All he wanted was some arms to carry on the fight but his plea fell on deaf ears. Apart from the few rifles picked up in a raid on a Free State patrol, the Fourth Brigade hadn't seen a new weapon since their last engagement with the British yet they were expected to keep two Free State armies from joining up.

In the end, he got the promise of some dynamite and an unspecified supply of ammunition once the leadership prevailed over a unit that had been jealously hoarding its arsenal for almost three years. He'd believe it when he'd see it. And with nothing more to show for his efforts, he set off for home across thirty miles of hostile territory.

A carter hid him under a load of oats being transported to the mill in Kilmallock and twice he rode his luck as bayonets stabbed into the trailer at checkpoints. The Staters were cocky now that every town, village and parish pump within a day's walk was under their control, but they were lazy too and, if they'd even been the slightest bit more thorough in their inspection, he would surely have been caught.

Another cart laden with hides carried him through the night out the Bruff Line through O'Rourke's Cross and on towards Newcastlewest and, while the greasy blood-caked stench of the pelts saved him from prying Free State eyes, he had almost suffocated from the fumes by the time the journey ended in Castlemahon. A third-generation Fenian hid him while he slept through the day on condition that he first burned his clothes and then soaked himself in the Deel until he had expunged the smell.

A few quiet words around the town conjured up a pair of trousers, a shirt and a jacket that fitted tolerably well over his big bony frame and a fine plate of bacon, curly cabbage and floury spuds was laid before him. Wolfing down the hot salty dinner and washing it down with a pint of plain porter before his astonished host, he realised that he hadn't had a decent meal in weeks.

Fed, slept and washed, he felt like a new man. Energy seeped back into joints that had been sapped by the rains, by the hunger of the hills, by the ever-encroaching range of the Free State patrols and by the fissured ineptitude of the Republican leadership. Just eight miles separated him from his comrades and he waited for nightfall to set out.

They told him that every approach to the Barna Gap, the gateway to the hills of West Limerick, was saturated with Free State patrols. But despite the awe in which they held him, they still wanted him out of the town. Word of the arrival of a Republican legend had whistled through the grapevine and someone somewhere was likely to get wind of his presence and might be tempted or impassioned to inform.

'Tis gone that way,' the old Fenian informed him. ''Twas way simpler when we were fighting John Bull, but now you can never be sure. A neighbour, even a friend you'd never suspected, might be thinking the other way.'

They found a motorcar going his way. An ailing woman up Shangolden way had grandly informed the family that she would rather die than be treated by a Freestate collaborator like Doctor Molyneaux and had summoned the physician of Castlemahon to her deathbed.

'Tis only in her head,' the doctor was saying. If he'd been a few years younger, he would have been up in the hills fighting alongside the Fourth Brigade. 'She's nowhere near as bad as she makes out. She's only looking for notice.' He waved his bag with the stethoscope protruding at a half-interested squad of soldiers. 'It's the same every year. Once the summer starts to decline, she takes to the notion that her number is up. Still, she always pays cash on the nail.'

Willie would have slipped out at Shanid Cross but they didn't dare stop as headlights approached them from the other direction. 'Molyneaux would have made a fortune out of her if his if his wife hadn't upstaged her years back when John Redmond came to town,' continued his driver. 'Then again, maybe he's the lucky man for it. She'd drive you to distraction if you if she had you at her beck and call every hour of the day.'

The oncoming vehicle, a lorryload of Freestaters on their way from Foynes to Newcastlewest, passed them by. 'They're bringing reinforcements in by boat from the other side of the Estuary. I'd say there's going to be a major push to secure the Barna Gap. ' The doctor stopped just beyond a dip in the road. 'Here, hop out and the best of luck to you. It's the safest place you'll get around here.'

Willie jumped through the hedge and looked up the steep climb into the hills. If he kept on walking straight ahead through the fields, he was less than an hour from safety. He'd be quicker still if he followed the boreen to his left that rose diagonally across the slope but he'd seen Freestaters patrolling it a week earlier.

And less than a quarter of a mile away to his right lay the Reidy farmhouse.

The moon had gone down. The rustling wind would mask his footsteps. There was no sign of activity around.

It was still madness.

But he desperately wanted to see her.

The yard was dark, silent and empty. The dog cocked an eye open, recognised who it was and fell back asleep. Willie clung to the shadows, hunched under the sill and tapped his knuckles softly on the window.

The curtains opened, the candle flickered and cast its shadow over the contours of her face, the sweep of her hair and the white folds of her nightdress. 'It's all right,' Josie whispered under the raised sash. 'I'm on my own. Come around to the door.'

He had her in his arms before she had opened it fully and they crashed over a chair as they stumbled back through the kitchen. 'God Almighty!' she panted into his ear, still locked in embrace as they rolled on the flagstones. 'You're making some noise for a man on the run.'

They staggered to their feet and he held her again, this time more slowly, stroking her hair and her ear and her neck.

'All washed and scrubbed for the occasion. Willie Hartnett! You do know how to treat a lady after all.' Then a tear rolled down her cheek. 'Oh My God, Willie! I've been so worried.'

They sat on the hob by the range, she on his lap, burying her head in his shoulder and quivering with sobs of relief and he submerged himself in the flood of her words.

'They come every day,' she was telling him, pouring out anything that came into her head just to reassure herself that he was there. 'Just after sunrise. Five or six of them in a lorry. They milk the cows and they bring it down to the creamery and they do anything that needs to be done in the yard or out in the fields. And I go off to the school in the morning and I come back in the evening and I pass them by without saying a word and they don't bother me in the slightest.'

How he had missed the beat of her voice, rich and soft when it flowed and those dainty little breaths as she hopped from one thought to the next.

'Maybe Ned thinks he's helping me out. Maybe he's staking his claim to the property. I've no idea what he's up to. He still hasn't answered the letter the solicitor sent him and, if you ask me, I think he's afraid to. He doesn't know whether I'm enemy or family and he hasn't the guts to find out.'

Her heart was pumping against his.

'Not that I care one way or the other. He can have the place as far as I'm concerned. The house as well. Philip Hurley will sell me his cottage. He's moved into his wife's place in Foynes since he got married.'

She shivered again. 'God, the nights are getting right cold now. How do ye stick it up in the hills?' She rose to her feet and led him into her bedroom.

It was still dark. She'd drag it out as long as she could. Ned's Free State soldiers wouldn't turn up for at least another hour.

His chest rose and fell as he soaked in the luxury of sleep in a real bed and she threaded her fingers over muscle and bone and nestled her cheek against the bristle of his chin. Way down below the bedclothes, her legs twined around his and she felt them shudder for a moment and then relax before his great big arm looped around her shoulder.

'Just hold me,' she whispered.

'Mmm ... mmm.' It could have been a sigh or a snore.

'Let me dream for a moment that you'll never go away.'

His lips brushed over her eyes and down her nose and her tongue reached out to meet them and she shut everything from her mind as his grasp tightened.

She should have heard the dog barking.

The door crashed open. She couldn't tell how many of them were behind the Tilly lamp but she saw the pairs of uniformed hands sprout from the darkness to drag him from her embrace and she saw his fists floor a few of them before they pinned him down, trussed him around a post with a rope, stuck a pistol in his ear and stuffed something in his mouth so that he couldn't even say goodbye.

'No!' she screamed as she rose to her feet. 'No! No! No!'

They brushed her aside. 'Will someone shut her up!' barked a gruff Dublin accent.

She rose again, tears streaming from her eyes as they lifted him out like a coffin, and she jumped forward through a pair of them to fling her arms around his legs in a forlorn attempt to hold him.

'Get her off me, for Jesus sake!' roared the Dubliner.

'Be careful you don't mark her!' shouted another. 'She's General Reidy's sister!'

They had to drop Willie on the ground as they yanked her away. For one fleeting moment in the light of the swinging lamp, she met his eyes and they melted with love and sorrow before they picked him up again and lifted him, still buck naked, outside into the cold night like an animal captured by the hunt.

'Oh my sweet Jesus up in Heaven!' she wailed as they hurried out into the yard. 'Will they ever leave us alone?'

46

ANY SPARE TIME Josie had was spent in trying to track down her brother. He hadn't been in Shanagolden since the day the Freestaters arrived and he hadn't been seen in Newcastlewest either since he'd departed for Dublin for the opening of the new Dáil. And if he was still around, no one was going to tell her. General Ned Reidy was far too important a figure in the Government for his movements to be disclosed when the foundations of the state were under attack, and it didn't matter a damn if she was friend, neighbour or family. Now that the Public Safety Act had come into force and the Irregulars hadn't crawled out of the hills in surrender, they could never be too careful.

Over a week had gone by as she cycled home from her day at the school. Some of those she passed would nod sympathetically; others would turn their faces awkwardly away. The entire parish was aware of Willie's capture yet, with the area swarming with soldiers, reaction was confined to the silent gesture. As the Civil War bit ever deeper, sympathies were hidden, curiosity was shelved and if anyone knew anything of importance, they went out of their way to conceal it.

Even the children were in on the act. The class knew of Miss Reidy's plight but no one, not even Eddie Costelloe who normally couldn't keep quiet for a moment, dared to open their mouths in case they might give something away. Instead, they decided to be good and never, in her six years of teaching, had she faced more attentive or more considerate pupils. It only added to her distraction. Philip Hurley had suggested she take some time off, but she couldn't face the thought of spending the entire day back in the house being watched by the soldiers sent out to work the farm.

The detail was clearing the ditch on the far side of the front field as she came up the lane. The yard was as empty as ever. Even the dog had taken his leave to chase a romantic notion.

Willie had just disappeared. All trace of him ended at the farm gate through which he'd been spirited off into the night. He could be dead or he could be alive; he could be in jail or have escaped back to the hills. Stories were circulating of Republican leaders like Tom Barry being sprung from Free State internment camps. Rumours were doing the rounds of private executions by a unit they called the Dublin Guard, formed around of the elite group that Michael Collins had set up to assassinate British intelligence agents.

'Psst. Ma'am! Miss Reidy!'

She turned to see a gawky young soldier stick his head out of the milking shed, the same one she'd noticed more than once admiring her from afar.

'The ... the ... the big push is starting,' he stammered. 'Any day now.'

Was he gloating or just making a fool of himself?

'We ... we'll be securing the road to Kerry ... d'you understand?'

Or telling her that he was leaving?

'I'd say you might find your brother ... I mean General Reidy that is ... he should be in Limerick for the next few days ... aah ... in Cruise's Hotel. That'd be where the Southern Division have set up their headquarters.'

'Thanks,' she whispered. And to his obvious embarrassment, she planted a light kiss on his cheek. He was still blushing when the sergeant came around bawling at him to get the lead out.

She had never felt so alone. It wasn't that Josie was a stranger to Limerick. Five years of boarding school had unlocked its sights, its sounds, its smells and its stories to her, but the city now buzzing with green uniforms, green lorries and green recruitment posters had been taken over by a power that she couldn't comprehend. Neither stranger nor friend, neither an occupying force, nor one of their own, it had won the race to grab the reins of control.

And unlike the British, whose latter days had been riddled with doubt, this new army swaggered with the certainty of success. Even though most of them had only weeks of experience, soldiers straightened their shoulders and pushed out their chests as they marched in full uniform without fear of ambush. Gone were the peaked caps, the homemade bandoliers and the threadbare overcoats of the original recruits. The ragtaggle look had been left to the men in the hills.

Everyone around them knew which side was winning and, with the city being further away from the front line of continuing resistance and big enough to escape the constraints of immediate familiarity, opinions could be expressed more openly in Limerick than in Shanagolden. In the maelstrom of comings and goings at the railway station, she heard the Holy Biddies and the Holy Joes welcoming the joint statement of the bishops excommunicating anyone who failed to accept the government's authority, the merchants and professionals insisting on a short sharp campaign against anarchy, the taunts of Free State treachery, the complaints that one load of oppressors had been replaced by another, the pleas to let bygones be bygones and look to the future and the clatter everywhere of an army on the move.

A Cumann na mBan source told her that there were no reports of Willie being held in the jail. Another revealed that official executions would begin within days. A third confirmed that Ned was still in town and had been spotted down at Cruise's Hotel on several occasions. Though depleted by arrest and defection, the network of messengers was still intact, but such was the overwhelming Free State presence in the city that the women's wing of the IRA could no longer move about freely in the open. Back home in Shanagolden, defeat was implied. Here in the city, it was rubbed in with a vengeance.

She could feel the stares all around her as she walked down to the heavily guarded section of O'Connell Street in front of Cruise's. Bullswool popped out everywhere she looked, polished leather, brass buttons and pips, eyes sunken underneath the peaks of caps, chests bound inside Sam Brownes and webbing, all indistinguishable from one another, as if to proclaim that no matter how many of them were shot at, there would always be others to take their place.

'You have no authorisation,' they told her at the barricade.

'I'm here to see General Reidy.' The title stuck in her gullet.

An officer popped his head out of a little hut hidden between the hoardings. 'Who told you he's here, madam?'

'I'm his sister.'

'Tell me another.' He rose from his hidey-hole but she walked straight through him with such determination that no one tried to restrain her. The guard at the entrance failed to stop her either and she was past the reception and halfway down the corridor to the open door of a large suite when a great spawg of a hand grabbed her by the shoulder.

There he was, looking right important as he hid behind a desk laden with a mountain of paper, a jug of water and three telephones, each with a different coloured ribbon tied around the mouthpiece. She tried to break free and, on hearing her vain slaps, he raised his head from a document he was reading and swivelled around his chair.

'It's all right, Séamus. She is my sister.' He waved the man-mountain away and she slammed the door behind her as she entered.

'Where is he?' she demanded.

'Who?'

'Don't play games with me, Ned.' She leaned her balled fists on the desk. 'What are ye doing to him?'

'Who?' he repeated.

'Willie. And don't bother trying to look so surprised. Your lackeys arrested him over a week ago.'

'Are you sure?'

'Of course I'm sure.' She knew he was bluffing from the way he arched his back away from her in his chair. 'I was in bed with him when they took him away. Enjoying him. I bet they didn't tell you that, did they?' The colour rose in his face. 'Or are you as big a snob as your father was?'

'Believe me, Josie, this is the first I've ever heard of it.'

'And nobody knows where he is.' She slapped at the heap of papers in front of her, scattering them all over the carpet. 'Have ye killed him already?'

'We're not like the Black and Tans.' All offended, he was. And then all concerned. She'd nearly have believed him only she knew him better. 'We don't kill our prisoners.'

'So where is he then?'

667

'I told you I don't know. But I'll look into it.' He picked up a pencil and absently scribbled on a sheet of paper as if he was jotting down the details of a tiresome supplicant. 'He might be detained. After all, he is the commander of the Irregulars in West Limerick ...'

'Don't you dare call them Irregulars, you jumped-up traitor! They're the army that won Ireland its freedom ...'

'Whatever you say. Let's not get into that.' He dropped the pencil and clasped his hands together. 'Look, Josie, do you seriously think I want to see him harmed? Willie and myself go back farther than anyone else in this awful Civil War.'

But he wouldn't meet her eyes and so she leaned even closer. 'I'll hold you to that, Ned Reidy. As God is my witness.'

He shrank before her. All contact was lost. She no longer had any family.

Willie had lost all track of time. Not having seen the light of day since they tossed him into the cellar, he could no longer tell whether it was day or evening or night and the long periods spent in total darkness between interrogations disrupted his remaining sense of perspective. Sometimes he'd wake up from a fitful shivering sleep convinced that he'd been imprisoned for months. Other times, memories would merge into one another and he'd think that he'd been held for only a matter of hours.

The footsteps were returning. With a supreme effort of willpower, he forced himself to sit upright on the slab and not to cower in the corner. Every inch of movement screamed against joints creaking from the beatings, from the damp and from the cold. But he was damned if he'd let them think he was afraid.

The sudden illumination disoriented him and he staggered blindly towards its source as they kicked him upright and out towards the door. The batons prodded him along a long illuminated corridor and, as his eyes adjusted their focus, he could see the alternating stripes of caked mud and caked blood covering a body that hadn't worn a stitch of clothing since his capture.

A side door opened long enough to let him hear the singing. He wasn't alone in this dungeon.

'Take it down from the mast, Irish traitors.

It's the flag we Republicans claim.

It shall never belong to Freestaters

Who have brought on it nothing but shame ...'

'Shut those bastards up, for Christ's sake!' roared the leader of his escort.

He hoped they saw him smiling. A balled fist swung towards his jaw but the sergeant grabbed it before it could connect. 'Not his face, you fool! Somewhere it can't be seen.'

A bent knee jabbed into his stomach. He kept grinning through the pain and he was still grinning as they bundled him into another bare room with a table and two chairs.

This time he was faced by an officer who fancied himself as a master of the more cerebral arts of questioning. Maybe he'd been raised on a diet of spiffing detective novels where dashing sleuths outwitted dim criminals with the sharpness of their superior intellects.

A facetious nod dismissed the thugs with the sandbags. A full packet of Craven As and a box of matches were tossed on the centre of the table. His interrogator pulled out a cigarette and made a big show of lighting it and letting the full flavour of Virginia waft under his nose.

They were wasting their time. Willie's smile beamed all the broader to let the Freestater know that he didn't smoke.

'Now, let's not be silly.' The officer collected his cigarettes and stuffed them back into his pocket. 'If you agree to surrender, you're a free man and nothing will happen to you. In fact, you'll be recognised as one of the great leaders in the fight for freedom and you'll have the right to a full army pension based on a colonel's salary. That's quite a tidy sum, in case you don't know.'

Willie focused his attentions on a spot on the wall where the damp was spreading its web across the plaster.

'Of course, I'm sure you're aware of the alternative, Colonel Hartnett. You were reported to be in possession of a service pistol at the time of your arrest. A military court will certainly find you guilty.' The fingers reached for another smoke and lit it off the butt of the first. 'The sentence is mandatory. Execution, as a common criminal. Burial in quicklime in an unmarked grave. A sordid end that will blacken your reputation forever.'

He closed his eyes and thought of Josie.

'Your soul will be damned to Hell.'

He could smell the scent of her body.

'All you have to do is sign your name to this document. Instruct your brigade to lay down their arms.'

They were desperate. They were still afraid to move into the hills.

'Then all of Limerick will be at peace.'

He could feel the softness of her touch.

'Do you hear me? We've the power to take it out on your family. We've ways of getting after your woman.'

'Take it down from the mast, Irish traitors,' he wheezed.

It's the flag we Republicans claim ...'

'Men!' shouted the officer. 'Take this stupid fool away.'

The sandbags swung against his chest, against his shoulders, against his buttocks and his thighs, across his back, piling more agony on existing pain. Before he passed out, Willie gloated in the triumph of provoking the smug officer and his henchmen into a tremor of vindictive fury.

Much to Patie Fitzgibbon's surprise, the Fourth Brigade had been resupplied. The column had all but fallen apart when news filtered through of Willie's capture and over half of them left to join better-armed and better-positioned units in Kerry. More would have buried the rifle and drifted back home had a Free State patrol not shot dead two comrades from another brigade after they had surrendered. And while anger regrouped those remaining under Patie's command, morale was still at rock-bottom until a cart appeared from nowhere in the middle of a wet night laden with crates of dymainite and ammunition, rolls of wire, boxes of detonators, a half-dozen captured Lee-Enfield rifles and a side of bacon. From a raid on a quarry in Kerry, the driver had intimated before directing his ass back into the mists from which they had sprung.

The arms were a Godsend, the contact even more so. They hadn't been forgotten. Knowing that comrades on the other side of the mountains were depending on them helped them to focus on something worth fighting for. So they forgot about the damp and the hunger and the cold, about localised rivalries and the niggling little rows that had filled up the boredom, and they began to accept that they could be led by someone other than Willie.

The first mine that they laid, hidden inside a barricade of debris strewn across the road between Ardagh and Carrickerry, caught a Free State column edging its way into the hills and, while it didn't inflict any casualties, it wrecked the lead lorry of the convoy and caused the enemy to turn back to the safety of the plains. A small victory and a temporary one at that, but it was their first successful operation since they'd taken to the hills.

They built on it as quickly as they could. Travelling through the twilight and working through the nights, they sealed off the other roads and the railway line leading from Limerick to Kerry and kept the ever-growing numbers of the opposing army frustrated on the lowlands below. And if the brigade had had more men and more guns at their disposal, they could have hidden in the hills behind their traps to attack the Freestaters during the first moments of confusion but, with only limited numbers, the best they could do was to guess which was the most likely route of the advance and concentrate all their resources there. In fact, if the other side had known how stretched Patie's group was, they would have long since gone on the offensive and would have flooded into Kerry without meeting any serious resistance.

But then it all came crashing down. Out late in the evening on the high road leading down from Knockanimpuha, the tail of the column got detached as it was cut across by a Free State patrol. Five of the lads didn't make it back to their hideout. They heard the pistol shots crack through the darkenss and they were afraid to count them.

When they awoke not long after sunrise, the lowlands below spewed black smoke into the crisp late autumn air from burning cottages and flaming haystacks. And way off in the distance, a convoy of vehicles was forming on the road out of Newcastlewest.

The loss of a quarter of their number had already unnerved them. The sight of an overwhelming enemy made them realise that they were all on their own, the only Republican presence along the Free State's march into Kerry.

'We're going nowhere, lads,' Mossy Noonan was saying. 'They know there's no one else up here except ourselves. They must have taken one of the lads prisoner and tortured it out of him.'

'Are you giving up as well?' Jimmy McCarthy was asking.

'No. I'll keep fighting as long as I'm ordered to.'

And who's running the show? Patie asked himself. Liam Lynch, Éamon de Valera, the Army Council, generals and commandants they'd never seen?

The convoy was on the move. 'They're heading for the Barna Gap, Patie,' Dick Mullane was telling him. 'We'll be there ahead of them if we move now.'

So he let himself be led into leading. With Dick shouting in his ear as they sprinted down the slopes of Sugar Hill to what they'd always known would be the scene of their final battle, he directed the fifteen of them still standing to positions they knew by heart. And with two separate mines hidden in culverts along the road climbing up the Gap before its descent to Abbeyfeale, they might just hit the convoy hard enough to make it think of turning back.

Through the field glasses, Patie watched the invasion take shape, the relentless line of lorries pushing each other forward. Some of the soldiers jumped out to lighten the load as the long straight ended and they bit into the incline. Engines roaring at the challenge of gravity, the convoy slowed to walking pace, sitting ducks for an ambush.

'Even more than I expected,' muttered Dick. 'A lot more.' The lead lorry edged ever closer. Soldiers hopped back up over the tailboard. 'Christ! The mine hasn't gone off. Will we leave it, Patie?'

They still had the second charge, primed to a firing box instead of to a trip wire. Only half as effective. Only half the confusion. Nowhere near enough to stop a steamrolling army.

And they'd have nowhere left to run.

'No. Let them have it.'

'Yaaah! Let them have it!'

Patie blasted the whistle and picked out the driver of the lead lorry as the armoured car behind shot upright and bounced back into the following vehicle. Five rounds into the scattering Freestaters and he whistled again. As they ran like the clappers into the furze and the heather, the second mine made its belated explosion.

They dragged him from his dungeon, hosed him down, shaved off his hair and the beard sprouting on his chin and threw some rags on him that were a few sizes too small. Like he'd done most times he woke up, Willie prepared himself for the worst. Life had reduced itself to cheating a few extra moments from his captors.

The cells along the side passage were empty again. No singing or shouting from comrades he'd never seen. Pain stabbed through his ankles and his knees as he climbed the stone stairs and he stumbled against the wall for support. The kick up the backside was no more than half-hearted.

A civilian awaited him this time, a big Dubliner with a bowler hat parked in front of him on the desk. Willie vaguely remembered the face as one of a Brotherhood group who were always to be seen circulating around Michael Collins back when everyone was fighting the Tans.

'Seven of our men murdered yesterday in the Barna Gap. Seven brave Irish soldiers. More of them wounded.' Blazes of hatred filled the eyes. 'In cold blood. By your so-called comrades.' But the voice managed to contain emotion to a quiver. 'Seven families who will never see their sons again. Butchered. Maimed. Blown to bits. Left to die like dogs.'

He rose from his desk to spit into Willie's face. 'I hope ye're proud of yerselves now, ye cowards. Ye've dragged the name of Ireland into the gutter.'

Sunlight edged through the window. A shaft brushed off his cheek where the gob of spit had landed. A warmth that he'd forgotten tingled his skin.

674

'Ye'll roast in Hell when ye die. Ye've been damned. The Church has damned ye.'

No mention of signing a document of surrender. The Freestaters must have made it through the Gap. He wondered how many of his own men had been killed.

'The country has turned its back on ye. The world has turned its back on ye. God has turned His back on ye.'

'You must have trouble sleeping at night. More trouble even than I have.'

They didn't strike him, just bundled him out the door and handcuffed him to another seven prisoners already chained together. He looked around at his surroundings. He'd been in Foynes all the time, right beside the old RIC barracks that the Fourth Brigade had attacked during its first action of the Tan War, just down the road from where half the county had greeted him and Ned Reidy on their return home from jail after the Rising.

He'd been dying to find out how long he'd been held. The man beside him told him the date. Five weeks and two days, somewhere around the midpoint in the range of his speculations. The length of his beard had been the most reliable indication.

He couldn't take his eyes off the sunlight streaming up the main street over the low early-morning haze. Just a slight breeze danced in from the Shannon with a little sting of cold to remind them of the season. After the dead dank air of his dungeon, he sniffed long draughts of its freshness.

The lorry arrived and they were herded up over the tailboard. Out they went in the direction of Limerick, the few passers-by averting their gaze as if they'd seen a ghost train and they and their guards sunk into silence. There was nothing left to say.

An old grey-bearded man stood at Robertstown Cross and blessed himself as the cargo of prisoners turned inland towards

675

Shanagolden. There was no one on the road when they stopped. Willie had expected somewhere more remote like a quarry or a lane leading to one of the creeks of the Estuary.

The lorry reversed to point back towards Foynes. Two of their guards leaped out to poke through the hedges.

'Nothing!' they shouted to the civilian who had come around from the cab. The prisoners were ordered out and marched up to an upturned hay float covered with branches that was blocking the road to Shanagolden.

'I don't have to tell ye that that's a trap mine,' the civilian was shouting behind them. 'See, Hartnett, you can't trust your mates. One of them is an informer. I'll leave it to yourself to guess which one of them it is.' One of the soldiers handcuffed the prisoner at the other end of the line from Willie to the float. 'Now, start looking.'

'What do we do now?' asked the man beside him.

'Look for the trip wire.'

'You mean disarm it?'

The rifle barrel pressed into Willie's back. 'Under the circumstances, I don't think we've much choice.'

'I see it,' said someone further down the line.

'Good!' shouted the civilian. 'Now, who's going to volunteer to dismantle it?'

The prisoners looked at each other.

'If ye don't, we'll have to shoot ye for trying to escape!'

Willie looked back. A Lewis machine gun pointed at them from over the tailboard. Life was now down to seconds. 'I'll do it.' He'd take the last few on offer.

'Ever the hero, Hartnett! Kelly! Make sure the rest of them don't wander!'

The next two in line had to crouch down beside him as he gently poked through the branches and lengths of timber that had been shoved under the float. He recognised it instantly as Patie Fitzgibbon's handiwork. The detonator would be a distance from the charge with at least two false trails of wire running from both.

Strapped underneath the winch, the sticks of dynamite were easy to spot. Eeny, meeny, miney, mo? Trusting his instincts, he eased his hand further inside, brushed past a wire blocking his access and held his breath.

Nothing happened. He'd found one of the red herrings.

His fingers dug into the macadam, scooping out a channel that gave him sight of the detonator and allowed him to trace the wire leading back to the charge. He'd need his other hand to hold the contact open while he slipped his finger under the spring.

'I can't get at it,' he shouted back as he emerged from the float. The soldiers guarding them had taken cover in the ditches on the sides of the road. 'You'll have to uncuff me.'

'Why would I bother?' replied the civilian.

Willie heard the shot ring out. And as the world around him slowed down, he saw the prisoner beside him toppling over on the trip wire and he saw the flash and he heard the bang and he smelled the smart whack of hot sulphur in his nose and he felt the draught of dust splattering against his face while forces beyond his comprehension pulled his body in opposing directions.

The telephone was ringing in the office outside as Ned Reidy was eating his breakfast. He ignored it as he finished off the helping of rashers, sausages, fried eggs, pudding and kidneys. They cooked them well in Cruise's Hotel.

An orderly removed his plate and passed it to the waiter standing by the trolley. Fingers of fresh hot toast were passed to the table to be spread with melting butter and, if he so desired, with marmalade from a little glass pot. Tea poured into the bone china cup. A housemaid opened the curtains to allow shafts of pale sunlight to enter.

White linen, white silver and a tradition of deferential service stretching back a century or two. A few years back, they were reserved solely for the gentry.

The newspaper arrived. Ned glanced over the front page. As had been the case every morning since the Public Safety Act came into force, news was divided into reports of major advances made by the defenders of the State and accounts of appalling atrocities committed by its enemies. Now that language had been redistributed by edict of his Cabinet colleagues, his side, the National Army or troops, could attack, commandeer and arrest. The opposition, now to be referred to under pain of arrest as the Irregulars or criminal elements, could only fire at, seize or kidnap.

The phone sounded again. This time, it refused to ring out while he drained the last sups of tea, chewed the last piece of toast and dabbed the serviette over the film of bacon grease and the traces of egg on the corners of his lips.

He knew what it was about. He hadn't slept a wink during the night.

The orderly knew too, as did the waiter and the housemaid. He was left alone to open the dividing door, pad to his desk and watch the receiver wobble to the ringing.

'I see,' was all he could say to the message from Foynes.

Successful advance from Newcastlewest to Abbeyfeale. Coast road cleared from Foynes to Glin. Mines removed in Carrickerry, Mountdavid, Knockanimpuha, Gortdroma. Resistance routed and its leadership dealt with.

Job done. West Limerick had been conquered. Two months of stalemate had ended as the offensive resumed its momentum. They were sure of their victory now.

It would look great in the newspapers. They didn't have to go into the details.

There was no alternative, he reminded himself. They had to end the nightmare as quickly as possible. If the country was to be at peace, there could be only the one authority.

Outside on the streets, the city was coming to life. Carts rolled out from the bakeries, the laundries and the breweries. Workers streamed towards their shops, their offices and their factories past the cries of newsboys and the pleas of beggars. Doors opened, shutters were removed, awnings rolled down, sawdust swept out. A ship's siren sounded down on the quays.

He returned to his desk, sat down and stared at the telegram. Congratulations from the Government on a successful operation.

His secretary dropped in a stack of notes. Reqests for meetings from the College of Surgeons and the College of Physicians staking out their patches under the new regime, from the chairman of a committee on the treatment of tuberculosis that had carried on regardless throughout three years of insurrection and civil war, from the Archbishop of Dublin on ensuring that Government health policies would not contravene Catholic teaching.

A pile of documents waited to be signed. Ministerial orders, appointments, disbursement of public funds from an exchequer already emptied by the insatiable demands of the military. He pushed them aside.

'Oh, sweet Jesus!' he sobbed as he buried his head in hands. 'Oh, Willie! What have we become?'

Nicholas Sullivan woke to the sound of the explosion. Bessie was already in the kitchen, cleaning up after her own breakfast and setting the table for his. It had been almost midnight when he'd arrived home from meeting an art dealer in Limerick who had expressed an interest in his painting of Shanid Castle. With the direct route back to Shanagolden closed off because of trap mines, the hackney at the Foynes train station had been reluctant to carry him and only relented when he'd squeezed four times the normal fare for taking him by the back way through Carrowclough.

A lorry rolled past. 'That's the second one,' she told him. 'They must be clearing the road.'

He spread sugar over his porridge.

'And about time too,' she added. 'They could have done it weeks ago if they'd put their minds to it.'

He ventured outside. Another lorry passed by the gate on its way back to the town. Grim-faced soldiers sat back in the trailer with tunics unbuttoned at the neck and clutching spades between their feet. Some were covered in bloodstains although none of them appeared to be wounded.

Curiosity tempted Sullivan to walk up to the checkpoint at the bend in the road but caution held him to the spot. After losing seven of their colleagues the day before in an ambush beyond Newcastlewest, they were certain to be in a trigger-happy mood. Instead, he went around to the back of the house to the studio that he'd set up in the shed. The light wasn't great, too low in the sky to give the illumination he wanted for adding the finishing touches to a landscape, but it was the best he'd get for the time of year. He'd want to hurry though. Wisps of gathering cloud threatened to relegate the morning into grey.

He set up the easel, then remembered that he'd forgotten his pipe. An envelope was lying on the sitting room table with a

Newfoundland stamp on it. Peter Callaghan was looking for an experienced outside policeman to investigate allegations of corruption against leading political figures of the Dominion. Sullivan would be his own boss and, as long as they weren't outrageous, he could name his own terms and conditions.

A few years back, he might have been tempted. Now it would mean him leaving colours and contours and moods that he'd only just begun to discover. He put the letter aside in his writing bureau away from Bessie's attentions. If he was going to decide one way or the other, he wanted to be sure of his own views first.

Of course, he'd spend the whole morning thinking about the offer and his mind wouldn't be on the painting. So he went out the front door instead, intent on a short walk into the town to clear his head. Across the road, a pair of soldiers were half-heartedly poking the hedge. Ears attuned by a lifetime in the constabulary picked up snatches of conversation.

'A waste of time, I'm telling you. We won't find anyone else.'

'They're saying one of them is missing.'

'How do they know? Sure aren't most of them in bits.'

'They counts the heads.'

'I swear to God, I think you're enjoying it.'

They looked up as he stepped out the gate, one suspicious and threatening, the other melting with guilt. Dried blood spattered their tunics and mud caked their fingers. The bigger of the two approached him with the implied claim that his Free State uniform, and not the one Sullivan had retired from, now carried weight in the land.

Realising that he'd been supplanted by a swagger he hadn't seen since the Tans had disappeared off into the twilight, the old policeman gave way and pottered back to his studio. He lit up his pipe and sucked in a few draughts of soothing tobacco before paring the tip of the turkey quill that he used for stippling his

681

heavy brush strokes. A movement on the floor caught his eye. Through the powder stains on the death-pale face and the head shorn of its hair, he recognised the features of Willie Hartnett.

Bending down to catch the incoherent mumbles, he saw the splinters of wood protruding from the body. 'Blown clear ... huugh! ... blown clear.' The hand moved, then a second one beside it, not his at all, another man's stump torn apart at the elbow and handcuffed to Hartnett's wrist.

Fighting down the heave in his stomach, Sullivan propped the head up on a sketchbook and hurried back into the house for blankets, for a pillow, for bandages, for water, for a towel, for whatever else broke through the addle of his rummaging before Bessie dropped her embroidery and took everything in hand while he cycled into the town to get the priest, the doctor and Miss Reidy.

Willie knew that his strength was ebbing but he wasn't yet ready to give in. Thrown clear of the blast by some freak of geometry, he'd seen the Freestaters bury whatever they could find of the rest of the prisoners. And having watched them from the bottom of a ditch as they scoured the hedges and the fields for the last unaccounted body, he knew that his escape had meant something.

When he'd pulled one splinter from his calf, the blood began to flow again so, ignoring the pain, he left the rest of the wood where it was, heaved himself up to ground level and crawled on his hands and knees in the direction of what he hoped was Shanagolden. Voices were still drifting past but they seemed to be out on the road and, from the mood of them, appeared to be going through the motions of obeying an order rather than actively engaging in a search.

The whitewashed wall appeared out of nowhere and it scratched some memory in the back of his mind but he couldn't remember whether it might be the home of an enemy or a friend. A figure was moving from the shed to the house and he was on the point of calling for help when he felt a hot spurt deep in his belly and he realised that his guts were seeping again. It took every ounce of effort to drag himself across the yard and rest inside the door of the shed.

Knowing that if he dropped off he would never wake up again, he fought the smothering fatigue. The man returned. Now he remembered who he was. He wanted to tell him what had happened but Inspector Sullivan went away again and a woman took his place.

Another dart shot through his leg. His insides were falling apart but he clung on, fastening his eyes on a picture of the sun setting over Shanid Castle. He'd never thought of it like that before, rising over centuries of marching armies, his own being just one of many.

Phlegm, or was it blood, cloaked his voice. He tried to spit it out.

'Tóg go bog é,' she was saying. 'Tá an sagart ag teacht.'

He didn't need help now. He needed a listening ear.

'Ego te absolvo a peccatis tuis in nomine Patris, et Filii, et Spiritus Sancti ...' A thumb dabbed oil his lips.

His chest cleared. 'Connie ... Freestaters ... Tied eight of us to a mine ... Blew us up ...'

He heard the door open again. He felt the hands cradling his head. 'Josie ... I came back to say goodbye.'

He heard her crying. He heard Father Connie asking him if he would take Josie as his wife. He gasped assent. He heard no more.

'I pronounce you man and wife,' Father Connie was saying. But she had already felt his life slip away. The head flopped back in her arms and she held it against her breasts as the red stain flooded her dress. Josie had never realised how warm blood could be.

'He's gone to a better place.' Mrs. Sullivan laid a hand on her shoulder. Her husband hunted a Free State soldier from the door and a line of mourners began to enter and fall to their knees. For one long moment, Josie took in everything around her. The Rosary mumbled. An old woman began to keen.

The loss hit her like a train. 'Oh my sweet Willie!' she wailed. 'We never got time together.' This time he'd never come back

47

IT WAS LIKE a rerun of Dan Hourigan's funeral. A lone piper led the procession down the length of the village from the church. Willie's beret and gloves lay over the Tricolour and the Shanagolden jersey on the coffin carried by his brothers and neighbours. Right behind it, old Joe Hartnett held Josie by the arm. Dick Mullane, Patie Fitzgibbon, Jimmy McCarthy and Mossy Noonan led the Fourth Brigade guard of honour in full IRA uniform and holding their rifles aloft.

Ned Reidy had been ordered to prevent the occasion from turning into a Republican show of force. Even if he had been willing to obey it, there was nothing he could have done. Half of Limerick had turned up to pay their respects.

Instead, his troops massed at the crossroads and left a path for their enemies to proceed. With Father Greaney and Inspector Sullivan acting as intermediaries, both sides had come to an agreement. Regardless of what the armchair strategists in Dublin might want, Ned was not going to inflict further sorrow on Shanagolden.

He waited until the Army had settled into position before stepping out of the limousine and he stood head bowed and hands joined as the coffin marched past. Most of the mourners ignored him; a few threw him darts of hate.

The rain returned and he let it drizzle down on his bare head as they packed into the cemetery that he'd agreed not to enter while they buried his childhood friend. He could hear the prayers and the lamentations, he could hear Philip Hurley's graveside oration, he could hear the keening and the sobbing from the other side of the wall.

Some day, he hoped they might understand. Willie Hartnett's life was the price of a better tomorrow, one half of the bargain of closure.

The volley of shots rang out. Fighting back the tears, General Ned Reidy stood to attention and saluted. Behind him, a battalion of Free Sate soldiers followed suit.

The Army wanted Ned to lead the mop up in Tipperary as it doused the flickering embers of the Civil War. The Government wanted him in Dublin to kick the Department of Public Health into shape. Cumann na nGaedhal, formed out of the pro-Treaty faction of Sinn Féin, wanted his help in setting up the party. He had every excuse to stay away from Shanagolden.

He had every reason to as well. While censored newspapers reported that a prematurely-exploding trap mine had wiped out a gang of Irregular desperados intent on slaughtering an Army patrol, every dog and devil in West Limerick knew how Willie and his seven comrades had met their Maker.

But other forces kept drawing home. Every Saturday morning, the big black limousine drove down the Coast Road and dropped him at the door of the farmhouse. His Cabinet colleagues and his Army comrades insisted on providing an armed guard wherever he went but he'd shoo them away the moment he stepped out of the State car and told them that he didn't want to see them again until they came back to collect him on the Monday.

Some admired his courage for standing up for the rule of law. Others dismissed it as the same reckless bravado that had led Michael Collins to his grave. The corner boys and the old Biddies reckoned he was making sure that he got his hands on the farm. But he was only staying in the house to prevent the property from falling into ruin. The day after Willie was laid to rest, Josie had moved out into Philip Hurley's old home even though he had let her know that she could have the entire estate of their father.

But whatever they thought, no one ever said it to Ned's face. When he listened to representations in the afternoon in the little room that Thomas Hennessy had set up for his constituency visits, when he called around to every pub in the town in the evening or when he turned up at Mass the following morning, he was treated with nothing more than politeness or deference. He'd been excluded from the inner thoughts of the parish and news of its goings-on only came to him second-hand through police reports or through the filter of Hennessy. Long before Ned himself became aware of it, everyone else in Shanagolden knew that Dick Mullane, Jimmy McCarthy and Mossy Noonan had disappeared, that Josie was expecting Willie's child, that Patie Fitzgibbon was still lurking in the hills with a price on his head, that Hennessy had bought up the ruin of Jack Noonan's premises.

He'd become a ghost in his home town, hearing, seeing, sensing everything that was happening around him but unable to take part. And like any haunting spirit, he was tied by shackles that wouldn't let him leave. Come Sunday evening, he'd try his best and put away a bottle of whiskey in a solitary session in the emptiness of Ballycormick House. But it never worked. When he'd wake in the small hours of the morning with his tongue stuck to the roof of his mouth and his head throbbing to the tortures of malt, he could the hear voices calling and he'd walk out into the damp moments of dawn to meet the other presence of Shanagolden.

There, down by the bend as the road snaked away towards Foynes, the cairn of rocks stood where the crater had been roughly filled in. 'I gcomóradh Liam Ó hAirtnéada, Ceannfort an 4adh Cathalán Luimnighe Óglaigh na hÉireann, do fuair bás ar son na hÉireann ar an 14adh lá de Shamhain 1922,' the rough Gaelic script proclaimed the death of a chieftain and listed the other seven names that would never be forgotten. Underneath, a fading red rose lay at the base of a small wooden cross inscribed 'Liam Ó hAirtnéada T.D., Clashganniff, Shanagolden, 10/08/1894 - 14/11/1922, husband of Josie, an Irish Volunteer. You will always be with me, my darling Willie.'

Ned would kneel for a few moments, thumbing his beads and waiting for it to come. If it wasn't to be that week, it would be another. It had taken Willie's death to bring an end to their war. It would take his own to create the conditions for peace.

The fighting was over in West Limerick. The Republic had lost; the cause that had called them put back for another day. Patie was on his own now, living off his wits as the dragnet of Free State patrols penned him inside the hills between Shanagolden and Ballyhahill. If he had listened to reason, he would have followed Dick, Mossy and Jimmy to Chicago where they had teamed up with a bootlegger friend of Jack Noonan. But he couldn't take leave of the soil of his birth until he answered the voice summoning him to the bend in the road.

Hands joined in prayer, Ned begged for forgiveness at Willie's memorial. On the hillside above him, Patie picked his spot and fired.